BRIDGERTON

TO SIR PHILLIP, WITH LOVE

AND

WHEN HE WAS WICKED

By Julia Quinn

The Bridgerton Prequels

Because of Miss Bridgerton
The Girl with the Make-Believe Husband
The Other Miss Bridgerton
First Comes Scandal

The Bridgerton Series

The Duke and I
The Viscount Who Loved Me
An Offer from a Gentleman
Romancing Mister Bridgerton
To Sir Phillip, With Love
When He Was Wicked
It's in His Kiss
On the Way to the Wedding
The Bridgertons: Happily Ever After

Anthologies

The Further Observations of Lady Whistledown
Lady Whistledown Strikes Back

The Smythe-Smith Quartet

Just Like Heaven
A Night Like This
The Sum of All Kisses
The Secrets of Sir Richard Kenworthy

The Bevelstoke Series

The Secret Diaries of Miss Miranda Cheever
What Happens in London
Ten Things I Love About You

The Two Dukes of Wyndham

The Lost Duke of Wyndham
Mr. Cavendish, I Presume

Agents of the Crown

To Catch an Heiress
How to Marry a Marquis

The Lyndon Sisters

Everything and the Moon
Brighter Than the Sun

The Splendid Trilogy

Splendid
Dancing at Midnight
Minx

BRIDGERTON

TO SIR PHILLIP, WITH LOVE

AND

WHEN HE WAS WICKED

JULIA QUINN

AVON
An Imprint of HarperCollins*Publishers*

"To Sir Phillip, With Love: The 2nd Epilogue" was originally published as an e-book.

"When He Was Wicked: The 2nd Epilogue" was originally published as an e-book.

Originally published separately as *To Sir Phillip, With Love* and *When He Was Wicked* in the United States by Avon Books in 2003 and 2004.

Bridgerton Family Tree designed by Emily Cotler, Waxcreative Design

Library of Congress Cataloging-in-Publication Data has been applied for.

ISBN 978-0-06-338366-1

2 SKY 24

Table of Contents

Bridgerton FAMILY TREE

Violet Ledger 1766- *m.* **EDMUND** 1764-1803

- **ANTHONY** 1784- *m.* **Kate Sheffield** 1793-
  The Viscount Who Loved Me
  BOOK 2
  - Edmund 1815
  - Charlotte 1822
  - Miles 1817
- **BENEDICT** 1786- *m.* **Sophie Beckett** 1794-
  An Offer From a Gentleman
  BOOK 3
  - Charles 1818
  - William 1822
  - Alexander 1820
- **COLIN** 1791- *m.* **Penelope** 1796- **Featherington**
  Romancing Mister Bridgerton
  BOOK 4
- **DAPHNE** 1792- *m.* **Simon Basset** 1784-
  Duke of Hastings
  The Duke And I
  BOOK 1
  - Amelia 1814
  - Belinda 1815
  - Caroline 1816
  - David 1817
- **ELOISE** 1796-
  featuring
  Sir Phillip Crane 1794-
  m. 1 Marina Thompson 1794-1823
  To Sir Phillip, With Love
  BOOK 5
  - Oliver 1816
  - Amanda 1816
- **FRANCESCA** 1797- *m.* John Stirling
  8th Earl of Kilmartin
  1792-1820
  When He Was Wicked
  BOOK 6
- **GREGORY** 1801-
  On the Way to the Wedding
  BOOK 8
- **HYACINTH** 1803-
  It's in His Kiss
  BOOK 7

BRIDGERTON

TO SIR PHILLIP, WITH LOVE

For Stefanie and Randall Hargreaves—
You opened your home, you showed us your town,
you stored our stuff, and when we arrived,
you had a care package waiting on the porch.
And when I really needed someone,
I knew exactly who to call.

And also for Paul, this time Because.
It's always really Because.

Prologue

February 1823
Gloucestershire, England

It was ironic, really, that it had happened on such a sunny day.

The first sunny day in, what had it been—six straight weeks of gray skies, accompanied by the occasional sprinkling of light snow or rain? Even Phillip, who'd thought himself impervious to the vagaries of the weather, had felt his spirits lighten, his smile widen. He'd gone outside—he'd had to. No one could remain indoors during such a splendid display of sunshine.

Especially in the middle of such a gray winter.

Even now, more than a month after it had happened, he couldn't quite believe that the sun had had the temerity to tease him so.

And how was it that he'd been so blind that he'd not expected it? He'd lived with Marina since the day of their marriage. Eight long years to know the woman. He should have expected it. And in truth . . .

Well, in truth, he *had* expected it. He just hadn't wanted to admit to the expectation. Perhaps he was just trying to delude himself, protect himself, even. To hide from the obvious, hoping that if he didn't think about it, it would never happen.

But it did. And on a sunny day, to boot. God certainly had a sick sense of humor.

He looked down at his glass of whiskey, which was, quite inexplicably, empty. He must have drunk the damned thing, and yet he had no memory of doing so. He didn't feel woozy, at least not as woozy as he should have been. Or even as woozy as he wanted to be.

He stared out the window at the sun, which was slipping low on the horizon. It had been another sunny day today. That probably explained his exceptional melancholy. At least he hoped it did. He wanted an explanation, needed one, for this awful tiredness that seemed to be taking over.

Melancholy terrified him.

More than anything. More than fire, more than war, more than hell itself. The thought of sinking into sadness, of being like *her* . . .

Marina had been melancholy. Marina had spent her entire life, or at least the entire life he'd known, melancholy. He couldn't remember the sound of her laughter, and in truth, he wasn't sure that he'd ever known it.

It had been a sunny day, and—

He squeezed his eyes shut, not certain whether the motion was meant to urge the memory or dispel it.

It had been a sunny day, and . . .

"Never thought you'd feel the likes of that on your skin again, eh, Sir Phillip?"

Phillip Crane turned his face to the sun, closing his eyes as he let the warmth spread over his skin. "It's perfect," he murmured. "Or it would be, if it weren't so bloody cold."

Miles Carter, his secretary, chuckled. "It's not as cold as that. The lake hasn't frozen this year. Just a few patchy spots."

Reluctantly, Phillip turned away from the sun and opened his eyes. "It isn't spring, though."

"If you were wishing for spring, sir, perhaps you should have consulted a calendar."

Phillip regarded him with a sideways glance. "Do I pay you for such impertinence?"

"Indeed. And rather handsomely, too."

Phillip smiled to himself as both men paused to enjoy the sun for a few moments longer.

"I thought you didn't mind the gray," Miles said conversationally, once they'd resumed their trek to Phillip's greenhouse.

"I don't," Phillip said, striding along with the confidence of a natural athlete. "But just because I don't mind an overcast sky doesn't mean I don't prefer the sun." He paused, thought for a moment. "Be sure to tell Nurse Millsby to take the children outside today. They'll need warm coats, of course, and hats and mittens and the like, but they ought to get a little sun on their faces. They've been cooped up far too long."

"As have we all," Miles murmured.

Phillip chuckled. "Indeed." He glanced over his shoulder at his greenhouse. He probably ought to take care of his correspondence now, but he had some seeds he needed to sort through, and truly, there was no reason he couldn't conduct his business with Miles in an hour or so. "Go on," he said to Miles. "Find Nurse Millsby. You and I can deal later. You know you hate the greenhouse, anyway."

"Not this time of year," Miles said. "The heat is rather welcome."

Phillip arched a brow as he inclined his head toward Romney Hall. "Are you calling my ancestral home drafty?"

"All ancestral homes are drafty."

"True enough," Phillip said with a grin. He rather liked Miles. He'd hired him six months earlier to help with the mountains of paperwork and details that seemed to accumulate from the running of his small property. Miles was quite good. Young, but good. And his dry sense of humor was certainly welcome in a house where laughter was never in abundance. The servants would never dare joke with Phillip, and Marina . . . well, it went without saying that Marina did not laugh or tease.

The children sometimes made Phillip laugh, but that was a different sort of humor, and besides, most of the time he did not know what to say to them. He tried, but then he felt too awkward, too big, too strong, if such a thing were possible. And then he just found himself shooing them off, telling them to go back to their nurse.

It was easier that way.

"Go on, then," Phillip said, sending Miles off on a task he probably should have done himself. He hadn't seen his children yet today, and he supposed he ought to, but he didn't want to spoil the day by saying something stern, which he inevitably seemed to do.

He'd find them while they were off on their nature walk with Nurse Millsby. That would be a good idea. Then he could point out some sort of plant and tell them about it, and everything would remain perfectly simple and benign.

Phillip entered his greenhouse and shut the door behind him, taking a welcome breath of the moist air. He'd studied botany at Cambridge, taken a first, even, and in truth, he'd probably have taken up an academic life if his older brother had not died at Waterloo, thrusting the second-born Phillip into the role of landowner and country gentleman.

He supposed it could have been worse. He could have been landowner and city gentleman, after all. At least here he was able to pursue his botanical pursuits in relative serenity.

He bent over his workbench, examining his latest project—a strain of peas that he was trying to breed to grow fatter and plumper in the pod. No luck yet, though. This latest batch was not just shriveled but had even turned yellow, which had not been the expected result at all.

Phillip frowned, then allowed himself a small smile as he moved to the back of the greenhouse to gather his supplies. He never minded too terribly when his experiments did not produce the expected outcome. In his opinion, necessity had never been the mother of invention.

Accidents. It was all about accidents. No scientist would admit to it, of course, but most great invention occurred while one was attempting to solve some other problem entirely.

He chuckled as he swept the shriveled peas aside. At this rate, he'd cure gout by the end of the year.

Back to work. Back to work. He bent over his seed collection, smoothing them out so that he could examine them all. He needed just the right one for—

He looked up and out the freshly washed glass. A movement across the field caught his eye. A flash of red.

Red. Phillip smiled to himself as he shook his head. It must be Marina. Red was her favorite color, something that he'd always found odd. Anyone who spent any time with her would have surely thought she'd prefer something darker, more somber.

He watched as she disappeared into the wooded copse, then got back to work. It was rare for Marina to venture outside. These days she didn't often leave the confines of her bedchamber. Phillip was happy to see her out in the sun. Maybe it would restore her spirits. Not completely, of course. Phillip didn't think even the sun had the ability to do that. But maybe a bright, warm day would be enough to draw her out for a few hours, bring a small smile to her face.

Heaven knew the children could use that. They visited their mother in her room almost every evening, but it wasn't enough.

And Phillip knew that this lack was not made up for by him.

He sighed, a wave of guilt washing over him. He was not the sort of father they needed, he knew that. He tried to tell himself that he was doing his best, that he was succeeding in what was his only goal when it came to parenthood—that he *not* behave in the manner of his own father.

But still he knew it wasn't enough.

With resolute motions, he pushed himself away from his workbench. The seeds could wait. His children could probably wait, too, but that didn't mean they should. And he ought to take them on their nature walk, not Nurse Millsby, who didn't know a deciduous tree from a coniferous and would most likely tell them that a rose was a daisy and . . .

He glanced out the window again, reminding himself that it was February. Nurse Millsby wasn't likely to locate any sort of flower in this weather, but still, it didn't excuse the fact that *he* ought to take the children on their nature walk. It was the one sort of children's activity at which he truly excelled, and he ought not shirk the responsibility.

He strode out of the greenhouse but then stopped, not even a third of the way back to Romney Hall. If he was going to fetch the children, he ought to take them out to see their mother. They craved her company, even when she did nothing more than pat them on the head. Yes, they should find Marina. That would be even more beneficial than a nature walk.

But he knew from experience that he ought not make assumptions about Marina's state of mind. Just because she'd ventured outside did not mean that she was feeling well. And he hated when the children saw her in one of her moods.

Phillip turned around and headed out toward the copse where he'd seen Marina disappear just a few moments earlier. He walked with nearly twice the speed of Marina; it wouldn't take very long to catch up to her and ascertain her mood. He could be back at the nursery before the children set out with Nurse Millsby.

He walked through the woods, easily following Marina's path. The ground was moist, and Marina must have been wearing heavy boots, because her prints had sunk into the earth with clear definition. They led down the slight incline and out of the woods, then onto a grassy patch.

"Damn," Phillip muttered, the word barely audible as the wind picked up around him. It was impossible to see her footprints on the grass. He used his hand to shade his eyes from the sun and scanned the horizon, looking for a telltale scrap of red.

Not near the abandoned cottage, nor at Phillip's field of experimental grains, nor at the large boulder that Phillip had spent so many hours clambering upon when he was a child. He turned north, his eyes narrowing when he finally saw her. She was heading toward the lake.

The lake.

Phillip's lips parted as he stared down at her form, moving slowly toward the water's edge. He wasn't quite frozen; it was more that he was . . . suspended . . . as his mind took in the strange sight. Marina didn't swim. He didn't even know if she could. He supposed she was aware that there was a lake on the grounds, but in truth, he'd never known her to go there, not in the eight years they'd been married. He started walking toward her, his feet somehow recognizing what his mind refused to accept. As she stepped into the shallows, he picked up speed, still too far to do anything but call out her name.

But if she heard him, she made no indication, just continued her slow and steady progress into the depths.

"Marina!" he screamed, now breaking into a run. He was still a good minute away, even moving at top speed. "Marina!"

She reached the point where the bottom dropped off, and then she dropped off, too, disappearing under the gunmetal gray of the surface, her red cloak floating along the top for a few seconds before being sucked under after her.

He yelled her name again, even though she couldn't possibly hear. He skidded and stumbled down the hill leading to the lake, then had just enough presence of mind to yank off his coat and boots before diving into the freezing-cold water. She'd been under barely a minute; his mind recognized that that was probably not enough time to drown, but every second it took him to find her was one second toward her death.

He'd swum in the lake countless times, knew exactly where the bottom dropped off, and he reached that critical point with swift, even strokes, barely noticing the drag of the water against his heavy clothes.

He could find her. He *had* to find her.

Before it was too late.

He dove down, his eyes scanning the murky water. Marina must have kicked up some of the sand from the bottom, and he had surely done the same, because the fine silt was swirling around him, the puffy opaque clouds making it difficult to see.

But in the end, Marina was saved by her one colorful quirk, and Phillip pumped through the water, down to the bottom where he saw the red of her cloak floating through the water like a languorous kite. She did not fight him as he pulled her to the surface; indeed, she had already lost consciousness and was nothing more than a dead weight in his arms.

They broke out into the air, and he took great, big gasps to fill his burning lungs. For a moment he could do nothing but breathe, his body recognizing that it had to save itself before he could save anyone else. Then he pulled her along to the shore, careful to keep her face above water, even though she didn't seem to be breathing.

Finally, they reached the water's edge, and he dragged her upon the narrow strip of dirt and pebbles that separated the water from the grass. With frantic movements he felt in front of her face for air, but there was none emerging from her lips.

He didn't know what to do, hadn't thought he'd ever have to save someone from drowning, so he just did what seemed most sensible and heaved her over his lap, face down, whacking her on the back. Nothing happened at first, but after the fourth violent thrust, she coughed, and a stream of murky water erupted from her mouth.

He turned her over quickly. "Marina?" he asked urgently, lightly slapping her face. "Marina?"

She coughed again, her body wracked by spasmodic tremors. Then she began to suck in air, her lungs forcing her to live, even when her soul desired something else.

"Marina," Phillip said, his voice shaking with relief. "Thank God." He didn't love her, had never really loved her, but she was his wife, and she was the mother of his children, and she was, deep down, beneath her unshakable cloak of sorrow and despair, a good and fine person. He may not have loved her, but he did not want her death.

She blinked, her eyes unfocused. And then, finally, she seemed to realize where she was, who he was, and she whispered, "No."

"I've got to get you back to the house," he said gruffly, startled by how angry he was over that single word.

No.

How dare she refuse his rescue? Would she give up on life just because she was *sad*? Did her melancholy amount to more than their two children? In the balance of life, did a bad mood weigh more than their need for a mother?

"I'm taking you home," he bit out, heaving her none too gently into his arms. She was breathing now, and clearly in possession of her faculties, misguided though they may be. There was no need to treat her like a delicate flower.

"No," she sobbed quietly. "Please don't. I don't want . . . I don't . . ."

"You're going home," he stated, trudging up the hill, oblivious to the chill wind turning his sodden clothes to ice; oblivious, even, to the rocky soil pressing into his unshod feet.

"I can't," she whispered, with what seemed like her last ounce of energy.

And as Phillip carried his burden home, all he could think was how apt those words were.

I can't.

In a way, it seemed to sum up her entire life.

By nightfall, it became apparent that fever might succeed where the lake had failed.

Phillip had carried Marina home as quickly as he was able, and, with the aid of Mrs. Hurley, his housekeeper, had stripped her of her icy garments and tried to warm her beneath the goose-down quilt that had been the centerpiece of her trousseau eight years earlier.

"What happened?" Mrs. Hurley had gasped when he staggered through the kitchen door. He hadn't wanted to use the main entrance, where he might be seen by his children, and besides, the kitchen door was closer by a good twenty yards.

"She fell in the lake," he said gruffly.

Mrs. Hurley gave him a look that was somehow dubious and sympathetic all at the same time, and he knew that she knew the truth. She had worked for the Cranes since their marriage; she knew Marina's moods.

She had shooed him out of the room once they had Marina in bed, insisting that he change his own clothing before he caught his death as well. He had returned, though, to Marina's side. That was his place as her husband, he thought guiltily, a place he had avoided in recent years.

It was depressing to be with Marina. It was *hard.*

But now wasn't the time to shirk his duties, and so he sat at her bedside throughout the day and into the night. He mopped her brow when she began to perspire, tried to pour lukewarm broth down her throat when she was calm.

He told her to fight, even though he knew his words fell on deaf ears.

Three days later she was dead.

It was what she'd wanted, but that was little comfort as Phillip faced his children, twins, just turned seven years old, and tried to explain that their mother was gone. He sat in their nursery, his large frame too big for any of their tot-sized chairs. But he sat, anyway, twisted like a pretzel, and forced himself to meet their gazes as he wrenched out the words.

They said little, which was unlike them. But they didn't look surprised, which Phillip found disturbing.

"I—I'm sorry," he choked out, once he reached the end of his speech. He loved them so much, and he failed them in so many ways. He barely knew how to be a father to them; how in hell was he meant to take on the role of mother as well?

"It's not your fault," Oliver said, his brown eyes capturing his father's with an intensity that was unsettling. "She fell in the lake, didn't she? You didn't push her."

Phillip only nodded, unsure of how to respond.

"Is she happy now?" Amanda asked softly.

"I think so," Phillip said. "She gets to watch you all the time now from heaven, so she must be happy."

The twins seemed to consider that for quite some time. "I hope she's happy," Oliver finally said, his voice more resolute than his expression. "Maybe she won't cry anymore."

Phillip felt his breath catch in his throat. He hadn't realized that they had heard Marina's sobs. She only seemed to sink so low late at night; their room was directly above hers, but he'd always assumed they'd already fallen asleep when their mother started to cry.

Amanda nodded her agreement, her little blond head bobbing up and down. "If she's happy now," she said, "then I'm glad she's gone."

"She's not gone," Oliver cut in. "She's dead."

"No, she's gone," Amanda persisted.

"It's the same thing," Phillip said flatly, wishing he had something to tell them other than the truth. "But I think she's happy now."

And in a way, that was the truth, too. It was what Marina had wanted, after all. Maybe it was all she had wanted all along.

Amanda and Oliver were quiet for a long while, both keeping their eyes on the floor as their legs swung from their perch on Oliver's bed. They looked so small, sitting there on a bed that was clearly too high for them. Phillip frowned. How was it that he'd never noticed this before? Shouldn't they be on lower beds? What if they fell off in the night?

Or maybe they were too big for all that. Maybe they didn't fall out of bed any longer. Maybe they never had.

Maybe he truly was an abominable father. Maybe he should know these things.

Maybe . . . maybe . . . He closed his eyes and sighed. Maybe he should stop thinking quite so much and simply try his best and be happy with that.

"Are you going to go away?" Amanda asked, raising her head.

He looked into her eyes, so blue, so like her mother's. "No," he whispered fiercely, kneeling before her and taking her tiny hands in his own. They looked so small in his grasp, so fragile.

"No," he repeated. "I'm not going away. I'm not ever going away. . . ."

Phillip looked down at his whiskey glass. It was empty again. Funny how a whiskey glass could go empty even after one filled it four times.

He hated remembering. He wasn't sure what was the worst. Was it the dive underwater or the moment Mrs. Hurley had turned to him and said, "She's gone"?

Or was it his children, the sorrow on their faces, the fear in their eyes?

He lifted the glass to his lips, letting the final drops slide into his mouth. The worst part was definitely his children. He'd told them he wouldn't ever leave them, and he hadn't—he wouldn't—but his simple presence wasn't enough. They needed more. They needed someone who knew how to be a parent, who knew how to speak to them and understand them and get them to mind and behave.

And since he couldn't very well get them another father, he supposed he ought to think about finding them a mother. It was too soon, of course. He couldn't marry anyone until his prescribed period of mourning was completed, but that didn't mean he couldn't look.

He sighed, slumping in his seat. He needed a wife. Almost any wife would do. He didn't care what she looked like. He didn't care if she had money. He didn't care if she could do sums in her head or speak French or even ride a horse.

She just had to be happy.

Was that so much to want in a wife? A smile, at least once a day. Maybe even the sound of her laughter?

And she had to love his children. Or at least pretend so well that they never knew the difference.

It wasn't so much to ask for, was it?

"Sir Phillip?"

Phillip looked up, cursing himself for having left his study door slightly ajar. Miles Carter, his secretary, was poking his head in.

"What is it?"

"A letter, sir," Miles said, walking forward to hand him an envelope. "From London."

Phillip looked down at the envelope in his hand, his brows rising at the obviously feminine slant to the handwriting. He dismissed Miles with a nod, then picked up his letter opener and slid it under the wax. A single sheet of paper slipped out. Phillip rubbed it between his fingers. High quality. Expensive. Heavy, too, a clear sign that the sender need not economize to reduce franking costs.

Then he turned it over and read:

No. 5, Bruton Street
London

Sir Phillip Crane—

I am writing to express my condolences on the loss of your wife, my dear cousin Marina. Although it has been many years since I last saw Marina, I remember her fondly and was deeply saddened to hear of her passing.

Please do not hesitate to write if there is anything I can do to ease your pain at this difficult time.

Yrs,
Miss Eloise Bridgerton

Phillip rubbed his eyes. Bridgerton . . . Bridgerton. Did Marina have Bridgerton cousins? She must have done, if one of them was sending him a letter.

He sighed, then surprised himself by reaching for his own stationery and quill. He'd received precious few condolence notes since Marina had died. It seemed most of her friends and family had forgotten her since her marriage. He supposed he shouldn't be upset, or even surprised. She'd rarely left her bedchamber; it was easy to forget about someone one never saw.

Miss Bridgerton deserved a reply. It was common courtesy, or even if it wasn't (and Phillip was quite certain he didn't know the full etiquette of one's wife dying), it still somehow seemed like the right thing to do.

And so, with a weary breath, he put his quill to paper.

Chapter 1

May 1824
Somewhere on the road from London to Gloucestershire
The middle of the night

Dear Miss Bridgerton—

Thank you for your kind note at the loss of my wife. It was thoughtful of you to take the time to write to a gentleman you have never met. I offer you this pressed flower as thanks. It is naught but the simple red campion (Silene dioica), but it brightens the fields here in Gloucestershire, and indeed seems to have arrived early this year.

It was Marina's favorite wildflower.

Sincerely,
Sir Phillip Crane

Eloise Bridgerton smoothed the well-read sheet of paper across her lap. There was little light by which to see the words, even with the full moon shining through the windows of the coach, but that didn't really matter. She had the entire letter memorized, and the delicate pressed flower, which was actually more pink than red, was safely protected between the pages of a book she'd nipped from her brother's library.

She hadn't been too terribly surprised when she'd received a reply from Sir Phillip. Good manners dictated as much, although even Eloise's mother, surely the supreme arbiter of good behavior, said that Eloise took her correspondence a bit too seriously.

It was common, of course, for ladies of Eloise's station to spend several hours each week writing letters, but Eloise had long since fallen into the habit of taking that amount of time each day. She enjoyed writing notes, especially to people she hadn't seen in years (she'd always liked to imagine their surprise when they opened her envelope), and so she pulled out her pen and paper for most any occasion—births, deaths, any sort of achievement that deserved congratulations or condolences.

She wasn't sure why she kept sending her missives, just that she spent so much time writing letters to whichever of her siblings were not in residence in London at the time, and it seemed easy enough to pen a short note to some far-off relative while she was seated at her escritoire.

And although everyone penned a short note in reply—she was a Bridgerton, of course, and no one wanted to offend a Bridgerton—never had anyone enclosed a gift, even something so humble as a pressed flower.

Eloise closed her eyes, picturing the delicate pink petals. It was hard to imagine a man handling such a fragile bloom. Her four brothers were all big, strong men, with broad shoulders and large hands that would surely mangle the poor thing in a heartbeat.

She had been intrigued by Sir Phillip's reply, especially his use of the Latin, and she had immediately penned her own response.

Dear Sir Phillip—

Thank you so very much for the charming pressed flower. It was such a lovely surprise when it floated out of the envelope. And such a precious memento of dear Marina, as well.

I could not help but notice your facility with the flower's scientific name. Are you a botanist?

Yours,
Miss Eloise Bridgerton

It was sneaky of her to end her letter with a question. Now the poor man would be forced to respond again.

He did not disappoint her. It had taken only ten days for Eloise to receive his reply.

Dear Miss Bridgerton—

Indeed I am a botanist, trained at Cambridge, although I am not currently connected with any university or scientific board. I conduct experiments here at Romney Hall, in my own greenhouse.

Are you of a scientific bent as well?

Yours,
Sir Phillip Crane

Something about the correspondence was thrilling; perhaps it was simply the excitement of finding someone not related to her who actually seemed eager to conduct a written dialogue. Whatever it was, Eloise wrote back immediately.

Dear Sir Phillip—

Heavens, no, I have not the scientific mind, I'm afraid, although I do have a fair head for sums. My interests lie more in the humanities; you may have noticed that I enjoy penning letters.

Yours in friendship,
Eloise Bridgerton

Eloise hadn't been certain about signing with such an informal salutation, but she decided to err on the side of daring. Sir Phillip was obviously enjoying the correspondence as much as she; surely he wouldn't have finished his missive with a question, otherwise?

Her answer came a fortnight later.

My dear Miss Bridgerton—

Ah, but it is a sort of friendship, isn't it? I confess to a certain measure of isolation here in the country, and if one cannot have a smiling face across one's breakfast table, then one might at least have an amiable letter, don't you agree?

I have enclosed another flower for you. This one is Geranium pratense, more commonly known as the meadow cranesbill.

With great regard,
Phillip Crane

Eloise remembered that day well. She had sat in her chair, the one by the window in her bedchamber, and stared at the carefully pressed purple flower for what seemed like an eternity. Was he attempting to *court* her? Through the post?

And then one day she received a note that was quite different from the rest.

My dear Miss Bridgerton—

We have been corresponding now for quite some time, and although we have never formally met, I feel as if I know you. I hope you feel the same.

Forgive me if I am too bold, but I am writing to invite you to visit me here at Romney Hall. It is my hope that after a suitable period of time, we might decide that we will suit, and you will consent to be my wife.

You will, of course, be properly chaperoned. If you accept my invitation, I will make immediate plans to bring my widowed aunt to Romney Hall.

I do hope you will consider my proposal.

Yours, as always,
Phillip Crane

Eloise had immediately tucked the letter away in a drawer, unable to even fathom his request. He wanted to marry someone he didn't even *know*?

No, to be fair, that wasn't entirely true. They did know one another. They'd said more in the course of a year's correspondence than many husbands and wives did during the entire course of a marriage.

But still, they'd never *met.*

Eloise thought about all of the marriage proposals she'd refused over the years. How many had there been? At least six. Now she couldn't even remember why she'd refused some of them. No reason, really, except that they weren't . . .

Perfect.

Was that so much to expect?

She shook her head, aware that she sounded silly and spoiled. No, she didn't need someone perfect. She just needed someone perfect for her.

She knew what the society matrons said about her. She was too demanding, worse than foolish. She'd end up a spinster—no, they didn't say that anymore. They said she already *was* a spinster, which was true. One didn't reach the age of eight and twenty without hearing that whispered behind one's back.

Or thrown in one's face.

But the funny truth was, Eloise didn't mind her situation. Or at least she hadn't, not until recently.

It had never occurred to her that she'd always be a spinster, and besides, she enjoyed her life quite well. She had the most marvelous family one could imagine—seven brothers and sisters in all, named alphabetically, which put her right in the middle at E, with four older and three younger. Her mother was a delight, and she'd even stopped nagging Eloise about getting married. Eloise still held a prominent place in society; the Bridgertons were universally adored and respected (and occasionally feared), and Eloise's sunny and irrepressible personality was such that everyone sought out her company, spinsterish age or no.

But lately . . .

She sighed, suddenly feeling quite a bit older than her twenty-eight years. Lately she hadn't been feeling so sunny. Lately she'd been starting to think that maybe those crotchety old matrons were right, and she *wasn't* going to find herself a husband. Maybe she had been too picky, too determined to follow the example of her older brothers and sister, all of whom had found a deep and passionate love with their spouses (even if it hadn't necessarily been there at the outset).

Maybe a marriage based on mutual respect and companionship was better than none at all.

But it was difficult to talk about these feelings with anyone. Her mother had spent so many years urging her to find a husband; as much as Eloise adored her, it would be difficult to eat crow and say that she should have listened. Her brothers would have been no help whatsoever. Anthony, the eldest, would probably have taken it upon himself to personally select a suitable mate and then browbeat the poor man into submission. Benedict was too much of a dreamer, and besides, he almost never came down to London anymore, preferring the quiet of the country. As for Colin—well, that was another story entirely, quite worthy of its own paragraph.

She supposed she should have talked to Daphne, but every time she went to see her, her elder sister was so bloody *happy*, so blissfully in love with her husband and her life as mother to her brood of four. How could someone like that possibly offer useful advice to one in Eloise's position? And Francesca seemed half a world away, off in Scotland. Besides, Eloise didn't think it fair to bother her with her silly woes. Francesca had been widowed at the age of twenty-three, for heaven's sake. Eloise's fears and worries seemed terribly inconsequential by comparison.

And maybe all this was why her correspondence with Sir Phillip had become such a guilty pleasure. The Bridgertons were a large family, loud and boisterous. It was nearly impossible to keep anything a secret, especially from her sisters, the youngest of whom—Hyacinth—could probably have won the war against Napoleon in half the time if His Majesty had only thought to draft her into the espionage service.

Sir Phillip was, in his own strange way, hers. The one thing she'd never had to share with anyone. His letters were bundled and tied with a purple ribbon, hidden at the bottom of her middle desk drawer, tucked underneath the piles of stationery she used for her many letters.

He was her secret. *Hers.*

And because she'd never actually met him, she'd been able to create him in her mind, using his letters as the bones and then fleshing him out as she saw fit. If ever there was a perfect man, surely it had to be the Sir Phillip Crane of her imagination.

And now he wanted to meet? *Meet?* Was he mad? And ruin what had to be the perfect courtship?

But then the impossible had occurred. Penelope Featherington, Eloise's closest friend for nearly a dozen years, had married. And what's more, she'd married *Colin*. Eloise's brother!

If the moon had suddenly dropped from the sky and landed in her back garden, Eloise could not have been more surprised.

Eloise was happy for Penelope. Truly, she was. And she was happy for Colin, too. They were quite possibly her two most favorite people in the entire world, and she was thrilled that they had found happiness. No one deserved it more.

But that didn't mean that their marriage hadn't left a hollow spot in her life.

She supposed that when she'd been considering her life as a spinster, and trying to convince herself that it was what she really wanted, Penelope had always been there in the image, spinster right beside her. It was acceptable—almost daring, even—to be twenty-eight and unmarried as long as Penelope was twenty-eight and unmarried, as well. It wasn't that she hadn't *wanted* Penelope to find a husband; it was just that it had never seemed even the least bit likely. *Eloise* knew that Penelope was wonderful and kind and smart and witty, but the gentlemen of the *ton* had never seemed to notice. In all her years in society—eleven in all—Penelope had not received one proposal of marriage. Nor even a whiff of interest.

In a way, Eloise had counted on her to remain where she was, what she was—first and foremost, Eloise's friend. Her companion in spinsterhood.

And the worst part—the part that left Eloise wracked with guilt—was that *she'd* never given a thought to how Penelope might feel if she married first, which, in truth, she'd always supposed she would do.

But now Penelope had Colin, and Eloise could see that the match was a splendid thing. And she was alone. Alone in the middle of crowded London, in the middle of a large and loving family.

It was hard to imagine a lonelier spot.

Suddenly Sir Phillip's bold proposal—tucked away at the very bottom of her bundle, at the bottom of the middle drawer, locked away in a newly purchased safebox, just so that Eloise wouldn't be tempted to look at it six times a day—well, it seemed a bit more intriguing.

More intriguing by the day, frankly, as she grew more and more restless, more dissatisfied with the lot in life that she had to admit she'd chosen.

And so one day, after she'd gone to visit Penelope, only to be informed by the butler that Mr. and Mrs. Bridgerton were not able to receive visitors (uttered in such a way that even Eloise knew what it meant), she made a decision. It was time to take her life into her own hands, time to control her destiny, rather than attending ball after ball in the vain hope that the perfect man would suddenly materialize before her, never mind that there was never anybody new in London, and after a full decade out in society, she'd already met everyone of the appropriate age and gender to marry.

She told herself that this did not mean she *had* to marry Sir Phillip; she was merely investigating what seemed like it might be an excellent possibility. If they did not suit, they would not have to marry; she'd made no promises to him, after all.

But if there was one thing about Eloise, it was that when she made a decision, she acted upon it quickly. No, she reflected with a rather impressive (in her opinion, at least) display of self-honesty, there were *two* things about her that colored her every action—she liked to act quickly and she was tenacious. Penelope had once described her as akin to a dog with a bone.

And Penelope had not been joking.

Once Eloise got her claws into an idea, not even the full force of the Bridgerton family could sway her from her intended goal. (And the Bridgertons constituted a mighty force, indeed.) It was probably just dumb luck that her goals and those of her family had never crossed purposes before, at least not over anything important.

Eloise knew that they would never countenance her going off blindly to meet a man she'd never met. Anthony would have probably demanded that Sir Phillip come to London to meet the entire family en masse, and Eloise couldn't imagine a single scenario more likely to scare off a prospective suitor. The men who'd previously sought her favor were at least familiar with the London scene and knew what they were getting into; poor Sir Phillip, who had—by his own admission in his letters—not set foot in London since his school days, and never participated in the social season, would be ambushed.

So the only option was for her to travel to Gloucestershire, and, as she came to realize after pondering the problem for a few days, she had to do it in secret. If her family knew of her plans, they might very well forbid her to go. Eloise was a worthy opponent, and she might prevail in the end, but it would be a long and painful battle. Not to mention that if they did allow her to go, whether after a protracted battle over the subject or not, they would insist upon sending at least two of their ranks to accompany her.

Eloise shuddered. Those two would most probably be her mother and Hyacinth.

Good gad, no one could fall in love with those two around. No one could even form a mild but lasting attachment, which Eloise thought she might actually be willing to settle for this go-around.

She decided that she would make her escape during her sister Daphne's ball. It was to be a grand affair, with hordes of guests, and just the right amount of noise and confusion to allow her absence to go unnoticed for a good six hours, maybe more. Her mother had always insisted that they be punctual—early, even—when a family member was hosting a social event, so they would surely arrive at Daphne's no later than eight. If she slipped away early on, and the ball did not wind down until the wee hours of the morning . . . well, it would be nearly dawn before anyone realized she was gone, and she could be halfway to Gloucestershire.

And if not halfway, then far enough to ensure that they wouldn't find it too terribly easy to follow her trail.

In the end, it had all proven almost frighteningly easy. Her entire family had been distracted by some grand announcement Colin planned to make, and so all she'd had to do was excuse herself to the ladies' retiring room, slip out the back, and walk the short distance to her own home, where she'd hidden her bags in the back garden. From there, she needed only to walk to the corner, where she'd arranged to have a hired coach waiting.

Goodness, if she'd known it would be this easy to make her own way in the world, she would have done so years ago.

And now here she was, rolling toward Gloucestershire, rolling toward destiny, she supposed—or hoped, she wasn't sure which—with nothing but a few changes of clothing and a pile of letters written to her by a man she'd never met.

A man she hoped she could love.

It was thrilling.

No, it was terrifying.

It was, she reflected, quite possibly the most foolhardy thing she'd done in her life, and she had to admit that she'd made a few foolish decisions in her day.

Or it might just be her only chance at happiness.

Eloise grimaced. She was growing fanciful. That was a bad sign. She needed to approach this adventure with all the practicality and pragmatism with which she always tried to make her decisions. There was still time to turn around. What did she know about this man, really? He'd said quite a lot over the course of a year's correspondence—

He was thirty years of age, two years her elder.

He had attended Cambridge and studied botany.

He had been married to her fourth cousin Marina for eight years, which meant that he'd been twenty-one at his wedding.

He had brown hair.

He had all of his teeth.

He was a baronet.

He lived at Romney Hall, a stone structure built in the eighteenth century near Tetbury, Gloucestershire.

He liked to read scientific treatises and poetry but not novels and definitely not works of philosophy.

He liked the rain.

His favorite color was green.

He had never traveled outside of England.

He did not like fish.

Eloise fought a bubble of nervous laughter. He didn't like *fish*? That was what she knew about him?

"Surely a sound basis for marriage," she muttered to herself, trying to ignore the panic in her voice.

And what did he know about her? What could have possibly led him to propose marriage to a total stranger?

She tried to recall what she had included in her many letters—

She was twenty-eight.

She had brown hair (chestnut, really) and all of her teeth.

She had gray eyes.

She came from a large and loving family.

Her brother was a viscount.

Her father had died when she was but a child, incomprehensibly brought down by a humble bee sting.

She had a tendency to talk too much. (Good God, had she really put that into writing?)

She liked to read poetry and novels but certainly not scientific treatises or works of philosophy.

She had traveled to Scotland, but that was all.

Her favorite color was purple.

She did not like mutton and positively detested blood pudding.

Another little burst of panicked laughter passed over her lips. Put that way, she thought with no small bit of sarcasm, she seemed a fine catch indeed.

She glanced out the window, as if that might possibly give her an indication as to where they were on the road from London to Tetbury.

Rolling green hills looked like rolling green hills looked like rolling green hills, and she could be in Wales, for all she knew.

Frowning, she looked down at the paper in her lap and refolded Sir Phillip's letter. Fitting it back into the ribbon-tied bundle she kept in her valise, she then tapped her fingers against her thighs in a nervous gesture.

She had reason to be nervous.

She had left home and all that was familiar, after all.

She was traveling halfway across England, and no one knew.

No one.

Not even Sir Phillip.

Because in her haste to leave London, she'd neglected to tell him she was coming. It wasn't that she'd *forgotten*; rather, she'd sort of . . . pushed the task aside until it was too late.

If she told him, then she was committed to the plan. This way, she still had the chance to back out at any moment. She told herself it was because she liked to have choices and options, but the truth was, she was quite simply terrified, and she had feared a total loss of her courage.

Besides, he was the one who had requested the meeting. He would be happy to see her.

Wouldn't he?

Phillip rose from bed and pulled open the draperies in his bedchamber, revealing another perfect, sunny day.

Perfect.

He padded over to his dressing room to find some clothes, having long since dismissed the servants who used to perform these duties. He couldn't explain it, but after Marina had died, he hadn't wanted anyone bustling into his bedroom in the morning, yanking open his curtains, and selecting his garments.

He'd even dismissed Miles Carter, who had tried so hard to be a friend after Marina's passing. But somehow the young secretary just made him feel worse, and so he'd sent him on his way, along with six months' pay and a superb letter of reference.

He'd spent his marriage with Marina looking for someone to talk to, since she was so often absent, but now that she was gone, all he wanted was his own company.

He supposed he must have alluded to this in one of his many letters to the mysterious Eloise Bridgerton, because he had sent off his proposal of not-quite-marriage-but-maybe-something-leading-up-to-it over a month ago, and the silence on her part had been deafening, especially since she usually responded to his letters with charming alacrity.

He frowned. The mysterious Eloise Bridgerton wasn't really *so* mysterious. In her letters she seemed quite open and honest and possessed of a positively *sunny* disposition, which, when it all came down to it, was all he really insisted upon in a wife this time around.

He yanked on a work shirt; he planned to spend most of the day in the greenhouse, up to his elbows in dirt. He was rather disappointed that Miss Bridgerton had obviously decided he was some sort of deranged lunatic to be avoided at all costs. She had seemed the perfect solution to his problems. He desperately needed a mother for Amanda and Oliver, but they'd grown so unmanageable that he couldn't imagine any woman willingly agreeing to cleave unto him in marriage and thus bind herself to those two little devils for life (or at least until they reached majority).

Miss Bridgerton was eight and twenty, however; quite obviously a spinster. And she'd been corresponding with a complete stranger for over a year; surely she was a little desperate? Wouldn't she appreciate the chance to find a husband? He had a home, a respectable fortune, and was only thirty years of age. What more could she want?

He muttered several annoyed phrases as he thrust his legs into his rough woolen trousers. Obviously she wanted *some*thing more, else she would have had the courtesy to at least write back and decline.

THUMP!

Phillip glanced up at the ceiling and grimaced. Romney Hall was old and solid and very well built, and if his ceiling was thumping, then his children had dropped (pushed? hurled?) something very large indeed.

THUMP!

He winced. That one sounded even worse. Still, their nurse was up there with them, and she always managed them better than he did. If he could just get his boots on in under a minute, he could be out of the house before they inflicted too much more damage, and thus he could pretend none of it was happening.

He reached for his boots. Yes, excellent idea. Out of earshot, out of mind.

He donned the rest of his ensemble with impressive speed and dashed out into the hall, making quick strides toward the stairs.

"Sir Phillip! Sir Phillip!"

Damn. His butler was after him now.

Phillip pretended he didn't hear.

"Sir Phillip!"

"Curse it," he muttered. There was no way he could ignore that bellow unless he was willing to suffer the torture of his servants hovering over him, concerned about his apparent hearing loss.

"Yes," he said, turning around slowly, "Gunning?"

"Sir Phillip," Gunning said, clearing his throat. "We have a caller."

"A caller?" Phillip echoed. "Was that the source of the, ah . . ."

"Noise?" Gunning supplied helpfully.

"Yes."

"No." The butler cleared his throat. "That would have been your children."

"I see," Phillip murmured. "How silly of me to have hoped otherwise."

"I don't believe they broke anything, sir."

"That's a relief and a change."

"Indeed, sir, but there is the caller to consider."

Phillip groaned. Who on earth was visiting at this time of the morning? It wasn't like they were used to receiving callers even during reasonable hours.

Gunning attempted a smile, but one could see that he was out of practice. "We used to have callers, do you recall?"

That was the problem with butlers who'd worked for the family since before one was born. They tended to think highly of sarcasm.

"Who is this caller?"

"I'm not entirely certain, sir."

"You're not certain?" Phillip asked disbelievingly.

"I didn't inquire."

"Isn't that what butlers are meant to do?"

"Inquire, sir?"

"Yes," Phillip ground out, wondering if Gunning was trying to see how red in the face his employer could get without actually collapsing to the floor in an apoplectic fit.

"I thought I'd let you inquire, sir."

"You thought you'd let me inquire." This one came out as a statement, Phillip having realized the futility of asking questions.

"Yes, sir. She's here to see you, after all."

"So are all of our callers, and that has never stopped you from ascertaining their identities before."

"Well, actually, sir—"

"I'm quite certain—" Phillip tried to interrupt.

"We don't have callers, sir," Gunning finished, quite clearly winning the conversational battle.

Phillip opened his mouth to point out that they *did* have callers, there was one downstairs that very moment; but really, what was the point? "Fine," he said, thoroughly irritated. "I'll go downstairs."

Gunning beamed. "Excellent, sir."

Phillip stared at his butler in shock. "Are you unwell, Gunning?"

"No, sir. Why do you ask, sir?"

It didn't seem quite polite to point out that the broad smile made Gunning look a bit like a horse, so Phillip just muttered, "It's nothing," and headed down the stairs.

A caller? Who would be calling? No one had come to visit in nearly a year, since the neighbors had finished making their obligatory condolence calls. He supposed he couldn't really blame them for staying away; the last time one of them had come to visit, Oliver and Amanda had smeared strawberry jam on the chairs.

Lady Winslet had left in a fit of temper quite beyond anything Phillip would have thought healthy for a woman of her years.

Phillip frowned as he reached the bottom of the stairs and turned into the entry hall. It was a she, wasn't it? Hadn't Gunning said his visitor was a she?

Who the devil—

He stopped short; stumbled, even.

Because the woman standing in his entry hall was young, and quite pretty, and when she looked up to meet his gaze, he saw that she had the largest, most achingly beautiful gray eyes he'd ever seen.

He could drown in those eyes.

And Phillip did not, as one might imagine, even *think* the word *drown* lightly.

Chapter 2

. . . and then, I'm sure you will not be surprised to hear, I talked far too much. I simply couldn't stop talking, but I suppose that is what I do when I am nervous. One can only hope I have less cause for nerves as the rest of my life unfolds.

—from Eloise Bridgerton to her brother Colin, upon the occasion of Eloise's debut into London society

Then she opened her mouth.

"Sir Phillip?" she asked, and before he even had a chance to nod in the affirmative, she said, at quite the speed of lightning, "I'm so terribly sorry to arrive unannounced, but I really had no other option, and to be honest, if I'd sent notice, it probably would have arrived behind me, making the notice really quite moot, as I'm sure you'll agree, and . . ."

Phillip blinked, certain he was supposed to be following what she was saying but no longer able to make out where one word ended and the next began.

". . . a long journey, and I'm afraid I didn't sleep, and so I must beg you to forgive my appearance and . . ."

She was making him dizzy. Would it be rude if he sat down?

". . . didn't bring very much, but I had no choice, and . . ."

This had clearly gone on far too long, with no sign, in truth, that it would ever end. If he allowed her to speak for one moment longer, he was quite certain that he would suffer an inner ear imbalance, or perhaps she would swoon from lack of breath and hit her head on the floor. Either way, one of them would be injured and in debilitating pain.

"Madam," he said, clearing his throat.

If she heard him, she gave no indication, instead saying something about the coach that had apparently conveyed her to his doorstep.

"Madam," he said, a little louder this time.

". . . but then I—" She looked up, blinking those devastating gray eyes at him, and for a moment he felt frighteningly off balance. "Yes?" she asked.

Now that he had her attention, he seemed to have forgotten why he'd sought it. "Er," he asked, "who *are* you?"

She stared at him for a good five seconds, her lips parting with surprise, and then she finally answered, "Eloise Bridgerton, of course."

Eloise was fairly certain she was talking too much, and she *knew* she was talking too fast, but she tended to do that when she was nervous, and while she prided herself on the fact that she was rarely nervous, now seemed like a rather deserving time to explore that emotion, and besides, Sir Phillip—if indeed he was the large bear of a man standing before her—was not *at all* what she had expected.

"*You're* Eloise Bridgerton?"

She looked up into his gaping face and felt the first stirrings of annoyance. "Well, of course I am. Who else would I be?"

"I could not possibly imagine."

"You did invite me," she pointed out.

"And you did not respond to my invitation," he returned.

She swallowed. He had a point there. A rather large one, if one wanted to be fair, which she didn't. Not just then, anyway.

"I didn't really have the opportunity," she hedged, and then, when it seemed from his expression that that wasn't enough explanation, she added, "as I mentioned when I spoke earlier."

He stared at her for longer than made her comfortable, his dark eyes inscrutable, and then he said, "I didn't understand a word you said."

She felt her mouth form an oval of . . . surprise? No, annoyance. "Weren't you listening?" she asked.

"I *tried*."

Eloise pursed her lips. "Very well, then," she said, counting to five in her head—in Latin—before adding, "My apologies. I am sorry to have arrived unannounced. It was dreadfully ill-bred of me."

He was silent for a full three seconds—Eloise counted that as well—before saying, "I accept your apology."

She cleared her throat.

"And of course"—he coughed, glancing around as if in search of someone who might save him from her—"I am delighted that you are here."

It would probably be impolite to point out that he sounded *anything* but delighted, so Eloise just stood there, staring at his right cheekbone as she tried to decide what she *could* say without insulting him.

Eloise considered it a sad state of affairs that she—who generally had something to say for any occasion—couldn't think of a thing.

Luckily, he saved their awkward silence from growing to monumental proportions by asking, "Is this all of your luggage?"

Eloise straightened her shoulders, delighted to move on to a comparatively trivial topic. "Yes. I didn't really—" She broke herself off. Did she really need to tell him that she'd stolen away from home in the middle of the night? It didn't seem to speak well of her, or of her family, for that matter. She wasn't sure why, but she didn't want him to know that she had, for all intents and purposes, run away. She wasn't certain why she thought so, but she had a distinct feeling that if he knew the truth, he'd pack her up and send her back to London posthaste. And while her meeting with Sir Phillip had not thus far proven to be the stuff of romance and bliss she'd imagined it to be, she was not yet prepared to give up.

Especially when that meant running back to her family with her tail between her legs.

"This is all I have," she said firmly.

"Good. I, er . . ." He looked around again, this time a little desperately, which Eloise did not find flattering in the least. "Gunning!" he bellowed.

The butler appeared so quickly that he must have been eavesdropping. "Yes, sir?"

"We . . . ah . . . need to prepare a room for Miss Bridgerton."

"I have already done so," Gunning assured him.

Sir Phillip's cheeks colored slightly. "Good," he grunted. "She will be staying here for . . ." He looked to her in askance.

"A fortnight," she supplied, hoping that was about the right amount of time.

"A fortnight," Sir Phillip reiterated as if the butler wouldn't have heard her reply. "We will do everything in our power to make her comfortable, of course."

"Of course," the butler agreed.

"Good," Sir Phillip said, still looking somewhat uncomfortable with the entire situation. Or if not uncomfortable, precisely, then perhaps weary, which might have been even worse.

Eloise was disappointed. She'd pictured him as a man of easy charm, rather like her brother Colin, who possessed a dashing smile and always knew what to say in any situation, awkward or otherwise.

Sir Phillip, on the other hand, looked as if he'd rather be anywhere else but where he was, which Eloise did not find encouraging, as his present surroundings included her. And what's more, he was supposed to be making at least some effort to make her acquaintance and determine if she would make him an acceptable wife.

And his efforts had better be good ones indeed, because if it was true that first impressions were the most accurate, she rather doubted that she would determine that *he* would make an acceptable husband.

She smiled at him through gritted teeth.

"Would you like to sit down?" he blurted out.

"That would be quite pleasing, thank you."

He looked around with a blank expression on his face, giving Eloise the impression he barely knew his way around his own house. "Here," he mumbled, motioning to a door at the end of the hall, "the drawing room."

Gunning coughed.

Sir Phillip looked at him and scowled.

"Perhaps you intended to order refreshments, sir?" the butler asked solicitously.

"Er, yes, of course," Sir Phillip replied, clearing his throat. "Of course. Er, perhaps . . ."

"A tea tray, perhaps?" Gunning suggested. "With muffins?"

"Excellent," Sir Phillip muttered.

"Or perhaps if Miss Bridgerton is hungry," the butler continued, "I could have a more extensive breakfast prepared."

Sir Phillip swung his gaze over to Eloise.

"Muffins will be lovely," she said, even though she *was* hungry.

Eloise allowed Sir Phillip to take her arm and lead her to the drawing room, where she sat on a sofa covered in striped blue satin. The room was neat and clean, but the furnishings were shabby. The entire house had a vague neglected quality to it, as if the owner had run out of money, or perhaps just didn't care.

Eloise tended to think that it was the latter. She supposed it was possible that Sir Phillip was short of funds, but the grounds had been magnificent, and she had seen enough of his greenhouse as she was driving in to realize that it was in excellent condition. Given that Sir Phillip was a botanist, that might explain the great care given to the exterior while the interior was left to fade.

Clearly, he needed a wife.

She folded her hands in her lap, then watched as he took a seat across from her, folding his large frame into a chair that had obviously been designed for one much smaller than he.

He looked most uncomfortable and (and Eloise had enough brothers to recognize the signs) rather like he wanted desperately to curse, but Eloise decided it was his own fault for choosing that chair, and so she smiled at him in what she hoped was a polite and encouraging manner, waiting for him to begin the conversation.

He cleared his throat.

She leaned forward.

He cleared his throat again.

She coughed.

He cleared his throat once more.

"Do you need some tea?" she finally asked, unable to bear even the thought of one more *ahem*.

He looked up gratefully, although Eloise wasn't certain whether that was due to her offer of tea or her merciful breaking of the silence. "Yes," he said, "that would be lovely."

Eloise opened her mouth to reply, then remembered she was in *his* house and had no business offering tea. Not to mention that he ought to have remembered that fact as well. "Right," she said. "Well, I'm sure it will be here soon."

"Right," he agreed, shifting in his seat.

"I'm sorry to have come by unannounced," she murmured, even though she'd already said as much. But something *had* to be said; Sir Phillip might be well used to awkward pauses, but Eloise was the sort who liked to fill any silence.

"It's quite all right," he said.

"It's not, actually," she replied. "It was terribly ill-mannered of me to do so, and I apologize."

He looked startled at her frankness. "Thank you," he murmured. "It is no problem, I assure you. I was merely . . ."

"Surprised?" she offered.

"Yes."

She nodded. "Yes, well, anyone would have been. I should have thought of that, and I truly am sorry for the inconvenience."

He opened his mouth, but then closed it, instead glancing out the window. "It's a sunny day," he said.

"Yes, it is," Eloise agreed, thinking that quite obvious.

He shrugged. "I imagine it will still rain by nightfall."

She wasn't quite certain how to respond to that, so she just nodded, surreptitiously studying him while his gaze was still fixed on the window. He was bigger than she'd imagined him, rougher-looking, less urbane. His letters had been so charming and well written; she'd pictured him to be more . . . smooth. More slender, perhaps, certainly not given to fat, but still, less muscled. He looked as if he worked outside like a laborer, especially in those rough trousers and shirt with no cravat. And even though he'd written that his hair was brown, she'd always imagined him as a dark blond, looking rather like a poet (why she always pictured poets with blond hair she did not know). But his hair was exactly as he'd described it—brown, a rather dark shade, actually, bordering on black, with an unruly wave to it. His eyes were brown, much the same shade as his hair, so dark they were utterly unreadable.

She frowned. She hated people she couldn't figure out in a heartbeat.

"Did you travel all night?" he inquired politely.

"I did."

"You must be tired."

She nodded. "I am, quite."

He stood, motioning gallantly to the door. "Would you prefer to rest? I don't wish to keep you here if you'd rather sleep."

Eloise was exhausted, but she was also ferociously hungry. "I'll have just a bite to eat first," she said, "and then I would be grateful to accept your hospitality and rest."

He nodded and started to sit down, trying to fold himself back into the ridiculously small chair, then finally muttering something under his breath, turning to her with a slightly more intelligible, "Excuse me," and moving to another, larger chair.

"I beg your pardon," he said, once he was settled.

Eloise just nodded at him, wondering when she had ever found herself in a more awkward situation.

He cleared his throat. "Er, was your journey a pleasant one?"

"Indeed," she replied, mentally giving him credit for at least trying to keep up a conversation. One good turn deserved another, so she made her contribution with, "You have a lovely home."

He raised a brow at that, giving her a look that said he didn't believe her false flattery for a second.

"The grounds are magnificent," she added hastily. Who would have thought that he'd actually know his furnishings were faded? Men never noticed such things.

"Thank you," he said. "I am a botanist, as you know, and so I spend a great deal of my time out-of-doors."

"Were you planning to work outside today?"

He answered in the affirmative.

Eloise offered him a tentative smile. "I'm sorry to have disrupted your schedule."

"It is nothing, I assure you."

"But—"

"You really needn't apologize again," he cut in. "For anything."

And then there was that awful silence again, with both of them looking longingly at the door, waiting for Gunning to return with salvation in the form of a tea tray.

Eloise tapped her hands against the cushion of the sofa in a manner that her mother would have deemed horribly ill-bred. She looked over at Sir Phillip and was somewhat gratified to see that he was doing the same. Then he caught her looking and quirked an irritating half-smile as his gaze dropped down to her restless hand.

She stilled herself immediately.

She looked over at him, silently daring—imploring?—him to *say* something. Anything.

He didn't.

This was killing her. She had to break the silence. This was not natural. It was too awful. People were meant to *talk*. This was—

She opened her mouth, driven by a desperation she didn't quite understand. "I—"

But before she could continue on with a sentence she fully intended to make up as she went along, a bloodcurdling scream ripped through the air.

Eloise jumped to her feet. "What was—"

"My children," Sir Phillip said, letting out a haggard sigh.

"You have *children*?"

He noticed that she was standing and rose wearily to his feet. "Of course."

She gaped at him. "You never said you had children."

His eyes narrowed. "Is that a problem?" he asked, quite sharply.

"Of course it isn't!" she said, bristling. "I adore children. I have more nieces and nephews than I can count, and I can assure you that I am their *favorite* aunt. But that does not excuse the fact that you did not mention their existence."

"That is impossible," he said, shaking his head. "You must have overlooked it."

Her chin jerked back so suddenly it was a wonder she didn't snap her neck. "That is not," she said haughtily, "the sort of thing I would overlook."

He shrugged, clearly dismissing her protest.

"You never mentioned them," she said, "and I can prove it."

He crossed his arms, giving her a patently disbelieving look.

She marched to the door. "Where is my valise?"

"Right where you left it, I imagine," he said, watching her with a condescending expression. "Or more likely already up in your room. My servants are not *that* inattentive."

She turned to him with a scowl. "I have every single one of your letters with me, and I can assure you, not one of them contains the words, 'my children.' "

Phillip's lips parted in surprise. "You saved my letters?"

"Of course. Didn't you save mine?"

He blinked. "Uh . . ."

She gasped. "You didn't save them?"

Phillip had never understood women and half the time was quite willing to put aside all current medical thought and declare them a separate species altogether. He fully accepted that he rarely knew what one was supposed to say to them, but this time even he knew he had blundered badly. "I'm sure I have some of them," he tried.

Her jaw clamped into a straight angry line.

"Most of them, I'm sure," he added hastily.

She looked mutinous. Eloise Bridgerton, he was coming to realize, had a formidable will.

"It's not that I would have disposed of them," he said, trying to dig his way out of his bottomless pit. "It is just that I'm not certain precisely where I put them."

He watched with interest as she gained control of her anger, then let out a short breath. Her eyes, however, remained a stormy gray. "Very well," she said. "It hardly signifies, anyway."

Exactly his opinion, Phillip thought, but even he was smart enough not to say so.

Besides, her tone made it quite clear that in her opinion, it did signify. A great deal.

Another scream rent the air, followed by a resounding crash. Phillip winced. It sounded like furniture.

Eloise glanced toward the ceiling, as if expecting plaster to start spinning down at any moment. "Shouldn't you go to them?" she asked.

He should, but by all that was holy, he didn't want to. When the twins were out of control, no one could manage them, which, Phillip supposed, was the definition of "out of control." It was his opinion that it was generally easier to let them run wild until they dropped from exhaustion (which usually didn't take too long) and deal with them then. It probably wasn't the most beneficial course of action, and certainly nothing that any other parent would have recommended, but a man only had so much energy to deal with two eight-year-olds, and he feared he'd run out of his a good six months ago.

"Sir Phillip?" Eloise prodded.

He let out a breath. "You're right, of course." It certainly wouldn't do to appear a disinterested parent in front of Miss Bridgerton, whom he was trying to woo, however clumsily, into the position of mother to the two hellions presently attempting the complete destruction of his home. "If you will excuse me," he said, giving her a nod as he stepped into the hall.

"Oliver!" he bellowed. "Amanda!"

He wasn't sure, but he thought he heard Miss Bridgerton stifle a horrified laugh.

A wave of irritation washed over him, and he glared at her, even though he knew he shouldn't. He supposed she thought she could do a better job with those two hellions.

He strode to the stairs and yelled the twins' names again. On the other hand, maybe he shouldn't be so uncharitable. He rather hoped—no, fervently prayed—that Eloise Bridgerton could do a better job with the twins than he could.

Good God, if she could teach them to mind, he would bloody well kiss the ground she walked upon on a thrice-daily schedule.

Oliver and Amanda rounded the corner in the staircase and descended the rest of the way down to the hall, looking not a bit sheepish.

"What," Phillip demanded, "was that all about?"

"What was what all about?" Oliver replied cheekily.

"The screaming," Phillip ground out.

"That was Amanda," Oliver said.

"It certainly was," she agreed.

Phillip waited for further elucidation, and when it appeared that none was forthcoming, he added, "And *why* was Amanda screaming?"

"It was a frog," she explained.

"A frog."

She nodded. "Indeed. In my bed."

"I see," Phillip said. "Do you have any idea how it got there?"

"I put it there," she replied.

He swung his gaze off of Oliver, to whom he'd addressed his question, and back to Amanda. "You put a frog in your own bed?"

She nodded.

Why why *why*? He cleared his throat. "Why?"

She shrugged. "I wanted to."

Phillip felt his chin thrust forward in disbelief. "You wanted to?"

"Yes."

"Put a frog in your bed?"

"I was trying to grow tadpoles," she explained.

"In your bed?"

"It seemed warm and cozy."

"I helped," Oliver put in.

"Of that I had no doubt," Phillip said in a tight voice. "But why did you scream?"

"I didn't scream," Oliver said indignantly. "Amanda did."

"I was asking Amanda!" Phillip said, just barely resisting the urge to throw his arms up in defeat and retire to his greenhouse.

"You were looking at me, sir," Oliver said. And then, as if his father were too dim to understand what he meant, he added, "When you asked the question."

Phillip took a deep breath before schooling his features into what he hoped was a patient expression and turned back to Amanda. "Why, *Amanda*, did you scream?"

She shrugged. "I forgot I put the frog there."

"I thought she was going to *die*!" Oliver put in, most dramatically.

Phillip decided not to pursue that statement. "I thought," he said, crossing his arms and leveling his sternest gaze at his children, "that we had said no frogs in the house."

"No," Oliver said (with vehement nodding from Amanda), "you said no *toads*."

"No amphibians of any kind," Phillip ground out.

"But what if one of them is dying?" Amanda asked, her pretty blue eyes filling with tears.

"Not even then."

"But—"

"You may tend to it outside."

"What if it's cold and freezing and only needs my care and a warm bed inside the house?"

"Frogs are supposed to be cold and freezing," Phillip shot back. "It's why they are amphibians."

"But what if—"

"*No!*" he bellowed. "No frogs, toads, crickets, grasshoppers, or animals of any kind in the house!"

Amanda started gulping for air. "But but but—"

Phillip let out a long sigh. He never knew what to say to his children, and now his daughter looked as if she might dissolve into a pool of tears. "For the love of—" He caught himself just in time and softened his voice. "What is it, Amanda?"

She gasped, then sobbed, "What about Bessie?"

Phillip felt around unsuccessfully for a wall to sag against. "Naturally," he ground out, "I did not intend to include our beloved spaniel in that statement."

"Well, I wish you'd said so," Amanda sniffed, looking surprisingly—and suspiciously—recovered. "You made me extremely sad."

Phillip gritted his teeth. "I am sorry I made you feel sad."

She nodded at him like a queen.

Phillip groaned. When had the twins gained the upper hand in the conversation? Surely a man of his size and (he'd like to think, anyway) intellect, ought to be able to manage two eight-year-olds.

But no, once again, despite his best intentions, he'd lost all control of the conversation and now he was actually apologizing to *them*.

Nothing made him feel more like a failure.

"Right, then," he said, eager to be done. "Run along. I'm very busy."

They stood there for a moment, just looking up at him with wide, blinking eyes. "All day?" Oliver finally asked.

"All day?" Phillip echoed. What the devil was he talking about?

"Are you going to be busy all day?" Oliver amended.

"Yes," he said sharply, "I am."

"What if we went on a nature walk?" Amanda suggested.

"I can't," he said, even though part of him wanted to. But the twins were so vexing, and they were sure to force him to lose his temper, and nothing terrified him more.

"We could help you in the greenhouse," Oliver said.

Destroy it was more like it. "No," Phillip said. He honestly didn't think he could answer to his temper if they ruined his work.

"But—"

"I can't," he snapped, hating the tone of his voice.

"But—"

"And who is this?" came a voice from behind him.

He turned around. It was Eloise Bridgerton, sticking her nose into what was assuredly not her business, and this after arriving on his doorstep without even so much as a hint of warning.

"I beg your pardon," he said to her, not bothering to hide the irritation in his voice.

She ignored him and faced the twins. "And who might you be?" she asked.

"Who are you?" Oliver demanded.

Amanda's eyes narrowed into slits.

Phillip allowed himself his first true grin of the morning and crossed his arms. Yes, let's see how Miss Bridgerton handled *this*.

"I am Miss Bridgerton," she said.

"You're not our new governess, are you?" Oliver asked, with suspicion bordering on venom.

"Heavens, no," she replied. "What happened to your last governess?"

Phillip coughed. Loudly.

The twins took the hint. "Er, nothing," Oliver said.

Miss Bridgerton didn't look the least bit fooled by the air of innocence the twins were trying to convey, but she wisely did not choose to pursue the subject, and instead just said, "I am your guest."

The twins pondered that for a moment, and then Amanda said, "We don't want any guests."

Followed by Oliver's, "We don't *need* any guests."

"Children!" Phillip interjected, not really wanting to take Miss Bridgerton's side after she'd been so meddlesome, but really having no other choice. He couldn't let his children be so rude.

The twins crossed their arms in unison and gave Miss Bridgerton the cut direct.

"That's it," Phillip boomed. "You will apologize to Miss Bridgerton at once."

They stared at her mutinously.

"Now!" he roared.

"Sorry," they mumbled, but no one could ever have mistaken them for meaning it.

"Back to your room, the both of you," Phillip said sharply.

They marched off like a pair of proud soldiers, noses in the air. It would have been quite an impressive sight, if Amanda hadn't turned around at the bottom of the stairs and stuck out her tongue.

"Amanda!" he bellowed, striding toward her.

She tore up the stairs with the speed of a fox.

Phillip held himself very still for several moments, his hands fisted and shaking at his sides. Just once—*once!*—he would like his children to behave and mind and not answer a question with a question and be polite to guests and not stick out their tongues, and—

Just once, he'd like to feel that he was a good father, that he knew what he was doing.

And not raise his voice. He hated when he raised his voice, hated the flash of terror he thought he saw in their eyes.

Hated the memories it brought back for him.

"Sir Phillip?"

Miss Bridgerton. Damn, he'd almost forgotten she was there. He turned around. "Yes?" he asked, mortified that she'd witnessed his humiliation. Which of course made him irritated with her.

"Your butler brought the tea tray," she said, motioning to the drawing room.

He gave her a curt nod. He needed to get outside. Away from his children, away from the woman who'd seen what a terrible father he was to them. It had started to rain, but he didn't care.

"I hope you enjoy your breakfast," he said. "I will see you after you have rested."

And then he made haste out the door, making his way to his greenhouse, where he could be alone with his nonspeaking, non-misbehaving, nonmeddlesome plants.

Chapter 3

. . . you will see why I could not accept his suit. He was too churlish by half and positively possessed of a foul temper. I should like to marry someone gracious and considerate, who treats me like a queen. Or at the very least, a princess. Surely that is not too much to ask.

—from Eloise Bridgerton to her dear friend Penelope Featherington, sent by messenger after Eloise received her first proposal of marriage

By afternoon, Eloise was almost convinced that she had made a terrible mistake.

And in truth, the sole reason she was only *almost* convinced was that the only thing she hated more than making mistakes was the admission thereof. So she was trying to maintain a proverbial stiff upper lip and forcing herself to pretend that this ghastly situation might all work itself out in the end.

She had been left stunned—openmouthed, even—when Sir Phillip had departed with barely more than an "Enjoy your food" and then stalked out the door. She had traveled halfway across England, answering *his* invitation to come and visit, and he left her alone in the drawing room a mere half hour after she arrived?

She hadn't expected him to fall in love at first sight and drop to his knees, professing his undying devotion, but she'd hoped for a little bit more than a curt "Who are you?" and "Enjoy your food."

Or maybe she *had* expected him to fall in love at the first sight of her. She'd built an elaborate dream around her image of this man—an image which she now knew to be untrue. She'd let herself mold him into the perfect man, and it hurt so much to learn that he wasn't just imperfect, he was quite close to abysmal.

And the worst was—she had only herself to blame. Sir Phillip had never misrepresented himself in his letters (although she did think he ought to have mentioned that he was a father, especially before he'd proposed marriage).

Her dreams had been just that—dreams. Wishful illusions, all of her own making. If he wasn't what she'd expected, that was her fault. She'd been expecting something that didn't even exist.

And she should have known better.

What's more, he didn't seem to be a very good father, which was as black a mark as anyone could get in her book.

No, she wasn't being fair. She shouldn't judge him so quickly on that score. The children didn't look ill-treated or malnourished or anything so dire, but Sir Phillip clearly had no idea how to manage them. He had handled them all wrong this morning, and it was clear from the way they behaved that his relationship with them was distant at best.

Good heavens, they had practically begged him to spend the day with them. Any child who actually received enough attention from his parents would never act in such a way. Eloise and her siblings had spent half their childhood trying to avoid their parents—lack of supervision being, of course, more conducive for mischief.

Her own father had been splendid. She had been only seven when he'd died, but she remembered him well, from the stories he wove at bedtime to the hikes they had taken across the fields of Kent, sometimes with all the Bridgertons in tow, sometimes just with one lucky child, chosen for some special alone time with Father.

It was clear to her that if she hadn't suggested to Sir Phillip that he find out why his children were screaming and knocking over the furniture, he would have left them to their own devices. Or, more to the point, left them to be someone else's problem. And by the end of their conversation, it was apparent that Sir Phillip's main aim in life was to avoid his children.

Which Eloise did not approve of at all.

She pushed herself off her bed, forcing herself upright even though she was bone-tired. But every time she laid down, something began to quicken in her lungs, and she felt herself gasping in that awful precursor to not just tears, but true, body-shaking sobs. If she didn't get up and do something, she wasn't going to be able to control herself.

And she didn't think she could bear herself if she cried.

She wrenched the window open, even though it was still gray and drizzling outside. There was no wind, so the rain ought not to blow in, and what she really needed right now was a bit of fresh air. A slap of cold on her face might not make her feel better, but it certainly wasn't going to make her feel worse.

From her window she could see Sir Phillip's greenhouse. She assumed that was where he was, since she hadn't heard him here in the house, stomping about and bellowing at his children. The glass was fogged up and the only thing she could see was a blurry curtain of green—his beloved plants, she supposed. What sort of man was he, that he preferred plants to people? Certainly not anyone who appreciated a fine conversation.

She felt her shoulders sag. Eloise had spent half her life in search of a fine conversation.

And if he was such a hermit, why had he bothered to write her back? He had worked just as hard as she had to perpetuate their correspondence. Not to mention his proposal. If he hadn't wanted company, he had no business inviting her here.

She took a few deep breaths of the misty air and then forced herself to stand up straight. She wasn't certain what she was expected to do with herself all day. She'd taken a nap already; exhaustion had quickly won out over misery. But no one had come by to inform her of lunch or of any other plans that might extend to her as a houseguest.

If she stayed here, in this slightly drab and drafty room, she was going to go mad. Or at the very least cry herself into oblivion, which was something she did not tolerate in others, so the thought of doing it herself was horrifying.

There was no reason she couldn't explore the house a bit, was there? And maybe she could find herself some food along the way. She'd eaten all four muffins on the tea tray this morning, all with as much butter and marmalade as she could politely slather on, but she was still famished. At this point she thought she might be willing to commit violence for a ham sandwich.

She changed her clothing, donning a dress of peach muslin that was pretty and feminine without being too frilly. And most importantly, it was easy to get on and off, surely a critical factor when one had run from home without a lady's maid.

A quick glance in the mirror told her that she looked presentable, if no picture of ravishing beauty, and so she stepped out into the hall.

Only to be immediately confronted by the eight-year-old Crane twins, looking very much as if they'd been lying in wait for hours.

"Good afternoon," Eloise said, waiting for them to come to their feet. "How nice of you to greet me."

"We're not here to *greet* you," Amanda blurted out, grunting when Oliver elbowed her in the ribs.

"You're not?" Eloise asked, trying to sound surprised. "Are you here, then, to show me to the dining room? I'm quite hungry, I must say."

"No," Oliver said, crossing his arms.

"Not even that?" Eloise mused. "Let me guess. You're here to take me to your room and show me your toys."

"No," they said, in unison.

"Then it must be to take me on a tour of the house. It's quite large and I might lose my way."

"No."

"No? You wouldn't want me to lose my way, would you?"

"No," Amanda said. "I mean yes!"

Eloise feigned incomprehension. "You want me to lose my way?"

Amanda nodded. Oliver just tightened his arms across his chest and speared her with a sullen stare.

"Hmmm. That's interesting, but it hardly explains your presence right here outside my door, does it? I'm not likely to get lost in the company of you two."

Their lips parted in befuddled surprise.

"You do know your way around the house, don't you?"

"Of course," Oliver grunted, followed by Amanda's, "We're not babies."

"No, I can see that," Eloise said with a thoughtful nod. "Babies wouldn't be allowed to wait by themselves outside my door, after all. They'd be quite busy with nappies and bottles and the like."

They had nothing to add to that.

"Does your father know you're here?"

"He's busy."

"Very busy."

"He's a very busy man."

"Much too busy for *you*."

Eloise watched and listened with interest as the twins shot off their lightning-fast statements, falling all over themselves to demonstrate how busy Sir Phillip was.

"So what you're telling me," Eloise said, "is that your father is busy."

They stared at her, momentarily dumbfounded by her calm retelling of the facts, then nodded.

"But that still doesn't explain your presence," Eloise mused. "Because I don't think your father sent you here in his stead. . . ." She waited until they shook their heads in the negative, then added, "Unless . . . I know!" she said in an excited voice, allowing herself a mental smile over her cleverness. She had nine nephews and nieces. She knew *exactly* how to talk to children. "You're here to tell me you have magical powers and can predict the weather."

"No," they said, but Eloise heard a giggle.

"No? That's a shame, because this constant drizzle is miserable, don't you think?"

"No," Amanda said, quite forcefully. "Father likes the rain, and so do we."

"He likes the rain?" Eloise asked in surprise. "How very odd."

"No, it's not," Oliver replied, his stance defensive. "My father isn't odd. He's perfect. Don't say mean things about him."

"I didn't," Eloise replied, wondering what on earth was going on now. At first she'd merely thought the twins were here to frighten her away. Presumably, they had heard that their father was thinking of marrying her and wanted no part of a stepmother, especially given the stories Eloise had been told by the housemaid of the succession of poor, abused governesses who had come and gone.

But if that were the simple truth, wouldn't they want her to think there was something wrong with Sir Phillip? If they wanted her gone, wouldn't they be trying to convince her that he would be a terrible candidate for marriage?

"I assure you, I harbor no ill will toward any of you," Eloise said. "In fact, I barely know your father."

"If you make Father sad, I will . . . I will . . ."

Eloise watched the poor little boy's face grow red with frustration as he fought for words and bravado. Carefully, gently, she crouched next to him until her face was on a level with his and said, "Oliver, I promise you, I am not here to make your father sad." He said nothing, so she turned to his twin and asked, "Amanda?"

"You need to go," Amanda blurted out, her arms crossed so tightly that her face was turning red. "We don't want you here."

"Well, I'm not going anywhere for at least a week," Eloise told them, keeping her voice firm. The children needed sympathy, and probably a great deal of love as well, but they also needed a bit of discipline and a clear idea of who was in charge.

And then, out of nowhere, Oliver hurled himself forward and pushed her hard, with both hands against her chest.

Her balance was precarious, crouching as she was on the balls of her feet. Eloise toppled over backward, landing most inelegantly on her bottom and rolling back until she was quite certain the twins had received a nice look at her petticoats.

"Well," she declared, rising to her feet and crossing her arms as she stared sternly down at them. They had both taken several steps back and were staring at her with a mixture of glee and horror, as if they couldn't quite believe that one of them had had the nerve to push her over. "That," Eloise continued, "was inadvisable."

"Are you going to hit us?" Oliver asked. His voice was defiant, but there was a hint of fright there, as if someone *had* hit them before.

"Of course not," Eloise said quickly. "I don't believe in striking children. I don't believe in striking anyone." *Except people who strike children*, she added to herself.

They looked somewhat relieved to hear it.

"I might remind you, however," Eloise continued, "that you struck me first."

"I pushed you," he corrected.

She allowed herself a tiny groan. She ought to have anticipated that one. "If you do not want people striking you, you ought to practice the same philosophy."

"The Golden Rule," Amanda piped up.

"Exactly," Eloise said with a wide smile. She rather doubted she'd changed the course of their lives with one little lesson, but nonetheless it was nice to hope that something she'd said provoked some consideration.

"But doesn't that mean," Amanda said thoughtfully, "that you should go home?"

Eloise felt her small moment of elation crumbling to dust, as she tried to imagine what leap of logic Amanda was about to embark upon to explain why Eloise should be banished to the Amazon.

"We're home," Amanda said, sounding exceedingly supercilious for an eight-year-old. Or maybe she was supercilious as *only* an eight-year-old could be. "So you should go home."

"It doesn't work that way," Eloise said sharply.

"Yes, it does," Amanda replied with a smug little nod. "Do unto others as you would like done to you. *We* haven't gone to your house, so you shouldn't come to ours."

"You're very clever, did you know that?" Eloise asked.

Amanda looked as if she wanted to nod, but she was clearly too suspicious of Eloise's compliment to accept it.

Eloise bent down so that they were face-to-face, all three of them. "But I," she said to them in a very serious—and slightly defiant—voice, "am very clever, too."

They stared at her with wide eyes, their mouths hanging slack as they regarded this person who was clearly so different from any other adult they'd ever met.

"Do we understand each other?" Eloise asked, straightening her spine and smoothing her hands along her skirts in a deceptively casual manner.

They said nothing, so she decided to answer for them. "Good," she said. "Now, then, would you like to show me where the dining room is? I'm famished."

"We have lessons," Oliver said.

"You do?" Eloise asked, arching her brows. "How interesting. Then you must return to them at once. I imagine you've fallen behind after spending so long waiting outside my door."

"How did you know—" Amanda's question was cut short by Oliver's elbow in her ribs.

"I have seven brothers and sisters," Eloise answered, deciding that Amanda's question deserved an answer, even if her brother hadn't allowed her to finish her sentence. "There isn't much about this sort of warfare that I don't already know."

But as the twins scurried down the hall, Eloise was left chewing her lower lip in apprehension. She had a feeling she shouldn't have ended their encounter with such a challenge. She had practically dared Oliver and Amanda to find a way to evict her from the premises.

And while she was quite certain they wouldn't succeed—she was a Bridgerton, after all, and made of sterner stuff than those two even knew existed—she had a feeling that they would throw every fiber of their being into the task.

Eloise shuddered. Eels in the bed, hair dipped in ink, jam on chairs. It had all been done to her at one point or another, and she didn't particularly relish a repeat performance—and certainly not by a pair of children twenty years her junior.

She sighed, wondering what it was she had gotten herself into. She had better find Sir Phillip and get to the task of deciding whether they would suit. Because if she really was leaving in a week or two, never to see any of the Cranes again, she wasn't sure that she wanted to put herself through the trouble of mice and spiders and salt in the sugar bowl.

Her stomach rumbled. Whether it was the thought of salt or sugar that did it, Eloise didn't know. But it was definitely time to find something to eat. And better sooner than later, before the twins had a chance to figure out how to poison her food.

Phillip knew that he'd blundered badly. But deuce it, the bloody woman had given him no warning. If she'd only alerted him of her arrival, he could have prepared himself, thought of a few poetic things to say. Did she really think he'd scribbled all those letters without laboring over every word? He'd never sent out the first draft of any of his missives (although he always wrote it on his best paper, each time hoping that this would be the time he'd get it right on the first try).

Hell, if she'd given him warning, he might have even summoned a romantic gesture or two. Flowers would have been nice, and heaven knew, if there was one thing he was good at, it was flowers.

But instead, she'd simply appeared before him as if conjured from a dream, and he'd mucked everything up.

And it hadn't helped that Miss Eloise Bridgerton was *not* what he had expected.

She was a twenty-eight-year-old spinster, for heaven's sake. She was supposed to be unattractive. Horse-faced, even. Instead she was—

Well, he wasn't exactly certain how one could describe her. Not beautiful, precisely, but still somehow stunning, with thick chestnut hair and eyes of the clearest, crispest gray. She was the sort of woman whose expressions made her beautiful. There was intelligence in her eyes, curiosity in the way she cocked her head to the side. Her features were unique, almost exotic, with her heart-shaped face and wide smile.

Not that he'd seen much of that smile. His less-than-legendary charm had seen to that.

He jammed his hands into a pile of moist soil and scooped some into a small clay pot, leaving it loosely packed for optimal root growth. What the devil was he going to do now? He'd pinned his hopes on his mirage of Miss Eloise Bridgerton, based upon the letters she'd sent to him over the past year. He didn't have time (nor, in truth, the inclination) to court a prospective mother for the twins, so it had seemed perfect (not to mention almost easy) to woo her through letters.

Surely an unmarried woman rapidly approaching the age of thirty would be gratified to receive a proposal of marriage. He hadn't expected her to accept his offer without meeting with him, of course, and he wasn't prepared to formally commit to the idea without making her acquaintance, either. But he *had* expected that she would be someone who was at least a little bit desperate for a husband.

Instead, she'd arrived looking young and pretty and smart and self-confident, and good God, but *why* would a woman like that want to marry someone she didn't even know? Not to mention tie herself to a decidedly rural estate in the farthest corner of Gloucestershire. Phillip might know less than nothing about fashion, but even he could tell that her garments had been well made and most probably of the latest style. She was going to expect trips to London, an active social life, friends.

None of which she was likely to find here at Romney Hall.

It seemed almost useless to even try to make her acquaintance. She wasn't going to stay, and he'd be foolish to get his hopes up.

He groaned, then cursed for good measure. Now he was going to have to court some other woman. Curse it, now he was going to have to *find* some other woman to court, which was going to be nearly as difficult. No one in the district would even look at him. All of the unmarried ladies knew about the twins, and there wasn't a one of them willing to take on the responsibility of his little devils.

He'd pinned all of his hopes on Miss Bridgerton, and now it seemed that he was going to have to give up on her as well.

He set his pot down too hard on a shelf, wincing as the clatter of it rang through the greenhouse.

With a loud sigh, he dunked his muddy hands into a bucket of already dirtied water to wash them off. He'd been rude this morning. He was still rather irritated that she'd come out here and wasted his time—or if she hadn't wasted it yet, she was almost certainly *going* to waste it, since she wasn't likely to turn around and leave this evening.

But that didn't excuse his behavior. It wasn't her fault he couldn't manage his own children, and it certainly wasn't her fault that this failing always put him in a foul mood.

Wiping his hands on a towel he kept by the door, he strode out into the drizzle and made his way to the house. It was probably time for luncheon, and it wouldn't hurt anyone to sit down with her at the table and make polite conversation.

Plus, she was *here*. After all his effort with the letters, it seemed foolish not to at least see if they might get on well enough for marriage. Only an idiot would send her packing—or allow her to leave—without even ascertaining her suitability.

It was unlikely that she would stay, but not, he reckoned, impossible, and he might at least give it a try.

He made his way through the misty drizzle and into the house, wiping his feet on the mat that the housekeeper always left out for him near the side entrance. He was a mess, as he always was after working in the greenhouse, and the servants were used to him in such a state, but he supposed he ought to clean up before finding Miss Bridgerton and inviting her to eat with him. She was from London and would surely object to sitting at table with a man who was less than perfectly groomed.

He cut through the kitchen, nodding genially at a maid washing carrots in a tub of water. The servants' stairs were just outside the other kitchen door and—

"Miss Bridgerton!" he said in surprise. She was sitting at a table in the kitchen, halfway through a very large ham sandwich and looking remarkably at home on her perch on a stool. "What are you doing here?"

"Sir Phillip," she said, nodding at him.

"You don't have to eat in the kitchen," he said, scowling at her for no reason other than that she was not where he'd expected her to be.

That and the fact that he'd actually intended to change his clothes for lunch—something with which he did not ordinarily bother—for her benefit, and here she'd caught him a mess, anyway.

"I know," she replied, cocking her head and blinking those devastating gray eyes at him. "But I was looking for food and company, and this seemed the best place to find both."

Was that an insult? He couldn't be certain, and her eyes looked innocent, so he decided to ignore it and said, "I was just on my way to change into cleaner attire and invite you to share my lunch with me."

"I would be happy to remove myself to the breakfast room and finish my sandwich there, if you wish to join me," Eloise said. "I'm sure Mrs. Smith wouldn't mind making another sandwich for you. This one is delicious." She looked over at the cook. "Mrs. Smith?"

"It's no trouble at all, Miss Bridgerton," the cook said, leaving Phillip nearly gaping at her. It was quite the friendliest tone of voice he had ever heard emerge from her lips.

Eloise edged herself off her stool and picked up her plate. "Shall we?" she said to Phillip. "I have no objection to your attire."

Before he even realized that he had not agreed to her plan, Phillip found himself in the breakfast room, seated across from her at the small round table he used far more often than the long, lonely one in the formal dining room. A maid had carried Miss Bridgerton's tea service, and after inquiring if he wanted some, Miss Bridgerton herself had expertly prepared him a cup.

It was an unsettling feeling, this. She had maneuvered him quite neatly to serve her purposes, and somehow it didn't quite matter that he'd *intended* to ask her to lunch with him in this very manner. He liked to think he was at least nominally in charge in his own home.

"I met your children earlier," Miss Bridgerton said, lifting her teacup to her lips.

"Yes, I was there," he replied, pleased that she had initiated the conversation. Now he didn't have to.

"No," she corrected, "after that."

He looked up in question.

"They were waiting for me," she explained, "outside my bedchamber door."

An awful feeling began to churn and roll in his stomach. Waiting for her with what? A bag of live frogs? A bag of *dead* frogs? His children had not been kind to their governesses, and he did not imagine they'd be much more charitable to a female guest who was obviously there in the role of prospective stepmother.

He coughed. "I trust you survived the encounter?"

"Oh, yes," she said. "We have reached an understanding of sorts."

"An understanding?" He eyed her warily. "Of sorts?"

She waved away his question as she chewed on her food. "You needn't worry about me."

"Need I worry about my children?"

She looked up at him with an inscrutable smile. "Of course not."

"Very well." He looked down at the sandwich that had been placed in front of him and took a healthy bite. Once he'd swallowed, he looked her straight in the eye and said, "I must apologize for my greeting this morning. I was less than gracious."

She nodded regally. "And I apologize for arriving unheralded. It was quite ill-bred of me."

He nodded back. "You, however, apologized for that this morning, while I did not."

She offered him a smile, a genuine one, and he felt his heart lurch. Good God, when she smiled it transformed her entire face. In all the time he'd been corresponding with her, he'd never dreamed that she would take his breath away.

"Thank you," she murmured, her cheeks flushing with the barest hint of pink. "That was very gracious of you."

Phillip cleared his throat and shifted uneasily in his seat. What was wrong with him, that he was less comfortable with her smiles than he was with her frowns? "Right," he said, coughing one more time to cover the gruffness in his voice. "Now that we have that out of the way, perhaps we should address your reason for being here."

Eloise set her sandwich down and regarded him with obvious surprise. Clearly, she hadn't expected him to be so direct. "You were interested in marriage," she said.

"Are you?" he countered.

"I'm here," she said simply.

He looked at her assessingly, his eyes searching hers until she squirmed in her seat. "You are not what I expected, Miss Bridgerton."

"Under the circumstances, I would not think it inappropriate for you to use my given name," she said, "and you are not what I expected, either."

He sat back in his seat, looking at her with the vaguest hint of a smile. "And what did you expect?"

"What did *you* expect?" Eloise countered.

He gave her a look that told her he'd noticed she'd avoided his question, then said, quite bluntly, "I didn't expect you to be so pretty."

Eloise felt herself lurch back slightly at the unexpected compliment. She hadn't been looking her best that morning, and even if she had—well, she'd never been considered one of the beauties of the *ton*. Bridgerton women were generally thought to be attractive, vivacious, and personable. She and her sisters were popular, and they'd all received more than one offer of marriage, but men seemed to like them because they *liked* them, not because they were struck dumb by their beauty.

"I . . . ah . . ." She felt herself flushing, which mortified her, which of course caused her cheeks to redden even more. "Thank you."

He nodded graciously.

"I am not certain why my appearance would have come as a surprise to you," she said, thoroughly annoyed with herself for reacting so strongly to his flattery. Heavens, one would think she had never been paid a compliment before. But he was just sitting there, *looking* at her. Looking, and staring, and . . .

She shivered.

And it wasn't the least bit drafty. Could one shiver from feeling too . . . *hot*?

"You yourself wrote that you are a spinster," he said. "There must be some reason you have never married."

"It was not because I received no offers," she felt compelled to inform him.

"Obviously not," he said, tilting his head in her direction as a gesture of compliment. "But I cannot help but be curious as to why a woman like you would feel the need to resort to . . . well . . . *me*."

She looked at him, really looked at him for the first time since she'd arrived. He was quite handsome in a rough, slightly unkempt sort of way. His dark hair looked in dire need of a good trim, and his skin showed signs of a faint tan, which was impressive considering how little sunshine they'd enjoyed lately. He was large and muscular, and sat in his chair with a careless, athletic sort of grace, legs sprawled in a manner that would not have been acceptable in a London drawing room.

And the look on his face told her that he didn't much care that his manners were not de rigeur. It wasn't the same sort of defiant attitude she saw so often among young men of the *ton*. She'd met so many men of that kind—the ones who made such a point of defying convention, and then spoiled the effect by going out of their way to make sure that everyone knew how daring and scandalous they were.

But with Sir Phillip it was different. Eloise would have bet good money that it would simply never have occurred to him to care that he wasn't sitting in a properly formal manner, and it certainly wouldn't have occurred to him to make sure that other people knew he didn't care.

It made Eloise wonder if that was the mark of a truly self-confident person, and if so, why did he need to resort to *her*? Because from what she'd seen of him, curt manners this morning aside, he shouldn't have had too much trouble finding himself a wife.

"I am here," she said, finally remembering that he had asked her a question, "because after refusing *several* offers of marriage"—she knew that a better person would have been more modest and not taken such pains to emphasize the word "several," but she just couldn't help herself—"I find that I still desire a husband. Your letters seemed to indicate that you might be a good candidate. It seemed shortsighted not to meet with you and find out if that was indeed true."

He nodded. "Very practical of you."

"What about you?" she countered. "You were the one who initially brought up the topic of marriage. Why couldn't you simply find yourself a wife among the women here?"

For a moment he did nothing but blink, looking at her as if he couldn't quite believe she hadn't figured it out for herself. Finally, he said, "You've met my children."

Eloise nearly choked on the bite of sandwich she'd just started to chew. "I beg your pardon?"

"My children," he said flatly. "You've met them. Twice, I think. You told me so."

"Yes, but what . . ." She felt her eyes grow wide. "Oh, no, don't tell me they've scared away every prospective wife in the district?"

The look he leveled at her was grim. "Most of the women in the area refuse to even enter the ranks of the prospectives."

She scoffed. "They're not that bad."

"They need a mother," he said baldly.

She raised her brows. "Surely you can find a more romantic way to convince me to be your wife."

Phillip sighed wearily, running a hand through his already ruffled hair. "Miss Bridgerton," he said, then corrected himself with, "Eloise. I'm going to be honest with you, because, to be frank, I have neither the energy nor the patience for fancy romantic words or cleverly constructed stories. I need a wife. My children need a mother. I invited you here to see if you would be willing to assume such a role, and indeed, if you and I would suit."

"Which one?" she whispered.

He clenched his hands, his knuckles brushing the tablecloth. What was it about women? Did they speak in some sort of *code*? "Which one . . . what?" he asked, impatience coloring his voice.

"Which one do you want," she clarified, her voice still soft. "A wife or a mother?"

"Both," he said. "I should think that was obvious."

"Which one do you want *more*?"

Phillip stared at her for a long while, aware that this was an important question, quite possibly one that could signal the end of his unusual courtship. Finally, he just offered her a helpless shrug and said, "I'm sorry, but I don't know how to separate the two."

She nodded, her eyes serious. "I see," she murmured. "I expect you are right."

Phillip let out a long breath he wasn't even aware he'd been holding. Somehow—God Himself only knew how—he'd answered correctly. Or at the very least, not incorrectly.

Eloise fidgeted slightly in her seat, then motioned to the half-eaten sandwich on his plate. "Shall we continue with our meal?" she suggested. "You've been in your greenhouse all morning. I'm sure you must be quite famished."

Phillip nodded and took a bite of his food, all of a sudden feeling quite pleased with life. He still wasn't certain that Miss Bridgerton was going to consent to become Lady Crane, but if she did . . .

Well, he didn't think he would have any objections.

But wooing her wasn't going to be as easy as he'd anticipated. It was clear to him that he needed her more than the other way around. He'd been counting on her being a desperate spinster, which was clearly not the case, despite her advanced years. Miss Bridgerton, he suspected, had a number of options in her life, of which he was only one.

But still, something must have compelled her to leave her home and travel all the way out to Gloucestershire. If her life in London was so perfect, why, then, had she left?

But as he watched her across the table, watched her face transform with a mere smile, it occurred to him—he didn't much care why she'd left.

He just needed to make sure that she stayed.

Chapter 4

. . . so sorry to hear that Caroline is colicky and giving you fits. And of course it is too bad that neither Amelia nor Belinda is amenable to her arrival. But you must look upon the bright side, dear Daphne. It would all have been so much more difficult had you birthed twins.

—from Eloise Bridgerton to her sister the Duchess of Hastings, one month after the birth of Daphne's third child

Phillip whistled to himself as he walked through the main hall toward the staircase, inordinately pleased with his life. He'd spent the better part of the afternoon in the company of Miss Bridgerton—no, *Eloise*, he reminded himself—and he was now convinced she'd make an excellent wife. She was quite clearly intelligent, and with all those brothers and sisters (not to mention nephews and nieces) she'd told him about, surely she'd know how to manage Oliver and Amanda.

And, he thought with a wolfish smile, she was rather pretty, and more than once this afternoon he'd caught himself looking at her, wondering how she'd feel in his arms, whether she'd respond to his kiss.

His body tightened at the thought. It had been so long since he'd been with a woman. More years than he cared to count.

More years, quite honestly, than any man would care to admit to.

He'd not availed himself of any of the services offered by the barmaids at the local public inn, preferring his women more freshly washed and, in truth, not quite so anonymous.

Or maybe *more* anonymous. None of those barmaids were likely to leave the village during their lifetime, and Phillip enjoyed his time at the public inn too much to ruin it by constantly having to run into women with whom he'd once lain and no longer cared to.

And before Marina's death—well, he'd never even considered being unfaithful to her, despite the fact that they'd not shared a bed since the twins were quite young.

She'd been so melancholy following their birth. Marina had always seemed fragile and overly pensive, but it was only after Oliver and Amanda had arrived that she'd sunk into her own world of sorrow and despair. It had been horrifying for Phillip, watching the life behind her eyes slip away, day by day, until all that was left was an eerie flatness, the barest shadow of the woman who had once existed.

He knew that women couldn't have relations immediately following childbirth, but even once she was physically healed he couldn't have even imagined forcing himself upon her. How was one supposed to lust after a woman who always looked as if she might cry?

When the twins were a bit older, and Phillip had thought—hoped, really—that Marina was getting better, he had visited her in her bedchamber.

Once.

She had not refused him, but nor had she taken part in his lovemaking. She'd just lain there, doing nothing, her head turned to the side, her eyes open, barely blinking.

It was almost as if she hadn't been there at all.

He'd left feeling soiled, morally corrupt, as if he'd somehow violated her, even though she had never uttered the word *no*.

And he had never touched her again.

His needs weren't so great that he needed to slake them upon a woman who lay beneath him like a corpse.

And he never wanted to feel again as he had that final night. Once he'd returned to his own room, he'd promptly emptied the contents of his stomach, shaking and trembling, disgusted with himself. He had behaved like an animal, desperately trying to rouse in her some sort—any sort—of response. When that had proven impossible, he'd grown angry with her, wanted to punish her.

And that had terrified him.

He'd been too rough. He didn't think he'd hurt her, but he hadn't been gentle. And he never wanted to see that side of himself again.

But Marina was gone.

Gone.

And Eloise was different. She wasn't going to cry at the drop of a hat or shut herself in her room, picking at her food and crying into her pillow.

Eloise had spirit. Backbone.

Eloise was *happy*.

And if that wasn't a good criterion for a wife, he didn't know what was.

He paused at the base of the stairs to check his pocket watch. He had told Eloise that supper would be at seven and that he would meet her outside her door to take her down to the dining room. He didn't want to be early and appear too eager.

On the other hand, it wouldn't do to be late. There was little to be gained in making her think he was disinterested.

He snapped his watch shut and rolled his eyes. He was behaving no better than a green boy. This was ridiculous. He was master of his own house and an accomplished scientist. He ought not to be counting minutes just so he could best win a woman's favor.

But even as he thought that, he opened his watch for one more check. Three minutes prior to seven. Excellent. That would give him just enough time to ascend the stairs and meet her outside her door with precisely one minute to spare.

He grinned, enjoying his warm flush of desire at the thought of her in an evening gown. He hoped it was blue. She would look lovely in blue.

His smile deepened. She would look lovely in nothing at all.

Except when he found her, upstairs in the hall outside her bedchamber, her hair had gone white.

As, it seemed, had the rest of her.

Bloody hell. "Oliver!" he bellowed. "Amanda!"

"Oh, they're long gone," Eloise bit off. She looked up at him with fuming eyes. Fuming eyes which, he couldn't help but note, were the only part of her not covered with a remarkably thick coating of flour.

Well, good for her for closing them in time. He'd always admired quick reflexes in a woman.

"Miss Bridgerton," he said, his hand moving forward to help her, then retracting as he realized there *was* no helping her. "I cannot begin to express—"

"*Don't* apologize for them," she snapped.

"Right," he said. "Of course. But I promise you . . . I will . . ."

His words trailed off. Truly, the look in her eyes would have been enough to silence Napoleon himself.

"Sir Phillip," she said . . . slowly, tightly, looking very much as if she might launch herself at him in a furious frenzy. "As you can see, I'm not quite ready for supper."

He took a self-preservational step back. "I gather the twins paid you a visit," he said.

"Oh, yes," she replied, with no small measure of sarcasm. "And then scampered away. The little cowards themselves are nowhere to be found."

"Well, they wouldn't be far," he mused, allowing her the well-deserved insult to his children while he tried to carry on a conversation as if she didn't look like some sort of hideous ghostly apparition.

Somehow it seemed the best course of action. Or at the very least, the one least likely to result in her wrapping her fingers around his throat.

"They'd want to see the results, of course," he said, taking another discreet step back as she coughed, sending up a swirling cloud of flour. "I don't suppose you heard any laughter when the flour came down? Cackling, perhaps?"

She glared at him.

"Right." He winced. "Sorry for that. Stupid joke."

"It was difficult," she said, so tightly he wondered if her jaw might snap, "to hear anything but the sound of the bucket hitting my head."

"Damn," he muttered, following her line of sight until his eyes fell on a large metal bucket lying on its side on the carpet, with a small amount of flour still inside. "Are you hurt?"

She shook her head.

He reached out and took her head in his hands, trying to inspect her skin for bumps or bruises.

"Sir Phillip!" she yelped, attempting to squirm out of his grasp. "I must ask you to—"

"Be still," he ordered, smoothing his thumbs over her temples, feeling for welts. It was an intimate gesture, and one he found oddly satisfying. She seemed just the right height next to him, and had she been clean, he wasn't sure he'd have been able to stop himself from leaning down and dropping a soft kiss on her brow.

"I'm fine," she practically grunted, wrenching herself free. "The flour weighed more than the bucket."

Phillip leaned down and righted the bucket, testing its weight in his hand. It was fairly light and shouldn't have caused too much damage, but still, it wasn't the sort of thing with which one wanted to be struck on the head.

"I shall survive, I assure you," she bit out.

He cleared his throat. "I imagine you will want a bath?"

He *thought* she said, "I imagine I will want those two little wretches on the end of a rope," but the words came out under her breath, and just because that was what he would have said—well, it didn't mean *she* was as uncharitably inclined.

"I'll have one drawn for you," he said quickly.

"Don't bother. The water from my last bath is still in the tub."

He winced. His children's timing couldn't have been more on the spot. "Nonetheless," he said hastily, "I shall see that it is warmed with a few fresh buckets."

He winced again at her glare. Bad choice of words.

"I'll just see to that now," he said.

"Yes," she replied tautly. "Do that."

He strode down the hall to give the order to a maid, except that the minute he turned the corner, he saw that a half dozen servants were already gaping at them, and had in fact set up a betting pool on how long the twins would last before Phillip tanned their hides.

After sending them on their way with instructions to draw a new bath immediately, he returned to Eloise's side. He was already dusted with flour, so he saw no harm in taking her hand. "I'm terribly sorry," he murmured, now trying not to laugh. His immediate reaction had been fury, but now . . . well, she did look rather ridiculous.

She glared at him, clearly sensing his change of mood.

He quickly assumed a sober mien. "Perhaps you should return to your room?" he suggested.

"And sit where?" she snapped.

She had a point. She was likely to ruin anything she touched, or at the very least necessitate a thorough cleaning.

"I'll just keep you company, then," he said, trying to sound jovial.

She gave him a look that was decidedly unamused.

"Right," he said, in an attempt to fill the silence with something other than flour. He glanced up over the door, impressed with the twins' handiwork, despite the unfortunate results. "I wonder how they did it," he mused.

Her mouth fell open. "Does it matter?"

"Well," he said, seeing from her face that this was not the most advisable avenue of conversation, but continuing nonetheless with, "I certainly can't condone their actions, but it was obviously quite cleverly done. I don't see where they attached the bucket, and—"

"They rested it on the top of the door."

"I beg your pardon?"

"I have seven brothers and sisters," she said dismissively. "Do you think I've never seen this prank before? They opened the door—just a crack—and then carefully placed the bucket."

"And you didn't hear them?"

She glared at him.

"Right," he said hastily. "You were in the bath."

"I don't suppose," she said in a haughty voice, "that you intend to imply that this was my fault for not having heard them."

"Of course not," he said—very quickly. Judging from the murderous look in Miss Bridgerton's eyes, he was fairly certain that his health and welfare were directly dependent upon the speed with which he agreed with her. "Why don't I leave you to your . . ."

Was there really a good way to describe the process of cleaning several pounds of flour off one's person?

"Will I see you at supper?" he asked, deciding that a change of subject was most definitely in order.

She nodded, once, briefly. There wasn't a great deal of warmth in that nod, but Phillip reckoned he should be happy that she wasn't planning to leave the county that night.

"I will instruct the cook to keep supper warm," he said. "And I will see to punishing the twins."

"No," she said, halting him in his tracks. "Leave them to me."

He turned around slowly, a bit unnerved by the tone of her voice. "What, precisely, do you plan to do with them?"

"With them, or *to* them?"

Phillip had never thought the day would come when he'd be frightened by a woman, but as God was his witness, Eloise Bridgerton scared the living wits out of him.

The look in her eyes was positively diabolical.

"Miss Bridgerton," he said, crossing his arms, "I must ask. What do you intend to do to my children?"

"I'm pondering my options."

He considered that. "May I depend upon their still being alive tomorrow morning?"

"Oh, yes," she replied. "Alive, and with every limb intact, I assure you."

Phillip stared at her for several moments, then let his lips spread into a slow, satisfied smile. He had a feeling that Eloise Bridgerton's vengeance—whatever it might be—would be exactly what his children needed. Surely anyone with seven brothers and sisters would know how to wreak havoc in the most cunning, underhanded, and ingenious manner.

"Very well, Miss Bridgerton," he said, almost glad they'd dumped a bucket of flour on her. "They are all yours."

An hour later, just after he and Eloise sat down for supper, the screaming began.

Phillip actually dropped his spoon; Amanda's shrieks had a more terrified tenor than usual.

Eloise didn't even pause as she placed a spoonful of turtle soup between her lips. "She's fine," she murmured, delicately wiping her mouth with her serviette.

The rapid patter of little feet thundered overhead, signaling that Amanda was racing toward the steps.

Phillip half rose in his seat. "Perhaps I should—"

"I put a fish in her bed," Miss Bridgerton said, not quite smiling, but nonetheless looking rather pleased with herself.

"A fish?" he echoed.

"Very well, it was a rather big fish."

The tadpole in his mind quickly grew into a toothy shark, and he found himself choking on air. "Er," he couldn't help but ask, "where did you find a fish?"

"Mrs. Smith," she said, as if his cook handed out large trout every day of the week.

He forced himself to sit back down. He wasn't going to run to save Amanda. He wanted to; he did possess the odd paternal instinct, after all, and she was shrieking as if the fires of hell were licking at her toes.

But his daughter had made her bed; now it was time to lie in the one Miss Bridgerton had stunk up for her. He dipped his spoon in his soup, lifted it a few inches, then paused. "And what did you place in Oliver's bed?"

"Nothing."

He quirked a brow in question.

"It will keep him in suspense," she explained coolly.

Phillip cocked his head toward her in salute. She was good. "They'll retaliate, of course," he felt honor-bound to warn her.

"I'll be ready." She sounded unconcerned. Then she looked up at him, straight in the eye, momentarily startling him with her direct gaze. "I suppose they know that you invited me here for the purpose of asking me to be your wife."

"I never said anything to them."

"No," she murmured, "you wouldn't."

He looked over at her sharply, unable to discern if she meant that as an insult. "I don't feel the need to keep my children apprised of my personal matters."

She shrugged, a delicate little motion that he found infuriating.

"Miss Bridgerton," he said, "I don't need your advice on how to raise my children."

"I didn't say a word on the subject," she returned, "although I might point out that you do appear rather desperate to find them a mother, which would seem to indicate that you *do* want help."

"Until you agree to take on that role," he bit off, "you may keep your opinions to yourself."

She speared him with a frosty stare, then turned her attention back to her soup. After only two spoonfuls, however, she looked back up at him defiantly, and said, "They need discipline."

"Do you think I don't know that?"

"They also need love."

"They get love," he muttered.

"And attention."

"They get that, too."

"From *you*."

Phillip might have been aware that he was far from being a perfect father, but he was damned if he would allow someone else to say so. "And I suppose you have deduced their state of shameful neglect during the *twelve hours* since your arrival."

She snorted her disdain. "It hardly required twelve hours to listen to them this morning, begging you to spend a paltry few minutes in their company."

"They did nothing of the sort," he retorted, but he could feel the tips of his ears growing hot, as they always did when he was lying. He *didn't* spend enough time with them, and he was mortified that she'd managed to figure that out in such a short amount of time.

"They practically begged you not to be busy *all day*," she shot back. "If you spent a bit more time with them—"

"You don't know anything about my children," he hissed. "And you don't know anything about me."

She stood abruptly. "Clearly," she said, heading for the door.

"Wait!" he called, jumping to his feet. Damn. How had this happened? Barely an hour ago he'd been convinced that she would become his wife, and now she was practically on her way back to London.

He let out a frustrated breath. Nothing had the ability to turn his temper like his children, or the discussion thereof. Or, to be more precise, the discussion of his failings as their father.

"I'm sorry," he said, meaning it, too. Or at least meaning it enough not to want her to leave. "Please." He held out his hand. "Don't go."

"I'll not be treated like an imbecile."

"If there is one thing I've learned in the twelve hours since your arrival," he said, purposefully repeating his earlier words, "it's that you're no imbecile."

She regarded him for a few more seconds, then placed her hand in his.

"At the very least," he said, not even caring that he sounded as if he were pleading with her, "you must stay until Amanda arrives."

Her brows rose in question.

"Surely you'll want to savor your victory," he murmured, then added under his breath, "I know I would."

She allowed him to reseat her, but they had only one more minute together before Amanda came shrieking into the room, her nursemaid hot on her heels.

"Father!" Amanda wailed, throwing herself onto his lap.

Phillip embraced her awkwardly. It was some time since he'd done so, and he'd forgotten how it felt. "Whatever can be the problem?" he asked, giving her a pat on the back for good measure.

Amanda pulled her face out of its burrowed position in his neck and pointed one furious, shaking finger at Eloise. *"It's her,"* she said, as if referring to the devil himself.

"Miss Bridgerton?" Phillip asked.

"She put a fish in my bed!"

"And you dumped flour on her head," he said sternly, "so I'd say you're even."

Amanda's little mouth fell open. "But you're my father!"

"Indeed."

"You're supposed to take my side!"

"When you're in the right."

"It was a *fish*," she sobbed.

"So I smell. You'll want a bath, I imagine."

"I don't want a bath!" she wailed. "I want you to punish her!"

Phillip smiled at that. "She's rather big for punishing, wouldn't you agree?"

Amanda stared at him with horrified disbelief, and then finally, her lower lip shaking, she gasped, "You need to tell her to leave. *Right now!*"

Phillip set Amanda down, rather pleased with how the entire encounter was progressing. Maybe it was Miss Bridgerton's calm presence, but he seemed to have more patience than usual. He felt no urge to snap at Amanda, or to avoid the issue altogether by banishing her to her room. "I beg your pardon, Amanda," he said, "but Miss Bridgerton is my guest, not yours, and she will remain here as long as I wish."

Eloise cleared her throat. Loudly.

"Or," Phillip amended, "as long as she wishes to remain."

Amanda's entire face scrunched in thought.

"Which doesn't mean," he said quickly, "that you may torture her in an attempt to force her away."

"But—"

"No buts."

"But—"

"What did I just say?"

"But she's *mean*!"

"I think she's very clever," Phillip said, "and I wish I'd put a fish in your bed months ago."

Amanda stepped back in horror.

"Go to your room, Amanda."

"But it smells bad."

"You have only yourself to blame."

"But my bed—"

"You'll have to sleep on the floor," he replied.

Face quivering—entire body quivering, truth be told—she dragged herself toward the door. "But . . . but . . ."

"Yes, Amanda?" he asked, in what he thought to be an impressively patient voice.

"But she didn't punish Oliver," the little girl whispered. "That wasn't very fair of her. The flour was his idea."

Phillip raised his brows.

"Well, it wasn't *only* my idea," Amanda insisted. "We thought it up together."

Phillip actually chuckled. "I wouldn't worry about Oliver if I were you, Amanda. Or rather," he said, giving his chin a thoughtful stroke with his fingers, "I *would* worry. I suspect Miss Bridgerton has plans for him yet."

That seemed to satisfy Amanda, and she mumbled a barely articulate "Good night, Father," before allowing her nursemaid to lead her from the room.

Phillip turned back to his soup, feeling very pleased with himself. He couldn't remember the last time he'd emerged from a run-in with one of the twins in which he'd felt he'd handled everything just right. He took a sip, then, still holding his spoon, looked over at Eloise and said, "Poor Oliver will be quaking in his boots."

She appeared to be trying hard not to grin. "He won't be able to sleep."

Phillip shook his head. "Not a wink, I should think. And you should watch your step. I'd wager he'll set some sort of trap at his door."

"Oh, I have no plans to torture Oliver this evening," she said with a blithe wave of her hand. "That would be far too easy to predict. I prefer the element of surprise."

"Yes," he said with a chuckle. "I can see that you would."

Eloise answered him with a smug expression. "I would almost consider leaving him in perpetual agony, except that it really wouldn't be fair to Amanda."

Phillip shuddered. "I hate fish."

"I know. You wrote me as much."

"I did?"

She nodded. "Odd that Mrs. Smith even had any in the house, but I suppose the servants like it."

They descended into silence, but it was a comfortable, companionable sort of quietude. And as they ate, moving through the courses of the supper as they chatted about nothing in particular, it occurred to Phillip that perhaps marriage wasn't supposed to be so hard.

With Marina he'd always felt like he was tiptoeing around the house, always fearful that she was going to descend into one of her bouts with melancholia, always disappointed when she seemed to withdraw from life, and indeed, almost disappear.

But maybe marriage was supposed to be easier than that. Maybe it was supposed to be like this. Companionable. Comfortable.

He couldn't remember the last time he had spoken with anyone about his children, or the raising thereof. His burdens had always been his alone, even when Marina had been alive. Marina herself had been a burden, and he was still wrestling with the guilt he felt at his relief that she was gone.

But Eloise . . .

He looked across the table at the woman who had so unexpectedly fallen into his life. Her hair glowed almost red in the flickering candlelight, and her eyes, when she caught him staring at her, sparkled with vitality and just a hint of mischief.

She was, he was coming to realize, exactly what he needed. Smart, opinionated, bossy—they weren't the sort of things men usually looked for in a wife, but Phillip so desperately needed someone to come to Romney Hall and fix things. Nothing was quite right, from the house to his children to the slightly hushed pall that had hung over the place when Marina had been alive, and sadly had not lifted even after her death.

Phillip would gladly cede some of his husbandly power to a wife if she would only make everything right again. He'd be more than happy to disappear into his greenhouse and let her be in charge of everything else.

Would Eloise Bridgerton be willing to take on such a role?

Dear God, he hoped so.

Chapter 5

. . . implore you, Mother, you MUST punish Daphne. It is NOT FAIR that I am the only one sent to bed without pudding. And for a week. A week is far too long. Especially since it was all mostly Daphne's idea.

—from Eloise Bridgerton to her mother, left upon Violet Bridgerton's night table during Eloise's tenth year

It was strange, Eloise thought, how much could change in a single day.

Because now, as Sir Phillip was escorting her through his home, ostensibly viewing the portrait gallery but really just prolonging their time together, she was thinking—

He might make a perfectly fine husband after all.

Not the most poetic way to phrase a concept that ought to have been full of romance and passion, but theirs wasn't a typical courtship, and with only two years remaining until her thirtieth birthday, Eloise couldn't really afford to be fanciful.

But still, there was something . . .

In the candlelight, Sir Phillip was somehow more handsome,

perhaps even a little dangerous-looking. The rugged planes of his face seemed to angle and shadow in the flickering light, lending him a more sculptured look, almost like the statues she'd visited at the British Museum. And as he stood next to her, his large hand possessively at her elbow, his entire presence seemed to envelop her.

It was odd, and thrilling, and just a little bit terrifying.

But gratifying, too. She'd done a crazy thing, running off in the middle of the night, hoping to find happiness with a man she'd never met. It was a relief to think that maybe it hadn't all been a complete mistake, that maybe she'd gambled with her future and won.

Nothing would have been worse than slinking back to London, admitting failure, and having to explain to her entire family what she'd done.

She didn't want to have to admit that she'd been wrong, to herself or anyone else.

But mostly to herself.

Sir Phillip had proven to be an enjoyable supper companion, even if he wasn't quite so glib or conversational as she was used to.

But he obviously possessed a sense of fair play, which Eloise deemed essential in any spouse. He had accepted—even admired—her fish-in-the-bed technique with Amanda. Many of the men Eloise had met in London would have been horrified that a gently bred lady would even think of resorting to such underhanded tactics.

And maybe, just maybe, this would work. Marriage to Sir Phillip did seem a harebrained scheme when she allowed herself to think about it in a logical manner, but it wasn't as if he were a *complete* stranger—they had been corresponding for over a year, after all.

"My grandfather," Phillip said mildly, gesturing to a large portrait.

"He was quite handsome," Eloise said, even though she could barely see him in the dim light. She motioned to the picture to the right. "Is that your father?"

Phillip nodded once, curtly, the corners of his lips tightening.

"And where are you?" she asked, sensing that he didn't wish to talk about his father.

"Over here, I'm afraid."

Eloise followed his direction to a portrait of Phillip as a young boy of perhaps twelve years, posing with someone who could only have been his brother.

His older brother.

"What happened to him?" she asked, since he had to be dead. If he lived, Phillip could not have inherited his house or baronetcy.

"Waterloo," he answered succinctly.

Impulsively, she placed her hand over his. "I'm sorry."

For a moment she didn't think he was going to say anything, but eventually he let out a quiet, "No one was sorrier than I."

"What was his name?"

"George."

"You must have been quite young," she said, counting back to 1815 and doing the math in her head.

"Twenty-one. My father died two weeks following."

She thought about that. At twenty-one, she was supposed to have been married. All young ladies of her station were expected to have been married by then. One would think that would confer a measure of adulthood, but now twenty-one seemed impossibly young and green, and far too innocent to have inherited a burden one had never thought to receive.

"Marina was his fiancée," he said.

Her breath rushed over her lips, and she turned to him, her hand falling away from his. "I didn't know," she said.

He shrugged. "It doesn't matter. Here, would you like to see her portrait?"

"Yes," Eloise replied, discovering that she did indeed wish to see Marina. They had been cousins, but distant ones, and it had been years since they'd visited with one another. Eloise remembered dark hair and light eyes—blue, maybe—but that was all. She and Marina had been of an age, and so they had been thrust together at family gatherings, but Eloise didn't recall their ever having very much in common. Even when they were barely older than Amanda and Oliver, their differences had been clear. Eloise had been a boisterous child, climbing trees and sliding down banisters, always following her older siblings, begging them to allow her to take part in whatever they were doing.

Marina had been quieter, almost contemplative. Eloise remembered tugging on her hand, trying to get her to come outside and play. But Marina had just wanted to sit with a book.

Eloise had taken note of the pages, however, and she was quite convinced that Marina never moved beyond page thirty-two.

It was a strange thing to remember, she supposed, except that her nine-year-old self had found it so astounding—why would someone choose to stay inside with a book when the sun was shining, and then not even read it? She'd spent the rest of the visit whispering with her sister Francesca, trying to figure out just what it was that Marina was doing with that book.

"Do you remember her?" Phillip asked.

"Just a little," Eloise replied, not sure why she didn't wish to share her memory with him. And anyway, it was the truth. That was the sum of her recollections of Marina—that one week in April over twenty years earlier, whispering with Francesca as Marina stared at a book.

Eloise allowed Phillip to lead her over to Marina's portrait. She had been painted seated, on some sort of ottoman, with her dark red skirts artfully arranged about her. A younger version of Amanda was on her lap, and Oliver stood at her side, in one of those poses young boys were always forced to assume—serious and stern, as if they were miniature adults.

"She was lovely," Eloise said.

Phillip just stared at the image of his dead wife, then, almost as if it required a force of will, turned his head and walked away.

Had he loved her? Did he love her still?

Marina should have been his brother's bride; everything seemed to suggest that Phillip had been given her by default.

But that didn't mean he didn't love her. Maybe he had been secretly in love with her while she had been engaged to his brother. Or maybe he had fallen in love after the wedding.

Eloise stole a look at his profile as he stared sightlessly at a painting on the wall. There had been emotion on his face when he had looked at Marina's portrait. She wasn't sure what he had felt for her, but it was definitely still something. It had only been a year, she reminded herself. A year might make up the official period of mourning, but it wasn't very long to get past the death of a loved one.

Then he turned. His eyes hit hers, and she realized she'd been staring at him, mesmerized by the planes of his face. Her lips parted with surprise, and she wanted to look away, felt as if she ought to blush and stammer at having been caught, but somehow she could not. She just stood there, transfixed, breathless, as a strange heat spread across her skin.

He was ten feet away, at the very least, and it felt as if they were touching.

"Eloise?" he whispered, or at least she thought he did. She saw his lips form the word more than she actually heard his voice.

And then somehow the moment was broken. Maybe it was his whisper, maybe the creak of a windblown tree outside. But Eloise was finally able to move—to think—and she quickly turned back to Marina's portrait, firmly affixing her gaze on her late cousin's serene face. "The children must miss her," Eloise said, needing to say something, anything that would restart the conversation—and restore her composure.

For a moment Phillip said nothing. And then, finally: "Yes, they've missed her for a long time."

It seemed to Eloise a rather odd way to phrase it. "I know how they feel," she said. "I was quite young when my father died."

He looked over at her. "I didn't realize."

She shrugged. "It's not something I talk about a great deal. It was a long time ago."

He crossed back to her side, his steps slow and methodical. "Did it take you very long to get over it?"

"I'm not certain it's something you ever do get over," she said. "Completely, that is. But no, I don't think about him every day, if that's what you want to know."

She turned away from Marina's portrait; she'd been focusing on it for too long and was beginning to feel oddly intrusive. "I think it was more difficult for my older brothers," she said. "Anthony—he is the eldest and was already a young man when it happened—had a particularly difficult time with it. They were very close. And my mother, of course." She looked over at him. "My parents loved each other very much."

"How did she react to his passing?"

"Well, she cried a great deal at first," Eloise said. "I'm sure we weren't meant to know. She always did it in her room at night, after she thought we were all asleep. But she missed him dreadfully, and it couldn't have been easy with seven children."

"I thought there were eight of you."

"Hyacinth was not yet born. I believe my mother was eight months along."

"Good God," she thought she heard him murmur.

Good God was right. Eloise had no idea how her mother had managed.

"It was unexpected," she told him. "He was stung by a bee. A bee. Can you imagine that? He was stung by a bee, and then— Well, I don't need to bore you with the details. Here," she said briskly, "let us leave. It's too dark in here to see the portraits properly, anyway."

It was a lie, of course. It *was* too dark, but Eloise couldn't have cared less about that. Talking about her father's death always made her feel a bit strange, and she just didn't feel like standing there surrounded by paintings of dead people.

"I should like to see your greenhouse," she said.

"Now?"

Put that way, it did seem an odd request. "Tomorrow, then," she said, "when it's light."

His lips curved into a hint of a smile. "We can go now."

"But we won't be able to see anything."

"We won't be able to see everything," he corrected. "But the moon is out, and we'll take a lantern."

She glanced doubtfully out the window. "It's cold."

"You can take a coat." He leaned down with a gleam in his eye. "You're not afraid, are you?"

"Of course not!" she retorted, knowing he was baiting her but falling for it, anyway.

He quirked a brow in a most provoking manner.

"I'll have you know I'm the least cowardly woman you're ever likely to encounter."

"I'm sure you are," he murmured.

"Now you're being patronizing."

He did nothing but chuckle.

"Very well," she said gamely, "lead the way."

"It's so warm!" Eloise exclaimed as Phillip shut the greenhouse door behind her.

"It's actually usually warmer than this," he told her. "The glass allows the sun to warm the air, but except for this morning, it's been quite overcast for the past few days."

Phillip often visited his greenhouse at night, toiling by the light of a lantern when he could not sleep. Or, before he'd been widowed, to keep him busy so that he would not consider entering Marina's bedchamber.

But he had never asked anyone to accompany him in the dark; even during the day, he almost always worked alone. Now he was seeing it all through Eloise's eyes—the magic in the way the pearlescent moonlight threw shadows across the leaves and fronds. During the day, a walk through the greenhouse wasn't so very different from a walk through any wooded area in England, with the exception of the odd rare fern or imported bromeliad.

But now, with the cloak of night playing tricks on the eyes, it was as if they were in some secret, hidden jungle, with magic and surprise lurking around every corner.

"What is this?" Eloise asked, peering down at eight small clay pots, arranged in a line across his workbench.

Phillip walked to her side, absurdly pleased that she seemed truly curious. Most people just feigned interest, or didn't even bother to pretend and made a quick escape. "It's an experiment I've been working on," he said, "with peas."

"The kind we eat?"

"Yes. I'm trying to develop a strain that will grow fatter in the pod."

She peered down at the pots. Nothing was sprouting yet; he'd only planted the seeds a week ago. "How curious," she murmured. "I had no idea one could do that."

"I have no idea if one can," he admitted. "I've been trying for a year."

"With no success? How very frustrating."

"I've had some success," he admitted, "just not as much as I'd like."

"I tried to grow roses one year," she told him. "They all died."

"Roses are more difficult than most people think," he said.

Her lips twisted slightly. "I noticed you have them in abundance."

"I have a gardener."

"A botanist with a gardener?"

He'd heard that question before, many times. "It's no different than a dressmaker with a seamstress."

She considered that for a moment, then moved farther into the greenhouse, stopping to peer at various plants and scold him for not keeping up with her with the lantern.

"You're a bit bossy this evening," he said.

She turned, caught that he was smiling—half-smiling, at least—and offered him a wicked grin. "I prefer to be called 'managing.' "

"A managing sort of female, eh?"

"I'm surprised you didn't deduce as much from my letters."

"Why do you think I invited you?" he countered.

"You want someone to manage your life?" she asked, tossing the words over her shoulder as she moved flirtatiously away from him.

He wanted someone to manage his children, but now didn't

seem like the best time to bring them up. Not when she was looking at him as if . . .

As if she wanted to be kissed.

Phillip had taken two slow, predatory steps in her direction before he even realized what he was doing.

"What is this?" she asked, pointing to something.

"A plant."

"I know it's a plant," she said with a laugh. "If I'd—" But then she looked up, caught the gleam in his eyes, and quieted.

"May I kiss you?" he asked. He would have stopped if she'd said no, he supposed, but he didn't allow her much opportunity, closing the distance between them before she could reply.

"May I?" he repeated, so close that his words were whispered across her lips.

She nodded, the motion tiny but sure, and he brushed his mouth against hers, gently, softly, as one was supposed to kiss a woman one thought one might marry.

But then her hands stole around and touched his neck, and God help him, but he wanted more.

Much more.

He deepened the kiss, ignoring her gasp of surprise as he parted her lips with his tongue. But even that wasn't what he wanted. He wanted to feel her, her warmth, her vitality, up and down the length of him, around him, through him, infusing him.

He slid his hands around her, settling one against her upper back, even as another daringly found the lush curve of her bottom. He pressed her against him, hard, not caring that she would feel the evidence of his desire. It had been so long. So damned long, and she was so soft and sweet in his arms.

He wanted her.

He wanted all of her, but even his passion-hazed mind knew that that was impossible this evening, and so he was determined to have the next best thing, which was just the feel of her, the sensation of her in his arms, the heat of her running along the entire length of his body.

And she was responding. Hesitantly, at first, as if she wasn't quite sure what she was doing, but then with greater ardor, making innocently seductive little sounds from the back of her throat.

It drove him wild. *She* drove him wild.

"Eloise, Eloise," he murmured, his voice hoarse and raspy with need. He sank one hand into her hair, tugging at it until her coiffure loosened and one thick chestnut lock slid out to form a seductive curlicue on her breastbone. His lips moved to her neck, tasting her skin, exulting when she arched back and offered him greater access. And then, just when he'd started to sink down, his knees bending as his lips trailed over her collarbone, she wrenched herself away.

"I'm sorry," she blurted out, her hands flying up to the neckline of her dress even though it wasn't the least bit out of place.

"I'm not," he said baldly.

Her eyes widened at his bluntness. He didn't care. He'd never been particularly fancy with words, and it was probably best that she learned that now, before they did anything permanent.

And then she surprised him.

"It was a figure of speech," she said.

"I beg your pardon?"

"I said I was sorry. I wasn't, really. It was a figure of speech."

She sounded remarkably composed and almost schoolteacherish, for a woman who had just been so soundly kissed.

"People say things like that all the time," she continued, "just to fill the silence."

Phillip was coming to realize that she wasn't the sort of woman who liked silence.

"It's rather like when one—"

He kissed her again.

"Sir Phillip!"

"Sometimes," he said with a satisfied smile, "silence is a good thing."

Her mouth fell open. "Are you saying I talk too much?"

He shrugged, having too much fun teasing her to do anything else.

"I'll have you know that I have been *much* quieter here than I am at home."

"That's difficult to imagine."

"Sir Phillip!"

"Shhh," he said, reaching out and taking her hand, then taking it again, more firmly this time, when she snatched it away. "We need a bit of noise around here."

Eloise woke the following morning as if she were still wrapped in a dream. She hadn't expected him to kiss her.

And she hadn't expected to like it quite so much.

Her stomach let out an angry growl, and she decided to make her way down to the breakfast room. She had no idea if Sir Phillip would be there. Was he an early riser? Or did he like to remain abed until noon? It seemed silly that she didn't know these things about him when she was seriously contemplating marriage.

And if he was there, waiting for her over a plate of coddled eggs, what would she say to him? What did one say to a man after he'd had his tongue in one's ear?

Never mind that it had been a very nice tongue, indeed. It was still quite beyond scandalous.

What if she got there and could barely manage "Good morning?" He'd surely find that amusing, after teasing her about her loquaciousness the night before.

It almost made her laugh. She, who could carry on a conversation about nothing in particular and frequently did, wasn't sure what she was going to say when she next saw Sir Phillip Crane.

Of course, he *had* kissed her. That changed everything.

Crossing the room, she checked to make sure that her door was firmly shut before she opened it. She didn't think that Oliver and Amanda would try the same trick twice, but one never knew. She didn't particularly relish the thought of another flour bath. Or worse. After the fish incident, they were probably thinking more along the lines of something liquid. Something liquid and smelly.

Humming softly to herself, she stepped out into the hall and turned to the right to make her way to the staircase. The day seemed filled with promise; the sun had actually been peeking out through the clouds this morning when she'd looked out the window, and—

"Oh!"

The shriek ripped itself right out of her throat as she plunged forward, her foot caught behind something that had been strung out across the hall. She didn't even have a chance to try to regain her balance; she had been walking quickly, as was her habit, and when she fell, she fell hard.

And without even the time to use her hands to break her fall.

Tears burned her eyes. Her chin—dear God, her chin felt like it was on fire. The side of it, at least. She had just managed to twist her head ever so slightly to the side before she fell.

She moaned something incoherent, the sort of noise one makes when one hurts so badly that one simply cannot keep it all inside. And she kept waiting for the pain to subside, thinking that this would be like a stubbed toe, which throbs mercilessly for a few seconds and then, once the surprise of it is over, slides into nothing more than a dull ache.

But the pain kept burning. On her chin, on the side of her head, on her knee, and on her hip.

She felt beaten.

Slowly, with great effort, she forced herself up onto her hands and knees, and then into a sitting position. She allowed herself to lean against the wall and lifted her hand to cradle her cheek, taking quick bursts of breath through her nose to try to control the pain.

"Eloise!"

Phillip. She didn't bother to look up, didn't want to move from her curled-up position.

"Eloise, my God," he said, triple-stepping the last few stairs as he rushed to her side. "What happened?"

"I fell." She hadn't meant to whimper, but it came out that way, anyway.

With a tenderness that seemed out of place on a man of his size, he took her hand in his and pulled it from her cheek.

The next words he said were not ones that were often uttered in Eloise's presence.

"You need a piece of meat on that," he said.

She looked up at him with watery eyes. "Am I bruised?"

He nodded grimly. "You may have a blackened eye. It's still too soon to tell."

She tried to smile, tried to put a game face on it, but she just couldn't manage it.

"Does it hurt very badly?" he asked softly.

She nodded, wondering why the sound of his voice made her want to cry even more. It reminded her of when she was small and she'd fallen from a tree. She'd sprained her ankle, quite badly, but somehow she'd managed not to cry until she'd made it back home.

One look from her mother and she'd begun to sob.

Phillip touched her cheek gingerly, his features pulling into a scowl when she winced.

"I'll be fine," she assured him. And she would. In a few days.

"What happened?"

And of course she knew exactly what had happened. Something had been strung across the hall, put in place to make her trip and fall. It didn't require very much intelligence to guess who had done it.

But Eloise didn't want to get the twins in trouble. At least not the sort of trouble they were likely to find themselves in once Sir Phillip got hold of them. She didn't think they'd intended to cause quite so much harm.

But Phillip had already spied the thin length of twine, tightly drawn across the hall and tied around the legs of two tables, both of which had been tugged toward the center of the hall when Eloise had tripped.

Eloise watched as he knelt down, touching the string and twisting it around his fingers. He looked over at her, not with question in his eyes, but rather grim statement of fact.

"I didn't see it," she said, even though that was quite obvious.

Phillip didn't take his eyes off hers, but his fingers kept twisting the string until it tautened and snapped.

Eloise sucked in her breath. There was something almost terrifying in the moment. Phillip didn't seem aware that he'd broken the string, barely cognizant of his strength.

Or the strength of his anger.

"Sir Phillip," she whispered, but he never heard her.

"Oliver!" he bellowed. "Amanda!"

"I'm sure they didn't mean to injure me," Eloise began, not certain why she was defending them. They'd hurt her, that was true, but she had a feeling her punishment would be considerably less painful than anything coming from their father.

"I don't care what they meant," Phillip snapped. "Look how close you landed to the stairs. What if you'd fallen?"

Eloise eyed the stairs. They were close, but not close enough for her to have taken a tumble. "I don't think . . ."

"They must answer for this," he said, his voice deadly low and shaking with rage.

"I'll be fine," Eloise said. Already the stinging pain was giving way to a duller ache. But it still hurt, enough so that when Sir Phillip lifted her into his arms, she let out a little cry.

And his fury grew.

"I'm putting you in bed," he said, his voice rough and curt.

Eloise offered no disagreement.

A maid appeared on the landing, gasping when she saw the darkening bruise on Eloise's face.

"Get me something for this," Sir Phillip ordered. "A piece of meat. Anything."

The maid nodded and ran off as Phillip carried Eloise into her room. "Are you hurt anywhere else?" he asked.

"My hip," Eloise admitted as he settled her on top of her covers. "And my elbow."

He nodded grimly. "Do you think you've broken anything?"

"No!" she said quickly. "No, I—"

"I'll need to check, anyway," he said, brushing aside her protests as he lightly examined her arm.

"Sir Phillip, I—"

"My children just nearly killed you," he said, without a trace of humor in his eyes. "I should think you could dispense with the *sir*."

Eloise swallowed as she watched him cross the room to the door, his strides long and powerful. "Get me the twins immediately," he said, presumably to some servant hovering outside in the hall. Eloise couldn't imagine that the children hadn't heard his earlier bellow, but she also couldn't blame them for attempting to delay judgment day at the hands of their father.

"Phillip," she said, trying to coax him back into the room with the sound of her voice, "leave them to me. I was the injured party, and—"

"They are my children," he said, his voice harsh, "and I will punish them. God knows it's long past due."

Eloise stared at him with growing horror. He was nearly shaking with rage, and while she could have happily swatted the children on their bottoms herself, she didn't think he ought to be meting out punishment in his state.

"They hurt you," Phillip said in a low voice. "That is not acceptable."

"I'll be fine," she assured him again. "In a few days I won't even—"

"That is not the point," he said sharply. "If I had . . ." He stopped, tried again with, "If I hadn't . . ." He stopped, beyond words, and leaned against the wall, his head hanging back as his eyes searched the ceiling—for what, she didn't know. Answers, she supposed. As if one could find answers with the simple upward sweep of the eyes.

He turned, looked at her, his eyes grim, and Eloise saw something on his face she hadn't expected to see there.

And that was when she realized it—all that rage in his voice, in the shaking of his body—it wasn't directed at the children. Not really, and certainly not entirely.

The look on his face, the bleakness in his eyes—it was self-loathing.

He didn't blame his children.

He blamed himself.

Chapter 6

. . . should not have let him kiss you. Who knows what liberties he will attempt to take the next time you meet? But what's done is done, I suppose, so all there is left is to ask: Was it lovely?

—from Eloise Bridgerton to her sister Francesca, slid under the door of her bedroom the night Francesca met the Earl of Kilmartin, whom she would marry two months later

When the children entered the room, half dragged and half pushed by their nursemaid, Phillip forced himself to remain rigidly in his position against the wall, afraid that if he went to them he'd beat them both within an inch of their lives.

And even more afraid that when he was through, he wouldn't regret his actions.

So instead he just crossed his arms and stared, letting them squirm under the heat of his fury, while he tried to figure out what the hell he meant to say.

Finally, Oliver spoke up, his voice trembling as he said, "Father?"

Phillip said the only thing that came to mind, the only thing that seemed to matter. "Do you see Miss Bridgerton?"

The twins nodded, but they didn't quite look at her. At least not at her face, which was beginning to purple around the eye.

"Do you notice anything amiss about her?"

They said nothing, forcing a silence until a maid appeared in the doorway with a "Sir?"

Phillip acknowledged her arrival with a nod, then strode to take hold of the piece of meat she'd brought for Eloise's eye.

"Hungry?" he snapped at his children. When they didn't reply, he said, "Good. Because sadly, none of us will be eating this, will we?"

He crossed the room to the bed, then sat down gently at Eloise's side. "Here," he said, still too angry for his voice to be anything but gruff. Brushing aside her efforts to help, he set the meat against her eye, then arranged a piece of cloth over it so that she would not have to dirty her fingers while keeping it in place.

Then, when he was done, he walked over to where the twins were cowering, and stood in front of them, arms crossed. And waited.

"Look at me," he ordered, when neither removed their gaze from the floor.

When they did, he saw terror in their eyes, and it sickened him, but he didn't know how else he was supposed to act.

"We didn't mean to hurt her," Amanda whispered.

"Oh, you didn't?" he bit off, turning on them both with palpable fury. His voice was icy, but his face clearly showed his anger, and even Eloise shrank back in her bed.

"You didn't think she might possibly be hurt when she tripped over the string?" Phillip continued, his sarcasm lending him a controlled air that was even more frightening. "Or perhaps you realized correctly that the string itself wasn't likely to cause injury, but it didn't occur to you that she might be hurt when she actually fell."

They said nothing.

He looked at Eloise, who had lifted the meat from her face and was gingerly touching her cheekbone. The bruise under her eye seemed to be worsening by the minute.

The twins had to learn that they couldn't continue like this. They needed to learn that they had to treat people with more respect. They needed to learn . . .

Phillip swore under his breath. They needed to learn *some*thing.

He jerked his head toward the door. "You will come with me." He walked into the hall, turned back at them, and snapped, "Now."

And as he led them from the room, he prayed that he could control himself.

Eloise tried not to listen, but she couldn't seem to stop herself from straining her ears. She didn't know where Phillip was taking the children—it could be the next room, it could be the nursery, it could be outside. But one thing was certain. They were going to be punished.

And while she thought they *should* be punished—what they had done was inexcusable and they were certainly old enough to have realized that—she still found herself oddly worried for them. They had looked terrified when Phillip had led them away, and there was that niggling memory from the day before, when Oliver had blurted out the question, "Are you going to hit us?"

He had recoiled when he'd said it, as if he were expecting to be hit.

Surely Sir Phillip didn't . . . No, that was impossible, Eloise thought. It was one thing to give children a spanking at a time like this, but surely he didn't strike his children habitually.

She couldn't have made such a misjudgment about a person. She had let the man kiss her the night before, kissed him in return, even. Surely she would have felt that something was wrong, sensed an inner cruelty if Phillip were the sort who beat his children.

Finally, after what seemed like an eternity, Oliver and Amanda filed in, looking somber and red-eyed, followed by a grim-faced Sir Phillip, whose job at the rear was clearly to keep the children walking at a pace that exceeded that of a snail.

The children shuffled over to her bedside, and Eloise turned her head so that she could see them. She couldn't see out of her left eye with the meat covering it, and of course that was the side the children had chosen.

"We're sorry, Miss Bridgerton," they mumbled.

"Louder," came their father's sharply worded directive.

"We're sorry."

Eloise gave them a nod.

"It won't happen again," Amanda added.

"That's certainly a relief to hear," Eloise said.

Phillip cleared his throat.

"Father says we must make it up to you," Oliver said.

"Er . . ." Eloise wasn't exactly certain how they meant to do that.

"Do you like sweets?" Amanda blurted out.

Eloise looked at her, blinking her good eye in confusion. "Sweets?"

Amanda's chin shook up and down.

"Well, yes, I suppose I do. Doesn't everyone?"

"I have a box of lemon drops. I've saved them for months. You can have them."

Eloise swallowed against the lump in her throat as she watched Amanda's tortured expression. There was something wrong with these children. Or if not with them, then for them. Something wasn't right in their lives. With all of her nieces and nephews, Eloise had seen enough happy children to know this. "That will be all right, Amanda," she said, her heart wrenching. "You may keep your lemon drops."

"But we have to give you something," Amanda said, casting a fearful glance at her father.

Eloise was about to tell her that that wasn't necessary, but then, as she watched Amanda's face, she realized that it was. In part, of course, because Sir Phillip had obviously insisted upon it, and Eloise wasn't about to undermine his authority by saying otherwise. But also because the twins needed to understand the concept of making amends. "Very well," Eloise said. "You may give me an afternoon."

"An afternoon?"

"Yes. Once I'm feeling better, you and your brother may give me an afternoon. There is much here at Romney Hall with which I'm unfamiliar, and I imagine you two know every last corner of the house and grounds. You may take me on a tour. Provided, of course," she added, because she did value her health and well-being, "that you promise there will be no pranks."

"None," Amanda said quickly, her chin bobbing in an earnest nod. "I promise."

"Oliver," Phillip growled, when his son did not speak quickly enough.

"There will be no pranks that afternoon," Oliver muttered.

Phillip strode across the room and grabbed his son by the collar.

"Ever!" Oliver said in a strangled voice. "I promise! We shall leave Miss Bridgerton completely alone."

"Not completely, I hope," Eloise said, glancing up at Phillip and hoping he correctly interpreted that to mean, *You may now put down the child.* "After all, you do owe me an afternoon."

Amanda offered her a tentative smile, but Oliver's scowl remained firmly in place.

"You may leave now," Phillip said, and the children fled through the open doorway.

The two adults remained in silence for a full minute after they left, both staring at the door with hollow, weary expressions. Eloise felt drained, and wary, almost as if she'd been dropped into a situation she didn't quite understand.

A burst of nervous laughter almost escaped her lips. What was she thinking? Of *course* she had been dropped into a situation she didn't understand, and she was lying to herself if she thought she knew what to do.

Phillip walked over to the bed, but when he got there, he stood rather stiffly. "How are you?" he asked Eloise.

"If I don't remove this meat soon," she said quite frankly, "I think I might be sick."

He picked up the platter the meat had arrived upon and held it out. Eloise put the steak down, grimacing at the wet, slopping sound it made. "I believe I would like to wash my face," she said. "The smell is rather overwhelming."

He nodded. "First let me look at your eye."

"Do you have very much experience with this sort of thing?" she asked, glancing at the ceiling when he asked her to look up.

"A bit." He pressed gently against the ridge of her cheekbone with his thumb. "Look right."

She did. "A bit?"

"I boxed at university."

"Were you good?"

He turned her head to the side. "Look left. Good enough."

"What does *that* mean?"

"Close your eye."

"What does that *mean*?" she persisted.

"You're not closing your eye."

She did, shutting them both, because whenever she winked only one eye she ended up squeezing it far too tightly. "What does it mean?"

She couldn't see him, but she could feel him pause. "Has anyone ever told you you can be a bit stubborn?"

"All the time. It's my only flaw."

She heard his smile in the tenor of his breath. "The only one, eh?"

"The only one worth commenting upon."

She opened her eyes. "You didn't answer my question."

"I've quite forgotten what it was."

She opened her mouth to repeat it, then realized he was teasing her, so she scowled instead.

"Close your eye again," he said. "I'm not yet finished." When she obeyed his command, he added, "*Good enough* meant I never had to fight if I didn't want to."

"But you weren't the champion," she surmised.

"You can open your eye now."

She did, then blinked when she realized how close he still was.

He stepped back. "I wasn't the champion."

"Why not?"

He shrugged. "I didn't care about it enough."

"How does it look?" she asked.

"Your eye?"

She nodded.

"I don't think there is anything to be done to stop the bruising."

"I didn't think I hit my eye," she said, letting out a frustrated sigh. "When I fell. I thought I hit my cheek."

"You don't have to hit your eye to bruise there. I can see from your face that you landed right here"—he touched her cheekbone, right where she'd hit, but he was so gentle that she felt no pain—"and that's close enough for the bleeding to spread to the eye area."

She groaned. "I'm going to look a fright for weeks."

"It might not take weeks."

"I have brothers," she said, giving him a look that said she knew what she was talking about. "I've seen blackened eyes. Benedict had one that didn't completely fade away for two months."

"What happened to him?" Phillip asked.

"My other brother," she said wryly.

"Say no more," he said. "I had a brother of my own."

"Beastly creatures," she muttered, "the lot of them." But there was love in her voice as she said it.

"Yours probably won't take that long," he said, helping her to stand so that she could make her way to the washbasin.

"But it might."

Phillip nodded, then, once she was splashing the smell of the meat off her skin, said, "We need to get you a chaperone."

She froze. "I'd quite forgotten."

He let several seconds go by before replying, "I hadn't."

She picked up a towel and patted herself dry. "I'm sorry. It's my fault, of course. You had written that you would arrange for a chaperone. In my haste to leave London, I quite forgot that you would need time to make the arrangements."

Phillip watched her closely, wondering if she realized that she had slipped and said more than she'd probably meant to. It was difficult to imagine a woman such as Eloise—open, bright, and extremely talkative—as having secrets, but she had been quite close-lipped about her reasons for coming to Gloucestershire.

She'd said that she was looking for a husband, but he suspected that her reasons had as much to do with what she'd left behind in London as they did with what she hoped to find here in the country.

And then she'd said—*in my haste.*

Why had she left in a hurry? What had happened there?

"I have already contacted my great-aunt," he said, helping her back into her bed even though she quite clearly wanted to do it herself. "I sent her a letter the morning you arrived. But I doubt she could be here any earlier than Thursday. She only lives in Dorset, but she's not the sort to leave her home at the drop of a hat. She will want time to pack, I'm sure, and do all those things"—he waved his hand about in a slightly dismissive manner—"that women need to do."

Eloise nodded, her expression serious. "It's only four days. And you've a great many servants. It's not as if we're alone together at some remote hunting box."

"Nonetheless, your reputation could be seriously compromised should people learn of your visit."

She let out a long exhale, then lifted her shoulders in a fatalistic gesture. "Well, there isn't much I can do about it now." She motioned to her eye. "If I returned, my current appearance would cause more comment than the fact that I left in the first place."

He nodded slowly, signaling his agreement even as his mind flew off in other directions. Was there a reason she was so unconcerned for her reputation? He'd not spent much time in society, but it was his experience that unmarried ladies, regardless of their age, were always concerned for their reputations.

Was it possible that Eloise's reputation had been ruined before she'd arrived on his doorstep?

And more to the point, did he care?

He frowned, unable to answer the latter question just yet. He knew what he wanted—no, make that what he *needed*—in a wife, and it had little to do with purity and chastity and all those other ideals that proper young ladies were meant to embody.

He needed someone who could step in and make his life easy and uncomplicated. Someone who would run his house and mother his children. He was quite frankly pleased to have found in Eloise a woman for whom he felt a great deal of desire as well, but even if she'd been ugly as a crone—well, he'd have been happy to marry a crone as long as she was practical, efficient, and good with his children.

But if all that were true, why did he feel rather annoyed by the possibility that Eloise had had a lover?

No, not annoyed, precisely. He couldn't quite put his finger on the correct word for his feelings. Irritated, he supposed, the way one was irritated by a pebble in one's shoe or a mild sunburn.

It was that feeling that something wasn't quite right. Not dreadfully, catastrophically wrong, but just not . . . *right*.

He watched her settle herself against the pillows. "Do you want me to leave you to your rest?" he asked.

She sighed. "I suppose, although I'm not tired. Bruised, perhaps, but not tired. It's barely eight in the morning."

He glanced at a clock on a shelf. "Nine."

"Eight, nine," she said, shrugging off the difference. "Whichever, it's still morning." She looked longingly out the window. "And it's finally not raining."

"Would you prefer to sit in the garden?" he inquired.

"I'd prefer to *walk* in the garden," she replied pertly, "but my hip does ache a bit. I suppose I should try to rest for a day."

"More than a day," he said gruffly.

"You're most probably right, but I can assure you I won't be able to manage it."

He smiled. She wasn't the sort of woman who would ever choose to spend her days sitting quietly in a drawing room, working on her embroidery or sewing, or whatever it was women were supposed to do with needles and thread.

He looked over at her as she fidgeted. She wasn't the sort of woman who would ever choose to sit still, period.

"Would you like to take a book with you?" he asked.

Her eyes clouded with disappointment. He knew that she'd expected him to accompany her to the garden, and heaven knew, part of him wanted to, but somehow he felt he had to get away, almost as a measure of self-preservation. He still felt off balance, desperately ill-at-ease from having had to spank the children.

It seemed that every fortnight they did something that required punishment, and he didn't know what else to do. But he drew no pleasure from the act. He hated it, absolutely hated it, felt almost as if he might retch every time, and yet what was he supposed to do when they misbehaved that badly? The little things he tried to brush aside, but when they glued their governess's hair to her bedsheets while she slept, how was he supposed to brush aside *that*? Or what about the time they had broken an entire shelf of terra-cotta pots in his greenhouse? They had claimed it was an accident, but Phillip knew better. And the look in their eyes as they protested their innocence told him that even they hadn't thought he'd actually believe them.

And so he disciplined them in the only way he knew how, although thus far he'd been able to avoid using anything other than his hand. When, that is, he did anything at all. Half the time—more than half, really—he was so overcome by memories of his own father's brand of discipline that he just stumbled away, shaking and sweating, horrified by the way his hand itched to swat them on their behinds.

He worried that he was too lenient. He probably was, since the children didn't seem to be getting any better. He told himself he needed to be more stern, and once he'd even strode out to the stables and grabbed the whip . . .

He shuddered at the memory. It was after the glue incident, and they'd had to cut away Miss Lockhart's hair just to free her, and he'd been so angry—so unbelievably, overpoweringly angry. His vision had gone red, and all he'd wanted to do was punish them, and make them behave, and teach them how to be good people, and he'd snatched the whip . . .

But it had burned in his hands, and he'd dropped it in horror, afraid of what he would become if he actually used it.

The children had gone unpunished for an entire day. Phillip had fled to his greenhouse, shaking with disgust, hating himself for what he'd almost done.

And for what he was unable to do.

Make his children better people.

He didn't know how to be a father to them. That much was clear. He didn't know how, and maybe he simply wasn't suited to the task. Maybe some men were born knowing what to say and how to act, and some of them simply couldn't do a good job of it no matter how hard they tried.

Maybe one needed a good father oneself to know how to be the same.

Which had left him doomed from birth.

And now here he was, trying to make up for his deficiencies with Eloise Bridgerton. Perhaps he could finally stop feeling so guilty about being such a bad father if he could only provide them with a good mother.

But nothing was ever as simple as one wanted it to be, and Eloise, in the single day she'd been in residence, had managed to turn his life upside down. He'd never expected to want her, at least not with the intensity he felt every time he stole a glance at her. And when he'd seen her on the floor—why was it that his first thought had been terror?

Terror for her well-being, and, if he was honest, terror that the twins might have convinced her to leave.

When poor Miss Lockhart had been glued to the bed, Phillip's first emotion had been rage at his children. With Eloise, he'd spared only the merest of thoughts for them until he'd assured himself that she was not seriously injured.

He hadn't wanted to care about her, hadn't wanted anything other than a good mother for his children. And now he didn't know what to do about it.

And so even though a morning in the garden with Miss Bridgerton sounded like heaven, somehow he couldn't quite allow himself the pleasure.

He needed some time alone. He needed to think. Or rather, to *not* think, since the thinking just left him angry and confused. He needed to bury his hands in some dirt and prune some plants, and shut himself away until his mind was no longer screaming with all of his problems.

He needed to escape.

And if he was a coward, so be it.

Chapter 7

. . . have never been so bored in all of my life. Colin, you must come home. It is interminably boring without you, and I don't think I can bear such boredom another moment. Please do return, for I have clearly begun to repeat myself, and nothing could be more of a bore.

—from Eloise Bridgerton to her brother Colin, during her fifth season as a debutante, sent (but never received) while Colin was traveling in Denmark

Eloise spent the entire day in the garden, lounging on an exceedingly comfortable chaise that she was quite convinced had been imported from Italy, since it was her experience that neither the English nor the French had any clue as to how to fashion comfortable furniture.

Not that she normally spent a great deal of time pondering the construction of chairs and sofas, but stuck outside by herself in the Romney Hall garden, it wasn't as if she had anything else to ponder.

No, not a thing. Not a single thing to think about other than the comfortable chaise beneath her, and maybe the fact that Sir Phillip was an ill-mannered beast for leaving her alone for the entire day after his two little monsters—whose existence, she added into her thoughts with a mental flourish, he had never seen fit to reveal in his correspondence—had given her a blackened eye.

It was a perfect day, with a blue sky and a light breeze, and Eloise didn't have a single thing in the world to think about.

She had never been so bored in her life.

It wasn't in her nature to sit still and watch the clouds float by. She would much rather be out *doing* something—taking a walk, inspecting a hedgerow, anything other than just sitting like a lump on the chaise, staring aimlessly at the horizon.

Or if she *had* to sit here, at least she could have done so in the company of another person. She supposed the clouds might have been more interesting if she weren't quite so alone, if someone were here to whom she might say, *Goodness, but that one looks rather like a rabbit, don't you think?*

But no, she'd been left quite on her own. Sir Phillip was off in his greenhouse—she could see it from here, even see him moving about from time to time—and while she really wanted to get up and join him, if for no other reason than the fact that his plants had to be more interesting than the blasted clouds, she wasn't about to give him the satisfaction of seeking him out.

Not after he'd rejected her so abruptly this morning. Good heavens, the man had practically fled from her company. It had been the oddest thing. She'd thought they were dealing with each other rather well, and then he'd grown quite abrupt, making up some sort of excuse about how he needed to work and fleeing the room as if she were plagued.

Odious man.

She picked up the book she'd selected from the library and held it resolutely in front of her face. She was going to read the blasted thing this time if it killed her.

Of course, that was what she'd told herself the last four times she'd picked it up. She never managed to get past a single sentence—a paragraph if she was really disciplined—before her mind wandered and the text on the page grew unfocused and, it went without saying, unread.

Served her right, she supposed, for being so irritated with Sir Phillip that she hadn't paid any attention in the library and she'd snatched up the first book she'd seen.

The Botany of Ferns? What had she been thinking?

Even worse, if he saw her with it, he'd surely think she'd chosen it because she wanted to learn more about his interests.

Eloise blinked with surprise when she realized that she had reached the end of her page. She didn't recall a single sentence, and in fact wondered if perhaps her eyes had only slid along the words without actually reading the letters.

This was ridiculous. She thrust the book aside and stood up, taking a few steps to test out the tenderness of her hip. Allowing herself a satisfied smile when she realized that the pain wasn't bad at all, and in fact couldn't even be called anything beyond mild discomfort, she walked all the way to the riotous mass of rosebushes off to the north, leaning forward to sniff the buds. They were still tightly closed—it was early in the season, after all—but maybe they'd have a scent, and—

"*What the devil are you doing?*"

Eloise just managed to avoid falling into the rosebush as she turned around. "Sir Phillip," she said, as if that weren't completely obvious.

He looked irate. "You're supposed to be sitting down."

"I was sitting down."

"You were supposed to *stay* sitting down."

She decided the truth would make an excellent explanation. "I was bored."

He glanced over at the chaise in the distance. "Didn't you get a book from the library?"

She shrugged. "I finished it."

He quirked a brow in patent disbelief.

She returned his expression with an arch look of her own.

"Well, you need to sit down," he said gruffly.

"I'm perfectly fine." She patted her hip gently. "It hardly hurts at all now."

He stared at her for some time, his expression irritable, as if he wanted to say something but didn't know what. He must have left the greenhouse in a hurry, because he was quite filthy, with dirt along his arms, under every fingernail, and streaked quite liberally on his shirt. He looked a fright, at least by the standards Eloise had grown used to in London, but there was something almost appealing about him, something rather primitive and elemental as he stood there scowling at her.

"I can't work if I have to worry about you," he grumbled.

"Then don't work," she replied, thinking the solution quite obvious.

"I'm in the middle of something," he muttered, sounding, in Eloise's opinion, at least, rather like a sullen child.

"Then I'll accompany you," she said, brushing past him on the way to the greenhouse. Really, how did he expect them to decide if they would suit if they didn't spend any time together?

He reached out to grab her, then remembered that his hand was covered with dirt. "Miss Bridgerton," he said sharply, "you can't—"

"Couldn't you use the help?" she interrupted.

"No," he said, and in such a tone that she really couldn't continue the argument along those lines.

"Sir Phillip," she ground out, completely losing patience with him, "may I ask you a question?"

Visibly startled by her sudden turn of conversation, he just nodded—once, curtly, the way men liked to do when they were annoyed and wanted to pretend they were in charge.

"Are you the same man you were last night?"

He looked at her as if she were a lunatic. "I beg your pardon."

"The man I spent the evening with last night," she said, just barely resisting the urge to cross her arms as she spoke, "the one with whom I shared a meal and then toured the house and greenhouse, actually *spoke* to me, and in fact, seemed to enjoy my company, astonishing as it might seem."

He did nothing but stare at her for several seconds, then muttered, "I enjoy your company."

"Then why," she asked, "have I been sitting alone in the garden for three hours?"

"It hasn't been three hours."

"It doesn't matter how long—"

"It's been forty-five *minutes*," he said.

"Be that as it may—"

"Be that as it *is*."

"Well," she declared, mostly because she suspected he might have been correct, which put her in something of an awkward position, and *well*, seemed all she could say without embarrassing herself further.

"Miss Bridgerton," he said, his clipped voice a reminder that just the night before he'd been calling her Eloise.

And kissing her. "As you might have guessed," he continued sharply, "this morning's episode with my children has left me in a foul mood. I thought merely to spare you my company, such as it is."

"I see," she said, rather impressed with the supercilious edge to her voice.

"Good."

Except that she was quite certain she *did* see. That he was lying, to be precise. Oh, his children had put him in a foul mood, that much was true, but there was something else at work as well.

"I will leave you to your work, then," she said, motioning to the greenhouse with a gesture that was meant to seem as if she were waving him away.

He eyed her suspiciously. "And what do you plan to do?"

"I suppose I shall write some letters and then go for a walk," she replied.

"You will *not* go for a walk," he growled.

Almost, Eloise thought, as if he actually *cared* about her.

"Sir Phillip," she replied, "I assure you that I am perfectly fine. I'm quite certain I look a great deal worse than I feel."

"You had better look worse than you feel," he muttered.

Eloise scowled at him. It was a blackened eye, after all, and thus only a temporary blight on her appearance, but truly, he didn't need to *remind* her that she looked a fright.

"I shall remain out of your way," she told him, "which is all that really matters, correct?"

A vein began to twitch in his temple. Eloise took great pleasure in that.

"Go," she said. And when he didn't, she turned and began to walk through a gate to another segment of the garden.

"Stop this instant," Sir Phillip ordered, closing the distance between them with a single step. "You may *not* go for a walk."

Eloise wanted to ask him if he intended to tie her down, but she held her tongue, fearing that he might actually approve of the suggestion.

"Sir Phillip," she said, "I fail to see how— Oh!"

Grumbling something about foolish women (and using another adjective which Eloise considered considerably less complimentary), Sir Phillip scooped her into his arms and strode over to the chaise, where he dumped her quite unceremoniously back onto the cushion.

"Stay there," he ordered.

She sputtered, trying to find her voice after his unbelievable display of arrogance. "You can't—"

"Good God, woman, you could try the patience of a saint."

She glared at him.

"What," he asked with weary impatience, "would it take to keep you from moving from this spot?"

"I can't think of a thing," she answered, quite honestly.

"Fine," he said, his chin jutting out in a furiously stubborn manner. "Hike the entire countryside. Swim to France."

"From Gloucestershire?" she asked, her lips twitching.

"If anyone could figure out a way to do it," he said, "it would be you. Good day, Miss Bridgerton."

And then he stalked off, leaving Eloise exactly where she'd been ten minutes earlier. Sitting on the chaise, so surprised by his sudden departure that she quite forgot that she'd meant to get up and leave.

If Phillip hadn't already been convinced that he had made an ass of himself earlier that day, Eloise's short missive informing him that she intended to take supper in her room that evening made it quite clear.

Considering she'd complained that she had no company, her decision to pass the evening by herself was a pointed insult, indeed.

He ate alone, in silence, as he had for so many months. Years, really, since Marina had rarely left her room to dine when she'd been alive. One would have thought he'd have grown used to it, but now he was restless and uncomfortable, ever aware of the servants, who all knew that Miss Bridgerton had rejected his company.

He grumbled to himself as he chewed his beefsteak. He knew that one was supposed to ignore the servants and go about daily life as if they didn't exist, or if they did, as if they were an entirely different species altogether. And while he had to admit he didn't have much interest in their lives outside of Romney Hall, the fact remained that they had interest in his, and he rather detested being the subject of gossip.

Which he surely would be tonight, as they gathered for supper in the alcove off the kitchen.

He took a vicious bite of his roll. He hoped they had to eat that damned fish from Amanda's bed.

He made his way through the salad and the poultry and the pudding, even though the soup and the meat had proven quite enough. But there was always the chance that Eloise would change her mind and join him for supper. It didn't seem likely, given her stubborn streak, but if she decided to bend her will, he wanted to be present when it happened.

When it became apparent that this was nothing but wishful thinking on his part, he considered going up to her, but even out here in the country, that was quite inappropriate, and besides, he doubted she wanted to see him.

Well, that wasn't quite true. He rather thought that she *did* want to see him, but she wanted him humbled and apologetic. And even if he didn't utter a single word resembling either *I'm* or *sorry*, his very appearance would be tantamount to eating crow.

Which wouldn't be the worst thing in the world, considering that he'd already decided he'd be willing to wrap himself around her feet and beg her piteously to marry him if she would only consent to stay and mother his children. This, even though he had botched it up completely this afternoon—and morning, really, if one were to be honest about it.

But wanting to woo a woman didn't mean one actually knew how to go about it.

His brother had been the one born with all the charm and flair, always knowing what to say and how to act. George would never have even noticed that the servants were eyeing him as if they were going to gossip about him ten minutes later, and in truth, the point was moot, because all that the servants had ever had to say was along the lines of, "That Master George is such a rascal." All said with a smile and a blush, of course.

Phillip, on the other hand, had been quieter, more thoughtful, and certainly less suited to the role of father and lord of the manor. He'd always planned to leave Romney Hall and never look back, at least while his father was still alive. George was to marry Marina and have a half dozen perfect children, and Phillip would be the gruff and slightly eccentric uncle who lived over in Cambridge, spending all his time in his greenhouse, conducting experiments that no one else understood or in truth even cared about.

That was how it was supposed to be, but it had all changed on a battlefield in Belgium.

England had won the war, but that had been little comfort to Phillip when his father had dragged him back to Gloucestershire, determined to mold him into a proper heir.

Determined to change him into George, who had always been his favorite.

And then his father had died. Right there, right in front of Phillip, his heart gave out in a screaming rage, surely exaggerated by the fact that his son was now too large to be hauled over his knee and beaten with a paddle.

And Phillip became Sir Phillip, with all the rights and responsibilities of a baronet.

Rights and responsibilities he had never, ever wanted.

He loved his children, loved them more than life itself, so he supposed he was glad for the way it had all turned out, but he still felt as if he were failing. Romney Hall was doing well—Phillip had introduced several new agricultural techniques he'd learned at university, and the fields were turning a profit for the first time since . . . well, Phillip didn't know since when. They certainly hadn't earned any money while his father had been alive.

But the fields were only fields. His children were human beings, flesh and blood, and every day he grew more convinced that he was failing them. Every day seemed to bring worse trouble (which terrified him; he couldn't imagine what could possibly be worse than Miss Lockhart's glued hair or Eloise's blackened eye) and he had no idea what to do. Whenever he tried to talk to them, he seemed to say the wrong thing. Or do the wrong thing. Or not do anything, all because he was so scared that he'd lose his temper.

Except for that one time. Supper last night with Eloise and Amanda. For the first time in recent memory, he'd handled his daughter *exactly* right. Something about Eloise's presence had calmed him, lent him a clarity of thought he usually lacked when it came to his children. He was able to see the humor in the situation, where he usually saw nothing but his own frustration.

Which was all the more reason he needed to make sure Eloise stayed and married him. And all the more reason he wasn't going to go to her tonight and try to make amends.

He didn't mind eating crow. Hell, he would have eaten an entire flock if that was what it took.

He just didn't want to muck up the situation any worse than it already was.

Eloise rose quite early the following morning, which wasn't surprising, since she'd crawled into bed at only half eight the night before. She'd regretted her self-imposed exile almost the moment after she'd sent the note down to Sir Phillip informing him of her decision to take supper in her room.

She'd been thoroughly annoyed with him earlier in the day, and she'd allowed her irritation to rule her thinking. The truth was, she hated eating by herself, hated sitting alone at a table with nothing to do but stare at her food and guess how many bites it might take to finish one's potatoes. Even Sir Phillip in his most obstinate and uncommunicative of moods would have been better than nothing.

Besides, she still wasn't convinced that they wouldn't suit, and dining apart wasn't going to offer her any further insight into his personality and temperament.

He could be a bear—and a grumpy one, at that—but when he smiled . . . Eloise suddenly understood what all those young ladies were talking about when they'd waxed rhapsodic over her brother Colin's smile (which Eloise found rather ordinary; it was *Colin*, after all).

But when Sir Phillip smiled, he was transformed. His dark eyes assumed a devilish twinkle, full of humor and mischief, as if he knew something she didn't. But that wasn't what sent her heart fluttering. Eloise was a Bridgerton, after all. She'd seen plenty of devilish twinkles and prided herself on being quite immune to them.

When Sir Phillip looked at her and smiled, there was an air of shyness to it, as if he weren't quite used to smiling at women. And she was left with the feeling that he was a man who, if all the pieces of their puzzle fell together in just the right way, might someday come to treasure her. Even if he never loved her, he would value her and not take her for granted.

And it was for that reason that Eloise was not yet prepared to pack her bags and leave, despite his rather gruff behavior of the previous day.

Stomach growling, she made her way down to the breakfast room, only to be informed that Sir Phillip had already come and gone. Eloise tried not to be discouraged. It didn't mean he was trying to avoid her; it was entirely possible, after all, that he had assumed she was not an early riser and had elected not to wait for her.

But when she peeked into his greenhouse and found it empty, she declared herself stymied and went looking for other company.

Oliver and Amanda owed her an afternoon, didn't they? Eloise marched resolutely up the stairs. There was no reason they couldn't make it a morning, instead.

"You want to go swimming?"

Oliver was looking at her as if she were mad.

"I do," Eloise replied with a nod. "Don't you?"

"No," he said.

"I do," Amanda piped up, sticking her tongue out at her brother when he shot her a ferocious glare. "I love to swim, and so does Oliver. He's just too cross with you to admit it."

"I don't think they should go," replied their nursemaid, a rather stern-looking woman of indeterminate years.

"Nonsense," Eloise said breezily, disliking the woman immediately. She looked the sort to tug on ears and rap hands. "It is unseasonably warm and a bit of exercise will be quite healthful."

"Nevertheless—" the nursemaid said, her testy voice demonstrating her irritation at having her authority challenged.

"I shall give them lessons while we go about it," Eloise continued, using the tone of voice her mother used when it was clear she would brook no argument. "They are currently without a governess, aren't they?"

"Indeed," the nurse said, "the two little monsters glued—"

"Whatever the reason for her departure," Eloise interrupted, quite certain she didn't want to know what they had done to their last governess, "I'm sure it has been a monstrous burden upon you to assume both roles these last few weeks."

"Months," the nursemaid bit off.

"Even worse," Eloise agreed. "One would think you deserve a free morning, wouldn't one?"

"Well, I wouldn't mind a brief trip into town. . . ."

"Then it's settled." Eloise glanced down at the children and allowed herself a small moment of self-congratulation. They were staring at her in awe. "Off you go," she said to the nurse, bustling her out the door. "Enjoy your morning."

She shut the door behind the still-bewildered nurse and turned to face the children.

"You are very clever," Amanda said breathlessly.

Even Oliver couldn't help but nod his agreement.

"I hate Nurse Edwards," Amanda said.

"Of course you don't," Eloise said, but her heart wasn't into the statement; she hadn't much liked Nurse Edwards, either.

"Yes, we do," Oliver said. "She's horrid."

Amanda nodded. "I wish we could have Nurse Millsby back, but she had to leave to care for her mother. She's sick," she explained.

"Her mother," Oliver said, "not Nurse Millsby."

"How long has Nurse Edwards been here?" Eloise asked.

"Five months," Amanda said glumly. "Five very long months."

"Well, I'm sure she's not as bad as all that," Eloise said, intending to say more, but closing her mouth when Oliver interrupted with—

"Oh, she is."

Eloise wasn't about to disparage another adult, especially one who was meant to have some authority over them, so instead she decided to sidestep the issue by saying, "It doesn't matter this morning, does it, because you have me instead."

Amanda reached out shyly and took her hand. "I like you," she said.

"I like you, too," Eloise replied, surprised by the tears forming in the corners of her eyes.

Oliver said nothing. Eloise wasn't insulted. It took some people longer to warm up to a person than others. Besides, these children had a right to be wary. Their mother had left them, after all. Granted, it was through death, but they were young; all they would know was that they had loved her and she was gone.

Eloise remembered well the months following the death of her father. She had clung to her mother at every opportunity, telling herself that if she just kept her nearby (or even better, holding her hand), then her mother couldn't leave, either.

Was it any wonder that these children resented their new nursemaid? They had probably been cared for by Nurse Millsby since birth. Losing her so soon after Marina's death must have been doubly difficult.

"I'm sorry we blackened your eye," Amanda said.

Eloise squeezed her hand. "It looks much worse than it actually is."

"It looks dreadful," Oliver admitted, his little face beginning to show signs of remorse.

"Yes, it does," Eloise agreed, "but it's starting to grow on me. I think I look rather like a soldier who's been to battle—and won!"

"You don't look like you've won," Oliver said, one corner of his mouth twisting in a dubious expression.

"Nonsense. Of course I do. Anyone who actually comes home from battle wins."

"Does that mean Uncle George lost?" Amanda asked.

"You father's brother?"

Amanda nodded. "He died before we were born."

Eloise wondered if they knew that their mother was originally to have married him. Probably not. "Your uncle was a hero," she said with quiet respect.

"But not Father," Oliver said.

"Your father couldn't go to war because he had too many responsibilities here," Eloise explained. "But this is a very serious conversation for such a fine morning, don't you think? We should be out swimming and having a grand time."

The twins quickly caught her enthusiasm, and in no time they were changed into their bathing costumes and headed across the fields to the lake.

"We must practice our arithmetic!" Eloise called out as they skipped ahead.

And much to her surprise, they actually did. Who would have known that sixes and eights could be so much fun?

Chapter 8

. . . how fortunate you are to be at school. We girls have been presented with a new governess, and she is misery personified. She drones on about sums from dawn until dusk. Poor Hyacinth now breaks into tears every time she hears the word "seven." (Although I must confess that I don't understand why one through six do not elicit similar reactions.) I don't know what we shall do. Dip her hair in ink, I suppose. (Miss Haversham's, that is, not Hyacinth's, although I would never rule out the latter.)

—from Eloise Bridgerton to her brother Gregory, during his first term as a student at Eton

When Phillip returned from the rose garden, he was surprised to find his home quiet and empty. It was a rare day when the air wasn't exploding with the sound of some overturned table or shriek of outrage.

The children, he thought, pausing to savor the silence. Clearly, they had been vacated from the premises. Nurse Edwards must have taken them out for a walk.

And, he supposed, Eloise would still be abed, although in truth it was already nearly ten, and she did not seem the sort to laze the day away under her covers.

Phillip stared down at the roses in his hand. He'd spent an hour choosing exactly the right ones; Romney Hall boasted three rose gardens, and he'd had to go to the far one to find the early-blooming varieties. He'd then painstakingly picked them, careful to snip at the exact right spot so as to encourage further blooming, and then meticulously sliced away each thorn.

Flowers he could do. Green plants he could do even better, but somehow he didn't think Eloise would find much romance in a fistful of ivy.

He wandered over to the breakfast room, expecting to see food laid out, awaiting Eloise's arrival, but the sideboard was tidy and spotless, signaling that the morning meal had come to an end. Phillip frowned and stood in the middle of the room for a moment, trying to figure out what he ought to do next. Eloise had obviously already arisen and eaten breakfast, but deuced if he knew where she was.

Just then a maid came through, holding a feather duster and a rag. She bobbed a quick curtsy when she saw him.

"I'll need a vase for these," he said, holding up the flowers. He'd hoped to hand them to Eloise directly, but he didn't feel like clutching them all morning while he hunted her down.

The maid nodded and started to leave, but he stopped her with, "Oh, and do you happen to know where Miss Bridgerton might have gone off to? I noticed that breakfast has been cleared."

"Out, Sir Phillip," the maid said. "With the children."

Phillip blinked in surprise. "She went out with Oliver and Amanda? Willingly?"

The maid nodded.

"That's interesting." He sighed, trying not to envision the scene. "I hope they don't kill her."

The maid looked alarmed. "Sir Phillip?"

"It was a joke . . . ah . . . Mary?" He didn't mean to finish his sentence on a questioning note, but the truth was, he wasn't quite certain of her name.

She nodded in such a way that he couldn't be sure whether he'd gotten it right or she was just being polite.

"Do you happen to know where they went?" he asked.

"Down to the lake, I believe. To go swimming."

Phillip's skin went cold. "Swimming?" he asked, his voice sounding disembodied and hollow to his ears.

"Yes. The children were wearing their bathing costumes."

Swimming. Dear God.

For a year now, he'd avoided the lake, always taken the long route around, just to spare himself the sight of it. And he had forbidden the children from ever visiting the site.

Or had he?

He'd told Nurse Millsby not to allow them near the water, but had he remembered to do the same with Nurse Edwards?

He took off at a run, leaving the floor littered with roses.

"Last one in is a hermit crab!" Oliver shrieked, tearing into the water at top speed, only to laugh when it reached his waist and he was forced to slow down.

"I'm not a hermit crab. *You're* a hermit crab!" Amanda yelled back as she splashed around in the shallower depths.

"You're a *rotten* hermit crab!"

"Well, you're a *dead* hermit crab!"

Eloise laughed as she waded through the water a few yards away from Amanda. She hadn't brought a bathing costume—indeed, who would have thought she might need one?—so she had tied her skirt and petticoat up, baring her legs to just above her knees. It was an awful lot of leg to be showing, but that hardly mattered in the company of two eight-year-olds.

Besides, they were having far too much fun tormenting each other to give her legs even a passing glance.

The twins had warmed up to her during their walk down to the lake, laughing and chattering the entire way, and Eloise wondered if all they truly needed was a bit of attention. They'd lost their mother, their relationship with their father was distant at best, and then their beloved nurse had left them. Thank heavens they had each other.

And maybe, perhaps, her.

Eloise bit her lip, not sure whether she ought even to be allowing her thoughts to veer in that direction. She hadn't yet decided whether she wanted to marry Sir Phillip, and much as these two children seemed to need her—and they did need her, she just knew they did—she couldn't make her decision based on Oliver and Amanda.

She wasn't going to be marrying *them*.

"Don't go any deeper!" she called out, mindful that Oliver had been inching away.

He pulled the sort of face boys do when they think they are being mollycoddled, but she noticed that he took two large steps back toward the shore.

"You should come in further, Miss Bridgerton," Amanda said, sitting down on the lake bottom and then squealing, "Oh! It's cold!"

"Why did you sit down, then?" Oliver said. "You knew how cold it was."

"Yes, but my feet were used to it," she replied, hugging her arms to her body. "It didn't feel so cold anymore."

"Don't worry," he told her with a supercilious grin, "your bottom will get used to it soon, too."

"Oliver," Eloise said sternly, but she was fairly certain she'd ruined the effect by smiling.

"He's right!" Amanda exclaimed, turning to Eloise with an expression of surprise. "I can't feel my bottom at all anymore."

"I'm not so sure that's a good thing," Eloise said.

"You should swim," Oliver prodded. "Or at least go as far as Amanda. You've barely got your feet wet."

"I don't have a bathing costume," Eloise said, even though she'd explained this to them at least six times already.

"I think you don't know how to swim," he said.

"I assure you I know very well how to swim," she returned, "*and* that you're not likely to provoke a demonstration while I'm wearing my third-best morning dress."

Amanda looked over at her and blinked a few times. "I should like to see your first- and second-best. That's a very pretty frock."

"Why, thank you, Amanda," Eloise said, wondering who picked out the young girl's clothing. The crotchety Nurse Edwards, probably. There was nothing wrong with what Amanda was wearing, but Eloise would wager that no one had ever thought to offer her the fun of choosing her own garments. She smiled at Amanda and said, "If you would like to go shopping sometime, I would be happy to take you."

"Oh, I should adore that," Amanda said breathlessly. "Above all else. Thank you!"

"Girls," Oliver said disdainfully.

"You'll be glad for us someday," Eloise remarked.

"Eh?"

She just shook her head with a smile. It would be some time before he thought girls were good for anything other than tying their plaits together.

Oliver just shrugged and went back to hitting the surface of the water with the heel of his hand at just the right angle so as to splash the maximum amount of water on his sister.

"Stop it!" Amanda hollered.

He cackled and splashed some more.

"Oliver!" Amanda stood up and advanced menacingly toward him. Then, when walking proved too slow, she dove in and began to swim. He shrieked with laughter and swam away, coming up for air only long enough to taunt her.

"I'll get you yet!" Amanda growled, stopping for a moment to tread water.

"Don't go too far out!" Eloise called, but it really wasn't very important. It was clear that both children were excellent swimmers. If they were like Eloise and her siblings, they'd probably been swimming since age four. The Bridgerton children had spent countless summer hours splashing around in the pond near their home in Kent, although, in truth, the swimming had been curtailed after the death of their father. When Edmund Bridgerton had been alive, the family had spent most of their time in the country, but once he was gone, they had found themselves in town more often than not. Eloise had never known if it was because her mother preferred town or simply that their home in the country held too many memories.

Eloise adored London and had certainly enjoyed her time there, but now that she was here in Gloucestershire, splashing in a pond with two boisterous young children, she realized how much she'd missed the country way of living.

Not that she was prepared to give up London and all the friends and amusements it offered, but still, she was beginning to think she didn't need to spend *quite* so much time in the capital.

Amanda finally caught up with her brother and launched herself on top of him, causing them both to go under. Eloise watched carefully; she could see a hand or foot break the surface every few seconds until they both came up for air, laughing and gasping and vowing to beat each other in what was clearly extremely important warfare.

"Be careful!" Eloise called out, mostly because she felt she should. It was strange to find herself in the position of authoritative adult; with her nieces and nephews she got to be the fun and permissive aunt. "Oliver! Do *not* pull your sister's hair!"

He stopped but then immediately moved to the collar of her bathing costume, which could not have been comfortable for Amanda, and indeed, she began to sputter and cough.

"Oliver!" Eloise yelled. "Stop that at once!"

He did, which surprised and pleased her, but Amanda used the momentary reprieve to jump on top of him, sending him under while she sat on his back.

"Amanda!" Eloise yelled.

Amanda pretended not to hear.

Oh, blast, now she was going to have to wade out there to put an end to it herself, and she was going to be completely soaked in the process. "Amanda, stop that this instant!" she called out, making one last attempt to save her dress and her dignity.

Amanda did, and Oliver came up gasping, "Amanda Crane, I'm going to—"

"No, you're not," Eloise said sternly. "Neither one of you is going to kill, maim, attack, or even hug the other for at least thirty minutes."

They were clearly appalled that Eloise had even mentioned the possibility of a hug.

"Well?" Eloise demanded.

They were completely silent, then Amanda asked, "Then what *will* we do?"

Good question. Most of Eloise's own memories of swimming involved the same sort of war games. "Maybe we'll dry off and rest for a spell," she said.

They both looked horrified by the suggestion.

"We certainly ought to work on lessons," Eloise added. "Perhaps a bit more arithmetic. I did promise Nurse Edwards that we would do something constructive with our time."

That suggestion went over about as well as the first.

"Very well," Eloise said. "What do you suggest we do?"

"I don't know," came Oliver's muttered reply, punctuated by Amanda's shoulder shrug.

"Well, there is certainly no point in standing here doing nothing," Eloise said, planting her hands on her hips. "Aside from the fact that it's exceedingly boring, we're likely to fr—"

"*Get out of the lake!*"

Eloise whirled around, so surprised by the furious roar that she slipped and fell in the water. Drat and blast, there went her dry intentions and her dress. "Sir Phillip," she gasped, thankful that she'd broken her fall with her hands and had not landed on her bottom. Still, the front of her dress was completely soaked.

"Get out of the water," Phillip growled, striding into the lake with astonishing force and speed.

"Sir Phillip," Eloise said, her voice cracking with surprise as she staggered to her feet, "what—"

But he had already grabbed both of his children, his arms

wrapped around each of their rib cages, and was hauling them to shore. Eloise watched with fascinated horror as he set them none-too-gently down on the grass.

"I told you never, ever to go near the lake," he yelled, shaking each by a shoulder. "You know you're supposed to stay away. You—"

He stopped, clearly shaken by something, and by the need to catch his breath.

"But that was last year," Oliver whimpered.

"Did you hear me rescind the order?"

"No, but I thought—"

"You thought wrong," Phillip snapped. "Now get back to the house. Both of you."

The two children recognized the deadly serious intent in their father's eyes and quickly fled up the hill. Phillip did nothing as they left, just watched them run, and then, as soon as they were out of earshot, he turned to Eloise with an expression that caused her to take a step back and said, "What the hell did you think you were doing?"

For a moment she could say nothing; his question seemed too ludicrous for a reply. "Having a spot of fun," she finally said, probably with a bit more insolence than she ought.

"I do not want my children near the lake," he bit off. "I have made those wishes clear—"

"Not to me."

"Well, you should have—"

"How was I meant to know that you wanted them to stay away from the water?" she asked, interrupting him before he could accuse her of irresponsibility or whatever it was he was going to say. "I told their nurse where we intended to go, *and* what we intended to do, and she gave no indication that it was forbidden."

She could see from his face that he knew he had no valid argument, and it was making him all the more furious. Men. The day they learned to admit to a mistake was the day they became women.

"It's a hot day," she continued, her voice clipping along in the way it always did when she was determined not to lose an argument.

Which, for Eloise, generally meant any argument.

"I was trying to mend the breach," she added, "since I don't particularly relish the thought of another blackened eye."

She said it to make it him feel guilty, and it must have worked, since his cheeks turned ruddy and he muttered something that might have been an assurance under his breath.

Eloise paused for a few seconds to see if he would say more, or, even better, say something with a tone that approached intelligible speech, but when he did nothing but glare at her, she continued with, "I thought that doing something *fun* might go a long way. Heaven knows," she muttered, "the children could use a spot of fun."

"What are you saying?" he asked, his voice angry and low.

"Nothing," she said quickly. "Just that I didn't see any harm in going swimming."

"You put them in danger."

"Danger?" she sputtered. "From swimming?"

Phillip said nothing, just glared at her.

"Oh, for heaven's sake," she said dismissively. "It would only have been dangerous if I couldn't swim."

"I don't care if *you* can swim," he bit off. "I only care that my children can't."

She blinked. Several times. "Yes, they can," she said. "In fact, they're both quite proficient. I'd assumed you'd taught them."

"What are you talking about?"

Her head tilted slightly, perhaps out of concern, perhaps out of curiosity. "Didn't you know they could swim?"

For a moment, Phillip felt as if he couldn't breathe. His lungs tightened and his skin prickled, and his body seemed to freeze into a hard, cold statue.

It was awful.

He was awful.

Somehow this moment seemed to crystallize all of his failings. It wasn't that his children could swim, it was that he hadn't *known* they could swim. How could a father not know such a thing about his own children?

A father ought to know if his children could ride a horse. He ought to know if they could read and count to one hundred.

And for the love of God, he ought to know if they could swim.

"I—" he said, his voice giving out after a single word. "I—"

She took a step forward, whispering, "Are you all right?"

He nodded, or at least he thought he nodded. Her voice was ringing in his head—*Yes they can yes they can they can they can*—and it didn't even matter what she was saying. It had been the tone. Surprise, and maybe even a hint of disdain.

And he hadn't *known.*

His children were growing and changing and he didn't know them. He saw them, he recognized them, but he didn't know who they were.

He felt himself take a gasp of air. He didn't know what their favorite colors were.

Pink? Blue? Green?

Did it matter, or did it only matter that he didn't know?

He was, in his own way, every bit as awful a father as his own had been. Thomas Crane may have beaten his children to within an inch of their lives, but at least he knew what they were up to. Phillip ignored and avoided and pretended—anything to keep his distance and avoid losing his temper. Anything to stop him from becoming his father all over again.

Except maybe distance wasn't always such a good thing.

"Phillip?" Eloise whispered, laying a hand on his arm. "Is something the matter?"

He stared at her, but he still felt blinded, and his eyes couldn't seem to focus.

"I think you should go home," she said, slowly and carefully. "You don't look well."

"I'm—" He meant to say *I'm fine*, but the words didn't quite come out. Because he wasn't fine, and he wasn't good, and these days he wasn't even sure what he was.

Eloise chewed on her lower lip, then hugged her arms to her chest and glanced up at the sky as a shadow passed over her.

Phillip followed her gaze, watched as a cloud slid over the sun, dropping the temperature of the air at least ten degrees. He looked at Eloise, his breath catching in his throat as she shivered.

Phillip felt colder than he ever had in his life. "You need to get inside," he said, grabbing her arm and attempting to haul her up the hill.

"Phillip!" she yelped, stumbling along behind him. "I'm fine. Just a little chilled."

He touched her skin. "You're not just a little chilled, you're bloody well freezing." He yanked off his coat. "Put this on."

Eloise didn't argue, but she did say, "Truly, I'm fine. There is no need to *run*."

The last word came out halfway strangled as he yanked her forward, nearly off her feet. "Phillip, *stop*," she yelped. "Please, just let me walk."

He halted so quickly that she stumbled, whirling around and hissing, "I will not be responsible for your freezing yourself into a lung fever."

"But it's May."

"I don't care if it's bloody July. You will not remain in those wet clothes."

"Of course not," Eloise replied, trying to sound reasonable, since it was quite clear that argument was simply going to make him dig his heels in even further. "But there is no reason I cannot *walk*. It's only ten minutes back to the house. I'm not going to die."

She hadn't thought that blood could literally drain from a person's face, but she had no idea how else to describe the sudden blanching of his skin.

"Phillip?" she asked, growing alarmed. "What is wrong?"

For a moment she didn't think he was going to answer, and then, almost as if he weren't aware that he was making a noise, he whispered, "I don't know."

She touched his arm and gazed up at his face. He looked confused, almost dazed, as if he'd been dropped into a theatrical play and didn't know his lines. His eyes were open, and they were on her, but she didn't think he saw anything, just a memory of something that must have been very awful indeed.

Her heart broke for him. She knew bad memories, knew how they could squeeze a heart and haunt one's dreams until one was afraid to blow out the candle.

Eloise had, at the age of seven, watched her father die, shrieked and sobbed as he'd gasped for air and collapsed to the ground, then beaten against his chest when he could no longer speak, begging him to wake up and *say* something.

It was obvious now that he'd already been dead by that point, but somehow that made the memory even worse.

But Eloise had managed to put that behind her. She didn't know how—it was probably all due to her mother, who had come to her side every night and held her hand and told her it was all right to talk about her father. And it was all right to miss him.

Eloise still remembered, but it no longer haunted her, and she hadn't had a nightmare in over a decade.

But Phillip . . . his was a different story. Whatever had happened to him in the past, it was still very much with him.

And unlike Eloise, he was facing it alone.

"Phillip," she said, touching his cheek. He didn't move, and if she hadn't felt his breath on her fingers, she would have sworn he was a statue. She said his name again, stepping even closer.

She wanted to erase that shattered look from his eyes; she wanted to heal him.

She wanted to make him the person she knew he was, deep down in his heart.

She whispered his name one last time, offering him compassion and understanding and the promise of help, all in one single word. She hoped he heard; she hoped he listened.

And then, slowly, his hand covered hers. His skin was warm and rough, and he pressed her hand against his cheek, as if he were trying to sear her touch into his memory. Then he moved her hand to his mouth and kissed her palm, intensely, almost reverently, before sliding it down to his chest.

Across his beating heart.

"Phillip?" she whispered, question in her voice even though she knew what he intended to do.

His free hand found the small of her back, and he pulled her to him, slowly but surely, with a firmness she could not deny. And then he touched her chin and tilted her face to his, stopping only to whisper her name before capturing her mouth in a kiss that was blinding in its intensity. He was hungry, needy, and he kissed her as if he would die without her, as if she were his very food, his air, his body and soul.

It was the type of kiss a woman could never forget, the sort Eloise had never even dreamed possible.

He pulled her even closer, until the entire length of her body was pressed up against his. One of his hands traveled down her back to her bottom, cupping her, pulling her against him until she gasped at the intimacy of it.

"I need you," he groaned, the words sounding as if they were ripped from his throat. His lips slid off her mouth to her cheek, then down her neck, teasing and tickling as they went.

She was melting. *He* was melting her, until she didn't know who she was or what she was doing.

All she wanted was him. More of him. All of him.

Except . . .

Except not like this. Not when he was using her like some sort of succor to heal his wounds.

"Phillip," she said, somehow finding the strength to pull back. "We can't. Not like this."

For a moment she didn't think he would let her go, but then, abruptly, he did. "I'm sorry," he said, breathing hard. He looked dazed, and she didn't know if that was from the kiss or simply from the tumultuous events of the morning.

"Don't apologize," she said, instinctively smoothing her skirts, only to find them wet and unsmoothable. But she ran her hands along them anyway, feeling nervous and uncomfortable in her own body. If she didn't move, didn't force herself into some sort of meaningless motion, she was afraid she would launch herself back into his arms.

"You should go back to the house," he said, his voice still low and hoarse.

She felt her eyes widen with surprise. "Aren't you coming as well?"

He shook his head and said in an oddly flat voice, "You won't freeze. It's May, after all."

"Well, yes, but . . ." She let her words trail off, since she didn't really know what to say. She supposed she'd been hoping he'd interrupt her.

She turned to walk up the hill, then stopped when she heard his voice, quiet and intent behind her.

"I need to think," he said.

"About what?" She shouldn't have asked, shouldn't have intruded, but she'd never been able to mind her own business.

"I don't know." He shrugged helplessly. "Everything, I suppose."

Eloise nodded and continued back to the house.

But the bleak look in his eyes haunted her all day.

Chapter 9

. . . we all miss Father, especially this time of year. But think how lucky you were to have had eighteen years with him. I remember so little, and I do wish he could have known me, and all that I've grown up to be.

—from Eloise Bridgerton to her brother Viscount Bridgerton, upon the occasion of the tenth anniversary of their father's death

Eloise was purposefully late for supper that evening. Not by much—it was not in her nature to be tardy, especially since it was a trait she didn't care to tolerate in others. But after the events of that afternoon, she had no idea if Sir Phillip was even going to show up for supper, and she couldn't bear the thought of waiting in the drawing room, trying not to twiddle her thumbs as she wondered if she was to dine alone.

At precisely ten minutes past seven, she reckoned she could assume that if he wasn't waiting for her, he wasn't joining her, and she could then proceed to the dining room on her own and act as if she'd planned to eat by herself all the while.

But much to her surprise and, if she was honest, her great relief as well, Phillip was standing by the window when she entered the drawing room, elegantly dressed in evening kit that was, if not the very latest in style, obviously well made and tailored to perfection. Eloise noticed that his attire was strictly black and white, and she wondered if he was still in partial mourning for Marina, or if perhaps that was simply his preference. Her brothers rarely wore the peacock colors that were so popular among a certain set of the *ton*, and Sir Phillip didn't seem the type, either.

Eloise stood in the doorway for a moment, staring at his profile, wondering if he'd even seen her. And then he turned, murmured her name, and crossed the room.

"I hope you will accept my apologies for this afternoon," he said, and although his voice was reserved, she could see the entreaty in his eyes, sense that her forgiveness was very much desired.

"No apology is necessary," she said quickly, and it was the truth, she supposed. How could she know if he should apologize when she didn't even understand what had transpired?

"It is," he said haltingly. "I overreacted. I—"

She said nothing, just watched his face as he cleared his throat.

He opened his mouth, but it was several seconds before he said, "Marina nearly drowned in that lake."

Eloise gasped, not realizing that her hand had flown up to cover her mouth until she felt her fingers on her lips.

"She wasn't a strong swimmer," he explained.

"I'm so sorry," she whispered. "Were you—" How to ask it without appearing morbidly curious? There was no way to avoid it, and she couldn't help herself; she had to know. "Were you there?"

He nodded grimly. "I pulled her out."

"How lucky for her," Eloise murmured. "She must have been terrified."

Phillip said nothing. He didn't even nod.

She thought about her father, thought about how helpless she had felt when he'd collapsed to the ground in front of her. Even as a child, she'd been the sort who needed to *do* things. She'd never been one of life's observers; she'd always wanted to take action, to fix things, to fix people, even. And the one time it had all truly mattered, she'd been impotent.

"I'm glad you were able to save her," she murmured. "It would have been horrible for you if you hadn't."

He looked at her oddly, and she realized how strange her words had been, so she added, "It's . . . very difficult . . . when someone dies, and you can only watch, and you can't do anything to stop it." And then, because the moment seemed to call for it, and she felt oddly connected to this man standing so quiet and stiff in front of her, she said softly, and perhaps a bit mournfully as well, "I know."

He looked at her, the question clearly in his eyes.

"My father," she said simply.

It wasn't something she shared with many people; in fact, her good friend Penelope was probably the only person outside her immediate family who knew that Eloise had been the sole witness to her father's strange and untimely death.

"I'm sorry," he murmured.

"Yes," she said wistfully. "So am I."

And then he said the oddest thing. "I didn't know my children could swim."

It was so unexpected, such a complete non sequitur, that it was all she could do to blink and say, "I beg your pardon?"

He held out his arm to lead her to the dining room. "I didn't know they could swim," he repeated, his voice bleak. "I don't even know who taught them."

"Does it matter?" Eloise asked softly.

"It does," he said bitterly, "because *I* should have done so."

It was difficult to look at his face. She couldn't recall ever seeing a man so pained, and yet in an odd way it warmed her heart. Anyone who cared so much for his children—even if he didn't quite know how to act around them—well, he had to be a good man. Eloise knew that she tended to see the world in blacks and whites, that she sometimes leapt to judgment because she didn't stop to analyze the gradations of gray, but of this she was certain.

Sir Phillip Crane was a good man. He might not be perfect, but he was good, and his heart was true.

"Well," she said briskly, since that was her manner, and she preferred to deal with problems by charging ahead and fixing them rather than stopping to lament, "there's nothing to be done about it now. They can't very well unlearn what they already know."

He stopped, looked at her. "You're right, of course." And then, more softly, "But no matter who did the teaching, I should have known they were able."

Eloise agreed with him, but he was so obviously distressed, a scolding seemed inappropriate, not to mention unfeeling. "You still have time, you know," she said softly.

"What," he said, his mocking tone turned upon himself, "to teach them the backstroke so that they might expand their repertoire?"

"Well, yes," she said, her tone slightly sharp, since she'd never had much patience for self-pity, "but also to learn other things about them. They're charming children."

He looked at her dubiously.

She cleared her throat. "They do misbehave on occasion—"

One of his brows shot up.

"Very well, they misbehave quite often, but truly, all they want is a little attention from you."

"They told you this?"

"Of course not," she said, smiling at his naïveté. "They're only eight. They're not going to say it in so many words. But it's quite clear to me."

They'd reached the dining room, so Eloise took the seat held out for her by a footman. Phillip sat across from her, put his hand on his wineglass, then drew it back. His lips moved, but very slightly, as if he had something to say but wasn't quite certain how to phrase it. Finally, after Eloise had taken a sip of her own wine, he asked, "Did they enjoy it? Swimming, I mean."

She smiled. "Very much. You should take them."

He closed his eyes and held them that way, not for very long, but still, more than a blink. "I don't think I'd be able," he said.

She nodded. She knew the power of memories. "Perhaps somewhere else," she suggested. "Surely there must be another lake nearby. Or even a mere pond."

He waited for her to pick up her spoon, then dipped his own in his soup. "That's a fine idea. I think . . ." He stopped, cleared his throat. "I think I could do that. I shall ponder where we might go."

There was something so heartbreaking about his expression—the uncertainty, the vulnerability. The awareness that even though he wasn't sure he was doing the right thing, he was going to try to do it anyway. Eloise felt her heart lurch, skip a beat, even, and she wanted to reach across the table and touch his hand. But of course she couldn't. Even if the table weren't a foot longer than the length of her arm, she couldn't. So in the end, she just smiled and hoped that her manner was reassuring.

Phillip ate a bit of his soup, then dabbed at his mouth with his napkin and said, "I hope that you will join us."

"Of course," Eloise said, delighted. "I would be desolate if I weren't invited."

"I'm quite certain you overstate," he said with a wry twist to his lips, "but nonetheless, we would be honored, and to be quite honest, *I* would be relieved to have you there." At her curious expression, he added, "The outing is certain to be a successful one with your presence."

"I'm sure you—"

He stopped her midsentence. "We will all enjoy ourselves much better with your accompaniment," he said quite emphatically, and Eloise decided to stop arguing and graciously accept the compliment. He was, in all likelihood, correct. He and his children were so unused to spending time together that they would probably benefit from having Eloise along to smooth the way.

Eloise found she didn't mind the idea one bit. "Perhaps tomorrow," she suggested, "if the fine weather holds out."

"I think it will," Phillip said conversationally. "The air didn't feel changeable."

Eloise glanced at him as she sipped her soup, a chicken broth with bits of vegetables that needed a touch more salt. "Do you predict the weather, then?" she asked, quite certain her skepticism showed on her face. She had a cousin who was convinced he could predict the weather, and every time she listened to him, she ended up soaked to the skin or freezing her toes off.

"Not at all," he replied, "but one can—" He stopped, craned his neck a bit. "What was that?"

"What was what?" Eloise answered, but as the words left her lips, she heard what Phillip must have heard. Argumentative voices, growing louder by the second. Heavy footfall.

A forceful stream of invective was followed by a yelp of terror that could only have come from the butler . . .

And then Eloise *knew*.

"Oh, dear God," she said, her grip on her spoon growing slack until the soup dribbled off, splashing back into her bowl.

"What the devil?" Phillip asked, standing up, obviously preparing to defend his home against invasion.

Except that he had no idea what sort of invaders he was about to face. What sort of annoying, meddlesome, and diabolical invaders he was going to have to meet in, oh, approximately ten seconds.

But Eloise did. And she knew that *annoying*, *meddlesome*, and *diabolical* meant nothing compared to *furious*, *unreasonable*, and *downright large* when it came to Phillip's imminent safety.

"Eloise?" Phillip asked, his brows shooting up when they both heard someone bellow her name.

She felt the blood drain from her body. Positively felt it, *knew* it had happened, even though she couldn't see it pooling about her feet. There was no way she could survive a moment such as this, no way she could make it through without killing someone, preferably someone to whom she was quite closely related.

She stood, her fingers gripping the table. The footsteps (which, to be honest, sounded rather like a rabid horde) grew closer.

"Someone you know?" Phillip asked, quite mildly for someone who was about to face his demise.

She nodded, and somehow managed to eke out the words: "My brothers."

It occurred to Phillip (as he was pinned up against the wall with two sets of hands around his throat) that Eloise might have given him a bit more warning.

He didn't need *days*, although that would have been nice, if still insufficient against the collective strength of four very large, very angry, and, from the looks of them, rather closely related men.

Brothers. He should have considered that. It was probably best to avoid courting a woman with brothers.

Four of them, to be precise.

Four. It was a wonder he wasn't dead already.

"Anthony!" Eloise shrieked. "Stop!"

Anthony, or at least Phillip presumed he was Anthony—they hadn't exactly bothered to go through the necessary introductions—tightened his grip on Phillip's neck.

"Benedict," Eloise pleaded, turning her attention to the largest of the lot. "Be reasonable."

The other one—well, the other one squeezing his throat; there were two others, but they were just standing around glowering—loosened his grip slightly to turn around and look at Eloise.

Which was a huge mistake, since, in their haste to rip every limb from his body, none of them had yet looked at her long enough to see that she sported a nasty blackened eye.

Which of course they would think *he* was responsible for.

Benedict let out an unholy growl and jammed Phillip against the wall so tightly that his feet came off the ground.

Wonderful, Phillip thought. *Now I really am going to die.* The first squeeze was merely uncomfortable, but this . . .

"Stop!" Eloise yelled, hurling herself onto Benedict's back and yanking his hair. Benedict howled as his head jerked backward, but unfortunately Anthony's strangulatory grip held firm, even as Benedict was forced to let go to fight off Eloise.

Who was, Phillip noted as well as he could, given his lack of oxygen, fighting like a fury crossed with a banshee, crossed with Medusa herself. Her right hand was still pulling out Benedict's hair, even as her left arm wrapped around his throat, with her forearm lodged quite neatly up under his chin.

"Good Christ," Benedict cursed, whirling around as he tried to dislodge his sister. "Someone get her off of me!"

Not surprisingly, none of the other Bridgertons rushed to his aid. In fact, the one back against the wall looked rather amused by the whole thing.

Phillip's vision began to curl and turn black at the edges, but he couldn't help but admire Eloise's fortitude. It was a rare woman who knew how to fight to win.

Anthony's face suddenly appeared very close to his. "Did . . . you . . . hit her?" he growled.

As if he could speak, Phillip thought woozily.

"No!" Eloise cried out, momentarily taking her attention off tearing Benedict's hair out. "Of course he didn't hit me."

Anthony looked over at her with a sharp expression as she resumed pummeling Benedict. "There's no *of course* about it."

"It was an accident," she insisted. "He had nothing to do with it." And then, when none of her brothers made any indication that they believed her, she added, "Oh, for heaven's sake. Do you really think that *I* would defend someone who'd struck me?"

That seemed to do the trick, and Anthony abruptly let go of Phillip, who promptly sagged to the floor, gasping for breath.

Four of them. Had she told him she had four brothers? Surely not. He would never have considered marriage to a woman with four brothers. Only a fool would shackle himself to such a family.

"What did you do to him?" Eloise demanded, jumping off Benedict and hurrying to Phillip's side.

"What did he do to *you*?" one of the other brothers demanded. The one who, Phillip realized, had punched him in the chin right before the others had decided to strangle him instead.

She shot him a scathing look. "What are *you* doing here?"

"Protecting my sister's honor," he shot back.

"As if I need protection from you. You're not even twenty!"

Ah, thought Phillip, he must be the one whose name began with G. George? No, that wasn't right. Gavin? No . . .

"I'm twenty-three," the young one bit off, with all the irritability of a younger sibling.

"And I'm twenty-eight," she snapped. "I didn't need your help when you were in nappies, and I don't need it now."

Gregory. That's right. Gregory. She'd said as much in one of her letters. Ah, damn. If he knew that, then he must have known about the flock of brothers. He really had no one to blame but himself.

"He wanted to come along," said the one in the corner, the only one who hadn't yet tried to kill Phillip. Phillip decided he liked this one best, especially when he wrapped his hand around Gregory's forearm to prevent the younger man from launching himself at Eloise.

Which, Phillip thought, feeling rather ironically-minded there on the floor, was nothing more than she deserved. Nappies, indeed.

"Well, you should have stopped him," Eloise said, oblivious to Phillip's mental defection. "Do you have any idea how mortifying this is?"

Her brothers stared at her, quite rightly, in Phillip's opinion, as if she'd gone mad.

"You lost the right," Anthony bit off, "to feel mortified, embarrassed, chagrined, or in fact any emotion other than blindingly stupid when you ran off without a word."

Eloise looked a bit mollified but still muttered, "It's not as if I would listen to anything he has to say."

"As opposed to us," the one who had to be Colin murmured, "with whom you are the soul of meekness and obeisance."

"Oh, for the love of God," Eloise said under her breath, sounding rather fetchingly unladylike to Phillip's stinging ears.

Stinging? Had someone boxed his ears? It was difficult to recall. Four-to-one odds against did tend to muddle one's memory.

"You," snapped the one Phillip was almost certain was Anthony, with a finger jabbed in Phillip's direction, "don't go anywhere."

As if that were even worth contemplating.

"And you," Anthony said to Eloise, his voice even deadlier, although Phillip wouldn't have thought it possible, "what the hell did you think you were doing?"

Eloise tried to sidestep the question with one of her own. "What are you doing here?"

And succeeded, because her brother actually answered her. "Saving you from ruin," he yelled. "For the love of God, Eloise, do you have any idea how worried we've been?"

"And here I'd thought you hadn't even noticed my departure," she tried to joke.

"Eloise," he said, "Mother is beside herself."

That sobered her in an instant. "Oh, no," she whispered. "I didn't think."

"No, you didn't," Anthony replied, his stern tone exactly what one would expect from a man who'd been the head of his family for twenty years. "I ought to take a whip to you."

Phillip started to intervene, because, really, he couldn't countenance a whipping, but then Anthony added, "Or at the very least, a muzzle," and Phillip decided that brother knew sister very well, indeed.

"Where do you think you're going?" demanded Benedict, and Phillip realized that he must have started to stand before plopping back to his rather impotent position on the floor.

Phillip looked to Eloise. "Perhaps introductions are in order?"

"Oh," Eloise said, gulping. "Yes, of course. These are my brothers."

"I'd gathered," he said, his voice as dry as dust.

She shot him an apologetic look, which, Phillip thought, was really the least she could do after nearly getting him tortured and killed, then turned to her brothers and motioned to each in turn, saying, "Anthony, Benedict, Colin, Gregory. These three," she added, motioning to A, B, and C, "are my elders. This one"—she waved dismissively at Gregory—"is an infant."

Gregory looked near ready to throttle her, which suited Phillip just fine, since it deflected the murderous intentions off *him*.

And then Eloise finally turned back to Phillip and said to her brothers, "Sir Phillip Crane, but I expect you know that already."

"You left a letter in your desk," said Colin.

Eloise closed her eyes in agony. Phillip thought he saw her lips form the words, *Stupid*, *stupid*, *stupid*.

Colin smiled grimly. "You ought to be more careful in the future, should you decide to run off again."

"I'll remember that," Eloise shot back, but she was losing her fire.

"Would now be a good time to stand?" Phillip inquired, directing his question to no one in particular.

"*No*."

It was difficult to discern which Bridgerton brother spoke the loudest.

Phillip remained on the floor. He didn't tend to think himself a coward, and he was, if he did say so himself, quite proficient with his fists, but hell, there were *four* of them.

Boxer he might be. Suicidal fool he was not.

"How did you get that eye?" Colin asked quietly.

Eloise paused before answering, "It was an accident."

He considered her words for a moment. "Would you care to expand upon that?"

Eloise swallowed uncomfortably and glanced down at Phillip, which he really wished she wouldn't do. It only made *them* (as he was coming to think of the quartet) even more convinced that he was the one responsible for her injury.

A misapprehension that could only lead to his death and dismemberment. They didn't seem the sorts to allow anyone to lay a hand on their sisters, much less blacken an eye.

"Just tell them the truth, Eloise," Phillip said wearily.

"It was his children," she said, wincing on the words. But Phillip didn't worry. As close as they'd come to strangling him, they didn't seem the sort to harm innocent children. And certainly Eloise would not have said anything if she'd thought it might place Oliver and Amanda in peril.

"He has children?" Anthony asked, eyeing him with a slightly less derogatory expression.

Anthony, Phillip decided, must be a father as well.

"Two," Eloise replied. "Twins, actually. A boy and a girl. They're eight."

"My felicitations," Anthony murmured.

"Thank you," Phillip answered, feeling rather old and weary in that moment. "Sympathies are probably more to the point."

Anthony looked at him curiously, almost—but not quite—smiling.

"They weren't especially keen on my presence here," Eloise said.

"Smart children," Anthony said.

She shot him a decidedly unamused look. "They set a trip wire," she said. "Rather like the one Colin"—she turned to spear him with a hostile glare—"set for me in 1804."

Colin's lips twisted into a disbelieving expression. "You remember the *date*?"

"She remembers everything," Benedict commented.

Eloise turned to glare at *him*.

Aching throat notwithstanding, Phillip was actually beginning to enjoy the interaction.

Eloise turned back to Anthony, regal as a queen. "I fell," she said simply.

"On your eye?"

"On my hip, actually, but I didn't have time to break my fall, and I hit my cheek. I imagine the bruising spread to the eye area."

Anthony looked down at Phillip with a ferocious expression. "Is she telling the truth?"

Phillip nodded. "On my brother's grave. The children will own up to it as well, should you feel the need to interrogate them."

"Of course not," Anthony said gruffly. "I would never—" He cleared his throat, then ordered, "Stand up." But he tempered his tone by offering Phillip his hand.

Phillip took it, having already decided that Eloise's brother would make a far finer ally than enemy. He eyed the four male Bridgertons warily, though, and his stance was defensive. He stood no chance if all four decided to charge at him at once, and he wasn't convinced that that was not still a likely possibility.

At the end of the day, he was going to find himself either dead or married, and he wasn't quite prepared to let the Bridgerton brothers take the matter to a vote.

And then, after Anthony silenced his four younger siblings with nothing more than a stare, he turned to Phillip and said, "Perhaps you should tell me what happened."

Out of the corner of his eye, Phillip saw Eloise open her mouth to interrupt, then close it again, sitting down on a chair with an expression that, if it wasn't meek, was at least meeker than anything he'd ever expected to see gracing her face.

Phillip decided that he needed to learn how to glare like Anthony Bridgerton. He'd have his children in line in no time.

"I don't think Eloise will be interrupting us now," Anthony said mildly. "Please, go on."

Phillip glanced over at Eloise. She looked about ready to explode. But still, she held her tongue, which seemed a remarkable feat indeed, for one such as her.

Phillip briefly recounted the events that had led to Eloise's arrival at Romney Hall. He told Anthony about the letters, beginning with Eloise's letter of condolence, and how they had begun a friendly correspondence, pausing in his story only when Colin shook his head and murmured, "I always wondered what she was writing up in her room."

When Phillip looked at him quizzically, he held up his hands and added, "Her fingers. They were always ink-stained, and I never knew why."

Phillip finished his tale, concluding with, "So, as you see, I was looking for a wife. From the tone of her letters, she seemed intelligent and reasonable. My children, as you will come to realize should you remain long enough to meet them, can be rather, er"—he searched for the least unflattering adjective—"rambunctious," he said, satisfied with his word choice. "I'd been hoping she would be a calming influence on them."

"Eloise?" Benedict snorted, and Phillip could see from their expressions that the other three brothers agreed with his assessment.

And while Phillip might smile at Benedict's comment about Eloise remembering everything, and even *agree* with Anthony about the muzzle, it was becoming apparent that the Bridgerton males did not hold their sister in the regard she deserved. "Your sister," he said, his voice coming off sharp, "has been a marvelous influence upon my children. You would do well not to disparage her in my presence."

He'd probably just issued his own death warrant. There were four of them, after all, and it wasn't in his best interest to be insulting. But even if they had charged halfway across the country to protect Eloise's virtue, there was no way he was going to stand here and listen to them snort and snuff and make a mockery of her.

Not Eloise. Not in front of him.

But to his great surprise, not a one of them had a retort, and in fact Anthony, who was still clearly the one in charge, held him with a level stare, assessing him as if he were peeling the layers back until he could see what lay hidden in his core.

"We have a great deal to talk about, you and I," Anthony said quietly.

Phillip nodded. "I expect you will need to speak with your sister as well."

Eloise shot him a grateful look. He wasn't surprised. He couldn't imagine she would take well to being left out of any decisions pertaining to her life. Hell, she wasn't the sort to take well to being left out of anything.

"Yes," Anthony said, "I do. In fact, I think we shall conduct our interview first, if you don't mind."

As if Phillip was stupid enough to argue with one Bridgerton while three more were glaring at him. "Please use my study," he offered. "Eloise can show you the way."

It was the wrong thing to say. None of the brothers cared to be reminded that Eloise had been in residence long enough to know her way around.

Anthony and Eloise left the room without another word, leaving Phillip alone with the remaining Bridgerton brothers.

"Mind if I sit?" Phillip asked, since he suspected he was going to be stuck here in the dining room for some time.

"Go right ahead," Colin said expansively. Benedict and Gregory just continued to glare. Colin, Phillip noted, didn't look particularly eager to strike up a friendship, either. He might have been marginally more amiable than his brothers, but his eyes showed a sharp shrewdness that Phillip rather thought he ought not underestimate.

"Please," Phillip said, motioning to the food still on the table, "eat."

Benedict and Gregory scowled at him as if he'd offered poison, but Colin sat across from him and plucked a crusty roll off a plate.

"They're quite good," Phillip said, even though he'd not had the opportunity to partake that evening.

"Good," Colin muttered, taking a bite. "I'm famished."

"How can you think of food?" Gregory said angrily.

"I always think of food," Colin replied, his eyes searching the table until he located the butter. "What else is there?"

"Your wife," Benedict drawled.

"Ah, yes, my wife," Colin said with a nod. He turned to Phillip, leveled a hard stare at him, and said, "Just so that you are aware, I would have rather spent the night with my wife."

Phillip couldn't think of a reply that might not hint at insult to the absent Mrs. Bridgerton, so he just nodded and buttered a roll of his own.

Colin took a huge bite, then spoke with his mouth full, the etiquette breach a clear insult to his host. "We've only been married a few weeks."

Phillip raised one of his brows in question.

"Still newlyweds."

Phillip nodded, since some sort of response seemed to be required.

Colin leaned forward. "I *really* did not want to leave my wife."

"I see," Phillip murmured, since truly, what else could he have said?

"Do you understand what he's saying?" Gregory demanded.

Colin turned and sent a chilling look at his brother, who was clearly too young to have mastered the fine art of nuance and circumspect speech. Phillip waited until Colin had turned back to the table, offered him a plate of asparagus (which he took), then said, "I gather you miss your wife."

There was a beat of silence, and then Colin said, after sending one last disdainful glance at his brother, "Indeed."

Phillip looked over at Benedict, since he was the only one uninvolved in the latest spat.

Big mistake. Benedict was flexing his hands, still looking as if he regretted not strangling him when he had his chance.

Phillip then turned his gaze to Gregory, whose arms were crossed angrily over his chest. His entire body practically quivered with fury, perhaps aimed at Phillip, perhaps at his family, who'd been treating him like a green boy all evening. Phillip's glance was not met with favor. Gregory's chin jutted angrily out, his teeth clenched, and—

And Phillip had had enough of that. He looked back to Colin.

Colin was still working on his food, having somehow managed to charm the servants into bringing him a bowl of soup. He'd set down his spoon, though, and was presently examining his other hand, idly flexing each finger in turn, murmuring a word as each pointed out toward Phillip.

"Miss. My. Wife."

"Bloody hell," Phillip finally burst out. "If you're going to break my legs, would you just go ahead and do it now?

Chapter 10

. . . you will never know how unfortunate you are, dearest Penelope, to have sisters only. Brothers are ever so much more fun.

—from Eloise Bridgerton to Penelope Featherington, following a midnight ride in Hyde Park with her three older brothers

"Here are your choices," Anthony said, sitting behind Phillip's desk as if he owned the place. "You can marry him in one week, or you can marry him in two."

Eloise's mouth fell open into a horrified oval. "Anthony!"

"Did you expect me to suggest an alternative?" he asked mildly. "I suppose we might stretch it to three, given a sufficiently compelling reason."

She hated when he spoke like that, as if he were reasonable and wise, and she were nothing more than a recalcitrant child. It was far better when he ranted and raved. Then, at least, she could pretend he was mad in the head and she was a poor, beleaguered innocent.

"I don't see why you would object," he continued. "Didn't you come here with the intention to marry him?"

"No! I came here with the intention to *find out* if he was suitable for marriage."

"And is he?"

"I don't know," she said. "It's only been two days."

"And yet," Anthony said, idly examining his fingernails in the dim candlelight, "that's still more than enough time to ruin your reputation."

"Does anyone know I was gone?" she quickly asked. "Outside the family, that is."

"Not yet," he admitted, "but someone will find out. Someone always finds out."

"There was supposed to be a chaperone," Eloise said sullenly.

"Was there?" he asked, his voice perfectly conversational, as if he were asking if there was supposed to have been lamb for dinner, or maybe a hunting expedition arranged for his entertainment.

"She's coming soon."

"Hmmm. Too bad for her I arrived first."

"Too bad for everyone," Eloise muttered.

"What was that?" he asked, but again he used that awful voice, the one that made it clear he'd heard every word.

"Anthony," Eloise said, and his name came out like a plea, even though she had no idea what it was she was pleading for.

He turned to her, his dark eyes blazing, the force of his stare so violent that it was only then that she realized she ought to have been grateful he'd been pretending to examine his fingernails.

She took a step back. Anyone would have when faced with Anthony Bridgerton in such a fury.

But when he spoke, his voice was even and controlled. "You've made yourself a rather messy little bed here," he said, his cadence slow and precise. "I'm afraid you're going to have to lie in it."

"You would have me marry a man I don't know?" she whispered.

"Is that even the truth?" Anthony responded. "Because you seemed to know him very well indeed in the dining room. You certainly leapt to his defense at every conceivable opportunity."

Anthony was talking her into a corner, and it was driving her mad. "It's not enough for marriage," she insisted. "At least not yet."

But Anthony wasn't the sort to let up. "If not now, then when? One week? Two?"

"Stop!" she burst out, wanting to throw her hands over her ears. "I can't think."

"You *don't* think," he corrected. "If you'd taken one moment to think, to use that tiny portion of your brain reserved for common sense, you would never have run off."

She crossed her arms, looking away. She had no argument, and it was killing her.

"What are you going to do, Eloise?" Anthony asked.

"I don't know," she muttered, hating how stupid she sounded.

"Well," he said, still continuing in that awful, reasonable voice, "that puts us in a bit of a bind, doesn't it?"

"Can't you just say it?" she asked, her fists clenching against her rib cage. "Do you have to end everything with a question?"

He smiled humorlessly. "And here I thought you'd appreciate my soliciting your opinion."

"You're being condescending and you know it."

He leaned forward, thunder in his eyes. "Do you have any idea how much effort it requires to keep my temper in check?"

Eloise thought it best not to hazard a guess.

"You ran off in the middle of the night," he said, rising to his feet, "without a word, without even a note—"

"I left a note!" she burst out.

He looked at her with patent disbelief.

"I did!" she insisted. "I left it on the side table in the front hall. Right next to the Chinese vase."

"And this mysterious note said . . ."

"It said not to worry, that I was fine and would contact you all within a month."

"Ah," Anthony said mockingly. "*That* would have set my mind at ease."

"I don't know why you didn't get it," Eloise muttered. "It probably got mixed up with a pile of invitations."

"For all we knew," Anthony continued, taking a step toward her, "you'd been kidnapped."

Eloise paled. She'd never even considered that her family might think such a thing. It had never occurred to her that her note might go astray.

"Do you know what Mother did?" Anthony asked, his voice deathly serious. "*After* nearly collapsing with worry?"

Eloise shook her head, dreading the answer.

"She went to the bank," Anthony continued. "Do you know why?"

"Could you just tell me?" Eloise asked wearily. She hated the questions.

"She went there," he said, walking toward her in a terrifying manner, "to make sure that all her funds were in the proper order so that she could withdraw them *should she need to ransom you*!"

Eloise shrank back at the fury in her older brother's voice. *I left a note*, she wanted to say again, but she knew it would come out the wrong way. She'd been wrong, and she'd been foolish, and she didn't want to compound her stupidity by trying to excuse it.

"Penelope was the one who finally figured out what you'd done," Anthony said. "We asked her to search your room, since she's probably spent more time there than any of the rest of us."

Eloise nodded. Penelope had been her closest friend—still was, in fact, even though she'd married Colin. They'd spent countless hours up in her room, talking about anything and everything. Phillip's letters were the only secret Eloise had ever kept from her.

"Where did she find the letter?" Eloise asked. Not that it mattered, but she couldn't help her curiosity.

"It had fallen behind your desk." Anthony crossed his arms. "Along with a pressed flower."

Somehow that seemed fitting. "He's a botanist," she whispered.

"I beg your pardon?"

"A botanist," she said, more loudly this time. "Sir Phillip. He took a first at Cambridge. He would have been an academic if his brother hadn't died at Waterloo."

Anthony nodded, digesting that fact, and the fact that she knew it. "If you tell me that he's a cruel man, that he will beat you, that he will insult you and demean you, I will not force your hand. But before you speak, I want you to consider my words. You are a Bridgerton. I don't care who you marry or what your name becomes when you stand up before a priest and say your vows. You will always be a Bridgerton, and we behave with honor and honesty, not because it is expected of us, but because *that is what we are.*"

Eloise nodded, swallowing as she fought the tears that were stinging in her eyes.

"So I will ask you right now," he said. "Is there any reason you cannot marry Sir Phillip Crane?"

"No," she whispered. She didn't even hesitate. She wasn't ready for this, wasn't yet ready for the marriage, but she wouldn't sully the truth by hesitating on her answer.

"I thought not."

She stood still, almost deflated, not certain what to do or say next. She turned, aware that Anthony had to know she was crying, but not wanting him to see her tears, nonetheless. "I'll marry him," she said, choking on the words. "It's just that I—I'd wanted—"

He held silent for a moment, respecting her distress, but then, when she did not continue, he asked, "What did you want, Eloise?"

"I'd hoped for a love match," she said, so softly she barely heard herself.

"I see," he said, his hearing superb as always. "You should have thought of that before you ran off, shouldn't you?"

She hated him in that moment. "You have a love match. You should understand."

"*I*," he said, the tone of his voice indicating that he did not appreciate her trying to make the conversation about him, "married my wife after we were caught in a compromising position by the biggest bloody gossip in England."

Eloise let out a long breath, feeling stupid. It had been so many years since Anthony had married. She'd forgotten the circumstances.

"I didn't love my wife when I married her," he continued, "or," he added, his voice growing a bit softer, more gruff and nostalgic, "if I did, I did not yet realize it."

Eloise nodded. "You were very lucky," she said, wishing she knew if she could be that lucky with Phillip.

And then Anthony surprised her, because he didn't scold, and he didn't reprimand. All he said was, "I know."

"I felt lost," she whispered. "When Penelope and Colin married . . ." She sank into a chair, letting her head drop into her hands. "I'm a terrible person. I must be a terrible person, horrible and shallow, because when they married, all I could think about was myself."

Anthony sighed, and he crouched beside her. "You're not a terrible person, Eloise. You know that."

She looked up at him, wondering when it was that this man, her brother, had become so wise. If he'd yelled one more word, spent one more minute speaking to her in that mocking voice, she would have broke. She would have broke, or she would have hardened, but either way, something between them would have been ruined.

But here he was, Anthony of all people, who was arrogant and proud and every inch the arch nobleman he'd been born to be, kneeling at her side, placing his hand on hers, and speaking with a kindness that nearly broke her heart.

"I was happy for them," she said. "I *am* happy for them."

"I know you are."

"I should have felt nothing but joy."

"If you had, you wouldn't be human."

"Penelope became my *sister*," she said. "I should have been happy."

"Didn't you say that you were?"

She nodded. "I am. I am. I know that I am. I'm not just saying it."

He smiled benignly and waited for her to continue.

"It's just that I suddenly felt so lonely, and so *old*." She looked up at him, wondering if he could possibly understand. "I never thought I would be left behind."

He chuckled. "Eloise Bridgerton, I don't think anyone would *ever* make the mistake of leaving you behind."

She felt her lips curve into a wobbly smile, marveling that her brother of all people could actually say the *exact* right thing. "I suppose I never really thought I'd always be a spinster," she said. "Or, if I was, then at least that Penelope would always be one, too. It wasn't very kind of me, and I don't even think I really thought about it much, but—"

"But that's just how it was," he said, doing her the kindness of finishing the sentiment. "I don't think even Penelope ever thought she'd marry. And to be honest, I doubt Colin did, either. Love can rather creep up on a person, you know."

She nodded, wondering if it could creep up on her. Probably not. She was the sort of person who would need it whacked over the head.

"I'm glad they're married," Eloise said.

"I know you are. I am, too."

"Sir Phillip," she said, motioning toward the door, even though he was actually down the hall and around two corners in the dining room. "We had been corresponding for over a year. And then he mentioned marriage. And he did it in such a sensible manner. He didn't propose, he just inquired if I might like to visit, to see if we would suit. I told myself he was mad, that I couldn't even consider such an offer. Who would marry someone she didn't know?" She let out a shaky little laugh. "And then Colin and Penelope announced their engagement. It was as if my entire world flipped sideways. And that was when I started thinking about it. Every time I looked at my desk, at the drawer where I kept his letters, it was as if they were burning a hole right through the wood."

Anthony said nothing, just squeezed her hand, as if he understood.

"I had to do something," she said. "I couldn't just sit and wait for life to happen to me any longer."

A chuckle burst from her brother's throat. "Eloise," he said, "that is the last thing I would ever worry about on your behalf."

"Anth—"

"No, let me finish," he said. "You're one of the special ones, Eloise. Life never *happens* to you. Trust me on this. I've watched you grow up, had to be your father at times when I wanted only to be your brother."

Her lips parted as something squeezed around her heart. He was right. He *had* been a father to her. It was a role neither of them had wanted for him, but he had done it for years, without complaint.

And this time she squeezed his hand, not because she loved him, but because it was only now that she realized how very much she did.

"*You* happen to life, Eloise," Anthony said. "You've always made your own decisions, always been in control. It might not always feel that way, but it's true."

She closed her eyes for a moment, shaking her head as she said, "Well, I was trying to make my own decisions when I came here. It seemed a good plan."

"And maybe," Anthony said quietly, "you'll find that it was indeed a good plan. Sir Phillip seems an honorable sort."

Eloise couldn't hide her peevish expression. "You were able to deduce this while you had your hands wrapped around his throat?"

He shot her a superior look. "You'd be surprised what men can deduce about one another while fighting."

"You call that fighting? It was four against one!"

He shrugged. "I never said it was *fair* fighting."

"You're incorrigible."

"An interesting adjective considering *your* recent activities."

Eloise felt herself flush.

"Very well," Anthony said, his brisk tone signaling a change of topic. "Here is what we are going to do."

And Eloise knew that whatever he said, it was what she'd be doing. His voice was that resolute.

"You will pack your bags immediately," Anthony said, "and we will all travel to My Cottage and remain there for a week."

Eloise nodded. My Cottage was the rather odd name of Benedict's home, situated not too far from Romney Hall in Wiltshire. He lived there with his wife Sophie and their three sons. It wasn't a particularly large home, but it was comfortable, and there was certainly enough room for a few extra Bridgertons.

"Your Sir Phillip may come visit each day," Anthony continued, and Eloise understood his words perfectly to mean, *Your Sir Phillip* will *come visit each day*.

She nodded again.

"If, at the end of the week, I determine that he is good enough to marry my sister, you will do so. Immediately."

"You're certain you can judge the measure of a man's character in one week?"

"It rarely takes longer," Anthony stated. "And if I'm unsure, we'll merely wait another sennight."

"Sir Phillip might not care to marry me," Eloise felt compelled to point out.

Anthony leveled a hard stare at her face. "He hasn't that option."

Eloise gulped.

One of Anthony's brows rose into an arrogant arch. "Do we understand each other?"

She nodded. His plan seemed reasonable—more reasonable, in fact, than most older brothers would have allowed—and if something went horribly wrong, if she decided that she couldn't possibly marry Sir Phillip Crane, well then, she had a week to figure out how to get out of it. A lot could happen in a week.

Just look at the last one.

"Shall we return to the dining room?" Anthony queried. "I imagine you're hungry, and if we tarry much longer, Colin is sure to have eaten our host out of house and home."

Eloise nodded. "Either that, or they've all killed him by now."

Anthony paused to consider that. "It would save me the expense of a wedding."

"Anthony!"

"It's a joke, Eloise," he said, giving his head a weary shake. "Come along, now. Let's make sure your Sir Phillip still resides among the ranks of the living."

"And then," Benedict was saying as Anthony and Eloise reentered the dining room, "the tavern wench arrived and she had the *biggest*—"

"Benedict!" Eloise exclaimed.

Benedict looked over at his sister with a supremely guilty expression, yanked back his hands, which were demonstrating the size of what was clearly an impossibly endowed female, and muttered, "Sorry."

"You're married," Eloise scolded.

"But not blind," Colin said with a grin.

"You're married, too!" she accused.

"But not blind," he said again.

"Eloise," Gregory said with what was quite possibly the most annoying use of condescension she'd ever had cause to hear, "there are some things that are impossible not to see. Especially," he added, "when you're a man."

"It's true," admitted Anthony. "I saw it myself."

Eloise gasped as she looked from brother to brother, looking for some sane spot in this cesspool of madness. Her eyes fell on Phillip, who, by the looks of him, not to mention his slightly inebriated state, had formed a lifelong bond with her brothers during the short time she'd been closeted away with Anthony.

"Sir Phillip?" she asked, waiting for him to say something acceptable.

But he just offered her a loopy grin. "I know who they're talking about," he said. "Been to that inn any number of times. Lucy's quite famous in these parts."

"Even I've heard of her," Benedict said, with a knowing nod. "I'm only an hour away on horseback. Less, if you push hard."

Gregory leaned toward Phillip, his blue eyes gleaming with interest as he asked, "So, did you? Ever?"

"Gregory!" Eloise practically yelled. This was really too much. Her brothers should never have been talking about such things in front of her, but even more, the last thing she wanted to know was whether Sir Phillip had tupped a tavern wench with bosoms the size of soup tureens.

But Phillip just shook his head. "She's married," he said. "As was I."

Anthony turned to Eloise and whispered in her ear, "He'll do."

"I'm glad you have such high standards for your beloved sister," she muttered.

"I told you," Anthony remarked, "I've seen Lucy. This is a man with restraint."

She planted her hands on her hips and looked her older brother squarely in the eye. "Were *you* tempted?"

"Of course not! Kate would slit my throat."

"I'm not talking about what Kate would do to you if you strayed, although I'm of the opinion that she would not start at your throat—"

Anthony winced. He knew it was true.

"—I want to know if you were tempted."

"No," he admitted, shaking his head. "But don't tell anyone. I used to be considered something of a rake, after all. Wouldn't want people to think I was completely tamed."

"You're appalling."

He grinned. "And yet, my wife still loves me to distraction, which is all that really matters, isn't it?"

Eloise supposed he was right. She sighed. "What are we going to do about them?" She motioned to the quartet of men sitting around the dining room table, which was littered with empty dishes. Phillip, Benedict, and Gregory were sitting back and relaxing, looking quite sated. Colin was still eating.

Anthony shrugged. "I don't know what you want to do, but I'm going to join them."

Eloise just stood in the doorway, watching as he sat down and poured himself a glass of wine. The conversation had thankfully moved on from Lucy and her tremendous bosoms, and now they were talking about boxing. Or at least that's what she assumed they were talking about. Phillip was demonstrating some sort of hand maneuver to Gregory.

Then he punched him in the face.

"So sorry," Phillip said, patting Gregory on the back. But Eloise noticed that the right corner of his mouth was curving ever so slightly into a smile. "Won't hurt for long, I'm sure. *My* chin's feeling better already."

Gregory grunted something that was clearly meant to mean that it didn't hurt, but he rubbed his chin nonetheless.

"Sir Phillip?" Eloise said loudly. "Might I have a word?"

"Of course," he said, standing up immediately, although in all truth, *all* of the men should have been standing, since she'd never vacated her position in the doorway.

Phillip walked to her side. "Is something amiss?"

"I was worried they were going to kill you," she hissed.

"Oh." He smiled, that lopsided, three-glasses-of-wine sort of smile. "They didn't."

"I see that," she ground out. "What happened?"

He looked back over at the table. Anthony was eating the meager scraps that Colin had left behind (almost certainly only because he hadn't realized they were there), and Benedict was tipping back in his chair, trying to balance it on two legs. Gregory was humming to himself, his eyes closed as he smiled beatifically, presumably thinking of Lucy, or, more likely, certain large and squishy parts of Lucy.

Phillip turned back to her and shrugged.

"When," Eloise said with exaggerated patience, "did you all become the best of friends?"

"Oh," he said, nodding. "Funny thing, actually. I asked them to break my legs."

Eloise just stared at him. As long as she lived, she'd never understand men. She had four brothers, and quite frankly should have understood them better than most women, and maybe it had taken all of her twenty-eight years to come to this realization, but men were, quite simply, freaks.

Phillip shrugged again. "It seemed to break the ice."

"Clearly."

She stared at him, and he stared at her, and all the while she could see Anthony staring at them both, and then suddenly Phillip seemed to sober.

"We'll have to marry," he said.

"I know."

"They really will break my legs if I don't."

"That's not all they would do," she grumbled, "but even so, a lady might like to think she's been chosen for a reason other than osteopathic health."

He blinked at her in surprise.

"I'm not stupid," she muttered. "I've studied Latin."

"Right," he said slowly, in that way men do when they are trying to cover up the fact that they're not sure what to say.

"Or at least," she tried desperately, searching for something that might be even loosely interpreted as a compliment, "if not a reason *other*, then perhaps a reason *in addition*."

"Right," he said, nodding, but still not saying anything more.

Her eyes narrowed. "How much wine have you drunk?"

"Only three." He stopped, considered that. "Maybe four."

"Glasses or bottles?"

He didn't seem to know the answer to that.

Eloise looked over at the table. There were four bottles of wine littered among the remains of supper. Three were empty.

"I wasn't gone that long," she said.

He shrugged. "It was either drink with them or let them break my legs. It seemed a fairly straightforward decision."

"Anthony!" she called out. She'd had enough of Phillip. She'd had enough of them all, of everything, of men, of marriage, of broken legs and empty wine bottles. But most of all, she'd had enough of herself, of feeling so out of control, so helpless against the tides of her life.

"I want to go," she said.

Anthony nodded and grunted, still chewing the solitary piece of chicken that Colin had missed.

"*Now*, Anthony."

And he must have heard the crack in her voice, the hollow note that choked on the syllables, because he stood immediately and said, "Of course."

Eloise had never been so glad to see the inside of a carriage in all her life.

Chapter 11

. . . cannot abide a man who drinks to excess. Which is why I'm sure you will understand why I could not accept Lord Wescott's offer.

—from Eloise Bridgerton to her brother Benedict, upon refusing her second proposal of marriage

"No!" gushed Sophie Bridgerton, Benedict's petite and almost ethereal-looking wife. "They didn't!"

"They did," Eloise said grimly, as she sat back in her lawn chair and sipped a cup of lemonade. "And then they all got drunk!"

"Fiends," Sophie muttered, leading Eloise to realize that what she'd really been sick of the night before was that horribly chummish and collegial manner of men. Clearly, all she'd needed was one sensible female with whom she might disparage the lot of them.

Sophie scowled. "Don't tell me they were talking about that poor Lucy woman again."

Eloise gasped. "You know about her?"

"Everyone knows about her. Heaven knows, one can't *miss* her if you pass in the street."

Eloise stopped, thought, tried to imagine. She couldn't.

"Truth be told," Sophie said, whispering under her breath even though there wasn't a soul nearby who might hear, "I feel sorry for the woman. All that unwanted attention, and, well, it can't be good for her back."

Eloise tried to stifle her laugh, but a little snort made it through.

"Posy once even asked her about it!"

Eloise's mouth fell open. Posy was Sophie's stepsister, who had lived for several years with the Bridgertons before marrying the rather jolly vicar who lived just five miles from Benedict and Sophie. She was also, quite honestly, the friendliest person of Eloise's acquaintance, and if anyone was going to befriend a married serving wench with large bosoms, it would have been her.

"She's in Hugh's parish," Sophie explained, referring to Posy's husband. "So of course they would have met."

"What did she say?" Eloise asked.

"Posy?"

"No. Lucy."

"Oh. I don't know." Sophie pulled a face. "Posy wouldn't tell me. Can you believe that? I don't think Posy has kept a secret from me in all her life. She said she couldn't betray the confidence of a parishioner."

Eloise thought that rather noble of Posy.

"It doesn't concern me, of course," Sophie said, with all the confidence of a woman who knows she is loved. "Benedict would never stray."

"Of course not," Eloise said quickly. Benedict and Sophie's love story was legendary in their family. It had been one of the reasons Eloise had refused so many proposals of marriage. She'd wanted that kind of love and passion and drama. She'd wanted more than, "I have three homes, sixteen horses, and forty-two hounds," which is what one of her suitors had informed her when he asked for her hand.

"But," Sophie continued, "I don't think it's so much to ask that he manage to keep his mouth closed when she walks by."

Eloise was about to offer her firm and vehement agreement when she saw Sir Phillip walking across the lawn in her direction.

"Is that him?" Sophie asked, smiling.

Eloise nodded.

"He's very handsome."

"Yes, I suppose," Eloise said slowly.

"You suppose?" Sophie snorted with impatience. "Don't play coy with me, Eloise Bridgerton. I was once your lady's maid, and I know you better than anyone ought."

Eloise forbore to point out that Sophie had been her lady's maid for all of two weeks before she and Benedict had come to their senses and decided to marry. "Very well," she allowed, "he's quite handsome, if you like the rough, rural sort."

"Which you do," Sophie said pertly.

To her complete mortification, Eloise felt herself blush. "Perhaps," she muttered.

"And," Sophie said approvingly, "he brought flowers."

"He's a botanist," Eloise said.

"That doesn't make the gesture any less sweet."

"No, just easier."

"Eloise," Sophie said disapprovingly, "stop this right now."

"Stop what?"

"Trying to cut the poor man down before he even has a chance."

"That's not what I was doing at all," Eloise protested, but she knew she was lying the moment the words left her lips. She hated that her family was trying to run her life, no matter how well intentioned they were, and it had left her feeling sullen and uncooperative.

"Well, I think the flowers are very sweet," Sophie declared firmly. "I don't care if he had eight thousand different varieties available to him. He still thought to bring them."

Eloise nodded, hating herself. She wanted to feel better, wanted to be all smiles and cheer and optimism, but she just couldn't manage it.

"Benedict didn't give me all the details," Sophie continued, ignoring Eloise's distress. "You know how men are. They never tell you what you want to know."

"What do you want to know?"

Sophie looked over at Sir Phillip, gauging how long she'd have before he reached their side. "Well, for one thing, is it true you'd not met him before you ran off?"

"Not face-to-face, no," Eloise admitted. It all sounded so stupid when she recounted the tale. Who would have thought that she, a Bridgerton, would run away to a man she'd never met?

"Well," Sophie said, her voice matter-of-fact, "if it all works out in the end, what a romantic tale it will be."

Eloise swallowed uncomfortably. It was still too soon to know if it would "all work out in the end." She rather suspected—no, in truth she was quite certain—that she'd find herself married to Sir Phillip, but who knew what sort of marriage it would be? She didn't love him, not yet, anyway, and he didn't love her, and she'd thought that would be all right, but now that she was here in Wiltshire, trying not to notice how Benedict looked at Sophie, she was wondering if she'd made a terrible mistake.

And did she really want to wed a man who was looking primarily for a mother for his children?

If one didn't have love, was it better, then, to be alone?

Unfortunately, the only way to answer these questions was to marry Sir Phillip and see how it went. And if it didn't go well . . .

She'd be stuck.

The easiest way out of marriage was death, and frankly, that wasn't something Eloise cared to contemplate.

"Miss Bridgerton."

Phillip was standing in front of her, holding out a bouquet of white orchids. "I brought these for you."

She smiled at him, heartened by the slightly nervous, giddy feeling that arose within her at his appearance. "Thank you," she murmured, taking them and smelling the blooms. "They're lovely."

"Wherever did you find orchids?" Sophie asked. "They're exquisite."

"I grew them," he answered. "I keep a greenhouse."

"Yes, of course," Sophie said. "Eloise mentioned that you are a botanist. I do like to garden myself, although I must say that most of the time I haven't the least idea what I'm doing. Our caretakers here consider me the bane of their existence, I'm sure."

Eloise cleared her throat, aware that she had not yet made introductions. "Sir Phillip," she said, motioning to her sister-in-law, "this is Benedict's wife, Sophie."

He bowed over her hand, murmuring, "Mrs. Bridgerton."

"I'm very pleased to meet you," Sophie said in her most friendly manner. "And please, do use my Christian name. I'm told you already do so with Eloise, and furthermore, it sounds as if you are practically a member of the family already."

Eloise flushed.

"Oh!" Sophie exclaimed, instantly embarrassed. "I did not mean that in relation to you, Eloise. I would never assume— Oh, dear. What I meant to say was that I meant it because the men . . ." Her cheeks turned a deep red as she looked down at her hands. "Well," she mumbled, "I'd heard there was a great deal of wine."

Phillip cleared his throat. "A detail I'd prefer not to remember."

"The fact that you remember at all is remarkable," Eloise said sweetly.

He looked over at her, his expression clearly indicating that he had not been taken in by her sugary tone. "You're too kind."

"Does your head ache?" she asked.

He winced. "Like the devil."

She should have been concerned. She should have been kind, especially since he'd gone to the trouble of bringing her rare orchids. But she couldn't help feeling it was no more than he deserved, so she said (quietly, but still said it), "Good."

"Eloise!" Sophie said disapprovingly.

"How is Benedict feeling?" Eloise asked her sweetly.

Sophie sighed. "He's been a bear all morning, and Gregory hasn't even risen from bed."

"I seemed to have fared well by comparison, then," Phillip said.

"Except for Colin," Eloise told him. "He never feels the aftereffects of alcohol. And of course Anthony drank little last night."

"Lucky man."

"Would you care for something to drink, Sir Phillip?" Sophie asked, adjusting her bonnet so that it better shaded her eyes. "Of the benign, nonintoxicating variety, of course, given the circumstances. I would be happy to have someone bring you a glass of lemonade."

"That would be most appreciated. Thank you." He watched as she rose and walked up the slight incline to the house, then sat in her place across from Eloise.

"It is good to see you this morning," he said, clearing his throat. He was never the most talkative of men, and he was clearly making no exceptions this morning, despite the rather extraordinary circumstances that had led to this moment.

"And you," she murmured.

He shifted in his seat. It was too small for him; most chairs were. "I must apologize for my behavior last night," he said stiffly.

She looked over at him, staring into his dark eyes for just a moment before her gaze slid down to a patch of grass beside him. He seemed sincere; he probably was. She didn't know him well—certainly not well enough to marry, although it seemed that point was now moot—but he didn't seem the sort to make false apologies. Still, she wasn't quite ready to fall all over him with gratitude, so when she answered, she did so in a sparing fashion. "I have brothers," she said. "I am used to it."

"Perhaps, but I am not. I assure you I do not make a habit of overimbibing."

She nodded, accepting his apology.

"I have been thinking," he said.

"As have I."

He cleared his throat, then tugged at his cravat, as if it had suddenly grown too tight. "We will, of course, have to marry."

It was nothing more than she knew, but there was something awful in the way he said it. Maybe it was the lack of emotion in his voice, as if she were a problem he had to solve. Or maybe it was the way he said it so matter-of-factly, as if she had no choice (which, in truth, she did not, but she didn't care to be reminded of that).

Whatever it was, it made her feel strange, and itchy, as if she needed to jump out of her skin.

She had spent her adult life making her own choices, had considered herself the luckiest of females because her family had allowed her to do so. Maybe that was why it now felt so unbearable to be forced onto a path before she was ready.

Or maybe it was unbearable because she was the one who had set this entire farce into motion. She was furious with herself, and it was making her snippy with everyone.

"I'll do my best to make you happy," he said gruffly. "And the children need a mother."

She smiled weakly. She'd wanted her marriage to be about more than just children.

"I'm sure you'll be a great help," he said.

"A great help," she echoed, hating the way it sounded.

"Wouldn't you agree?"

She nodded, mostly because she was afraid that if she opened her mouth, she might scream.

"Good," he said. "Then it's all settled."

It's all settled. For the rest of her life, that would be her grand proposal of marriage. *It's all settled.* And the worst part of it was—she had no right to complain. She was the one who'd run off without giving Phillip enough time to arrange for a chaperone. She was the one who'd been so eager to make her own destiny. She was the one who'd acted without thinking, and now all she had to show for it was—

It's all settled.

She swallowed. "Wonderful."

He looked at her, blinking in confusion. "Aren't you happy?"

"Of course," she said hollowly.

"You don't sound happy."

"I'm happy," she snapped.

Phillip muttered something under his breath.

"What did you say?" she asked.

"Nothing."

"You said something."

He gave her an impatient look. "If I'd meant for you to hear it, I would have said it out loud."

She sucked in her breath. "Then you shouldn't have said it at all."

"Some things," Phillip muttered, "are impossible to keep inside."

"What did you *say*?" she demanded.

Phillip raked his hand through his hair. "Eloise—"

"Did you insult me?"

"Do you really want to know?"

"Since it appears we are to be wed," she bit off, "yes."

"I don't recall my exact words," Phillip shot back, "but I believe I may have uttered the words *women* and *lack of sense* in the same breath."

He shouldn't have said it. He *knew* he shouldn't have said it; it would have been rude under any circumstances, and it was especially wrong right now. But she had pushed and pushed and pushed and wouldn't back down. It was like she'd sliced a needle under his skin, and then decided to jab just for the fun of it.

And besides, why was she in such a terrible mood, anyway? All he'd done was state the facts. They *would* have to marry, and frankly, she should have been glad that if she'd been compromised, at least it had been with a man who was willing to do the right thing and wed her.

He didn't expect gratitude. Hell, this was as much his fault as it was hers; he was the one who'd issued the initial invitation, after all. But was it too much to expect a smile and a pleasant mood?

"I'm glad we had this conversation," Eloise said quite suddenly. "This has been good."

He looked up, instantly suspicious. "I beg your pardon."

"Very beneficial," she said. "One should always understand one's spouse before one marries, and—"

He groaned. This was not going to end well.

"And," she added sharply, glaring at his groan, "it is certainly provident that I now know how you feel about my gender."

He was the sort who usually walked away from conflict, but really, this was too much. "If I recall correctly," he shot back, "I never did tell you exactly what I thought of women."

"I inferred it," she retorted. "The phrase 'lack of sense' pointed me in the correct direction."

"Did it?" he drawled. "Well, I'm thinking differently now."

Her eyes narrowed. "What do you mean?"

"I mean that I've changed my mind. I've decided I don't have difficulties with women in general, after all. It's *you* I find insufferable."

She drew back, clearly affronted.

"Has no one called you insufferable before?" He found that difficult to believe.

"No one who wasn't related to me," she grumbled.

"You must live in a very polite society." He squirmed in his seat again; really, did no one make chairs for large men anymore? "Either that," he muttered, "or you've simply terrified everyone into bending to your every whim."

She flushed, and he couldn't tell if it was because she was embarrassed by his spot-on assessment of her personality or just because she was angry beyond words.

Probably both.

"I'm sorry," she muttered.

He turned to her in surprise. "I beg your pardon?" He couldn't have heard correctly.

"I said I'm sorry," she repeated, making it clear that she was not going to say the words a third time, so he'd better be listening well.

"Oh," he said, too stunned to say much of anything else. "Thank you."

"You're welcome." Her tone was less than gracious, but she seemed to be trying hard, nonetheless.

For a moment he said nothing. Then he had to ask. "What for?"

She looked up, obviously irritated that that hadn't been the end of it. "Did you have to ask?" she grumbled.

"Well, yes."

"I am sorry," she ground out, "because I am in a horrid mood and have been behaving badly. And if you ask *how* I have been behaving badly, I swear I will get up and walk away and you will never see me again, because I assure you, this apology is difficult enough without my having to explain it further."

Phillip decided he couldn't possibly hope for more. "Thank you," he said softly. He held his tongue for a minute, quite possibly the longest minute of his life, then he decided he might as well just go ahead and say it.

"If it makes you feel any better," he told her, "I had decided we would suit before your brothers arrived. I was already planning to ask you to be my wife. Properly, with a ring and whatever else it is I'm supposed to do. I don't know. It's been a long while since I've proposed marriage to anyone, and last time wasn't under normal circumstances in any case."

She looked up at him, surprise in her eyes . . . and perhaps a little bit of gratitude as well.

"I'm sorry that your brothers came along and made it all happen faster than you are ready for," he added, "but I'm not sorry that it's happening."

"You're not?" she whispered. "Really?"

"I'll give you as long as you need," he said, "within reason, of course. But I cannot—" He glanced up the hill; Anthony and Colin were ambling down toward them, followed by a footman carrying a tray of food. "I cannot speak for your brothers. I daresay they won't care to wait as long as you might prefer. And quite frankly, if you were my sister, I'd have marched you to a church last night."

She looked up the hill at her brothers; they were still at least a half a minute away. She opened her mouth, then closed it in obvious thought. Finally, after several seconds, during which he could practically see the wheels of her mind churning and turning, she blurted out, "Why did you decide we would suit?"

"I beg your pardon?" It was a stalling tactic, of course. He hadn't expected such a direct question.

Although heaven knew why not. This was Eloise, after all.

"Why did you decide we would suit?" she repeated, her voice pointed and undeniable.

But of course that would be how she would ask it. There was nothing subtle or deniable about Eloise Bridgerton. She would never skirt around an issue when she could just walk right in and stick her nose directly into the heart of the matter.

"I . . . ah . . ." He coughed, cleared his throat.

"You don't know," she stated, sounding disappointed.

"Of course I know," he protested. No man liked to be told he didn't know his own mind.

"No, you don't. If you did, you wouldn't be sitting there choking on air."

"Good God, woman, do you have a charitable bone in your body? A man needs time to formulate an answer."

"Ah," came Colin Bridgerton's ever-genial voice. "Here's the happy couple."

Phillip had never been so glad to see another human being in all his life. "Good morning," he said to the two Bridgerton men, inordinately pleased to have escaped Eloise's interrogation.

"Hungry?" Colin inquired as he sat in the chair next to Phillip. "I took the liberty of having the kitchen prepare breakfast alfresco."

Phillip looked over at the footman and wondered if he ought to offer to help. The poor man looked nearly ready to collapse under the weight of the food.

"How are you this morning?" Anthony asked as he sat down on the cushioned bench next to Eloise.

"Fine," she replied.

"Hungry?"

"No."

"Cheerful?"

"Not for you."

Anthony turned to Phillip. "She's usually more conversational."

Phillip wondered if Eloise would hit him. It wouldn't be more than he deserved.

The tray of food came down on the table with a loud clatter, followed by the footman's abject apology for being so clumsy, followed by Anthony's assurance that it was no trouble at all, that Hercules himself could not carry enough food to suit Colin.

The two Bridgerton brothers served themselves, then Anthony turned to Eloise and Phillip and said, "The two of you certainly seem well suited this morning."

Eloise looked at him with open hostility. "When did you reach that conclusion?"

"It only took a moment," he said with a shrug. He looked at Phillip. "It was the bickering, actually. All the best couples do it."

"I'm glad to hear it," Phillip murmured.

"My wife and I often have similar conversations before she comes around to my way of thinking," Anthony said affably.

Eloise shot him a peevish expression.

"Of course, my wife might offer a different interpretation," he added with a shrug. "I *allow* her to think that I'm coming 'round to her way of thinking." He turned back to Phillip and smiled. "It's easier that way."

Phillip stole a glance at Eloise. She appeared to be working very hard to hold her tongue.

"When did you arrive?" Anthony asked him.

"Just a few minutes ago," he replied.

"Yes," Eloise said. "He proposed marriage, I'm sure you'll be happy to hear."

Phillip coughed with surprise at her sudden announcement. "I beg your pardon?"

Eloise turned to Anthony. "He said, 'We'll have to marry.' "

"Well, he's right," Anthony replied, settling a level stare directly on her face. "You do have to marry. And my compliments to him for not beating around the bush about it. I'd think you of all people would appreciate direct conversation."

"Scone, anyone?" Colin asked. "No? More for me, then."

Anthony turned to Phillip and said, "She's just a bit irritated because she hates being ordered about. She'll be fine in a few days."

"I'm fine right now," Eloise ground out.

"Yes," Anthony murmured, "you look fine."

"Don't you have somewhere to *be*?" Eloise asked. Through her teeth.

"An interesting question," her brother replied. "One might say that I ought to *be* in London, with my wife and children. In fact, if I did have somewhere else to *be*, I imagine that would be it. But strangely enough, I seem to be here. In Wiltshire. Where, when I woke in my comfortable bed *in London* three days ago, I would never have guessed I would be." He smiled blandly. "Any other questions?"

She was quiet at that.

Anthony handed an envelope to Eloise. "This arrived for you."

She looked down, and Phillip could see that she instantly recognized the handwriting.

"It's from Mother," Anthony said, even though it was clear she already knew that.

"Do you want to read it?" Phillip asked.

She shook her head. "Not now."

Which meant, he realized, not in front of her brothers.

And then suddenly he knew what he had to do.

"Lord Bridgerton," he said to Anthony, standing up, "might I request a moment alone with your sister?"

"You just had a moment alone with her," Colin said between bites of bacon.

Phillip ignored him. "My lord?"

"Of course," Anthony said, "if she's agreeable."

Phillip grabbed Eloise's hand and yanked her to her feet. "She's agreeable," he said.

"Mmmm," Colin remarked. "She looks very agreeable."

Phillip decided then and there that *all* the Bridgertons ought to be fitted with muzzles. "Come with me," he said to Eloise, before she had a chance to argue.

Which of course she would, since she was Eloise, and she would never smile politely and follow when an argument was a possibility.

"Where are we going?" she gasped, once he had pulled her away from her family and was striding across the lawn, unmindful of how she had to run to keep up.

"I don't know."

"You don't *know*?"

He stopped so quickly that she crashed into him. It was rather nice, actually. He could feel every last bit of her, from her breasts to her thighs, although she recovered all too quickly and stepped away before he could savor the moment.

"I've never been here before," he said, explaining it to her as if she were a small child. "I'd have to be a bloody clairvoyant to know where I'm going."

"Oh," she said. "Well then, lead the way."

He pulled her back to the house, making his way to a side door. "Where does this go?" he asked.

"Inside," she replied.

He gave her a sarcastic look.

"Through Sophie's writing room to the hall," Eloise expounded.

"Is Sophie in her writing room?"

"I doubt it. Didn't she go to fetch you lemonade?"

"Good." He pulled the door open, muttering a quick thanks that it was unlocked, and poked his head inside. The room was empty, but the door to the hall was open, so he strode across and pulled it shut. When he turned back around, Eloise was still standing in the open doorway to the outside, watching him with a blend of curiosity and amusement.

"Shut the door," he ordered.

Her brows rose. "I beg your pardon?"

"Shut it." It wasn't a tone of voice he used often, but after a year of floating along, of feeling lost amid the currents of his life, he was finally taking control.

And he knew exactly what he wanted.

"Shut the door, Eloise," he said in a low voice, moving slowly across the room toward her.

Her eyes widened. "Phillip?" she whispered. "I—"

"Don't talk," he said. "Just shut the door."

But she was frozen in place, staring at him as if she didn't know him. Which, in truth, she didn't. Hell, he wasn't so sure he knew himself any longer.

"Phillip, you—"

He reached behind her and shut the door for her, turning the lock with a loud and ominous click.

"What are you doing?" she asked.

"You were worried," he said, "that we might not suit."

Her lips parted.

He stepped forward. "I think it's time I showed you that we do."

Chapter 12

. . . and how did you know that you and Simon were well-suited for marriage? For I vow I have not met a man about which I might say the same, and this after three long seasons on the Marriage Mart.

—from Eloise Bridgerton to her sister the Duchess of Hastings, upon refusing her third proposal of marriage

Eloise had time to breathe—barely—before his mouth came down on hers. And it was a good thing she did, because it didn't feel as if he had any plans to release her until, oh, the next millennium.

But then, abruptly, he drew back, his large hands cradling her face. And he looked at her.

Just looked at her.

"What?" she asked, uncomfortable with his scrutiny. She knew she was considered to be attractive, but she was no legendary beauty, and he was examining her as if he wanted to catalogue her every feature.

"I wanted to see you," he whispered. He touched her cheek, then smoothed his thumb down the line of her jaw. "You're always in motion. I don't get to just *see* you."

Her legs turned wobbly, and her lips parted, but she couldn't seem to make them work, couldn't seem to do anything other than stare up into his dark eyes.

"You're so beautiful," he murmured. "Do you know what I thought when I saw you the first time?"

She shook her head, desperate for his words.

"I thought I could drown in your eyes. I thought"—he moved in closer, his words now as much breath as sound—"I could drown in *you*."

She felt herself swaying toward him.

He touched her lips, tickling the tender skin with his forefinger. The motion sent ripples of pleasure throughout her, right down to the center of her being, to places forbidden even to her.

And she realized that she had never really understood the power of desire until that very moment. Never really understood what it was at all.

"Kiss me," she whispered.

He smiled. "You always order me about."

"Kiss me."

"Are you sure?" he murmured, his mouth curved into a teasing smile. "Because once I do, I might not be able to—"

She grabbed the back of his head and yanked him down.

He chuckled against her lips, his arms tightening around her with uncompromising strength. She opened her mouth, welcoming his invasion, moaning with pleasure as his tongue swept in, exploring her warmth. He nibbled and licked, slowly stirring a fire within her, all the while pressing her closer and closer against him until his heat poured through her clothing, wrapping her in a haze of desire.

His hands stole around her back, then down to her derriere, squeezing and kneading, then tilting her up until—

She gasped. She was twenty-eight years old, old enough to have heard indiscreet whispers. She knew what his hardness meant. She'd just never expected it to feel quite so hot, so insistent.

She jerked back, the motion more instinct than anything else, but he wouldn't let her go, pulled her closer and groaned, rubbing her against him. "I want to be inside you," he groaned in her ear.

Her legs completely gave out.

It didn't matter, of course; he just held her even tighter, then sank her onto the sofa, coming down atop her until the full length of him pressed her into the soft, cream-colored cushions. He was heavy, but his weight was thrilling, and she could do nothing but loll her head back as his lips left hers to travel down the column of her throat.

"Phillip," she moaned, and then again, as if his name were the only word left to her.

"Yes," he grunted, "yes." His words seemed torn from his throat, and she had no idea what he was talking about, only that whatever he was saying yes to, she wanted it, too. She wanted everything. Anything he wanted, anything possible.

She wanted everything that was possible and everything impossible, too. There was no more reason, only sensation. Only need and desire and this overwhelming sense of *now*.

This wasn't about yesterday and it wasn't about tomorrow. This was now, and she wanted it all.

She felt his hand on her ankle, rough and callused as it moved up her leg until it reached the edge of her stocking. He didn't pause, did nothing to implicitly ask her permission, but she gave it anyway, urging her legs apart until he settled more firmly between them, giving him more room to caress, more space to tickle her skin.

He moved up and up and up, pausing every now and then to squeeze, and she thought she might die from the waiting. She was on fire, burning for him, feeling strange and wet and so completely unlike herself she thought she might dissolve into a pool of nothingness.

Or evaporate completely. Or maybe even explode.

And then, just when she was quite convinced that nothing could be stranger, nothing could wind her even tighter than she was, he touched her.

Touched her.

Touched her where no one had ever touched her, where she didn't dare touch herself. Touched her so intimately, so tenderly that she had to bite her lip to keep from screaming his name.

And as his finger slid inside, she knew that in that moment she no longer belonged to herself.

She was his.

Sometime later, much later, she'd be herself again, back in control, with all her powers and faculties, but for now she was his. In this moment, for this second, she lived for him, for all he could make her feel, for every last whisper of pleasure, each moan of desire.

"Oh, Phillip," she gasped, his name a plea, a promise, a question. It was whatever she needed to say to make sure he didn't stop. She had no idea where this was all heading, whether she'd even be the same person when it was done, but it had to go *some*where. She couldn't possibly continue in this state forever. She was wound so tight, so tense that she'd surely shatter.

She was near the end. She had to be.

She needed something. She needed release, and she knew that only he could give it to her.

She arched to him, pressed up with a power she would never have imagined she possessed, actually lifting them both off the sofa with her need. Her hands found his shoulders, biting into his muscles, then moved down to the small of his back in an effort to pull him even closer against her.

"Eloise," he groaned, sliding his other hand up her skirt until it found her backside. "Do you have any idea—"

And then she had no idea what he did—he probably didn't know, either—but her entire body went impossibly tense. She couldn't speak, couldn't even breathe as her mouth opened into a silent scream of surprise and delight and a hundred other things all rolled into one. And then, just when she thought she couldn't possibly survive even a second longer, she shuddered and collapsed beneath him, panting with exhaustion, so limp and spent she couldn't have moved even her littlest finger.

"Oh, my God," she finally said, the blasphemy the only words coursing through her mind. "Oh, my God."

His hands tightened on her backside.

"Oh, my God."

His hand moved, came up to stroke her hair. He was gentle, achingly gentle, even though his body was rigid and tense.

Eloise just lay there, wondering if she'd ever be able to move again, breathing against him as she felt his breath on her temple. Eventually he shifted and moved, mumbling something about being too heavy for her, and then there was nothing but air, and when she looked to the side, he was kneeling next to the sofa, smoothing her skirts back down.

It seemed a rather tender and gentlemanly gesture, given her recent wantonness.

She looked into his face, knowing she must have the silliest smile on hers. "Oh, Phillip," she sighed.

"Is there a washroom?" he asked hoarsely.

She blinked, noticing for the first time that he looked rather strained. "A washroom?" she echoed.

He nodded stiffly.

She pointed to the door leading to the hall. "Out and to the right," she said. It was hard to believe he needed to relieve himself right after such a thrilling encounter, but who was she to attempt to understand the workings of the male body?

He walked to the door, put his hand on the knob, then turned around. "Do you believe me now?" he asked, one of his brows rising into an impossibly arrogant arch.

Her lips parted in confusion. "About what?"

He smiled. Slowly. And all he said was, "We'll suit."

Phillip had no idea how long it would take Eloise to regain her composure and restore her appearance. She'd looked quite delectably disheveled when he'd left her on the sofa in Sophie Bridgerton's little office. He never could understand the intricacies of a woman's toilette, and was quite certain he never would, but he was fairly sure she was going to need to redress her hair at the very least.

As for him, he required less than a minute in the washroom to find his release; he was wound that tight from his encounter with Eloise.

Dear God, she was magnificent.

It had been so long since he'd been with a woman. He'd known that when he finally found one he wanted to bed that his body would react strongly. He'd had more years than he'd cared to count with only his hand to satisfy his needs; a female body seemed like pure bliss.

And heaven knew he had imagined one often enough.

But this had been different, not at all what he'd pictured in his mind. He'd been mad for her. For *her*. For the sounds that escaped her throat, for the scent of her skin, for the way his body seemed to fit perfectly in the crook of hers. Even though he'd had to finish off himself, he'd still felt more, and more intensely, than he'd ever thought possible.

He'd thought almost any female body would do, but it was now quite clear to him that there was a reason he'd never availed himself of the services of the whores and barmaids who'd expressed their willingness. There was a reason he'd never found himself a discreet widow.

He'd needed more.

He'd needed Eloise.

He wanted to sink himself into her and never come out.

He wanted to own her, to possess her, and then to lay back and let her torture him until he screamed.

He'd had fantasies before. Hell, every man did. But now his fantasy had a face, and he feared he was going to find himself walking around with a constant erection if he didn't learn how to control his thoughts.

He needed a wedding. Fast.

He groaned, giving his hands a quick wash in the basin. She didn't know she'd left him in such a state. She didn't even realize. She'd just looked at him with that blissful smile, too caught in her own passion to notice that he was ready to explode.

He pushed open the door, his feet moving quickly along the marble floor as he made his way back to the lawn. He'd have plenty of time to explode soon enough. And when he did, she'd be right there along with him.

The thought brought a smile to his lips, and very nearly sent him back into the washroom.

"Ah, there he is," Benedict Bridgerton said as Phillip walked toward him across the lawn. Phillip saw the gun in his hand and stopped in his tracks, wondering if he ought to be worried. Benedict couldn't possibly know what had just happened in his wife's office, could he?

Phillip swallowed, thinking hard. No, there was no way. And besides, Benedict was smiling.

Of course, he could be the sort who would enjoy picking off the spoiler of his sister's innocence . . .

"Er, good morning," Phillip said, glancing at everyone else in an attempt to gauge the situation.

Benedict nodded his greeting, then said, "Do you shoot?"

"Of course," Phillip replied.

"Good." He jerked his head toward a target. "Join us."

Phillip noted with relief that the target seemed to be firmly in place, indicating that *he* would not have to play that role. "I didn't bring a pistol," he said.

"Of course not," Benedict replied. "Why would you? We're all friends here." His brows rose. "Aren't we?"

"One would hope."

Benedict's lips curved, but it wasn't the sort of smile that inspired confidence in one's well-being. "Don't worry about the pistol," he said. "We'll provide one."

Phillip nodded. If this was to be how he was to prove his manhood to Eloise's brothers, so be it. He could shoot as well as the best of them. It had been one of those manly pursuits his father had been so insistent he learn. He'd spent countless hours outside Romney Hall, his arm outstretched until his muscles burned, holding his breath as he aimed for whatever it was his father was out to destroy. Every shot was accompanied by a fervent prayer that his aim would be true.

If he hit the target, his father wouldn't hit him. It was as simple—and desperate—as that.

He walked over to a table with several pistols on it, murmuring his hellos to Anthony, Colin, and Gregory. Sophie was sitting about ten or so yards away, her nose in a book.

"Let's get on with this," Anthony said, "before Eloise returns." He looked over at Phillip. "Where *is* Eloise?"

"She went off to read the letter from your mother," Phillip lied.

"I see. Well, that won't take long," Anthony said with a frown. "We'd better hurry, then."

"Maybe she'll want to reply," Colin said, picking up a gun and examining it. "That'll buy us a few extra minutes. You know Eloise. She's always writing someone a letter."

"Indeed," Anthony replied. "Got us into this mess, didn't it?"

Phillip just looked at him with an inscrutable smile. He was far too pleased with himself this morning to rise to any bait Anthony Bridgerton cared to offer.

Gregory chose a gun. "Even if she replies, she'll be back soon. She's fiendishly fast."

"At writing?" Phillip queried.

"At everything," Gregory said grimly. "Let's shoot."

"Why are you all so eager to get started without Eloise?" Phillip asked.

"Er, no reason," Benedict said, at precisely the same moment Anthony mumbled, "Who said anything about that?"

They all had, of course, but Phillip didn't remind them of it.

"Age before beauty, old chap," Colin said, slapping Anthony on the back.

"You're too kind," Anthony murmured, stepping up to a chalk line someone had drawn in the grass. He lifted his arm, took aim, and fired.

"Well done," Phillip said, once the footman had brought forth the bull's-eye. Anthony had not hit dead center, but he was only an inch off.

"Thank you." He set his pistol down. "How old are you?"

Phillip blinked at the unexpected question, then replied, "Thirty."

Anthony jerked his head toward Colin. "You're after Colin, then. We always do these things by age. It's the only way to keep track."

"By all means," Phillip said, watching as Benedict and Colin took their turns. They were both good shots, neither dead center, but certainly close enough to kill a man, had that been their goal.

Which, thankfully, it didn't seem to be, at least not that morning.

Phillip selected a pistol, tested its weight in his hand, then stepped up to the chalk line. It had only been recently that he'd stopped thinking of his father every time he took aim at a target. It had taken years, but he'd finally allowed himself to realize that he actually liked shooting, that it didn't have to be a chore. And then suddenly his father's voice, so often at the back of his mind, always yelling, always criticizing, was gone.

He lifted his arm, his muscles rock steady, and fired.

He squinted toward the target. It looked good. The footman brought it forward. One-half inch, at most, off the center. Closer than anyone else thus far.

The target went back, and Gregory took his turn, proving himself to be Phillip's equal.

"We do five rounds," Anthony told Phillip. "Best out, and if there's a tie, the leaders face off."

"I see," Phillip said. "Any particular reason?"

"No," Anthony said, picking up his gun. "Just that we've always done it this way."

Colin looked at Phillip with deadly serious eyes. "We take our games seriously."

"I'm gathering."

"Do you fence?"

"Not well," Phillip said.

One corner of Colin's mouth turned up. "Excellent."

"Be quiet," Anthony barked, looking testily over at them. "I'm trying to aim."

"Such need for silence will not serve you well at a time of crisis," Colin remarked.

"Shut up," Anthony bit off.

"If we were attacked," Colin continued, one of his hands moving expressively as he wove his tale, "it would be quite noisy, and frankly, I find it disturbing to think—"

"Colin!" Anthony bellowed.

"Don't mind me," Colin said.

"I'm going to kill him," Anthony announced. "Does anyone mind if I kill him?"

No one did, although Sophie did look up and mention something about blood and messes and not wanting to have to clean up.

"It's an excellent fertilizer," Phillip said helpfully, since, after all, that was his area of expertise.

"Ah." Sophie nodded and turned back to her book. "Kill him, then."

"How's that book, darling?" Benedict called out to her.

"It's quite good, actually."

"Will you all *shut up*?" Anthony ground out. Then, his cheeks coloring slightly, he turned to his sister-in-law and mumbled, "Not you, of course, Sophie."

"Glad to be exempted," she said cheerfully.

"Do try not to threaten my wife," Benedict said mildly.

Anthony turned to his brother and skewered him with a glare. "The lot of you should be drawn and quartered," he grunted.

"Except for Sophie," Colin reminded him.

Anthony turned to him with a deadly expression. "You do realize this gun is loaded, don't you?"

"Lucky for me fratricide is considered quite beyond the pale."

Anthony clamped his mouth shut and turned back toward the target. "Round two," he called out, taking aim.

"*Waaaaaaait!*"

All four Bridgerton men sagged and turned around, groaning as they saw Eloise careening down the hill.

"Are you shooting?" she demanded, stumbling to a halt.

No one answered. No one really needed to. It was quite obvious.

"Without me?"

"We're not shooting," Gregory said. "Just standing about with guns."

"Near a target," Colin added helpfully.

"You're shooting."

"Of course we're shooting," Anthony snapped. He flicked his head off to the right. "Sophie is by herself. You should keep her company."

Eloise planted her hands on her hips. "Sophie is reading a book."

"A good one, too," Sophie put in, returning her attention to the pages.

"You should read a book, too, Eloise," Benedict suggested. "They're very improving."

"I don't need any improving," she shot back. "Give me a gun."

"I'm not giving you a gun," Benedict retorted. "We don't have enough to go around."

"We can share," Eloise ground out. "Have you ever tried sharing? It's very improving."

Benedict scowled at her in a manner that wasn't particularly fitting for a man of his years.

"I think," Colin said, "that what Benedict was trying to say is that he's as improved as he's ever going to be."

"For certain," Sophie said, not even raising her eyes from her book.

"Here," Phillip said magnanimously, handing his gun to Eloise, "have mine." The four Bridgerton men groaned, but he decided he rather enjoyed annoying them.

"Thank you," Eloise said graciously. "From Anthony's bark of 'Round two' I deduce that you've each taken one shot?"

"Indeed," Phillip replied. He looked over at her brothers, all of whom wore dejected expressions. "What's wrong?"

Anthony just shook his head.

Phillip looked to Benedict.

"She's a freak of nature," Benedict muttered.

Phillip looked back at Eloise with renewed interest. She didn't look particularly freakish to him.

"I'm dropping out," Gregory muttered. "I haven't eaten breakfast yet."

"You'll have to ring for more," Colin told him. "I already finished it all."

Gregory let out an annoyed sigh. "It's a wonder I haven't starved," he grumbled, "younger brother that I am."

Colin shrugged. "You've got to be quick if you want to eat."

Anthony looked at the two of them with disgust. "Did the two of you grow up in an orphanage?" he asked.

Phillip bit his lip to contain his smile.

"Are we going to shoot?" Eloise demanded.

"*You* certainly are," Gregory said, slumping against a tree. "I'm leaving to eat."

He stayed, though, watching his sister with a bored expression as she lifted her arm and, without even appearing to aim, fired.

Phillip blinked in surprise as the footman brought forth the target.

Dead center.

"Where did you learn to do that?" he asked, trying not to gape.

She shrugged. "I couldn't tell you. I've always been able to do it."

"Freak of nature," Colin muttered. "Clearly."

"I think it's splendid," Phillip said.

Eloise looked at him with glowing eyes. "Do you really?"

"Of course. Should I ever need to defend my home, I shall know who to send out to the front line."

She beamed. "Where's the next target?"

Gregory threw his arms up in disgust. "I forfeit. I'm getting something to eat."

"Get something for me, too," Colin called out.

"Of course," Gregory muttered.

Eloise turned to Anthony. "Is it your turn now?"

He took the gun from her hands and set it on the table to be reloaded. "As if it matters."

"We have to do all five rounds," she said officiously. "You were the one who made the rules."

"I know," he said glumly. He lifted his arm and fired off a shot, but his heart clearly was not into it, and he was off by five inches.

"You're not even trying!" Eloise accused.

Anthony just turned to Benedict and said, "I hate shooting with her."

"Your turn," Eloise said to Benedict.

He took his turn, as did Colin, both men putting in a bit more effort than Anthony had, but still coming up off the mark.

Phillip stepped up to the chalk line, pausing only to listen as Eloise said, "Don't you decide to give up."

"I wouldn't dream of it," he murmured.

"Good. It's no fun to play with *bad sports*." She directed the last two words quite vehemently toward her brothers.

"That's the point," Benedict said.

"They do this every time," Eloise said to Phillip. "They shoot badly until I decide the match isn't worth it, and *then* they all have fun."

"Be quiet," Phillip told her, lips twitching. "I'm aiming."

"Oh." She shut her mouth with alacrity, watching with interest as he focused on the target.

Phillip took his shot, allowing himself a slow, satisfied smile as the target was brought forward.

"Perfect!" Eloise exclaimed, clapping her hands together. "Oh, Phillip, that was wonderful!"

Anthony muttered something under his breath that he probably ought not to have said in his sister's presence, then added, directing his words to Phillip, "You are going to marry her, aren't you? Because frankly, if you get her off our hands and allow her to shoot with you so that she doesn't pester us, I'll gladly double her dowry."

Phillip was quite certain at that point that he'd wed her for nothing, but he just grinned and said, "It's a deal."

Chapter 13

. . . and as I'm sure you can imagine, they were all possessed of a most foul temper. Is it my fault I am so superior? I think not. No more, I suppose, than it is their fault they were born men and thus without the barest hint of common sense or innate good manners.

—from Eloise Bridgerton to Penelope Featherington, after trouncing six men (three not related to her) in a shooting match

The following day Eloise traveled to Romney Hall for lunch, along with Anthony, Benedict, and Sophie. Colin and Gregory had declared that the rest of the family had the situation well enough in hand and decided to return to London, Colin back to his new wife, and Gregory back to whatever it was the young unmarried men of the *ton* did to fill their daily lives.

Eloise was happy to see them go; she loved her brothers, but truly, the four of them at once was more than any woman ought to be expected to bear.

She was feeling optimistic as she stepped down from the carriage; the previous day had gone far better than she could ever have hoped. Even if Phillip hadn't taken her into Sophie's office to prove to her that they "would suit" (Eloise could now think of those words only as if they were in quotations), the day would have been a success. Phillip had more than held his own against the collective force of the Bridgerton brothers, which had left her feeling quite pleased and more than a little proud.

Funny how it hadn't occurred to her until then that she could never marry a man who couldn't square off with each and any of her brothers and emerge unscathed.

And in Phillip's case, he'd taken on all four at once. Most impressive.

Eloise still had reservations about the marriage, of course. How could she not? She and Phillip had developed a sense of mutual respect and hopefully even affection, but they were not in love, and Eloise had no way of knowing if they ever would be.

Still, she was convinced that she was doing the right thing by marrying him. She had little choice in the matter, of course; it was either marry Phillip or face complete ruin and a life alone. But even so, she thought he would make a fine husband. He was honest and honorable, and if he was at times too quiet, at least he seemed to have a sense of humor, which Eloise felt was essential for any prospective spouse.

And when he kissed her . . .

Well, it was quite obvious that he knew exactly how to turn her knees to butter.

And the rest of her as well.

Eloise was, of course, a pragmatic. She always had been, and she knew that passion was not enough to sustain a marriage.

But, she thought with a wicked smile, surely it couldn't hurt.

Phillip checked the clock on the mantel for about the fifteenth time in as many minutes. The Bridgertons were due to arrive at half noon, and it was already thirty-five past the hour. Not that five minutes was anything to worry about when one had to travel over country roads, but still, it was deuced hard to keep Oliver and Amanda neat and tidy and, above all, well behaved as they waited with him in the drawing room.

"I hate this jacket," Oliver said, tugging on his little coat.

"It's too small," Amanda told him.

"I *know*," he replied, with clear disdain. "If it weren't too small, I wouldn't have complained."

Phillip rather thought he'd have found something else to complain about, but there seemed little reason to express this opinion.

"And anyway," Oliver continued, "your dress is too small, too. I can see your ankles."

"You're supposed to be able to see my ankles," Amanda said, frowning down at her lower legs.

"Not so much of them."

She looked down again, this time with an expression of alarm.

"You're only eight years old," Phillip said in a weary voice. "The dress is perfectly suitable." Or at least he hoped it was, little that he knew of such things.

Eloise, he thought, her name echoing through his head like the answer to his prayers. Eloise would know these things. She would know if a child's dress was too short and when a girl should start wearing her hair up and even whether a boy should attend Eton or Harrow.

Eloise would know all these things.

Thank God.

"I think they're late," Oliver announced.

"They're not late," Phillip said automatically.

"I think they *are* late," Oliver said. "I can read the clock now, you know."

Phillip didn't know, which depressed him. It was rather like the swimming thing. Too much like it, really.

Eloise, he reminded himself. Whatever his failings as a father, he was making up for all of that by marrying the perfect mother for them. He was, for the first time since their birth, doing the exact right thing for his children, and the sense of relief was almost overwhelming.

Eloise. She couldn't get here soon enough.

Hell, he couldn't marry her soon enough. How did one procure a special license, anyway? It hadn't been the sort of thing he'd ever thought he'd need to know, but the last thing he wanted to do was wait several weeks to have banns read.

Weren't weddings meant to be held on Saturday mornings? Could they manage it by this Saturday? It was only two days away, but if they could get that special license . . .

Phillip caught Oliver by the collar as he tried to race out the door. "No," he said firmly. "You will wait here for Miss Bridgerton. And you will do so quietly, without incident, and with a smile on your face."

Oliver made at least some attempt to settle down at the mention of Eloise's name, but his "smile" (performed obediently at his father's order) was a ghastly stretch of the lips that left Phillip feeling like he'd just had an audience with an anemic gorgon.

"That wasn't a smile," Amanda immediately said.

"It was, too."

"No. Your lips didn't even curve up. . . ."

Phillip sighed as he attempted to block his ears from the inside out. He'd talk to Anthony Bridgerton about the special license this afternoon. It seemed like the sort of thing the viscount would know about.

Saturday couldn't come soon enough. He could turn the twins over to Eloise during the day, and . . .

He smiled to himself. She could turn herself over to *him* at night.

"Why are you smiling?" Amanda demanded.

"I'm not smiling," Phillip said, feeling himself begin to—dear *God*—blush.

"You *are* smiling," she accused. "And now your cheeks are turning pink."

"Don't be silly," he muttered.

"I'm not silly," she insisted. "Oliver, look at Father. Don't his cheeks look pink?"

"One more word about my cheeks," Phillip threatened, "and I'm going to . . ."

Hell, he'd been about to say *horsewhip*, but they all knew he would never do that.

". . . do something," he finished, in a lame attempt at a threat.

Amazingly, it worked, and they held still and silent for a moment. Then Amanda swung her legs from her perch on the sofa and knocked over a footstool.

Phillip looked at the clock.

"Oops," she said, jumping down and then bending over to right it. "Oliver!" she howled.

Phillip tore his eyes away from the minute hand, which was, inexplicably, not even to the eight. Amanda was sprawled on the floor, glaring at her brother.

"He pushed me," Amanda said.

"Did not."

"Did too."

"Did—"

"Oliver," Phillip cut in. "*Some*one pushed her, and I'm fairly certain it was not I."

Oliver chewed on his lower lip, having forgotten to consider the fact that his culpability would be quite obvious. "Maybe she fell over on her own," he suggested.

Phillip just stared at him, hoping that the ferocious expression would be enough to nip *that* idea in the bud.

"Very well," Oliver admitted. "I pushed her. I'm sorry."

Phillip blinked with surprise. Maybe he was getting better at fatherhood. He couldn't recall the last time he'd heard an unsolicited apology.

"You can push me back," Oliver said to Amanda.

"Oh, no," Phillip said quickly. Bad idea. Very, very bad idea.

"All right," Amanda said brightly.

"No, Amanda," Phillip said, jumping to his feet. "Do not—"

But she'd already pressed both of her little hands to her brother's chest and heaved.

Oliver went tumbling back with a loud burst of laughter. "Now I get to push *you*!" he yelled with glee.

"You will *not* push your sister!" Phillip roared, jumping over an ottoman.

"She pushed me!" Oliver hollered.

"Because you asked her to, you miserable little wretch." Phillip swung his hand out to grab Oliver's sleeve before he slithered away, but the sneaky little bugger was slippery as an eel.

"Push me!" Amanda squealed. "Push me!"

"Do not push her!" Phillip yelled. Visions of his drawing room floated ominously in his brain, the image strewn with broken furniture and overturned lamps.

Good God, and with the Bridgertons due at any moment.

He reached Oliver just as Oliver reached Amanda, and the three of them went tumbling down, taking two cushions off the sofa with them. Phillip thanked the Lord for small favors. At least the cushions were not breakable.

Crash.

"What the devil?"

"I think it was the clock," Oliver gulped.

How on earth they'd managed to topple the clock off the mantel, Phillip would never know. "The two of you are hereby banished to your rooms until you're sixty-eight," he hissed.

"Oliver did it," Amanda said quickly.

"I don't give a—care who did it," Phillip bit off. "You *know* that Miss Bridgerton is expected at any—"

"Ahem."

Phillip turned slowly to the doorway, horrified—but not surprised—to see Anthony Bridgerton standing there, Benedict, Sophie, and Eloise right behind him.

"My lord," Phillip said, his voice too curt. Really, he should have been more gracious—it wasn't the viscount's fault that his children were just one transgression short of being complete monsters—but Phillip just couldn't manage good cheer at the moment.

"Perhaps we're interrupting?" Anthony said mildly.

"Not at all," Phillip replied. "As you can see, we're merely . . . ah . . . rearranging the furniture."

"And doing an excellent job of it," Sophie said brightly.

Phillip shot her a grateful smile. She seemed like the type of woman who always went out of her way to make others feel more comfortable, and at the moment he could have kissed her for it.

He rose, stopping to right the overturned ottoman as he did so, then grabbed both of his children by the arms and hauled them to their feet. Oliver's little cravat was now completely undone, and Amanda's hair clip hung limply near her ear. "May I present my children," he said, with all the dignity he could muster, "Oliver and Amanda Crane."

Oliver and Amanda mumbled their greetings, both looking rather uncomfortable at being paraded before so many adults. Either that, or maybe they were actually shamefaced for their abominable behavior, unlikely as that seemed.

"Very well," Phillip said, once the twins had done their duty. "You can run along now."

They looked at him with woeful expressions.

"What now?"

"Can we stay?" Amanda asked in a small voice.

"No," Phillip answered. He'd invited the Bridgertons over for lunch and a tour of his greenhouse, and he needed the children to disappear back to the nursery if either endeavor was to be successful.

"Please?" Amanda pleaded.

Phillip studiously avoided looking at his guests, aware that they were all witnessing his supreme lack of command over his children. "Nurse Edwards is waiting for you in the hall," he said.

"We don't like Nurse Edwards," Oliver said. Amanda nodded beside him.

"Of course you like Nurse Edwards," Phillip said impatiently. "She's been your nurse for months."

"But we don't *like* her."

Phillip looked over at the Bridgertons. "Excuse me," he said in a clipped voice. "I apologize for the interruption."

"It's no bother," Sophie said quickly, her face taking on a maternal air as she assessed the situation.

Phillip guided the twins to the far corner of the room, then crossed his arms and stared down at them. "Children," he said sternly, "I have asked Miss Bridgerton to be my wife."

Their eyes lit up.

"Good," he grunted. "I see that you agree with me that this is a superior idea."

"Will she—"

"Don't interrupt me," Phillip interrupted, too impatient by now to deal with any of their questions. "I want you to listen to me. I still need to gain approval from her family, and for that I need to entertain them and offer them lunch, and all this without children underfoot." It was almost the truth, at least. The twins didn't need to know that Anthony had practically ordered the wedding and that approval was no longer an issue.

But Amanda's lower lip started wobbling, and even Oliver looked upset. "What now?" Phillip asked wearily.

"Are you ashamed of us?" Amanda asked.

Phillip sighed, feeling utterly sick of himself. Dear God, how had it come to this? "I'm not—"

"May I be of assistance?"

He looked over at Eloise as if she were his savior. He watched in silence as she knelt down near his children, telling them something in a voice so soft that he couldn't understand the words, only the gentle quality of the tone.

The twins said something which was obviously in protest, but Eloise cut them off, gesticulating with her hands as she spoke. Then, to his complete and utter amazement, the twins said their farewells and walked out into the hall. They didn't look especially happy to go, but they did it all the same.

"Thank God I'm marrying you," Phillip said under his breath.

"Indeed," she murmured, brushing past him with a secretive smile as she walked back to her family.

Phillip followed her and immediately apologized to Anthony, Benedict, and Sophie for his children's behavior. "They have been difficult to manage since their mother passed," he explained, trying to put it in the most excusable terms possible.

"There is nothing more difficult than the death of a parent," Anthony said quietly. "Please, do not feel any need to apologize on their behalf."

Phillip nodded his thanks, grateful for the older man's understanding. "Come," he said to the group, "let's go on to lunch."

But as he led them to the dining room, Oliver's and Amanda's faces loomed large in his mind. Their eyes had been sad as they'd walked away.

He'd seen his children obstinate, insufferable, even in full-fledged tantrums, but he'd not seen them sad since their mother had died.

It was very troubling.

After lunch and a tour through the greenhouse, the quintet broke into two groups. Benedict had brought along an artist's pad, so he and Sophie remained near the house, chattering contentedly as he sketched the exterior. Anthony, Eloise, and Phillip decided to take a walk around the grounds, but Anthony very discreetly allowed Eloise and Phillip to tarry a good many yards behind, affording the affianced couple the opportunity to speak with some privacy.

"What did you say to the children?" Phillip immediately asked.

"I don't know," Eloise said quite honestly. "I just tried to act like my mother." She shrugged. "It seemed to work."

He thought about that. "It must be nice to have parents one can emulate."

She looked at him curiously. "Didn't you?"

He shook his head. "No."

She hoped he would say more, gave him time, even, but he did not speak. Finally, she decided to press the matter and asked, "Was it your mother or your father?"

"What do you mean?"

"Which of your parents was so difficult?"

He looked at her for a long moment, his dark eyes inscrutable as his brows ever-so-slightly came together. Then he said, "My mother died at my birth."

She nodded. "I see."

"I doubt you do," he said in a tight, hollow voice, "but I appreciate your trying."

They walked along, keeping their pace slow, not wanting to come within earshot of Anthony, even though neither broke the silence for several minutes. Finally, as they turned along the path toward the back side of the house, Eloise uttered the question she'd been dying to ask all day—

"Why did you take me into Sophie's study yesterday?"

He spluttered and stumbled. "I should think that would be obvious," he mumbled, his cheeks turning pink.

"Well, yes," Eloise said, blushing as she realized exactly what it was she had asked. "But surely you didn't think *that* was going to happen."

"A man can always hope," he muttered.

"You don't mean that!"

"Of course I do. But," he added, looking rather like he couldn't believe he was having this conversation, "as it happens, no, it never crossed my mind that matters would get quite so out of hand." He gave her a sly, sideways sort of look. "I'm not sorry, however, that they did."

She felt her cheeks turn hot. "You still haven't answered my question."

"I haven't?"

"No." She knew she was being persistent to the point of unseemliness, but as matters went, this seemed an important one to press. "Why did you take me in there?"

He stared at her for a full ten seconds, presumably to ascertain if she was daft, then shot a quick look at Anthony to make sure he was out of earshot before answering, "Well, if you must know, yes, I did intend to kiss you. You were yapping on about the marriage and asking me all sorts of ridiculous questions." He planted his hands on his hips and shrugged. "It seemed a good way to prove once and for all that we are well suited."

She decided to let his description of her as a yapping female pass. "But passion is surely not enough to sustain a marriage," she persisted.

"It's certainly a good start," he muttered. "May we talk of something else?"

"No. What I'm trying to say—"

He snorted and rolled his eyes. "You are always trying to say something."

"It's what makes me charming," she said peevishly.

He looked at her with exaggerated patience. "Eloise. We are well suited and will enjoy a perfectly pleasant and amiable marriage. I don't know what else to say or do to prove it."

"But you don't love me," she said, her voice soft.

That seemed to knock the wind out of him, and he just stopped and stared at her for the longest moment. "Why do you say things like that?" he asked.

She shrugged helplessly. "Because it's important."

For a moment he did nothing but stare. "Hasn't it ever occurred to you that every thought and feeling doesn't need to be given voice?"

"*Yes,*" she said, a lifetime of regrets wrapped into that single syllable. "All the time." She looked away, discomforted by the odd, hollow sensation rumbling in her throat. "I can't seem to help myself, though."

He shook his head, obviously perplexed, which didn't surprise her. Half the time she perplexed herself. *Why* had she forced the issue? Why couldn't she ever be subtle, coy? Her mother had once told her that she could catch more flies with honey than a sledgehammer, but Eloise never could learn to keep her thoughts to herself.

She had practically asked Sir Phillip if he loved her, and his silence was as much of an answer as *no* would have been. Her heart twisted. She hadn't really thought he would contradict her, but her disappointment was proof that some tiny part of her had been hoping that he'd drop to his knees and cry out that he did love her, that he cherished her, and was in fact quite certain that he would die without her.

Which was all nothing but rot, and she didn't know why she'd even wished for it, when she didn't love him, either.

But she could. She had this feeling that if she gave it enough time, she could love this man. And maybe she'd just wanted him to say the same.

"Did you love Marina?" she asked, the words crossing her lips before she'd even had a chance to ponder the wisdom of asking. She winced. There she went again, asking questions that were far too personal.

It was a wonder he hadn't thrown up his arms and run screaming in the opposite direction already.

He didn't answer for the longest moment. They just stood there, watching one another, trying to ignore Anthony, who was studiously examining a tree some thirty yards away. Finally, in a low voice, Phillip said, "No."

Eloise didn't feel elated; she didn't feel sorrow. She didn't feel anything at all at his pronouncement, which surprised her. But she did let out a long breath, one she hadn't realized she'd been holding. And she did feel rather glad that she now knew.

She hated the not knowing. About anything.

And so she really shouldn't have been surprised when she whispered, "Why did you marry her?"

A rather blank expression washed over his eyes, and finally he just shrugged and said, "I don't know. It seemed like the right thing to do."

She nodded. It all made so much sense. It was exactly the sort of thing he would do. Phillip was always doing the right thing, the honorable thing, apologizing for his transgressions, shouldering everyone's burdens . . .

Honoring his brother's promises.

And then she had one more question. "Did you . . ." she whispered, almost losing her nerve. "Did you feel passion for her?" She knew she shouldn't ask, but after that afternoon, she had to know. The answer didn't matter—or at least she told herself it didn't.

But she had to know.

"No." He turned away, began to walk, his long stride forcing her to jump to attention and follow. But then, just when she'd gathered enough speed to catch up, he stopped, causing her to stumble and put her hands out against his arm just to keep her balance.

"I have a question for you," he said, his voice abrupt.

"Of course," she murmured, surprised by his sudden change of demeanor. Still, it was only fair. She'd practically interrogated the poor man.

"Why did you leave London?" he asked.

She blinked in surprise. She hadn't been expecting something with such an easy answer. "To meet you, of course."

"Balderdash."

Her mouth fell open at his palpable disdain.

"That's why you came," he said, "not why you left."

It hadn't occurred to her until that very minute that there was a difference, but he was right. He'd had nothing to do with why she'd left London. He'd just provided an easy means of escape, a way to leave without feeling she was running away.

He'd given her something to run to, which was so much easier to justify than running *from*.

"Did you have a lover?" he asked, his voice low.

"No!" she answered, loud enough so that Anthony actually turned around, forcing her to smile and wave at him, assuring him that all was well. "Just a bee," she called out.

Anthony's eyes widened, and he started to stride in their direction.

"It's gone now!" Eloise called quickly, shooing him away. "Nothing about it!" She turned to Phillip and explained, "He's rather morbidly afraid of bees." She grimaced. "I forgot. I should have said it was a mouse."

Phillip looked over at Anthony, curiosity on his face. Eloise wasn't surprised; it was difficult to imagine that a man such as her brother was afraid of bees, but it did make sense, seeing as how their father had died after being stung by one.

"You didn't answer my question."

Damn. She'd thought she'd got him off the subject. "How could you even ask it?" she asked.

Phillip shrugged. "How could I not? You ran away from home, not bothering to tell your family where you were going—"

"I left a note," she interrupted.

"Yes, of course, the note."

Her mouth fell open. "Don't you believe me?"

He nodded. "I do, actually. You're much too organized and officious to leave without making sure all of your loose ends were tied up."

"It's not my fault it got shuffled into Mother's invitations," she muttered.

"The note is not the issue," he stated, crossing his arms.

Crossing his arms? She clenched her teeth together. It made her feel a child, and there was nothing she could do or say about it, because she had a feeling that whatever he was about to say concerning her recent behavior, he was right.

Much as it pained her to admit it.

"The fact of the matter," he continued, "is that you fled London like a criminal in the middle of the night. It simply occurred to me that something might have happened to . . . ah . . . stain your reputation." At her peevish expression, he added, "It's not an unreasonable conclusion to reach."

He was right, of course. Not about her reputation—that was still as pure and clean as snow. But it did look odd, and frankly, it was a wonder he hadn't inquired after it already.

"If you had a lover," he said quietly, "it won't change my intentions."

"It's not that at all," she said quickly, mostly just to make him stop talking about it. "It was . . ." Her voice trailed off, and she sighed. "It was . . ."

And then she told him everything. All about the marriage proposals she'd received, and the ones Penelope hadn't, and the plans they'd jokingly made to grow old and spinsterish together. And she told him how guilty she'd felt when Penelope and Colin had married, and she couldn't stop thinking about herself and how alone she was.

She told him all that and more. She told him what was in her mind and what was in her heart, and she told him things she'd never told another soul. And it occurred to her that for a woman who opened her mouth every other second, there was an awful lot inside of her that she'd never shared.

And then, when she was done (and, in truth, she didn't even realize she'd finished; she just kind of ran out of energy and dwindled off into silence), he reached out and took her hand.

"It's all right," he said.

And it was, she realized. It actually was.

Chapter 14

. . . I grant that Mr. Wilson's face does have a certain amphibious quality, but I do wish you would learn to be a bit more circumspect in your speech. While I would never consider him an acceptable candidate for marriage, he is certainly not a toad, and it ill-behooved me to have my younger sister call him thus, and in his presence.

—from Eloise Bridgerton to her sister Hyacinth, upon refusing her fourth offer of marriage

Four days later, they were married. Phillip had no idea how Anthony Bridgerton had managed it, but he'd procured a special license, allowing them to be wed without banns and on a Monday, which, Eloise assured him, was no worse than Tuesday or Wednesday, just that it wasn't Saturday, as was proper.

Eloise's entire family, minus her widowed sister in Scotland, who hadn't had time to make the journey, had trooped out to the country for the wedding. Normally, the ceremony would have taken place in Kent, at the Bridgerton family seat, or at the very least in London, where the family attended church regularly at St. George's in Hanover Square, but such arrangements were not possible on such a hastened schedule, and this wasn't an ordinary sort of wedding in any case. Benedict and Sophie had offered their home for the reception, but Eloise had felt that the twins would be more comfortable at Romney Hall, so they'd held the ceremony at the parish church down the lane, followed by a small, intimate reception on the lawn outside Phillip's greenhouse.

Later in the day, just as the sun was beginning to dip in the sky, Eloise found herself in her new bedchamber with her mother, who was busying herself by pretending to tuck away items in Eloise's hastily gathered trousseau. It all, of course, had been taken care of by Eloise's lady's maid (brought up from London with the family) earlier that morning, but Eloise didn't comment upon her mother's idle busywork. It seemed like Violet Bridgerton simply needed something to do while she talked.

Eloise, of all people, understood that need perfectly.

"I should complain that I'm being denied my proper moment of glory as the mother of the bride," Violet said to her daughter as she folded her lacy veil and placed it gently on top of a bureau, "but in truth I'm just happy to see you a bride."

Eloise smiled gently at her mother. "You'd quite despaired of it, hadn't you?"

"Quite." But then she cocked her head to the side and added, "Actually, no. I always thought you might surprise us in the end. You frequently do."

Eloise thought of all those years since her debut, all those rejected marriage proposals. All those weddings they'd attended, with Violet watching another of her friends marrying off another of their daughters to another fabulously eligible gentleman.

Another gentleman, of course, who could now no longer marry Eloise, Lady Bridgerton's famously on-the-shelf spinster daughter.

"I'm sorry if I've disappointed you," Eloise whispered.

Violet gazed at her with a wise expression. "My children never disappoint me," she said softly. "They merely . . . astonish me. I believe I like it that way."

Eloise found herself lurching forward to hug her mother. She felt awkward doing so; she didn't know why, since hers was a family that had never discouraged such displays of affection in the privacy of their own home. Maybe it was because she was so perilously close to tears; maybe it was because she sensed her mother was the same. But she felt an awkward girl again, all gangly arms and legs and bony elbows and a mouth that always opened when it should be closed.

And she wanted her mother.

"There, there," Violet said, sounding very much as she had years ago, when fussing over a skinned knee or bruised feelings. "Now," she said, her face turning pink. "Now, then."

"Mother?" Eloise murmured. She looked very strange indeed, as if she'd eaten bad fish.

"I dread this," Violet muttered.

"Mother?" Surely she couldn't have heard correctly.

Violet took a deep, fortifying breath. "We have to have a little talk." She leaned back, looked her daughter in the eye, then added, "*Do* we have to have a little talk?"

Eloise wasn't certain whether her mother was asking her if she knew of the details *of* intimacy or if she actually knew them . . . intimately. "Uhhh . . . I haven't . . . ah . . . If you mean . . . That is to say, I'm still . . ."

"Excellent," Violet said with a heartfelt sigh. "But do you—that is to say, are you aware . . . ?"

"Yes," Eloise said quickly, eager to spare both of them undue embarrassment. "I don't believe I need anything explained."

"Excellent," Violet said again, her sigh even more heartfelt. "I must say, I do detest this part of motherhood. I can't even recall what I said to Daphne, just that I spent the entire time blushing and stammering, and honestly, I have no idea if she left the encounter any better informed than when she arrived." The corners of her mouth turned down. "Probably not, I'm afraid."

"She seems to have adapted to married life quite well," Eloise murmured.

"Yes, she has. Hasn't she?" Violet said brightly. "Four little children and a husband who dotes upon her. One certainly can't hope for more."

"What did you say to Francesca?" Eloise asked.

"I beg your pardon?"

"Francesca," Eloise repeated, referring to her younger sister who had married six years earlier—and was tragically widowed two years after that. "What did you say to her when she married? You mentioned Daphne, but not Francesca."

Violet's blue eyes clouded, as they always did when she thought of her third daughter, widowed so young. "You know Francesca. I expect she could have told me a thing or two."

Eloise gasped.

"I don't mean it *that* way, of course," Violet hastened to add. "Francesca was as innocent as . . . well, as innocent as you are, I imagine."

Eloise felt her cheeks grow hot and thanked her maker for the cloudy day, which left the room somewhat darkened. That and the fact that her mother was busy inspecting a torn hem on her dress. She was *technically* untouched, of course, and she'd certainly pass inspection if examined by a physician, but she didn't feel quite so innocent any longer.

"But you know Francesca," Violet continued, shrugging and

looking back up when she realized that there was nothing she could do about the hem. "She's so sly and knowing. I expect she bribed some poor housemaid into explaining it all to her years earlier."

Eloise nodded. She didn't want to tell her mother that she and Francesca had in fact pooled their pin money to bribe the housemaid. It had been worth every penny, however. Annie Mavel's explanation had been detailed and, Francesca had later informed her, absolutely correct.

Violet smiled wistfully, then reached up and touched her daughter's cheekbone, right near the corner of her eye. The skin was still slightly discolored, but the purple had faded through blue and green to a rather sickly (but certainly less unsightly) shade of yellow. "Are you certain you'll be happy?" she asked.

Eloise smiled ruefully. "It's a little late to wonder, don't you think?"

"It might be too late to do anything about it, but it's never too late to wonder."

"I think I'll be happy," Eloise said. *I hope so*, she added, but just in her mind.

"He seems a nice man."

"He's a very nice man."

"Honorable."

"He is that."

Violet nodded. "I think you'll be happy. It might take time until you realize it, and you might doubt yourself at first, but you'll be happy. Just remember—" She stopped, chewing on her lip.

"What, Mother?"

"Just remember," she said slowly, as if she were choosing each word with great care, "that it takes time. That's all."

What takes time? Eloise wanted to scream.

But her mother had already stood up and was briskly smoothing her skirts, "I expect I shall have to usher the family out, or they will never leave." She fiddled with a bow on her dress as she turned slightly away. One of her hands reached up to her face, and Eloise tried not to notice that she was brushing aside a tear.

"You're very impatient," Violet said, facing the door. "You always have been."

"I know," Eloise said, wondering if this was a scolding, and if so, *why* was her mother choosing to do it now?

"I always loved that about you," Violet said. "I always loved everything about you, of course, but for some reason I always found your impatience especially charming. It was never because you wanted *more*, it was because you wanted everything."

Eloise wasn't so sure that sounded like such a good trait.

"You wanted everything for everyone, and you wanted to know it all and learn it all, and . . ."

For a moment Eloise thought her mother might be done, but then Violet turned around and added, "You've never been satisfied with second-best, and that's good, Eloise. I'm glad you never married any of those men who proposed in London. None of them would have made you happy. Content, maybe, but not happy."

Eloise felt her eyes widen with surprise.

"But don't let your impatience become all that you are," Violet said softly. "Because it isn't, you know. There's a great deal more to you, but I think sometimes you forget that." She smiled, the gentle, wise smile of a mother saying goodbye to her daughter. "Give it time, Eloise. Be gentle. Don't push too hard."

Eloise opened her mouth but found herself entirely incapable of speech.

"Be patient," Violet said. "Don't push."

"I . . ." Eloise had meant to say *I won't*, but her words fell away, and all she could do was stare at her mother's face, only now realizing what it truly meant that she was married. She'd been thinking so much about Phillip that she hadn't thought of her family.

She was leaving them. She would always have them in all the ways that mattered, but still, she was leaving.

And she hadn't realized until that very moment how often she sat down with her mother and just talked. Or how very precious those moments were. Violet always seemed to know just what her children needed, which was remarkable, really, since there were eight of them—eight very different souls, each with unique hopes and dreams.

Even Violet's letter—the one she'd written and asked Anthony to give to her at Romney Hall—it was exactly right, precisely what Eloise had needed to hear. Violet could have scolded, she could have hurled accusations; she would have been perfectly within her rights to do either—or more.

But all she'd written was, "I hope you are well. Please remember that you are my daughter and you will always be my daughter. I love you."

Eloise had bawled. Thank goodness she'd forgotten to read it until late in the night, when she was able to do so in the privacy of her room at Benedict's house.

Violet Bridgerton had never wanted for anything, but her true wealth lay in her wisdom and her love, and it occurred to Eloise, as she watched Violet turn back to the door, that she was more than just her mother—she was everything that Eloise aspired to be.

And Eloise couldn't believe it had taken her this long to realize it.

"I imagine you and Sir Phillip will want some privacy," Violet said, placing her hand on the doorknob.

Eloise nodded even though her mother couldn't see the gesture. "I shall miss you all."

"Of course you will," Violet said, her brisk tone obviously her way of recovering her composure. "And we shall miss you. But you won't be far. And you'll live so close to Benedict and Sophie. And Posy, too. I expect I shall be coming out this way more often for visits now that I have two more grandchildren to spoil."

Eloise brushed away tears of her own. Her family had accepted Phillip's children instantly and unconditionally. She had expected no less, but still, it warmed her heart more than she would ever have imagined. Already the twins were playing raucously with the Bridgerton grandchildren, and Violet had insisted that they call her Grandmama. They had agreed with alacrity, especially after Violet had produced an entire bag of peppermint drops that she claimed must have fallen into her valise back in London.

Eloise had already said her goodbyes to her family, so when her mother departed, she felt well and truly Lady Crane. Miss Bridgerton would have returned to London with the rest of the family, but Lady Crane, wife of a Gloucestershire landowner and baronet, remained here at Romney Hall. She felt strange and different and chided herself for it. One would think, at twenty-eight, that marriage would not seem such a momentous step. After all, she wasn't a green girl, and hadn't been for some time.

Still, she told herself, she had every right to feel that her life had changed forever. She was married, for heaven's sake, and the mistress of her own home. Not to mention mother to two children. None of her siblings had had to take on the responsibilities of parenthood so suddenly.

But she was up to the task. She had to be. She squared her shoulders, looking determinedly at her reflection in the mirror as she brushed her hair. She was a Bridgerton, even if it was no longer her legal surname, and she was up to anything. And as she wasn't the sort to tolerate an unhappy life, then she would simply have to make certain that hers was anything but.

A knock sounded at the door, and when Eloise turned around, Phillip had entered the room. He closed the door behind him but remained where he was, presumably to offer her a bit of time to collect herself.

"Wouldn't you like your maid for that?" he asked, nodding toward her hairbrush.

"I told her to take a free evening," Eloise said. She shrugged. "It seemed odd to have her here, almost an intrusion, I think."

He cleared his throat as he tugged at his cravat, a motion that had become endearingly familiar. He was never quite at home in formal attire, she realized, always tugging or shifting and quite obviously wishing he was in his more comfortable work clothes.

How strange to have a husband with an actual vocation. Eloise had never thought to marry a man like that. Not that Phillip was in trade, but still, his work in the greenhouse was certainly something more than what most of the idle young men of her acquaintance had to fill their lives.

She liked it, she realized. She liked that he had a purpose and a calling, liked that his mind was sharp and engaged in intellectual inquiry rather than horses and gambling.

She liked *him*.

It was a relief, that. What a bind she would have been in if she didn't.

"Would you like a few more minutes?" he asked.

She shook her head. She was ready.

A rush of air blew past his lips. Eloise thought she might have heard the words "Thank God," and then she was in his arms, and he was kissing her, and whatever else she'd been thinking, it was gone.

Phillip supposed that he should have devoted a bit more of his mental energy to his wedding, but the truth was, he couldn't keep his mind on the events of the day, not when the events of the night loomed tantalizingly close. Every time he looked at Eloise, every time he even sniffed her scent, which seemed to be everywhere, standing out among all the delicate perfumes of the Bridgerton women, he felt a telltale tightening in his body, a shiver of anticipation as he recalled what it felt like to have her in his arms.

Soon, he told himself, forcing his body to relax, then thanking God that he was actually successful in the endeavor. *Soon*.

And then soon became now, and they were alone, and he couldn't quite believe how lovely she was with her long, chestnut hair cascading in soft waves down her back. He had never seen it down, he realized, never imagined the length of it when it had been tucked away in a tidy little bun at the nape of her neck.

"I always wondered why women kept their hair up," he murmured, once he'd finished with his seventh kiss.

"It's expected, of course," Eloise said, looking puzzled at the comment.

"That's not why," he said. He touched her hair, ran his fingers through it, then lifted it to his face and breathed in the scent. "It's for the protection of other men."

Her eyes flew to his with surprise and confusion. "Surely you mean the protection *from*."

He shook his head slowly. "I'd have to kill anyone who saw you thus."

"Phillip." Her tone was meant to be scolding, he was quite sure of that, but she was blushing and looking rather absurdly pleased by his statement.

"No one who saw this could resist you," he said, winding a length of her silky hair around his fingers. "I'm quite sure of it."

"Many men have found me quite resistible," she said, offering him a self-deprecating smile as she looked up at him. "Quite a lot, actually."

"They're fools," he said simply. "And besides, it [illegible] proves my point, does it not? This"—he held one long thick lock up [illegible] their faces, then tickled it against his lips, breathing in its heady scent—"has been hidden away in a bun for years."

"Since I was sixteen," she said.

He tugged her toward him, gently but inexorably. "I'm glad. You'd never have been mine if you'd tugged out your hairpins. Someone else would have snatched you up years ago."

"It's just hair," she whispered, her voice a little trembly.

"You're right," he agreed. "You must be, because on anyon[illegible]se, I don't think it would be nearly so intoxicating. It must be [illegible]" he whispered, letting the strands drop from his fingers. "On[illegible]."

He cradled her face in his hands, tilting it slightly to [illegible]ide so that he might more easily kiss her. He knew what h[illegible]s tasted like, had kissed them, in fact, just minutes earlier. [illegible]ven with that, he was startled by her sweetness, by the war[illegible] her breath and her mouth, and the way his body turned t[illegible]rom one simple kiss.

Except that it would never be just a simp[illegible]s. Not with her.

His fingers found the fastenin[illegible]gown, small fabric-covered buttons marching do[illegible]Turn around," he ordered, breaking the kiss. H[illegible]experienced at seduction that he could slip them fr[illegible]eir loops without the advantage of sight.

[illegible] he rather [illegible]yed this—this slow disrobing, each button [illegible]er half inch of creamy skin.

She was his, he realized, sliding one finger down her spine before attending to the third-to-last button. His for eternity. It was hard to imagine how he had been so lucky, but he resolved not to wonder at his good fortune, just to enjoy it.

Another button. This one revealed a square of flesh near the base of her spine.

He touched her. She shivered.

His fingers went to the last button. He didn't really need to attend to it; her dress was more than loose enough to slip from her shoulders. But somehow he needed to do this right, to disrobe her properly, to savor the moment.

Besides, this last one revealed the curve of her buttocks.

He wanted to kiss her. He wanted to kiss her right there. Right at the top of her cleft while she stood facing the other way, shivering not from cold but from excitement.

He leaned toward her, pressed his lips to the back of her neck as both of his hands found her shoulders. There were some things that were too wicked for an innocent like Eloise.

But she was his. His wife. And she was fire and passion and energy all wrapped into one. She wasn't Marina, he reminded himself, delicate and breakable, unable to express emotion other than sorrow.

She wasn't Marina. It seemed necessary to remind himself of this, not just now, but continually, throughout the day, each time he looked at her. She wasn't Marina, and he didn't need to hold his breath around her, afraid of his own words, afraid of his facial expressions, afraid of anything that might cause her to sink into herself, into her own despair.

This was Eloise. *Eloise.* Strong, magnificent Eloise.

Unable to stop himself, he sank to his knees, holding Eloise's hips firmly between his hands when she let out a soft murmur of surprise and tried to turn around.

And he kissed her. Right there, at the base of her spine, in the spot that had tempted him so, he kissed her. And then—he didn't know why; his experience with women had been limited, but his imagination was clearly making up for that lack—he ran his tongue along that central line, down her spine to the beginning of her cleft, tasting the sweet saltiness of her skin, stopping—but not removing his lips—when she moaned, putting her hands out against the wall to support herself when she could no longer stand.

"Phillip," she gasped.

He rose and turned her around, leaning down until they were nearly nose to nose. "It was there," he said helplessly, as if that would explain everything. And in truth, that was all the explanation there was. It was there, that tantalizing little patch of skin, pink and peachy and waiting for a kiss.

She was there, and he had to have her.

He kissed her mouth again as he let her gown slide from her body. She'd been married in blue, a pale version of the color that made her eyes look deeper and more tempestuous than ever, rather like a cloudy sky just before a rainstorm.

It was a heavenly dress—he'd heard her sister Daphne say that to her earlier that day. But it was even more heavenly to rid her of it.

She wasn't wearing a chemise, and he knew that she was bared to him, heard her suck in her breath as the tips of her breasts grazed the fine linen of his shirt. But instead of looking, he ran his hand along the side of her breast, his knuckles lightly nuzzling the side of the swell. Then, as he continued to kiss her, his hand curved around until he was cupping her, feeling the exquisite weight of her in his fingers.

"Phillip," she moaned, the word sinking into his mouth like a benediction.

He moved his hand again until he covered her, her pert nipple sliding between his fingers. And as he squeezed—gently, reverently—he could, after all, hardly believe this had all come to pass.

And then he couldn't wait any longer. He had to see her, to see every bit of her and watch her face as he did so. He pulled back, breaking their kiss with a whispered promise that he'd be back.

He sucked in his breath as he gazed down at her. It was not yet dark, and the last vestiges of sunlight still filtered in through the windows, bathing her skin in a red-gold glow. Her breasts were larger than he'd imagined, full and round and plump, and it was all he could do not to sweep her into bed that very moment. He could feast forever on those breasts, love them and worship them until . . .

Dear God, who was he trying to fool? Until his own need grew too intense, and he had to have her, to plunge into her, devour her.

With shaking fingers, he went to work on his own buttons, watching her watching him as he tore the shirt from his body. And then he forgot, and he turned . . .

And she gasped.

He froze.

"What happened?" she whispered.

He didn't know why he was so surprised by the moment, by the fact that he would have to explain. She was his wife, and she was going to see him naked every day for the rest of his life, and if anyone was going to know the nature of his scars, it would be her.

He was able to avoid them, as they were quite out of his sight on his back, but Eloise would not be so lucky.

"I was whipped," he said, not turning around. He should probably spare her the sight, but she was going to have to get used to it sometime.

"Who did this to you?" Her voice was low and angry, and her outrage warmed his heart.

"My father." Phillip well remembered the day. He had been twelve, home from school, and his father had forced him to accompany him on a hunt. Phillip was a good horseman, but not good enough for the jump his father had taken ahead of him. He'd tried it, though, knowing he'd be branded a coward if he did not make the attempt.

He'd fallen, of course. Been thrown, really. Miraculously, he'd walked away without injury, but his father had been livid. Thomas Crane possessed a very narrow vision of English manhood, and it did not include tumbles off horseback. His sons would ride and shoot and fence and box and excel and excel and excel.

And God help them if they did not.

George had made the jump, of course. George was always a hair better at all things sporting. And George was also two years his elder, two years bigger, two years stronger. He'd tried to intercede, to save Phillip from punishment, but then Thomas had just whipped him as well, berating him for meddling. Phillip needed to learn how to be a man, and Thomas would not tolerate anyone interfering, even George.

Phillip wasn't sure what had been different about the punishment that day; usually his father used a belt, which, over a shirt, left no marks. But they'd already been out by the stables, and the whip was handy, and his father had been so damned angry, even angrier than normal.

When the whip sliced through Phillip's shirt, Thomas didn't stop.

It was the only time his father's beatings had left visible scars.

And Phillip was stuck with the reminder for the rest of his life.

He glanced over at Eloise, who was watching him with an oddly intense look in her eyes. "I'm sorry," he said, even though he wasn't. There was nothing to be sorry for, save for having forced her into the horror of his childhood.

"I'm not sorry," she growled, her eyes narrow and fierce.

His eyes widened with surprise.

"I'm furious."

And then he couldn't help it. He laughed. He threw his head back and laughed. She was absolutely perfect, naked and angry, ready to march down to hell itself to drag his father out for a tongue-lashing.

She looked slightly alarmed at his oddly timed laughter, but then she smiled, too, as if recognizing the importance of the moment.

He took her hand and, desperate for her to touch him, brought it to his heart, pressing it flat until her fingers spread out, sinking into the soft, springy hair on his chest.

"So strong," she whispered, her hand sliding gently along his skin. "I had no idea it was such difficult work, toiling away in the greenhouse."

He felt like a boy of sixteen, so pleased was he by her compliment. And the memory of his father quietly slipped away. "I do work outside, too," he said gruffly, unable to simply say thank you.

"With the laborers?" she murmured.

He looked at her with amusement. "Eloise Bridgerton—"

"Crane," she corrected.

A burst of pleasure shot through him at her words. "Crane," he repeated. "Don't tell me you've been harboring secret fantasies about the farm laborers."

"Of course not," she said, "although . . ."

There was no way he was going to let those words trail off into oblivion. "Although?" he prompted.

She looked a little sheepish. "Well, they do look terribly . . . *elemental* . . . out there in the sun, toiling away."

He smiled. Slowly, like a man about to feast upon his dream come true. "Oh, Eloise," he said, bringing his lips to her neck and moving down, down, down. "You have no idea of elemental. No idea at all."

And then he did what he'd been dreaming of for days—well, one of the things he'd been dreaming of—and he took her nipple into his mouth, running his tongue around the edge before closing around to suck.

"Phillip!" she nearly shrieked, sinking into him.

He swept her into his arms and carried her to the bed, already turned down and waiting for the newlyweds. He laid her atop the sheets, stopping to enjoy the sight of her before attending to her stockings, which were all that was left on her body. Her hands went instinctively to cover her sex, and he allowed her her modesty, knowing that his turn would come soon.

He looped his fingers under the edge of one stocking, caressing her through the whisper-fine silk before sliding it down her leg. She moaned as he passed her knee, and he couldn't help looking up and asking, "Ticklish?"

She nodded. "And more."

And more. He loved that. He loved that she felt more, that she wanted more.

The other stocking was disposed of more quickly, and then he stood beside her, his fingers moving to the fastenings on his trousers. He paused for a moment and looked at her, waiting for her to tell him with her eyes that she was ready.

And then, with a speed and agility he'd never dreamed he possessed, he'd stripped himself of his remaining garments and laid down beside her. She stiffened for a moment, then relaxed as he stroked her, his lips making shushing sounds as they moved to her temple, and then to her lips.

"There is nothing to be afraid of," he murmured.

"I'm not afraid," she said.

He drew back, looked her in the face. "You're not?"

"Nervous, but not afraid."

He shook his head in wonder. "You are magnificent."

"I keep telling everyone that," she said with a nonchalant shrug, "but you seem to be the only one to believe me."

He chuckled at that, shaking his head in wonder, barely able to believe that here he was, on his wedding night, and he was laughing. Twice now, she had made him laugh, and he was beginning to realize that this was a gift. An amazing, priceless gift, one that he was truly blessed to receive.

Intercourse had always been about need, about his body and his lust and whatever it was that made him a man. It had never been about this joy, this wonder at discovering another person.

He took her face in his hands and kissed her again, this time with all the feeling and emotion coursing through him. He kissed her mouth, then he kissed her cheek, then her neck. And he moved down, exploring her body, from her shoulders to her belly to the side of her hip.

He skipped only one place, one place he would have very much liked to explore, but he decided that would come later, when she was ready.

When *he* was ready. Marina had never let him kiss her there—no, that wasn't fair; in truth, he'd never even asked. It had just seemed so wrong as she lay beneath him, still and silent, as if she were performing a duty. There had been women before his marriage, but they'd been of the experienced sort, and he'd never wanted to be quite so intimate with them.

Later, he promised himself as he stopped, briefly, to nuzzle her curls.

Soon. Definitely soon.

He wrapped his large hands around her calves, then slid them up, nudging her legs apart so that he could settle between them. He was hard, *really* hard, afraid he was going to embarrass himself, and so he took deep breaths as he touched her opening, trying to calm his blood so that he would be able to make this last long enough for her to enjoy herself.

"Oh, Eloise," he said, although in truth it was more of a grunt. He wanted her more than anything, more than life itself, and he had no idea how he was going to last.

"Phillip?" she asked, her voice sounding vaguely alarmed.

He pulled back so that he could see her face.

"You're very big," she whispered.

He smiled. "Don't you know that's *exactly* what a man wishes to hear?"

"I'm sure," she said, nibbling on her lower lip. "It does seem the sort of thing you'd brag about while you're racing horses and playing cards and being competitive for no particular reason."

He wasn't sure whether he was shaking with laughter or dismay. "Eloise," he managed to say, "I assure you—"

"How much is it going to hurt?" she blurted out.

"I don't know," he said honestly. "I've never been in your position. A little, I imagine. I hope not too much."

She nodded, seeming to appreciate his candor. "I keep . . ." Her words trailed off.

"Tell me," he urged.

For several seconds she did nothing but blink, then she said, "I keep getting swept away, like the other day, but then I see you, or I feel you, and I can't *imagine* how this will work, and I worry I'll be torn apart, and I lose it. The magic," she explained. "I lose the magic."

And then he decided—to hell with it. Why should he wait? Why should *she* wait? He leaned down, kissed her quickly on the mouth. "Wait right here," he said. "Don't go anywhere."

Before she could ask questions—and she was Eloise, so of course she had questions—he slithered down, and spread her legs wide, the way he'd lain awake imagining at night, and kissed her.

She screamed.

"Good," he murmured, his words disappearing into the very heart of her. His hands held her firm; he had no choice, she was squirming and bucking like a wild woman. He licked and kissed, and he tasted every inch, every tantalizing crevice. He was voracious, and he devoured her, thinking that this had to be quite simply the *best* thing he'd ever done in his entire life, and dear *God*, he was thankful he was a married man now and could do it as often as he liked.

He'd heard other men talk about it, of course, but never ever had he dreamed it would be this good. He was a hairbreadth away from losing himself completely, and she hadn't even touched him. Not that he would have wanted her to at that moment—the way she was gripping the sheets, her knuckles white and straining, hell, she would have ripped him in two.

He should have let her finish, should have kissed her until she exploded into his mouth, but at that point his own needs took over, and he simply had no choice. This was his wedding night, and when he spilled himself, it was going to be into her, not the sheets, and dear God, but if he didn't feel her squeezing around him soon, he was quite certain he was going to burst into flame.

And so he lifted himself, ignoring her cry of distress as he removed his lips, and he moved up, settling his member against her one more time, then using his fingers to part her even more as he pushed forward.

She was wet—very, very wet, a mix of her and him, and it was nothing like he'd ever felt before. He slid right in, her passage somehow easy and tight at the same time.

She gasped his name, and he gasped hers, and then, unable to keep his pace slow, he plunged forward, breaking through her last barrier until he was embedded to the hilt. And maybe he should have stopped, maybe he should have asked if she was all right, if she felt any pain, but he just couldn't. It had been so damned long, and he needed her so damned much, and once his body began to move there wasn't a thing he could do to stop it.

He was fast and he was rough, but she must have liked it because she was fast and rough beneath him, her hips grinding against his with needy force as her fingers bit into his back.

And when she moaned, it wasn't his name. It was, "More!"

He slid his fingers beneath her, grabbing on to her buttocks, squeezing hard as he tilted her up to allow him even easier entry, and the change of position must have done something to change the way he was rubbing her, or maybe she had just reached her limit, because she arched beneath him, going so stiff she shook, and then a cry was ripped from her throat as he felt her muscles convulse around him.

He could take no more. With one final shout he plunged forward, shuddering and shaking as he emptied himself, claiming her finally and indelibly as his own.

Chapter 15

. . . I cannot believe that you will not tell me more. As your elder sister (by a full year, I should not have to remind you) I am owed a certain measure of respect, and while I appreciate your informing me that Annie Mavel's account of married love was correct, I should have liked a few details beyond that brief account. Surely you are not so wrapped in your own bliss that you cannot spare a few words (adjectives, in particular, would be helpful) for your beloved sister.

—from Eloise Bridgerton to her sister the Countess of Kilmartin, two weeks after Francesca's wedding

One week later, Eloise was sitting in the small parlor that had recently been converted into an office for her, chewing on the end of her pencil as she attempted to go over the household accounts. She was supposed to be counting funds, and bags of flour, and the servants' wages, and the like, but in truth all she could count was the number of times she and Phillip had made love.

Thirteen, she thought. No, fourteen. Well, fifteen, actually, if she counted that time when he hadn't actually gone inside of her, but they'd both . . .

She blushed, even though there wasn't a soul in the room besides her, and it wasn't as if anyone would have known what she was thinking, anyway.

But good God, had she really *done* that? Kissed him *there*?

She hadn't even known such a thing was possible. Annie Mavel certainly hadn't described anything like that when she'd delivered her little lesson to Eloise and Francesca all those years ago.

Eloise scrunched her face as she thought back. She wondered if Annie Mavel had even known such things were possible. It was difficult to imagine Annie doing it, but then, it was difficult to imagine *anyone* doing it, most especially herself.

It was amazing, she thought, utterly amazing and beyond wonderful to have a husband who was so mad for her. They didn't see one another too terribly often during the day—he had his work, after all, and she had hers, of a sort—but at night, after he'd given her five minutes for her toilette (it had started at twenty, but it seemed to be getting progressively shorter, and she could even hear his footsteps pacing outside the door during the scant minutes he now allowed her) . . .

At night, he pounced upon her like a man possessed. A starving man, really. His energy seemed endless, and he was always trying new things, positioning her in new ways, teasing and tormenting until she was screaming and begging, never sure whether it was for him to stop or keep going.

He'd said that he hadn't felt passion for Marina, but Eloise found that hard to believe. He was a man of *hearty* appetites (it was a silly word, but she could not think of any other way to describe it), and the things he did with his hands . . .

And his mouth . . .

And his teeth . . .

And his tongue . . .

She blushed again. The things he did—well, a woman would have to be half dead not to respond.

She looked back down at the columns in her ledger. The numbers hadn't miraculously added themselves up while she daydreamed, and every time Eloise tried to concentrate they began swimming around before her eyes. She glanced out the window; she couldn't see Phillip's greenhouse from her position, but she knew it was just around the corner, and that he was in it, toiling away, snipping leaves and planting seeds and whatever else it was that he did there all day.

All day.

She frowned. It was actually a very apt phrase. Phillip did spend the entire day in the greenhouse, often even having his midday meal brought in on a tray. She knew it wasn't terribly abnormal for man and wife to lead separate lives during the day (and, for many couples, at night as well), but they had only been married one week.

And in truth, she was in many ways still learning who her new husband was. The marriage had come about so precipitously; she really knew very little about him. Oh, she knew he was honest and honorable and would treat her well, and now she knew that he possessed a carnal side that she would never have dreamed lurked beneath his reserved exterior.

But aside from what she had learned about his father, she didn't know his experiences, his opinions, what had happened in his life to make him the man he now was. She tried, sometimes, to draw him out in conversation, and she sometimes succeeded, but more often than not, her attempts melted away.

Because he never seemed to want to talk when he could kiss. And that, inevitably, led to his nudging her into the bedroom, where words were forgotten.

And on the few occasions when she did manage to engage him in conversation, it proved to be nothing more than an exercise in frustration. She would ask his opinion on anything relating to the household, for example, and he would just shrug and tell her that she should handle it how she saw fit. Sometimes she wondered if he'd married her just to gain a housekeeper.

And, of course, a warm body in his bed.

But there could be more. Eloise knew there could be more to a marriage, knew there could be more *in* a marriage. She couldn't recall much of her parents' union, but she'd seen her siblings with their spouses, and she thought she and Phillip might find the same bliss if they would only spend a little time together outside the bedroom.

She stood abruptly and walked to the door. She should talk to him. There was no reason she couldn't go to the greenhouse and talk to him. Maybe he'd even appreciate it if she asked about his work.

She wasn't going to interrogate him, exactly, but surely there could be no harm in a question or two, peppered into the conversation. And if he even hinted that she was bothering him or making it difficult to work, she'd leave immediately.

But then she heard her mother's voice echoing in her head.

Don't push, Eloise. Don't push.

It took willpower she'd never thought she possessed, since it went against her every last natural inclination, but she stopped, turned around, and sat back down.

She'd never known her mother to be wrong about anything truly important, and if Violet had seen fit to give advice on her wedding night, Eloise rather suspected she ought to pay it careful attention.

This, she thought with a grumpy frown, must have been what her mother had meant when she'd said to give it time.

She jammed her hands under her bottom, as if to keep them from reaching forward and leading her back toward the door. She glanced out the window, then had to avert her gaze because even though she couldn't see the greenhouse, she knew it was right there, just around the corner.

This was not, she thought through clenched teeth, her natural state. She'd never been the sort who could sit still and smile while she did so. She was meant to be moving, doing, exploring, questioning. And if she were to be honest—bothering, pestering, and stating her opinions to anyone who would listen as well.

She frowned, sighing. Put that way, she didn't sound a terribly attractive person.

She tried to remember her mother's wedding-night speech. Surely there was something positive in there as well. Her mother loved her, after all. She must have said *some*thing good. Hadn't there been something about her being charming?

She sighed. If she recalled correctly, her mother had said she found her impatience charming, which wasn't really the same as finding someone's *good* temperament charming.

How awful this was. She was eight and twenty, for heaven's sake. She'd sailed through her entire life feeling perfectly happy with who she was and how she conducted herself.

Well, almost perfectly happy. She knew she talked too much and was perhaps a little too direct at times, and very well, not everybody liked her, but most people did, and she'd long since decided that that was fine with her.

So why now? Why was she suddenly so unsure of herself, so fearful of doing or saying the wrong thing?

She stood. She couldn't stand this—the indecision, the lack of action. She'd heed her mother's advice and give Phillip a bit of privacy, but by God, she couldn't sit here doing nothing one moment longer.

She looked down at the incomplete ledgers. Oh, dear. If she'd been doing what she was *supposed* to be doing, she wouldn't have been doing nothing, would she?

With a little huff of irritation, she slammed the ledgers shut. It didn't really matter if she could be adding her sums, because she knew herself well enough to know that she *wouldn't* be adding them, even if she sat here, so she might as well go off and do something else.

The children. That was it. She'd become a wife a week ago, but she'd also become a mother. And if anyone needed interfering in their lives, it was Oliver and Amanda.

Buoyed by her newfound sense of purpose, she strode out the door, feeling once again like her old self. She needed to oversee their lessons, make sure they were learning properly. Oliver was going to need to prepare himself for Eton, where he really ought to enroll in the fall term.

And then there was their clothing. They'd quite outgrown everything in their wardrobes, and Amanda deserved something prettier, and . . .

She sighed with contentment as she hurried up the stairs. Already she was ticking off her projects on her fingers, mentally planning for the dressmaker and the tailor, not to mention devising the wording for the advertisement she intended to place to secure the services of a few more tutors, because they desperately needed to learn French and the pianoforte, and, of course, sums—and were they too young for long division?

Feeling rather jaunty, she pushed open the door to the nursery, and then . . .

She stopped short, trying to figure out what was going on.

Oliver's eyes were red, as if he'd been crying, and Amanda was sniffling, wiping her nose with the back of her hand. Both were taking those hiccuppy gasps of breath that one does when one is upset.

"Is something wrong?" Eloise asked, looking first at the children and then at their nurse.

The twins said nothing, but they looked at her with wide, imploring eyes.

"Nurse Edwards?" Eloise asked.

The nurse's lips were twisted into an unpleasant frown. "They are merely sulking because they were punished."

Eloise nodded slowly. It wasn't the least bit surprising that Oliver and Amanda might do something requiring punishment, but nonetheless, there was something wrong about what she was seeing. Maybe it was the broken look in their eyes, as if they'd tried defiance and had given up on it.

Not that she wanted to encourage defiance, especially not against their nurse, who needed to maintain her position of authority in the schoolroom, but nor did she ever want to see this expression in their eyes—so totally humbled, so meek and sorrowful.

"Why were they punished?" Eloise asked.

"Disrespectful speech," came their nurse's immediate reply.

"I see." Eloise sighed. The twins probably had deserved punishment; they did often speak with disrespect and it was something she herself had scolded them about on several occasions. "And what punishment was meted out?"

"They were rapped on the knuckles," Nurse Edwards said, her back ramrod stiff.

Eloise forced herself to unclench her jaw. She didn't like corporal punishment, but at the same time, rapped knuckles were a staple in all the best schools. She was quite certain all of her brothers had had their knuckles rapped on numerous occasions at Eton; she couldn't imagine they had made it through all those years without a number of disciplinary transgressions.

Still, she didn't like the look in the children's eyes, so she took Nurse Edwards aside and said softly, "I understand their need for discipline, but if you must do this again, I must ask that you do it more softly."

"If I do it softly," the nurse said quite sharply, "they won't learn their lesson."

"I will be the judge of their learned lessons," Eloise said, bristling at the nurse's tone. "And I am no longer asking. I am telling you, they are children, and you must be more gentle."

Nurse Edwards's lips pursed, but she nodded. Once, sharply, to show that she would do as asked, but that she disagreed—and disapproved of Eloise's interference.

Eloise turned back to the children and said in a loud voice, "I am quite certain they have learned their lesson for today. Perhaps they might take a short break with me."

"We are practicing our penmanship," Nurse Edwards said. "We can't afford to take any time off. Especially not if I am meant to act as both nurse and governess."

"I assure you that I plan to address that problem with all possible haste," Eloise said. "And as for today, I will be happy to practice penmanship with the children. You may be assured that they will not fall behind."

"I do not think—"

Eloise speared her with a glare. She was not a Bridgerton for nothing, and by God, she knew how to deal with recalcitrant servants. "You need only to inform me of your lesson plans."

The nurse looked exceedingly grumpy, but she informed Eloise that today they were practicing *M*, *N*, and *O*. "*Both* uppercase and lowercase," she added sharply.

"I see," Eloise said, giving her voice a supercilious lilt. "I am fairly certain that I am qualified in that particular area of scholarly pursuit."

Nurse Edwards's face turned red at the sarcasm. "Will that be all?" she bit off.

Eloise nodded. "Indeed. You are dismissed. Do enjoy your free time—surely you don't get enough of it, serving double duty as you do, as both nurse and governess—and please return to see to their lunch."

Head held high, Nurse Edwards left the room.

"Well then," Eloise announced, turning her attention to the two children, who were still sitting at their little table, gazing up at her as if she were a minor deity, come down to earth for the sole purpose of saving children from evil witches. "Shall we—"

But she couldn't finish her question, because Amanda had launched herself at her, throwing her arms around her midsection with enough force to knock her back against the wall. And Oliver soon followed.

"There, there," Eloise said, patting their hair in confusion. "Whatever could be wrong?"

"Nothing," came Amanda's muffled reply.

Oliver pulled back and stood straight like the little man people were always telling him to be. Then he ruined the effect by wiping his nose with the back of his hand.

Eloise handed him a handkerchief.

He used it, nodded his thanks, and said, "We like you better than Nurse Edwards."

Eloise couldn't imagine liking anyone worse than Nurse Edwards, and she privately vowed to look into finding a replacement as soon as possible. But she wasn't going to say anything to the children about this; they would almost certainly relate the information to the nurse, who would either give her notice immediately, leaving them all in a terrible bind, or take her frustration and ire out on the children, which wouldn't do at all.

"Let's sit down," she said, steering them toward the table. "I don't know about the rest of you, but *I* don't want to have to face her if we haven't practiced our *M*s, *N*s, and *O*s."

And she thought to herself—*I really must speak with Phillip about this.*

She looked down at Oliver's hands. They didn't look abused, but one of the knuckles looked a little bit red. It might have been her imagination, but still . . .

She needed to talk to Phillip. As soon as she was able.

Phillip hummed to himself as he carefully transplanted a seedling, well aware that prior to his marriage, he had always labored in complete and utter silence.

He had never felt like whistling before, he realized, never once wanted to sing softly to himself or hum. But now . . . well, now it seemed as if music were simply in the air, all around him. He felt more relaxed, too, and the constant knots of tension in his shoulders had started to dissolve.

Marrying Eloise was, quite simply, the best thing he could have done. Hell, he'd even go so far as to say it was the best thing he'd *ever* done.

He was, for the first time in recent memory, happy.

It seemed such a simple thing now, to be happy. And he wasn't even sure that he'd realized he wasn't happy before. He had certainly laughed on occasion, and enjoyed himself from time to time—it wasn't, as it had been for Marina, that he'd been completely and constantly unhappy.

But he hadn't been *happy*. Not in the way he was now, waking up each day with the feeling that the world was indeed a wonderful place and that it would still be a wonderful place when he went to bed that night and still yet again when he got up the following morning.

He couldn't remember the last time he'd felt like that. Probably not since his university days, when he'd had his first taste of the thrill of intellectual discovery—and he was far enough away from his father that he didn't have to worry about the constant threat of the rod.

It was difficult to count the ways that Eloise had improved his life. There was, of course, their time in the bedroom, which was quite beyond anything he might have imagined. If he'd even dreamed that sexual intercourse could be so splendid, there was no way he would have remained celibate for so long. No way he could have, quite frankly, if his current appetite was any indication.

But he simply hadn't known. Lovemaking certainly hadn't been like that with Marina. Or with any of the women he'd fumbled with as a university lad, before his marriage.

But if he were honest with himself—and that was a difficult task, considering how completely besotted his body was with Eloise's—the intercourse wasn't the main reason for his current sense of contentment.

It was this feeling—this knowledge, really—that he had finally, and truly, for the first time since he'd become a father, done the absolute right thing for the twins.

He'd never be a perfect father. He knew that, and even if he hated it, he accepted it. But he had finally done the next best thing, and gotten them the perfect mother.

It was as if a thousand pounds of guilt had been lifted from his shoulders.

No wonder his muscles finally felt unknotted and relaxed.

He could go into his greenhouse in the morning and *not worry.* He couldn't remember the last time he'd done that, simply gone in and worked without cringing every time he heard a loud noise or shriek. Or been able to concentrate on his work without his mind wandering into guilt, unable to focus on anything other than his lacks as a father.

But now he walked in and forgot all his cares. Hell, he had no cares.

It was splendid. Magical.

A relief.

And if sometimes his wife looked at him as if she wanted him to say something different or do something different—well, he chalked that up to the simple fact that he was a man and she was a woman, and his sort would never understand her sort, and truly, he ought just to be grateful that Eloise almost always said exactly what she meant, which was a very good thing, since he wasn't constantly left guessing what was expected of him.

What was that thing his brother had always said— Beware a woman asking questions. You will never answer correctly.

Phillip smiled to himself, enjoying the memory. Put that way, there was no reason to worry if occasionally their conversations dwindled off into nothingness. Most of the time they dwindled right into bed, which was perfectly fine by him.

He looked down at the bulge forming in his breeches. Damn. He was going to have to stop thinking about his wife in the middle of the day. Or at the very least, find a way to get discreetly back to the house in his condition and find her quickly.

But then, almost as if she'd known he was standing there thinking how perfect she was, and she wanted to prove it one more time, she opened the door to the greenhouse and poked her head in.

Phillip looked around and wondered why he'd built the structure entirely of glass. He might need to install some sort of privacy screen if she was going to come visiting on a regular basis.

"Am I intruding?"

He thought about that. She was, actually; he was quite in the middle of something, but he realized he didn't mind. Which was odd and rather pleasing at the same time. He'd always been irritated by interruptions before. Even when it was someone whose company he enjoyed, after a few minutes he found himself wishing they would just leave so that he could get back to whatever project he'd had to put aside for their benefit. "Not at all," he said, "if you are not offended by my appearance."

She looked at him, taking in the dirt and mud, including the smudge he was rather certain he sported on his left cheek, and she shook her head. "It's no problem at all."

"What is troubling you?"

"It's the children's nurse," she said without preamble. "I don't like her."

That was not what he expected. He set down his spade. "You don't? What's wrong with her?"

"I don't know exactly. I just don't like her."

"Well, that's hardly a reason to terminate her employment."

Eloise's lips thinned slightly, a sure sign, he was coming to realize, that she was irritated. She said, "She rapped the children across the knuckles."

He sighed. He didn't like the thought of someone striking his children, but then again, it was just a knuckle rap. Nothing that didn't occur in every schoolroom across the country. And, he thought resignedly, his children were not exactly models of good behavior. And so, wanting to groan, he asked, "Did they deserve it?"

"I don't know," Eloise admitted. "I wasn't there. She said they spoke to her disrespectfully."

Phillip felt his shoulders sag a bit. "Unfortunately," he said, "I do not find that difficult to believe."

"No, of course not," Eloise said. "I'm sure they were little beasts. But still, something didn't seem right."

He leaned back against his workbench, tugging her hand until she tumbled against him. "Then look into it."

Her lips parted with surprise. "Don't *you* want to look into it?"

He shrugged. "I'm not the one with concerns. I've never had cause to doubt Nurse Edwards before, but if you feel uncomfortable, by all means, you should investigate. Besides, you're better at this sort of thing than I am."

"But"—she squirmed slightly as he pulled her against him and nuzzled her neck—"you're their father."

"And you're their mother," he said, his words coming out thick and hot against her skin. She was intoxicating, and he was aching with desire, and if he could only get her to stop talking, he could probably maneuver her to the bedroom, where they could have considerably more fun. "I trust your judgment," he said, thinking that would placate her—and besides, it was the truth. "It's why I married you."

Clearly, his answer surprised her. "It's why you . . . *what*?"

"Well, this, too," he murmured, trying to figure out just how much he could fondle her with so many clothes between them.

"Phillip, stop!" she cried out, wrenching herself away.

What the devil? "Eloise," he asked—cautiously, since it was his experience, limited though it was, that one should always tread carefully with a woman in a temper—"what is wrong?"

"What is *wrong*?" she demanded, her eyes flashing dangerously. "How can you even ask that?"

"Well," he said slowly, and with just a touch of sarcasm, "it might be because I don't know what is wrong."

"Phillip, this is not the time."

"To ask you what is wrong?"

"No!" she nearly shrieked.

Phillip took a step back. Self-preservation, he thought wryly. Surely that had to be what the male side of marital spats was all about. Self-preservation and nothing else.

She began waving her arms in a bizarre fashion. "To do this."

He looked around. She was waving at the workbench, at the pea plants, at the sky above, winking in through the panes of glass. "Eloise," he said, his voice deliberately even, "I am not an unintelligent man, but I have no idea what you're talking about."

Her mouth fell open, and he knew he was in trouble. "You don't *know*?" she asked.

He probably should have heeded his own warnings about self-preservation, but some little devil—some annoyed male devil, he was sure—forced him to say, "I don't read minds, Eloise."

"It is not the time," she finally ground out, "to be intimate."

"Well, of course not," he agreed. "We haven't a bit of privacy.

But"—he smiled just thinking about it—"we could always go back to the house. I know it's the middle of the day, but—"

"That is not what I meant at all!"

"Very well," he said, crossing his arms. "I give up. What do you mean, Eloise? Because I assure you, I haven't a clue."

"Men," she muttered.

"I'll take *that* as a compliment."

Her glare could have frozen the Thames. It quite froze off his desire, which irritated him no end, since he'd been looking forward to getting rid of it in another fashion altogether.

"It wasn't meant as such," she said.

He leaned back against the workbench, his casual posture meant to irritate her. "Eloise," he said calmly, "try to afford a small measure of respect for my intelligence."

"It is difficult," she shot back, "when you display so little."

That was *it*. "I don't even know why we are arguing!" he exploded. "One minute you were willing in my arms, and the next you're shrieking like a banshee."

She shook her head. "I was never willing in your arms."

It was as if the bottom dropped out of his world.

She must have seen the shock on his face, because she quickly added, "Today. I meant just today. Just now, actually."

His body sagged with relief, even as the rest of him seethed with anger.

"I was trying to talk with you," she explained.

"You're always trying to talk with me," he pointed out. "That's all you ever do. Talk talk talk."

She drew back. "If you didn't like it," she said in a snippy voice, "you shouldn't have married me."

"It wasn't as if I had a choice in the matter," he bit off. "Your brothers were ready to castrate me. And just so you don't paint me completely black, I don't *mind* your talking. Just not, for the love of God, all of the time."

She looked like she was trying to say something utterly clever and cutting, but all she could do was gape like a fish and make sounds like, "Unh! Unh!"

"Every now and then," he said, feeling quite superior, "you might consider shutting your mouth and using it for some other purpose."

"You," she fumed, "are insufferable."

He raised his brows, knowing it would irritate her.

"I'm sorry you find my propensity for speech so offensive," she ground out, "but I was trying to talk to you about something important, and you tried to kiss me."

He shrugged. "I always try to kiss you. You're my wife. What the hell else am I supposed to do?"

"But sometimes it's not the right time," she said. "Phillip, if we want to have a good marriage—"

"We do have a good marriage," he interrupted, his voice defensive and bitter.

"Yes, of course," she said quickly, "but it can't always be about . . . you know."

"No," he said, deliberately obtuse. "I don't know."

Eloise ground her teeth together. "Phillip, don't be like this."

He said nothing, just tightened his already crossed arms and stared at her face.

She closed her eyes, and her chin bobbed slightly forward as her lips moved. And he realized that she was talking. She wasn't making a sound, but she was still talking.

Dear God, the woman never stopped. Even now she was talking to herself.

"What are you doing?" he finally asked.

She didn't open her eyes as she said, "Trying to convince myself it's all right to ignore my mother's advice."

He shook his head. He would never understand women.

"Phillip," she finally said, just when he'd decided that he was going to leave and let her talk to herself in private. "I very much enjoy what we do in bed—"

"That's nice to hear," he bit off, still too irritated to be gracious.

She ignored his lack of civility. "But it can't be just about that."

"It?"

"Our marriage." She blushed, clearly uncomfortable with such frank speech. "It can't be just about making love."

"It can certainly be a great deal about it," he muttered.

"Phillip, why won't you discuss this with me? We have a problem, and we need to talk about it."

And then something within him simply snapped. He was convinced that his was the perfect marriage, and she was *complaining*? He'd been so sure he'd gotten it right this time. "We've been married one week, Eloise," he ground out. "One week. What do you expect of me?"

"I don't know. I—"

"I'm just a man."

"And I'm just a woman," she said softly.

For some reason, her quiet words only irritated him more. He leaned forward, deliberately using his size to intimidate her. "Do you know how long it had been since I'd lain with a woman?" he hissed. "Do you have any idea?"

Her eyes grew impossibly wide, and she shook her head.

"Eight years," he bit off. "Eight long years with nothing but my own hand for comfort. So the next time I seem to be enjoying myself while I'm driving into you, please do excuse my immaturity and my *maleness*—" He spoke the word as she might, with sarcasm and anger. "I'm simply having a ripping good time after a long dry spell."

And then, unable to bear her for one moment longer—

No, that wasn't true. He was unable to bear himself.

Either way, he left.

Chapter 16

. . . you do have the right of it, dearest Kate. Men are so easy to manage. I cannot imagine ever losing an argument with one. Of course, had I accepted Lord Lacye's proposal, I should not have had even the opportunity. He rarely speaks, which I do find most odd.

—from Eloise Bridgerton to her sister-in-law Viscountess Bridgerton, upon refusing her fifth offer of marriage

Eloise remained in the greenhouse for nearly an hour, unable to do anything but stare off into space, wondering—

What had happened?

One minute they were talking—very well, they were arguing, but in a relatively reasonable and civilized manner—and the next he was out of his head, his face pinched with fury.

And then he'd left. Left. He actually *walked away* from her in the middle of an argument and left her standing there in his greenhouse, her mouth hanging open and her pride more than pricked.

He'd walked away. That was what really bothered her. How could someone walk away in the middle of an argument?

Granted, she'd been the one to instigate the discussion—oh, very well, argument—but still, nothing had transpired that warranted such a storming off on his part.

And the worst of it was, she didn't know what to do.

All her life, she'd known what to do. She hadn't always turned out to be *right*, but at least she'd felt sure of herself when she had made her decisions. And as she sat there on Phillip's workbench, feeling utterly confused and inept, she realized that for her, at least, it was a great deal better to act and be wrong than it was to feel helpless and impotent.

And as if all that weren't enough, she couldn't get her mother's voice out of her head. *Don't push, Eloise. Don't push.*

And all she could think was— She *hadn't* pushed. Good heavens, what had she done but come to him with a concern about his children? Was it so very wrong to actually want to *speak* rather than race off to the bedroom? She supposed it might be wrong, if the couple in question never spent any intimate time together, but they had . . . they were . . .

It had just been that morning!

No one could say that they had any problems in the bedroom. No one.

She sighed and slumped. She'd never felt so alone in all her life. Funny, that. Who'd have thought she'd have to go and get married—join her life for *eternity* with another person—in order to feel alone?

She wanted her mother.

No, she didn't want her mother. She definitely didn't want her mother. Her mother would be kind and understanding and everything a mother should be, but a talk with her mother would just leave her feeling like a small child, not like the adult she was supposed to be.

She wanted her sisters. Not Hyacinth, who was barely one and twenty and knew nothing of men, but one of her married sisters. She wanted Daphne, who always knew what to say, or Francesca, who never said what one wanted to hear but always managed to eke out a smile nonetheless.

But they were too far away, in London and Scotland respectively, and Eloise was *not* going to run off. She'd made her bed when she'd married, and she was quite contentedly lying in it every night with Phillip. It was just the days that were a bit off.

She wasn't going to play the coward and leave, even if only for a few days.

But Sophie was near, just an hour away. And if they weren't sisters by birth—well, they were sisters of the heart.

Eloise looked out the door. It was too cloudy to see the sun, but she was fairly sure it wasn't much past noon. Even with the travel time, she could spend most of the day with Sophie and be back by supper.

Her pride didn't want anyone to know she was miserable, but her heart wanted a shoulder to cry on.

Her heart won out.

Phillip spent the next several hours stomping across his fields, viciously yanking weeds from the ground.

Which kept him fairly busy, since he wasn't in a cultivated area, which meant that pretty much every bit of growth could be classified as a weed, if one was so inclined.

And he *was* so inclined. He was more than inclined. If he had his way, he'd yank every damned plant from the earth.

And he, a botanist.

But he didn't want to plant things right now, didn't want to watch anything bloom or grow. He wanted to kick and maim and destroy. He was angry and frustrated and cross with himself and cross with Eloise and he was quite prepared to be upset with anyone who happened across his path.

But after an afternoon of this, of kicking and stomping, and yanking the heads off wildflowers and tearing blades of grass down the middle, he sat on a rock and let his head hang in his hands.

Hell.

What a muck.

What a bloody muck, and the really ironic bit of it was—he'd thought they were happy.

He'd thought his marriage perfect, and all this time—oh, very well, it had only been a week, but it had been a week of, in his opinion, perfection. And she'd been miserable.

Or if not miserable, then not happy.

Or maybe a little bit happy, but certainly not caught up in blissful rapture, as he had been.

And now he had to go and *do* something about it, which was the last thing he wanted to do. Talking with Eloise, actually asking questions and trying to deduce what was wrong, not to mention figuring out what to do to fix it—it was just the sort of thing he always bungled.

But he didn't have much of a choice, did he? He'd married Eloise in part—well, more than in part; almost in whole, in truth—because he'd wanted her to take charge, to take over all the annoying little tasks in his life, to free him up for the things that really mattered. The fact that he was growing to care for her had been an unexpected bonus.

He suspected, however, that one's marriage didn't count as an annoying little task, and he couldn't just leave it to Eloise. And as painful as a heart-to-heart discussion was, he was going to have to bite the bullet and give it a go.

He was quite certain he'd botch it up but good, but at least he could say he'd tried.

He groaned. She was probably going to ask him about his *feelings*. Was there no woman alive who understood that men did not talk about feelings? Hell, half of them didn't even have feelings.

Or maybe he could take the easy way out and simply apologize. He wasn't certain what he'd be apologizing for, but it would appease her and make her happy, and that was all that mattered.

He didn't want Eloise to be unhappy. He didn't want her to regret her marriage, even for one moment. He wanted his marriage back to the way he'd thought it was—easy and comfortable by day, fiery and passionate by night.

He trudged up the hill back to Romney Hall, rehearsing what he'd say in his mind and scowling over how asinine it all sounded.

But his efforts were moot, anyway, because when he arrived at the house and found Gunning, all the butler had to say was, "She's not here."

"What do you mean, she's not here?" Phillip demanded.

"She's not here, sir. She went to her brother's house."

Phillip's stomach clenched. "Which brother?"

"I believe the one who lives close by."

"You believe?"

"I'm rather certain," Gunning corrected.

"Did she say when she planned to return?"

"No, sir."

Phillip swore viciously under his breath. Surely Eloise hadn't *left* him. She wasn't the sort to bail out on a sinking ship, at least not without making sure every last passenger had left safely before her.

"She did not bring a bag, sir," Gunning said.

Oh, now, *that* made him feel good. His butler felt the need to reassure him that he'd not been abandoned by his wife. "That will be all, Gunning," Phillip said through gritted teeth.

"Very good, sir," Gunning said. He inclined his head, as he always did when he excused himself, and left the room.

Phillip stood in the hall for several minutes, stock-still, his hands fisted angrily at his sides. What the devil was he supposed to do now? He wasn't about to go running after Eloise. If she so desperately wanted to be out of his company, then by God that's what he would give her.

He started to walk to his office, where he could stew and fume in private, but then, when he was just a few steps away from the door, he stopped, glancing at the large grandfather clock at the end of the hall. It was a bit past three, just about the time the twins usually took their afternoon snack. Before they'd married, Eloise had accused him of not taking enough interest in their welfare.

He planted his hands on his hips, his foot pivoting slightly, as if unsure which way to turn. He might as well go up to the nursery and spend a few unexpected minutes with his children. It wasn't as if he had anything better to do with his time, stuck here waiting for his errant wife to return. And when she did get back—well, she wouldn't have anything to complain about, not after he'd twisted himself into one of those tiny chairs and eaten milk and biscuits with the twins.

With a decisive turn, he headed up the stairs to the nursery, located on the top floor of Romney Hall, tucked neatly away under the eaves. It was the same set of rooms in which he'd grown up, with the same furniture and toys, and presumably the same crack in the ceiling over the small beds, the one that looked like a duck.

Phillip frowned as he stepped off the final stair onto the third-floor hallway. He probably ought to see if that crack was still there, and if it was, inquire what his children thought it looked like. George, his brother, had always sworn it resembled a pig, but Phillip had never understood how he'd mistaken the bill for a snout.

Phillip shook his head. Good heavens, how anyone could mistake a duck for a pig, he'd never know. Even the—

He stopped short, just two doors down from the nursery. He'd heard something, and he wasn't quite certain what it was, except that he didn't like it. It was . . .

He listened again.

It was a whimper.

His first inclination was to storm forward and burst through the nursery door, but he held himself back when he realized that the door was ajar by two inches, and so he crept forward instead, peeking through the crack as unobtrusively as he could.

It required only half a second to realize what was happening.

Oliver was curled up in a ball on the floor, shaking with silent sobs, and Amanda was standing in front of a wall, bracing herself with her tiny little hands, whimpering as her nurse beat her across the back with a large, heavy book.

Phillip slammed through the door with a force that nearly took it off its hinges. "What the hell do you think you're doing?" he nearly roared.

Nurse Edwards turned around in surprise, but before she could open her mouth to speak, Phillip snatched the book away and hurled it behind him against the wall.

"Sir Phillip!" Nurse Edwards cried out in shock.

"How dare you strike these children," he said, his voice shaking with fury. "And with a book."

"I was told—"

"And you did it where no one would see." He felt himself growing hot, agitated, itching to lash out. "How many children have you beaten, making sure to leave the bruises where no one would see?"

"They spoke disrespectfully," Nurse Edwards said stiffly. "They had to be punished."

Phillip stepped forward, close enough so that the nurse was forced to retreat. "I want you out of my house," he said.

"You told me to discipline the children as I see fit," Nurse Edwards protested.

"Is this how you see fit?" he hissed, using every ounce of his restraint to hold his arms at his sides. He wanted to swing them wildly, to lash out, to grab a book and beat this woman just as she had done to his children.

But he held on to his temper. He had no idea how, but he did it.

"You beat them with a book?" he continued furiously. He looked over at his children; they were cowering in a corner, presumably as scared of their father in such a mood as they were of their nurse. It sickened him that they were seeing him this way, so close to a total loss of control, but there was nothing more he could do to rein himself in.

"There was no switch," Nurse Edwards said haughtily.

Wrong thing to say. Phillip felt his skin grow even hotter, fought against the red haze that had begun to cloud his vision. There *had* been a switch in the nursery; the hook it had hung upon was still there, right by the window.

Phillip had burned it the day of his father's funeral, had stood in front of the fire and watched it turn to ash. He hadn't been satisfied with just tossing it in; he'd needed to see it destroyed, completely and forever.

And he thought of that switch, thought of the hundreds of times it had been used upon him, thought of the pain, of the indignity, of all the effort he had used, trying to keep himself from crying out.

His father had hated crybabies. Tears only resulted in another round with the switch. Or with the belt. Or the riding crop. Or, when there was nothing else available, his father's hand.

But never, Phillip thought with a strange sort of detachment, a book. Probably his father had never thought of it.

"Get out," Phillip said, his voice barely audible. And then, when Nurse Edwards did not immediately respond, he roared it. "Get out! Get out of this house!"

"Sir Phillip," she protested, scooting away from him, out of reach of his long, strong arms.

"Get out! Get out! Get out!"

He didn't know where it was all coming from anymore. From somewhere deep inside, never tamed, but held down by sheer force of will.

"I need to gather my things!" she cried out.

"You have one half hour," Phillip said, his voice low but still quavering with the exertion of his outburst. "Thirty minutes. If you have not departed by then, I will throw you out myself."

Nurse Edwards hesitated at the door, started to walk through, then turned around. "You are ruining those children," she hissed.

"They are mine to ruin."

"Have it your way, then. They are nothing but little monsters, anyway, ill-tempered, misbehaved—"

Had she no care for her own safety? Phillip's control was dangling by one very thin thread, and he was this close to grabbing the damned woman by the arm and hurling her out the door himself.

"Get out," he growled, for what he prayed was the last time. He couldn't hold on much longer. He stepped forward, punctuating his words with movement, and finally—*finally*—she ran from the room.

For a moment Phillip simply held still, trying to calm himself, to calm his breathing and wait for his rushing blood to settle down. His back was to the twins, and he dreaded turning around. He was dying inside, ravaged by guilt that he'd hired that woman, that monster, to care for his children. And he'd been too busy trying avoid them to see that they were suffering.

Suffering in the same way he had.

Slowly, he turned around, terrified of what he'd see in their eyes.

But when he raised his gaze off the floor and looked into their faces, they hurled into motion, launching themselves at him with almost enough force to knock him over.

"Oh, Daddy!" Amanda cried out, using an endearment she hadn't uttered for ages. He'd been "Father" for years now, and he'd forgotten how sweet the other sounded.

And Oliver—he was hugging him, too, his small, thin arms wrapped tightly around Phillip's waist, his face buried against his shirt so that his father would not see him cry.

But Phillip could feel it. The tears soaked through his shirt, and every sniffle rumbled against his belly.

His arms went around his children, tightly, protectively. "Shhhh," he crooned. "It's all right. I'm here now." They were words he'd never said, words he'd never imagined saying; he'd never thought that his presence might be the one to make everything all right. "I'm sorry," he choked out. "I'm so sorry."

They had told him they didn't like their nurse; he hadn't listened.

"It's not your fault, Father," Amanda said.

It was, but there seemed little point in belaboring the fact. Not now, not when the time was ripe for a fresh start.

"We'll find you a new nurse," he assured them.

"Someone like Nurse Millsby?" Oliver asked, sniffling as his tears finally subsided.

Phillip nodded. "Someone just like her."

Oliver looked at him with great sincerity. "Can Miss—Mother help to choose?"

"Of course," Phillip replied, tousling his hair. "I expect she'll want a say. She is a woman of a great many opinions, after all."

The children giggled.

Phillip allowed himself a smile. "I see you two know her well."

"She does like to talk," Oliver said hesitantly.

"But she is terribly clever!" Amanda put in.

"Indeed she is," Phillip murmured.

"I rather like her," Oliver said.

"As do I," his sister added.

"I'm glad to hear that," Phillip told them. "Because I do believe she is here to stay."

And so am I, he added silently. He'd spent years avoiding his children, fearing that he'd make a mistake, terrified that he'd lose his temper. He'd thought he was doing the best thing for them, keeping them at arm's length, but he'd been wrong. So very wrong.

"I love you," he said to them, hoarsely, with great emotion. "You know that, don't you?"

They nodded, their eyes bright.

"I will always love you," he whispered, crouching down until they were all of a level. He drew them close, savoring their warmth. "I will always love you."

Chapter 17

. . . regardless, Daphne, I do not think you should have run off.

—from Eloise Bridgerton to her sister the Duchess of Hastings, during Daphne's brief separation from her husband, mere weeks into their marriage

The ride to Benedict's was rutted and bumpy, and by the time Eloise stepped down at her brother's front steps, her mood had gone from bad to foul. To make matters worse, when the butler opened the door he looked at her as if she were a madwoman.

"Graves?" Eloise finally asked, when it became clear that he was beyond speech.

"Are they expecting you?" he asked, still gaping.

"Well, no," Eloise said, looking quite pointedly beyond him into the house, since that, after all, was where she wanted to be.

It had started to drizzle, and she was not dressed for the rain.

"But I hardly think . . ." she began.

Graves stepped aside, belatedly remembering himself and allowing her entrance. "It's Master Charles," he said, referring to Benedict and Sophie's eldest son, just five and a half years old. "He's quite ill. He—"

Eloise felt something awful and acidic rise in her throat. "What is wrong?" she asked, not even bothering to temper her urgency. "Is he . . ." Good heavens, how did one ask if a young child was dying?

"I'll get Mrs. Bridgerton," Graves said, swallowing convulsively. He turned and scurried up the stairs.

"Wait!" Eloise called out, wanting to ask him more, but he was already gone.

She slumped into a chair, feeling sick with worry, and then, as if that weren't enough, rather disgusted with herself for having been even the least bit dissatisfied with her own lot in life. Her troubles with Phillip, which in truth weren't even troubles at all but nothing more than small irritants—well, they seemed very small and insignificant next to *this*.

"Eloise!"

It was Benedict, not Sophie, who came down the stairs. He looked haggard, his eyes red-rimmed, his skin pale and pasty. Eloise knew better than to ask him how long it had been since he'd slept; the question would be beyond annoying, and besides, the answer was right there on his face—he hadn't closed his eyes for days.

"What are you doing here?" he asked.

"I came for a visit," she said. "Just to say hello. I had no idea. What is wrong? How is Charles? I saw him just last week. He looked fine. He— What is wrong?"

Benedict required several seconds to muster the energy to speak. "He has a fever. I don't know why. On Saturday, he woke up fine, but by luncheon he was—" He sagged against the wall, closing his eyes in agony. "He was burning up," he whispered. "I don't know what to do."

"What did the doctor say?" Eloise asked.

"Nothing," Benedict said in a hollow voice. "Nothing of use, anyway."

"May I see him?"

Benedict nodded, his eyes still closed.

"You need to rest," Eloise said.

"I can't," he said.

"You must. You're no good to anyone like this, and I'd wager Sophie is no better."

"I made her sleep an hour ago," he said. "She looked like death."

"Well, you don't look any better," Eloise told him, keeping her tone purposefully brisk and businesslike. Sometimes that was what people needed at times like this—to be ordered about, told what to do. Compassion would only make her brother cry, and neither of them wanted to be witness to that.

"You must go to bed," Eloise ordered. "*Now*. I'll care for Charles. Even if you sleep only an hour, you'll feel so much better."

He didn't reply; he'd fallen asleep standing up.

Eloise quickly took charge. She directed Graves to put Benedict to bed, and she took over the sickroom, trying not to gasp when she first stepped in and saw her small nephew.

He looked tiny and frail in the large bed; Benedict and Sophie had had him moved to their bedchamber, where there was more room for people to tend to him. His skin was flushed, but his eyes, when he opened them, were glassy and unfocused, and when he wasn't lying unnaturally still, he was thrashing about, mumbling incoherently about ponies and treehouses and marzipan candy.

It made Eloise wonder what she would mumble incoherently about, were she ever to be gripped by a fever.

She mopped his brow, and she turned him and helped the maids change his sheets, and she didn't notice as the sun slipped below the horizon. She just thanked the heavens that Charles did not worsen under her care, because according to the servants, Benedict and Sophie had been at his side for two days straight, and Eloise did not want to have to wake either of them up with bad news.

She sat in the chair by the bed, and she read to him from his favorite book of children's tales, and she told him stories of when his father was young. And she doubted that he heard a word, but it all made her feel better, because she couldn't just sit there and do nothing.

And it wasn't until eight in the evening, when Sophie finally rose from her stupor and asked after Phillip, that it occurred to her that she ought to send a note, that he might be growing worried.

So she scrawled something short and hasty and resumed her vigil. Phillip would understand.

By eight in the evening, Phillip realized that one of two things had happened to his wife. She had either perished in a carriage accident, or she had left him.

Neither prospect was terribly appealing.

He didn't *think* she would have left him; she seemed mostly happy in their marriage, despite their quarrel that afternoon. And besides, she hadn't taken any of her belongings with her, although that didn't mean much; most of her belongings had yet to arrive from her home in London. It wasn't as if she'd be leaving much behind here at Romney Hall.

Just a husband and two children.

Good God, and he'd just said to them this afternoon— *I do believe she's here to stay.*

No, he thought savagely, Eloise would not leave him. She would never do such a thing. She didn't have a cowardly bone in her body, and she would never slink off and abandon their marriage. If she was displeased in some way, she'd tell him so, right to his face and without mincing words.

Which, he realized, yanking on his coat as he practically hurled himself out the front door, meant that she was dead in some ditch on the Wiltshire road. It had been raining steadily all evening, and the roads between his house and Benedict's were not well tended to begin with.

Hell, it would almost be better if she'd left him.

But as he rode up the drive to My Cottage, Benedict Bridgerton's absurdly named house, soaking wet and in a terrible temper, it was starting to look more like Eloise had decided to abandon her marriage.

Because she hadn't been lying in a ditch by the side of the road, and there hadn't been any sign of any sort of carriage accident, and furthermore, she hadn't been holed up at either of the two inns along the way.

And as there was only one route between his home and Benedict's, it wasn't as if she were in some other inn on some other road, and this entire farce could be chalked up to nothing more than a big misunderstanding.

"Temper," he said under his breath as he stomped up the front steps. "Temper."

Because he had never been so close to losing his.

Maybe there was a logical explanation. Maybe she hadn't wanted to drive home in the rain. It wasn't *that* bad, but it was more than a drizzle, and he supposed she might not have cared to travel.

He lifted up the knocker on the door and slammed it down. Hard.

Maybe the carriage had broken a wheel.

He banged the knocker again.

No, that couldn't explain it. Benedict could easily have sent her home in his carriage.

Maybe . . .

Maybe . . .

His mind searched fruitlessly for some other reason why she would be here with her brother and not at home with her husband. He couldn't think of one.

The curse that hissed out of his mouth was one he had not uttered in years.

He reached up for the knocker again, this time prepared to yank the damned thing off the door and hurl it through the window, but just then the door opened, and Phillip found himself staring at Graves, whom he had met less than a fortnight earlier, during his farce of a courtship.

"My wife?" Phillip practically growled.

"Sir Phillip!" the butler gasped.

Phillip didn't move, even though the rain was streaming down his face. Damned house didn't have a portico. Whoever heard of such a thing, in England, of all places?

"My wife," he bit off again.

"She's here," Graves assured him. "Come in."

Phillip stepped in. "I want my wife," he said again. "Now."

"Let me get your coat," Graves said.

"I don't give a damn about my coat," Phillip snapped. "I want my wife."

Graves froze, his hands still poised to take Phillip's coat. "Did you not receive Lady Crane's note?"

"No, I did not receive a note."

"I thought you'd arrived rather quickly," Graves murmured. "You must have crossed with the messenger. You'd better come in."

"I am in," Phillip reminded him testily.

Graves let out a long breath, almost a sigh, which was remarkable for a butler bred not to show even a hint of emotion. "I think you will be here for some time," he said softly. "Take off your coat. Get dry. You will want to be comfortable."

Phillip's anger suddenly slid into bone-deep terror. Had something happened to Eloise? Good God, if anything— "What is going on?" he whispered.

He'd just found his children. He wasn't ready to lose his wife.

The butler just turned to the stairs with sad eyes. "Come with me," he said softly.

Phillip followed, each step filling him with dread.

Eloise had, of course, attended church nearly every Sunday of her life. It was what was expected of her, and it was what good, honest people did, but in truth she'd never been a particularly God-fearing or religious sort. Her mind tended to wander during the sermons, and she sang along with the hymns not out of any great sense of spiritual uplifting but rather because she very much liked the music, and church was the only acceptable place for a tin ear like herself to raise her voice in song.

But now, tonight, as she looked down upon her small nephew, she prayed.

Charles hadn't worsened, but he hadn't improved, and the doctor, who had come and gone for the second time that day, had pronounced it "in God's hands."

Eloise hated that phrase, hated how doctors resorted to it when faced with illness beyond their skills, but if the physician was correct, and it was indeed in God's hands, then by the heavens above, that was to whom she would appeal.

When she wasn't placing a cooling cloth on Charles's forehead or spooning lukewarm broth down his throat, that was. But there was only so much to be done, and most of her time in the sickroom was spent rather helplessly in vigil.

And so she just sat there, her hands folded tightly in her lap, whispering, "Please. *Please.*"

And then, as if the wrong prayer had been answered, she heard a noise in the doorway, and somehow it was Phillip, even though she'd only sent the messenger an hour earlier. He was soaked from the rain, his hair plastered inelegantly against his forehead, but he was the dearest sight she'd ever seen, and before she had a clue what she was doing, she'd run across the room and thrown herself into his arms.

"Oh, Phillip," she sobbed, finally allowing herself to cry. She'd been so strong all day, forcing herself to be the rock that her brother and sister-in-law needed. But now Phillip was here, and as his arms came around her, he felt so solid and good, and for once she could allow someone else to be strong for her.

"I thought it was you," Phillip whispered.

"What?" she asked, confused.

"The butler—he didn't explain until we were up the stairs. I thought it was—" He shook his head. "Never mind."

Eloise said nothing, just looked up at him, a tiny, sad smile on her face.

"How is he?" he asked.

She shook her head. "Not good."

He looked over at Benedict and Sophie, who had risen to greet him. They looked rather "not good" as well.

"How long has he been this way?" Phillip asked.

"Two days," Benedict replied.

"Two and a half," Sophie corrected. "Since Saturday morning."

"You need to get dry," Eloise said, pulling away from him. "And now I do, too." She looked ruefully down at her dress, now soaked through the front from Phillip's wet clothing. "You'll end up in no better a state than Charles."

"I'm fine," Phillip said, brushing past her as he came to the little boy's bedside. He touched his forehead, then shook his head and glanced back at his parents. "I can't tell," he said. "I'm too cold from the rain."

"He's feverish," Benedict confirmed grimly.

"What have you done for him?" Phillip asked.

"Do you know something of medicine?" Sophie asked, her eyes filling with desperate hope.

"The doctor bled him," Benedict answered. "It didn't seem to help."

"We've been giving him broth," Sophie said, "and cooling him when he grows too hot."

"And warming him when he grows too cold," Eloise finished miserably.

"Nothing seems to work," Sophie whispered. And then, in front of everyone, she simply crumpled. Collapsed against the side of the bed and sobbed.

"Sophie," Benedict choked out. He dropped to his knees beside her and held her as she wept, and Phillip and Eloise both looked away as they realized that he was crying, too.

"Willow bark tea," Phillip said to Eloise. "Has he had any?"

"I don't think so. Why?"

"It's something I learned at Cambridge. It used to be given for pain, before laudanum became so popular. One of my professors insisted that it also helped to reduce fever."

"Did you give the tea to Marina?" Eloise asked.

Phillip looked at her in surprise, then remembered that she still thought Marina had died of lung fever, which, he supposed, was mostly true. "I tried," he answered, "but I couldn't get much down her throat. And besides, she was much sicker than Charles." He swallowed, remembering. "In many ways."

Eloise looked up into his face for a long moment, then turned briskly to Benedict and Sophie, who were quiet now, but still kneeling on the floor together, lost in their private moment.

Eloise, however, being Eloise, had little reverence for private moments at such a time, and so grabbed her brother's shoulder and turned him around. "Do you have any willow bark tea?" she asked him.

Benedict just looked at her, blinking, and then finally said, "I don't know."

"Mrs. Crabtree might," Sophie said, referring to one half of the old couple who had cared for My Cottage before Benedict had married, when it had been nothing more than an occasional place for him to lay his head. "She always has things like that. But she and Mr. Crabtree went to visit their daughter. They won't be home for several days."

"Can you get into their house?" Phillip asked. "I will recognize it if she has it. It won't be a tea. Just the bark, which we'll soak in hot water. It might help to bring down the fever."

"Willow bark?" Sophie asked doubtfully. "You mean to cure my son with the bark of a *tree*?"

"It certainly can't hurt him now," Benedict said gruffly, striding toward the door. "Come along, Crane. We have a key to their cottage. I will take you there myself." But as he reached the doorway, he turned to Phillip and asked, "Do you know what you are about?"

Phillip answered the only way he knew how. "I don't know. I hope so."

Benedict stared him in the face, and Phillip knew that the older man was taking his measure. It was one thing for Benedict to allow him to marry his sister. It was quite another to let him force strange potions down his son's throat.

But Phillip understood. He had children, too.

"Very well," Benedict said. "Let's go."

And as Phillip hurried out of the house, all he could do was pray that Benedict Bridgerton's trust in him had not been misplaced.

In the end it was difficult to say whether it was the willow bark or Eloise's whispered prayers or just dumb luck, but by the following morning Charles's fever had broken, and although the boy was still weak and listless, he was indubitably on the mend. By noontime, it was clear that Eloise and Phillip were no longer needed and in fact were getting in the way, and so they climbed into their carriage and headed home, both eager to collapse into their large, sturdy bed and, for once, do nothing but sleep.

The first ten minutes of the ride home were spent in silence. Eloise, astonishingly, found herself too tired to speak. But even in her exhaustion, she was too restless, too tightly wound from the stress and worry of the previous night to sleep. And so she contented herself with staring out the window at the dampened countryside. It had stopped raining right about the time Charles's fever broke, suggesting a divine intervention that might have pointed to Eloise's prayers as the young boy's savior, but as Eloise stole a glance at her husband, sitting beside her in the carriage with his eyes closed (although not, she was quite certain, asleep), she knew it was the willow bark.

She didn't know how she knew, and she was quite cognizant of the fact that she could never prove it, but her nephew's life had been saved by a cup of tea.

And to think how unlikely it was that Phillip had even been

at her brother's house that evening. It had been quite a singular chain of events. If she hadn't gone in to see the twins, if she hadn't gone to tell Phillip that she didn't like their nurse, if they hadn't quarreled . . .

Put that way, little Charles Bridgerton was quite the luckiest little boy in Britain.

"Thank you," she said, not realizing that she'd intended to speak until the words left her lips.

"For what?" Phillip murmured sleepily, without opening his eyes.

"Charles," she said simply.

Phillip did open his eyes at that, and he turned to her. "It might not have been my doing. We'll never know if it was the willow bark."

"*I* know," she said firmly.

His lips curved into the barest of smiles. "You always do."

And she thought to herself— Was this what she'd been waiting for her entire life? Not the passion, not the gasps of pleasure she felt when he joined her in bed, but *this*.

This sense of comfort, of easy companionship, of sitting next to someone in a carriage and knowing with every fiber of your being that it was where you belonged.

She placed her hand on his. "It was so awful," she said, surprised that she had tears in her eyes. "I don't think I have ever been so scared in my life. I can't imagine what it must have been like for Benedict and Sophie."

"Nor I," Phillip said softly.

"If it had been one of our children . . ." she said, and she realized it was the first time she'd said that. *Our* children.

Phillip was silent for a long time. When he spoke, he was looking out the window. "The entire time I was watching Charles," he said, his voice suspiciously hoarse, "all I kept thinking was, thank God it's not Oliver or Amanda." And then he turned back to her, his face pinched with guilt. "But it shouldn't be anyone's child."

Eloise squeezed his hand. "I don't think there is anything wrong with such feelings. You're not a saint, you know. You're just a father. A very good one, I think."

He looked at her with an odd expression, and then he shook his head. "No," he said gravely, "I'm not. But I hope to be."

She cocked her head. "Phillip?"

"You were right," he said, his mouth tightening into a grim line. "About their nurse. I didn't want anything to be wrong, and so I paid no attention, but you were right. She was beating them."

"What?"

"With a book," he continued, his voice almost dispassionate, as if he'd already used up all of his emotions. "I walked in and she was beating Amanda with a book. She had already finished with Oliver."

"Oh, no," Eloise said, as tears—of sorrow *and* anger—filled her eyes. "I never dreamed. I didn't like her, of course. And she'd rapped them on the knuckles, but . . . *I've* been rapped on the knuckles. Everyone has been rapped on the knuckles." She slumped in her seat, guilt weighing her shoulders down. "I should have realized. I should have seen."

Phillip snorted. "You've barely been in residence a fortnight. I've been living with that bloody woman for months. If I didn't see, why should you have done?"

Eloise had nothing to say to this, nothing at least that would not make her already guilt-ridden husband feel worse. "I assume you dismissed her," she finally said.

He nodded. "I told the children you would help to find a replacement."

"Of course," she said quickly.

"And I—" He stopped, cleared his throat, and looked out the window before continuing. "I—"

"What is it, Phillip?" she asked softly.

He didn't turn back to her when he said, "I'm going to be a better father. I've pushed them away for too long. I was so afraid of becoming my father, of being like him, that I—"

"Phillip," Eloise murmured, laying her hand on his, "you're not like your father. You could never be."

"No," he said, his voice hollow, "but I thought I could. I got a whip once. I went to the stables and I grabbed the whip." His head fell into his hands. "I was so angry. So bloody angry."

"But you didn't use it," she whispered, knowing that her words were true. They had to be.

He shook his head. "But I wanted to."

"But you didn't," she said again, keeping her voice as firm as she was able.

"I was so angry," he said again, and she wasn't even sure he'd heard her, so lost was he in his own memory. But then he turned to her, and his eyes pierced hers. "Do you understand what it is to be terrified by your own anger?"

She shook her head.

"I'm not a small man, Eloise," he said. "I could hurt someone."

"So could I," she replied. And then, at his dry look, she added, "Well, maybe not you, but I'm certainly big enough to hurt a child."

"You would never do that," he grunted, turning away.

"Neither would *you*," she repeated.

He was silent.

And then, suddenly, she understood. "Phillip," she said softly, "you said you were angry, but . . . with *whom* were you angry?"

He looked at her uncomprehendingly. "They glued their governess's hair to the sheets, Eloise."

"I know," she said, with a dismissive wave of her hand. "I'm quite certain I would have wanted to throttle them both, had I been present. But that's not what I asked." She waited for him to make some sort of response. When he did not, she added, "Were you angry with them because of the glue, or were you angry with yourself, because you didn't know how to make them mind?"

He didn't say anything but they both knew the answer.

Eloise reached out and touched his hand. "You're nothing like your father, Phillip," she repeated. "Nothing."

"I know that now," Phillip said softly. "You have no idea how badly I wanted to tear that bloody Nurse Edwards from limb to limb."

"I can imagine," Eloise said, snorting as she settled back in her seat.

Phillip felt his lips twitch. He had no idea why, but there was something almost funny in his wife's tone, something comforting, even. Somehow they had found humor in a situation where there ought not to be any. And it felt good.

"She deserved nothing less," Eloise added with a shrug. And then she turned and looked at him. "But you didn't touch her, did you?"

He shook his head. "No. And if I managed to keep my temper with her, then I'm damn well not ever going to lose it with my children."

"Of course not," Eloise said, as if it had never been an issue. She patted his hand, then glanced out the window, clearly unconcerned.

Such faith in him, Phillip realized. Such faith in his inner goodness, in the quality of his soul, when he'd been wracked by doubt for so many years.

And then he felt he had to be honest, had to come clean, and before he knew what he was about, he blurted out, "I thought you'd left me."

"Last night?" She turned to him in shock. "Whyever would you think that?"

He shrugged self-deprecatingly. "Oh, I don't know. It might be because you left for your brother's house and never came back."

She hmmphed at that. "It's clear now why I was detained, and besides, I would never leave you. You should know that."

He quirked a brow. "Should I?"

"Of course you should," she said, looking rather cross with him. "I made a vow in that church, and I assure you I do not take such things lightly. Besides, I made a commitment to Oliver and Amanda to be their mother, and I would never turn my back on that."

Phillip regarded her steadily, then murmured, "No. No, you wouldn't. Silly of me not to have thought of that."

She sat back and crossed her arms. "Well, you should have done. You know me better than that." And then, when he did not say anything more, she added, "Those poor children. They have already lost one mother through no fault of their own. I'm certainly not going to run off and make them go through all that again."

She turned to him with a supremely irritated expression. "I cannot believe you even thought that of me."

Phillip was beginning to wonder the same thing himself. He'd only known Eloise—Dear God, could it possibly have been only two weeks? It felt, in many ways, like a lifetime. Because he did feel he knew her, inside and out. She'd always have her secrets, of course, as all people did, and he was quite certain he'd never *understand* her, since he couldn't imagine ever understanding anyone female.

But he knew her. He was quite certain he knew her. And he should have known better than to have worried that she'd abandoned their marriage.

It must have been panic, pure and simple. And, he supposed, because it was better to think she'd left him than to imagine her dead in a ditch by the side of the road. With the former he could at least storm her brother's house and drag her home.

If she'd died . . .

He was unprepared for the pain he felt in his gut at the mere thought.

When had she come to mean so much to him? And what was he going to do to keep her happy?

Because he needed her happy. Not just, as he'd been telling himself, because a happy Eloise meant that his life would continue to run smoothly. He needed her happy because the mere thought of her unhappy was like a knife in his heart.

The irony was well aimed, indeed. He'd told himself, over and over, that he'd married her to be a mother to his children, but just now, when she'd declared that she would never leave their marriage, that her commitment to the twins was too strong—

He'd felt jealous.

He'd actually felt jealous of his own children. He'd wanted her to mention the word *wife*, and all he'd heard was mother.

He wanted her to want him. Him. Not just because she'd made a vow in a church, but because she was quite convinced she could not live without him. Maybe even because she loved him.

Loved him.

Dear God, when had this happened? When had he come to want so much from marriage? He'd married her to mother his children; they both knew that.

And then there was the passion. He was a man, for God's sake, and he'd not lain with a woman for eight years. How could he not be drunk on the feel of Eloise's skin next to his, on the sound of her whimpers and moans when she exploded around him?

On the pure force of his own pleasure every time he entered her?

He'd found everything he'd ever wanted in a marriage. Eloise ran his life to perfection by day and warmed his bed with the skill of a courtesan by night. She fulfilled his every desire so well that he hadn't noticed that she'd done something more.

She'd found his heart. She'd touched it, changed it. Changed him.

He loved her. He hadn't been looking for love, hadn't even given a thought to it, but there it was, and it was the most precious thing imaginable.

He was at the dawn of a new day, the first page of a new chapter of his life. It was thrilling. And terrifying. Because he did not want to fail. Not now, not when he'd finally found everything he needed. Eloise. His children. Himself.

It had been years since he'd felt comfortable in his own skin, since he'd trusted his instincts. Since he'd looked in the mirror without avoiding his own gaze.

He glanced out the window. The carriage was slowing down, pulling up alongside Romney Hall. Everything looked gray—the skies, the stone of the house, the windows, which reflected the clouds. Even the grass seemed a little less green without the sun to brighten its hue.

It suited his contemplative mood perfectly.

A footman appeared to help Eloise down, and once Phillip had hopped down beside her, she turned to him and said, "I'm exhausted, and you look the same. Shall we go take a nap?"

He was just about to agree, since he was exhausted, but then, just before the words could leave his lips, he shook his head and said, "You go along without me."

She opened her mouth to question him, but he silenced her with a gentle squeeze on her shoulder. "I'll be up shortly," he said. "But right now, I think I want to hug my children."

Chapter 18

. . . I do not tell you often enough, dear Mother, how very grateful I am that I am yours. It is a rare parent who would offer a child such latitude and understanding. It is an even rarer one who calls a daughter friend. I do love you, dear Mama.

—from Eloise Bridgerton to her mother, upon refusing her sixth offer of marriage

When Eloise awoke from her nap, she was surprised to see that the sheets on the other side of the bed were neat and unrumpled. Phillip had been just as tired as she had been, probably more so, since he had ridden all the way to Benedict's house the night before, in the wind and rain, no less.

After she'd tidied herself, she set about to locate him, but he was nowhere to be found. She told herself not to worry, that they'd had a difficult few days, that he probably just needed some time to himself, to think.

Just because she tended not to prefer solitude didn't mean everyone else agreed with her.

She laughed humorlessly to herself. That was a lesson she'd been trying—unsuccessfully—to learn her entire life.

And so she forced herself to stop looking for him. She was married now, and suddenly she understood what it was her mother had been trying so hard to tell her on her wedding night. Marriage was about compromise, and she and Phillip were very different people. They might be perfect for one another, but that didn't mean they were the same. And if she wanted him to change some of his ways for her, well then, she was going to have to do the same for him.

She didn't see him for the rest of the day, not when she took tea in the afternoon, not when she bade the twins good night, and not at supper, which she was forced to take by herself, feeling very small and very alone at the large mahogany table. She dined in silence, ever aware of the watchful eyes of the footmen, both of whom smiled at her sympathetically as they brought forth her food.

Eloise smiled back, because she did believe in being polite in all things, but inside she was sighing with resignation. It was a sad state of affairs when the footmen (*men*, for goodness' sakes, who were normally oblivious to another's distress) felt sorry for you.

But then again, here she was, only one week into her marriage and dining alone. Who wouldn't have pitied her?

Besides, the last the servants knew, Sir Phillip had raged out the door to fetch his wife, who had presumably fled to her brother's house after a horrible row.

Put that way, Eloise thought with a sigh, it wasn't quite so surprising that Phillip might have thought she'd left him.

She ate sparingly, not wanting to prolong the meal any longer than was necessary, and when she finished her obligatory two bites of pudding, she rose, fully intending to take herself off to bed, where, she presumed, she would pass her time as she had all day—alone.

But as she stepped into the hall, she found herself restless, not quite ready to retire. And so she began to walk, somewhat aimlessly, through the house. It was a chilly night for late May, and she was glad she'd brought a shawl. Eloise had spent time in many grand country homes, where all the fireplaces were lit at night, leaving the house in a blaze of light and warmth, but Romney Hall, while snug and comfortable, held no such delusions of self-importance, and so most of the rooms were kept closed off for the night, with the fireplaces only lit when needed.

And blast it, it was *cold.*

She pulled her shawl closer around her shoulders as she walked along, rather enjoying finding her way with only the dim moonlight to guide her. But then, as she approached the portrait gallery, she saw the unmistakable light of a lantern.

Someone was there, and she knew, even before she'd taken another step forward, that it was Phillip.

She approached quietly, glad that she'd worn her soft-soled slippers, and peered through the doorway.

The sight she saw nearly broke her heart.

Phillip was standing there, stock-still, in front of Marina's portrait. He moved not at all, save for the occasional blink of his eyes. He just stood there, looking at her, looking at his dead wife, and the expression on his face was so bleak and sorrowful that Eloise almost gasped.

Had he lied to her when he'd said that he hadn't loved Marina? When he'd said he hadn't felt passion?

And did it matter? Marina was dead. It wasn't as if she was a true competitor for Phillip's affections. And even if she was, did it matter? Because he didn't love Eloise, either, and she didn't—

Or maybe, she realized, in one of those flashes that knock the very breath from one's lungs, she did.

It was hard to imagine when it had happened, or even how it had happened, but this feeling she had for him, this affection and respect, had grown into something deeper.

And oh, how she wanted him to feel the same way.

He needed her. Of that she was quite sure. He needed her maybe even more than she needed him, but that wasn't it. She loved being needed, being wanted, being indispensable, even, but there was more to her feelings.

She loved the way he smiled, slightly lopsided, a little boyish, and with a little lilt of surprise, as if he couldn't quite believe in his own happiness.

She loved the way he looked at her, as if she were the most beautiful woman in the world, when she knew, quite patently, that she was not.

She loved the way he actually listened to what she had to say, and the way he didn't allow her to cow him. She even loved the way he told her she talked too much, because he almost always did it with a smile, and because, of course, it was true.

And she loved the way he still listened to her, even after he told her she talked too much.

She loved the way he loved his children.

She loved his honor, his honesty, and his sly sense of humor.

And she loved the way she fit into his life, and the way he fit into hers.

It was comfortable. It was right.

And this, she finally realized, was where she belonged.

But he was standing there, staring at a portrait of his dead wife, and from the way he was so still and unmoving . . . well, God only knew how long he'd been doing that. And if he still loved her . . .

She choked back a wave of guilt. Who was she to feel anything but sorrow on behalf of Marina? She had died so young, so unexpectedly. And she'd lost what Eloise considered every mother's God-given right—to watch her children grow up.

To feel jealous of a woman like that was unconscionable.

And yet . . .

And yet Eloise must not be as good a person as she ought, because she couldn't watch this scene, couldn't watch Phillip staring at the portrait of his first wife without envy squeezing around her heart. She'd just realized she loved this man, and would, to the very last of her days. *She* needed him, not a dead woman.

No, she thought fiercely. He didn't still love Marina. Maybe he'd never loved Marina. He'd said the morning before that he hadn't been with a woman for eight years.

Eight *years*?

It sank in, finally.

Good God.

She'd spent the past two days in such a flurry of emotion that she hadn't really stopped and thought—really thought—about what he'd said.

Eight years.

It was not what she would have expected. Not from a man such as Phillip, who clearly enjoyed—no, clearly *needed*—the physical aspects of married love.

Marina had only been dead for fifteen months. If Phillip had gone without a woman for eight years, that meant they hadn't shared a bedroom since the twins had been conceived.

No . . .

Eloise did some mental arithmetic. No, it would have been after the twins had been born. A little bit after.

Of course, Phillip could have been off in his dates, or perhaps exaggerating, but somehow Eloise didn't think so. She rather thought he knew exactly when he and Marina had last slept together, and she feared, especially now that she had pinpointed the date of it, that it had been a terrible occasion indeed.

But he had not betrayed her. He had remained faithful to a woman from whose bed he'd been banned. Eloise wasn't surprised, given his innate sense of honor and dignity, but she didn't think she would have thought less of him if he had sought comfort elsewhere.

And the fact that he hadn't—

It made her love him all the more.

But if his time with Marina had been so difficult and disturbing, why had he come here tonight? Why was he staring at her portrait, standing there as if he couldn't move from the spot? Gazing upon her as if he were pleading with her, begging her for something.

Begging the favor of a dead woman.

Eloise couldn't stand it any longer. She stepped forward and cleared her throat.

Phillip surprised her by turning instantly; she'd thought that he was so completely lost in his own world that he would not hear her. He didn't say anything, not even her name, but then . . .

He held out his hand.

She walked forward and took it, not knowing what else to do, not even knowing—as strange as it seemed—what to say. So she just stood beside him and stared up at Marina's portrait.

"Did you love her?" she asked, even though she'd asked him before.

"No," he said, and she realized that a small part of her must have still been very worried, because the rush of relief she felt at his denial was surprising in its force.

"Do you miss her?"

His voice was softer, but it was sure. "No."

"Did you hate her?" she whispered.

He shook his head, and he sounded very sad when he said, "No."

She didn't know what else to ask, wasn't sure what she *should* ask, so she just waited, hoping he would speak.

And after a very long while, he did.

"She was sad," he said. "She was always sad."

Eloise looked up at him, but he did not return the glance. His eyes were on Marina's portrait, as if he had to look at her while he spoke about her. As if maybe he owed her that.

"She was always somber," he continued, "always a bit too serene, if that makes any sense, but it was worse after the twins were born. I don't know what happened. The midwife said it was normal for women to cry after childbirth but that I shouldn't worry, that it would clear away in a few weeks."

"But it didn't," Eloise said softly.

He shook his head, then harshly brushed one dark lock of hair aside when it fell onto his brow. "It just got worse. I don't know how to explain it. It was almost as if . . ." He shrugged helplessly as he searched for words, and when he continued, he was whispering. "It was almost as if she'd disappeared. . . . She rarely left her bed. . . . I never saw her smile. . . . She cried a lot. A great deal."

The sentences came forth, not in a rush, but one at a time, as if each piece of information were being brought forth from his memory in slow succession. Eloise didn't say anything, didn't feel it her place to interrupt him or to try to inject her feelings on a matter she knew nothing about.

And then, finally, he turned away from Marina to Eloise, and looked her squarely in the eye.

"I tried everything to make her happy. Everything in my power. Everything I knew. But it wasn't enough."

Eloise opened her mouth, made a small sound, the beginnings of a murmur meant to assure him that he'd done his best, but he cut her off.

"Do you understand, Eloise?" he asked, his voice growing louder, more urgent. "It wasn't enough."

"It wasn't your fault," she said softly, because even though she hadn't known Marina as an adult, she knew Phillip, and she knew that had to be the truth.

"Eventually I just gave up," he said, his voice flat. "I stopped trying to help her at all. I was so sick and tired of beating my head against a wall where she was concerned. And all I tried to do was protect the children, and keep them away when she was in a really bad spell. Because they loved her so much." He looked at her pleadingly, maybe for understanding, maybe for something else Eloise didn't understand. "She was their mother."

"I know," she said softly.

"She was their mother, and she didn't . . . she couldn't . . ."

"But *you* were there," Eloise said fervently. "You were there."

He laughed harshly. "Yes, and a fat lot of good that did them. It's one thing to be born with one dreadful parent, but to have two? I would never have wished that on my children, and yet . . . here we are."

"You are not a bad father," Eloise said, unable to keep the scolding tone out of her voice.

He just shrugged and turned back to the portrait, clearly unable to consider her words.

"Do you know how much it hurt?" he whispered. "Do you have any idea?"

She shook her head, even though he'd turned away.

"To try so hard, so damned hard, and never succeed? Hell—" He laughed, a short, bitter sound, full of self-loathing. "Hell," he said again, "I didn't even like her and it hurt so much."

"You didn't like her?" Eloise asked, her surprise pitching her words into a different register.

His lips quirked ironically. "Can you like someone you don't even know?" He turned back to her. "I didn't know her, Eloise. I was married to her for eight years, and I never knew her."

"Maybe she didn't let you know her."

"Maybe I should have tried harder."

"Maybe," Eloise said, infusing her voice with all the surety and conviction she could, "there was nothing more you could have done. Some people are born melancholy, Phillip. I don't know why, and I doubt anyone knows why, but that's just the way they are."

He looked at her sardonically, his dark eyes clearly dismissing her opinion, and so she leapt back in with, "Don't forget, I knew her, too. As a child, long before you even knew she existed."

Phillip's expression changed then, and his gaze grew so intense upon her face that she nearly squirmed under the pressure of it.

"I never heard her laugh," Eloise said softly. "Not even once. I've been trying to remember her better since I met you, trying to recall why my memories of her always seemed so strange and odd, and I think that's it. She never laughed. Whoever heard of a child who doesn't laugh?"

Phillip was silent for a few moments, then he said, "I don't think I ever heard her laugh, either. Sometimes she would smile, usually when the children came to see her, but she never laughed."

Eloise nodded. And then she said, "I'm not Marina, Phillip."

"I know," he said. "Believe me, I know. It's why I married you, you know."

It wasn't quite what she wanted to hear, but she stifled her disappointment and allowed him to continue.

The creases in his forehead deepened, and he rubbed them hard. He looked so burdened, so tired of his responsibilities. "I just wanted someone who wasn't going to be sad," he said. "Someone who would be present for the children, someone who wouldn't—"

He cut himself off, turned away.

"Someone who wouldn't what?" she asked urgently, sensing that this was important.

For the longest time she thought he wasn't going to answer, but then, just when she'd quite given up on him, he said, "She died of influenza. You know that, don't you?"

"Yes," she said, since his back was to her and he wouldn't see her nod.

"She died of influenza," he repeated. "That's what we told everyone—"

Eloise suddenly felt very sick, because she knew, absolutely *knew* what he was going to say.

"Well, it was the truth," he said bitterly, surprising her with his words. She'd been so sure he was going to say that they'd been lying all the while.

"It's the truth," he said again. "But it wasn't all of the truth. She did die of influenza, but we never told anyone why she fell ill."

"The lake," Eloise whispered, her words coming forth unbidden. She hadn't even realized she'd been thinking them until she spoke.

He nodded grimly. "She didn't fall in by accident."

Her hand flew to cover her mouth. No wonder he'd been so upset that she'd taken the children there. She felt awful. Of course she didn't know, couldn't have known, but still . . .

"I got her just in time," he said. "Just in time to save her from drowning, that is. Not in time to save her from lung fever three days later." He choked back bitter laughter. "Not even my famed willow bark tea could do the job for *her*."

"I'm so sorry," Eloise whispered, and she was, even though Marina's death had, in so many ways, made her own happiness possible.

"You don't understand," he said, not looking at her. "You couldn't possibly."

"I have never known someone who took their own life," she said cautiously, not certain if these were the words one was meant to say in such a situation.

"That's not what I mean," he said, almost snapped, really. "You don't know what it's like to feel trapped, stuck, hopeless. To try so hard and never, *ever*"—he turned to her then, and his eyes were flashing fire—"break through. I tried. Every day I tried. I tried for me and I tried for Marina, and most of all for Oliver and Amanda. I did everything I knew how, everything everyone told me to do, and nothing, not one thing made it work. I tried, and she cried, and then I tried again and again and again, and all she ever did was dig herself deeper into her damned bed and pull up the covers over her head. She lived in darkness with her curtains drawn and the lights dimmed and then she picked the one goddamned sunny day to go and kill herself."

Eloise's eyes widened.

"A sunny day," he said. "We'd had a bloody month of overcast skies, and then finally the sun came out, and she had to kill herself." He laughed, but the sound was short and bitter. "After everything she'd done, she had to go and ruin sunny days for me."

"Phillip," Eloise said, placing her hand on his arm.

But he just shook her off. "And if that weren't enough, she couldn't even kill herself properly. Well, no," he said harshly, "I suppose that was *my* fault. She would have been quite good and dead if I hadn't come along and forced her to torture us all for three more days, wondering if she might live or die." He crossed his arms and snorted in disgust. "But of course she died. I don't know why we even held out hope. She didn't fight it at all, didn't use even an ounce of energy to fight the illness. She just laid there and let it claim her, and I kept waiting for her to smile, as if she were finally happy because now she'd succeeded in the one thing she wanted to do."

"Oh, my God," Eloise whispered, sickened by the image. "Did she?"

He shook his head. "No. She didn't have even the energy for that. She just died with the same expression on her face she always had. Empty."

"I'm so sorry," Eloise said, even though she knew her words could never be enough. "No one should have to go through something like that."

He stared at her for the longest time, his eyes searching hers, looking for something, searching for an answer that she wasn't sure she had. Then he turned abruptly away and walked to the window, staring out at the inky night sky. "I tried so hard," he said, his voice quiet with resignation and regret, "and still, every day I wished I were married to someone else." His head tipped forward, until his forehead was leaning against the glass. "Anyone else."

He was silent for a very long time. Too long, in Eloise's estimation, and so she stepped forward, murmuring his name, just to hear his response. Just to know that he was all right.

"Yesterday," he said, his voice abrupt, "you said we have a problem—"

"No," she cut in, as quickly as she was able. "I didn't mean—"

"You said we have a problem," he repeated, his voice so low and forceful she didn't think he'd hear another interruption even if she tried. "But until you live through what I lived through," he continued, "until you've been trapped in a hopeless marriage, to a hopeless spouse, until you've gone to bed alone for years wishing for nothing more than the touch of another human being . . ."

He turned around, stepped toward her, his eyes alight with a fire that humbled her. "Until you've lived through all that," he said, "don't you *ever* complain about what we have. Because to me . . . to me . . ." He choked on the words, but he barely paused before he continued. "This—us—is heaven. And I can't bear to hear you say otherwise."

"Oh, Phillip," she said, and then she did the only thing she knew to do. She closed the distance between them and threw her arms around him and held on for all she was worth. "I'm so sorry," she murmured, her tears soaking into his shirt. "I'm so sorry."

"I don't want to fail again," he choked out, burying his face in the crook of her neck. "I can't—I couldn't—"

"You won't," she vowed. "*We* won't."

"You've got to be happy," he said, his words sounding as if they'd been ripped from his throat. "You have to be. Please say—"

"I *am*," she assured him. "I am. I promise you."

He pulled back and took her face in his hands, forcing her to look deeply into his eyes. He seemed to be searching for something in her expression, desperately seeking confirmation, or maybe absolution, or maybe just a simple promise.

"I *am* happy," she whispered, covering his hands with her own. "More than I ever dreamed possible. And I am proud to be your wife."

His face seemed to tighten, and his lower lip began to quiver. Eloise caught her breath. She'd never seen a man cry, never really even thought it possible, but then a tear rolled slowly down his cheek, settling into the dimple at the corner of his mouth until she reached out and brushed it away.

"I love you," he said, choking on the words. "I don't even care if you don't feel the same way. I love you and . . . and . . ."

"Oh, Phillip," she whispered, reaching up and touching the tears on his face. "I love you, too."

His lips moved as if trying to form words, and then he gave up on speech, and he reached out for her, crushing her to him with a strength and intensity that humbled her. He buried his face in her neck, murmuring her name over and over again, and then his words became kisses, and he moved along her skin until he found her mouth.

How long they stood there, kissing as if the world were to end that very night, Eloise would never know. Then he swept her into his arms and carried her out of the portrait gallery and up the stairs, and before she knew it, she was on her bed, and he was on top of her.

And his lips had never left hers.

"I need you," he said hoarsely, pulling her dress from her body with shaking fingers. "I need you like I need breath. I need you like food, like water."

She tried to say she needed him, too, but she couldn't, not when his mouth had closed around her nipple, not when he was sucking in such a way that made her feel it down in her belly, a warm, slow heat that curled and grew, taking her hostage until she could do nothing but reach for this man, her husband, and give herself to him with everything that she had.

He lifted himself away from her, just long enough to yank off his own clothing, and then he rejoined her, this time lying beside her. He pulled her to him until they were belly to belly, and then he stroked her hair, softly, gently, and his other hand splayed at the small of her back.

"I love you," he whispered. "I want nothing more than to grab you and—" He swallowed. "You have no idea how much I want you right now."

Her lips curved. "I think I have some idea."

That made him smile. "My body is dying. It's like nothing I've ever felt, and yet . . ." He leaned in closer and brushed his lips across hers. "I had to stop. I had to tell you."

She couldn't speak, could barely breathe. And she felt the tears coming, burning in her eyes until they spilled out, flowing over his hands.

"Don't cry," he whispered.

"I can't help it," she said, her voice shaking. "I love you so much. I didn't think—I'd always hoped, but I guess I never really thought—"

"I never thought, either," he said, and they both knew what they were thinking—

I never thought it would happen to me.

"I'm so lucky," he said, and his hands moved, sliding down her rib cage, over her belly, and then around to her backside. "I think I've waited my entire life for you."

"I know I've been waiting for you," Eloise said.

He squeezed and pulled her against him, nearly burning her with his touch. "I'm not going to be able to go slowly," he said, his voice shaking. "I think I used up my entire allotment of willpower just now."

"Don't go slowly," she said, sliding onto her back and pulling him atop her. She spread her legs, opening until he settled between them, his sex coming to rest right at the opening of her womanhood. Her hands found his hair and sank in, pulling his head down until his mouth was right at hers. "I don't want it slow," she said.

And then, in a single fluid motion, so fast that it took her breath away, he was inside her, embedded to the hilt, knocking against her womb with enough force to jolt a surprised little "Oh!" from her lips.

He smiled wickedly. "You said you wanted it fast."

She responded by curling her legs around his, locking him to her. She tilted her hips, which pulled him in even deeper, and smiled back. "You're not doing anything," she said to him.

And then he did.

All words were lost as they moved. They weren't graceful, and they didn't move as one. Their bodies weren't in tune, and the sounds they made were not musical or lovely.

They just moved, with need and fire and total abandon, reaching for each other, reaching for the summit. The wait was not long. Eloise tried to make it last, tried to hold out, but there was no way. With every stroke, Phillip unleashed a fire within her that could not be denied. And then finally, when she couldn't contain herself one moment longer, Eloise cried out and arched beneath him, lifting them both from the bed with the force of her fulfillment. Her body quivered and shook, and she gasped for breath, and all she could do was clutch his back, her fingers surely leaving bruises on his skin as she clung to him.

And then, before she could even fall back down to earth, Phillip cried out, and he slammed forward over and over again, emptying himself within her until he collapsed, the full weight of him pinning her into the mattress.

But she didn't mind. She loved the feel of him atop her, loved the heaviness, loved the smell and the taste of the sweat on his skin.

She loved *him*.

It was that simple.

She loved him, and he loved her, and if there was anything more, anything else important in her world, it just didn't matter. Not right there, not right then.

"I love you," he whispered, finally rolling off her and allowing her lungs to fill with air.

I love you.

It was all she needed.

Chapter 19

. . . days are filled with endless amusements. I shop and attend luncheons and pay calls (and have calls paid upon me). In the evenings I usually attend a ball or musicale, or perhaps a smaller party. Sometimes I remain at home with my own company and read a book. Truly, it is a full and lively existence; I have no cause for complaint. What more, I often ask, could a lady want?

—from Eloise Bridgerton to Sir Phillip Crane,
six months into their unusual correspondence

For the rest of her days, Eloise would remember the following week as one of the most magical of her life. There were no stupendous events, no bursts of fine weather, no birthdays, no extravagant gifts or unexpected visitors.

But still, even though it all seemed, on the outside at least, very ordinary . . .

Everything changed.

It wasn't the sort of thing that hit one like a thunderbolt, or even, Eloise thought with a wry smile, like a slammed door or high

C at the opera. It was a slow, creeping kind of change, the sort of thing that begins without one realizing it, and ends before one even knows it has begun.

It started a few mornings after she'd come across Phillip in the portrait gallery. When she woke, he was sitting fully dressed at the foot of the bed, staring at her with an indulgent smile on his face.

"What are you doing there?" Eloise asked, tucking the sheets under her arms as she scooted into a sitting position.

"Watching you."

Her lips parted with surprise, and then she couldn't help but smile. "It can't be very interesting."

"To the contrary. I can't think of anything that could keep my attention for so long."

She blushed, mumbling something about his being silly, but in truth, his words made her want to yank him right back into bed. She had a feeling he wouldn't resist—he never did—but she put a hold on her desire, since he had, after all, got himself completely dressed, and she rather thought he'd done so for a reason.

"I brought you a muffin," he said, holding out a plate.

Eloise thanked him and took his proffered dish. While she was munching away (and wishing he'd thought to bring something to drink as well), he said, "I thought we might go on an outing today."

"You and I?"

"Actually," he said, "I thought the four of us might go."

Eloise froze, her teeth lodged in the muffin, and looked at him. This was, she realized, the first time he'd suggested such a thing. The first time, to her knowledge, at least, that he'd reached out to his children rather than setting them aside, hoping that someone else would see to them.

"I think that's a fine idea," she said softly.

"Good," he said, rising to his feet. "I'll leave you to your morning routine and inform that poor housemaid you bullied into acting as their nurse that we will be taking them for the day."

"I'm sure she'll be relieved," Eloise said. Mary hadn't really wanted to take the position as nursemaid, even on a temporary basis. None of the servants had; they all knew the twins too well. And poor long-haired Mary vividly recalled having to burn the bedsheets after they'd been unable to remove the last governess's glued-on hair.

But there was nothing else to be done, and Eloise had extracted a promise from both children that they would treat Mary with the respect due to, say, the queen, and so far they had been living up to their word. Eloise even had her fingers crossed that Mary might relent and agree to the position on a permanent basis. It did pay better than cleaning, after all.

Eloise looked over at the door and was surprised to see Phillip standing quite still, frowning. "What is wrong?" she asked.

He blinked, then looked in her direction, his brows still pulled down in thought. "I'm not sure what to do."

"I believe the doorknob will turn in either direction," she teased.

He shot her a look, then said, "There are no fairs or events occurring in the village. What should we do with them?"

"Anything," Eloise said, smiling at him with all the love in her heart. "Or nothing at all. It doesn't matter, really. All they want is you, Phillip. All they want is you."

Two hours later Phillip and Oliver were standing outside the Larkin's Fine Tailor and Dressmaker in the village of Tetbury, waiting somewhat impatiently while Eloise and Amanda completed their purchases inside.

"Did we have to go *shopping*?" Oliver groaned, as if he'd been asked to wear pigtails and a frock.

Phillip shrugged. "It is what your mother wished to do."

"Next time, it's the men's turn to pick," Oliver grumbled. "If I'd known having a mother would mean *this* . . ."

Phillip had to force himself not to laugh. "Men must make sacrifices for the women we love," he said in serious tones, patting his son on the shoulder. "It's the way of the world, I'm afraid."

Oliver let out a long-suffering sigh, as if he'd been making such sacrifices on a daily basis.

Phillip looked through the window. Eloise and Amanda showed no signs of wrapping up their business. "But as pertains to the issue of shopping, and who gets to decide upon the next joint activity," he said, "I agree wholeheartedly."

Just then, Eloise poked her head outside. "Oliver?" she asked. "Would you care to come in?"

"No," Oliver replied, shaking his head emphatically.

Eloise pursed her lips. "Allow me to rephrase," she said. "Oliver, I would like you to come in."

Oliver looked up to his father, his eyes pleading.

"I'm afraid you must do as she says," Phillip said.

"So many sacrifices," Oliver grumbled, shaking his head as he hauled himself up the steps.

Phillip coughed to cover a laugh.

"Are you coming, too?" Oliver asked.

Hell, no, Phillip almost said, but managed to catch himself in time to change it to, "I need to remain outside to watch the carriage."

Oliver's eyes narrowed. "Why does the carriage need watching?"

"Er, strain on the wheels," Phillip mumbled. "All our packages, you know."

He was unable to hear what Eloise said under her breath, but the tone was not complimentary.

"Run along, Oliver," he said, patting his son on the back. "Your mother needs you."

"And you, too," Eloise said sweetly, just to torture him, he was sure. "You need new shirts."

Phillip groaned. "Can't we have the tailor come out to the house?"

"Don't you want to choose the fabric?"

He shook his head and said, quite grandly, "I trust you implicitly."

"I think he needs to watch the carriage," Oliver said, still hovering in the threshold.

"He's going to need to watch his back," Eloise muttered, "if he doesn't—"

"Oh, very well," Phillip said. "I'll come in. But only for a moment." He found himself standing in the women's half of the shop, a frilly, feminine place if ever there was one, and shuddered. "Anything more, and I'm likely to perish of claustrophobia."

"A big, strong man like you?" Eloise said in a mild voice. "Nonsense." And then she looked up at him and motioned to him with her chin to come close.

"Yes?" he asked, wondering what this was all about.

"Amanda," she whispered, nodding toward a door at the back of the room. "When she comes out, make a fuss."

He looked about the store doubtfully. He might as well have been in China, so out of place did he feel. "I'm not very good at fussing."

"Learn," she ordered, then turned her attention to Oliver with a: "Now it's your turn, Master Crane. Mrs. Larkin—"

Oliver's groan would have done a dying man justice. "I want Mr. Larkin," he protested. "Like Father."

"You would like to see the tailor?" Eloise asked.

Oliver nodded vigorously.

"Really?"

He nodded again, although without quite as much conviction.

"Even though," Eloise continued, with enough inflection to put her on the Drury Lane stage, "not an hour ago you vowed that wild horses could not drag you inside a storefront unless there were guns or toy soldiers in the window?"

Oliver's mouth went slack, but he nodded. Barely.

"You're good," Phillip murmured in her ear as he watched Oliver drag himself through the doorway that separated Mr. Larkin's half of the store from Mrs. Larkin's.

"It's all a matter of showing them how much worse the alternative is," Eloise said. "Getting fitted by Mr. Larkin is tedious, but *Mrs. Larkin*—now, that would be wretched."

An indignant howl rent the air, and Oliver came running back in—straight to Eloise, which left Phillip feeling a little bereft. He wanted his children to run to him, he realized.

"He stuck me with a pin!" Oliver declared.

"Were you squirming?" Eloise asked, without even batting an eyelash.

"No!"

"Not even a little bit?"

"Only the tiniest bit."

"Right, then," Eloise said. "Don't move next time. I assure you that Mr. Larkin is very good at his job. If you don't move, you won't get jabbed. It's as simple as that."

Oliver digested that, then turned to Phillip with a pleading look in his eyes. It was rather nice to be perceived as an ally, but Phillip wasn't going to contradict Eloise and undermine her authority. Especially not when he agreed with her wholeheartedly.

But then Oliver surprised him. He didn't beg to be set free from Mr. Larkin's clutches, and he didn't say something horrid about Eloise, which, Phillip was sure, he would have done just a few weeks earlier, about any adult who thwarted his wishes.

Oliver just looked up at him and asked, "Will you come with me, Father? Please."

Phillip opened his mouth to reply, but then, inexplicably, had to stop. His eyes began to sting with unshed tears, and he realized that he was, quite simply, overcome.

It wasn't just the moment, the fact that his son wanted his company for a male rite of passage. Oliver had begged his company before.

But this was the first time that Phillip felt truly able to say yes, confident that if he went, he would do the right thing and say the right words.

And even if he didn't, it wouldn't matter. He wasn't his father, would never be—*could* never be like him. He couldn't afford to be a coward, to keep pushing his children toward other people, all because he was worried he'd make a mistake.

He *would* make mistakes. It was inevitable. But they wouldn't be huge ones, and with Eloise at his side, he was quite confident he could do anything.

Even manage the twins.

He placed his hand on Oliver's shoulder. "I would be delighted to accompany you, son." He cleared his throat, which had gone hoarse on the final word. Then he bent down and whispered, "The last thing we want is women over on the men's side."

Oliver nodded his vigorous agreement.

Phillip straightened, preparing to follow his son back to Mr. Larkin's side of the establishment. Then he heard Eloise, clearing her throat behind him. He turned, and she was gesturing with her head toward the back of the room.

Amanda.

Looking very grown up in her new lavender frock, showing just a hint of the woman she would one day become.

For the second time in as many minutes, Phillip's eyes began to burn.

This was what he'd been missing. In his fear, in his self-doubt, he'd been missing this.

They'd been growing up without him.

Phillip patted his son on the shoulder to signal that he'd be right back, and then crossed the room to his daughter's side. Without a word, he picked up her hand and kissed it. "You, Miss Amanda Crane," he said, his heart in his eyes, his voice, his smile, "are the most beautiful girl I have ever seen."

Her eyes grew wide and her lips formed a tiny little *O* of sheer delight. "What about Miss—Mother?" she whispered frantically.

Phillip looked over at his wife, who appeared close to tears herself, and then turned back to Amanda, leaning over to whisper in her ear, "Let's make a deal, you and I. You can think your mother is the most beautiful woman alive. But I get to think it's you."

And later that night, after he'd tucked them into bed, kissed each on the forehead, and headed for the door, he heard his daughter whisper, "Father?"

He turned. "Amanda?"

"This was the best day ever, Father," she whispered.

"Ever," Oliver agreed.

Phillip nodded. "For me as well," he said softly. "For me as well."

It started with a note.

Later that night, as Eloise finished her supper and her plate was cleared away, she realized that there had been a piece of paper tucked underneath, folded twice until it formed a small rectangle.

Her husband had excused himself, claiming that he needed to find a book that contained a poem they had been discussing over pudding, and so, with no one watching her, not even the footman, who was busy transporting the dishes to the kitchen, Eloise unfolded the paper.

I have never been good with words,

it said, in Phillip's unmistakable handwriting. And then, smaller, in the corner:

Proceed to your office.

Intrigued, she stood and exited the dining room. A minute later she entered her office.

And there, in the middle of her desk, was another piece of paper.

But it all started with a letter, did it not?

Followed by instructions to take herself to the sitting room. She did, this time having to concentrate quite hard on keeping her half walk, half skip from turning into a full-fledged run.

A small piece of paper, again folded twice, sat on a red cushion positioned at the very center of the sofa.

And so if it started with words, it ought to continue with them, too.

This time she was directed to the front hall.

But there are no words to thank you for all you have given me, so I will use the only ones at my disposal, and I will tell you the only way I know how.

And at the bottom corner of the note, she was directed to her bedroom.

Eloise headed up the stairs slowly, her heart beating with anticipation. This was her final destination, she was sure of it. Phillip would be waiting for her, waiting to take her hand, to lead her into their future together.

It had, she realized, all started with a note. Something so innocent, so innocuous, and it had grown into this, a love so full and rich she could barely contain it.

She reached the upstairs hall and on quiet feet made her way to the bedroom door. It was slightly ajar, just an inch or so, and with shaking hand she pushed it open, all the way—

And she gasped.

For there, on the bed, were flowers. Hundreds and hundred of blooms, some clearly out of season, picked from Phillip's special collection in his greenhouse. And written in blossoms of red, against the backdrop of white and pink petals:

I LOVE YOU.

"Words aren't enough," Phillip said softly, stepping out of the shadows behind her.

She turned to him, barely cognizant of the tears trickling down her cheeks. "When did you do this?"

He smiled. "Surely you'll allow me a few secrets."

"I—I—"

He took her hand, pulled her close. "Speechless?" he murmured. "You? I must be better at this than I thought."

"I love you," she said, choking on the words. "I love you so much."

His arms came around her, and as she laid her cheek against his chest, his chin came down to rest gently on her head. "Today," he said softly, "the twins told me it was the best day ever. And I realized they were right."

Eloise nodded, beyond words.

"But then," he continued, "I realized they were wrong."

She looked up at him, a question in her eyes.

"I couldn't choose a day," he confessed. "Any day with you, Eloise. Any day with you."

He touched her chin, brought his lips to hers. "Any week," he murmured, "any month, any hour."

He kissed her then, softly, but with all the love in his soul. "Any moment," he whispered, "as long as I'm with you."

Epilogue

There is so much I hope to teach you, little one. I hope that I may do so by example, but I feel the need to put the words to paper as well. It is a quirk of mine, one which I expect you will recognize and find amusing by the time you read this letter.

Be strong.

Be diligent.

Be conscientious. There is never anything to be gained by taking the easy road. (Unless, of course, the road is an easy one to begin with. Roads sometimes are. If that should be the case, do not forge a new, more difficult one. Only martyrs go out looking for trouble.)

Love your siblings. You have two already, and God willing, there will be more. Love them well, for they are your blood, and when you are unsure, or times are difficult, they will be the ones to stand by your side.

Laugh. Laugh out loud, and laugh often. And when circumstances call for silence, turn your laugh into a smile.

Don't settle. Know what you want and reach for it.

And if you don't know what you want, be patient. The answers will come to you in time, and you may find that your heart's desire has been right under your nose all the while.

And remember, always remember that you have a mother and a father who love each other and love you.

I feel you growing restless. Your father is making strange gasping sounds and will surely lose his temper altogether if I do not move from my escritoire to my bed.

Welcome to the world, little one. We are all so delighted to make your acquaintance.

—from Eloise, Lady Crane,
to her daughter Penelope,
upon the occasion of her birth

Dear Reader,

Have you ever wondered what happened to your favorite characters after you closed the final page? Wanted just a little bit more of a favorite novel? I have, and if the questions from my readers are any indication, I'm not the only one. So after countless requests from Bridgerton fans, I decided to try something a little different, and I wrote a "2nd Epilogue" for each of the novels. These are the stories that come after *the stories.*

At first, the Bridgerton 2nd Epilogues were available exclusively online; later they were published (along with a novella about Violet Bridgerton) in a collection called The Bridgertons: Happily Ever After. *Now, for the first time, each 2nd Epilogue is being included with the novel it follows. I hope you enjoy Phillip and Eloise as they continue their journey.*

Warmly,
Julia Quinn

To Sir Phillip, With Love: The 2nd Epilogue

I am not the most patient of individuals. And I have almost no tolerance for stupidity. Which was why I was proud of myself for holding my tongue this afternoon, while having tea with the Brougham family.

The Broughams are our neighbors, and have been for the past six years, since Mr. Brougham inherited the property from his uncle, also named Mr. Brougham. They have four daughters and one extremely spoiled son. Luckily for me the son is five years younger than I am, which means I shall not have to entertain notions of marrying him. (Although my sisters Penelope and Georgiana, nine and ten years my junior, will not be so lucky.) The Brougham daughters are all one year apart, beginning two years ahead of me and ending two behind. They are perfectly pleasant, if perhaps a touch too sweet and gentle for my taste. But lately they have been too much to bear.

This is because I, too, have a brother, and he is not five years younger than they are. In fact, he is my twin, which makes him a matrimonial possibility for any of them.

Unsurprisingly, Oliver did not elect to accompany my mother, Penelope, and me to tea.

But here is what happened, and here is why I am pleased with myself for not saying what I wished to say, which was: *Surely you must be an idiot.*

I was sipping my tea, trying to keep the cup at my lips for as long as possible so as to avoid questions about Oliver, when Mrs. Brougham said, "It must be so very intriguing to be a twin. Tell me, dear Amanda, how is it different than not being one?"

I should hope that I do not have to explain why this question was so asinine. I could hardly tell her what the difference was, as I have spent approximately one hundred percent of my life as a twin and thus have precisely zero experience at not being one.

I must have worn my disdain on my face because my mother shot me one of her legendary warning looks the moment my lips parted to reply. Because I did not wish to embarrass my mother (and not because I felt any need to make Mrs. Brougham feel cleverer than she actually was), I said, "I suppose one always has a companion."

"But your brother is not here now," one of the Brougham girls said.

"My father is not always with my mother, and I would imagine that she considers him to be her companion," I replied.

"A brother is hardly the same as a husband," Mrs. Brougham trilled.

"One would hope," I retorted. Truly, this was one of the more ridiculous conversations in which I had taken part. And Penelope looked as if she would have questions when we returned home.

My mother gave me another look, one that said she knew exactly what sort of questions Penelope would have, and she did not wish to answer them. But as my mother had always said she valued curiosity in females . . .

Well, she'd be hoisted by her own petard.

I should mention that, petard hoistings aside, I am convinced that I have the finest mother in England. And unlike being a non-twin, about which I have no knowledge, I do know what it's like to have a different mother, so I am fully qualified, in my opinion, to make the judgment.

My mother, Eloise Crane, is actually my stepmother, although I only refer to her as such when required to for purposes of clarification. She married my father when Oliver and I were eight years old, and I am quite certain she saved us all. It is difficult to explain what our lives were like before she entered them. I could certainly describe events, but the *tone* of it all, the feeling in our house . . .

I don't really know how to convey it.

My mother—my original mother—killed herself. For most of my life I did not know this. I thought she died of a fever, which I suppose is true. What no one told me was that the fever was brought on because she tried to drown herself in a lake in the dead of winter.

I have no intention of taking my own life, but I must say, this would not be my chosen method.

I know I should feel compassion and sympathy for her. My current mother was a distant cousin of hers and tells me that she was sad her entire life. She tells me that some people are like that, just as others are unnaturally cheerful all the time. But I can't help but think that if she was going to kill herself, she might as well have done it earlier. Perhaps when I was a toddler. Or better yet, an infant. It certainly would have made my life easier.

I asked my uncle Hugh (who is not really my uncle, but he is married to the stepsister of my current mother's brother's wife *and* he lives quite close *and* he's a vicar) if I would be going to hell for such a thought. He said no, that frankly, it made a lot of sense to him.

I do think I prefer his parish to my own.

But the thing is, now I have memories of her. Marina, my first mother. I don't *want* memories of her. The ones I have are hazy and muddled. I can't recall the sound of her voice. Oliver says that might be because she hardly spoke. I can't remember whether she spoke or not. I can't remember the exact shape of her face, and I can't remember her smell.

Instead I remember standing outside her door, feeling very small and frightened. And I remember tiptoeing a great deal, because we knew we mustn't make noise. I remember always feeling rather nervous, as if I knew something bad were about to happen.

And indeed it did.

Shouldn't a memory be specific? I would not mind a memory of a moment, or of a face, or a sound. Instead I have vague feelings, and not even happy ones at that.

I once asked Oliver if he had the same memories, and he just shrugged and said he didn't really think about her. I am not sure if I believe him. I suppose I probably do; he does not often think deeply about such things. Or perhaps more accurately, he does not think deeply about anything. One can only hope that when he marries (which surely will not come soon enough for the sisters Brougham) that he will choose a bride with a similar lack of thoughtfulness and sensibility. Otherwise, she shall be miserable. He won't be, of course; he wouldn't even notice her misery.

Men are like that, I'm told.

My father, for example, is remarkably unobservant. Unless, of course, you happen to be a plant, and then he notices everything. He is a botanist and could happily toddle about in his greenhouse all day. He seems to me a most unlikely match for my mother, who is vivacious and outgoing and never at a loss for words, but when they are together it is obvious that they love each other very much. Last week I caught them kissing in the garden. I was aghast. Mother is nearly forty, and Father older than that.

But I have digressed. I was speaking of the Brougham family, more specifically of Mrs. Brougham's foolish query about not being a twin. I was, as previously mentioned, feeling rather pleased with myself for not having been rude, when Mrs. Brougham said something that *was* of interest.

"My nephew comes to visit this afternoon."

Every one of the Brougham girls popped straighter in her seat. I swear, it was like some children's game with snaps. Bing bing bing bing . . . Up they went, from perfect posture to preternaturally erect.

From this I immediately deduced that Mrs. Brougham's nephew must be of marriageable age, probably of good fortune, and perhaps of pleasing features.

"You did not mention that Ian was coming to visit," one of the daughters said.

"He's not," replied Mrs. Brougham. "He is still at Oxford, as you well know. Charles is coming."

Poof. The daughters Brougham deflated, all at once.

"Oh," said one of them. "Charlie."

"Today, you say," said another, with a remarkable lack of enthusiasm.

And then the third said, "I shall have to hide my dolls."

The fourth said nothing. She just resumed drinking her tea, looking rather bored by the whole thing.

"Why do you have to hide your dolls?" Penelope asked. In all truth, I was wondering the same thing, but it seemed too childish a question for a lady of nineteen years.

"That was twelve years ago, Dulcie," Mrs. Brougham said. "Good heavens, you've a memory of an elephant."

"One does not forget what he did to my dolls," Dulcie said darkly.

"What did he do?" Penelope asked.

Dulcie made a slashing motion across her throat. Penelope gasped, and I must confess, there was something rather gruesome in Dulcie's expression.

"He is a beast," said one of Dulcie's sisters.

"He is *not* a beast," Mrs. Brougham insisted.

The Brougham girls all looked at us, shaking their heads in silent agreement, as if to say, *Do not listen to her.*

"How old is your nephew now?" my mother asked.

"Two and twenty," Mrs. Brougham replied, looking rather grateful for the question. "He was graduated from Oxford last month."

"He is a year older than Ian," explained one of the girls.

I nodded, even though I could hardly use Ian—whom I had never met—as a reference point.

"He's not as handsome."

"Or as nice."

I looked at the last Brougham daughter, awaiting her contribution. But all she did was yawn.

"How long will he be staying?" my mother asked politely.

"Two weeks," Mrs. Brougham answered, but she really only got out "Two wee" before one of her daughters howled with dismay.

"Two weeks! An entire fortnight!"

"I was hoping he could accompany us to the local assembly," Mrs. Brougham said.

This was met by more groans. I must say, I was beginning to grow curious about this Charles fellow. Anyone who could inspire such dread among the Brougham daughters must have something to recommend him.

Not, I hasten to add, that I dislike the Brougham daughters. Unlike their brother, none of them was granted every wish and whim, and thus they are not at all unbearable. But they are—how shall I say it—placid and biddable, and therefore not a natural sort of companion for me (about whom such adjectives have never been applied). Truthfully, I don't think I had ever known any of them to express a strong opinion about anything. If all four of them detested someone that much—well, if nothing else, he would be interesting.

"Does your nephew like to ride?" my mother asked.

Mrs. Brougham got a crafty look in her eye. "I believe so."

"Perhaps Amanda would consent to showing him the area." With that, my mother smiled a most uncharacteristically innocent and sweet smile.

Perhaps I should add that one of the reasons I am convinced that mine is the finest mother in England is that she is rarely innocent and sweet. Oh, do not misunderstand—she has a heart of gold and would do anything for her family. But she grew up the fifth in a family of eight, and she can be marvelously devious and underhanded.

Also, she cannot be bested in conversation. Trust me, I have tried.

So when she offered me up as a guide, I could do nothing but say yes, even as three out of four Brougham sisters began to snicker. (The fourth still looked bored. I was beginning to wonder if there might be something wrong with her.)

"Tomorrow," Mrs. Brougham said delightedly. She clapped her hands together and beamed. "I shall send him over tomorrow afternoon. Will that do?"

Again, I could say nothing but yes, and so I did, wondering what exactly I had just consented to.

The following afternoon I was dressed in my best riding habit and was lolling about the drawing room, wondering if the mysterious Charles Brougham would actually make an appearance. If he didn't, I thought, he'd be entirely within his rights. It would be rude, of course, as he was breaking a commitment made on his behalf by his aunt, but all the same, it wasn't as if he'd asked to be saddled with the local gentry.

Pun unintended.

My mother had not even tried to deny that she was playing matchmaker. This surprised me; I would have thought she'd put up at least a feeble protest. But instead she reminded me that I had refused a season in London and then began to expound upon the lack of appropriately aged, eligible gentlemen here in our corner of Gloucestershire.

I reminded her that she had not found *her* husband in London.

She then said something that began with "Be that as it may" and then veered off so quickly and with such twists and turns that I could not follow a thing she said.

Which I am fairly certain was her intention.

My mother wasn't precisely upset that I had said no to a season; she was rather fond of our life in the country, and heaven knows my father would not survive in town for more than a week. Mother called me unkind for saying so, but I believe that she secretly agreed with me—Father would get distracted by a plant in the park, and we'd never find him again. (He's a bit distractable, my father.)

Or, and I confess this is more likely, he would say something utterly inappropriate at a party. Unlike my mother, my father does not have the gift of polite conversation, and he certainly does not see the need for double entendre or cunning twists of phrase. As far as he is concerned, a body ought to say what a body means.

I do love my father, but it is clear that he should be kept away from town.

I could have had a season in London, if I wished. My mother's family is extremely well connected. Her brother is a viscount, and her sisters married a duke, an earl, and a baron. I should be admitted to all of the most exclusive gatherings. But I really didn't wish to go. I should have no freedom whatsoever. Here I may take walks or go for a ride by myself so long as I tell someone where I am going. In London a young lady may not so much as touch her toe to her front steps without a chaperone.

I think it sounds dreadful.

But back to my mother. She did not mind that I had refused the season because this meant that she would not have to be apart from my father for several months. (Since, as we have determined, he would have to be left at home.) But at the same time, she was genuinely concerned for my future. To that end, she had launched into a bit of a crusade. If I would not go to the eligible gentlemen, she would bring them to me.

Hence Charles Brougham.

At two o'clock he had still not arrived, and I must confess, I was growing irritable. It was a hot day, or at least as hot as it gets in Gloucestershire, and my dark green habit, which had felt so stylish and jaunty when I had donned it, was beginning to itch.

I was beginning to wilt.

Somehow my mother and Mrs. Brougham had forgotten to set a time for the nephew's arrival, so I had been obligated to be dressed and ready at noon precisely.

"What time would you say marks the end of the afternoon?" I asked, fanning myself with a folded-up newspaper.

"Hmmm?" My mother was writing a letter—presumably to one of her many siblings—and wasn't really listening. She looked quite lovely sitting there by the window. I have no idea what my original mother would have looked like as an older woman, since she did not deign to live that long, but Eloise had not lost any of her beauty. Her hair was still a rich, chestnut color and her skin unlined. Her eyes are difficult to describe—rather changeable in color, actually.

She tells me that she was never considered a beauty when she was young. No one thought she was unattractive, and she was in fact quite popular, but she was never designated a diamond of the first water. She tells me that women of intelligence age better.

I find this interesting, and I do hope it bodes well for my own future.

But at present I was not concerned for any future outside that of the next ten minutes, after which I was convinced I would perish from the heat. "The afternoon," I repeated. "When would you say it ends? Four o'clock? Five? Please say it isn't six."

She finally glanced up. "What are you talking about?"

"Mr. Brougham. We did say the afternoon, did we not?"

She looked at me blankly.

"I may stop waiting for him once the afternoon passes into evening, may I not?"

Mother paused for a moment, her quill suspended in air. "You should not be so impatient, Amanda."

"I'm not," I insisted. "I'm *hot*."

She considered that. "It is warm in here, isn't it?"

I nodded. "My habit is made of wool."

She grimaced, but I noticed she did not suggest that I change. She was not going to sacrifice a potential suitor for anything as inconsequential as the weather. I resumed fanning myself.

"I don't think his name is Brougham," Mother said.

"I beg your pardon?"

"I believe he is related to Mrs. Brougham, not mister. I don't know what her family name is."

I shrugged.

She went back to her letter. My mother writes an inordinate number of letters. About what, I cannot imagine. I would not call our family dull, but we are certainly ordinary. Surely her sisters have grown bored of *Georgiana has mastered French conjugation* and *Frederick has skinned his knee.*

But Mother likes to receive letters, and she says that one must send to receive, so there she is at her desk, nearly every day, recounting the boring details of our lives.

"Someone is coming," she said, just as I was beginning to nod off on the sofa. I sat up and turned toward the window. Sure enough, a carriage was rolling up the drive.

"I thought we were meant to go for a ride," I said, somewhat irritably. Had I sweltered in my riding habit for nothing?

"You were," Mother murmured, her brow knitting together as she watched the carriage draw near.

I did not think that Mr. Brougham—or whoever was in the carriage—could see into the drawing room through the open window, but just in case, I maintained my dignified position on the sofa, tilting my head ever so slightly so that I could observe the events in the front drive.

The carriage came to a halt and a gentleman hopped down, but his back was to the house and I could see nothing of him other than his height (average) and his hair (dark). He then reached up and assisted a lady down.

Dulcie Brougham!

"What is she doing here?" I said indignantly.

And then, once Dulcie had both feet safely on the ground, the gentleman aided another young lady, and then another. And then another.

"Did he bring all of the Brougham girls?" my mother asked.

"Apparently so."

"I thought they hated him."

I shook my head. "Apparently not."

The reason for the sisters' about-face became clear a few moments later, when Gunning announced their arrival.

I do not know what Cousin Charles *used* to look like, but now . . . well, let us just say that any young lady would find him pleasing. His hair was thick and with a bit of wave, and even from across the room I could see that his eyelashes were ridiculously long. His mouth was the sort that always looks as if it is about to smile, which in my opinion is the best sort of mouth to have.

I am not saying that I felt anything other than polite interest, but the Brougham sisters were falling all over themselves to be the one on his arm.

"Dulcie," my mother said, walking forth with a welcoming smile. "And Antonia. And Sarah." She took a breath. "And Cordelia, too. What a pleasant surprise to see all of you."

It is a testament to my mother's skills as a hostess that she did indeed sound pleased.

"We could not let dear Cousin Charles come over by himself," Dulcie explained.

"He does not know the way," added Antonia.

It could not have been a simpler journey—one had only to ride into the village, turn right at the church, and it was only another mile until our drive.

But I did not say this. I did, however, look over at Cousin Charles with some sympathy. It could not have been an entertaining drive.

"Charles, dear," Dulcie was saying, "this is Lady Crane, and Miss Amanda Crane."

I bobbed a curtsy, wondering if I was going to have to climb into that carriage with all five of them. I hoped not. If it was hot in here, it would be beastly in the carriage.

"Lady Crane, Amanda," Dulcie continued, "my dear cousin Charles, Mr. Farraday."

I cocked my head at that. My mother was correct—his name was not Brougham. Oh dear, did that mean he *was* related to Mrs. Brougham? I found Mr. Brougham the more sensible of the two.

Mr. Farraday bowed politely, and for the briefest of moments, his eyes caught mine.

I should say at this point that I am not a romantic. Or at least I do not think I am a romantic. If I were, I would have gone to London for that season. I would have spent my days reading poetry and my nights dancing and flirting and making merry.

I certainly do not believe in love at first sight. Even my parents, who are as much in love as anyone I know, tell me that they did not love each other instantly.

But when my eyes met Mr. Farraday's . . .

As I said, it was not love at first sight, since I do not believe in such things. It was not anything at first sight, really, but there was something . . . a shared recognition . . . a sense of humor. I'm not certain how to describe it.

I suppose, if pressed, that I would say it was a sense of knowing. That somehow I already knew him. Which was of course ridiculous.

But not as ridiculous as his cousins, who were trilling and frilling and fluttering about. Clearly they had decided that Cousin Charles was no longer a beast, and if anyone was going to marry him, it was going to be one of them.

"Mr. Farraday," I said, and I could feel the corners of my mouth pinching in an attempt to hold back a smile.

"Miss Crane," he said, wearing much the same expression. He bent over my hand and kissed it, much to the consternation of Dulcie, who was standing right next to me.

Again, I *must* stress that I am not a romantic. But my insides did a little flip when his lips touched my skin.

"I am afraid that I am dressed for a ride," I told him, motioning to my riding habit.

"So you are."

I glanced ruefully at his cousins, who were most assuredly not dressed for any sort of athletic endeavor. "It's such a lovely day," I murmured.

"Girls," my mother said, looking squarely at the Brougham sisters, "why don't you join me while Amanda and your cousin go for a ride? I did promise your mother that she would show him the area."

Antonia opened her mouth to protest, but she was no match for Eloise Crane, and indeed she did not make even a sound before my mother added, "Oliver will be down shortly."

That settled it. They sat, all four of them, in a neat row on the sofa, descending as one, with identically placid smiles on their faces.

I almost felt sorry for Oliver.

"I did not bring my mount," Mr. Farraday said regretfully.

"That is no matter," I replied. "We have an excellent stable. I'm certain we can find something suitable."

And off we went, out the drawing room door, then out of the house, then around the corner to the back lawn, and then—

Mr. Farraday sagged against the wall, laughing. "Oh, thank you," he said, with great feeling. "Thank you. Thank you."

I was not sure if I should feign ignorance. I could hardly acknowledge the sentiment without insulting his cousins, which I did not wish to do. As I have mentioned, I do not dislike the Brougham sisters, even if I found them a bit ridiculous that afternoon.

"Tell me you can ride," he said.

"Of course."

He motioned to the house. "None of them can."

"That's not true," I replied, puzzled. I knew I had seen them on horseback at some point.

"They can sit in a saddle," he said, his eyes flashing with what could only be a dare, "but they cannot ride."

"I see," I murmured. I considered my options and said, "I can."

He looked at me, one corner of his mouth tilted up. His eyes were a rather nice shade of green, mossy with little brown flecks. And again, I got that odd sense of being in accord.

I hope I am not being immodest when I say that there are a few things I do quite well. I can shoot with a pistol (although not with a rifle, and not as well as my mother, who is freakishly good). I can add up sums twice as quickly as Oliver, provided I have pen and paper. I can fish, and I can swim, and above all, I can ride.

"Come with me," I said, motioning toward the stables.

He did, falling into step beside me. "Tell me, Miss Crane," he said, his voice laced with amusement, "with what were you bribed for your presence this afternoon?"

"You think your company was not enough reward?"

"You did not know me," he pointed out.

"True." We turned onto the path toward the stables, and I was happy to feel that the breeze was picking up. "As it happens, I was outmaneuvered by my mother."

"You admit to being outmaneuvered," he murmured. "Interesting."

"You don't know my mother."

"No," he assured me, "I am impressed. Most people would not confess to it."

"As I said, you don't know my mother." I turned to him and smiled. "She is one of eight siblings. Besting her in any sort of devious matter is nothing short of a triumph."

We reached the stables, but I paused before entering. "And what about you, Mr. Farraday?" I asked. "With what were you bribed for your presence this afternoon?"

"I, too, was thwarted," he said. "I was told I'd escape my cousins."

I let out a snort of laughter at that. Inappropriate, yes, but unavoidable.

"They attacked just as I was departing," he told me grimly.

"They are a fierce lot," I said, utterly deadpan.

"I was outnumbered."

"I thought they didn't like you," I said.

"So did I." He planted his hands on his hips. "It was the only reason I consented to the visit."

"What exactly did you do to them when you were children?" I asked.

"The better question would be—what did they do to me?"

I knew better than to claim that he held the upper hand because of his gender. Four girls could easily trounce one boy. I had gone up against Oliver countless times as a child, and although he would never admit it, I bested him more often than not.

"Frogs?" I asked, thinking of my own childhood pranks.

"That was me," he admitted sheepishly.

"Dead fish?"

He didn't speak, but his expression was clearly one of guilt.

"Which one?" I asked, trying to imagine Dulcie's horror.

"All of them."

I sucked in my breath. "At the same time?"

He nodded.

I was impressed. I suppose most ladies would not find such things attractive, but I have always had an unusual sense of humor. "Have you ever done a flour ghosting?" I asked.

His eyebrows rose, and he actually leaned forward. "Tell me more."

And so I told him about my mother, and how Oliver and I had tried to scare her off before she'd married my father. We'd been utter beasts. Truly. Not just mischievous children, but utter and complete blights on the face of humanity. It's a wonder my father hadn't shipped us off to a workhouse. The most memorable of our stunts was when we'd rigged a bucket of flour above her door so that it would dust her when she stepped out into the hall.

Except that we'd filled the bucket quite high, so it was more of a coating than a dusting, and in fact more of a deluge than anything else.

We also hadn't counted on the bucket hitting her on the head.

When I said that my current mother's entry into our lives had saved us all, I meant it quite literally. Oliver and I were so desperate for attention, and our father, as lovely as he is now, had no idea how to manage us.

I told all this to Mr. Farraday. It was the strangest thing. I have no idea why I spoke so long and said so much. I thought it must be that he was an extraordinary listener, except that he later told me that he is not, that in fact he is a dreadful listener and usually interrupts too often.

But he didn't with me. He listened, and I spoke, and then I listened and he spoke, and he told me of his brother Ian, with his angelic good looks and courtly manners. How everyone fawns over him, even though Charles is the elder. How Charles never could manage to hate him, though, because when all was said and done, Ian was a rather fine fellow.

"Do you still want to go for a ride?" I asked, when I noticed that the sun had already begun to dip in the sky. I could not imagine how long we had been standing there, talking and listening, listening and talking.

To my great surprise Charles said no, let's walk instead.

And we did.

It was still warm later that night, and so after supper was done I took myself outside. The sun had sunk below the horizon, but it was not yet completely dark. I sat on the steps of the back patio, facing west so I could watch the last hints of daylight turn from lavender to purple to black.

I love this time of the night.

I sat there for quite some time, long enough so that the stars began to appear, long enough so that I had to hug my arms to my body to ward off the chill. I hadn't brought a shawl. I suppose I hadn't thought I'd be sitting outside for so long. I was just about to head back inside when I heard someone approaching.

It was my father, on his way home from his greenhouse. He was holding a lantern and his hands were dirty. Something about the sight of him made me feel like a child again. He was a big bear of a man, and even before he'd married Eloise, back when he didn't seem to know what to say to his own children, he'd always made me feel safe. He was my father, and he would protect me. He didn't need to say it, I just knew.

"You're out late," he said, sitting beside me. He set his lantern down and brushed his hands against his work trousers, shaking off the loose dirt.

"Just thinking," I replied.

He nodded, then leaned his elbows on his thighs and looked out at the sky. "Any shooting stars tonight?"

I shook my head even though he wasn't facing me. "No."

"Do you need one?"

I smiled to myself. He was asking if I had any wishes to be made. We used to wish on stars together all the time when I was small, but somehow we'd got out of the habit.

"No," I said. I was feeling introspective, thinking about Charles and wondering what it meant that I'd spent the whole of the afternoon with him and now could not wait to see him again tomorrow. But I didn't feel as if I needed any wishes granted. At least, not yet.

"I always have wishes," he remarked.

"You do?" I turned to him, my head tilting to the side as I took in his profile. I know that he'd been terribly unhappy before he'd met my current mother, but that was all well behind him. If ever a man had a happy and fulfilled life, it was he.

"What do you wish for?" I asked.

"The health and happiness of my children, first and foremost."

"That doesn't count," I said, feeling myself smile.

"Oh, you don't think so?" He looked at me, and there was more than a hint of amusement in his eyes. "I assure you, it's the first thing I think about in the morning, and the last before I lay myself down to sleep."

"Really?"

"I have five children, Amanda, and every one of them is healthy and strong. And as far as I know, you're all happy. It's probably dumb luck that you've all turned out so well, but I'm not going to tempt any fates by wishing for something else."

I thought about that for a moment. It had never occurred to me to wish for something I already had. "Is it scary being a parent?" I asked.

"The most terrifying thing in the world."

I don't know what I thought he might say, but it wasn't that. But then I realized—he was speaking to me as an adult. I don't know if he'd ever really done so before. He was still my father, and I was still his daughter, but I'd crossed some mysterious threshold.

It was thrilling and sad at the same time.

We sat together for a few minutes more, pointing out constellations and not saying anything of import. And then, just when I was about to head back inside he said, "Your mother said that you had a gentleman caller this afternoon."

"And four of his female cousins," I quipped.

He looked over at me with arched brows, a silent scolding for making light of the topic.

"Yes," I said. "I did."

"Did you like him?"

"Yes." I felt myself grow a bit light, as if my insides had gone fizzy. "I did."

He digested that, then said, "I'm going to have to get a very large stick."

"What?"

"I used to say to your mother that when you were old enough to be courted, I was going to have to beat away the gentlemen."

There was something almost sweet about that. "Really?"

"Well, not when you were very small. Then you were such a nightmare I despaired of anyone ever wanting you."

"Father!"

He chuckled. "Don't say you don't know it's true."

I couldn't contradict.

"But when you were a bit older, and I started to see the first hints of the woman you would become . . ." He sighed. "Good Lord, if ever being a parent is terrifying . . ."

"And now?"

He thought about that for a moment. "I suppose now I can only hope I raised you well enough to make sensible decisions." He paused. "And of course, if anyone even thinks about mistreating you, I shall still have that stick."

I smiled, then scooted over slightly, so that I could rest my head on his shoulder. "I love you, Father."

"I love you, too, Amanda." He turned and kissed me on the top of my head. "I love you, too."

I did marry Charles, by the way, and my father never once had to brandish a stick. The wedding occurred six months later, after a proper courtship and slightly improper engagement. But I am certainly not going to put into writing any of the events that made the engagement improper.

My mother insisted upon a premarital chat, but this was conducted the night before the wedding, by which time the information was no longer exactly timely, but I did not let on. I did, however, get the impression that she and my father might also have anticipated their marriage vows. I was shocked. Shocked. It seems most unlike them. Now that I have experienced the physical aspects of love, the mere thought of my parents . . .

It is too much to bear.

Charles's family home is in Dorset, rather close to the sea, but as his father is very much alive, we have let a home in Somerset, halfway between his family and mine. He dislikes town as much as I do. He is thinking of beginning a breeding program for horses, and it's the oddest thing, but apparently the breeding of plants and the breeding of animals are not entirely dissimilar. He and my father have become great friends, which is lovely, except that now my father visits quite often.

Our new home is not large and all of the bedrooms are quite near to one another. Charles has devised a new game he calls "See how quiet Amanda can be."

Then he proceeds to do all measure of wicked things to me—all whilst my father sleeps across the hall!

He is a devil, but I adore him. I can't help it. Especially when he . . .

Oh, wait, I wasn't going to put any such things in writing, was I?

Just know that I am smiling very broadly as I remember it.

And that it was *not* covered in my mother's premarital chat.

I suppose I should admit that last night I lost the game. I was not quiet at all.

My father did not say a word. But he departed rather unexpectedly that afternoon, citing some sort of botanical emergency.

I don't know that plants *have* emergencies, but as soon as he left, Charles insisted upon inspecting our roses for whatever it was my father said was wrong with his.

Except that for some reason he wanted to inspect the roses that were already cut and arranged in a vase in our bedroom.

"We're going to play a new game," he whispered in my ear. "See how noisy Amanda can be."

"How do I win?" I asked. "And what is the prize?"

I can be quite competitive, and so can he, but I think it is safe to say that we both won that time.

And the prize was lovely, indeed.

BRIDGERTON

WHEN HE WAS WICKED

For B.B., who kept me company throughout the writing of this book. The best things come to those who wait!

And also for Paul, even though he wanted to call it Love in the Time of Malaria.

Acknowledgments

The author wishes to thank Paul Pottinger, MD, and Philip Yarnell, MD, for their expertise in the fields of, respectively, infectious diseases and neurology.

Part One

March, 1820
London, England

Chapter 1

. . . I wouldn't call it a jolly good time, but it's not as bad as that. There are women, after all, and where there are women, I'm bound to make merry.

—from Michael Stirling to his cousin John, the Earl of Kilmartin, posted from the 52nd Foot Guards during the Napoleonic Wars

In every life there is a turning point. A moment so tremendous, so sharp and clear that one feels as if one's been hit in the chest, all the breath knocked out, and one knows, absolutely *knows* without the merest hint of a shadow of a doubt that one's life will never be the same.

For Michael Stirling, that moment came the first time he laid eyes on Francesca Bridgerton.

After a lifetime of chasing women, of smiling slyly as they chased him, of allowing himself to be caught and then turning the tables until he was the victor, of caressing and kissing and making love to them but never actually allowing his heart to become engaged, he took one look at Francesca Bridgerton and fell so fast and so hard into love it was a wonder he managed to remain standing.

Unfortunately for Michael, however, Francesca's surname was to remain Bridgerton a mere thirty-six hours longer; the occasion of their meeting was, lamentably, a supper celebrating her imminent wedding to his cousin.

Life was ironic that way, Michael liked to think in his more polite moods.

In his less polite moods, he used a different adjective entirely.

And his moods, since falling in love with his first cousin's wife, were not often polite.

Oh, he hid it well. It wouldn't do to be visibly out of sorts. Then some annoyingly perceptive soul might actually take notice, and—God forbid—*inquire* as to his welfare. And while Michael Stirling held a not unsubstantiated pride in his ability to dissemble and deceive (he had, after all, seduced more women than anyone cared to count, and had somehow managed to do it all without ever once being challenged to a duel)— Well, the sodding truth of it was that he'd never been in love before, and if ever there was a time that a man might lose his ability to maintain a façade under direct questioning, this was probably it.

And so he laughed, and was very merry, and he continued to seduce women, trying not to notice that he tended to close his eyes when he had them in bed, and he stopped going to church entirely, because there seemed no point now in even contemplating prayer for his soul. Besides, the parish church near Kilmartin dated to 1432, and the crumbling stones certainly couldn't take a direct strike of lightning.

And if God ever wanted to smite a sinner, he couldn't do better than Michael Stirling.

Michael Stirling, Sinner.

He could see it on a calling card. He'd have had it printed up, even—his was just that sort of black sense of humor—if he weren't convinced it would kill his mother on the spot.

Rake he might be, but there was no need to torture the woman who'd borne him.

Funny how he'd never seen all those other women as a sin. He still didn't. They'd all been willing, of course; you couldn't seduce an unwilling woman, at least not if you took seduction at the true sense of the word and took care not to confuse it with rape. They had to actually want it, and if they didn't—if Michael sensed even a hint of unease, he turned and walked away. His passions were never so out of control that he couldn't manage a quick and decisive departure.

And besides, he'd never seduced a virgin, and he'd never slept with a married woman. Oh very well, one ought to remain true to oneself, even while living a lie—he'd slept with married women, plenty of them, but only the ones whose husbands were rotters, and even then, not unless she'd already produced two male offspring; three, if one of the boys seemed a little sickly.

A man had to have rules of conduct, after all.

But this . . . This was beyond the pale. Entirely unacceptable. This was the one transgression (and he'd had many) that was finally going to blacken his soul, or at the very least—and this was assuming he maintained the strength never to act upon his desires—make it a rather deep shade of charcoal. Because this . . . this—

He coveted his cousin's wife.

He coveted John's wife.

John.

John, who, damn it all, was more of a brother to him than one of his own could ever have been. John, whose family had taken him in when his father had died. John, whose father had raised him and taught him to be a man. John, with whom—

Ah, bloody hell. Did he really need to do this to himself? He could spend a sennight cataloguing all the reasons why he was going straight to hell for having chosen John's wife with whom to fall in love. And none of it was ever going to change one simple fact.

He couldn't have her.

He could never have Francesca Bridgerton Stirling.

But, he thought with a snort as he slouched into the sofa and propped his ankle over his knee, watching them across their drawing room, laughing and smiling, and making nauseating eyes at each other, he *could* have another drink.

"I think I will," he announced, downing it in one gulp.

"What was that, Michael?" John asked, his hearing superb, as always, damn it.

Michael produced an excellent forgery of a smile and lifted his glass aloft. "Just thirsty," he said, maintaining the perfect picture of a bon vivant.

They were at Kilmartin House, in London, as opposed to Kilmartin (no House, no Castle, just Kilmartin), up in Scotland, where the boys had grown up, or the other Kilmartin House, in Edinburgh—not a creative soul among his forbearers, Michael had often reflected; there was also a Kilmartin Cottage (if one could call twenty-two rooms a cottage), Kilmartin Abbey, and, of course, Kilmartin Hall. Michael had no idea why no one had thought to offer their surname to one of the residences; "Stirling House" had a perfectly respectful ring to it, in his opinion. He supposed that the ambitious—and unimaginative—Stirlings of old had been so damned besotted with their newfound earldom that they couldn't think to put any other name on anything.

He snorted into his glass of whisky. It was a wonder he didn't drink Kilmartin Tea and sit on a Kilmartin-style chair. In fact, he probably would be doing just that if his grandmother had found a way to manage it without actually taking the family into trade. The old martinet had been so proud one would have thought she'd been born a Stirling rather than simply married into the name. As far as she'd been concerned, the Countess of Kilmartin (herself) was just as important as any loftier personage, and she'd more than once sniffed her displeasure when being led into supper after an upstart marchioness or duchess.

The Queen, Michael thought dispassionately. He supposed his grandmother had knelt before the Queen, but he certainly couldn't imagine her offering deference to any other female.

She would have approved of Francesca Bridgerton. Grandmother Stirling would surely have turned her nose up upon learning that Francesca's father was a mere viscount, but the Bridgertons were an old and immensely popular—and, when the fancy took them, powerful—family. Plus, Francesca's spine was straight and her manner was proud, and her sense of humor was sly and subversive. If she'd been fifty years older and not nearly so attractive, she would have made quite a fine companion for Grandmother Stirling.

And now Francesca was the Countess of Kilmartin, married to his cousin John, who was one year his junior but in the Stirling household always treated with the deference due the elder; he was the heir, after all. Their fathers had been twins, but John's had entered the world seven minutes before Michael's.

The most critical seven minutes in Michael Stirling's life, and he hadn't even been alive for them.

"What shall we do for our second anniversary?" Francesca asked as she crossed the room and seated herself at the pianoforte.

"Whatever you want," John answered.

Francesca turned to Michael, her eyes startlingly blue, even in the candlelight. Or maybe it was just that he knew how blue they were. He seemed to dream in blue these days. Francesca blue, the color ought to be called.

"Michael?" she said, her tone indicating that the word was a repetition.

"Sorry," he said, offering her the lopsided smile he so frequently affixed to his face. No one ever took him seriously when he smiled like that, which was, of course, the point. "Wasn't listening."

"Do you have any ideas?" she asked.

"For what?"

"For our anniversary."

If she'd had an arrow, she couldn't have jammed it into his heart any harder. But he just shrugged, since he was appallingly good at faking it. "It's not my anniversary," he reminded her.

"I know," she said. He wasn't looking at her, but she sounded like she rolled her eyes.

But she hadn't. Michael was certain of that. He'd come to know Francesca agonizingly well in the past two years, and he knew she didn't roll her eyes. When she was feeling sarcastic, or ironic, or sly, it was all there in her voice and the curious tip of her mouth. She didn't need to roll her eyes. She just looked at you with that direct stare, her lips curving ever so slightly, and—

Michael swallowed reflexively, then covered it with a sip of his drink. It didn't really speak well of him that he'd spent so much time analyzing the curve of his cousin's wife's lips.

"I assure you," Francesca continued, idly trailing the pads of her fingertips along the surface of the piano keys without actually pressing any into sound, "I'm well aware of whom I married."

"I'm sure you are," he muttered.

"Beg pardon?"

"Continue," he said.

Her lips pursed in a peevish crease. He'd seen her with that expression quite frequently, usually in her dealings with her brothers. "I was asking your advice," she said, "because you are so often merry."

"I'm so often merry?" he repeated, knowing that was how the world saw him—they called him the Merry Rake, after all—but hating the word on her lips. It made him feel frivolous, without substance.

And then he felt even worse, because it was probably true.

"You disagree?" she inquired.

"Of course not," he murmured. "I'm simply unused to being asked for advice regarding anniversary celebrations, as it is clear I have no talent for marriage."

"That's not clear at all," she said.

"You're in for it now," John said with a chuckle, settling back in his seat with that morning's copy of the *Times*.

"You have never tried marriage," Francesca pointed out. "How could you possibly know you have no talent for it?"

Michael managed a smirk. "I think it's fairly clear to all who know me. Besides, what need have I? I have no title, no property—"

"You have property," John interjected, demonstrating that he was still listening from behind his newspaper.

"Only a small bit of property," Michael corrected, "which I am more than happy to leave for your children, since it was given to me by John, anyway."

Francesca looked at her husband, and Michael knew exactly what she was thinking—that John had given him the property because John wanted him to feel he had something, a purpose, really. Michael had been at loose ends since decommissioning from the army several years back. And although John had never said so, Michael knew that he felt guilty for having not fought for England on the Continent, for remaining behind while Michael faced danger alone.

But John had been heir to an earldom. He had a duty to marry, be fruitful and multiply. No one had expected him to go to war.

Michael had often wondered if the property—a rather lovely and comfortable manor house with twenty acres—was John's form of penance. And he rather suspected that Francesca wondered the same.

But she would never ask. Francesca understood men with remarkable clarity—probably from growing up with all of those brothers. Francesca knew exactly what not to ask a man.

Which always left Michael a little worried. He thought he hid his feelings well, but what if she *knew*? She would never speak of it, of course, never even allude to it. He rather suspected they were, ironically, alike that way; if Francesca suspected he was in love with her, she would *never* alter her manner in any way.

"I think you should go to Kilmartin," Michael said abruptly.

"To Scotland?" Francesca asked, pressing gently against B-flat on the pianoforte. "With the season so close?"

Michael stood, suddenly rather eager to depart. He shouldn't have come over in any case. "Why not?" he asked, his tone careless. "You love it there. John loves it there. It's not such a long journey if your carriage is well sprung."

"Will you come?" John asked.

"I think not," Michael said sharply. As if he cared to witness their anniversary celebration. Truly, all it would do was remind him of what he could never have. Which would then remind him of the guilt. Or amplify it. Reminders were rather unnecessary; he lived with it every day.

Thou Shalt Not Covet Thy Cousin's Wife.

Moses must have forgotten to write that one down.

"I have much to do here," Michael said.

"You do?" Francesca asked, her eyes lighting with interest. "What?"

"Oh, you know," he said wryly, "all those things I have to do to prepare for a life of dissolution and aimlessness."

Francesca stood.

Oh God, she stood, and she was walking to him. This was the worst—when she actually touched him.

She laid her hand on his upper arm. Michael did his best not to flinch.

"I wish you wouldn't speak that way," she said.

Michael looked past her shoulder to John, who had raised his newspaper just high enough so that he could pretend he wasn't listening.

"Am I to become your project, then?" Michael asked, a bit unkindly.

She drew back. "We care about you."

We. *We.* Not *I*, not *John.* We. A subtle reminder that they were a unit. John and Francesca. Lord and Lady Kilmartin. She hadn't meant it that way, of course, but it was how he heard it all the same.

"And I care for you," Michael said, waiting for a plague of locusts to stream through the room.

"I know," she said, oblivious to his distress. "I could never ask for a better cousin. But I want you to be happy."

Michael glanced over at John, giving him a look that clearly said: *Save me.*

John gave up his pretense of reading and set the paper down. "Francesca, darling, Michael is a grown man. He'll find his happiness as he sees fit. *When* he sees fit."

Francesca's lips pursed, and Michael could tell she was irritated.

She didn't like to be thwarted, and she certainly did not enjoy admitting that she might not be able to arrange her world—and the people inhabiting it—to her satisfaction.

"I should introduce you to my sister," she said.

Good God. "I've met your sister," Michael said quickly. "All of them, in fact. Even the one still in leading strings."

"She's not in—" She cut herself off, grinding her teeth together. "I grant you that Hyacinth is not suitable, but Eloise is—"

"I'm not marrying Eloise," Michael said sharply.

"I didn't say you had to marry her," Francesca said. "Just dance with her once or twice."

"I've done so," he reminded her. "And that is all I am going to do."

"But—"

"Francesca," John said. His voice was gentle, but his meaning was clear. *Stop.*

Michael could have kissed him for his interference. John of course just thought that he was saving his cousin from needless feminine nagging; there was no way he could know the truth—that Michael was trying to compute the level of guilt one might feel for being in love with one's cousin's wife *and* one's wife's sister.

Good God, married to Eloise Bridgerton. Was Francesca trying to *kill* him?

"We should all go for a walk," Francesca said suddenly.

Michael glanced out the window. All vestiges of daylight had left the sky. "Isn't it a bit late for that?" he asked.

"Not with two strong men as escorts," she said, "and besides, the streets in Mayfair are well lit. We shall be perfectly safe." She turned to her husband. "What do you say, darling?"

"I have an appointment this evening," John said, consulting his pocket watch, "but you should go with Michael."

More proof that John had no idea of Michael's feelings.

"The two of you always have such a fine time together," John added.

Francesca turned to Michael and smiled, worming her way another inch into his heart. "Will you?" she asked. "I'm desperate for a spot of fresh air now that the rain has stopped. And I've been feeling rather odd all day, I must say."

"Of course," Michael replied, since they all knew that he had no appointments. His was a life of carefully cultivated dissolution.

Besides, he couldn't resist her. He knew he should stay away, knew he should never allow himself to be alone in her company. He would never act upon his desires, but truly, did he really need to subject himself to this sort of agony? He'd just end the day alone in bed, wracked by guilt and desire, in almost equal measures.

But when she smiled at him he couldn't say no. And he certainly wasn't strong enough to deny himself an hour in her presence.

Because her presence was all he was ever going to get. There would never be a kiss, never a meaningful glance or touch. There would be no whispered words of love, no moans of passion.

All he could have was her smile and her company, and pathetic idiot that he was, he was willing to take it.

"Just give me a moment," she said, pausing in the doorway. "I need to get my coat."

"Be quick about it," John said. "It's already after seven."

"I'll be safe enough with Michael to protect me," she said with a jaunty smile, "but don't worry, I'll be quick." And then she offered her husband a wicked smile. "I'm always quick."

Michael averted his eyes as his cousin actually blushed. Lord above, but he *truly* did not want to know the meaning behind *I'll be quick*. Unfortunately, it could have been any number of things, all of them deliciously sexual. And he was likely to spend the next hour cataloguing them all in his mind, imagining them being done to him.

He tugged at his cravat. Maybe he could get out of this jaunt with Francesca. Maybe he could go home and draw a cold bath. Or better yet, find himself a willing woman with long chestnut hair. And if he was lucky, blue eyes as well.

"I'm sorry about that," John said, once Francesca had left.

Michael's eyes flew to his face. Surely John would never mention Francesca's innuendo.

"Her nagging," John added. "You're young enough. You don't need to be married yet."

"You're younger than I," Michael said, mostly to be contrary.

"Yes, but I met Francesca." John shrugged helplessly, as if that ought to be explanation enough. And of course it was.

"I don't mind her nagging," Michael said.

"Of course you do. I can see it in your eyes."

And that was the problem. John *could* see it in his eyes. There was no one in the world who knew him better. If something was bothering him, John would always be able to tell. The miracle was that John didn't realize *why* Michael was distressed.

"I will tell her to leave you alone," John said, "although you should know that she only nags because she loves you."

Michael managed a tight smile. He certainly couldn't manage words.

"Thank you for taking her for a walk," John said, standing up. "She's been a bit peckish all day, with the rain. Said she's been feeling uncommonly closed in."

"When is your appointment?" Michael asked.

"Nine o'clock," John replied as they walked out into the hall. "I'm meeting Lord Liverpool."

"Parliamentary business?"

John nodded. He took his position in the House of Lords very seriously. Michael had often wondered if he'd have approached the duty with as much gravity, had he been born a lord.

Probably not. But then again, it didn't much matter, did it?

Michael watched as John rubbed his left temple. "Are you all right?" he asked. "You look a little . . ." He didn't finish the sentence, since he wasn't quite certain how John looked. Not right. That was all he knew.

And he knew John. Inside and out. Probably better than Francesca did.

"Devil of a headache," John muttered. "I've had it all day."

"Do you want me to call for some laudanum?"

John shook his head. "Hate the stuff. It makes my mind fuzzy, and I need my wits about me for the meeting with Liverpool."

Michael nodded. "You look pale," he said. Why, he didn't know. It wasn't as if it was going to change John's mind about the laudanum.

"Do I?" John asked, wincing as he pressed his fingers harder into the skin of his temple. "I think I'll lie down, if you don't mind. I don't need to leave for an hour."

"Right," Michael murmured. "Do you want me to have someone wake you?"

John shook his head. "I'll ask my valet myself."

Just then, Francesca descended the stairs, wrapped in a long velvet cloak of midnight blue. "Good evening, gentlemen," she said, clearly basking in the undivided male attention. But as she reached the bottom, she frowned. "Is something wrong, darling?" she asked John.

"Just a headache," John said. "It's nothing."

"You should lie down," she said.

John managed a smile. "I'd just finished telling Michael that I was planning to do that very thing. I'll have Simons wake me in time for my meeting."

"With Lord Liverpool?" Francesca queried.

"Yes. At nine."

"Is it about the Six Acts?"

John nodded. "Yes, and the return to the gold standard. I told you about it at breakfast, if you recall."

"Make sure you—" She stopped, smiling as she shook her head. "Well, you know how I feel."

John smiled, then leaned down and dropped a tender kiss on her lips. "I always know how you feel, darling."

Michael pretended to look the other way.

"Not always," she said, her voice warm and teasing.

"Always when it matters," John said.

"Well, *that* is true," she admitted. "So much for my attempts to be a lady of mystery."

He kissed her again. "I prefer you as an open book, myself."

Michael cleared his throat. This shouldn't be so difficult; it wasn't as if John and Francesca were acting any differently than was normal. They were, as so much of society had commented, like two peas in a pod, marvelously in accord, and splendidly in love.

"It's growing late," Francesca said. "I should go if I want that spot of fresh air."

John nodded, closing his eyes for a moment.

"Are you sure you're well?"

"I'm fine," he said. "Just a headache."

Francesca looped her hand into the crook of Michael's elbow. "Be sure to take some laudanum when you return from your meeting," she said over her shoulder, once they'd reached the door, "since I know you won't do it now."

John nodded, his expression weary, then headed up the stairs.

"Poor John," Francesca said, stepping outside into the brisk night air. She took a deep inhale, then let out a sigh. "I detest headaches. They always seem to lay me especially low."

"Never get them myself," Michael admitted, leading her down the steps to the pavement.

"Really?" She looked up at him, one corner of her mouth quirking in that achingly familiar way. "Lucky you."

It almost made Michael laugh. Here he was, strolling through the night with the woman he loved.

Lucky him.

Chapter 2

. . . and if it were as bad as that, I suspect you would not tell me. As for the women, do at least try to make sure they are clean and free of disease. Beyond that, do what you must to make your time bearable. And please, try not to get yourself killed. At the risk of sounding maudlin, I don't know what I would do without you.

—from the Earl of Kilmartin to his cousin Michael Stirling, sent in care of the 52nd Foot Guards during the Napoleonic Wars

For all his faults—and Francesca was willing to allow that Michael Stirling had many—he really was the *dearest* man.

He was a horrible flirt (she'd seen him in action, and even she had to admit that otherwise intelligent women lost all measure of sense when he chose to be charming), and he certainly didn't approach his life with the gravity that she and John would have liked him to, but even with all that, she couldn't help but love him.

He was the best friend John had ever had—until he'd married

her, of course—and over the last two years, he'd become her close confidant as well.

It was a funny thing, that. Who would have thought she'd have counted a man as one of her closest friends? She was not uncomfortable around men; four brothers tended to wring the delicacy out of even the most feminine of creatures. But she was not like her sisters. Daphne and Eloise—and Hyacinth, too, she supposed, although she was still a bit young to know for sure—were so open and sunny. They were the sorts of females who excelled at hunting and shooting—the kinds of pursuits that tended to get them labeled as "jolly good sports." Men always felt comfortable in their presence, and the feeling was, Francesca had observed, entirely mutual.

But she was different. She'd always felt a little different from the rest of her family. She loved them fiercely, and would have laid down her life for any one of them, but even though she looked like a Bridgerton, on the inside she always felt like a bit of a changeling.

Where the rest of her family was outgoing, she was . . . not shy, precisely, but a bit more reserved, more careful with her words. She'd developed a reputation for irony and wit, and she had to admit, she could rarely resist the opportunity to needle her siblings with a dry remark. It was done out of love, of course, and perhaps a touch of the desperation that comes from having spent far too much time with one's family, but they teased Francesca right back, so all was fair.

It was the way of her family. They laughed, they teased, they bickered. Francesca's contributions to the din were simply a touch quieter than the rest, a bit more sly and subversive.

She often wondered if part of her attraction to John had been the simple fact that he removed her from the chaos that was so often the Bridgerton household. Not that she didn't love him; she did. She adored him with every last breath in her body. He was her kindred spirit, so like her in so many ways. But it had, in a strange sort of fashion, been a relief to exit her mother's home, to escape to a more serene existence with John, whose sense of humor was precisely like hers.

He understood her, he anticipated her.

He completed her.

It had been the oddest sensation when she'd met him, almost as if she were a jagged puzzle piece finally finding its mate. Their first meeting hadn't been one of overwhelming love or passion, but rather filled with the most bizarre sense that she'd finally found the one person with whom she could completely be herself.

It had been instant. It had been sudden. She couldn't remember just what it was he'd said to her, but from the moment words first left his lips, she had felt at home.

And with him had come Michael, his cousin—although truth be told, the two men were much more like brothers. They'd been raised together, and they were so close in age that they'd shared everything.

Well, almost everything. John was the heir to an earldom, and Michael was just his cousin, and so it was only natural that the two boys would not be treated quite the same. But from what Francesca had heard, and from what she knew of the Stirling family now, they had been loved in equal measure, and she rather thought that was the key to Michael's good humor.

Because even though John had inherited the title and the wealth, and well, everything, Michael didn't seem to envy him.

He didn't envy him. It was amazing to her. He'd been raised as John's brother—John's older brother, even—and yet he'd never once begrudged John any of his blessings.

And it was for that reason that Francesca loved him best.

Michael would surely scoff if she tried to praise him for it, and she was quite certain that he would point to his many misdeeds (none of which, she feared, were exaggerated) to prove that his soul was black and he was a scoundrel through and through—but the truth of the matter was that Michael Stirling possessed a generosity of spirit and a capability for love that was unmatched among men.

And if she didn't find a wife for him soon, she was going to go mad.

"What," she said, aware that her voice was quite suddenly piercing the silence of the night, "is wrong with my sister?"

"Francesca," he said, and she could hear irritation—and, thankfully, a bit of amusement as well—in his voice, "I'm not going to marry your sister."

"I didn't say you had to marry her."

"You didn't have to. Your face is an open book."

She looked up at him, twisting her lips. "You weren't even looking at me."

"Of course I was, and anyway, it wouldn't matter if I weren't. I know what you're about."

He was right, and it scared her. Sometimes she worried that he understood her as well as John did.

"You need a wife," she said.

"Didn't you just promise your husband that you would stop pestering me about this?"

"I did not, actually," she said, giving him a rather superior glance. "He asked, of course—"

"Of course," Michael muttered.

She laughed. He could always make her laugh.

"I thought wives were supposed to accede to their husbands' wishes," Michael said, quirking his right brow. "In fact, I'm quite certain it's right there in the marriage vows."

"I'd be doing you a grave disservice if I found you a wife like *that*," she said, punctuating the sentiment with a well-timed and extremely disdainful snort.

He turned and gazed down at her with a vaguely paternalistic expression. He should have been a nobleman, Francesca thought. He was far too irresponsible for the duties of a title, but when he looked at a person like that, all superciliousness and certitude, he might as well have been a royal duke.

"Your responsibilities as Countess of Kilmartin do not include finding me a wife," he said.

"They should."

He laughed, which delighted her. She could always make him laugh.

"Very well," she said, giving up for now. "Tell me about something wicked, then. Something John would not approve of."

It was a game they played, even in John's presence, although John always made at least the pretense of discouraging them. But Francesca suspected that John enjoyed Michael's tales as much as she did. Once he'd finished with his obligatory admonitions, he was always all ears.

Not that Michael ever told them much. He was far too discreet for that. But he dropped hints and innuendo, and Francesca and John were always thoroughly entertained. They wouldn't trade their wedded bliss for anything, but who didn't like to be regaled with tales of debauchery and spice?

"I'm afraid I've done nothing wicked this week," Michael said, steering her around the corner to King Street.

"You? Impossible."

"It's only Tuesday," he reminded her.

"Yes, but not counting Sunday, which I'm sure you would not desecrate"—she shot him a look that said she was quite certain he'd already sinned in every way possible, Sunday or no—"that does leave you Monday, and a man can do quite a bit on a Monday."

"Not this man. Not this Monday."

"What did you do, then?"

He thought about that, then said, "Nothing, really."

"That's impossible," she teased. "I'm quite certain I saw you awake for at least an hour."

He didn't say anything, and then he shrugged in a way she found oddly disturbing and said, "I did nothing. I walked, I spoke, I ate, but at the end of the day, there was nothing."

Francesca impulsively squeezed his arm. "We shall have to find you something," she said softly.

He turned and looked at her, his strange, silvery eyes catching hers with an intensity she knew he didn't often allow to rise to the fore.

And then it was gone, and he was himself again, except she suspected that Michael Stirling wasn't at all the man he wished people to believe him to be.

Even, sometimes, her.

"We should return home," he said. "It's growing late, and John will have my head if I let you catch a chill."

"John would blame *me* for my foolishness, and well you know it," Francesca said. "This is just your way of telling me you have a woman waiting for you, probably draped in nothing but the sheets on her bed."

He turned to her and grinned. It was wicked and devilish, and she understood why half the *ton*—the female half, that was—fancied themselves in love with him, even with no title or fortune to his name.

"You said you wanted something wicked, didn't you?" he asked. "Did you want more detail? The color of the sheets, perhaps?"

She blushed, drat it all. She *hated* that she blushed, but at least the reaction was covered by the night. "Not yellow, I hope," she said, because she couldn't bear to let the conversation end on her embarrassment. "It makes you look sallow."

"I won't be wearing the sheets," he drawled.

"Nevertheless."

He chuckled, and she knew that he knew that she'd said it just to have the last word. And she thought he was going to allow her the small victory, but then, just when she was beginning to find relief in the silence, he said, "Red."

"I beg your pardon?" But of course she knew what he meant.

"Red sheets, I think."

"I can't believe you told me that."

"You asked, Francesca Stirling." He looked down at her, and one lock of midnight black hair fell onto his forehead. "You're just lucky I don't tell your husband on you."

"John would never worry over me," she said.

For a moment she didn't think he would reply, but then he said, "I know," and his voice was oddly grave and serious. "It's the only reason I tease you."

She'd been watching the pavement, looking for rough spots, but his tone was so serious she had to look up.

"You're the only woman I know who would never stray," he said, touching her chin. "You have no idea how much I admire you for that."

"I love your cousin," she whispered. "I would never betray him."

He brought his hand back to his side. "I know."

He looked so handsome in the moonlight, and so unbearably in need of love, that her heart nearly broke. Surely there was no woman who could resist him, not with that perfect face and tall, muscular body. And anyone who took the time to explore what was underneath would come to know him as she did—as a kind-hearted man, loyal and true.

With a hint of the devil, of course, but Francesca supposed that was what would attract the ladies in the first place.

"Shall we?" Michael said, suddenly all charm. He tilted his head back in the direction of home, and she sighed and turned around.

"Thank you for taking me out," she said, after a few minutes of companionable silence. "I wasn't exaggerating when I said I was going mad with the rain."

"You didn't say that," he said, immediately giving himself a mental kick. She'd said that she'd been feeling a bit odd, not that she'd been going mad, but only an idiot savant or a lovesick fool would have noticed the difference.

"Didn't I?" She scrunched her brow together. "Well, I was certainly thinking it. I've been rather sluggish, if you must know. The fresh air did me a great deal of good."

"Then I'm happy to have helped," he said gallantly.

She smiled as they ascended the front steps to Kilmartin House. The door opened as their feet touched the top stair—the butler must have been watching for them—and then Michael waited as Francesca was divested of her cloak in the front hall.

"Will you stay for another drink, or must you leave immediately for your appointment?" she inquired, her eyes glinting with the devil.

He glanced at the clock at the end of the hall. It was half eight, and while he had no place to be—there was no lady waiting for him, although he could certainly find one at the drop of a hat, and he rather thought he would—he didn't much feel like remaining here at Kilmartin House.

"I must go," he said. "I've much to do."

"You've nothing to do, and you know it," she said. "You just wish to be wicked."

"It's an admirable pastime," he murmured.

She opened her mouth to offer a retort, but just then Simons, John's recently hired valet, came down the stairs.

"My lady?" he inquired.

Francesca turned to him and inclined her head, indicating that he should proceed.

"I've rapped on his lordship's door and called his name—twice—but he seems to be sleeping quite soundly. Do you still wish me to wake him?"

Francesca nodded. "Yes. I'd love to let him sleep. He's been working so hard lately"—she directed this last bit at Michael—"but I know that this meeting with Lord Liverpool is very important. You should— No, wait, I'll rouse him myself. It will be better that way."

She turned to Michael. "I shall see you tomorrow?"

"Actually, if John hasn't yet left, I'll wait," he replied. "I came on foot, so I might as well avail myself of his carriage once he's done with it."

She nodded and hurried up the stairs, leaving Michael with nothing to do but hum under his breath as he idly examined the paintings in the hall.

And then she screamed.

Michael had no recollection of running up the stairs, but somehow there he was, in John and Francesca's bedchamber, the one room in the house he never invaded.

"Francesca?" he gasped. "Frannie, Frannie, what is—"

She was sitting next to the bed, clutching John's forearm, which was dangling over the side. "Wake him up, Michael," she cried. "Wake him up. Do it for me. Wake him up!"

Michael felt his world slip away. The bed was across the room, a good twelve feet away, but he *knew.*

No one knew John as well as he did. No one.

And John wasn't there in the room. He was gone. What was on the bed—

It wasn't John.

"Francesca," he whispered, moving slowly toward her. His limbs felt strange and funny and gruesomely sluggish. "Francesca."

She looked up at him with huge, stricken eyes. "Wake him up, Michael."

"Francesca, I—"

"Now!" she screamed, launching herself at him. "Wake him up! You can do it. Wake him up! Wake him up!"

And all he could do was stand there as she beat her fists against his chest, stand there as she grabbed his cravat and shook and yanked until he was gasping for breath. He couldn't even embrace her, couldn't offer her comfort, because he was every bit as devastated and confused.

And then suddenly the fire left her, and she collapsed in his arms, her tears soaking his shirt. "He had a headache," she whimpered. "That's all. He just had a headache. It was just a headache." She looked up at him, her eyes searching his face, looking for answers he'd never be able to give her. "It was just a headache," she said again.

And she looked broken.

"I know," he said, even though he knew it wasn't enough.

"Oh, Michael," she sobbed. "What am I to do?"

"I don't know," he said, because he didn't. Between Eton, Cambridge, and the army, he'd been trained for everything that the life of an English gentleman was supposed to offer. But he hadn't been trained for *this*.

"I don't understand," she was saying, and he supposed she was saying a lot of things, but none of it made any sense to his ears. He didn't even have the strength to stand, and together the two of them sank to the carpet, leaning against the side of the bed.

He stared sightlessly at the far wall, wondering why he wasn't crying. He was numb, and his body felt heavy, and he couldn't shake the feeling that his very soul had been ripped from his body.

Not John.

Why?

Why?

And as he sat there, dimly aware of the servants gathering just outside the open door, it occurred to him that Francesca was whimpering those very same words.

"Not John.

"Why?

"*Why*?"

"Do you think she might be with child?"

Michael stared at Lord Winston, a new and apparently over-eager appointee to the Committee for Privileges of the House of Lords, trying to make sense of his words. John had been dead barely a day. It was still hard to make sense of anything. And now here was this puffy little man, demanding an audience, prattling on about some sacred duty to the crown.

"Her ladyship," Lord Winston said. "If she's carrying, it will complicate everything."

"I don't know," Michael said. "I didn't ask her."

"You need to. I'm sure you're eager to assume control of your new holdings, but we really must determine if she's carrying. Furthermore, if she *is* pregnant, a member of our committee will need to be present at the birth."

Michael felt his face go slack. "I beg your pardon?" he somehow managed to say.

"Baby switching," Lord Winston said grimly. "There have been instances—"

"For God's sake—"

"It's for your protection as much as anyone's," Lord Winston cut in. "If her ladyship gives birth to a girl, and there is no one present to witness it, what is to stop her from switching the babe with a boy?"

Michael couldn't even bring himself to dignify this with an answer.

"You need to find out if she is carrying," Lord Winston pressed. "Arrangements will need to be made."

"She was widowed yesterday," Michael said sharply. "I will not burden her with such intrusive questions."

"There is more at stake here than her ladyship's feelings," Lord Winston returned. "We cannot properly transfer the earldom while there is doubt as to the succession."

"The devil take the earldom," Michael snapped.

Lord Winston gasped, drawing back in visible horror. "You forget yourself, my lord."

"I'm not your lord," Michael bit off. "I'm not anyone's—" He halted his words, sinking into a chair, trying very hard to get past the fact that he was perilously close to tears. Right here, in John's study, with this damnable little man who didn't seem to understand that a man had died, not just an earl, but a man, Michael wanted to cry.

And he would, he suspected. As soon as Lord Winston left, and

Michael could lock the door and make sure that no one could see him, he would probably bury his face in his hands and cry.

"Someone has to ask her," Lord Winston said.

"It won't be me," Michael said in a low voice.

"I will do it, then."

Michael leapt from his seat and pinned Lord Winston against the wall. "You will not approach Lady Kilmartin," he growled. "You will not even breathe the same air. Do I make myself clear?"

"Quite," the smaller man gurgled.

Michael let go, dimly aware that Lord Winston's face was beginning to turn purple. "Get out," he said.

"You will need—"

"Get out!" he roared.

"I will come back tomorrow," Lord Winston said, skittering out the door. "We will speak when you are in a calmer frame of mind."

Michael leaned against the wall, staring at the open doorway. Good God, how had it all come to this? John hadn't even been thirty. He was the picture of health. Michael might have been second in line for the earldom as long as John and Francesca's marriage remained childless, but no one had truly thought he'd ever inherit.

Already he'd heard that men in the clubs were calling him the luckiest man in Britain. Overnight, he'd gone from the fringe of aristocracy to its very epicenter. No one seemed to understand that Michael had never wanted this. Never.

He didn't want an earldom. He wanted his cousin back. And no one seemed to understand that.

Except, perhaps, Francesca, but she was so wrapped in her own grief that she could not quite comprehend the pain in Michael's heart.

And he would never ask her to. Not when she was so wrecked by her own.

Michael wrapped his arms against his chest as he thought of her. For the rest of his life, he would not forget the sight of Francesca's face once the truth had finally sunk in. John was not sleeping. He was not going to wake up.

And Francesca Bridgerton Stirling was, at the tender age of two and twenty, the saddest thing imaginable.

Alone.

Michael understood her despair better than anyone could ever imagine.

They'd put her to bed that night, he and her mother, who had hurried over at Michael's urgent summons. And she'd slept like a baby, with nary even a whimper, her body worn out from the shock of it all.

But when she'd awakened the next morning, she'd acquired the proverbial stiff upper lip, determined to remain strong and steadfast, handling the myriad details that had showered down upon the house at John's death.

The problem was, neither one of them had a clue what those details were. They were young; they had been carefree. They had never thought to deal with death.

Who knew, for example, that the Committee for Privileges would get involved? And demand a box seat at what ought to be a private moment for Francesca?

If indeed she was even carrying.

But bloody hell, *he* wasn't going to ask her.

"We need to tell his mother," Francesca had said earlier that morning. It was the first thing she'd said, actually. There was no preamble, no greeting, just, "We need to tell his mother."

Michael had nodded, since of course she was right.

"We need to tell your mother, too. They're both in Scotland; they won't know yet."

He nodded again. It was all he could manage.

"I'll write the notes."

And he nodded a third time, wondering what *he* was supposed to do.

That question had been answered when Lord Winston had come to call, but Michael couldn't bear to think about all that now. It seemed so distasteful. He didn't want to think of all he would gain at John's death. How could anyone possibly speak as if something *good* had come of all this?

Michael felt himself sinking down, down, sliding against the wall until he was sitting on the floor, his legs bent in front of him, his head resting on his knees. He hadn't wanted this. Had he?

He'd wanted Francesca. That was all. But not like this. Not at this cost.

He'd never begrudged John his good fortune. He'd never coveted the title, the money, or the power.

He'd merely coveted his wife.

Now he was meant to assume John's title, step into his shoes. And guilt was squeezing its merciless fist right around his heart.

Had he somehow wished for this? No, he couldn't have. He hadn't.

Had he?

"Michael?"

He looked up. It was Francesca, still wearing that hollow look, her face a blank mask that tore at his heart far more than her wailing sorrow ever could have done.

"I sent for Janet."

He nodded. John's mother. She would be devastated.

"And your mother as well."

She would be equally bereft.

"Is there anyone else you think—"

He shook his head, aware that he should get up, aware that propriety dictated that he rise, but he just couldn't find the strength. He didn't want Francesca to see him so weak, but he couldn't help it.

"You should sit down," he finally said. "You need to rest."

"I can't," she said. "I need to . . . If I stop, even for a moment, I will . . ."

Her words trailed off, but it didn't matter. He understood.

He looked up at her. Her chestnut hair was pulled back into a simple queue, and her face was pale. She looked young, barely out of the schoolroom, certainly too young for this sort of heartbreak.

"Francesca," he said, his word not quite a question, more of a sigh, really.

And then she said it. She said it without his having to ask.

"I'm pregnant."

Chapter 3

. . . I love him madly. Madly! Truly, I would die without him.

—from the Countess of Kilmartin to her sister Eloise Bridgerton, one week after Francesca's wedding

"I declare, Francesca, you are the healthiest expectant mother I have ever laid eyes upon."

Francesca smiled at her mother-in-law, who had just entered the garden of the St. James's mansion they now shared. Overnight, it seemed, Kilmartin House had become a household of women. First Janet had taken up residence, and then Helen, Michael's mother. It was a house full of Stirling females, or at least those who had acquired the name in marriage.

And it all felt so different.

It was strange. She would have thought that she'd sense John's presence, feel him in the air, see him in the surroundings they'd shared for two years. But instead, he was simply gone, and the influx of women had changed the tone of the house entirely. Francesca supposed that was a good thing; she needed the support of women right now.

But it was odd, living among women. There were more flowers now—vases everywhere, it seemed. And there was no longer any lingering smell of John's cheroot, or the sandalwood soap he'd favored.

Kilmartin House now smelled of lavender and rosewater, and every whiff of it broke Francesca's heart.

Even Michael had been strangely distant. Oh, he came to call—several times a week, if one cared to count, which Francesca had to admit she did. But he wasn't *there*, not in the way he had been before John's death. He wasn't the same, and she supposed she ought not to castigate him for that, even if only in her mind.

He was hurting, too.

She knew that. She reminded herself of it when she saw him, and his eyes were distant. She reminded herself of it when she didn't know what to say to him, and when he didn't tease her.

And she reminded herself of it when they sat together in the drawing room and had nothing to say.

She'd lost John, and now it seemed she'd lost Michael, too. And even with two mother hens fussing over her—three, if she counted her own, who came to call every single day—she was so lonely.

And sad.

No one had ever told her how sad she'd be. Who would have *thought* to tell her? And even if someone had, even if her mother, who had also been widowed young, had explained the pain, how could she have understood?

It was one of those things that had to be experienced to be understood. And oh, how Francesca wished she didn't belong to this melancholy club.

And where was Michael? Why couldn't he comfort her? Why didn't he realize how very much she needed him? Him, not his mother. Not anyone's mother.

She needed Michael, the one person who had known John the way she had, the only person who had loved him as fully. Michael was her one link to the husband she had lost, and she hated him for staying away.

Even when he was here at Kilmartin House, in the same dashed room as her, it wasn't the same. They didn't joke, and they didn't tease. They just sat there and looked sad and grief stricken, and when they spoke, there was an awkwardness that had never been there before.

Couldn't *anything* remain as it was before John had died? It had never occurred to her that her friendship with Michael might be killed off as well.

"How are you feeling, dear?"

Francesca looked up at Janet, belatedly realizing that her mother-in-law had asked her a question. Several, probably, and she'd forgotten to answer, lost in her own thoughts. She did that a lot lately.

"Fine," she said. "No different than I ever have done."

Janet shook her head in wonder. "It's remarkable. I've never heard of such a thing."

Francesca shrugged. "If it weren't for the loss of my courses, I'd never know anything was different."

And it was true. She wasn't sick, she wasn't hungry, she wasn't anything. A trifle more tired than usual, she supposed, but that could be the grief as well. Her mother told her that she'd been tired for a year after her father had died.

Of course her mother had had eight children to look after.

Francesca just had herself, with a small army of servants treating her like an invalid queen.

"You're very fortunate," Janet said, sitting down on the chair opposite Francesca's. "When I was carrying John, I was sick every single morning. And most afternoons as well."

Francesca nodded and smiled. Janet had told this to her before, several times. John's death had turned his mother into a magpie, constantly chattering on, trying to fill the silence that was Francesca's grief. Francesca adored her for it, for trying, but she suspected the only thing that would assuage her pain was time.

"I'm so pleased you're carrying," Janet said, leaning forward and impulsively squeezing Francesca's hand. "It makes it all a bit more bearable. Or I suppose a bit less unbearable," she added, not really smiling, but looking like she was trying to.

Francesca just nodded, afraid that speaking would loosen the tears in her eyes.

"I'd always wanted more children," Janet confessed. "But it wasn't to be. And when John died, I— Well, let's just say that no grandchild shall ever be loved more than the one you're carrying." She stopped, pretending to dab her handkerchief against her nose but really aiming for her eyes. "Don't tell anyone, but I don't care whether it's a boy or a girl. It's a piece of him. That's all that matters."

"I know," Francesca said softly, placing her hand on her belly. She wished there was some sign of the baby within. She knew it was too soon to feel movement; she wasn't even three months along, by her carefully calculated estimation. But all her dresses still fit perfectly, and her food still tasted just as it always had, and she simply wasn't experiencing any of the quirks and illnesses that other women had told her about.

She'd have been happy to have been casting up her accounts

each morning, if only so that she could imagine the baby was waving its hand with a cheerful, "I'm here!"

"Have you seen Michael recently?" Janet asked.

"Not since Monday," Francesca said. "He doesn't come to call very often anymore."

"He misses John," Janet said softly.

"So do I," Francesca replied, and she was horrified by the sharp edge to her voice.

"It must be very difficult for him," Janet mused.

Francesca just stared at her, her lips parting with surprise.

"I do not mean to say it is not difficult for you, too," Janet said quickly, "but think of the tenuousness of his position. He won't know if he's to be the earl for six more months."

"There is nothing I can do about that."

"No, of course not," Janet assured her, "but it does put him in awkward straits. I've heard more than one matron say that they simply can't consider him as a potential suitor for their daughters until and unless you give birth to a girl. It's one thing to marry the Earl of Kilmartin. It's quite another when it's his impoverished cousin. And no one knows which he will be."

"Michael isn't impoverished," Francesca said peevishly, "and besides, he would never marry while in mourning for John."

"No, I suppose not, but I do hope he starts looking," Janet said. "I do so want him to be happy. And of course if he is to be the earl, he shall have to beget an heir. Otherwise the title shall go to that awful Debenham side of the family." Janet shuddered at the thought.

"Michael will do what he must," Francesca said, although she wasn't so sure. It was difficult to imagine him marrying. It had always been difficult—Michael wasn't the sort to stay true to any woman for very long—but now it just seemed strange. For years, she had had John, and Michael had been their companion. Could she bear it if he married, and then she was the third wheel? Was her heart big enough to be happy for him while she was alone?

She rubbed her eyes. She felt very tired, and in truth a bit weak. A good sign, she supposed; she'd heard that pregnant women were supposed to be more tired than she usually was. She looked over at Janet. "I think I shall go upstairs and take a nap."

"An excellent idea," Janet said approvingly. "You need your rest."

Francesca nodded and stood, then grabbed the arm of the chair to steady herself when she swayed. "I don't know what is wrong with me," she said, attempting a wobbly smile. "I feel very unsteady. I—"

Janet's gasp cut her off.

"Janet?" Francesca looked at her mother-in-law with concern. She'd gone quite pale, and one shaking hand rose to meet her lips.

"What is it?" Francesca asked, and then she realized that Janet wasn't looking at her. She was looking at her chair.

With slowly dawning horror, Francesca looked down, forcing herself to look at the seat she'd just vacated.

There, in the middle of the cushion, was a small patch of red.

Blood.

Life would have been easier, Michael thought wryly, if he'd been given to drink. If ever there was a time to overindulge, to drown one's sorrows in the bottle, this was it.

But no, he'd been cursed with a robust constitution and a marvelous ability to hold his liquor with dignity and flair. Which meant that if he wanted to reach any sort of mind-numbing oblivion, he'd have to down the entire bottle of whisky sitting on his desk, and maybe even then some.

He looked out the window. It wasn't yet dark. Even he, dissolute rake that he tried to be, couldn't bring himself to drink an entire bottle of whisky before the sun went down.

Michael tapped his fingers against his desk, wishing he knew what to do with himself. John had been dead for six weeks now, but he was still living in his modest apartments in the Albany. He couldn't quite bring himself to take up residence in Kilmartin House. It was the residence of the earl, and that wouldn't be him for at least another six months.

Or maybe not ever.

According to Lord Winston, whose lectures Michael had eventually been forced to tolerate, the title would go into abeyance until Francesca delivered. And if she gave birth to a boy, Michael would remain in the same position he'd always been in—cousin to the earl.

But it wasn't Michael's peculiar situation that was keeping him away. He'd have been reticent to move into Kilmartin House even if Francesca hadn't been pregnant. She was still *there.*

She was still there, and she was still the Countess of Kilmartin, and even if he was the earl, with no questions attached to the title, she wouldn't be *his* countess, and he just didn't know if he could take the irony of it.

He'd thought that his grief might finally overtake his longing for her, that he might finally be with her and *not* want her, but no, his breath still caught every time she walked into the room, and his body tightened when she brushed past him, and his heart still ached with the pain of loving her.

Except now it was all wrapped in an extra layer of guilt—as if he hadn't had enough of *that* while John was alive. She was in pain, and she was grieving, and he ought to be comforting her, not lust-ing after her. Good God, John wasn't even cold in his grave. What kind of monster would lust after his wife?

His pregnant wife.

He was already stepping into John's shoes in so many ways. He would not complete the betrayal by taking his place with Francesca as well.

And so he stayed away. Not completely; that would have been too obvious, and besides, he couldn't do that, not with his mother and John's in residence at Kilmartin House. Plus, everyone was looking to him to manage the affairs of the earl, even though the title wasn't potentially to be his for another six months.

He did it, though. He didn't mind the details, didn't care that he was spending several hours per day looking after a fortune that might go to another. It was the least he could do for John.

And for Francesca. He couldn't bring himself to be a friend to her, not the way he ought, but he could make sure that her financial affairs were in order.

But he knew she didn't understand. She often came to visit him while he was working in John's study at Kilmartin House, poring over reports from various land stewards and solicitors. And he could tell that she was looking for their old camaraderie, but he just couldn't do it.

Call him weak, call him shallow. But he just couldn't be her friend. Not just yet, anyway.

"Mr. Stirling?"

Michael looked up. His valet was at the door, accompanied by a footman dressed in the unmistakable green and gold livery of Kilmartin House.

"A message for you," the footman said. "From your mother."

Michael held out his hand as the footman crossed the room,

wondering what it was this time. His mother summoned him to Kilmartin House every other day, it seemed.

"She said it was urgent," the footman added as he placed the envelope in Michael's hand.

Urgent, eh? That was new. Michael glanced up at the footman and valet, his steady gaze a clear dismissal, and then, once the room had been emptied, slid his letter-opener under the flap.

Come quickly, was all it said. *Francesca has lost the baby.*

Michael nearly killed himself rushing to Kilmartin House, racing on horseback at a breakneck pace, ignoring the shouts from the angry pedestrians he'd nearly decapitated in his haste.

But now that he was here, standing in the hall, he had no idea what to do with himself.

Miscarriage? It seemed such a womanly thing. What was he meant to do? It was a tragedy, and he felt horrible for Francesca, but what did they think he could say? Why did they want him here?

And then it hit him. He was the earl now. It was done. Slowly but surely, he was assuming John's life, filling every corner of the world that had once belonged to his cousin.

"Oh, Michael," his mother said, rushing into the hall. "I'm so glad you're here."

He embraced her, his arms awkwardly coming around her. And he said something utterly meaningless like, "Such a tragedy," but mostly he just stood there, feeling foolish and out of place.

"How is she?" he finally asked, once his mother stepped back.

"In shock," she replied. "She's been crying."

He swallowed, wanting desperately to loosen his cravat. "Well, that's to be expected," he said. "I—I—"

"She can't seem to stop," Helen interrupted.

"Crying?" Michael asked.

Helen nodded. "I don't know what to do."

Michael measured his breaths. Even. Slow. In and out.

"Michael?" His mother was looking up to him for a response. Maybe for guidance.

As if *he* would know what to do.

"Her mother came by," Helen said, when it became apparent that Michael was not going to speak. "She wants Francesca to go back to Bridgerton House."

"Does Francesca want to?"

Helen shrugged sadly. "I don't think she knows. It's all such a shock."

"Yes," Michael said, swallowing again. He didn't want to be here. He wanted to get out.

"The doctor said we're not to move her for several days, in any case," Helen added.

He nodded.

"Naturally, we called for you."

Naturally? There was nothing natural about it. He'd never felt so out of place, so completely at a loss for words or action.

"You're Kilmartin now," his mother said quietly.

He nodded again. Just once. It was as much of an acknowledgment as he could muster.

"I must say I—" Helen stopped, her lips pursing in an odd, jerky manner. "Well, a mother wants the world for her children, but I didn't—I never would have—"

"Don't say it," Michael said hoarsely. He wasn't ready for anyone to say this was a good thing. And by God, if anyone offered his congratulations . . .

Well, he wouldn't be responsible for the violence.

"She asked for you," his mother said.

"Francesca?" he asked, his eyes flying open with surprise.

Helen nodded. "She said she wanted you."

"I can't," he said.

"You have to."

"I can't." He shook his head, panic making his movements too quick. "I can't go in there."

"You can't abandon her," his mother said.

"She was never mine to abandon."

"Michael!" Helen gasped. "How can you say such a thing?"

"Mother," he said, desperately trying to redirect the conversation, "she needs a woman. What can I do?"

"You can be her friend," Helen said softly, and he felt eight again, scolded for a thoughtless transgression.

"No," he said, and his voice horrified him. He sounded like a wounded animal, pained and confused. But there was one thing he knew for certain. He couldn't see her. Not now. Not yet.

"Michael," his mother said.

"No," he said again. "I will . . . Tomorrow, I'll . . ." And he strode for the door with nothing more than a "Give her my best."

And then he fled, coward that he was.

Chapter 4

. . . I am sure it is not worth such high drama. I do not profess to know or understand romantic love between husband and wife, but surely it is not so all-encompassing that the loss of one would destroy the other. You are stronger than you think, dear sister. You would survive quite handily without him, moot point though it may be.

—from Eloise Bridgerton to her sister, the Countess of Kilmartin, three weeks after Francesca's wedding

The following month was, Michael was certain, the best approximation of hell on earth that any human being was likely to experience.

With every new ceremony, each and every document he found himself signing as Kilmartin, or "my lord" he was forced to endure, it was as if John's spirit was being pushed farther away.

Soon, Michael thought dispassionately, it would be as if he'd never existed. Even the baby—who was to have been the last piece of John Stirling left on earth—was gone.

And everything that had been John's was now Michael's.

Except Francesca.

And Michael intended to keep it that way. He would not—no, he *could* not offer his cousin that last insult.

He'd had to see her, of course, and he'd offered his best words of comfort, but whatever he'd said, it wasn't the right thing, and she'd just turned her head and looked at the wall.

He didn't know what to say. Frankly, he was more relieved that she was not injured than he was upset that the baby had been lost. The mothers—his, John's, and Francesca's—had felt compelled to describe the gore to him in appalling detail, and one of the maids had even trotted out the bloody sheets, which someone had saved to offer as proof that Francesca had miscarried.

Lord Winston had nodded approvingly but had then added that he would have to keep an eye on the countess, just to be sure that the sheets were truly hers, and that she wasn't actually increasing. This wouldn't be the first time someone had tried to circumvent the sacred laws of primogeniture, he'd added.

Michael had wanted to hurl the yappy little man out the window, but instead he'd merely shown him the door. He no longer had energy for that kind of anger, it seemed.

He still hadn't moved into Kilmartin House. He wasn't quite ready for it, and the thought of living there with all those women was suffocating. He'd have to do so soon, he knew; it was expected of the earl. But for now, he was content enough in his small suite of apartments.

And that was where he was, avoiding his duties, when Francesca finally sought him out.

"Michael?" she said, once his valet had shown her to his small sitting room.

"Francesca," he replied, shocked at her appearance. She'd never come here before. Not when John had been alive, and certainly not after. "What are you doing here?"

"I wanted to see you," she said.

The unspoken message being: *You're avoiding me.*

It was the truth, of course, but all he said was, "Sit down." And then belatedly: "Please."

Was this improper? Her being here in his apartments? He wasn't sure. The circumstances of their position were so odd, so completely out of order that he had no idea which rules of etiquette were currently governing them.

She sat, and did nothing but fiddle her fingers against her skirts for a full minute, and then she looked up at him, her eyes meeting his with heartbreaking intensity, and said, "I miss you."

The walls began to close in around him. "Francesca, I—"

"You were my friend," she said accusingly. "Besides John, you were my closest friend, and I don't know who you are any longer."

"I—" Oh, he felt like a fool, utterly impotent and brought down by a pair of blue eyes and a mountain of guilt.

Guilt for what, he wasn't even certain any longer. It seemed to come from so many sources, from such a variety of directions, that he couldn't quite keep track of it.

"What is wrong with you?" she asked. "Why do you avoid me?"

"I don't know," he replied, since he couldn't lie to her and say that he wasn't. She was too smart for that. But neither could he tell her the truth.

Her lips quivered, and then the lower one caught between her teeth. He stared at it, unable to take his eyes off her mouth, hating himself for the rush of longing that swept over him.

"You were supposed to be my friend, too," she whispered.

"Francesca, don't."

"I needed you," she said softly. "I still do."

"No you don't," he replied. "You have the mothers, and all your sisters as well."

"I don't want to talk to my sisters," she said, her voice growing impassioned. "They don't understand."

"Well, *I* certainly don't understand," he shot back, desperation lending an unpleasant edge to his voice.

She just stared at him, condemnation coloring her eyes.

"Francesca, you—" He wanted to throw up his arms but instead he just crossed them. "You—you *miscarried*."

"I am aware of that," she said tightly.

"What do I know of such things? You need to talk to a woman."

"Can't you say you're sorry?"

"I *did* say I was sorry!"

"Can't you mean it?"

What did she *want* from him? "Francesca, I *did* mean it."

"I'm just so angry," she said, her voice rising in intensity, "and I'm sad, and I'm upset, and I look at you and I don't understand why you're *not*."

For a moment he didn't move. "Don't you ever say that," he whispered.

Her eyes flashed with anger. "Well, you've a funny way of showing it. You never call, and you never speak to me, and you don't understand—"

"What do you want me to understand?" he burst out. "What *can* I understand? For the love of—" He stopped himself before he blasphemed and turned away from her, leaning heavily on the windowsill.

Behind him Francesca just sat quietly, still as death. And then, finally, she said, "I don't know why I came. I'll go."

"Don't go," he said hoarsely. But he didn't turn around.

She said nothing; she wasn't sure what he meant.

"You only just arrived," he said, his voice halting and awkward. "You should have a cup of tea, at least."

Francesca nodded, even though he still wasn't looking at her.

And they remained thus for several minutes, for far too long, until she could not bear the silence any longer. The clock ticked in the corner, and her only company was Michael's back, and all she could do was sit there and think and think and wonder why she'd come here.

What did she want from him?

And wouldn't her life be easier if she actually knew.

"Michael," she said, his name leaving her lips before she realized it.

He turned around. He didn't speak, but he acknowledged her with his eyes.

"I . . ." Why had she called out to him? What did she want? "I . . ."

Still, he didn't speak. Just stood there and waited for her to collect her thoughts, which made everything so much harder.

And then, to her horror, it spilled out. "I don't know what I'm supposed to do now," she said, hearing her voice break. "And I'm so angry, and . . ." She stopped, gasped—anything to halt the tears.

Across from her, Michael opened his mouth, but only barely, and even then, nothing came out.

"I don't know why this is happening," she whimpered. "What did I do? What did I ever do?"

"Nothing," he assured her.

"He's gone, and he isn't coming back, and I'm so . . . so . . ." She looked up at him, feeling the grief and the anger etching themselves into her face. "It isn't fair. It isn't fair that it's me and not someone else, and it isn't fair that it should be anyone, and it isn't fair that I lost the—" And then she choked, and the gasps became sobs, and all she could do was cry.

"Francesca," Michael said, kneeling at her feet. "I'm sorry. I'm so sorry."

"I know," she sobbed, "but it doesn't make it better."

"No," he murmured.

"And it doesn't make it fair."

"No," he said again.

"And it doesn't— It doesn't—"

He didn't try to finish the sentence for her. She wished he had; for years she wished he had, because maybe then he would have said the wrong thing, and maybe then she wouldn't have leaned into him, and maybe then she wouldn't have allowed him to hold her.

But oh, God, how she missed being held.

"Why did you go?" she cried. "Why can't you help me?"

"I want to— You don't—" And then finally he just said, "I don't know what to say."

She was asking too much of him. She knew it, but she didn't care. She was just so sick of being alone.

But right then, at least for a moment, she wasn't alone. Michael was there, and he was holding her, and she felt warm and safe for the first time in weeks. And she just cried. She cried weeks of tears. She cried for John and she cried for the baby she'd never know.

But most of all she cried for herself.

"Michael," she said, once she'd recovered enough to speak. Her voice was still shaky, but she managed his name, and she knew she was going to have to manage more.

"Yes?"

"We can't go on like this."

She felt something change in him. His embrace tightened, or maybe it loosened, but something was not quite the same. "Like what?" he asked, his voice hoarse and hesitant.

She drew back so she could see him, relieved when his arms fell away, and she didn't have to wriggle free. "Like this," she said, even though she knew he didn't understand. Or if he did, that he was going to pretend otherwise. "With you ignoring me," she continued.

"Francesca, I—"

"The baby was to have been yours in a way, too," she blurted out.

He went pale, deathly pale. So much so that for a moment she couldn't breathe.

"What do you mean?" he whispered.

"It would have needed a father," she said, shrugging helplessly. "I— You— It would have had to be you."

"You have brothers," he choked out.

"They didn't know John. Not the way you did."

He moved away, stood, and then, as if that weren't enough, backed up as far as he could, all the way to the window. His eyes flared slightly, and for a moment she could have sworn that he resembled a trapped animal, cornered and terrified, waiting for the finality of the kill.

"Why are you telling me this?" he said, his voice flat and low.

"I don't know," she said, swallowing uncomfortably. But she did know. She wanted him to grieve as she grieved. She wanted him to hurt in every way she hurt. It wasn't fair, and it wasn't nice, but she couldn't help it and she didn't feel like apologizing for it, either.

"Francesca," he said, and his tone was strange, hollow and sharp, and like nothing she'd ever heard.

She looked at him, but she moved her head slowly, scared by what she might see in his face.

"I'm not John," he said.

"I know that."

"I'm not John," he said again, louder, and she wondered if he'd even heard her.

"I know."

His eyes narrowed and focused on her with dangerous intensity. "It wasn't my baby, and I can't be what you need."

And inside of her, something started to die. "Michael, I—"

"I won't take his place," he said, and he wasn't shouting, but it sounded like maybe he wanted to.

"No, you couldn't. You—"

And then, in a startling flash of motion, he was at her side, and he'd grabbed her shoulders and hauled her to her feet. "I won't do it," he yelled, and he was shaking her, and then holding her still, and then shaking her again. "I can't be him. I won't be him."

She couldn't speak, couldn't form words, didn't know what to do.

Didn't know who he was.

He stopped shaking her, but his fingers bit into her shoulders as he stared down at her, his quicksilver eyes afire with something terrifying and sad. "You can't ask this of me," he gasped. "I can't do it."

"Michael?" she whispered, hearing something awful in her voice. Fear. "Michael, please let me go."

He didn't, but she wasn't even sure he'd heard her. His eyes were lost, and he seemed beyond her, unreachable.

"Michael!" she said again, and her voice was louder, panicked.

And then, abruptly, he did as she asked, and he stumbled back, his face a portrait of self-loathing. "I'm sorry," he whispered, staring at his hands as if they were foreign bodies. "I'm so sorry."

Francesca edged toward the door. "I'd better go," she said.

He nodded. "Yes."

"I think—" She stopped, choking on the word as she grasped the doorknob, clutching it like her salvation. "I think we had better not see each other for a while."

He nodded jerkily.

"Maybe . . ." But she didn't say anything more. She didn't know what *to* say. If she'd known what had just happened between them she might have found some words, but for now she was too bewildered and scared to figure it all out.

Scared, but why? She certainly wasn't scared of *him*. Michael would never hurt her. He'd lay down his life for her if the opportunity forced itself; she was quite sure of that.

Maybe she was just scared of tomorrow. And the day after that. She'd lost everything, and now it appeared she'd lost Michael as well, and she just wasn't sure how she was supposed to bear it all.

"I'm going to go," she said, giving him one last chance to stop her, to say something, to say *any*thing that might make it all go away.

But he didn't. He didn't even nod. He just looked at her, his eyes silent in their agreement.

And Francesca left. She walked out the door and out of his house. And then she climbed into her carriage and went home.

And she didn't say a word. She climbed up her stairs and she climbed into her bed.

But she didn't cry. She kept thinking she should, kept feeling like she might like to.

But all she did was stare at the ceiling.

The ceiling, at least, didn't mind her regard.

Back in his apartments in the Albany, Michael grabbed his bottle of whisky and poured himself a tall glass, even though a glance at the clock revealed the day to be still younger than noon.

He'd sunk to a new low, that much was clear.

But try as he might, he couldn't figure out what else he could have done. It wasn't as if he'd meant to hurt her, and he certainly hadn't stopped, pondered, and decided *Oh, yes, I do believe I shall act like an ass*, but even though his reactions had been swift and unconsidered, he didn't see how he might have behaved any other way.

He knew himself. He didn't always—or these days even often—like himself, but he knew himself. And when Francesca had turned to him with those bottomless blue eyes and said, "The baby was to have been yours in a way, too," she'd shattered him to his very soul.

She didn't know.

She had no idea.

And as long as she remained in the dark about his feelings for her, as long as she couldn't understand why he had no choice but to hate himself for every step he took in John's shoes, he couldn't be near her. Because she was going to keep saying things like that.

And he simply didn't know how much he could take.

And so, as he stood in his study, his body taut with misery and guilt, he realized two things.

The first was easy. The whisky was doing nothing to ease his pain, and if twenty-five-year-old whisky, straight from Speyside, didn't make him feel any better, nothing in the British Isles was going to do so.

Which led him to the second, which wasn't easy at all. But he had to do it. Rarely had the choices in his life been so clear. Painful, but painfully clear.

And so he set down his glass, two fingers of the amber liquid remaining, and he walked down the hall to his bedchamber.

"Reivers," he said, upon finding his valet standing at the wardrobe, carefully folding a cravat, "what do you think of India?"

Part Two

March, 1824
Four years later

Chapter 5

. . . you would enjoy it here. Not the heat, I should think; no one seems to enjoy the heat. But the rest would enchant you. The colors, the spices, the scent of the air—they can place one in a strange, sensuous haze that is at turns unsettling and intoxicating. Most of all, I think you would enjoy the pleasure gardens. They are rather like our London parks, except far more green and lush, and full of the most remarkable flowers you have ever seen. You have always loved to be out among nature; this you would adore, I am quite sure of it.

—from Michael Stirling (the new Earl of Kilmartin) to the Countess of Kilmartin, one month after his arrival in India

Francesca wanted a baby.

She had for quite some time, but it was only in recent months that she'd been able to admit as much to herself, to finally put words to the sense of longing that seemed to accompany her wherever she went.

It had started innocently enough, with a little pang in her heart upon reading a letter from her brother's wife Kate, the missive filled with news of their little girl Charlotte, soon to turn two and already incorrigible.

But the pang had grown worse, into something more akin to an ache, when her sister Daphne had arrived in Scotland for a visit, all four of her children in tow. It hadn't occurred to Francesca just how completely a gaggle of children could transform a home. The Hastings children had altered the very essence of Kilmartin, brought to it life and laughter that Francesca realized had been sadly lacking for years.

And then they left, and all was quiet, but it wasn't peaceful.

Just empty.

From that moment on, Francesca was different. She saw a nursemaid pushing a pram, and her heart ached. She spied a rabbit hopping across a field and couldn't help but think that she ought to be pointing it out to someone else, someone small. She traveled to Kent to spend Christmas with her family, but when night fell, and all of her nieces and nephews were tucked into bed, she felt too alone.

And all she could think was that her life was passing her by, and if she didn't do something soon, she'd die this way.

Alone.

Not unhappy—she wasn't that. Strangely enough, she'd grown into her widowhood and found a comfortable and contented pattern to her life. It was something she never would have believed possible during the awful months immediately following John's death, but she had, a bit through trial and error, found a place for herself in the world. And with it, a small measure of peace.

She enjoyed her life as Countess of Kilmartin—Michael had never married, so she retained the duties as well as the title. She loved Kilmartin, and she ran it with no interference from Michael;

his instructions upon leaving the country four years earlier had been that she should manage the earldom as she saw fit, and once the shock of his departure had worn off, she'd realized that that had been the most precious gift he could have bestowed upon her.

It had given her something to do, something to work toward.

A reason to stop staring at the ceiling.

She had friends, and she had family, both Stirling and Bridgerton, and she had a full life, in Scotland and London, where she spent several months of each year.

So she should have been happy. And she was, mostly.

She just wanted a baby.

It had taken some time to admit this to herself. It was a desire that seemed somewhat disloyal to John; it wouldn't be *his* baby, after all, and even now, with him gone four years, it was difficult to imagine a child without his features woven across its face.

And it meant, first and foremost, that she'd have to remarry. She'd have to change her name and pledge her troth to another man, to vow to make him first in her heart and her loyalties, and while the thought of that no longer struck pain in her heart, it seemed . . . well . . . strange.

But she supposed there were some things a woman simply had to get past, and one cold February day, as she was staring out a window at Kilmartin, watching the snow slowly wrap a shroud around the tree branches, she realized that this was one of them.

There were a lot of things in life to be afraid of, but strangeness ought not be among them.

And so she decided to pack her things and head down to London a bit early this year. She generally spent the season in town, enjoying time with her family, shopping and attending musicales, taking in plays and doing all the things that simply weren't available in the Scottish countryside. But this season would be different. She needed a new wardrobe, for one. She'd been out of mourning for some time, but she hadn't completely shrugged off the grays and lavenders of half-mourning, and she certainly hadn't paid the attention to fashion that a woman in her new position ought.

It was time to wear blue. Bright, beautiful, cornflower blue. It had been her favorite color years ago, and she'd been vain enough that she'd worn it fully expecting people to comment on how it matched her eyes.

She'd buy blue, and yes, pink and yellow as well, and maybe even—something in her heart shivered with anticipation at the thought—crimson.

She wasn't an unmarried miss this time around. She was an eligible widow, and the rules were different.

But the aspirations were the same.

She was going to London to find herself a husband.

It had been too long.

Michael knew that his return to Britain was well overdue, but it had been one of those things that was appallingly easy to put off. According to his mother's letters, which had found him with remarkable regularity, the earldom was thriving under Francesca's stewardship. He had no dependents who might accuse him of neglect, and by all accounts, everyone he'd left behind was faring rather better in his absence than they had when he'd been around to cheer them on.

So there was nothing to feel guilty about.

But a man could only run from his destiny for so long, and as he marked his third year in the tropics, he had to admit that the novelty of an exotic life had worn off, and to be completely frank, he was growing rather sick of the climate. India had given him a purpose, a place in life that went beyond the only two things at which he'd ever excelled—soldiering and making merry. He'd boarded a ship with nothing but the name of an army friend who'd moved to Madras three years earlier. Within a month he'd obtained a governmental post and found himself making decisions that mattered, implementing laws and policies that actually shaped the lives of men.

For the first time, Michael finally understood why John had been so enamored of his work in the British Parliament.

But India hadn't made him happy. It had given him a small measure of peace, which seemed rather paradoxical, since in the past few years he'd nearly met his demise three times, four if one counted that run-in with the knife-wielding Indian princess (Michael still maintained that he could have disarmed her without injury, but she did, he had to admit, have a rather murderous look in her eye, and he'd long since learned that one should never ever underestimate a woman who believes—however erroneously—herself scorned.)

Life-threatening episodes aside, however, his time in India had brought him a certain sense of balance. He'd finally done something for himself, made something *of* himself.

But most of all, India had brought him peace because he didn't have to live with the constant knowledge that Francesca was just around the corner.

Life wasn't necessarily better with thousands of miles between him and Francesca, but it certainly was easier.

It was past time, however, to face up to the rigors of having her in close proximity, and so he'd packed up his belongings, informed his rather relieved valet that they were going back to England, booked a luxurious starboard suite on the *Princess Amelia*, and headed home.

He'd have to face her, of course. There was no escaping that. He would have to look into the blue eyes that had haunted him relentlessly and try to be her friend. It was the one thing she'd wanted during the dark days after John's death, and it had been the only thing he had been completely unable to do for her.

But maybe now, with the benefit of time and the healing power of distance, he could manage it. He wasn't stupid enough to hope that she'd changed, that he'd see her and discover he no longer loved her—*that*, he was quite certain, would never happen. But Michael had finally grown used to hearing the words "Earl of Kilmartin" without looking over his shoulder for his cousin. And maybe now, with the grief no longer so raw, he could be with Francesca in friendship, without feeling as if he were a thief, plotting to steal what he'd coveted for so long.

And hopefully she, too, had moved on, and wouldn't ask him to fulfill John's duties in every way but one.

But all the same, he was glad that it would be March when he disembarked in London, too early in the year for Francesca to have arrived for the season.

He was a brave man; he'd proven that countless times, on and off the battlefield. But he was an honest man, too, honest enough to admit that the prospect of facing Francesca was terrifying in a way that no French battlefield or toothy tiger could ever be.

Maybe, if he was lucky, she'd choose not to come down to London for the season at all.

Wouldn't that be a boon.

It was dark, and she couldn't sleep, and the house was miserably cold, and the worst of it was, it was all her fault.

Oh, very well, not the dark. Francesca supposed she couldn't take the blame for that. Night was night, after all, and she was rather overreaching to think that she had anything to do with the sun going down. But it was her fault that the household hadn't been given adequate time to prepare for her arrival. She'd forgotten to send notice that she was planning to come down to London a month early, and as a result, Kilmartin House was still running with a skeleton staff, and the stores of coal and beeswax candles were perilously low.

All would be better on the morrow, after the housekeeper and butler made a mad dash to the Bond Street shops, but for now Francesca was shivering in her bed. It had been a miserably freezing day, with a blustery wind that made it far colder than was normal for early March. The housekeeper had attempted to move all the available coal to Francesca's grate, but countess or no, she couldn't allow the rest of the household to freeze at her expense. Besides, the countess's bedchamber was immense, and it had always been difficult to heat properly unless the rest of the house was warm as well.

The library. That was it. It was small and cozy, and if Francesca shut the door, a fire in its grate would keep the room nice and toasty. Furthermore, there was a settee on which she could lie. It was small, but then again, so was she, and it couldn't possibly be any worse than freezing to death in her bedroom.

Her decision made, Francesca leapt out of bed and dashed through the cold night air to her nightrobe, which was lying across the back of a chair. It wasn't nearly warm enough—Francesca hadn't thought to need anything bulkier—but it was better than nothing, and, she thought rather stoically, beggars couldn't be choosers, especially when their toes were falling off with cold.

She hurried downstairs, her heavy wool socks slipping and sliding on the polished steps. She tumbled down the last two, thankfully landing on her feet, then ran along the runner carpet to the library.

"Fire fire fire," she mumbled to herself. She'd ring for someone just as soon as she got to the library. They'd have a blaze roaring in no time. She'd regain feeling in her nose, her fingertips would lose that sickly blue color and—

She pushed open the door.

A short, staccato scream hurled itself across her lips. There was already a fire in the grate, and a man standing in front of it, idly warming his hands.

Francesca reached wildly for something—anything—that she might use as a weapon.

And then he turned.

"*Michael?*"

He hadn't known she'd be in London. Damn it, he hadn't even considered that she might be in London. Not that it would have made any difference, but at least he'd have been prepared. He might have schooled his features into a saturnine smirk, or at the very least made sure that he was impeccably dressed and wholeheartedly immersed in his role as the unrecoverable rake.

But no, there he was, just gaping at her, trying not to notice that she was wearing nothing but a dark crimson nightgown and dressing robe, so thin and sheer that he could see the outline of—

He gulped. Don't look. Do *not* look.

"Michael?" she whispered again.

"Francesca," he said, since he had to say something. "What are you doing here?"

And that seemed to snap her into thought and motion. "What am I doing here?" she echoed. "I'm not the one who's meant to be in India. What are *you* doing here?"

He shrugged carelessly. "Thought it was time to come home."

"Couldn't you have written?"

"To you?" he asked, quirking a brow. It was, and was meant to be, a direct hit. She hadn't penned him a single letter during his travels. He had sent her three letters, but once it became apparent that she didn't plan to answer, he'd conducted the rest of his correspondence through his mother and John's.

"To anyone," she replied. "Someone would have been here to greet you."

"You're here," he pointed out.

She scowled at him. "If we'd known you were coming, we would have readied the house for you."

He shrugged again. The motion seemed to embody the image he desperately needed to convey. "It's ready enough."

She hugged her arms to her body, effectively blocking his view of her breasts, which, he had to concede, was probably for the best. "Well, you might have written," she finally said, her voice hanging sharp in the night air. "It would only have been courteous."

"Francesca," he said, turning slightly away from her so that he could continue to rub his hands together by the fire, "do you have any idea how long it takes for mail to reach London from India?"

"Five months," she answered promptly. "Four, if the winds are kind."

Damn it, she was right. "Be that as it may," he said peevishly, "by the time I decided to return, there was little use in attempting forward notice. The letter would have gone out on the same ship I did."

"Really? I thought the passenger vessels were slower than the ones that take the mail."

He sighed, glancing at her over his shoulder. "They all take the mail. And besides, does it really matter?"

For a moment he thought she would answer in the affirmative, but then she said quietly, "No, of course not. The important thing is that you're home. Your mother will be thrilled."

He turned away so that she wouldn't see his humorless smile. "Yes," he murmured, "of course."

"And I—" She stopped, cleared her throat. "I am delighted to have you back as well."

She sounded as if she were trying very hard to convince herself of this, but Michael decided to play the gentleman for once and not point it out. "Are you cold?" he asked instead.

"Not very," she said.

"You're lying."

"Just a little."

He stepped to the side, making room for her closer to the fire. When he didn't hear her move toward him, he motioned toward the empty space with his hand.

"I should go back to my room," she said.

"For God's sake, Francesca, if you're cold, just come to the fire. I won't bite."

She gritted her teeth and stepped forward, joining him near the blaze. But she kept herself somewhat off to the side, maintaining a bit of distance between them. "You look well," she said.

"As do you."

"It's been a long time."

"I know. Four years, I believe."

Francesca swallowed, wishing this weren't so difficult. This was Michael, for heaven's sake. It wasn't supposed to be difficult. Yes, they'd parted badly, but that had been in the dark days immediately following John's death. They'd all been in pain then, wounded animals lashing out at anyone in their way. It was supposed to be different now. Heaven knew she'd thought of this moment often enough. Michael couldn't stay away forever, they'd all known that. But once her initial anger had passed, she'd rather hoped that when he did return, they'd be able to forget that anything unpleasant had ever passed between them.

And be friends again. She needed that, more than she'd ever realized.

"Do you have any plans?" she asked, mostly because the silence was too awful.

"For now, all I can think about is getting warm," he muttered.

She smiled in spite of herself. "It *is* exceptionally chilly for this time of year."

"I'd forgotten how damnably cold it can be here," he grumbled, rubbing his hands together briskly.

"One would think you'd never escape the memory of a Scottish winter," Francesca murmured.

He turned to her then, a wry smile tilting one corner of his mouth. He'd changed, she realized. Oh, there were the obvious differences—the ones everyone would notice. He was tan, quite scandalously so, and his hair, always midnight black, now sported a few odd strands of silver.

But there was more. He held his mouth differently, more tightly, if that made any sense, and his smooth, lanky grace seemed to have gone missing. He had always seemed so at ease, so comfortable in his skin, but now he was . . . taut.

Strained.

"You'd think," he murmured, and she just looked at him blankly, having quite forgotten what he was replying to until he added, "I came home because I couldn't stand the heat any longer, and now here I am, ready to perish from the cold."

"It will be spring soon," she said.

"Ah yes, spring. With its merely frigid winds, as opposed to the icy ones of winter."

She laughed at that, absurdly pleased to have anything to laugh about in his presence. "The house will be better tomorrow," she said. "I only just arrived this evening, and like you, I neglected to send advance notice. Mrs. Parrish assures me that the house will be restocked tomorrow."

He nodded, then turned around to warm his back. "What are you doing here?"

"Me?"

He motioned to the empty room, as if to make a point.

"I live here," she said.

"You usually don't come down until April."

"You know that?"

For a moment, he looked almost embarrassed. "My mother's letters are remarkably detailed," he said.

She shrugged, then inched a little closer to the fire. She ought not stand so near to him, but dash it, she was still rather cold, and her thin nightrobe did little to ward off the chill.

"Is that an answer?" he drawled.

"I just felt like it," she said insolently. "Isn't that a lady's prerogative?"

He turned again, presumably to warm his side, and then he was facing her.

And he seemed terribly close.

She moved, just an inch or so; she didn't want him to realize she'd been made uncomfortable by his nearness.

Nor did she want to admit the very same thing to herself.

"I thought it was a lady's prerogative to change her mind," he said.

"It's a lady's prerogative to do anything she wants," Francesca said pertly.

"Touché," Michael murmured. He looked at her again, more closely this time. "You haven't changed."

Her lips parted. "How can you say that?"

"Because you look exactly as I remembered you." And then, devilishly, he motioned toward her revealing nightwear. "Aside from your attire, of course."

She gasped and stepped back, wrapping her arms more tightly around her body.

It was a bit sick of him, but he was rather pleased with himself for having offended her. He'd needed her to step away, to move out of his reach. She was going to have to set the boundaries.

Because he wasn't sure he'd prove up to the task.

He'd been lying when he'd said she hadn't changed. There was something different about her, something entirely unexpected.

Something that shook him down to his very soul.

It was a sense about her—all in his mind, really, but no less devastating. There was an air of availability, a horrible, torturous knowledge that John was gone, really, truly gone, and the only thing stopping Michael from reaching out and touching her was his own conscience.

It was almost funny.

Almost.

And there she was, still without a clue, still completely unaware that the man standing next to her wanted nothing so much than to peel every layer of silk from her body and lay her down in front of the fire. He wanted to nudge her thighs apart, sink himself into her, and—

He laughed grimly. Four years, it seemed, had done little to cool his inappropriate ardor.

"Michael?"

He looked over at her.

"What's so funny?"

Her question, that's what. "You wouldn't understand."

"Try me," she dared.

"Oh, I think not."

"Michael," she prodded.

He turned to her and said with deliberate coolness, "Francesca, there are some things you will never understand."

Her lips parted, and for a moment she looked as if she'd been struck.

And he felt as horrid as if he'd done so.

"That was a terrible thing to say," she whispered.

He shrugged.

"You've changed," she said.

The sad thing was, he hadn't. Not in any of the ways that might have made his life easier to bear. He sighed, hating himself because he couldn't bear to have her hate him. "Forgive me," he said, running his hand through his hair. "I'm tired, and I'm cold, and I'm an ass."

She grinned at that, and for a moment they were transported back in time. "It's all right," she said kindly, touching his upper arm. "You've had a long journey."

He sucked in his breath. She used to do this all the time—touch his arm in friendship. Never in public, of course, and rarely even when it had just been the two of them. John would have been there; John was always there. And it had always—*always*—shaken him.

But never so much as now.

"I need to go to bed," he mumbled. He was usually a master at hiding his unease, but he just hadn't been prepared to see her this evening, and beyond that, he was damned tired.

She withdrew her hand. "There won't be a room ready for you. You should take mine. I'll sleep here."

"No," he said, with far more force than he'd intended. "I'll sleep here, or . . . hell," he muttered, striding across the room to yank on the bellpull. What the devil was the point of being the bloody Earl of Kilmartin if you couldn't have a bedchamber readied at any hour of the night?

Besides, ringing the bell would mean that a servant would arrive within minutes, which would mean that he would no longer be standing here alone with Francesca.

It wasn't as if they hadn't been alone together before, but never at night, and never with her in her nightgown, and—

He yanked the cord again.

"Michael," she said, sounding almost amused. "I'm sure they heard you the first time."

"Yes, well, it's been a long day," he said. "Storm in the Channel and all that."

"You'll have to tell me of your travels soon," she said gently.

He looked over at her, lifting a brow. "I would have written to you of them."

Her lips pursed for a moment. It was an expression he'd seen countless times on her face. She was choosing her words, deciding whether or not to spear him with her legendary wit.

And apparently she decided against it, because instead she said, "I was rather angry with you for leaving."

He sucked in his breath. Trust Francesca to choose stark honesty over a scathing retort.

"I'm sorry," he said, and he meant it, even though he wouldn't have changed any of his actions. He'd needed to leave. He'd *had* to leave. Maybe it meant he was a coward; maybe it meant he'd been less of a man. But he hadn't been ready to be the earl. He wasn't

John, could never be John. And that was the one thing everyone had seemed to want of him.

Even Francesca, in her own halfway sort of manner.

He looked at her. He was quite sure she still didn't understand why he'd left. She probably thought she did, but how could she? She didn't know that he loved her, couldn't possibly understand how damned guilty he felt at assuming John's life.

But none of that was her fault. And as he looked at her, standing fragile and proud as she stared at the fire, he said it again.

"I'm sorry."

She acknowledged his apology with the barest hint of a nod. "I should have written to you," she said. She turned to him then, her eyes filled with sorrow and perhaps a hint of their own apology. "But the truth was, I just didn't feel like it. Thinking of you made me think of John, and I suppose I needed not to think of him so much just then."

Michael didn't pretend to understand, but he nodded nonetheless.

She smiled wistfully. "We had such fun, the three of us, didn't we?"

He nodded again. "I miss him," he said, and he was surprised by how good it felt to voice that.

"I always thought it would be so lovely when you finally married," Francesca added. "You would have chosen someone brilliant and fun, I'm sure. What grand times the four of us would have had."

Michael coughed. It seemed the best course of action.

She looked up, broken from her reverie. "Are you catching a chill?"

"Probably. I'll be at death's door by Saturday, I'm sure."

She arched a brow. "I hope you don't expect me to nurse you."

Just the opening he needed to move their banter back to where he felt most comfortable. "Not necessary," he said with a wave of his hand. "I shouldn't need more than three days to attract a bevy of unsuitable women to attend to my every need."

Her lips pinched slightly, but she was clearly amused. "The same as ever, I see."

He gave her a lopsided grin. "No one ever really changes, Francesca."

She cocked her head to the side, motioning to the hall, where they could hear someone moving toward them on swift feet. The footman arrived, and Francesca took care of everything, allowing Michael to do nothing but stand by the fire, looking vaguely imperial as he nodded his agreement.

"Good night, Michael," she said, once the footman had left to do her bidding.

"Good night, Francesca," he said softly.

"It's good to see you again," she said. And then, as if she needed to convince one of them of it—he wasn't sure which, she added, "It truly is."

Chapter 6

. . . I'm sorry I haven't written. No, that's not true. I'm not sorry. I don't wish to write. I don't wish to think of—

—from the Countess of Kilmartin to the new Earl of Kilmartin, one day after the receipt of his first missive to her, torn to bits, then soaked with tears

By the time Michael arose the next morning, Kilmartin House seemed to be back up and running as befitted the home of an earl. There were fires in every grate, and a splendid breakfast had been laid out in the informal dining room, with coddled eggs, ham, bacon, sausage, toast with butter and marmalade, and his own personal favorite, broiled mackerel.

Francesca, however, was nowhere to be found.

When he inquired after her, he was given a folded note she'd left for him earlier that morning. It seemed she felt that tongues might wag at their living alone together at Kilmartin House, and so she had removed herself to her mother's residence at Number Five, Bruton Street, until either Janet or Helen arrived down from Scotland. She did, however, invite him to call upon her that day, as she was certain they had much to discuss.

And Michael supposed she was right, so once he'd finished with his breakfast (finding, much to his great surprise, that he rather missed the yogurts and dosas of his Indian morning meal), he stepped outside and made his way to Number Five.

He elected to walk; it wasn't very far, and the air had warmed appreciably since the icy gusts of the day before. But mostly, he just wanted to take in the cityscape, to remind himself of the rhythms of London. He'd never noticed the particular smells and sounds of the capital before, how the clip-clop of horses' hooves combined with the festive shout of the flower seller and low rumble of cultured voices. There was the sound of his feet on the pavement, and smell of roasting nuts, and the vague heft of soot in the air, all combining to make something that was uniquely London.

It was almost overpowering, which was strange, because he remembered feeling precisely the same way upon landing in India four years earlier. The humid air, redolent with spice and flowers, had shocked his every sense. It had felt almost like an assault, leaving him drowsy and disoriented. And while his reaction to London wasn't quite that dramatic, he still felt rather like the odd man out, his senses buffeted by smells and sounds that shouldn't have felt so unfamiliar.

Had he become a stranger in his own land? It seemed almost bizarre, and yet, as he walked along the crowded streets of London's most exclusive shopping district, he couldn't help but think that he stood out, that anyone glancing upon him must instantly know that he was different, removed from their very British existence.

Or, he allowed, as he caught sight of his reflection in a shop window, it could be the tan.

It would take weeks to fade. Months, maybe.

His mother was going to be scandalized.

The thought of it made him grin. He rather enjoyed scandalizing his mother. He'd never be so grown up that *that* ceased to be fun.

He turned on Bruton Street and walked past the last few homes to Number Five. He'd been there before, of course. Francesca's mother had always defined the word "family" in the widest of all possible manners, so Michael had found himself invited along with John and Francesca to any number of Bridgerton family events.

When he arrived, Lady Bridgerton was already in the green-and-cream drawing room, taking a cup of tea at her writing desk under the window. "Michael!" she exclaimed, rising to her feet with obvious affection. "How good to see you!"

"Lady Bridgerton," he said, taking her hand and gracing it with a gallant kiss.

"No one does that like you," she said approvingly.

"One has to cultivate one's best maneuvers," he murmured.

"And I can't tell you how much we ladies of a certain age appreciate your doing so."

"A certain age being . . ." He smiled devilishly. ". . . one and thirty?"

Lady Bridgerton was the sort of woman who grew lovelier with age, but the smile she gave him made her positively radiant. "You are *always* welcome in this house, Michael Stirling."

He grinned and sat in a high-backed chair when she motioned for him to do so.

"Oh, dear," she said with a slight frown. "I must apologize. I suppose I should be calling you Kilmartin now."

" 'Michael' is just fine," he assured her.

"I know that it's been four years," she continued, "but as I haven't seen you . . ."

"You may call me anything you wish," he said smoothly. It

was strange. He'd finally grown used to being called Kilmartin, adapted to the way his title had overtaken his surname. But that had been in India, where no one had known him as plain Mr. Stirling, and perhaps more importantly, no one had known John as the earl. Hearing his title on Violet Bridgerton's lips was a little unnerving, especially since she had, as was the custom for many mothers-in-law, habitually referred to John as her son.

But if she sensed any of his inner discomfort, she gave no indication. "If you are going to be so accommodating," she said, "then I must be as well. Please do call me Violet. It's well past time that you did."

"Oh, I couldn't," he said quickly. And he meant it. This was Lady Bridgerton. She was . . . Well, he didn't know what she was, but she couldn't possibly be *Violet* to him.

"I insist, Michael," she said, "and I'm certain you're already aware that I usually get my way."

There was no way he was going to win the argument, so he just sighed and said, "I don't know if I can kiss the hand of a Violet. It seems rather scandalously intimate, don't you think?"

"Don't you dare stop."

"Tongues will wag," he warned her.

"I believe my reputation can withstand it."

"Ah, but can mine?"

She laughed. "You are a rascal."

He leaned back in his chair. "It serves me well."

"Would you care for tea?" She motioned to the delicate china pot on the desk across the room. "Mine has gone cold, but I would be happy to ring for more."

"I'd love some," he admitted.

"I suppose you're spoiled for it now, after so many years in India," she said, standing and crossing the room to ring the bellpull.

"It's just not the same," he said, quickly rising to his feet as well. "I can't explain it, but nothing tastes quite like tea in England."

"The quality of the water, do you think?"

He smiled stealthily. "The quality of the woman pouring."

She laughed. "You, my lord, need a wife. Immediately."

"Oh, really? And why is that?"

"Because in your present state, you are clearly a danger to unmarried women everywhere."

He couldn't resist one last flirtation. "I hope you are including yourself in those ranks, Violet."

And then a voice from the door: "Are you flirting with my *mother*?"

It was Francesca, of course, impeccably turned out in a lavender morning dress adorned with a rather intricate stretch of Belgian lace. She looked as if she were very much trying to be stern with him.

And not entirely succeeding.

Michael allowed his lips to curve into a mysterious smile as he watched the two ladies take their seats. "I have traveled the world over, Francesca, and can say without qualification that there are few women with whom I'd rather flirt than your mother."

"I am inviting you to supper right now," Violet announced, "and I will not accept no for an answer."

Michael chuckled. "I'd be honored."

Across from him, Francesca murmured, "You are incorrigible."

He just flashed her an easy grin. This was good, he decided. The morning was proceeding exactly as he'd hoped, with he and Francesca falling into their old roles and habits. He was once again the reckless charmer and she was pretending to scold him, and all was as it had been back before John had died.

He'd been surprised last night. He hadn't expected to see her.

And he hadn't been able to make sure that his public persona was firmly in place.

And it wasn't as if it *all* was an act. He'd always been a bit reckless, and he probably *was* an irredeemable flirt. His mother certainly liked to say that he'd been charming the ladies since the age of four.

It was just that when he was with Francesca it was vitally important that that aspect of his personality remained at the forefront, so that she never suspected what lay underneath.

"What are your plans now that you are returned?" Violet asked.

Michael turned to her with what he knew had to be a blank expression. "I'm not certain, actually," he said, ashamed to admit to himself that that was true. "I imagine it will take me some time to understand just what exactly is expected of me in my new role."

"I'm sure Francesca can be of help in that quarter," Violet said.

"Only if she wishes it," Michael said quietly.

"Of course," Francesca said, moving slightly to the side when a maid came in with a tea tray. "I will assist you in any way you need."

"That was rather quick," Michael murmured.

"I'm mad for tea," Violet explained. "Drink it all day long. The maids keep water to near boiling on the stove at all times now."

"Will you have some?" Francesca asked, since she had taken charge of pouring.

"Yes, thank you," Michael replied.

"No one knows Kilmartin as Francesca does," Violet said, with all the pride of a mother hen. "She will prove invaluable to you."

"I am quite sure that you are correct," Michael said, accepting a cup from Francesca. She had remembered how he took it—milk, no sugar. For some reason this pleased him immensely. "She has been the countess for six years, and for four of them, she has had to be the earl as well." At Francesca's startled glance, he added, "In every way but in name. Oh, come now, Francesca, you must realize that it is true."

"I—"

"*And*," he added, "that it is a compliment. I owe you a greater debt than I could ever repay. I could not have stayed away so long had I not known that the earldom was in such capable hands."

Francesca actually blushed, which surprised him. In all the years he'd known her, he could count on one hand the times he had seen her cheeks go pink.

"Thank you," she mumbled. "It was no difficulty, I assure you."

"Perhaps, but it is appreciated all the same." He lifted his teacup to his lips, allowing the ladies to direct the conversation from there.

Which they did. Violet asked him about his time in India, and before he knew it he was telling them of palaces and princesses, caravans and curries. He left out the marauders and malaria, deciding they weren't quite the thing for a drawing-room conversation.

After a while he realized that he was enjoying himself immensely. Maybe, he thought, reflecting on the moment as Violet said something about an Indian-themed ball she'd attended the year before, just maybe he'd made the right decision.

It might actually be good to be home.

An hour later, Francesca found herself on Michael's arm, strolling through Hyde Park. The sun had broken through the clouds, and when she had declared that she could not resist the fine weather, Michael had had no choice but to offer to accompany her for a walk.

"It's rather like old times," she said, tilting her face up toward the sun. She'd most likely end up with a ghastly tan, or at the very least freckles, but she supposed she'd always look like pale porcelain next to Michael, whose skin marked him immediately as a recent returnee from the tropics.

"Walking, you mean?" he asked. "Or your expertly maneuvering me into accompanying you?"

She tried to maintain a straight face. "Both, of course. You used to take me out a great deal. Whenever John was busy."

"So I did."

They walked on in silence for a few moments, and then he said, "I was a bit surprised to find you gone this morning."

"I hope you understand why I had to leave," she said. "I didn't want to, of course; returning to my mother's home makes me feel as if I'm stepping right back into childhood." She felt her lips pinching together in distaste. "I adore her, of course, but I've grown rather used to maintaining my own household."

"Would you like me to take up residence elsewhere?"

"No, of course not," she said quickly. "You are the earl. Kilmartin House belongs to you. Besides, Helen and Janet are only a week behind me; they should arrive soon, and then I will be able to move back in."

"Chin up, Francesca. I'm sure you will endure."

She shot him a sideways glance. "It is nothing that you—or any man, for that matter—will understand, but I much prefer my status as a married woman to that of a debutante. When I'm at Number Five, with both Eloise and Hyacinth in residence, I feel as if I'm back in my first season, with all the attendant rules and regulations."

"Not all of them," he pointed out. "If that were true, you'd not be allowed out with me right now."

"True," she acceded. "Especially with you, I imagine."

"And just what is that supposed to mean?"

She laughed. "Oh, come now, Michael. Did you really think that your reputation would find itself whitewashed just because you left the country for four years?"

"Francesca—"

"You're a *legend*."

He looked aghast.

"It's true," she said, wondering why he was so surprised. "Goodness, women are still talking about you."

"Not to you, I hope," he muttered.

"Oh, to me above all others." She grinned wickedly. "They all want to know when you plan to return. And it's sure to be worse once word gets out that you're back. I must say, it's rather an odd role—confidante to London's most notorious rake."

"Confidante, eh?"

"What else would you call it?"

"No, no, confidante is a perfectly appropriate word. It's just that if you think I've confided *everything* in you . . ."

Francesca shot him a cross expression. This was so like him, letting his words trail off meaningfully, leaving her imagination feverish with questions. "I take it then," she muttered, "that you did not share with us all the news from India."

He just smiled. Devilishly.

"Very well. Allow me, then, to move the conversation to more respectable areas. What *do* you plan to do now that you are back? Will you take up your seat in Parliament?"

He appeared not to have considered that.

"It is what John would have wanted," she said, knowing that she was being fiendishly manipulative.

Michael looked at her grimly, and his eyes told her that he did not appreciate her tactics.

"You will have to marry as well," Francesca said.

"Do you plan to take on the role of my matchmaker?" he asked peevishly.

She shrugged. "If you desire it. I'm sure I couldn't possibly do a worse job of it than you."

"Good God," he grumbled, "I've been back one day. Do we need to address this now?"

"No, of course not," she allowed. "But soon. You're not getting any younger."

Michael just stared at her in shock. "I can't imagine permitting anyone else to speak to me in such a manner."

"Don't forget your mother," she said with a satisfied smile.

"You," he said rather forcefully, "are *not* my mother."

"Thank heavens for that," she returned. "I'd have expired of heart failure years ago. I don't know how she does it."

He actually halted in his tracks. "I'm not *that* bad."

She shrugged delicately. "Aren't you?"

And he was speechless. Absolutely speechless. It was a conversation they'd had countless times, but something was different now. There was an edge to her voice, a jab to her words that had never quite been there before.

Or maybe it was just that he'd never noticed it.

"Oh, don't look so shocked, Michael," she said, reaching across her body and patting him lightly on the arm. "Of course you have a terrible reputation. But you are endlessly charming, and so you are always forgiven."

Was this how she saw him, he wondered. And why was he surprised? It was exactly the image he'd cultivated.

"And now that you are the earl," she continued, "the mamas shall be falling all over themselves to pair you with their precious daughters."

"I feel afraid," he said under his breath. "Very afraid."

"You should," she said, with no sympathy whatsoever. "It will be a feeding frenzy, I assure you. You are fortunate that I took my mother aside this morning and made her swear not to throw Eloise or Hyacinth in your path. She would do it, too," she added, clearly relishing the conversation.

"I seem to recall that you used to find joy in throwing your sisters in my path."

Her lips twisted slightly. "That was years ago," she said, swishing her hand through the air as if she could wave his words away on the wind. "You would never suit."

He'd never had any desire to court either of her sisters, but nor could he resist the chance to give Francesca a wee verbal poke. "Eloise," he queried, "or Hyacinth?"

"Neither," she replied, with enough testiness to make him smile. "But I shall find you someone, do not fret."

"Was I fretting?"

She went on as if he hadn't spoken. "I think I shall introduce you to Eloise's friend Penelope."

"Miss Featherington?" he asked, vaguely recalling a slightly pudgy girl who never spoke.

"She's my friend as well, of course," Francesca added. "I believe you might like her."

"Has she learned to speak?"

She glared at him. "I'm going to ignore that comment. Penelope is a perfectly lovely and highly intelligent lady once one gets past her initial shyness."

"And how long does *that* take?" he muttered.

"I think she would balance you quite nicely," Francesca declared.

"Francesca," he said, somewhat forcefully, "you will not play matchmaker for me. Is that understood?"

"Well, some—"

"And don't you say that someone has to," he cut in. Really, she was the same open book she'd been years ago. She'd always wanted to manage his life.

"Michael," she said, the word coming out as a sigh that was far more long-suffering than she had a right to be.

"I have been back in town for one day," he said. "One day. I am tired, and I don't care if the sun is out—I'm still bloody cold, and my belongings haven't even been unpacked. Pray give me at least a week before you start planning my wedding."

"A week, then?" she said slyly.

"Francesca," he said, his voice laced with warning.

"Very well," she said dismissively. "But don't you dare say I didn't warn you. Once you are out in society, and the young ladies have you backed into a corner with their mamas coming in for the kill—"

He shuddered at the image. And at the knowledge that her prediction was probably correct.

"—you will be begging for my help," she finished, looking up at him with a rather annoyingly satisfied expression.

"I'm sure I will," he said, giving her a paternalistic smile that he knew she'd detest. "And when that happens, I promise you that I shall be duly prostrate with regretfulness, atonement, shamefacedness, and any other unpleasant emotion you care to assign to me."

And then she laughed, which warmed his heart far more than he should have let it. He could always make her laugh.

She turned to him and smiled, then patted his arm. "It's good to have you back."

"It's good to be back," he said. He'd said the words automatically, but he realized he'd meant them. It *was* good. Difficult, but good. But even difficult wasn't worth complaining over. It was certainly nothing he wasn't used to.

They were fairly deep in Hyde Park now, and the grounds were growing a bit more crowded. The trees were only just beginning to bud, but the air was still nippy enough that the people out strolling weren't looking for shade.

"I should have brought bread for the birds," Francesca murmured.

"At the Serpentine?" Michael asked with surprise. He'd often walked in Hyde Park with Francesca, and they had tended to avoid that area of the Serpentine's banks like the plague. It was always full of nursemaids and children, shrieking like little savages (often the nursemaids more so than the children) and Michael had at least one acquaintance who had found himself pelted in the head with a loaf of bread.

Seems no one had told the budding little cricket player that one was supposed to break the bread into more manageable—and less hazardous—segments.

"I like to toss bread in for the birds," Francesca said, a touch defensively. "Besides, there won't be too many children about today. It's still a bit cold yet."

"Never stopped John and me," Michael offered gamely.

"Yes, well, you're Scottish," she returned. "Your blood circulates quite well half frozen."

He grinned. "A hearty lot, we Scots." It was a bit of a joke, that. With so much intermarriage, the family was at least as much English as it was Scottish, perhaps even more so, but with Kilmartin firmly situated in the border counties, the Stirlings clung to their Scottish heritage like a badge of honor.

They found a bench not too far from the Serpentine and sat, idly watching the ducks on the water.

"You'd think they'd find a warmer spot," Michael said. "France, maybe."

"And miss out on all the food the children toss at them?" Francesca smiled wryly. "They're not stupid."

He just shrugged. Far be it from him to pretend any great knowledge of avian behavior.

"How did you find the climate in India?" Francesca queried. "Is it as hot as they say?"

"More so," he replied. "Or maybe not. I don't know. I imagine the descriptions are perfectly accurate. The problem is, no Englishman can truly understand what they mean until he gets there."

She looked at him quizzically.

"It's hotter than you could ever imagine," he said, spelling it out.

"It sounds . . . Well, I don't know how it sounds," she admitted.

"The heat isn't nearly so difficult as the insects."

"It sounds dreadful," Francesca decided.

"You probably wouldn't like it. Not for an extended stay, anyway."

"I'd like to travel, though," she said softly. "I'd always planned to."

She fell silent, nodding in a rather absentminded manner, her chin tilting up and down for so long that he was quite sure she'd forgotten she was doing it. Then he realized that her eyes were fixed off in the distance. She was watching something, but for the life of him he couldn't imagine what. There was nothing interesting in the vista, just a pinchfaced nursemaid pushing a pram.

"What are you looking at?" he finally asked.

She said nothing, just continued to stare.

"Francesca?"

She turned to him. "I want a baby."

Chapter 7

. . . had hoped to have received a note from you by now, but of course the post is notoriously unreliable when it must travel so far. Just last week I heard tale of the arrival of a mail pouch that was a full two years old; many of the recipients had already returned to England. My mother writes that you are well and fully recovered from your ordeal; I am glad to hear of it. My work here continues to challenge and fulfill. I have taken up residence outside the city proper, as do most Europeans here in Madras. Nonetheless, I enjoy visiting the city; it is rather Grecian in appearance; or rather, what I must imagine is Grecian, having never visited that country myself. The sky is blue, so blue it is nearly blinding, almost the bluest thing I have ever seen.

—from the Earl of Kilmartin to the Countess of Kilmartin, six months after his arrival in India

"I beg your pardon?"

She'd shocked him. He was sputtering, even. She hadn't made

her announcement to elicit this sort of reaction, but now that he was sitting there, his mouth hanging open and slack, she couldn't help but take a small amount of pleasure from the moment.

"I want a baby," she said with a shrug. "Is there something surprising in that?"

His lips moved before he actually made sound. "Well . . . no . . . but . . ."

"I'm twenty-six."

"I know how old you are," he said, a little testily.

"I'll be twenty-seven at the end of April. I don't think it's so odd that I might want a child."

His eyes still held a vaguely glazed sort of quality. "No, of course not, but—"

"And I shouldn't have to explain myself to you!"

"I wasn't asking you to," he said, staring at her as if she'd grown two heads.

"I'm sorry," she mumbled. "I overreacted."

He said nothing, which irritated her. At the very least, he could have contradicted her. It would have been a lie, but it was still the kind and courteous thing to do.

Finally, because the silence was simply unbearable, she muttered, "A lot of women want children."

"Right," he said, coughing on the word. "Of course. But . . . don't you think you might want a husband first?"

"Of course." She speared him with an aggravated glare. "Why do you think I came down to London early?"

He looked at her blankly.

"I am shopping for a husband," she said, speaking to him as if he were a halfwit.

"How mercenarily put," he murmured.

She pursed her lips. "It's what it is. And you had probably best get used to it for your own sake. It's precisely how the ladies will soon be talking about *you.*"

He ignored the latter part of her statement. "Do you have a particular gentleman in mind?"

She shook her head. "Not yet. I imagine someone will pop to the forefront once I start looking, though." She was trying to sound jolly about it, but the truth was, her voice was dropping in both tone and volume. "I'm sure my brothers have friends," she finally mumbled.

He looked at her, then slumped back slightly and stared at the water.

"I've shocked you," she said.

"Well . . . yes."

"Normally, I'd take great pleasure in that," she said, her lips twisting ironically.

He didn't reply, but he did roll his eyes slightly.

"I can't mourn John forever," she said. "I mean, I can, and I will, but . . ." She stopped, hating that she was near tears. "And the worst part of it is, maybe I can't even *have* children. It took me two years to conceive with John, and look how I mucked that up."

"Francesca," he said fiercely, "you mustn't blame yourself for the miscarriage."

She let out a bitter laugh. "Can you imagine? Marrying someone just so I could have a baby and then not having one?"

"It happens to people all the time," he said softly.

It was true, but it didn't make her feel any better. *She* had a choice. She didn't have to marry; she would be quite well provided for—and blessedly independent—if she remained a widow. If she married—no, *when* she married—she had to mentally commit to the idea—it wouldn't be for love. She wasn't going to have a marriage like the one she'd shared with John; a woman simply didn't find love like that twice in a lifetime.

She was going to marry for a baby, and there was no guarantee that she would get one.

"Francesca?"

She didn't look at him, just sat there and blinked, desperately trying to ignore the tears burning at the corners of her eyes.

Michael held out a handkerchief, but she didn't want to acknowledge the gesture. If she took the cloth, then she'd *have* to cry. There would be nothing stopping her.

"I must move on," she said defiantly. "I must. John is gone, and I—"

And then the strangest thing happened. Except *strange* wasn't really the right word. Shocking, perhaps, or altering, or maybe there wasn't a word for the type of surprise that stole the pulse from one's body, leaving one immobile, unable to breathe.

She turned to him. It should have been a simple thing. She'd certainly turned to Michael before, hundreds . . . no, thousands of times. He might have spent the last four years in India, but she knew his face, and she knew his smile. In truth, she knew everything about him—

Except this time was different. She turned to him, but she hadn't expected him to have already turned to her. And she hadn't expected him to be so close that she'd see the charcoal flecks in his eyes.

But most of all, she hadn't expected her gaze to drop to his lips. They were full, and lush, and finely molded, and she knew the shape as well as the shape of her own, except never before had she really *looked* at them, noticed the way they weren't quite uniform in color, or how the curve of his lower lip was really quite sensual, and—

She stood. So quickly that she nearly lost her balance. "I have to go," she said, stunned that her voice sounded like her own and not some freakish demon. "I have an appointment. I'd forgotten."

"Of course," he said, standing beside her.

"With the dressmaker," she added, as if details would make her lie more convincing. "All my clothes are in half-mourning colors."

He nodded. "They don't suit you."

"Kind of you to point it out," she said testily.

"You should wear blue," he said.

She nodded jerkily, still off balance and out of sorts.

"Are you all right?" he asked.

"I'm fine," she bit off. And then, because no one would ever have been fooled by her tone, she added, more carefully, "I'm fine. I assure you. I simply detest being tardy." That much was true, and he knew it of her, so hopefully he'd accept it as reason for her snappishness.

"Very well," he said collegially, and Francesca chattered all the way back to Number Five. She had to put up a good front, she realized rather feverishly. She couldn't possibly allow him to guess what had really transpired within her on the bench by the Serpentine.

She had known, of course, that Michael was handsome, even startlingly so. But it had all been an abstract sort of knowledge. Michael was handsome, just as her brother Benedict was tall, and her mother had beautiful eyes.

But suddenly . . . But now . . .

She'd looked at him, and she'd seen something entirely new.

She'd seen a *man*.

And it scared the very devil out of her.

Francesca tended to subscribe to the notion that the best course of action was more action, so when she returned to Number Five after her stroll, she sought out her mother and informed her that she needed to visit the modiste immediately. Best to make truth out of her lie as soon as possible, after all.

Her mother was only too delighted to see Francesca out of her half-mourning grays and lavenders, and so barely an hour passed before the two of them were comfortably ensconced in Violet's elegant carriage, on their way to the exclusive shops on Bond Street. Normally, Francesca would have bristled at Violet's interference; she was perfectly capable of picking out her own wardrobe, thank you very much, but today she found her mother's presence oddly comforting.

Not that her mother wasn't usually a comfort. Just that Francesca tended to favor her independent streak more often than not, and she rather preferred not to be thought of as "one of those Bridgerton girls." And in a very strange way, this trip to the dressmaker was rather discomfiting. It would have required full-fledged torture to get her to admit it, but Francesca was, quite simply, terrified.

Even if she hadn't decided it was time to remarry, shrugging off her widow's weeds signaled a huge change, and not one she was entirely sure she was ready for.

She looked down at her sleeve as she sat in the carriage. She couldn't see the fabric of her dress—it was covered by her coat—but she knew that it was lavender. And there was something comforting in that, something solid and dependable. She'd worn that color, or gray in its place, for three years now. And unrelenting black for a year before that. It had been a bit of a badge, she realized, a uniform of sorts. One never had to worry about who one was when one's clothing proclaimed it so loudly.

"Mother?" she said, before she even realized that she had a question to ask.

Violet turned to her with a smile. "Yes, dear?"

"Why did you never remarry?"

Violet's lips parted slightly, and to Francesca's great surprise, her eyes grew bright. "Do you know," Violet said softly, "this is the first time any of you has asked me that?"

"That can't be true," Francesca said. "Are you certain?"

Violet nodded. "None of my children has asked me. I would have remembered."

"No, no, of course you would," Francesca said quickly. But it was all so . . . odd. And unthinking, really. Why would no one have asked Violet about this? It seemed to Francesca quite the most burning question imaginable. And even if none of Violet's children had cared about the answer for their own personal curiosity, didn't they realize how important it was to Violet?

Didn't they want to *know* their mother? Truly know her?

"When your father died . . ." Violet said. "Well, I don't know how much you recall, but it was very sudden. None of us expected it." She gave a sad little laugh, and Francesca wondered if she'd ever be able to laugh about John's death, even if it was tinged with grief.

"A bee sting," Violet continued, and Francesca realized that even now, more than twenty years after Edmund Bridgerton's death, her mother still sounded surprised when she talked about it.

"Who would have thought it possible?" Violet said, shaking her head. "I don't know how well you remember him, but your father was a very large man. As tall as Benedict and perhaps even broader in the shoulders. You just wouldn't think that a bee . . ." She stopped, pulling out a crisp, white handkerchief and holding it to her lips as she cleared her throat. "Well, it was unexpected. I don't really know what else to say, except . . ." She turned to her daughter with achingly wise eyes. "Except I imagine you understand better than anyone."

Francesca nodded, not even trying to stem the burning sensation behind her eyes.

"Anyway," Violet said briskly, obviously eager to move forward, "after his death, I was just so . . . stunned. I felt as if I were walking in a haze. I'm not at all certain how I functioned that first year. Or even the ones directly thereafter. So I couldn't possibly even think of marriage."

"I know," Francesca said softly. And she did.

"And after that . . . well, I don't know what happened. Maybe I just didn't meet anyone with whom I cared to share my life. Maybe I loved your father too much." She shrugged. "Maybe I just never saw the need. I was in a very different position from you, after all. I was older, don't forget, and already the mother of eight children. And your father left our affairs in very good order. I knew we would never want for anything."

"John left Kilmartin in excellent order," Francesca said quickly.

"Of course he did," Violet said, patting her hand. "Forgive me. I did not mean to imply otherwise. But you don't have eight children, Francesca." Her eyes changed somehow, grew an even deeper blue. "And you've quite a lot of time ahead of you to spend it all alone."

Francesca nodded jerkily. "I know," she said. "I know. I know, but I can't quite . . . I can't . . ."

"You can't what?" Violet asked gently.

"I can't . . ." Francesca looked down. She didn't know why, but for some reason she couldn't take her eyes off the floor. "I can't rid myself of the feeling that I'm doing something wrong, that I'm dishonoring John, dishonoring our marriage."

"John would have wanted you to be happy."

"I know. I know. Of course he would. But don't you see—" She looked up again, her eyes searching her mother's face for something, she wasn't sure what—maybe approval, maybe just love, since there was something comforting in looking for something she already knew she'd find. "I'm not even looking for that," she added. "I'm not going to find someone like John. I've accepted that. And it feels so wrong to marry with less."

"You won't find someone like John, that is true," Violet said. "But you might find a man who will suit you equally well, just in a different way."

"You didn't."

"No, I didn't," she agreed, "but I didn't look very hard. I didn't look at all."

"Do you wish you had?"

Violet opened her mouth, but not a sound came out, not even breath. Finally she said, "I don't know, Francesca. I honestly don't know." And then, because the moment almost certainly needed a bit of laughter, she added, "I certainly didn't want any more children!"

Francesca couldn't help but smile. "I do," she said softly. "I want a baby."

"I thought that you did."

"Why did you never ask me about it?"

Violet tilted her head to the side. "Why did you never ask me about why I never remarried?"

Francesca felt her lips part. She shouldn't have been so surprised by her mother's perceptiveness.

"If you had been Eloise, I think I would have said something," Violet added. "Or any of your sisters, for that matter. But you—" She smiled nostalgically. "You're not the same. You never have been. Even as a child you set yourself apart. And you needed your distance."

Impulsively, Francesca reached out and squeezed her mother's hand. "I love you, did you know that?"

Violet smiled. "I rather suspected it."

"Mother!"

"Very well, of course I knew it. How could you not love me when I love you so very, very much?"

"I haven't said it," Francesca said, feeling rather horrified by her omission. "Not recently, anyway."

"It's quite all right." Violet squeezed her hand back. "You've had other things on your mind."

And for some reason that made Francesca giggle under her breath. "A bit of an understatement, I should say."

Violet just grinned.

"Mother?" Francesca blurted out. "May I ask you one more question?"

"Of course."

"If I don't find someone—not like John, of course, but still not equally suited to me. If I don't find someone like that, and I marry someone whom I rather like, but perhaps don't love . . . is that all right?"

Violet was silent for several moments before she answered. "I'm afraid only you will know the answer to that," she finally said. "I would never say no, of course. Half the *ton*—more than half, in truth—has marriages like that, and quite a few of them are perfectly content. But you will have to make your judgments for yourself when they arise. Everyone is different, Francesca. I suspect you know that better than most. And when a man asks for your hand, you will have to judge him on his merits and not by some arbitrary standard you have set out ahead of time."

She was right, of course, but Francesca was so sick of life being messy and complicated that it wasn't the answer she'd been seeking.

And none of it addressed the problem that lay most deeply

within her heart. What would happen if she actually did meet someone who made her feel the way she'd felt with John? She couldn't imagine that she would; truly, it seemed wildly improbable.

But what if she did? How could she live with herself then?

There was something rather satisfying about a foul mood, so Michael decided to indulge his completely.

He kicked a pebble all the way home.

He snarled at anyone who jostled him on the street.

He yanked open his front door with such ferocity that it slammed into the stone wall behind it. Or rather he would have done, if his sodding butler hadn't been so on his toes and had the door open before Michael's fingers could even touch the handle.

But he *thought* about slamming it open, which provided some satisfaction in and of itself.

And then he stomped up the stairs to his room—which still felt too bloody much like John's room, not that there was anything he could do about that just then—and yanked off his boots.

Or tried to.

Bloody hell.

"Reivers!" he bellowed.

His valet appeared—or really, it seemed rather more like he apparated—in the doorway.

"Yes, my lord?"

"Would you help me with my boots?" Michael ground out, feeling rather infantile. Three years in the army and four in India, and he couldn't remove his own damned boots? What was it about London that reduced a man to a sniveling idiot? He seemed to recall that Reivers had had to remove his boots for him the last time he'd lived in London as well.

He looked down. They *were* different boots. Different styles, he supposed, for different situations, and Reivers had always taken a stunningly ridiculous pride in his work. Of course he'd have wanted to outfit Michael in the very best of London fashion. He'd have—

"Reivers?" Michael said in a low voice. "Where did you get these boots?"

"My lord?"

"These boots. I do not recognize them."

"We have not yet received all of your trunks from the ship, my lord. You didn't have anything suitable for London, so I located these among the previous earl's belong—"

"*Jesus.*"

"My lord? I'm terribly sorry if these don't suit you. I remembered that the two of you were of a size, and I thought you'd want—"

"Just get them off. Now." Michael closed his eyes and sat in a leather chair—*John's* leather chair—marveling at the irony of it. His worst nightmare coming true, in the most literal of fashions.

"Of course, my lord." Reivers looked pained, but he quickly went to work removing the boots.

Michael pinched the bridge of his nose with his thumb and forefinger and let out a long breath before speaking again. "I would prefer not to use any items from the previous earl's wardrobe," he said wearily. Truly, he had no idea why John's clothing was still here; the lot of it should have been given to the servants or donated to charity years ago. But he supposed that was Francesca's decision to make, not his.

"Of course, my lord. I shall see to it immediately."

"Good," Michael grunted.

"Shall I have it locked away?"

Locked? Good God, it wasn't as if the stuff were toxic. "I'm sure it is all just fine where it is," Michael said. "Just don't use any of it for me."

"Right." Reivers swallowed, and his Adam's apple bobbed uncomfortably.

"What is it now, Reivers?"

"It's just that all of the previous Lord Kilmartin's accouterments are still here."

"Here?" Michael asked blankly.

"Here," Reivers confirmed, glancing about the room.

Michael sagged in his chair. It wasn't that he wanted to wipe every last reminder of his cousin off the face of this earth; *no one* missed John as much as he did, no one.

Well, except maybe Francesca, he allowed, but that was different.

But he just didn't know how he was meant to lead his life so completely and smotheringly surrounded by John's belongings. He held his title, spent his money, lived in his house. Was he meant to wear his damned shoes as well?

"Pack it all up," he said to Reivers. "Tomorrow. I don't wish to be disturbed this evening."

And besides, he probably ought to alert Francesca of his intentions.

Francesca.

He sighed, rising to his feet once the valet had departed. Christ, Reivers had forgotten to take the boots with him. Michael picked them up and deposited them outside the door. He was probably overreacting, but hell, he just didn't want to stare at John's boots for the next six hours.

After shutting the door with a decisive click, he padded aimlessly over to the window. The sill was wide and deep, and he leaned heavily against it, gazing through the sheer curtains at the blurry streetscape below. He pushed the thin fabric aside, his lips twisting into a bitter smile as he watched a nursemaid tugging a small child along the pavement.

Francesca. She wanted a baby.

He didn't know why he was so surprised. If he thought about it rationally, he really shouldn't have been. She was a woman, for God's sake; of course she'd want children. Didn't they all? And while he'd never consciously sat down and told himself that she'd pine away for John forever, he'd also never considered the idea that she might actually care to remarry one day.

Francesca and John. John and Francesca. They were a unit, or at least they had been, and although John's death had made it sadly easy to envision one without the other, it was quite something else entirely to think of one with another.

And then of course there was the small matter of his skin crawling, which was his general reaction to the thought of Francesca with another man.

He shuddered. Or was that a shiver? Damn, he hoped it wasn't a shiver.

He supposed he was simply going to have to get used to the notion. If Francesca wanted children, then Francesca needed a husband, and there wasn't a damned thing he could do about it. It would have been rather nice, he supposed, if she had come to this decision and taken care of the whole odious matter last year, sparing him the nausea of having to witness the entire courtship unfold. If she'd just gone and gotten herself married *last* year, then it would have been over and done with, and that would have been that.

End of story.

But now he was going to have to *watch*. Maybe even advise.

Bloody hell.

He shivered again. Damn. Maybe he was just cold. It was March, after all, and a chilly one at that, even with a fire in the grate.

He tugged at his cravat, which was starting to feel unaccountably tight, then yanked it off altogether. Christ, he felt like the very devil, all hot and cold, and queerly off balance.

He sat down. It seemed the best course of action.

And then he just gave up all pretense of being well, stripping off the rest of his clothing and crawling into bed.

It was going to be a long night.

Chapter 8

. . . ~~wonderful lovely nice~~ good to hear from you. I am glad you are faring well. John would have been proud. ~~I miss you~~. I miss him. ~~I miss you~~. Some of the flowers are still out. Isn't it nice that some of the flowers are still out?

—from the Countess of Kilmartin to the Earl of Kilmartin, one week after the receipt of his second missive to her, first draft, never finished, never sent

"Didn't Michael say that he would be joining us for supper this evening?"

Francesca looked up at her mother, who was standing before her with concerned eyes. She had been thinking the exact same thing, actually, wondering what was keeping him.

She'd spent the better part of the day dreading his arrival, even though he had absolutely no idea that she had been so distressed by that moment in the park. Good heavens, he probably didn't even realize there *had* been a "moment."

It was the first time in her life that Francesca was thankful for the general obtuseness of men.

"Yes, he did say that he would come," she replied, shifting slightly in her chair. She had been waiting for some time now in the drawing room with her mother and two of her sisters, idly passing the time until their supper guest arrived.

"Didn't we give him the time?" Violet asked.

Francesca nodded. "I confirmed it with him when he left me here after our stroll in the park." She was quite certain of the exchange; she clearly recalled feeling rather sick in her stomach when they had spoken of it. She hadn't wanted to see him again—not so quickly, anyway—but what could she do? Her mother had issued the invitation.

"He's probably just running late," said Hyacinth, Francesca's youngest sister. "I'm not surprised. His sort is always late."

Francesca turned on her instantly. "What is that supposed to mean?"

"I've heard all about his reputation."

"What has his reputation to do with anything?" Francesca asked testily. "And anyway, what would you know of it? He left England years before you made your bow."

Hyacinth shrugged, jabbing a needle into her extremely untidy embroidery. "People still speak of him," she said carelessly. "The ladies swoon like idiots at the mere mention of his name, if you must know."

"There's no other way to swoon," put in Eloise, who, although Francesca's elder by precisely one year, was still unmarried.

"Well, rake he may be," Francesca said archly, "but he has always been punctual to a fault." She never could countenance others speaking ill of Michael. She might sigh and moan and belabor his faults, but it was entirely unacceptable that Hyacinth, whose knowledge of Michael was based entirely on rumor and innuendo, would make such a sweeping judgment.

"Believe what you will," Francesca said sharply, because there was no way she was going to allow Hyacinth to have the last word, "but he would never be late to a supper here. He holds Mother in far too high regard."

"What about his regard for you?" Hyacinth said.

Francesca glared at her sister, who was smirking into her embroidery. "He—" No, she wasn't going to do this. She wasn't going to sit here and get into an argument with her younger sister, not when something might actually be wrong. Michael was, for all his wicked ways, faultlessly polite and considerate to the bone, or at least he had always been so in her presence. And he would never have arrived for supper—she glanced up at the mantel clock—over thirty minutes late. Not, at least, without sending word.

She stood, briskly smoothing down her dove gray skirts. "I am going to Kilmartin House," she announced.

"By yourself?" Violet asked.

"By myself," Francesca said firmly. "It is my home, after all. I hardly think that tongues will wag if I stop by for a quick visit."

"Yes, yes, of course," her mother said. "But don't stay too long."

"Mother, I am a widow. And I do not plan to spend the night. I merely intend to inquire as to Michael's welfare. I shall be just fine, I assure you."

Violet nodded, but from her expression, Francesca could see that she would have liked to have said more. It had been like this for years—Violet wanted to resume her role of mother hen to her young widowed daughter, but she held back, attempting to respect her independence.

She didn't always manage to resist interfering, but she tried, and Francesca was grateful for the effort.

"Do you want me to accompany you?" Hyacinth asked, her eyes lighting up.

"No!" Francesca said, surprise making her tone a bit more vehement than she'd intended it. "Why on earth would you want to?"

Hyacinth shrugged. "Curiosity. I'd like to meet the Merry Rake."

"You've met him," Eloise pointed out.

"Yes, but that was ages ago," Hyacinth said with a dramatic sigh, "before I understood what a rake was."

"You don't understand that now," Violet said sharply.

"Oh, but I—"

"You do *not*," Violet repeated, "understand what a rake is."

"Very well." Hyacinth turned to her mother with a sickly sweet smile. "I don't know what a rake is. I also don't know how to dress myself or wash my own teeth."

"I did see Polly helping her on with her evening gown last night," Eloise murmured from the sofa.

"No one can get into an evening gown on her own," Hyacinth shot back.

"I'm leaving," Francesca announced, even though she was quite certain no one was listening to her.

"What are you doing?" Hyacinth demanded.

Francesca stopped short until she realized that Hyacinth wasn't speaking to her.

"Just examining your teeth," Eloise said sweetly.

"Girls!" Violet exclaimed, although Francesca couldn't imagine that Eloise took too kindly to the generalization, being seven and twenty as she was.

And indeed she didn't, but Francesca took Eloise's irritation and subsequent rejoinder as an opportunity to slip out of the room and ask a footman to call up the carriage for her.

The streets were not very crowded; it was early yet, and the *ton* would not be heading out for parties and balls for at least another hour or two. The carriage moved swiftly through Mayfair, and in under a quarter of an hour Francesca was climbing the front steps of Kilmartin House in St. James's. As usual, a footman opened the door before she could even lift the knocker, and she hurried inside.

"Is Kilmartin here?" she asked, realizing with a small jolt of surprise that it was the first time she had referred to Michael as such. It was strange, she realized, and good, really, how naturally it had come to her lips. It was probably past time that they all grew used to the change. He was the earl now, and he'd never be plain Mr. Stirling again.

"I believe so," the footman replied. "He came in early this afternoon, and I was not made aware of his departure."

Francesca frowned, then gave a nod of dismissal before heading up the steps. If Michael was indeed at home, he must be upstairs; if he were down in his office, the footman would have noticed his presence.

She reached the second floor, then strode down the hall toward the earl's suite, her booted feet silent on the plush Aubusson carpet. "Michael?" she called out softly, as she approached his room. "Michael?"

There was no response, so she moved closer to his door, which she noticed was not quite all the way closed. "Michael?" she called again, only slightly louder. It wouldn't do to bellow his name through the house. Besides, if he was sleeping, she didn't wish to wake him. He was probably still tired from his long journey and had been too proud to indicate as such when Violet had invited him to supper.

Still nothing, so she pushed the door open a few additional inches. "Michael?"

She heard something. A rustle, maybe. Maybe a groan.

"Michael?"

"Frannie?"

It was definitely his voice, but it wasn't like anything she'd ever heard from his lips.

"Michael?" She rushed in to find him huddled in his bed, looking quite as sick as she'd ever seen another human being. John, of course, had never been sick. He'd merely gone to bed one evening and woken up dead.

So to speak.

"Michael!" she gasped. "What is wrong with you?"

"Oh, nothing much," he croaked. "Head cold, I imagine."

Francesca looked down at him with dubious eyes. His dark hair was plastered to his forehead, his skin was flushed and mottled, and the level of heat radiating from the bed quite took her breath away.

Not to mention that he smelled sick. It was that awful, sweaty, slightly putrid smell, the sort that, if it had a color, would surely be vomitous green. Francesca reached out and touched his forehead, recoiling instantly at the heat of it.

"This is *not* a head cold," she said sharply.

His lips stretched into a hideous approximation of a smile. "A really bad head cold?"

"Michael Stuart Stirling!"

"Good God, you sound like my mother."

She didn't particularly feel like his mother, especially not after what had happened in the park, and it was almost a bit of a relief to see him so feeble and unattractive. It took the edge off whatever it was she'd been feeling earlier that afternoon.

"Michael, what is wrong with you?"

He shrugged, then buried himself deeper under the covers, his entire body shaking from the exertion of it.

"Michael!" She reached out and grabbed his shoulder. None too gently, either. "Don't you dare try your usual tricks on me. I know exactly how you operate. You always pretend that nothing matters, that water rolls off your back—"

"It does roll off my back," he mumbled. "Yours as well. Simple science, really."

"Michael!" She would have smacked him if he weren't so ill. "You will not attempt to minimize this, do you understand me? I insist that you tell me right now what is wrong with you!"

"I'll be better tomorrow," he said.

"Oh, *right*," Francesca said, with all the sarcasm she could muster, which was, in truth, quite a bit.

"I will," he insisted, restlessly shifting positions, every movement punctuated with a groan. "I'll be fine for tomorrow."

Something about the phrasing of his words struck Francesca as profoundly odd. "And what about the day after that?" she asked, her eyes narrowing.

A harsh chuckle emerged from somewhere under the covers. "Why, then I'll be sick as a dog again, of course."

"Michael," she said again, dread forcing her voice low, "what is wrong with you?"

"Haven't you guessed?" He poked his head back out from under the sheet, and he looked so ill she wanted to cry. "I have malaria."

"Oh, my God," Francesca breathed, actually backing up a step. "Oh, my God."

"First time I've ever heard you blaspheme," he remarked. "Probably ought to be flattered it's over me."

She had no idea how he could be so flip at such a time. "Michael, I—" She reached out, then didn't reach out, unsure of what to do.

"Don't worry," he said, huddling closer into himself as his body was wracked with another wave of shudders. "You can't catch it from me."

"I can't?" She blinked. "I mean, of course I can't." And even if she could, that ought not to have stopped her from nursing him. He was Michael. He was . . . well, it seemed difficult precisely to define what he was to her, but they had an unbreakable bond, they two, and it seemed that four years and thousands of miles had done little to diminish it.

"It's the air," he said in a tired voice. "You have to breathe the putrid air to catch it. It's why they call it malaria. If you could get it from another person, we lot would have infected all of England by now."

She nodded at his explanation. "Are you . . . are you . . ." She couldn't ask it; she didn't know how.

"No," he said. "At least they don't think so."

She felt herself sag with relief, and she had to sit down. She couldn't imagine a world without him. Even while he'd been gone, she'd always known he was *there*, sharing the same planet with her, walking the same earth. And even in those early days following John's death, when she'd hated him for leaving her, even when she'd been so angry with him that she wanted to cry—she had taken some comfort in the knowledge that he was alive and well, and would return to her in an instant, if ever she asked it of him.

He was here. He was alive. And with John gone . . . Well, she didn't know how anyone could expect her to lose them both.

He shivered again, violently.

"Do you need medicine?" she asked, snapping to attention. "Do you *have* medicine?"

"Took it already," he chattered.

But she had to do *some*thing. She wasn't self-hating enough to think that there had been anything she could have done to prevent John's death—even in the worst of her grief she hadn't gone down *that* road—but she had always hated that the whole thing had happened in her absence. It was, in truth, the one momentous thing John had ever done without her. And even if Michael was only sick, and not dying, she was not going to allow him to suffer alone.

"Let me get you another blanket," she said. Without waiting for his reply, she rushed through the connecting door to her own suite and pulled the coverlet off her bed. It was rose pink and would most likely offend his masculine sensibilities once he reached a state of sensibility, but that, she decided, was *his* problem.

When she returned to his room, he was so still she thought he'd fallen asleep, but he managed to rouse himself enough to say thank you as she tucked the blanket over him.

"What else can I do?" she asked, pulling a wooden chair to the side of his bed and sitting down.

"Nothing."

"There must be something," she insisted. "Surely we're not meant to merely wait this out."

"We're meant," he said weakly, "to merely wait this out."

"I can't believe that's true."

He opened one eye. "Do you mean to challenge the entire medical establishment?"

She ground her teeth together and hunched over in her chair. "Are you certain you don't need more medicine?"

He shook his head, then moaned at the exertion of it. "Not for another few hours."

"Where is it?" she asked. If the only thing she could truly do was to locate the medication and be ready to dispense it, then by God, she would at least do that.

He moved his head slightly to the left. Francesca followed the motion toward a small table across the room, where a medicinal bottle sat atop a folded newspaper. She immediately rose and retrieved it, reading the label as she walked back to her chair. "Quinine," she murmured. "I've heard of that."

"Miracle medicine," Michael said. "Or so they say."

Francesca looked at him dubiously.

"Just look at me," he said with a lopsided—and feeble—grin. "Proof positive."

She inspected the bottle again, watching the powder shift as she tilted it. "I remain unconvinced."

One of his shoulders attempted to move in a blithe gesture. "I'm not dead."

"That's not funny."

"No, it's the *only* funny thing," he corrected. "We've got to take our laughter where we can. Just think, if I died, the title would go to—how does Janet always put it—that—"

"Awful Debenham side of the family," they finished together, and Francesca couldn't believe it, but she actually smiled.

He could always make her smile.

She reached out and took his hand. "We will get through this," she said.

He nodded, and then he closed his eyes.

But just when she thought he was asleep, he whispered, "It's better with you here."

The next morning Michael was feeling somewhat refreshed, and if not quite his usual self, then at least a damn sight better than he'd been the night before. Francesca, he was horrified to realize, was still in the wooden chair at his bedside, her head tilted drunkenly to the side. She looked uncomfortable in every way a body *could* look uncomfortable, from the way she was perched in the chair to the awkward angle of her neck and the strange spiral twist of her torso.

But she was asleep. Snoring, even, which he found rather endearing. He'd never pictured her snoring, and sad to say, he had imagined her asleep more times than he cared to count.

He supposed it had been too much to hope that he could hide his illness from her; she was far too perceptive and certainly far too nosy. And even though he would have preferred that she didn't worry over him, the truth was, he'd been comforted by her presence the night before. He shouldn't have been, or at least he shouldn't have allowed himself to be, but he just couldn't help it.

He heard her stir and rolled to his side to get a better look. He had never seen her wake up, he realized. He wasn't certain why he found that so strange; it wasn't as if he'd been privy to many of her private moments before. Maybe it was because in all of his daydreams, in all of his fantasies, he'd never quite pictured this—the low rumbling from deep in her throat as she shifted position, the small sigh of sound when she yawned, or even the delicate ballet of her eyelids as they fluttered open.

She was beautiful.

He'd known that, of course, had known that for years, but never before had he felt it quite so profoundly, quite so deeply in his bones.

It wasn't her hair, that rich, lush wave of chestnut that he was rarely so privileged as to see down. And it wasn't even her eyes, so radiantly blue that men had been moved to write poetry—much, Michael recalled, to John's everlasting amusement. It wasn't even in the shape of her face or the structure of her bones; if that were the case, he'd have been obsessed with the loveliness of all the Bridgerton girls; such peas in a pod they were, at least on the outside.

It was something in the way she moved.

Something in the way she breathed.

Something in the way she merely *was*.

And he didn't think he was ever going to get over it.

"Michael," she murmured, rubbing the sleep from her eyes.

"Good morning," he said, hoping she'd mistake the roughness in his voice for exhaustion.

"You look better."

"I feel better."

She swallowed and paused before she said, "You're used to this."

He nodded. "I wouldn't go so far as to say that I don't mind the illness, but yes, I'm used to it. I know what to do."

"How long will this continue?"

"It's hard to say. I'll get fevers every other day until I just . . . stop. A week in total, maybe two. Three if I'm fiendishly unlucky."

"And then what?"

He shrugged. "Then I wait and hope it never happens again."

"It can do that?" She sat up straight. "Just never come back?"

"It's a strange, fickle disease."

Her eyes narrowed. "*Don't* say it's like a woman."

"Hadn't even occurred to me until you brought it up."

Her lips tightened slightly, then relaxed as she asked, "How long has it been since your last . . ." She blinked. "What do you call them?"

He shrugged. "I call them attacks. Certainly feels like one. And it's been six months."

"Well, that's good!" She caught her lower lip between her teeth. "Isn't it?"

"Considering it had only been three before that, yes, I think so."

"How often has this happened?"

"This is the third time. All in all, it's not too bad compared with what I've seen."

"Am I meant to take solace in that?"

"I do," he said bluntly. "Model of Christian virtue that I am."

She reached out abruptly and touched his forehead. "You're much cooler," she remarked.

"Yes, I will be. It's a remarkably consistent disease. Well, at least when you're in the midst of it. It would be nice if I knew when I might expect an onset."

"And you'll really have another fever in a day's time? Just like that?"

"Just like that," he confirmed.

She seemed to consider that for a few moments, then said, "You won't be able to hide this from your family, of course."

He actually tried to sit up. "For God's sake, Francesca, *don't* tell my mother and—"

"They're expected any day now," she cut in. "When I left Scotland, they said they would be only a week behind me, and knowing Janet, that really means only three days. Do you truly expect them not to notice that you're rather conveniently—"

"Inconveniently," he cut in acerbically.

"Whichever," she said sharply. "Do you really think they won't notice that you're sick as death every other day? For heaven's sake, Michael, do credit them with a bit of intelligence."

"Very well," he said, slumping back against the pillows. "But no one else. I have no wish to become the freak of London."

"You're hardly the first person to be stricken with malaria."

"I don't want anyone's pity," he bit off. "Most especially yours."

She drew back as if struck, and of course he felt like an ass.

"Forgive me," he said. "That came out wrong."

She glared at him.

"I don't want your pity," he said repentantly, "but your care and your good wishes are most welcome."

Her eyes didn't meet his, but he could tell that she was trying to decide if she believed him.

"I mean it," he said, and he didn't have the energy to try to cover the exhaustion in his voice. "I am glad you were here. I have been through this before."

She looked over sharply, as if she were asking a question, but for the life of him, he didn't know what.

"I have been through this before," he said again, "and this time was . . . different. Better. Easier." He let out a long breath, relieved to have found the correct word. "Easier. It was easier."

"Oh." She shifted in her chair. "I'm . . . glad."

He glanced over at the windows. They were covered with heavy drapes, but he could see glimmers of sunlight peeking in around the sides. "Won't your mother be worried about you?"

"Oh, *no*!" Francesca yelped, jumping to her feet so quickly that her hand slammed into the bedside table. "Ow ow *ow*."

"Are you all right?" Michael inquired politely, since it was quite clear she'd done herself no real harm.

"Oh . . ." She was shaking her hand out, trying to stem the pain. "I'd forgotten all about my mother. She was expecting me back last night."

"Didn't you send her a note?"

"I did," she said. "I told her you were ill, but she wrote back and said she would stop by in the morning to offer her assistance. What time is it? Do you have a clock? Of course you have a clock." She turned frantically to the small mantel clock over the fireplace.

It had been John's room; it still was John's room, in so many ways. Of course she'd know where the clock was.

"It's only eight," she said with a relieved sigh. "Mother never rises before nine unless there is an emergency, and hopefully she won't count this as one. I tried not to sound too panicked in my note."

Knowing Francesca, it would have been worded with all the coolheaded calmness she was known for. Michael smiled. She'd probably lied and said she'd hired a nurse.

"There's no need to panic," he said.

She turned to him with agitated eyes. "You said you didn't want anyone to know you had malaria."

His lips parted. He had never dreamed that she would hold his wishes quite so close to her heart. "You would keep this from your mother?" he asked softly.

"Of course. It is your decision to tell her, not mine."

It was really quite touching, rather tender even—

"I think you're insane," she added sharply.

Well, maybe tender wasn't quite the right word.

"But I will honor your wishes." She planted her hands on her hips and regarded him with what could only be described as vexation. "How could you even think I would do otherwise?"

"I have no idea," he murmured.

"Really, Michael," she grumbled. "I do not know what is wrong with you."

"Swampy air?" he tried to joke.

She shot him A Look. Capitalized.

"I'm going back to my mother's," she said, pulling on her short gray boots. "If I don't, you can be sure she will show up here with the entire faculty of the Royal College of Physicians in tow."

He lifted a brow. "Is that what she did whenever you took ill?"

She let out a little sound that was half snort, half grunt, and all irritation. "I will be back soon. Don't go anywhere."

He lifted his hands, gesturing somewhat sarcastically to the sickbed.

"Well, I wouldn't put it past you," she muttered.

"Your faith in my superhuman strength is touching."

She paused at the door. "I swear, Michael, you make the most annoying deathly ill patient I have ever met."

"I live to entertain you!" he called out as she was walking down the hall, and he was quite certain that if she'd had something to throw at the door, she would have done so. With great vigor.

He settled back down against his pillows and smiled. He might make an annoying patient, but she was a crotchety nurse.

Which was just fine with him.

Chapter 9

. . . it is possible that our letters have crossed in the mail, but it does seem more likely that you simply do not wish to correspond. I accept that and wish you well. I shan't bother you again. I hope you know that I am listening, should you ever change your mind.

—from the Earl of Kilmartin to the Countess of Kilmartin, eight months after his arrival in India

It wasn't easy hiding his illness. The *ton* didn't present a problem; Michael simply turned down all of his invitations, and Francesca put it about that he wished to settle in at his new home before taking his place in society.

The servants were more difficult. They talked, of course, and often to servants from other households, so Francesca had had to make sure that only the most loyal retainers were privy to what went on in Michael's sickroom. It was tricky, especially since she wasn't even officially living at Kilmartin House, at least not until Janet and Helen arrived, which Francesca fervently hoped was soon.

But the hardest part, the people who were the most fiendishly curious and difficult to keep in the dark, had to be Francesca's family. It had never been easy maintaining a secret within the Bridgerton household, and keeping one from the whole lot of them was, to put it simply, a bloody nightmare.

"Why do you go over there every day?" Hyacinth asked over breakfast.

"I live there," Francesca replied, taking a bite of a muffin, which any reasonable person would have taken as a sign that she did not wish to converse.

Hyacinth, however, had never been known to be reasonable. "You live here," she pointed out.

Francesca swallowed, then took a sip of tea, the delay intended to preserve her composed exterior. "I sleep here," she said coolly.

"Isn't that the definition of where you live?"

Francesca slathered more jam on her muffin. "I'm eating, Hyacinth."

Her youngest sister shrugged. "So am I, but it doesn't prevent me from carrying on an intelligent conversation."

"I'm going to kill her," Francesca said to no one in particular. Which was probably a good thing, as there was no one else present.

"Who are you talking to?" Hyacinth demanded.

"God," Francesca said baldly. "And I do believe I have been given divine leave to murder you."

"Hmmph," was Hyacinth's response. "If it was that easy, I'd have asked permission to eliminate half the *ton* years ago."

Francesca decided just then that not all of Hyacinth's statements required a rejoinder. In fact, few of them did.

"Oh, Francesca!" came Violet's voice, thankfully interrupting the conversation. "There you are."

Francesca looked up to see her mother entering the breakfast room, but before she could say a word, Hyacinth piped up with, "Francesca was just about to kill me."

"Excellent timing on my part, then," Violet said, taking her seat. She turned to Francesca. "Are you planning to go over to Kilmartin House this morning?"

Francesca nodded. "I live there."

"I think she lives here," Hyacinth said, adding a liberal dose of sugar to her tea.

Violet ignored her. "I believe I will accompany you."

Francesca nearly dropped her fork. "Why?"

"I should like to see Michael," Violet said with a delicate shrug. "Hyacinth, will you please pass me the muffins?"

"I'm not sure what his plans are today," Francesca said quickly. Michael had had an attack the night before—his fourth malarial fever, to be precise, and they were hoping it would be the last of the cycle. But even though he would be much recovered by now, he would still most likely look dreadful. His skin—thank God—wasn't jaundiced, which Michael had told her was often a sign that the sickness was progressing to its fatal stage, but he still had that awful sickly air to him, and Francesca knew that if her mother caught one glimpse of him she would be horrified. And furious.

Violet Bridgerton did not like to be kept in the dark. Especially when it pertained to a matter about which one could use the term "life and death" without being accused of hyperbole.

"If he's not available I will simply turn around and go home," Violet said. "Jam please, Hyacinth."

"I'll come, too," Hyacinth said.

Oh, *God*. Francesca's knife skittered right across her muffin. She was going to have to drug her sister. It was the only solution.

"You don't mind if I come along, too, do you?" Hyacinth asked Violet.

"Didn't you have plans with Eloise?" Francesca said quickly.

Hyacinth stopped, thought, blinked a few times. "I don't think so."

"Shopping? At the milliner?"

Hyacinth took another moment to run through her memory. "No, in fact I'm quite certain I don't. I just purchased a new bonnet last week. Lovely one, actually. Green, with the most cunning ecru trim." She glanced down at her toast, regarded it for a moment, then reached for the marmalade. "I'm weary of shopping," she added.

"No woman is ever weary of shopping," Francesca said, a touch desperately.

"This woman is. Besides, the earl—" Hyacinth cut herself off, turning to her mother. "May I call him Michael?"

"You'll have to ask him," Violet replied, taking a bite of eggs.

Hyacinth turned back to Francesca. "He's been back in London an entire week, and I haven't even seen him. My friends have been asking me about him, and I don't have anything to say."

"It's not polite to gossip, Hyacinth," Violet said.

"It isn't gossip," Hyacinth retorted. "It's the honest dissemination of information."

Francesca actually felt her chin drop. "Mother," she said, shaking her head, "you really should have stopped at seven."

"Children, you mean?" Violet asked, sipping at her tea. "Sometimes I do wonder."

"Mother!" Hyacinth exclaimed.

Violet just smiled at her. "Salt?"

"It took her eight tries to get it right," Hyacinth announced, thrusting the salt cellar at her mother with a decided lack of grace.

"And does that mean that you, too, hope to have eight children?" Violet inquired sweetly.

"*God* no," Hyacinth said. With great feeling. And neither she nor Francesca could quite resist a chuckle after that.

"It's not polite to blaspheme, Hyacinth," Violet said, in much the same tone she'd used to tell her not to gossip.

"Why don't we stop by shortly after noon?" Violet asked Francesca, once the moment of levity had petered out.

Francesca glanced up at the clock. That would give her barely an hour to make Michael presentable. And her mother had said *we*. As in more than one person. As in she was actually going to bring Hyacinth, who had the capacity to turn any awkward situation into a living nightmare.

"I'll go now," Francesca blurted out, standing up quickly. "To see if he's available."

To her surprise, her mother stood also. "I will walk you to the door," Violet said. Firmly.

"Er, you will?"

"Yes."

Hyacinth started to rise.

"Alone," Violet said, without even giving Hyacinth a glance.

Hyacinth sat back down. Even she was wise enough not to argue when her mother was combining her serene smile with a steely tone.

Francesca allowed her mother to precede her out of the room, and they walked in silence until they reached the front hall, where she waited for a footman to retrieve her coat.

"Is there something you wish to tell me?" Violet asked.

"I don't know what you mean."

"I think you do."

"I assure you," Francesca said, giving her mother her most innocent look, "I don't."

"You have been spending a great deal of time at Kilmartin House," Violet said.

"I live there," Francesca pointed out, for what felt like the hundredth time.

"Not right now you don't, and I worry that people will talk."

"No one has said a word about it," Francesca returned. "I haven't seen a thing in the gossip columns, and if people were talking about it, I'm sure that one of us would have heard by now."

"Just because people are keeping quiet today doesn't mean they will do so tomorrow," Violet said.

Francesca let out an irritated exhale. "It's not as if I'm a never-married virgin."

"Francesca!"

Francesca crossed her arms. "I'm sorry to speak so frankly, Mother, but it is true."

The footman arrived just then with Francesca's coat and informed her that the carriage would be in front momentarily. Violet waited until he stepped outside to await its arrival, then turned to Francesca and asked, "What, precisely, is your relationship to the earl?"

Francesca gasped. "Mother!"

"It is not a silly question," Violet said.

"It is the silliest—no, quite the stupidest—question I have ever heard. Michael is my cousin!"

"He was your husband's cousin," Violet corrected.

"And he was my cousin as well," Francesca said sharply. "And my friend. Good heavens, of all people . . . I can't even imagine . . . Michael!"

But the truth was, she *could* imagine. Michael's illness had kept it all at bay; she'd been so busy caring for him and keeping him well that she'd managed to avoid thinking about that jolting moment in the park, when she'd looked at him and something had sparked to life within her.

Something she had been quite certain had died inside of her four years earlier.

But hearing her *mother* bring it up . . . Good God, it was mortifying. There was no way, no earthly way that she could feel an attraction to Michael. It was wrong. It was really wrong. It was . . . well, it was just *wrong*. There wasn't another word that described it better.

"Mother," Francesca said, keeping her voice carefully even, "Michael has not been feeling well. I told you that."

"Seven days is quite a long time for a head cold."

"Perhaps it is something from India," Francesca said. "I don't know. I think he is almost recovered. I have been helping him get settled here in London. He has been gone a very long time and as you've noted, he has many new responsibilities as the earl. I thought it my duty to help him with all of this." She looked at her mother with a resolute expression, rather pleased with her speech. But Violet just said, "I will see you in an hour," and walked away.

Leaving Francesca feeling very panicked indeed.

Michael was enjoying a few moments of peace and quiet—not that he'd been bereft of quiet, but malaria did little to allow a body peace—when Francesca burst through his bedroom door, wild-eyed and out of breath.

"You have two choices," she said, or rather, heaved.

"Only two?" he murmured, even though he hadn't a clue what she was talking about.

"Don't make jokes."

He hauled himself into a sitting position. "Francesca?" he asked gingerly, since it was his experience that one should always proceed with caution when a female was in a state. "Are you quite all—"

"My mother is coming," she said.

"Here?"

She nodded.

It wasn't an ideal situation but hardly something deserving of Francesca's feverish demeanor. "Why?" he inquired politely.

"She thinks—" She stopped, catching her breath. "She thinks—Oh, heavens, you won't believe it."

When she didn't expound upon this any further, he widened his eyes and held out his hands in an impatient gesture, as if to say—*Care to elaborate*?

"She thinks," Francesca said, shuddering as she turned to him, "that we are conducting an affair."

"After only a week back in London," he murmured thoughtfully. "I'm faster than I imagined."

"How can you joke about this?" Francesca demanded.

"How can you not?" he returned. But of course she could never laugh about such a thing. To her it was unthinkable. To him it was . . .

Well, something else entirely.

"I am horrified," she declared.

Michael just offered her a smile and a shrug, even though he was starting to feel a little pricked. Naturally, he did not expect Francesca to think of him in such a manner, but a reaction of horror didn't exactly make a fellow feel *good* about his manly prowess.

"What are my two choices?" he asked abruptly.

She just stared at him.

"You said I have two choices."

She blinked, and would have looked rather adorably befuddled if he weren't a bit too annoyed with her ire to credit her with anything that charitable. "I . . . don't recall," she finally said. "Oh, my heavens," she moaned. "What am I to do?"

"Settling down might be a good beginning," he said, sharply enough to make her head jerk back in his direction. "Stop and think, Frannie. This is *us*. Your mother will realize how foolish she's being once she takes the time to think about it."

"That's what I told her," she replied fervently. "I mean, for goodness' sake. Can you imagine?"

He could, actually, which had always been a bit of a problem.

"It is the most unfathomable thing," Francesca muttered, pacing across the room. "As if I—" She turned, gesturing to him with overblown motions. "As if *you*—" She stopped, planted her hands on her hips, then clearly gave up on trying to hold still and began to pace anew. "How could she even consider such a thing?"

"I don't believe I have ever seen you quite so put out," Michael commented.

She halted in her tracks and stared at him as if he were an imbecile. With two heads.

And maybe a tail.

"You really ought to endeavor to calm down," he said, even though he knew his words would have the exact opposite effect. Women hated to be told to calm down, especially women like Francesca.

"Calm down?" she echoed, turning on him as if possessed by an entire spectrum of furies. "Calm *down*? Good God, Michael, are you still feverish?"

"Not at all," he said coolly.

"Do you understand what I'm saying to you?"

"Quite," he bit off, about as politely as any man could after having his manhood impugned.

"It's insane," she said. "Simply insane. I mean, look at you."

Really, she might as well just grab a knife and apply it to his ballocks. "You know, Francesca," he said with studied mildness, "there are a lot of women in London who would be rather pleased to be, how did you say it, conducting an affair with me."

Her mouth, which had been hanging open after her latest outburst, snapped shut.

He lifted his brows and leaned back against his pillows. "Some would call it a privilege."

She glared at him.

"*Some* women," he said, knowing full well he should never bait her about such a subject, "might even engage in physical battle just for the mere opportunity—"

"Stop!" she snapped. "Good heavens, Michael, such an inflated view of your own prowess is not attractive."

"I'm told it's deserved," he said with a languid smile.

Her face burned red.

He rather enjoyed the sight. He might love her, but he hated what she did to him, and he was not so big of heart that he didn't occasionally take a bit of satisfaction in seeing her so tortured.

It was only a fraction of what *he* felt on a day-to-day basis, after all.

"I have no wish to hear about your amorous exploits," Francesca said stiffly.

"Funny, you used to ask about them all the time." He paused, watching her squirm. "What was it you always asked me?"

"I don't—"

"*Tell me something wicked*," he said, using his best trying-to-sound-as-if-he'd-just-thought-of-it voice, when of course he never forgot anything she said to him. "Tell me something wicked," he said again, more slowly this time. "That was it. You rather liked me when I was wicked. You were always so curious about my exploits."

"That was before—"

"Before what, Francesca?" he asked.

There was an odd pause before she spoke. "Before this," she muttered. "Before now, before everything."

"I'm supposed to understand that?"

Her answer was merely a glare.

"Very well," he said, "I suppose I should get ready for your mother's visit. It shouldn't be too much of a problem."

Francesca regarded him dubiously. "But you look terrible."

"I knew there was a reason I loved you so well," he said dryly. "One really needn't worry about falling into the sin of vanity with you about."

"Michael, be serious."

"Sadly, I am."

She scowled at him.

"I can rise to my feet now," he told her, "exposing you to parts of my body I would imagine you'd rather not see, or you can leave and await my glorious presence downstairs."

She fled.

Which puzzled him. The Francesca he knew didn't flee anything.

Nor, for that matter, would she have departed without at least making an attempt to get the last word.

But most of all, he couldn't believe she had let him get away with calling himself glorious.

Francesca never did have to suffer a visit from her mother. Not twenty minutes after she left Michael's bedchamber, a note arrived from Violet informing her that her brother Colin—who had been traveling in the Mediterranean for months—had just returned to London, and Violet would have to postpone her visit. Then, later that evening, much as Francesca had predicted at the onset of Michael's attack, Janet and Helen arrived in London, assuaging Violet's concerns about Francesca and Michael and their lack of a chaperone.

The mothers—as Francesca and Michael had long since taken to calling them—were thrilled at Michael's unexpected appearance, although one look at his sickly features propelled both of them into maternal tizzies of concern that had forced Michael to take Francesca aside and beg her not to leave him alone with either of the two ladies. In truth, the timing of their arrival was rather fortuitous, as Michael had a comparatively healthy day in their presence before being struck by another raging fever. Francesca had taken them aside before the next expected attack and explained the nature of the illness, so by the time they saw the malaria in all its horrible glory, they were prepared.

And unlike Francesca, they were more agreeable—no, downright eager—to keep his malady a secret. It was difficult to imagine that a wealthy and handsome earl might not be considered an excellent catch by the unmarried ladies of London, but malaria was never a mark in one's favor when looking for a wife.

And if there was one thing Janet and Helen were determined to see before the year was out, it was Michael standing at the front of a church, his ring firmly on the finger of a new countess.

Francesca was actually relieved to sit back and listen to the mothers harangue him about getting married. At least it took their attention off of *her*. She had no idea how they would react to her own marital plans—she rather imagined they would be happy for her—but the last thing she wanted was two more matchmaking mamas attempting to pair her up with every poor pathetic bachelor on the Marriage Mart.

Good heavens, she had enough to put up with, with her *own* mother, who was surely not going to be able to resist the temptation to meddle once Francesca made clear her desire to find a husband this year.

And so Francesca moved back to Kilmartin House, and the entire Stirling household turned itself into a little cocoon, with Michael declining all invitations with the promise that he would be out and about once he settled in from his long journey. The three ladies did occasionally go out in society, and although Francesca had expected questions about the new earl, even she was unprepared for the volume and frequency.

Everyone, it seemed, was mad for the Merry Rake, especially now that he'd shrouded himself with mystery.

Oh, and inherited an earldom. Mustn't forget that. Or the hundred thousand pounds that went with it.

Francesca shook her head as she thought about it. Truly Mrs. Radcliffe herself couldn't have devised a more perfect hero. It was going to be a madhouse once he was recovered.

And then, suddenly, he was.

Very well, Francesca supposed it wasn't that sudden; the fevers had been steadily decreasing in severity and duration. But it did seem that one day he still looked wan and pale, and the next he was his regular hale and hearty self, prowling about the house, eager to escape into the sunshine.

"Quinine," Michael said with a lazy shrug when she remarked upon his changed appearance at breakfast. "I'd take the stuff six times a day if it didn't taste so damned foul."

"Language, please, Michael," his mother murmured, spearing a sausage with her fork.

"Have you tasted the quinine, Mother?" he asked.

"Of course not."

"Taste it," he suggested, "and then we'll see how *your* language compares."

Francesca chuckled under her napkin.

"*I* tasted it," Janet announced.

All eyes turned to her. "You did?" Francesca asked. Even she hadn't been so daring. The smell alone had been enough for her to keep the bottle firmly corked at all times.

"Of course," Janet replied. "I was curious." She turned to Helen. "It really is foul."

"Worse than that awful concoction Cook made us take last year for the, er . . ." Helen gave Janet a look that clearly meant *you know what I mean.*

"Much worse," Janet affirmed.

"Did you reconstitute it?" Francesca asked. The powder was meant to be mixed with purified water, but she supposed that Janet might have simply put a bit on her tongue.

"Of course. Aren't I supposed to?"

"Some people like to mix it with gin," Michael said.

Helen shuddered.

"It could hardly be worse than on its own," Janet said.

"Still," Helen said, "if one is going to mix it with spirits, one might at least choose a nice whisky."

"And spoil the whisky?" Michael queried, helping himself to several spoonfuls of eggs.

"It can't be that bad," Helen said.

"It is," Michael and Janet said in unison.

"It's true," Janet added. "I can't imagine ruining a fine whisky that way. Gin would be a happy medium."

"Have you even tasted gin?" Francesca asked. It was not,

after all, considered a suitable spirit for the upper classes, most especially women.

"Once or twice," Janet admitted.

"And here I thought I knew everything about you," Francesca murmured.

"I have my secrets," Janet said airily.

"This is a very odd conversation for the breakfast table," Helen stated.

"True enough," Janet agreed. She turned to her nephew. "Michael, I am most pleased to see you up and about and looking so fine and healthy."

He inclined his head, thanking her for the compliment.

She dabbed the corners of her mouth daintily with her napkin. "But now you must attend to your responsibilities as the earl."

He groaned.

"Don't be so petulant," Janet said. "No one is going to hang you up by your thumbs. All I was going to say is that you must go to the tailor and make sure you have proper evening clothes."

"Are you certain I can't donate my thumbs instead?"

"They're lovely thumbs," Janet replied, "but I do believe they'd better serve all of humanity attached to your hands."

Michael met her eyes with a steady stare. "Let's see. I have on my schedule today—my first since rising from my sickbed, I might add—a meeting with the prime minister concerning my assumption of my seat in parliament, a meeting with the family solicitor so that I might review the state of our financial holdings, and an interview with our primary estate manager, who I'm told has come down to London with the express purpose of discussing the state of all seven of our family properties. At which point, might I inquire, do you wish me to squeeze in a visit to the tailor?"

The three ladies were speechless.

"Perhaps I should inform the prime minister that I shall have to move him until Thursday?" he asked mildly.

"When did you make all of these appointments?" Francesca asked, a bit ashamed that she was so surprised at his diligence.

"Did you think I'd spent the last fortnight staring at the ceiling?"

"Well, no," she replied, although in truth she didn't know what she'd thought he'd been doing. Reading, she supposed. That's what she would have done.

When no one said anything further, Michael pushed back his chair. "If you ladies will excuse me," he said, setting his napkin down, "I believe we have established that I have a busy day ahead of me."

But he'd not even risen from his seat before Janet said quietly, "Michael? The tailor."

He froze.

Janet smiled at him sweetly. "Tomorrow would be perfectly acceptable."

Francesca rather thought she heard his teeth grind.

Janet just tilted her head ever so slightly to the side. "You do need new evening clothes. Surely you would not dream of missing Lady Bridgerton's birthday ball?"

Francesca quickly forked a bite of eggs into her mouth so that he wouldn't catch her grinning. Janet was devious in the extreme. Her mother's birthday party was the one event that Michael would feel positively obligated to attend. Anything else he could shrug off without a care.

But Violet?

Francesca didn't *think* so.

"When is it?" he sighed.

"April eleventh," Francesca said sweetly. "Everyone will be there."

"Everyone?" he echoed.

"All the Bridgertons."

He brightened visibly.

"And everyone else," she added with a shrug.

He looked at her sharply. "Define 'everyone.' "

Her eyes met his. "Everyone."

He slumped in his seat. "Am I to get no reprieve?"

"Of course you are," Helen said. "You did, in fact. Last week. We called it malaria."

"And here I was looking forward to health," he muttered.

"Fear not," Janet said. "You will have a fine time, I'm sure."

"And perhaps meet a lovely lady," Helen put in helpfully.

"Ah, yes," Michael murmured, "lest we forget the real purpose of my life."

"It's not such a bad purpose," Francesca said, unable to resist the small chance to tease him.

"Oh, really?" he asked, swinging his head around to face her. His eyes settled on hers with startling accuracy, leaving Francesca with the extremely unpleasant sensation that perhaps she shouldn't have provoked him.

"Er, really," she said, since she couldn't back down now.

"And what are *your* purposes?" he asked sweetly.

Out of the corner of her eye, Francesca could see Janet and Helen watching the exchange with avid and unconcealed curiosity.

"Oh, this and that," Francesca said with a blithe wave of her hand. "Presently, just to finish my breakfast. It is most delicious, wouldn't you agree?"

"Coddled eggs with a side portion of meddling mothers?"

"Don't forget your cousin as well," she said, kicking herself under the table as soon as the words left her lips. Everything about his demeanor screamed not to provoke him, but she just couldn't help it.

There was little in this world she enjoyed more than provoking Michael Stirling, and moments like this were simply too delicious to resist.

"And how will you be spending your season?" Michael asked, tilting his head slightly into an obnoxiously patient expression.

"I imagine I'll begin by going to my mother's birthday party."

"And what will you be doing there?"

"Offering my felicitations."

"Is that all?"

"Well, I won't be inquiring after her age, if that's what you're asking," Francesca replied.

"Oh, no," Janet said, followed by Helen's equally fervent, "Don't do that."

All three ladies turned to Michael with identical expectant expressions. It was his turn to speak, after all.

"I'm leaving," he said, his chair scraping along the floor as he stood.

Francesca opened her mouth to say something provoking, since it was always her first inclination to tease him when he was in such a state, but she found herself without words.

Michael had changed.

It wasn't that he'd been irresponsible before. It was just that he'd been without responsibilities. And it hadn't really occurred to her how well he might rise to thc occasion once he returned to England.

"Michael," she said, her soft voice instantly gaining his attention, "good luck with Lord Liverpool."

His eyes caught hers, and something flashed there. A hint of appreciation, maybe of gratitude.

Or maybe it was nothing so precise. Maybe it was just a wordless moment of understanding.

The sort she'd had with John.

Francesca swallowed, uncomfortable with this sudden realization. She reached for her tea with a slow and deliberate movement, as if her control over her body might extend to her mind as well.

What had just happened?

He was just Michael, wasn't he?

Just her friend, just her longtime confidant.

Wasn't that all?

Wasn't it?

Chapter 10

. . . .

—nothing more than hatchmarks, caused by the tapping of the Countess of Kilmartin's pen against paper, two weeks after the receipt of the Earl of Kilmartin's third missive to her

"Is he here?"

"He's not here."

"Are you certain?"

"I'm quite certain."

"But he is coming?"

"He said he was."

"Oh. But when is he coming?"

"I'm sure I don't know."

"You don't?"

"No, I don't."

"Oh. Right. Well . . . Oh, look! I see my daughter. Lovely seeing you, Francesca."

Francesca rolled her eyes—not an affectation she espoused except under the most severe of circumstances—as she watched

Mrs. Featherington, one of the *ton*'s most notorious gossips, toddle off toward her daughter Felicity, who was chatting amiably with a handsome, albeit untitled, young man at the edge of the ballroom.

The conversation would have been amusing if it hadn't been the seventh—no eighth, mustn't forget her own mother—time she had been subjected to it. And the conversation was always the same, truly down to the very word, save for the fact that not everyone knew her well enough to use her given name.

Once Violet Bridgerton had let it be known that the elusive Earl of Kilmartin would be making his reappearance at her birthday party— Well, Francesca was quite sure she would never be safe from interrogation again, at least not from anyone with any attachment to an unmarried female.

Michael was the catch of the season, and he hadn't even shown up yet.

"Lady Kilmartin!"

She looked up. Lady Danbury was coming her way. A more crotchety and outspoken old lady had never graced the ballrooms of London, but Francesca rather liked her, so she just smiled as the countess approached, noticing that the partygoers on either side of her quickly fled to parts unknown.

"Lady Danbury," Francesca said, "how nice to see you this evening. Are you enjoying yourself?"

Lady D thumped her cane against the ground for no apparent reason. "I'd enjoy myself a dashed sight more if someone would tell me how old your mother is."

"I wouldn't dare."

"Pfft. What's the fuss? It's not as if she's as old as I am."

"And how old are *you*?" Francesca asked, her tone as sweet as her smile was sly.

Lady D's wrinkled face cracked into a smile. "Heh heh heh, clever one you are. Don't think I'm going to tell *you*."

"Then surely you will understand if I exercise the same loyalty toward my mother."

"Hmmph," Lady Danbury grunted by way of a response, thumping her cane against the floor for emphasis. "What's the use of a birthday party if no one knows what we're celebrating?"

"The miracle of life and longevity?"

Lady Danbury snorted at that, then asked, "Where's that new earl of yours?"

My, she was blunt. "He's not *my* earl," Francesca pointed out.

"Well, he's more yours than anyone else's."

That much was probably true, although Francesca wasn't about to confirm it with Lady Danbury, so she just said, "I imagine his lordship would take exception to being labeled as anyone's but his own."

"His lordship, eh? That's rather formal, don't you think? Thought the two of you were friends."

"We are," Francesca said. But that did not mean she would bandy about his given name in public. Truly, it wouldn't do to stir up any rumors. Not if she needed to keep her reputation pristine in her search for a husband of her own. "He was my husband's closest confidant," she said pointedly. "They were like brothers."

Lady Danbury looked disappointed with Francesca's bland characterization of her relationship with Michael, but all she did was pinch her lips as she scanned the crowd. "This party needs some livening up," she muttered, tapping her cane again.

"Do try not to say that to my mother," Francesca murmured. Violet had spent weeks on the arrangements, and truly, no one could find exception with the party. The lighting was soft and romantic, the music pure perfection, and even the food was good—no small achievement at a London ball. Francesca had already enjoyed two éclairs and had spent the time since plotting how to make her way back to the table of refreshments without appearing a complete glutton.

Except that she kept getting waylaid by inquisitive matrons.

"Oh, it's not your mother's fault," Lady D said. "She's not to blame for the overpopulation of dullards in our society. Good God, she bred eight of you, and not an idiot in the lot." She gave Francesca a pertinent glance. "That's a compliment, by the way."

"I'm touched."

Lady Danbury's mouth clamped together into a frighteningly serious line. "I'm going to have to do something," she said.

"About what?"

"The party."

An awful sensation took hold in Francesca's stomach. She'd never known Lady Danbury to actually ruin someone else's fête, but the old lady was clever enough to do some serious damage if she put her mind to it. "What, exactly, do you plan to do?" Francesca asked, trying to keep her voice free of panic.

"Oh, don't look at me like I'm about to kill your cat."

"I don't have a cat."

"Well, *I* do, and I assure you, I'd be mad as Hades if anyone tried to harm him."

"Lady Danbury, what on *earth* are you talking about?"

"Oh, I don't know," the old lady said with an irritated wave of her hand. "You can be sure that if I did, I'd have done it already. But I certainly wouldn't cause a scene at your mother's party." She lifted her chin sharply in the air and gifted Francesca with a disdainful sniff. "As if I would do anything to hurt your dear mama's feelings."

Somehow that did little to assuage Francesca's apprehension. "Right. Well, whatever you do, please be careful."

"Francesca Stirling," Lady D said with a sly smile, "are you worried for my welfare?"

"You, I have no qualms about whatsoever," Francesca replied pertly, "it's the rest of us for whom I tremble."

Lady Danbury let out a cackle of laughter. "Well said, Lady Kilmartin. I do believe you deserve a reprieve. From me," she added, in case Francesca didn't grasp her meaning.

"You *are* my reprieve," Francesca muttered.

But Lady D obviously didn't hear her as she looked out over the crowd, because she sounded quite singleminded as she declared, "I do believe I shall go pester your brother."

"Which one?" Not that they all couldn't use a bit of torture.

"That one." She pointed toward Colin. "Hasn't he just returned from Greece?"

"Cyprus, actually."

"Greece, Cyprus, it's all the same to me."

"Not to them, I imagine," Francesca murmured.

"Who? You mean the Greeks?

"Or the Cypriots."

"Pfft. Well, if one of them chooses to show up tonight they can feel free to explain the difference. Until then, I shall wallow in my ignorance." And with that, Lady Danbury thumped her cane against the floor one last time before turning toward Colin and bellowing, "Mr. Bridgerton!"

Francesca watched with amusement as her brother tried desperately to pretend that he hadn't heard her. She was rather pleased that Lady D had chosen to torture Colin a bit—he undoubtedly deserved it—but now that she was on her own again, she realized that Lady Danbury had provided her with a rather effective defense against the multitude of matchmaking mamas who saw her as their only link to Michael.

Good God, she could see three of them approaching already.

Time to escape. Now. Francesca quickly turned on her heel and started walking toward her sister Eloise, who was easy to spot by the bright green of her dress. In truth, she would have much rather bypassed Eloise entirely and headed straight out the door, but if she was serious about this marriage business, then she had to circulate and let it be known she was in the market for a new husband.

Not that anyone was likely to care one way or another until Michael finally showed his face. Francesca could have announced her plan to move to Africa and take up goat herding, and all anyone would have said was, "And will the earl be accompanying you?"

"Good evening!" Francesca said, joining the small group around her sister. It was all family—Eloise was chatting amiably with their two sisters-in-law, Kate and Sophie.

"Oh, hullo, Francesca," Eloise said. "Where's—"

"Don't *you* start."

"What's wrong?" Sophie asked, eyes all concern.

"If one more person asks me about Michael, I swear my head will explode."

"That would certainly change the tenor of the evening," Kate remarked.

"Not to mention the cleaning duties of the staff," Sophie added.

Francesca actually growled.

"Well, where *is* he?" Eloise demanded. "And don't look at me like—"

"—I'm trying to kill your cat?"

"I don't have a cat. What the devil are you talking about?"

Francesca just sighed. "I don't know. He said he would be here."

"If he's smart, he's probably hiding in the hall," Sophie said.

"Good God, you're probably right." Francesca could easily see him bypassing the ballroom entirely and ensconcing himself in the smoking saloon.

Away, in other words, from all females.

"It's still early," Kate put in helpfully.

"It doesn't feel early," Francesca grumbled. "I wish he'd just get here, so that people would stop asking me about him."

Eloise actually laughed, fiendish turncoat that she was. "Oh, my poor delusional Francesca," she said, "once he arrives the questions will redouble. They'll simply change from 'Where is he?' to 'Tell us more.' "

"I fear she's right," Kate said.

"Oh, God," Francesca groaned, looking for a wall to sag against.

"Did you just blaspheme?" Sophie asked, blinking in surprise.

Francesca sighed. "I seem to be doing quite a bit of it lately."

Sophie gave her a kindly look, then suddenly exclaimed, "You're wearing blue!"

Francesca looked down at her new evening gown. She was quite pleased with it actually, not that anyone had noticed besides Sophie. It was one of her favorite shades of blue, not quite royal and not quite marine. The gown was elegantly simple, with a neckline adorned with a softly draped swath of lighter blue silk. She felt like a princess in it, or if not a princess, then at the very least, not quite so much the untouchable widow.

"Are you out of mourning, then?" Sophie asked.

"Well, I've been out of mourning for a few years now," Francesca mumbled. Now that she had finally shrugged off her grays and lavenders, she felt a little silly for having clung to them for so long.

"We knew you were out and about," Sophie said, "but you never changed your clothing, and— Well, it's of no matter. I'm just so pleased to see you in blue!"

"Does this mean that you will consider remarrying?" Kate asked. "It *has* been four years."

Francesca winced. Trust Kate to get right to the point. But she couldn't keep her plans a secret forever, not if she wanted to meet with any success, so all she said was, "Yes."

For a moment no one spoke. And then of course, they spoke all at once, offering congratulations and advice and various other bits of nonsense that Francesca wasn't positive she wished to hear. But it was all said with the best and most loving of intentions, so she just smiled and nodded and accepted their good wishes.

And then Kate said, "We shall have to set this about, of course."

Francesca was aghast. "I beg your pardon?"

"The blue dress is an excellent signal of your intentions," Kate explained, "but do you really think the men of London are perceptive enough to grasp it? Of course not," she said, answering her own question before anyone else could. "I could dye Sophie's hair to black, and most of them wouldn't notice a thing."

"Well, Benedict would notice," Sophie pointed out loyally.

"Yes, well, he's your husband, and besides that, he's a painter. He's trained to actually notice things. Most men—" Kate cut herself off, looking rather irritated with the turn in the conversation. "You do see my point, don't you?"

"Of course," Francesca murmured.

"The fact of the matter," Kate continued, "is that most of humanity has more hair than wit. If you wish for people to be aware that you are on the Marriage Mart, you shall have to make it quite clear. Or rather, we shall have to make it clear for you."

Francesca had horrible visions of her female relatives, chasing down men until the poor fellows ran screaming for the doors. "What, precisely, do you mean to do?"

"Oh, goodness, don't cast up your dinner."

"Kate!" Sophie exclaimed.

"Well, you must admit that she looked as if she were about to."

Sophie rolled her eyes. "Well, yes, but you needn't have remarked upon it."

"I enjoyed the comment," Eloise put in helpfully.

Francesca speared her with a glare, since she was feeling the need to give *some*one a dirty look, and it was always easiest to do so with one's blood relatives.

"We shall be masters of tact and discretion," Kate said.

"Trust us," Eloise added.

"Well, I certainly can't stop you," Francesca said.

She noticed that even Sophie did not contradict her.

"Very well," she said. "I am off to obtain one last éclair."

"I think they're gone," Sophie said, giving her a sympathetic look.

Francesca's heart sank. "The chocolate biscuits?"

"Gone as well."

"What's left?"

"The almond cake."

"The one that tasted like dust?"

"That's the one," Eloise put in. "It was the only dessert Mother didn't sample ahead of time. I warned her, of course, but no one ever listens to me."

Francesca felt herself deflate. Pathetic as she was, the promise of a sweet was the only thing keeping her going just then.

"Cheer up, Frannie," Eloise said, her chin lifting a notch as she looked out over the crowd. "I see Michael."

And sure enough, there he was. Standing on the other side of the room, looking sinfully elegant in his black evening kit. He was surrounded by women, which didn't surprise Francesca in the least. Half were the sorts who were pursuing him for marriage, either for themselves or their daughters.

The other half, Francesca noted, were young and married, and clearly pursuing him for something else entirely.

"I'd forgotten how handsome he was," Kate murmured.

Francesca glared at her.

"He's very tanned," Sophie added.

"He was in India," Francesca said. "Of course he's tanned."

"You're rather short of temper this evening," Eloise said.

Francesca schooled her features into an impassive mask. "I'm just weary of being asked about him, that's all. He's not my favorite topic of conversation."

"Did the two of you have a falling out?" Sophie inquired.

"No, of course not," Francesca replied, realizing belatedly that she'd given the wrong impression. "But I have done nothing but speak of him all evening. At this point I would be quite delighted to comment on the weather."

"Hmmm."

"Yes."

"Right. Of course."

Francesca had no idea who'd said what, especially when she realized that all four of them were just standing there staring at Michael and his bevy of women.

"He *is* handsome." Sophie sighed. "All that delicious black hair."

"Sophie!" Francesca exclaimed.

"Well, he is," Sophie said defensively. "And you didn't say anything to Kate when she made the same comment."

"You're both married," Francesca muttered.

"Does that mean *I* might comment upon his good looks?" Eloise asked. "Spinster that I am."

Francesca turned to her sister in disbelief. "Michael is the last man you'd want to marry."

"Why is that?" This came from Sophie, but Francesca noticed that Eloise was listening closely for her answer as well.

"Because he's a terrible rake," Francesca said.

"Funny," Eloise murmured. "You flew quite off the handle when Hyacinth said the same thing a fortnight ago."

Trust Eloise to remember *every*thing. "Hyacinth didn't know what she was talking about," Francesca said. "She never does. And besides, we were talking about his punctuality, not his marriageability."

"And what renders him so unmarriageable?" Eloise asked.

Francesca leveled a serious stare at her older sister. Eloise was mad if she thought she should set her cap for Michael.

"Well?" Eloise prodded.

"He could never remain faithful to one woman," Francesca said, "and I doubt you'd be willing to put up with infidelities."

"No," Eloise murmured, "not unless he'd be willing to put up with severe bodily injury."

The four ladies fell silent at that, continuing their shameless perusal of Michael and his companions. He leaned down and murmured something in one of their ears, causing the lady in question to titter and blush, hiding her mouth behind her hand.

"He's quite a flirt," Kate said.

"A certain air about him," Sophie confirmed. "Those women haven't a chance."

He smiled at one of his companions then, a slow, liquid grin that caused even the Bridgerton women to sigh.

"Haven't we something better to do besides spy on Michael?" Francesca asked, disgusted.

Kate, Sophie, and Eloise looked at each other, blinking.

"No."

"No."

"I guess not," Kate concluded. "Not just now, anyway."

"You should go and talk to him," Eloise said, nudging Francesca with her elbow.

"Why on earth?"

"Because he's *here*."

"So are a hundred other men," Francesca replied, "all of whom I'd rather marry."

"I only see three I'd even consider promising to obey," Eloise muttered, "and I'm not even certain about them."

"Be that as it may," Francesca said, not wanting to grant Eloise the point, "my purpose here is to find a husband, so I hardly see how dancing attendance on Michael will be of any benefit."

"And I thought we were here to wish Mother a happy birthday," Eloise murmured.

Francesca glared at her. She and Eloise were the closest of all the Bridgertons in age—exactly one year apart. Francesca would have given her life for Eloise, of course, and there was certainly no other woman who knew more of her secrets and inner thoughts, but half the time she could have happily strangled her sister.

Including right now. Especially right now.

"Eloise is right," Sophie said to Francesca. "You should go over and greet Michael. It's only polite, considering his long stay abroad."

"It's not as if we haven't been living in the same house for over a week," Francesca said. "We've more than said our greetings."

"Yes, but not in public," Sophie replied, "and not at your family's home. If you don't go over and speak with him, everyone will comment upon it tomorrow. They will think there is a rift between the two of you. Or worse, that you do not accept him as the new earl."

"Of course I accept him," Francesca said. "And even if I didn't, what would it matter? The line of succession was hardly in doubt."

"You need to show everyone that you hold him in high esteem," Sophie said. Then she turned to Francesca with a quizzical expression. "Unless, of course, you don't."

"No, of course I do," Francesca said with a sigh. Sophie was right. Sophie was always right when it came to matters of propriety. She should go and greet Michael. He deserved an official and public welcome to London, as ludicrous as it seemed, given that she had spent the last few weeks nursing him through his malarial fevers. She just didn't relish fighting her way through his throng of admirers.

She'd always found Michael's reputation amusing. Probably because she felt rather removed from it all, above it, even. It had been a bit of an inside joke among the three of them—her, John, and Michael. He'd never taken any of the women seriously, and so she hadn't, either.

But now she wasn't watching from her comfortable, secure position as a happily married lady. And Michael was no longer just the Merry Rake, a ne'er-do-well who maintained his position in society through wit and charm.

He was an earl, and she was a widow, and she suddenly felt rather small and powerless.

It wasn't his fault, of course. She knew that, just as she knew . . . well, just as she knew that he'd make someone a terrible husband someday. But somehow she couldn't quite block her ire, if not with him then with the gaggle of giggling females around him.

"Francesca?" Sophie asked. "Do you want one of us to go with you?"

"What? No. No, of course not." Francesca drew herself up straight, embarrassed to have been caught woolgathering by her sisters. "I can see to Michael," she said firmly.

She took two steps in his direction, then turned back to Kate, Sophie, and Eloise. "After I see to myself," she said.

And with that, she turned to make her way to the ladies' retiring room. If she was going to have to smile and be polite amidst Michael's simpering women, she might as well do it without feeling she had to hop from foot to foot.

But as she departed, she heard Eloise's low murmur of, "Coward."

It took all of Francesca's fortitude not to turn around and impale her sister with a scathing retort.

Well, that and the fact that she rather feared Eloise was right.

And it was mortifying to think that she might have turned coward over Michael, of all people.

Chapter 11

. . . I have heard from Michael. Three times, actually. I have not yet responded. You would be disappointed in me, I'm sure. But I—

—from the Countess of Kilmartin to her deceased husband, ten months after Michael's departure for India, crumpled with a muttered, "This is madness," and tossed in the fire

Michael had spotted Francesca the moment he'd entered the ballroom. She was standing at the far side of the room, chatting with her sisters, wearing a blue gown and new hairstyle.

And he noticed the instant she left as well, exiting through the door in the northwest wall, presumably to go to the ladies' retiring room, which he knew was just down the hall.

Worst of all, he was quite certain he would be equally aware of her return, even though he was conversing with about a dozen other ladies, all of whom thought he was giving their little gathering his full attention.

It was like a sickness with him, a sixth sense. He couldn't be in a room with Francesca and not know where she was. It had been like this since the moment they'd met, and the only thing that made it bearable was that she hadn't a clue.

It was one of the things he had most enjoyed about India. She wasn't there; he never had to be *aware* of her. But she'd haunted him still. Every now and then he'd catch a glimpse of chestnut hair that caught the candlelight as hers did, or someone would laugh, and for a split second it sounded like hers. His breath would catch, and he would look for her, even though he *knew* she wasn't there.

It was hell, and usually worthy of a stiff drink. Or a night spent with his latest paramour.

Or both.

But that was over, and now he was back in London, and he was surprised by how easy it was to fall into his old role as the devil-may-care charmer. Nothing much had changed in town; oh, some of the faces were different, but the aggregate sum of the *ton* was the same. Lady Bridgerton's birthday fête was much as he had anticipated, although he had to admit that he was a little taken aback at the level of curiosity aroused by his reappearance in London. It seemed the Merry Rake had become the Dashing Earl, and within the first fifteen minutes of his arrival, he had been accosted by no fewer than eight—no make that nine, mustn't forget Lady Bridgerton herself—society matrons, all eager to court his favor and, of course, introduce him to their lovely and unattached daughters.

He wasn't quite sure if it was amusing or hell.

Amusing, he decided, for now at least. By next week he had no doubt it would be hell.

After another fifteen minutes of introductions, reintroductions, and only slightly veiled propositions (thankfully by a widow and not one of the debutantes or their mothers), he announced his intention to locate his hostess and excused himself from the crowd.

And then there she was. Francesca. Halfway across the room, of course, which meant that he'd have to make his way through the punishing crowd if he wanted to speak with her. She looked breathtakingly lovely in a deep blue gown, and he realized that for all her talk about buying herself a new wardrobe, this was the first he'd seen her out of her half-mourning colors.

Then it hit him again. She was finally out of mourning. She would remarry. She would laugh and flirt and wear blue and find a husband.

And it would probably all happen in the space of a month. Once she made clear her intention to remarry, the men would be beating down her door. How could anyone *not* want to marry her? She might not have been as youthful as the other women looking for husbands, but she had something the younger debutantes lacked—a sparkle, a vivacity, a gleam of intelligence in her eyes that brought something extra to her beauty.

She was still alone, standing in the doorway. Amazingly, no one else seemed to have noticed her entrance, so Michael decided to brave the crowds and make his way to her.

But she saw him first, and although she did not exactly smile, her lips curved, and her eyes flashed with recognition, and as she walked to him, his breath caught.

It shouldn't have surprised him. And yet it did. Every time he thought he knew everything about her, had unwillingly memorized every last detail, something inside her flickered and changed, and he felt himself falling anew.

He would never escape her, this woman. He would never escape her, and he could never have her. Even with John gone, it was impossible, quite simply wrong. There was too much there. Too much had happened, and he would never be able to shake the feeling that he had somehow stolen her.

Or worse, that he had wished for this. That he had wanted John gone and out of the way, wanted the title and Francesca and everything else.

He closed the distance between them, meeting her halfway. "Francesca," he murmured, making his voice smooth and personable, "it is a delight to see you."

"And you as well," she replied. She smiled then, but it was in an amused sort of fashion, and he had the unexpected sense that she was mocking him. But there seemed little to be gained by pointing this out; it would only demonstrate how attuned he was to her every expression. And so he just said, "Have you been enjoying yourself?"

"Of course. Have you?"

"Of course."

She quirked a brow. "Even in your present state of solitude?"

"I beg your pardon?"

She shrugged carelessly. "The last I saw of you, you were surrounded by women."

"If you saw me, why didn't you come over to save me?"

"Save you?" she said with a laugh. "Anyone could see that you were enjoying yourself."

"Is that so?"

"Oh, please, Michael," she said, giving him a pointed glance. "You live to flirt and seduce."

"In that order?"

She shrugged. "You're not the Merry Rake for nothing."

He felt his jaw clamping together. Her comment rankled, and then the fact that it did rankled some more.

She studied his face, closely enough to make him want to squirm with discomfort, and then her own erupted into a smile. "You don't like it," she said slowly, almost breathless with the realization. "Oh, my heavens, you don't like it."

She looked as if she'd just experienced an epiphany of biblical proportions, but as the whole thing was at his expense, all he could do was scowl.

Then she laughed, which made it even worse. "Oh, my," she said, actually holding her hand to her belly in mirth. "You feel like a fox at a hunt, and you don't like it one bit. Oh, this is simply too much. After all the women you've chased . . ."

She had it all wrong, of course. He didn't much care one way or another that the society matrons had labeled him the season's biggest catch and were pursuing him accordingly. That was just the sort of thing it was easy to maintain a sense of humor over.

He didn't care if they called him the Merry Rake. He didn't care if they thought him a worthless seducer.

But when Francesca said the same thing . . .

It was like acid.

And the worst of it was, he had no one to blame but himself. He had cultivated this reputation for years, spent countless hours teasing and flirting, and then making sure Francesca saw, so she would never guess the truth.

And maybe he had done it for himself, too, because if he was the Merry Rake, at least he was *some*thing. The alternative was to be nothing but a pathetic fool, hopelessly in love with another man's wife. And hell, he was *good* at being the man who could seduce with a smile. He might as well have something in life he could succeed at.

"You can't say I didn't warn you," Francesca said, sounding very pleased with herself.

"It's not so bad surrounding oneself with beautiful women," he said, mostly to irritate her. "Even better when it comes about so effortlessly."

It worked, because her face pinched just a bit around the mouth. "I'm sure it's more than delightful, but you must be careful not to forget yourself," she said sharply. "These are not your usual women."

"I wasn't aware I had usual women."

"You know exactly what I mean, Michael. Others may have called you a complete rogue, but I know you better than that."

"Oh, really?" And he almost laughed. She thought she knew him so well, but she knew nothing. She'd never know the full truth.

"You had standards four years ago," she continued. "You never seduced anyone who would be irreparably hurt by your actions."

"And what makes you think I'm about to start now?"

"Oh, I don't think you'd do anything like that on purpose," she said, "but before, you never even associated with young women looking for marriage. There wasn't even the possibility that you might make a misstep and accidentally ruin one of them."

The vague, prickling sense of irritation that had been simmering within him began to grow and boil. "Who do you think I am, Francesca?" he asked, his entire body stiff with something he couldn't quite put his finger on. He hated that she thought this of him, *hated* it.

"Michael—"

"Do you really think me so dim that I might *accidentally* ruin a young lady's reputation?"

Her lips parted, then quivered slightly before she replied. "Not dim, Michael, of course not. But—"

"Careless, then," he bit off.

"No, not that, either. I just think—"

"What, Francesca?" he asked ruthlessly. "What *do* you think of me?"

"I think you are one of the finest men I know," she said softly.

Damn. Trust her to unman him with a single sentence. He stared at her, just stared at her, trying to figure out what the *hell* she'd meant by that.

"I do," she said with a shrug. "But I also think you're foolish, and I think you can be fickle, and I think you're going to break more hearts this spring than I'll be able to count."

"It isn't your job to count them," he said, his voice quiet and hard.

"No, it isn't, is it?" She looked over at him and smiled wryly. "But I'm going to end up doing it all the same, won't I?"

"And why is that?"

She didn't seem to have an answer to that, and then, just when he was sure she would say no more, she whispered, "Because I won't be able to stop myself."

Several seconds passed. They just stood there, their backs to the wall, looking for all the world as if they were just watching the party. Finally, Francesca broke the silence and said, "You should dance."

He turned to her. "With you?"

"Yes. Once, at least. But you should also dance with someone eligible, someone you might marry."

Someone he might marry. Anyone but her.

"It will signal to society that you are at least open to the possibility of matrimony," Francesca added. When he made no comment, she asked, "Aren't you?"

"Open to matrimony?"

"Yes."

"If you say so," he said, somewhat flippantly. He had to be cavalier. It was the only way he could mask the bitterness sweeping over him.

"Felicity Featherington," Francesca said, motioning toward a very pretty young lady about ten yards away. "She'd be an excellent choice. Very sensible. She won't fall in love with you."

He looked down at her sardonically. "Heaven forbid I find love."

Francesca's lips parted and her eyes grew very wide. "Is that what you want?" she asked. "To find love?"

She looked delighted by the prospect. Delighted that he might find the perfect woman.

And there it was. His faith in a higher power reaffirmed. Truly, moments of this ironic perfection could not come about by accident.

"Michael?" Francesca asked. Her eyes were bright and shining, and she clearly wanted something for him, something wonderful and good.

And all he wanted was to scream.

"I have no idea," he said caustically. "Not a single, bloody clue."

"Michael . . ." She looked stricken, but for once, he didn't care.

"If you will excuse me," he said sharply, "I believe I have a Featherington to dance with."

"Michael, what is wrong?" she asked. "What did I say?"

"Nothing," he said. "Nothing at all."

"Don't be this way."

As he turned to her, he felt something wash over him, a numbness that somehow slid a mask back over his face, enabled him to smile smoothly and regard her with his legendary heavy-lidded stare. He was once again the rake, maybe not so merry, but every bit the urbane seducer.

"What way?" he asked, his lips twisting with the perfect mix of innocence and condescension. "I'm doing exactly what you asked of me. Dance with a Featherington, didn't you say? I'm following your instructions to the letter."

"You're angry with me," she whispered.

"Of course not," he said, but they both knew his voice was too easy, too suave. "I've merely accepted that you, Francesca, know best. Here I've been listening to my own mind and conscience all this time, but to what avail? Heaven knows where I'd be if I'd listened to you years ago."

Her breath gasped across her lips and she drew back. "I need to go," she said.

"Go, then," he said.

Her chin lifted a notch. "There are many men here."

"Very many."

"I need to find a husband."

"You should," he agreed.

Her lips pressed together and then she added, "I might find one tonight."

He almost gave her a mocking smile. She always had to have the last word. "You might," he said, at the very second he knew she thought the conversation had concluded.

By then she was just far enough away that she couldn't yell back one last retort. But he saw the way she paused and tensed her shoulders, and he knew she'd heard him.

He leaned back against the wall and smiled. One had to take one's simple pleasures where one could.

The next day Francesca felt perfectly horrid. And worse, she couldn't quell an extremely annoying quiver of guilt, even though Michael was the one who'd spoken so insultingly the night before.

Truly, what had she said to provoke such an unkind reaction on his part? And what right did he have to act so badly toward her?

All she had done was express a bit of joy that he might want to find a true and loving marriage rather than spend his days in shallow debauchery.

But apparently she'd been wrong. Michael had spent the entire night—both before and after their conversation—charming every woman at the party. It had gotten to the point where she had thought she might be ill.

But the worst of it was, she couldn't seem to stop herself from counting his conquests, just as she'd predicted the night before. *One*, *two*, *three*, she'd murmured, watching him enchant a trio of sisters with his smile. *Four*, *five*, *six*—there went two widows and a countess. It was disgusting, and Francesca was disgusted with herself for having been so mesmerized.

And then every now and then, he'd look at her. Just look at her with a heavy-lidded, mocking stare, and she couldn't help but think that he knew what she was doing, that he was moving from woman to woman just so that she could round her count up to the next dozen or so.

Why had she said that? What had she been thinking?

Or had she been thinking not at all? It seemed the only explanation. She certainly hadn't intended to tell him that she wouldn't be able to stop herself from tallying his broken hearts. The words had whispered over her lips before she'd even realized she was thinking them.

And even now, she wasn't sure what it meant.

Why did she care? Why on earth did she care how many ladies fell under his spell? She'd never cared before.

It was only going to get worse, too. The women were mad for Michael. If the rules of society were reversed, Francesca thought wryly, their drawing room at Kilmartin House would be overflowing with flowers, all addressed to the Dashing Earl.

It was still going to be dreadful. She would be inundated with visitors today, of that she was certain. Every woman in London would call upon her in hopes that Michael might stroll through the drawing room. Francesca was going to have to endure countless questions, occasional innuendo, and—

"Good heavens!" She stopped short, peering into the drawing room with dubious eyes. "What is all this?"

Flowers. Everywhere.

It was her nightmare come true. Had someone changed the rules of society and forgotten to tell her?

Violets, irises, and daisies. Imported tulips. Hothouse orchids. And roses. Roses everywhere. Of every color. The smell was almost overwhelming.

"Priestley!" Francesca called out, spying her butler across the room, setting a tall vase of snapdragons on a table. "What are all these flowers?"

He gave the vase one last adjustment, twisting one pink stalk so that it faced away from the wall, then turned and walked toward her. "They are for you, my lady."

She blinked. "Me?"

"Indeed. Would you care to read the cards? I have left them on the arrangements so that you would be able to identify each sender."

"Oh." It seemed all she could say. She felt rather like a simpleton, with her hand over her opened mouth, glancing back and forth at all the flowers.

"If you'd like," Priestley continued, "I could remove each card and note on the back which arrangement I took it from. Then you could read through them all at once." When Francesca didn't reply, he suggested, "Perhaps you would like to remove yourself to your desk? I would be happy to bring you the cards."

"No, no," she said, still feeling terribly distracted by all this. She was a widow, for heavens sake. Men weren't supposed to bring her flowers. Were they?

"My lady?"

"I . . . I . . ." She turned to Priestley, straightening her spine as she forced her mind back to clarity. Or tried. "I will just, ah, have a look at . . ." She turned to the nearest bouquet, a lovely and delicate arrangement of grape hyacinths and stephanotis. "A pale comparison to your eyes," the card read. It was signed by the Marquess of Chester.

"Oh!" Francesca gasped. Lord Chester's wife had died two years earlier. Everyone knew he was looking for a new bride.

Barely able to contain the oddly giddy feeling rising within her, she inched down toward an arrangement of roses and picked up the card, trying very hard not to appear too eager in front of the butler. "I wonder who this is from," she said with studied casualness.

A sonnet. From Shakespeare, if she remembered correctly. Signed by Viscount Trevelstam.

Trevelstam? They'd only been introduced but once. He was young, very handsome, and it was rumored that his father had squandered away most of the family fortune. The new viscount would have to marry someone wealthy. Or so everyone said.

"Good heavens!"

Francesca turned to see Janet behind her.

"What is this?" she asked.

"I do believe those were my exact words upon entering the room," Francesca murmured. She handed Janet the two cards, then watched her carefully as her eyes scanned the neatly handwritten lines.

Janet had lost her only child when John had died. How would she react to Francesca being wooed by other men?

"My goodness," Janet said, looking up. "You seem to be this season's Incomparable."

"Oh, don't be silly," Francesca said, blushing. Blushing? Good God, what was wrong with her? She didn't blush. She hadn't even blushed during her first season, when she really had been an Incomparable. "I'm far too old for that," she mumbled.

"Apparently not," Janet said.

"There are more in the hall," Priestley said.

Janet turned to Francesca. "Have you looked through all the cards?"

"Not yet. But I imagine—"

"That they're more of the same?"

Francesca nodded. "Does that bother you?"

Janet smiled sadly, but her eyes were kind and wise. "Do I wish you were still married to my son? Of course. Do I want you to spend the rest of your life married to his memory? Of course not." She reached out and clasped one of Francesca's hands in her own. "You are a daughter to me, Francesca. I want you to be happy."

"I would never dishonor John's memory," Francesca assured her.

"Of course not. If you were the sort who would, he'd never have married you in the first place. Or," she added with a sly look, "I would never have allowed him to."

"I would like children," Francesca said. Somehow she felt the need to explain it, to make sure that Janet understood that what she truly wanted was to be a mother, not necessarily a wife.

Janet nodded, turning away as she dabbed at her eyes with her fingertips. "We should read the rest of the these cards," she said, her brisk tone signaling that she'd like to move on, "and perhaps prepare ourselves for an onslaught of afternoon calls."

Francesca followed her as she sought out an enormous display of tulips and plucked the card free. "I rather think the callers will be women," Francesca said, "inquiring after Michael."

"You may be right," Janet replied. She held the card up. "May I?"

"Of course."

Janet scanned the words, then looked up and said, "Cheshire."

Francesca gasped, "As in the Duke of?"

"The very one."

Francesca actually placed her hand over her heart. "My word," she breathed. "The Duke of Cheshire."

"You, my dear, are clearly the catch of the season."

"But I—"

"What the devil is this?"

It was Michael, catching a vase he'd nearly overturned and looking extremely cross and put out.

"Good morning, Michael," Janet said cheerfully.

He nodded at her, then turned to Francesca and grumbled, "You look as if you're about to pledge allegiance to your sovereign lord."

"And that would be you, I imagine?" she shot back, quickly dropping her hand to her side. She hadn't even realized it was still over her heart.

"If you're lucky," he muttered.

Francesca just gave him a look.

He smirked right back in return. "And are we opening a flower shop?"

"No, but clearly we could," Janet replied. "They're for Francesca," she added helpfully.

"Of course they're for Francesca," he muttered, "although, good God, I don't know who would be idiot enough to send roses."

"I like roses," Francesca said.

"Everyone sends roses," he said dismissively. "They're trite and old, and"—he motioned to Trevelstam's yellow ones—"who sent this?"

"Trevelstam," Janet answered.

Michael let out a snort and swung around to face Francesca. "You're not going to marry *him*, are you?"

"Probably not, but I fail to see what—"

"He hasn't two shillings to rub together," he stated.

"How would you know?" Francesca asked. "You haven't even been back a month."

Michael shrugged. "I've been to my club."

"Well, it may be true, but it is hardly his fault," Francesca felt compelled to point out. Not that she felt any great loyalty to Lord Trevelstam, but still, she did try to be fair, and it was common knowledge that the young viscount had spent the last year trying to repair the damage his profligate father had done to the family fortunes.

"You're not marrying him, and that's final," Michael announced.

She *should* have been annoyed by his arrogance, but the truth was, she was mostly just amused. "Very well," she said, lips twitching. "I'll select someone else."

"Good," he grunted.

"She has many to choose from," Janet put in.

"Indeed," Michael said caustically.

"I'm going to have to find Helen," Janet said. "She won't want to miss this."

"I hardly think the flowers are going to fly out the window before she rises," Michael said.

"Of course not," Janet replied sweetly, giving him a motherly pat on the arm.

Francesca quickly swallowed a laugh. Michael would hate that, and Janet knew it.

"She does adore her flowers, though," Janet said. "May I take one of the arrangements up to her?"

"Of course," Francesca replied.

Janet reached for Trevelstam's roses, then stopped herself. "Oh, no, I had better not," she said, turning back around to face Michael and Francesca. "He might stop by, and we wouldn't want him to think we'd banished his flowers to some far corner of the house."

"Oh, right," Francesca murmured, "of course."

Michael just grunted.

"Nevertheless, I'd better go tell her about this," Janet said, and she turned and hurried up the stairs.

Michael sneezed, then glared at a particularly innocuous display of gladiolas. "We're going to have to open a window," he grumbled.

"And freeze?"

"I'll wear a coat," he ground out.

Francesca smiled. She wanted to grin. "Are you jealous?" she asked coyly.

He swung around and nearly leveled her with a dumbstruck expression.

"Not over *me*," she said quickly, almost blushing at the thought. "My word, not *that*."

"Then what?" he asked, his voice quiet and clipped.

"Well, just—I mean—" She motioned to the flowers, a clear display of her sudden popularity. "Well, we're both after much the same goal this season, aren't we?"

He just stared at her blankly.

"*Marriage*," she said. Good heavens, he was particularly obtuse this morning.

"Your point?"

She let out an impatient breath. "I don't know if you had thought about it, but I'd naturally assumed you would be the one to be relentlessly pursued. I never dreamed that I would . . . Well . . ."

"Emerge as a prize to be won?"

It wasn't the nicest way of putting it, but it wasn't exactly inaccurate, so she just said, "Well, yes, I suppose."

For a moment he said nothing, but he was watching her strangely, almost wryly, and then he said, his voice quiet, "A man would have to be a fool not to want to marry you."

Francesca felt her mouth form a surprised oval. "Oh," she said, quite at a loss for words. "That's . . . that's . . . quite the nicest thing you could have said to me just now."

He sighed and ran his hand through his hair. She decided not to tell him that he'd just deposited a streak of yellow pollen into the black strands.

"Francesca," he said, looking tired and weary and something else.

Regretful?

No, that was impossible. Michael wasn't the sort to regret anything.

"I would never begrudge you this. You . . ." He cleared his throat. "You should be happy."

"I—" It was the strangest moment, especially after their tense words the night before. She hadn't the faintest clue how to reply, and so she just changed the subject and said, "Your turn will come."

He looked at her quizzically.

"It already has, really," she continued. "Last night. I was besieged with far more admirers for your hand than for my own. If women could send flowers, we'd be completely awash with them."

He smiled, but the sentiment didn't quite reach his eyes. He didn't look angry, just . . . hollow.

And she was struck by what a strange observation that was.

"Er, last night," he said, reaching up and tugging at his cravat. "If I said anything to upset you . . ."

She watched his face. It was so dear to her, and she knew every last detail of it. Four years, it seemed, did little to smudge a memory. But something was different now. He'd changed, but she wasn't sure how.

And she wasn't sure why.

"Everything is fine," she assured him.

"Nonetheless," he said gruffly, "I'm sorry."

But for the rest of the day, Francesca wondered if he knew exactly what he was apologizing for. And she couldn't escape the feeling that she wasn't sure, either.

Chapter 12

. . . rather ridiculous writing to you, but I suppose after so many months in the East, my perspective on death and the afterlife has slid into something that would have sent Vicar MacLeish screaming for the hills. So far from England, it is almost possible to pretend that you are still alive and able to receive this note, just like the many I sent from France. But then someone calls out to me, and I am reminded that I am Kilmartin and you are in a place unreachable by the Royal Mail.

—from the Earl of Kilmartin to his deceased cousin, the previous earl, one year and two months after his departure for India, written to completion and then burned slowly over a candle

It wasn't that he *enjoyed* feeling like an ass, Michael reflected as he swirled a glass of brandy at his club, but it seemed that lately, around Francesca at least, he couldn't quite avoid acting like one.

There she had been at her mother's birthday party, so damned *happy* for him, so delighted that he had uttered the word *love* in her presence, and he had simply snapped.

Because he knew how her mind worked, and he knew that she was already thinking madly ahead, trying to select the perfect woman for him, and the truth was . . .

Well, the truth was just too pathetic for words.

But he'd apologized, and although he could swear up and down that he wasn't going to behave like an idiot again, he would probably find himself apologizing again sometime in the future, and she would most likely just chalk it all up to a cranky nature on his part, never mind that he'd been a model of good humor and equanimity when John had been alive.

He downed his brandy. Bugger it all.

Well, he'd be done with this nonsense soon. She'd find someone, marry the bloke, and move out of the house. They would remain friends, of course—Francesca wasn't the sort to allow otherwise—but he wouldn't see her every day over the breakfast table. He wouldn't even see her as often as he had before John's death. Her new husband would not permit her to spend so much time in his company, cousinly relationship or no.

"Stirling!" he heard someone call out, followed by the usual slight cough which preceded, "Kilmartin, I mean. So sorry."

Michael looked up to see Sir Geoffrey Fowler, an acquaintance of his from his days at Cambridge. "Nothing of it," he said, motioning to the chair across from him.

"Splendid to see you," Sir Geoffrey said, taking a seat. "I trust your journey home was uneventful."

The pair exchanged the most basic of pleasantries until Sir Geoffrey got to the point. "I understand that Lady Kilmartin is looking for a husband," he said.

Michael felt as if he'd been punched. Never mind the atrocious floral display in his drawing room; it still sounded rather distasteful coming from someone's lips.

Someone young, reasonably handsome, and obviously in the market for a wife.

"Er, yes," he finally replied. "I believe she is."

"Excellent." Sir Geoffrey rubbed his hands together in anticipation, leaving Michael with the overwhelming desire to smack his face.

"She will be quite choosy," Michael said peevishly.

Sir Geoffrey didn't seem to care. "Will you dower her?"

"What?" Michael snapped. Good God, he was now her nearest male relative, wasn't he? He'd probably have to give her away at her wedding.

Hell.

"Will you?" Sir Geoffrey persisted.

"Of course," Michael bit off.

Sir Geoffrey sucked in his breath appreciatively. "Her brother offered to do so as well."

"The Stirlings will care for her," Michael said stiffly.

Sir Geoffrey shrugged. "It appears the Bridgertons will as well."

Michael felt his teeth grinding to powder.

"Don't look so dyspeptic," Sir Geoffrey said. "With a double dowry, she'll be off your hands in no time. I'm sure you're eager to be rid of her."

Michael cocked his head, trying to decide which side of Sir Geoffrey's nose could better take a punch.

"She's got to be a burden on you," Sir Geoffrey continued blithely. "The clothes alone must cost a fortune."

Michael wondered what the legal ramifications were for strangling a knight of the realm. Surely nothing he couldn't live with.

"And then when *you* marry," Sir Geoffrey continued, obviously unaware that Michael was flexing his fingers and measuring his neck, "your new countess won't want her in the house. Can't have two hens in charge of the household, right?"

"Right," Michael said tightly.

"Very well, then," Sir Geoffrey said, standing up. "Good to speak with you, Kilmartin. I must be off. Need to go tell Shively the news. Not that I want the competition, of course, but this isn't likely to stay a secret for very long, anyway. I might as well be the one to let it out."

Michael frosted him with a glare, but Sir Geoffrey was too excited with his gossip to notice. Michael looked down at his glass. Right. He'd drunk it all. Damn.

He signaled to a waiter to bring him another, then sat back with every intention of reading the newspaper he'd picked up on the way in, but before he could even scan the headlines, he heard his name yet again. He made the minimum effort required to hide his irritation and looked up.

Trevelstam. Of the yellow roses. Michael felt the newspaper crumple between his fingers.

"Kilmartin," the viscount said.

Michael nodded. "Trevelstam." They knew each other; not closely, but well enough so that a friendly conversation was not unexpected. "Have a seat," he said, motioning to the chair across from him.

Trevelstam sat, setting his half-sipped drink on the table. "How do you fare?" he asked. "Haven't seen you much since your return."

"Well enough," Michael grunted. Considering that he was being forced to sit with some ninny who wanted to marry Francesca's dowry. No, make that her double dowry. The way gossip spread,

Trevelstam had probably already heard the news from Sir Geoffrey.

Trevelstam was slightly more sophisticated than Sir Geoffrey—he managed to make small talk for a full three minutes, asking about Michael's trip to India, the voyage back, et cetera et cetera et cetera. But then, of course, he got down to his true purpose.

"I called upon Lady Kilmartin this afternoon," he said.

"Did you?" Michael murmured. He hadn't returned home since leaving that morning. The last thing he had wanted was to be present for Francesca's parade of suitors.

"Indeed. She's a lovely woman."

"That she is," Michael said, glad his drink had arrived.

Then not so glad when he realized it had arrived two minutes earlier and he had already drunk it.

Trevelstam cleared his throat. "I'm sure you are aware that I intend to court her."

"I'm certainly aware of it now." Michael eyed his glass, trying to determine if there might be a few drops of brandy left after all.

"I wasn't certain whether I should inform you or her brother of my intentions."

Michael was quite certain that Anthony Bridgerton, Francesca's eldest brother, was quite capable of weeding out unsuitable marriage prospects, but nonetheless he said, "I am quite sufficient."

"Good, good," Trevelstam murmured, taking another sip of his drink. "I—"

"Trevelstam!" came a booming voice. "And Kilmartin, too!"

It was Lord Hardwick, big and beefy, and if not yet drunk, not exactly sober either.

"Hardwick," both men said, acknowledging his arrival.

Hardwick grabbed a chair, scraping it along the floor until it found a place at the table. "Good to see you, good to see you," he huffed. "Capital night, don't you think? Most excellent. Most excellent, indeed."

Michael had no idea what he was talking about, but he nodded, anyway. Better that than actually to ask him what he meant; Michael was quite certain he lacked the patience to listen to an explanation.

"Thistleswaite's over there setting bets on the Queen's dogs, and, oh! Heard about Lady Kilmartin, too. Good talk tonight," he said, nodding approvingly. "Good talk, indeed. Hate when it's quiet here."

"And how are the Queen's dogs faring?" Michael inquired.

"Out of mourning, I understand."

"The dogs?"

"No, Lady Kilmartin!" Hardwick chortled. "Heh heh heh. Good one, there, Kilmartin."

Michael signaled for another drink. He was going to need it.

"Wore blue the other night, she did," Hardwick said. "Everyone saw."

"She looked quite lovely," Trevelstam added.

"Indeed, indeed," Hardwick said. "Good woman. I'd go after her myself if I weren't already shackled to Lady Hardwick."

Small favors and all that, Michael decided.

"She mourned the old earl for how long?" Hardwick asked. "Six years?"

As the "old earl" had been but twenty-eight at the time of his death, Michael found the comment somewhat offensive, but there seemed little point in attempting to change Lord Hardwick's customary bad judgment and behavior at this late stage in his life—and from the size and ruddiness of him, he was clearly going to keel over at any time. Right now, in fact, if Michael was lucky.

He glanced across the table. Still alive.

Damn.

"Four years," he said succinctly. "My cousin died four years ago."

"Four, six, whatever," Hardwick said with a shrug. "It's still a bloody long time to black the windows."

"I believe she was in half-mourning for some time," Trevelstam put in.

"Eh? Really?" Hardwick took a swig of his drink, then wiped his mouth rather sloppily with a handkerchief. "All the same for the rest of us when you think about it. She wasn't looking for a husband 'til now."

"No," Michael said, mostly because Hardwick had actually stopped talking for a few seconds.

"The men are going to be after her like bees to honey," Hardwick predicted, drawing out the *bees* until it sounded like it ended with four Zs. "Bees to honey, I tell you. Everyone knows she was devoted to the old earl. Everyone."

Michael's drink arrived. Thank God.

"And there's been no whiff of scandal attached to her name since he died," Hardwick added.

"I should say not," Trevelstam said.

"Not like some of the widows out and about," Hardwick continued, taking another swig of his liquor. He chuckled lewdly and elbowed Michael. "If you know what I mean."

Michael just drank.

"It's like . . ." Hardwick leaned in, his jowls jiggling as his expression grew salacious. "It's like . . ."

"For God's sake, man, just spit it out," Michael muttered.

"Eh?" Hardwick said.

Michael just scowled.

"I'll tell you what it's like," Hardwick said with a leer. "It's like you're getting a virgin who knows what to do."

Michael stared at him. "What did you just say?" he asked, very quietly.

"I said—"

"I'd take care not to repeat that if I were you," Trevelstam quickly interjected, casting an apprehensive glance at Michael's darkening visage.

"Eh? It's no insult," Hardwick grunted, gulping down the rest of his drink. "She's been married, so you know she ain't untouched, but she hasn't gone and—"

"Stop *now*," Michael ground out.

"Eh? Everyone is saying it."

"Not in my presence," Michael bit off. "Not if they value their health."

"Well, it's better than saying she ain't like a virgin." Hardwick chortled. "If you know what I mean."

Michael lunged.

"Good God, man," Hardwick yelped, falling back onto the floor. "What the hell is wrong with you?"

Michael wasn't certain how his hands had come to be around Hardwick's neck, but he realized he rather liked them there. "You will never," he hissed, "utter her name again. Do you understand me?"

Hardwick nodded frantically, but the motion cut off his air even further, and his cheeks began to purple.

Michael let go and stood up, wiping his hands against each other as if attempting to rub away something foul. "I will not countenance Lady Kilmartin being spoken of in such disrespectful terms," he bit off. "Is that clear?"

Hardwick nodded. And so did a number of the onlookers.

"Good," Michael grunted, deciding now was a good time to get the hell out. Hopefully Francesca would already be in bed when he got home. Either that or out. Anything as long as he didn't have to see her.

He walked toward the exit, but as he stepped out of the room and into the hall, he heard his name being uttered yet again. He turned around, wondering what man was idiot enough to pester him in such a state.

Colin Bridgerton. Francesca's brother. Damn.

"Kilmartin," Colin said, his handsome face decorated with his customary half smile.

"Bridgerton."

Colin motioned lightly to the now overturned table. "That was quite a show in there."

Michael said nothing. Colin Bridgerton had always unnerved him. They shared the same sort of reputation—that of the devil-may-care rogue. But whereas Colin was the darling of the society mamas, who cooed over his charming demeanor, Michael had always been (or at least until he'd come into the title) treated with a bit more caution.

But Michael had long suspected there was quite a bit of substance under Colin's ever-jovial surface, and perhaps it was because they were alike in so many ways, but Michael had always feared that if anyone were to sense the truth of his feelings for Francesca, it would be this brother.

"I was having a quiet drink when I heard the commotion," Colin said, motioning to a private salon. "Come join me."

Michael wanted nothing more than to get the hell out of the club, but Colin was Francesca's brother, which made them relations of a sort, requiring at least the pretense of politeness. And so he gritted his teeth and walked into the private salon, fully intending to take his drink and leave in under ten minutes.

"Pleasant night, don't you think?" Colin said, once Michael was pretending to be comfortable. "Aside from Hardwick and all that." He sat back in his chair with careless grace. "He's an ass."

Michael gave him a terse nod, trying not to notice that Francesca's brother was watching him as he always did, his shrewd gaze carefully overlaid with an air of charming innocence. Colin cocked his head slightly to the side, rather as if, Michael thought acerbically, he were angling for a better look into his soul.

"Damn it all," Michael muttered under his breath, and he rang for a waiter.

"What was that?" Colin asked.

Michael turned slowly back to face him. "Do you want another drink?" he asked, his words as clear as he could manage, considering they had to squeeze through his clenched teeth.

"I believe I will," Colin replied, all friendliness and good cheer.

Michael didn't believe his façade for a moment.

"Do you have any plans for the remainder of the evening?" Colin asked.

"None."

"Neither do I, as it happens," Colin murmured.

Damn. Again. Was it really too much to wish for one bloody hour of solitude?

"Thank you for defending Francesca's honor," Colin said quietly.

Michael's first impulse was to growl that he didn't need to be thanked; it was his place as well as any Bridgerton's to defend

Francesca's honor, but Colin's green eyes seemed uncommonly sharp that evening, so he just nodded instead. "Your sister deserves to be treated with respect," he finally said, making sure that his voice was smooth and even.

"Of course," Colin said, inclining his head.

Their drinks arrived. Michael fought the urge to down his in one gulp, but he did take a large enough sip for it to burn down his throat.

Colin, on the other hand, let out an appreciative sigh and sat back. "Excellent whisky," he said with great appreciation. "Best thing about Britain, really. Or one of them at least. One just can't get anything like it in Cyprus."

Michael just grunted a response. It was all that seemed necessary.

Colin took another drink, clearly savoring the brew. "Ahhh," he said, setting his glass down. "Almost as good as a woman."

Michael grunted again, raising his glass to his lips.

And then Colin said, "You should just marry her, you know."

Michael nearly choked. "I beg your pardon?"

"Marry her," Colin said with a shrug. "It seems simple enough."

It was probably too much to hope that Colin was speaking of anyone but Francesca, but Michael took one desperate stab, anyway, and said, in quite the chilliest tone he could muster, "To whom, might I ask, do you refer?"

Colin lifted his eyebrows. "Do we really need to play this game?"

"I can't marry Francesca," Michael sputtered.

"Why not?"

"Because—" He cut himself off. Because there were a hundred reasons he couldn't marry her, none of which he could speak aloud. So he just said, "She was married to my cousin."

"Last I checked, there was nothing illegal in that."

No, but there was everything immoral. He'd wanted Francesca for so long, loved her for what felt like an eternity—even when John had been living. He had deceived his cousin in the basest way possible; he would not compound the betrayal by stealing his wife.

It would complete the ugly circle that had led to his being the Earl of Kilmartin, a title that was never supposed to have been his. *None* of it was supposed to be his. And except for those damned boots he'd forced Reivers to toss in a wardrobe, Francesca was the only thing left of John's that he *hadn't* made his own.

John's death had given him fabulous wealth. It had given him power, prestige, and the title of earl.

If it gave him Francesca as well, how could he possibly hang on to the thread of hope that he hadn't somehow, even if only in his dreams, wished for this to happen?

How could he live with himself then?

"She has to marry someone," Colin said.

Michael looked up, aware that he'd been silent with his thoughts for some time. And that Colin had been watching him closely all the while. He shrugged, trying to maintain a cavalier mien, even though he suspected it wouldn't fool the man across the table. "She'll do what she wants," he said. "She always does."

"She might marry hastily," Colin murmured. "She wants to have children before she's too old."

"She's not too old."

"No, but she might think she is. And she might worry that others will think she is, as well. She didn't conceive with your cousin, after all. Well, not successfully."

Michael had to clutch the end of the table to keep from rising. He could have had Shakespeare at his side to translate, and still not have been able to explain why Colin's remark infuriated him so.

"If she chooses too hastily," Colin added, almost offhandedly, "she might choose someone who would be cruel to her."

"Francesca?" Michael asked derisively. Maybe some other woman would be that foolish, but not his Francesca.

Colin shrugged. "It could happen."

"Even if it did," Michael countered, "she would never remain in such a marriage."

"What choice would she have?"

"This is *Francesca*," Michael said. Which really should have explained it all.

"I suppose you're right," Colin acceded, sipping at his drink. "She could always take refuge with the Bridgertons. We would certainly never force her to return to a cruel spouse." He set his glass down on the table and sat back. "Besides, the point is moot, anyway, is it not?"

There was something strange in Colin's tone, something hidden and provoking. Michael looked up sharply, unable to resist the impulse to search the other man's face for clues to his agenda. "And why is that?" he asked.

Colin took another sip of his drink. Michael noticed that the volume of liquid in the glass never seemed to go down.

Colin toyed with his glass for several moments before looking up, his gaze settling on Michael's face. To anyone else, it might have seemed a bland expression, but there was something in Colin's eyes that made Michael want to squirm in his seat. They were sharp and piercing, and although different in color, shaped precisely like Francesca's.

It was damned eerie, that.

"Why is the point moot?" Colin murmured thoughtfully. "Well, because you so clearly don't wish to marry her."

Michael opened his mouth for a quick retort, then slammed it shut when he realized—with more than considerable shock—that he'd been about to say, "Of course I do."

And he did.

He wanted to marry her.

He just didn't think he could live with his conscience if he did.

"Are you quite all right?" Colin asked.

Michael blinked. "Perfectly so, why?"

Colin's head tilted slightly to the side. "For a moment there, you looked . . ." He gave his head a shake. "It's nothing."

"What, Bridgerton?" Michael nearly snapped.

"Surprised," Colin said. "You looked rather surprised. Bit odd, I thought."

Dear God, one more moment with Colin Bridgerton, and the bloody bastard would have all of Michael's secrets laid open and bare. Michael pushed his chair back. "I need to be going," he said abruptly.

"Of course," Colin said genially, as if their entire conversation had consisted of horses and the weather.

Michael stood, then gave a curt nod. It wasn't a terribly warm farewell, considering that they were relations of a sort, but it was the best he could do under the circumstances.

"Think about what I said," Colin murmured, just when Michael had reached the door.

Michael let out a harsh laugh as he pushed through the door and into the hall. As if he'd be able to think about anything else.

For the rest of his life.

Chapter 13

. . . all at home is pleasant and well, and Kilmartin thrives under Francesca's careful stewardship. She continues to mourn John, but then of course, so do we all, as, I'm sure, do you. You might consider writing to her directly. I know that she misses you. I do pass along all of your tales, but I am certain you would relate them to her in a different fashion than you do to your mother.

—from Helen Stirling to her son, the Earl of Kilmartin, two years after his departure for India

The rest of the week passed in a supremely annoying blur of flowers, candy, and one appalling display of poetry, recited aloud, Michael recalled with a shudder, on his front steps.

Francesca, it seemed, was putting all the fresh-faced debutantes to shame. The number of men vying for her hand might not have been doubling every day, but it certainly felt like it to Michael, who was constantly tripping over some lovesick swain in the hall.

It was enough to make a man want to vomit. Preferably on the lovesick swain.

Of course he had his admirers as well, but as it was not suitable for a lady to call upon a gentleman, he generally only had to deal with them when he chose to do so, and not when they took it upon themselves to stop by unannounced and for no apparent reason other than to compare his eyes to—

Well, to whatever one would compare your average gray eyes. It was a stupid analogy, anyway, although Michael had been forced to listen to more than one man rhapsodize over Francesca's eyes.

Good God, didn't any of them have an original thought in his head? Forget that *everyone* made mention of her eyes; at the very least one of them could have had the creativity to compare them to something other than the water or the sky.

Michael snorted with disgust. Anyone who took the time to really look at Francesca's eyes would have realized that they were quite their own color.

As if the sky could even compare.

Furthermore, Francesca's nauseating parade of suitors was made all the more difficult to bear by Michael's complete inability to stop thinking about his recent conversation with her brother.

Marriage to Francesca? He had never even let himself think about such a notion.

But now it gripped him with a fervor and intensity that left him reeling.

Marriage to Francesca. Good God. Everything about it was wrong.

Except he wanted it so badly.

It was hell watching her, hell speaking to her, hell living in the same house. He'd thought it was difficult before—loving someone who could never be his—but this . . .

This was a thousand times worse.

Colin knew.

He had to know. Why would he have suggested it if he didn't?

Michael had held on to his sanity all these years for one reason and one reason only: No one knew he was in love with Francesca.

Except, apparently, he was to be denied even that last shred of dignity.

But now Colin knew, or at least he damn well suspected, and Michael couldn't quite quash this rising sense of panic within his chest.

Colin knew, and Michael was going to have to do something about it.

Dear God, what if he told Francesca?

That question was foremost in his mind, even now, as he stood slightly off to the side at the Burwick ball, nearly a week after his momentous meeting with Colin.

"She looks beautiful tonight, doesn't she?"

It was his mother's voice at his ear; he had forgotten to pretend that he wasn't watching Francesca. He turned to Helen and gave her a little bow. "Mother," he murmured.

"Doesn't she?" Helen persisted.

"Of course," he agreed, quickly enough so she might think he was just being polite.

"Green suits her."

Everything suited Francesca, but he wasn't about to tell his mother that, so he just nodded and made a murmur of agreement.

"You should dance with her."

"I'm sure I will," he said, taking a sip of his champagne. He *wanted* to march across the ballroom and forcibly remove her from her annoying little crowd of admirers, but he couldn't very well show such emotion in front of his mother. So he concluded with, "*After* I finish my drink."

Helen pursed her lips. "Her dance card will surely be filled by then. You should go now."

He turned to his mother and smiled, just the sort of devilish grin designed to take her mind off of whatever it was that had her so fixated. "Now why would I do that," he queried, setting his champagne flute down on a nearby table, "when I can dance with you instead?"

"You rascal," Helen said, but she didn't protest when he led her out on the floor.

Michael knew he'd pay for this tomorrow; already the society matrons were circling him for the kill, and there was nothing they liked better than a rake who doted upon his mother.

The dance was a lively one, which didn't allow for much conversation. And as he twisted and turned, dipped and bowed, he kept catching glances of Francesca, radiant in her emerald gown. No one seemed to notice that he was watching her, which suited him just fine, except that as the music reached its penultimate crescendo, Michael was forced to make one final turn away from her.

And when he turned back to face her again, she was gone.

He frowned. That didn't seem right. He supposed she could have darted out to the ladies' retiring room, but, pathetic fool that he was, he'd been watching her closely enough that he knew that she had done that just twenty minutes earlier.

He completed his dance with his mother, bade her farewell, then ambled casually over to the north side of the room, where he'd last seen Francesca. He had to move quickly, lest someone tried to waylay him. But he kept his ears open as he moved through the crowds. No one, however, seemed to be speaking of her.

When he reached her previous location, however, he noticed French doors, presumably to the back garden. They were curtained and closed, of course; it was only April, and not warm enough to be letting the night air in, even with a crowd of three hundred heating up the room. Michael was instantly suspicious; he'd lured too many women out to gardens himself not to be aware of what could happen in the dark of the night.

He slipped outside, making his exit unobtrusive. If Francesca was indeed out in the back garden with a gentleman, the last thing he wanted was a crowd trailing in his wake.

The rumble of the party seemed to pulsate through the glass doors, but even with that, the night felt quiet.

Then he heard her voice.

And it sliced his gut.

She sounded happy, he realized, more than content to be in the company of whatever man had lured her out into the dark. Michael couldn't make out her words, but she was definitely laughing. It was a musical, tinkling sound, and it ended in a soul-searing, flirtatious murmur.

Michael put his hand back on the knob. He should leave. She wouldn't want him here.

But he was rooted to the spot.

He'd never—ever—spied on her with John. Not once had he listened in on a conversation that wasn't meant to include him. If he stumbled within earshot, he had always removed himself immediately. But now—it was different. He couldn't explain it, but it was different, and he could not force himself to leave.

One more minute, he swore to himself. That was all. One more minute to assure that she was not in a dangerous situation, and—

"No, no."

Francesca's voice.

His ears pricked up and he took a few steps in the direction of her voice. She didn't sound upset, but she *was* saying no. Of course, she could be laughing about a joke, or maybe some inane piece of gossip.

"I really must— *No*!"

And that was all it took for Michael to move.

Francesca knew that she shouldn't have come outside with Sir Geoffrey Fowler, but he had been polite and charming, and she was feeling a trifle warm in the crowded ballroom. It was the sort of thing she'd never have done as an unmarried debutante, but widows weren't held to quite the same standards, and besides, Sir Geoffrey had said that he would leave the door ajar.

All had been perfectly pleasant for the first few minutes. Sir Geoffrey made her laugh, and he made her feel beautiful, and it was almost heartbreaking to realize how much she'd missed that. And so she had laughed and flirted, and allowed herself to melt into the moment. She wanted to feel like a woman again—maybe not in the fullest sense of the word, but still, was it so wrong to enjoy the heady intoxication of knowing that she was desired?

Maybe they were all after her now infamous double dowry, maybe they wanted the alignment with two of Britain's most notable families—Francesca was both a Bridgerton and a Stirling, after all. But for one lovely evening, she was going to let herself believe it was all about *her*.

But then Sir Geoffrey had moved closer. Francesca had backed up as discreetly as she was able, but he took another step in her direction, and then another, and before she knew it, her back was against a fat-trunked tree, and Sir Geoffrey's hands were planted against the bark, each uncomfortably close to her head.

"Sir Geoffrey," Francesca said, endeavoring to remain polite as long as she possibly could, "I'm afraid there has been a misunderstanding. I believe I would like to return to the party." She kept her voice light and friendly, not wishing to provoke him into something she would regret.

His head dipped an inch closer to hers. "Now, why would you want to do that?" he murmured.

"No, no," she said, ducking to the side as he came in closer, "people will be missing me." Dash it all, she was going to have to stamp on his foot, or worse, unman him in the manner her brothers had taught her back when she was a green girl. "Sir Geoffrey," she said, trying one last time for civility, "I really must—"

And then his mouth, wet and mushy and entirely unwelcome, landed on hers.

"—No!" she managed to squeal.

But he was quite determined to mash her with his lips. Francesca twisted this way and that, but he was stronger than she had realized, and he clearly had no intention of letting her escape. Still struggling, she maneuvered her leg so that she might jam her knee up into his groin, but before she could do that, Sir Geoffrey seemed to . . . quite simply . . . disappear.

"Oh!" The surprised sound flew from her lips of its own accord. There was a flurry of movement, a noise that sounded rather sickeningly like knuckles on flesh, and one very heartfelt cry of pain. By the time Francesca had any idea what was going on, Sir Geoffrey was sprawled on the ground, swearing most vehemently, and a large man loomed over him, his boot planted firmly on Sir Geoffrey's chest.

"Michael?" Francesca asked, unable to believe her eyes.

"Say the word," Michael said, in a voice she had never dreamed could cross his lips, "and I will crush his ribs."

"No!" Francesca said quickly. She'd not have felt the least bit guilty for kneeing Sir Geoffrey between the legs, but she didn't want Michael to *kill* the man.

And from the look on Michael's face, she was quite certain he would have happily done so.

"That's not necessary," she said, hurrying to Michael's side and then backing up when she saw the feral gleam in his eyes. "Er, perhaps we could just ask him to leave?"

For a moment Michael did nothing but stare at her. Hard, in the eyes, and with an intensity that robbed her of the ability to breathe. Then he ground his boot down into Sir Geoffrey's chest. Not too very much harder, but enough to make the supine man grunt with discomfort.

"Are you certain?" Michael bit off.

"Yes, please, there's no need to hurt him," Francesca said. Good heavens, this would be a nightmare if anyone caught them thus. Her reputation would be tarnished, and heaven knew what they'd say about Michael, attacking a well-respected baronet. "I shouldn't have come out here with him," she added.

"No, you shouldn't have done," Michael said harshly, "but that hardly gives him leave to force his attentions on you." Abruptly, he removed his boot from Sir Geoffrey's chest and hauled the quivering man to his feet. Grabbing him by his lapels, he pinned him against the tree and then jerked his own body forward until the two men were nearly nose to nose.

"Doesn't feel so good to be trapped, does it?" Michael taunted.

Sir Geoffrey said nothing, just stared at him in terror.

"Do you have something to say to the lady?"

Sir Geoffrey shook his head frantically.

Michael slammed his head back against the tree. "Think harder!" he growled.

"I'm sorry!" Sir Geoffrey squeaked.

Rather like a girl, Francesca thought dispassionately. She'd known he wouldn't make a good husband, but that clinched it.

But Michael was not through with him. "If you ever step within ten yards of Lady Kilmartin again, I will personally disembowel you."

Even Francesca flinched.

"Am I understood?" Michael ground out.

Another squeak, and this time Sir Geoffrey sounded like he might cry.

"Get out of here," Michael grunted, shoving the terrified man away. "And while you're at it, endeavor to leave town for a month or so."

Sir Geoffrey looked at him in shock.

Michael stood still, dangerously so, and then shrugged one insolent shoulder. "You won't be missed," he said softly.

Francesca realized she was holding her breath. He was terrifying, but he was also magnificent, and it shook her to her very core to realize that she'd never seen him thus.

Never dreamed he could *be* like this.

Sir Geoffrey ran off, heading across the lawn to the back gate, leaving Francesca alone with Michael, alone and, for the first time since she'd known him, without a word to say.

Except, perhaps, "I'm sorry."

Michael turned on her with a ferocity that nearly sent her reeling. "Don't apologize," he bit off.

"No, of course not," she said, "but I should have known better, and—"

"*He* should have known better," he said savagely.

It was true, and Francesca was certainly not going to take the blame for her attack, but at the same time, she thought it best not to feed his anger any further, at least not right now. She'd never seen him like this. In truth, she'd never seen anyone like this—wound so tightly with fury that he seemed as if he might snap into pieces. She'd thought he was out of control, but now, as she watched him, standing so still she was afraid to breathe, she realized that the opposite was true.

Michael was holding on to his control like a vise; if he hadn't, Sir Geoffrey would be lying in a bloody heap right now.

Francesca opened her mouth to say something more, something placating or even funny, but she found herself without words, without the ability to do anything but watch him, this man she'd thought she knew so well.

There was something mesmerizing about the moment, and she couldn't take her eyes off of him. He was breathing hard, obviously still struggling to control his anger, and he was, she realized with curiosity, not entirely *there*. He was staring at some far off horizon, his eyes unfocused, and he looked almost . . .

In pain.

"Michael?" she whispered.

No reaction.

"Michael?" This time, she reached out and touched him, and he flinched, whipping around so quickly that she stumbled backward.

"What is it?" he asked gruffly.

"Nothing," she stammered, not certain what it was she'd meant to say, not even certain if she'd *had* something to say other than his name.

He closed his eyes for a moment, then opened them, clearly waiting for her to say more.

"I believe I will go home," she said. The party no longer held appeal; all she wanted to do was cocoon herself where all was safe and familiar.

Because Michael was suddenly neither of those things.

"I will make your apologies inside," he said stiffly.

"I'll send the carriage back for you and the mothers," Francesca added. The last she'd looked, Janet and Helen were enjoying themselves immensely. She didn't want to cut their evening short.

"Shall I escort you through the back gate, or would you rather go through the ball?"

"The back gate, I think," she said.

And he did, the full distance to the carriage, his hand burning at her back the entire way. But when she reached the carriage, instead of accepting his assistance to climb up, she turned to him, a question suddenly burning on her lips.

"How did you know I was in the garden?" she inquired.

He didn't say anything. Or maybe he would have done, just not quickly enough to suit her.

"Were you watching me?" she asked.

His lips curved, not quite into a smile, not even into the beginnings of a smile. "I'm always watching you," he said grimly.

And she was left with *that* to ponder for the rest of the evening.

Chapter 14

. . . Did Francesca say that she misses me? Or did you merely infer it?

—from the Earl of Kilmartin to his mother, Helen Stirling, two years and two months after his departure for India

Three hours later, Francesca was sitting in her bedroom back at Kilmartin House when she heard Michael return. Janet and Helen had come home quite a bit earlier, and when Francesca had (somewhat purposefully) run into them in the hall, they'd informed her that Michael had chosen to round out his evening with a visit to his club.

Most likely to avoid *her*, she'd decided, even though there was no reason for him to expect to see her at such a late hour. Still, she had left the ball earlier that evening with the distinct impression that Michael did not desire her company. He had defended her honor with all the valor and purpose of a true hero, but she couldn't help but feel that it was done almost reluctantly, as if it was something he *had* to do, not something he wanted to do.

And even worse, that she was someone whose company he had

to endure, rather than the cherished friend she had always told herself she was.

That, she realized, hurt.

Francesca told herself that when he returned to Kilmartin House she would leave well enough alone. She would do nothing but listen at the door as he tramped down the hallway to his bedchamber. (She was honest enough with herself to admit that she was not above—and in fact fundamentally unable to resist—eavesdropping.) Then she would scoot over to the heavy oak door that connected their rooms (locked on both sides since her return from her mother's; she certainly didn't fear Michael, but proprieties were proprieties) and then listen there a few minutes longer.

She had no idea what she'd be listening for, or even why she felt the need to hear his footsteps as he moved about his room, but she simply had to do it. Something had changed tonight. Or maybe nothing had changed, which might have been worse. Was it possible that Michael had never been the man she'd thought he was? Could she have been so close to him for so long, counted him as one of her dearest friends, even when they'd been estranged, and still not *known* him?

She'd never dreamed that Michael might have secrets from her. From *her*! Everyone else, maybe, but not her.

And it left her feeling rather off balance and untidy. Almost as if someone had come up to Kilmartin House and shoved a pile of bricks under the south wall, setting the entire world at a drunken slant. No matter what she did, no matter what she thought, she still felt as if she were sliding. To where, she didn't know, and she didn't dare hazard a guess.

But the ground was most definitely no longer firm beneath her feet.

Her bedroom faced the front of Kilmartin House, and when all was quiet she could hear the front door close, provided the person closing it did so with enough force. It didn't need to be slammed, but—

Well, whatever firmness it required, Michael evidently was exercising it, because she heard the telltale thunk beneath her feet, followed by a low rumble of voices, presumably Priestley chatting with him as he took his coat.

Michael was home, which meant she could finally just go to bed and at least pretend to sleep. He was home, which meant that it was time to declare the evening officially over. She should put this behind her, move on, maybe pretend nothing had happened . . .

But when she heard his footsteps coming up the stairs, she did the one thing she never would have expected herself to do—

She opened her door and dashed out into the hall.

She had no idea what she was doing. Not even a clue. By the time her bare feet touched the runner carpet, she was so shocked at her own actions that she found herself somewhat frozen and out of breath.

Michael looked exhausted. And surprised. And heartstoppingly handsome with his cravat slightly loosened and his midnight hair falling in wavy locks over his forehead. Which left her wondering—When had she begun to notice how handsome he was? It had always been something that had simply been *there*, that she knew in an intellectual sense but never really took note of.

But now . . .

Her breath caught. Now his beauty seemed to fill the air around her, swirling about her skin, leaving her shivery and hot, all at the same time.

"Francesca," Michael said, her name more of a tired statement than anything else.

And of course she had nothing to say. It was so unlike her to do something like this, to rush in without thinking about what she was planning, but she didn't particularly feel like herself that evening. She was so unsettled, so off balance, and the only thought in her head (if indeed there had been any) before dashing out her door was that she had to *see* him. Just catch a glimpse and maybe hear his voice. If she could convince herself that he really *was* the person she thought she knew, then maybe she was still the same, too.

Because she didn't feel the same.

And it shook her to the core.

"Michael," she said, finally finding her voice. "I . . . Good evening."

He just looked at her, raising one brow at her remarkably meaningless statement.

She cleared her throat. "I wanted to make sure you were, er . . . all right." The ending sounded a little weak, even to her ears, but it was the best adjective she could come up with on such short notice.

"I'm fine," he said gruffly. "Just tired."

"Of course," she said. "Of course, of course."

He smiled, but entirely without humor. "Of course."

She swallowed, then tried to smile, but it felt forced. "I didn't thank you earlier," she said.

"For what?"

"For coming to my aid," she replied, thinking that ought to be obvious. "I would have . . . Well, I would have defended myself." At his wry glance, she added, somewhat defensively, "My brothers showed me how."

He crossed his arms and looked down at her in a vaguely paternalistic manner. "In that case, I'm sure you would have rendered him a soprano in no time."

She pinched her lips together. "Regardless," she said, deciding not to comment upon his sarcasm, "I very much appreciated not having to, er . . ." She blushed. Oh, God, she hated when she blushed.

"Knee him in the bollocks?" Michael finished helpfully, one corner of his mouth curving into a mocking smile.

"Indeed," she ground out, quite convinced that her cheeks had gone from pink straight to crimson, skipping all shades of rose, fuchsia, and red along the way.

"You're quite welcome," he said abruptly, giving her a nod that was meant to indicate the end of the conversation. "Now, if you will excuse me."

He moved as if heading for his bedroom door, but Francesca wasn't quite ready (and she was certain that the devil himself only knew why) to end the conversation. "Wait!" she called out, gulping when she realized that now she was going to have to *say* something.

He turned around, slowly and with a strange sense of deliberation. "Yes?"

"I . . . I just . . ."

He waited while she floundered, then finally said, "Can it wait until morning?"

"No! Wait!" And this time she reached out and grabbed his arm.

He froze.

"Why are you so angry with me?" she whispered.

He just shook his head, as if he couldn't quite believe her question. But he did not take his eyes off of her hand on his arm. "What are you talking about?" he asked.

"Why are you so angry with me?" she repeated, and she realized that she hadn't even realized she'd felt this way until the words had left her lips. But something wasn't right between them, and she had to know why.

"Don't be ridiculous," he muttered. "I'm not angry with you. I'm merely tired, and I want to go to bed."

"You are. I'm sure you are." Her voice was rising with conviction. Now that she'd said it, she knew it was true. He tried to hide it, and he'd become quite accomplished at apologizing when it slipped to the fore, but there was anger inside of him, and it was directed at her.

Michael placed his hand over hers. Francesca gasped at the heat of the contact, but then all he did was lift her hand off of his arm and allow it to drop. "I'm going to bed," he announced.

And then he turned his back on her. Walked away.

"No! You can't go!" She dashed after him, unthinking, unheedful . . .

Right into his bedroom.

If he hadn't been angry before, he was now. "What are you doing here?" he demanded.

"You can't just dismiss me," she protested.

He stared at her. Hard. "You are in my bedchamber," he said in a low voice. "I suggest you leave."

"Not until you explain to me what is going on."

Michael held himself perfectly still. His every muscle had frozen into a hard, stiff line, and it was a blessing, really, because if he'd allowed himself to move—if he'd felt even capable of moving—he would have lunged at her. And what he would do when he caught her was anyone's guess.

He'd been pushed to the edge. First by her brother, and then by Sir Geoffrey, and now by Francesca herself, standing in front of him without a bloody clue.

His world had been overturned by a single suggestion.

Why don't you just marry her?

It dangled before him like a ripe apple, a wicked possibility that shouldn't be his to take.

John, his conscience pounded. *John. Remember John.*

"Francesca," he said, his voice hard and controlled, "it is well past midnight, and you are in the bedchamber of a man to whom you are not married. I suggest you leave."

But she didn't. Damn her, she didn't even move. She just stood there, three feet past the still-open doorway, staring at him as if she'd never seen him before.

He tried not to notice that her hair was loose. He tried not to see that she was wearing her nightclothes. They were demure, yes, but still meant to be removed, and his gaze kept dipping to the silken hem, which brushed the top of her foot, allowing him a tantalizing peek at her toes.

Good God, he was staring at her toes. Her *toes*. What had his life come to?

"Why are you angry with me?" she asked again.

"I'm not," he snapped. "I just want you to get the h—" He caught himself at the last moment. "To get out of my room."

"Is it because I wish to remarry?" she asked, her voice choked with emotion. "Is that it?"

He didn't know how to answer, so he just glared at her.

"You think I'm betraying John," she said accusingly. "You think I should spend my days mourning your cousin."

Michael closed his eyes. "No, Francesca," he said wearily, "I would never—"

But she wasn't listening. "Do you think I don't mourn him?" she demanded. "Do you think I don't think about him each and every day? Do you think it feels *good* to know that when I marry, I'll be making a mockery of the sacrament?"

He looked at her. She was breathing hard, caught up in her anger and maybe her grief as well.

"What I had with John," she said, her entire body shaking now, "I'm not going to find with any of the men sending me flowers.

And it feels like a desecration—a selfish desecration that I'm even considering remarrying. If I didn't want a baby so . . . so *damned* much . . ."

She broke off, maybe from overemotion, maybe just at the shock of having actually cursed aloud. She just stood there, blinking, her lips parted and quivering, looking as if she might break at the merest touch.

He should have been more sympathetic. He should have tried to comfort her. And he would have done both of those things, if they had been in any other room besides his bedchamber. But as it was, it was all he could do just to control his breathing.

And himself.

She looked back up at him, her eyes huge and heartstoppingly blue, even in the candlelight. "You don't know," she said, turning away. She walked to a long, low bureau of drawers. She leaned heavily against it, her fingers biting into the wood. "You just don't know," she whispered, her back still to him.

And somehow that was more than he could take. She had barged her way in here, demanding answers when she didn't even understand the questions. She'd invaded his bedchamber, pushed him to the limit, and now she was just going to *dismiss* him? Turn her back on him and tell him *he* didn't know?

"Don't know what?" he demanded, just before he crossed the room. His feet were silent but swift, and before he knew it he was right behind her, close enough to touch, close enough to grab what he wanted and—

She whirled around. "You—"

And then she stopped. Didn't make another sound. Did nothing but allow her eyes to lock onto his.

"Michael?" she whispered. And he didn't know what she meant. Was it a question? A plea?

She stood there, stock still, the only sound her breath over her lips. And her eyes never left his face.

His fingers tingled. His body burned. She was close. As close as she'd ever stood to him. And if she were anyone else, he would have sworn that she wanted to be kissed.

Her lips were parted, her eyes were unfocused. And her chin seemed to tilt up, as if she were waiting, wishing, wondering when he would finally bend down and seal her fate.

He felt himself say something. Her name, maybe. His chest grew tight, and his heart pounded, and suddenly the impossible became the inevitable, and he realized that this time there was no stopping. This time it wasn't about his control or his sacrifice or his guilt.

This time was for him.

And he was going to kiss her.

When she thought about it later, the only excuse she could come up with was that she didn't know he was right behind her. The carpet was soft and thick, and she hadn't heard his footsteps over the roaring of blood in her ears. She didn't know all that, she *couldn't* have, because then she *never* would have whirled around, intending for all the world to silence him with a scathing retort. She was going to say something horrid and cutting, and intended to make him feel guilty and awful, but when she turned . . .

He was right there.

Close, so close. Mere inches away. It had been years since anyone had stood so close to her, and never, *ever* Michael.

She couldn't speak, couldn't think, couldn't do anything but breathe as she stared at his face, realizing with an awful intensity that she wanted him to kiss her.

Michael.

Good God, she wanted Michael.

It was like a knife slicing through her. She wasn't supposed to feel this. She wasn't supposed to want *anyone*. But Michael . . .

She should have walked away. Hell, she should have run. But something rooted her to the spot. She couldn't take her eyes off of his, couldn't help but moisten her lips, and when his hands settled on her shoulders, she didn't protest.

She didn't even move.

And maybe, just maybe she even leaned in a little, something within her recognizing this moment, this subtle dance between man and woman.

It had been so long since she'd swayed into a kiss, but it seemed that there were some things a body did not forget.

He touched her chin, raised her face just the barest hint.

Still, she didn't say no.

She stared at him, licked her lips, and waited . . .

Waited for the moment, the first touch, because as terrifying and wrong as it was, she knew it would feel like perfection.

And it did.

His lips touched hers in the barest, softest hint of a caress. It was the sort of kiss that seduced with subtlety, sent tingles through her body and left her desperate for more. Somewhere in the hazy back recesses of her mind, she knew that this was wrong, that it was more than wrong—it was insane. But she couldn't have moved if the fires of hell were licking at her feet.

She was mesmerized, transfixed by his touch. She couldn't quite bring herself to make another move, to invite him in any other manner than the soft sway of her body, but neither did she make any attempt to break the contact.

She just waited, breath baited, for him to do something more.

And he did. His hand found the small of her back and splayed there, his fingers tempting her with their intoxicating heat. He didn't exactly pull her toward him, but the pressure was there, and the space between them whispered away until she could feel the gentle scrape of his evening clothes through the silk of her dressing gown.

And she grew hot. Molten.

Wicked.

His lips grew more demanding, and hers parted, allowing him greater exploration. He took full advantage, his tongue swooping in in a dangerous dance, teasing and tempting, stoking her desire until her legs grew weak, and she had no choice but to grasp onto his upper arms, to hold him, to touch him of her own accord, to acknowledge that she was there in the kiss, too, that she was taking part.

That she wanted this.

He murmured her name, his voice hoarse with desire and need and something more, something pained, but all she could do was hold on to him, and let him kiss her, and God help her, kiss him back.

Her hand moved to his neck, reveling in the soft heat of his skin. His hair was slightly long these days and curled onto her fingers, thick and crisp, and— Oh, God, she just wanted to sink into it.

His hand slid up her back, leaving a trail of fire in its wake. His fingers caressed her shoulder, slid down her arm, and then over to her breast.

Francesca froze.

But Michael was too far gone to notice; he cupped her, moaning audibly as he squeezed.

"No," she whispered. This was too much, it was too intimate.

It was too . . . *Michael.*

"Francesca," he murmured, his lips trailing along her cheek to her ear.

"No," she said, and she wrenched herself free. "I can't."

She didn't want to look at him, but she couldn't *not* do it. And when she did, she was sorry.

His chin was dipped, and his face was slightly turned, but he was still staring at her, his eyes searing and intense.

And she was burned.

"I can't do this," she whispered.

He said nothing.

The words came faster, but not in greater numbers. "I can't. I can't. I can't . . . I . . . I—"

"Then go," he bit off. "Now."

She ran.

She ran to her bedroom, and then the next day she ran to her mother.

And then the day after that, she ran all the way to Scotland.

Chapter 15

. . . I am pleased that you are thriving in India, but I do wish you would consider returning home. We all miss you, and you do have responsibilities that cannot be fulfilled from abroad.

—from Helen Stirling to her son, the Earl of Kilmartin, two years and four months after his departure for India

Francesca had always been a rather good liar, and, Michael reflected as he read the short letter she'd left for Helen and Janet, she was even better when she could avoid face-to-face contact and do it in writing.

An emergency had arisen at Kilmartin, Francesca had written, describing the outbreak of spotted fever among the sheep in admirable detail, and it required her immediate attention. They weren't to worry, she assured them, she'd be back soon, and she promised to bring down some of Cook's splendid raspberry jam, which, as they all knew, was unmatched by any confection in London.

Never mind that Michael had never heard of a sheep contracting spotted fever, or any other farm animal for that matter. Where, one had to wonder, did the sheep show their spots?

It was all very neat, and all very easy, and Michael wondered if Francesca had even arranged for Janet and Helen to be out of town for the weekend just so that she could make her escape without having to make her farewells face to face.

And it *was* an escape. There was no doubting that. Michael didn't believe for one minute that there was an emergency up at Kilmartin. If that had been the case, Francesca would have felt duty bound to inform him of it. She might have been running the estate for years, but he was the earl, and she wasn't the sort to usurp or undermine his position now that he was back.

Besides, he had kissed her, and more than that, he had seen her face after he'd kissed her.

If she could have run to the moon, she would have done so.

Janet and Helen hadn't seemed too terribly concerned that she was gone, although they did chatter on (and on and on) about how they missed her company.

Michael just sat in his study, pondering methods of self-flagellation.

He had kissed her. *Kissed* her.

Not, he thought wryly, the best course of action for a man attempting to hide his true feelings.

Six years, he'd known her. Six years, and he'd kept everything beneath the surface, played his role to perfection. Six years, and he'd gone and ruined the whole thing with one simple kiss.

Except there hadn't been anything simple about it.

How was it possible that a kiss could exceed his every fantasy? And with six years to fantasize, he'd imagined some truly superior kisses.

But this . . . it was more. It was better. It was . . .

It was Francesca.

Funny how that changed everything. You could think about a woman every day for years, imagine what she might feel like in your arms, but it never, ever matched the real thing.

And now he was worse off than ever before. Yes, he'd kissed her; yes, it had been quite the most spectacular kiss of his life.

But yes, it was also all over.

And it wasn't going to happen again.

Now that it had finally happened, now that he had tasted perfection, he was in more agony than ever before. Now he knew exactly what he was missing; he understood with painful clarity just what it was that would never be his.

And nothing would ever be the same.

They would never be friends again. Francesca was not the sort of woman who could treat an intimacy lightly. And as she hated awkwardness of any kind, she would go out of her way to avoid his presence.

Hell, she'd gone all the way to Scotland just to be rid of him. A woman couldn't make her feelings much clearer than that.

And the note she'd penned to him— Well, it was far less conversational than the one she'd left for Janet and Helen.

It was wrong. Forgive me.

What the hell she thought she needed forgiveness for was beyond him. *He* had kissed *her*. She might have entered his bedchamber against his wishes, but he was man enough to know that she had not done so with the expectation that he might maul her. She had been concerned because she thought he was angry with her, for God's sake.

She had acted rashly, but only because she cared for him and valued their friendship.

And now he had gone and ruined *that*.

He still wasn't quite certain how it had happened. He'd been looking at her; he couldn't take his eyes off of her. The moment was seared in his brain—her pink silk dressing robe, the way her fingers had pinched together as she spoke to him. Her hair had been loose, hanging over one shoulder, and her eyes had been huge and wet with emotion.

And then she had turned away.

That was when it had happened. That was when everything had changed. Something had risen within him, something he couldn't possibly identify, and his feet had moved. Somehow he found himself across the room, inches away, close enough to touch, close enough to take.

Then she had turned back.

And he was lost.

There was no stopping himself at that point, no listening to reason. Whatever fist of control he'd kept wrapped around his desire for years had simply evaporated, and he had to kiss her.

It had been as simple as that. There had been no choice involved, no free will. Maybe if she'd said no, maybe if she'd backed up and walked away. But she did neither of those things; she just stood there, her breath the only sound between them, and waited.

Had she waited for the kiss? Or had she waited for him to come to his senses and step away?

It was no matter, he thought harshly, crumpling a piece of paper between his fingers. The floor around his desk was now littered with crumpled pieces of paper. He was in a destructive mood, and the sheets were easy targets. He picked up a creamy white card sitting on his blotter and glanced at it before readying his fingers for the kill. It was an invitation.

He stopped, then took a closer look. It was for tonight, and he'd probably answered in the affirmative. He was quite certain Francesca had planned to go; the hostess was a longtime friend of hers.

Maybe he should drag his pathetic self upstairs and dress for the evening. Maybe he should go out, find himself a wife. It probably wouldn't cure what ailed him, but it had to be done sooner or later. And it had to be better for the soul than sitting around and drinking behind his desk.

He stood, eyeing the invitation again. He sighed. He really didn't want to spend the evening socializing with a hundred people who were going to ask after Francesca. With his luck, the party would be full of Bridgertons, or even worse, Bridgerton females, who looked fiendishly alike with their chestnut hair and wide smiles. None held a candle to Francesca, of course—her sisters were almost too friendly, too sunny and open. They lacked Frannie's sense of mystery, the ironic twinkle that colored her eyes.

No, he didn't want to spend the evening among polite company.

And so he decided to take care of his problems as he had so many times before.

By finding himself a woman.

Three hours later, Michael was at the front door to his club, his mood stunningly foul.

He'd gone to La Belle Maison, which was, if one wanted to be honest about it, nothing but a brothel, but as far as brothels went, it was classy and discreet, and one could be assured that the women were clean and there of their own free will. Michael had been an occasional guest during the years he'd lived in London;

most men of his acquaintance had visited La Belle, as they liked to call it, at one point or another. Even John had gone, before he'd married Francesca.

He'd been greeted with great warmth by the madam, treated like a prodigal son. He had a reputation, she explained; and they'd missed his presence. The women had always adored him, frequently remarking that he was one of the few who seemed to care for their pleasure as well as his own.

For some reason, the flattery just left a sour taste in his mouth. He didn't feel like a legendary lover just then; he was sick of his rakish reputation and didn't much care if he pleased anyone that night. He just wanted a woman who might make his mind a delirious blank, even if only for a scant few minutes.

They had just the girl for him, the madam cooed. She was new and in great demand, and he would love her. Michael just shrugged and allowed himself to be led to a petite blond beauty that he was assured was the "very best."

He started to reach out for her, but then his hand dropped. She wasn't right. She was too blond. He didn't want a blond.

Quite all right, he was told, and out emerged a ravishing brunette.

Too exotic.

A redhead?

All wrong.

Out they came, one after another, but they were too young, too old, too buxom, too slight, and then finally he'd selected one at random, determined to just close his damned eyes and get it over with.

He'd lasted two minutes.

The door had shut behind him and he'd felt sick, almost panicked, and he realized he couldn't do it.

He couldn't make love to a woman. It was appalling. Emasculating. Hell, he might as well have grabbed a knife and eunuched himself.

Before, he had taken his pleasure with women to blot out *one* woman. But now that he'd tasted her, even with one fleeting kiss, he was ruined.

And so instead he'd come here, to his club, where he didn't have to worry about seeing anyone of the female persuasion. The aim, of course, was to wipe Francesca's face from his mind, and he was rather hoping that alcohol would work where the delectable girls of La Belle Maison had not.

"Kilmartin."

Michael looked up. Colin Bridgerton.

Damn.

"Bridgerton," he grunted. Damn damn damn. Colin Bridgerton was the last person he wanted to see right now. Even the ghost of Napoleon, come down to slice a rapier through his gullet, would have been preferable.

"Sit down," Colin said, motioning to the chair across from him.

There was no getting out of it; he could have lied and said he was meeting someone, but he still would have no excuse for not sitting with Colin to share a quick drink while he was waiting. And so Michael just gritted his teeth and sat, hoping that Colin had another engagement that would require his presence in—oh, about three minutes.

Colin picked up his tumbler, regarded it with curious diligence, then swirled the amber liquid around several times before taking a small sip. "I understand that Francesca has returned to Scotland."

Michael gave a grunt and a nod.

"Surprising, wouldn't you think? With the season still so young."

"I don't pretend to know her mind."

"No, no, of course you wouldn't," Colin said softly. "No man of any intelligence would pretend to know a female mind."

Michael said nothing.

"Still, it's only been . . . what . . . a fortnight since she came down?"

"Just over," Michael bit off. Francesca had returned to London the precise day that he had done.

"Right, of course. Yes, you'd know that, wouldn't you?"

Michael shot Colin a sharp look. What the hell was he getting at?

"Ah, well," Colin said, lifting one of his shoulders into a careless shrug. "I'm sure she'll be back soon. Not likely to find a husband up in Scotland, after all, and that is her aim for this spring, is it not?"

Michael nodded tersely, eyeing a table across the room. It was empty. So empty. So joyfully, blessedly empty.

He could picture himself a very happy man at that table.

"Not feeling very conversational this evening, are we?" Colin asked, breaking into his (admittedly tame) fantasies.

"No," Michael said, not appreciating the vague hint of condescension in the other man's voice, "*we* are not."

Colin chuckled, then took the last sip of his drink. "Just testing you," he said, leaning back in his chair.

"To see if I have spontaneously divided into two separate beings?" Michael bit off.

"No, of course not," Colin said with a suspiciously easy grin. "I can see that quite clearly. I was merely testing your mood."

Michael arched a brow in a most forbidding manner. "And you found it . . . ?"

"Rather as usual," Colin answered, undeterred.

Michael did nothing but scowl at him as the waiter arrived with their drinks.

"To happiness," Colin said, lifting his glass in the air.

I am going to strangle him, Michael decided right then and there. *I am going to reach across the table and wrap my hands around his throat until those annoying green eyes pop right out of his head.*

"No toast to happiness?" Colin asked.

Michael let out an incoherent grunt and downed his glass in one gulp.

"What are you drinking?" Colin asked conversationally. He leaned over and peered at Michael's glass. "Must be jolly good stuff."

Michael fought the urge to clock him over the head with his now empty tumbler.

"Very well," Colin said with a shrug, "I shall toast to my own happiness, then." He took a sip, leaned back, then touched his lips to the glass again.

Michael glanced at the clock.

"Isn't it a good thing I have nowhere to be?" Colin mused.

Michael let his glass drop down onto the table with a loud *thunk*. "Is there a point to any of this?" he demanded.

For a moment it looked like Colin, who could, by all accounts, talk anyone under the table when he so chose, would remain silent. But then, just when Michael was ready to give up on any guise of politeness and simply get up and leave, he said, "Have you decided what you're going to do?"

Michael held himself very still. "Meaning?"

Colin smiled, with just enough condescension that Michael wanted to punch him. "About Francesca, of course," he said.

"Didn't we just confirm that she has left the country?" Michael said carefully.

Colin shrugged. "Scotland's not so very far away."

"It's far enough," Michael muttered. Certainly far enough to make it abundantly clear that she didn't want anything to do with him.

"She'll be all alone," Colin said on a sigh.

Michael just narrowed his eyes and stared at him. Hard.

"I still think you should—" Colin broke himself off, quite on purpose, Michael was convinced. "Well, you know what I think," Colin finally finished, taking a sip of his drink.

And Michael just gave up on being polite. "You don't know a damned thing, Bridgerton."

Colin raised his brows at the snarl in Michael's voice. "Funny," he murmured, "I hear that very thing all day long. Usually from my sisters."

Michael was familiar with this tactic. Colin's neat sidestep was exactly the sort of maneuver he himself employed with such facility. And it was for probably this reason that his right hand had formed a fist under the table. Nothing had the power to irritate like the reflection of one's own behavior in someone else.

But oh God, Colin's face was so close.

"Another whisky?" Colin asked, effectively ruining Michael's lovely vision of blackened eyes.

Michael was in the perfect mood to drink himself into oblivion, but *not* in the company of Colin Bridgerton, so he just let out a terse, "No," and pushed his chair back.

"You do realize, Kilmartin," Colin said, his voice so soft it was almost chilling, "that there is no reason you can't marry her. None at all. Except, of course," he added, almost as an afterthought, "the reasons you manufacture for yourself."

Michael felt something tearing in his chest. His heart, probably, but he was growing so used to the feeling it was a wonder he still noticed it.

And Colin, damn his eyes, just wouldn't shut up.

"If you don't want to marry her," Colin said thoughtfully, "then you don't want to marry her. But—"

"She might say no," Michael heard himself say. His voice sounded rough, choked, foreign to his ears.

Dear God, if he'd jumped on the table and declared his love for Francesca, he couldn't have made it any more clear.

Colin's head tilted a fraction of an inch to the side, just enough to acknowledge that he'd heard the subtext in Michael's words. "She might," he murmured. "In fact, she probably will. Women often do, the first time you ask."

"And how many times have you proposed marriage?"

Colin smiled slowly. "Just once, actually. This afternoon, as a matter of fact."

It was the one thing—truly, the only thing—that Colin could have said to completely diffuse Michael's churning emotions. "I beg your pardon?" Michael asked, his jaw dropping in shock. This was Colin Bridgerton, the eldest of the unmarried Bridgerton brothers. He'd practically created a profession of avoiding marriage.

"Indeed," Colin said mildly. "Thought it was about time, although I suppose honesty is owed here, so I should probably admit that she did not force me to ask twice. If it makes you feel any better, however, it did take several minutes to wheedle the *yes* out of her."

Michael just stared.

"Her first reaction to my query was to fall to the pavement in surprise," Colin admitted.

Michael fought the impulse to look around to see if he'd somehow been trapped in a theatrical farce without his knowledge. "Er, is she well?" he asked.

"Oh, quite," Colin said, picking up his drink.

Michael cleared his throat. "Might I inquire as to the identity of the lucky lady?"

"Penelope Featherington."

The one who doesn't speak? Michael almost blurted out. Now there was an odd match if ever he'd seen one.

"Now you *really* look surprised," Colin said, thankfully with good humor.

"I did not realize you'd hoped to settle down," Michael hastily improvised.

"Neither did I," Colin said with a smile. "Funny how that works out."

Michael opened his mouth to congratulate him, but instead he heard himself asking, "Has anyone told Francesca?"

"I became engaged *this afternoon*," Colin reminded him, somewhat bemusedly.

"She'll want to know."

"I expect she will. I certainly tormented her enough as a child. I'm sure she will wish to devise some sort of wedding-related torture for me."

"Someone needs to tell her," Michael said forcefully, ignoring Colin's stroll through his childhood memories.

Colin leaned back in his seat with a casual sigh. "I imagine my mother will pen her a note."

"Your mother will be quite busy. It won't be the first thing on her agenda."

"I couldn't speculate."

Michael frowned. "Someone should tell her about it."

"Yes," Colin said with a smile, "someone should. I'd go myself—It's been an age since I've been up to Scotland. But of course I'm going to be a touch busy here in London, seeing as how

I'm getting married. Which is, of course, the entire reason for this discussion, is it not?"

Michael shot him an annoyed glance. He hated that Colin Bridgerton thought he was cleverly manipulating him, but he didn't see how he could disabuse him of that notion without admitting that he desperately wanted to travel to Scotland to see Francesca.

"When is the wedding to be?" he asked.

"I'm not entirely sure yet," Colin said. "Soon, I would hope."

Michael nodded. "Then Francesca will need to be informed right away."

Colin smiled slowly. "Yes, she will, won't she?"

Michael scowled.

"You don't have to marry her while you're up there," Colin said, "just inform her of my impending nuptials."

Michael revisited his earlier fantasy of strangling Colin Bridgerton and found the image even more tantalizing than before.

"I'll see you later," Colin said as Michael headed for the door. "Perhaps a month or so?"

Meaning that he fully expected Michael *not* to be in London anytime soon.

Michael swore under his breath, but he did nothing to contradict him. He might hate himself for it, but now that he had an excuse to go after Francesca, he couldn't resist making the trip.

The question was, would he be able to resist *her?*

And more to the point, did he even want to?

Several days later, Michael was standing at the front door of Kilmartin, his childhood home. It had been years since he'd stood here, more than four, to be precise, and he couldn't quite halt the catch in his throat when he realized that all of *this*—the house, the lands, the legacy—was his. Somehow it hadn't sunk in, perhaps in his brain, but not in his heart.

Springtime didn't seem to have arrived in the border counties of Scotland yet, and the air, while not biting, held a chill that had him rubbing his gloved hands together. The air was misty and the skies were gray, but there was something in the atmosphere that called to him, reminding his weary soul that *this*, not London and not India, was home.

But his sense of place was little comfort as he prepared for what lay ahead. It was time to face Francesca.

He had rehearsed this moment a thousand times since his conversation with Colin Bridgerton back in London. What he'd say to her, how he'd make his case. And he rather thought he'd figured it out. Because before he convinced Francesca, he'd had to convince himself.

He was going to marry her.

He'd have to get her to agree, of course; he couldn't very well force her into marriage. She'd probably come up with countless reasons why it was a mad idea, but in the end, he'd convince her.

They would marry.

Marry.

It was the one dream he'd never permitted himself to consider.

But the more he thought about it, the more it made sense. Forget that he loved her, forget that he'd loved her for years. She didn't need to know any of that; telling her would only make her feel awkward and then he'd feel like a fool.

But if he could present it to her in practical terms, explain why it made *sense* that they marry, he was sure he could warm her to the idea. She might not understand the emotions, not when she didn't feel them herself, but she had a cool head, and she understood sense.

And now that he'd finally allowed himself to imagine a life with her, he couldn't let it go. He *had* to make it happen. He had to.

And it would be good. He might not ever have all of her—her heart, he knew, would never be his—but he'd have most of her, and that would be enough.

It was certainly more than he had now.

And even half of Francesca— Well, that would be ecstasy.

Wouldn't it?

Chapter 16

. . . but as you have written, Francesca is managing Kilmartin with admirable skill. I do not mean to shirk my duties, and I assure you, had I not such an able stand-in, I would return immediately.

—from the Earl of Kilmartin to his mother, Helen Stirling, two years and six months after his departure for India, written with a muttered, "She never answered my question."

Francesca didn't like to think of herself as a coward, but when her choices were that and fool, she chose coward. Gladly.

Because only a fool would have remained in London—in the same house, even—as Michael Stirling after experiencing his kiss.

It had been . . .

No, Francesca wouldn't think about it. When she thought about it, she inevitably ended up feeling guilty and ashamed, because she wasn't supposed to feel like this about Michael.

Not Michael.

She hadn't planned to feel desire for *anyone*. Truly, the most she'd been hoping for with a husband was a mild, pleasant sensation—a kiss that felt nice against the lips but left her unaffected everywhere else.

That would have been enough.

But now . . . But this . . .

Michael had kissed her. He'd kissed her, and worse, she'd kissed him back, and since then all she could do was imagine his lips on hers, then imagine them everywhere else. And at night, when she was alone in her enormous bed, the dreams became more vivid, and her hand would creep down her body, only to halt before it reached its final destination.

She wouldn't— No, she couldn't fantasize about Michael. It was wrong. She would have felt terrible for feeling this kind of desire about anyone, but Michael . . .

He was John's cousin. His best friend. Her best friend, too. And she shouldn't have kissed him.

But, she thought with a sigh, it had been magnificent.

And that was why she'd had to choose coward over fool and run to Scotland. Because she had no faith in her ability to resist him again.

She'd been at Kilmartin for nearly a week now, trying to immerse herself in the regular, everyday life of the family seat. There was always much to do—accounts to review, tenants to visit—but she didn't find the same satisfaction she usually did in such tasks. The regularity of it should have been soothing, but instead, it just made her restless, and she couldn't force herself to focus, to center her mind on any one thing.

She was jittery and distracted, and half the time she felt as if she didn't know what to do with herself—in the most literal and physical sense. She couldn't seem to sit still, and so she had taken to leaving Kilmartin for hours on end, strapping on her most comfortable boots and trekking across the countryside until she was exhausted.

Not that it made her sleep any better at night, but still, at least she was trying.

And right now she was trying with great vigor, having just hauled herself up Kilmartin's biggest hill. Breathing hard from the exertion, she glanced up at the darkening sky, trying to gauge both the time and the likelihood that it would rain.

Late, and probably.

She frowned. She should head home.

She didn't have far to go, just down the hill and across one grassy field. But by the time she reached Kilmartin's stately front portico, it had begun to sprinkle, and her face was lightly dusted with misty droplets. She removed her bonnet and shook it out, thankful that she'd remembered to don it before leaving—she wasn't always that diligent—and was just heading upstairs to her bedchamber, where she thought she might indulge herself in some chocolate and biscuits, when Davies, the butler, appeared before her.

"My lady?" he said, clearly desiring her attention.

"Yes?"

"You have a visitor."

"A visitor?" Francesca felt her brow furrow in thought. Most everyone who came calling up at Kilmartin had already removed to Edinburgh or London for the season.

"Not precisely a visitor, my lady."

Michael. It had to be. And she couldn't say she was surprised, not exactly. She had thought he might follow her, although she'd assumed he'd do it right away or not at all. Now, after the passage of a sennight, she'd reckoned she might be safe from his attentions.

Safe from her own response to them.

"Where is he?" she asked Davies.

"The earl?"

She nodded.

"Waiting for you in the rose drawing room."

"Has he been here long?"

"No, my lady."

Francesca nodded her dismissal and then forced her feet to carry her down the hall to the drawing room. She shouldn't be dreading this quite so intensely. It was just Michael, for heaven's sake.

Except she had a sinking feeling that he would never be *just Michael* ever again.

Still, it wasn't as if she hadn't gone over what she might say a million times in her head. But all of her platitudes and explanations sounded rather inadequate now that she was faced with the prospect of actually uttering them aloud.

How nice to see you, Michael, she could say, pretending that nothing had happened.

Or— *You must realize that nothing will change*—even though, of course, everything had changed.

Or she could make good humor her guide and open with something like— *Can you believe the silliness of it all?*

Except that she rather doubted either of them had found it silly.

And so she just accepted that she was going to have make it all up as she went along, and she stepped through the doorway into Kilmartin's famed and lovely rose drawing room.

He was standing by the window—watching for her, perhaps?—and didn't turn when she entered. He looked travelworn, with slightly wrinkled clothing and ruffled hair. He wouldn't have ridden all the way to Scotland—only a fool or a man chasing someone to Gretna would do that. But she had traveled with Michael often enough to know that he'd probably joined the driver in front for a fair bit of the trip. He'd always hated closed carriages for long journeys and had more than once sat in the drizzle and rain rather than remain penned in with the rest of the passengers.

She didn't say his name. She could have done, she supposed. She wasn't buying herself very much time; he would turn around soon enough. But for now she just wanted to take the time to acclimate herself to his presence, to make sure that her breathing was under control, that she wasn't going to do something truly foolish like burst into tears, or, just as likely, erupt with silly, nervous laughter.

"Francesca," he said, without even turning around.

He'd sensed her presence, then. Her eyes widened, although she shouldn't have been surprised. Ever since he'd left the army he'd had an almost catlike ability to sense his surroundings. It was probably what had kept him alive during the war. No one, apparently, could attack him from behind.

"Yes," she said. And then, because she thought she should say more, she added, "I trust you had a pleasant journey."

He turned. "Very much so."

She swallowed, trying not to notice how handsome he was. He'd quite taken her breath away in London, but here in Scotland he seemed changed. Wilder, more elemental.

Far more dangerous to her soul.

"Is anything amiss in London?" she asked, hoping there was some sort of practical purpose to his visit. Because if there wasn't, then he had come just for *her*, and that scared the very devil out of her.

"Nothing amiss," he said, "although I do bear news."

She tilted her head, waiting for his reply.

"Your brother has become betrothed."

"Colin?" she asked in surprise. Her brother had been so committed to his life as a bachelor that she wouldn't have been shocked if he'd told her that the lucky fellow was actually her younger brother Gregory, even though he was nearly ten years Colin's junior.

Michael nodded. "To Penelope Featherington."

"To Penel—oh, my, that *is* a surprise. But lovely, I should say. I think she will suit him tremendously."

Michael took a step toward her, his hands remaining clasped behind his back. "I thought you would want to know."

And he couldn't have penned a letter? "Thank you," she said. "I appreciate your thoughtfulness. It's been a long time since we've had a wedding in the family. Not since—"

Mine, they both realized she'd been about to say.

The silence hung in the room like an unwanted guest, and then finally she broke it with, "Well, it has been a long time. My mother must be delighted."

"She is quite," Michael confirmed. "Or so your brother told me. I didn't have an opportunity to converse with her myself."

Francesca cleared her throat, then tried to feign comfort with the strange tableau by giving a little wave with one of her hands as she asked, "Will you stay long?"

"I haven't decided," he said, taking another step in her direction. "It depends."

She swallowed. "On what?"

He'd halved the distance between them. "On you," he said softly.

She knew what he meant, or at least she thought she did, but the last thing she wanted to do just then was acknowledge what had transpired in London, so she backed up a step—which was as far as she could go without actually fleeing the room—and pretended to misunderstand. "Don't be silly," she said. "Kilmartin is yours.

You may come and go as you please. I have no control over your actions."

His lips curved into a wry smile. "Is that what you think?" he murmured.

And she realized he'd halved the distance between them yet again.

"I'll have a room readied for you," she said hastily. "Which would you like?"

"It doesn't matter."

"The earl's bedchamber, then," she said, well aware that she was babbling now. "It's only right. I'll move down the hall. Or, er, to another wing," she added, mumbling.

He took another step toward her. "That may not be necessary."

Her eyes flew to his. What was he suggesting? Surely he didn't think that a single kiss in London would give him leave to avail himself of the connecting door between the earl's and countess's bedchambers?

"Shut the door," he said, nodding at the open doorway behind her.

She glanced backward, even though she knew exactly what she'd see there. "I'm not sure—"

"I am," he said. And then, in a voice that was velvet over steel he said, "Shut it."

She did. She was fairly certain it was a bad idea, but she did it anyway. Whatever he planned to say to her, she didn't particularly care to have it overheard by a fleet of servants.

But once her fingers left the doorknob she scooted around him and into the room, setting a more comfortable distance—and an entire seating group—between them.

He looked amused by her actions, but he did not mock her for them. Instead, he merely said, "I have given matters a great deal of thought since you left London."

As had she, but there seemed little point in mentioning it.

"I hadn't meant to kiss you," he said.

"No!" she said, too loudly. "I mean, no, of course not."

"But now that I have . . . Now that *we* have . . ."

She winced at his use of the plural. He wasn't going to allow her to pretend that she hadn't been a willing participant.

"Now that it is done," he said, "I'm sure you understand that everything is changed."

She looked up at him then; she'd been quite intently focusing on the pink-and-cream fleur-de-lis pattern on the damask-covered sofa. "Of course," she said, trying to ignore the way her throat was beginning to tighten.

His fingers wrapped around the mahogany edge of a Hepplewhite chair. Francesca glanced down at his hands; his knuckles had gone white.

He was nervous, she realized with surprise. She hadn't expected that. She didn't know that she had ever seen him nervous before. He was always such a model of urbane elegance, his charm easy and smooth, his wicked wit always a whisper from his lips.

But now he looked different. Stripped down. Nervous. It made her feel . . . not better, precisely, but maybe not so much like the only fool in the room.

"I have given the matter a great deal of thought," he said.

He was repeating himself now. This was very strange.

"And I have come to a conclusion that surprised even me," he continued, "although now that I have reached it, I am quite convinced it is the best course of action."

With his every word, she felt more in control, less ill at ease. It wasn't that she *wanted* him to feel badly—well, maybe she did; it was only fair after how *she'd* spent the last week. But there was something rather relieving in the knowledge that the awkwardness was not one-sided, that he'd been as disturbed and shaken as she.

Or if not, at least that he had not been unaffected.

He cleared his throat, then moved his chin slightly, stretching his neck. "I believe," he said, his gaze suddenly settling on hers with remarkable clarity, "that we should be married."

What?

Her lips parted.

What?

And then, finally, she said it. "*What*?"

Not *I beg your pardon.* Not even the more succinct *Excuse me.* Just *What?*

"If you listen to my arguments," he said, "you will see that it makes sense."

"Are you mad?"

He drew back slightly. "Not at all."

"I can't marry you, Michael."

"Why not?"

Why not? Because . . . Because . . . "Because I can't!" she finally burst out. "For heaven's sake, you of all people ought to understand the insanity of such a suggestion."

"I will allow that on first reflection, it seems highly irregular, but if you simply listen to my arguments, you will see the sense in it."

She gaped at him. "How can it make sense? I can't think of anything that makes *less* sense!"

"You won't have to move," he said, ticking the items off on his fingers, "and you will retain your title and position."

Convenient, both items, but hardly reason enough to marry *Michael*, who . . . well . . . *Michael.*

"You will be able to enter into the marriage knowing that you will be treated with care and respect," he added. "It could take months to reach the same conclusion about another man, and even then, could you really be certain? Early impressions can be deceiving, after all."

She searched his face, trying to see if there was anything, *anything* behind his words. There had to be some sort of reason for this, because she just couldn't grasp that he was proposing. It was mad. It was . . .

Good God, she wasn't sure what it was. Was there a word to apply to something that quite simply removed the earth from beneath one's feet?

"I will give you children," he said softly. "Or at least, I will try."

She blushed. She felt it in an instant, her cheeks turning a furiously hot pink. She didn't want to imagine herself in bed with him. She'd spent the last week desperately trying not to do that.

"What will you gain?" she whispered.

He appeared momentarily startled by her query, but he quickly recovered and said, "I will have a wife who has been running my estates for years. I am certainly not so proud that I would not take advantage of your superior knowledge."

She nodded. Just once, but it was enough to signal for him to continue.

"I already know you and trust you," he said. "And I am secure in the knowledge that you will not stray."

"I can't think about this right now," she said, bringing her hands to her face. Her head was spinning with it all, and she had the horrible sensation that it would never quite recover.

"It makes sense," Michael said. "You need only consider—"

"No," she said, desperately searching for a resolute tone. "It would never work. You know that." She turned away, not wanting to look at him. "I can't believe you would even consider it."

"I couldn't either," he admitted, "when the idea first came to me. But once it did, I couldn't let it go, and I soon realized it made perfect sense."

She pressed her fingers into her temples. For God's sake, why did he keep carping on about sense? If he uttered the word one more time she thought she might scream.

And how could he be so calm? She wasn't certain how she thought he *ought* to act; she'd certainly never imagined *this* moment. But something about his bloodless recitation of a proposal gnawed at her. He was so cool, so collected. A bit nervous, perhaps, but with his emotions completely even and unengaged.

Whereas she felt as if her world might spin right off its axis.

It wasn't fair.

And for that moment at least, she hated him for making her feel that way.

"I'm going upstairs," she said abruptly. "I'll have to talk with you about it in the morning."

She almost made it. She was more than halfway to the door when she felt his hand on her arm, his grasp gentle and yet holding her with unrelenting strength.

"Wait," he said, and she could not move.

"What do you want?" she whispered. She wasn't looking at him, but she could see his face in her mind, the way his midnight hair fell over his forehead, his heavy-lidded eyes, framed with lashes so long they could make an angel weep.

And his lips. Most of all, she could see his lips, perfectly shaped, finely molded, perpetually curved into that devilish expression of his, as if he *knew* things, understood the world in a way that more innocent mortals never would.

His hand traveled up her arm until it reached her shoulder, and then one of his fingers traced a feather-light line down the side of her neck.

His voice, when it came, was low and husky, and she felt it right in the very center of her being.

"Don't you want another kiss?"

Chapter 17

. . . yes, of course. Francesca is a wonder. But you already knew that, didn't you?

—from Helen Stirling to her son, the Earl of Kilmartin, two years and nine months after his departure for India

Michael wasn't certain when it had become apparent to him that he would have to seduce her. He'd tried to appeal to her mind, to her innate sense of the practical and wise, and it wasn't working.

And it couldn't be about emotion, because that, he knew, was one-sided.

So it would have to be passion.

He wanted her— Oh, God, he wanted her. With an intensity he hadn't even imagined before he'd kissed her the week previous in London. But even as his blood raced with desire and need and, yes, love, his mind was sharp and calculating, and he knew that if he was to bind her to him, he would need to do it with this. He would have to claim her in a way she could not deny. He couldn't just try to convince her with words and thoughts and ideas. She could attempt to talk herself out of that, pretend the feelings weren't there.

But if he made her his, left his imprint on her in the most physical way possible, he would be with her always.

And she would be his.

She slipped out from beneath his fingers, edging backward until she'd put a few paces between them.

"Don't you want another kiss, Francesca?" he murmured, moving toward her with predatory grace.

"It was a mistake," she said, her voice shaky. She scooted back a few inches farther, stopping only when she bumped into the edge of a table.

He moved forward. "Not if we marry."

"I can't marry you, you know that."

He took her hand, idly rubbed the skin with his thumb. "And why is that?"

"Because I . . . you . . . you're you."

"True," he said, lifting her hand to his mouth and kissing her palm. Then he flicked his tongue along her wrist, just because he could. "And for the first time in a very long while," he said, glancing up at her through his lashes, "there is no one I'd rather be just now."

"Michael . . ." she whispered, arching backwards.

But she wanted him. He could hear it in her breath.

"Michael no, or Michael yes?" he murmured, kissing the inside of her elbow.

"I don't know," she moaned.

"Fair enough." He moved higher, nudging at her chin until she had no choice but to loll back.

And he had no choice but to make love to her neck.

He kissed her slowly, thoroughly, sparing no inch of skin his sensual onslaught. He moved up to the line of her jaw, then over to her earlobe, then back down to the edge of her bodice, grasping it between his teeth. He heard Francesca gasp, but she didn't tell him to stop, so he just pulled and pulled and pulled until one breast popped free.

God, he loved current women's fashions.

"Michael?" she whispered.

"Shhh." He didn't want to have to answer any questions. He didn't want her thinking enough to ask one.

He ran his tongue along the underside of her breast, tasting the salty-sweet essence of her skin, then reached out and cupped her. He'd touched her through her dress the first time they'd kissed, and he'd thought that was heaven, but nothing compared to the feel of her, hot and bare, in his hand.

"Oh, my," she moaned. "Oh . . ."

He blew lightly on her nipple. "Shall I kiss you?" He looked up. He knew he was taking a chance with this, waiting for her answer. He probably shouldn't even have posed the question, but even though his intent was to seduce, he couldn't quite bring himself to do it without at least one affirmative word from her.

"Shall I?" he murmured again, sweetening the deal with one light flick of his tongue across her nipple.

"Yes!" she burst out. "Yes, for God's sake, yes!"

He smiled. Slowly, languidly, savoring the moment. And then, after letting her quiver with anticipation for one second longer than was probably fair, he leaned in and took her into his mouth, pouring years and years of desire onto the one breast, centering it wickedly onto one innocent nipple.

She wasn't going to stand a chance.

"Oh, my God!" she gasped, grasping the edge of the table for purchase as her entire body arched back. "Oh, my God. Oh, Michael. Oh, my God."

He took advantage of her passion to slide his hands around her hips and lift her up until she was seated on the table, her legs parting for him as he stepped into their feminine cradle.

Satisfaction raced through his veins, even as his body screamed for its own pleasure. He loved that he could do this to her, make her scream and moan and cry out with desire. She was so strong, always so cool and composed, and yet right now she was simply and purely his, a slave to her own needs, captive to his expert touch.

He kissed, he licked, he nibbled, he tugged. He tortured her until he thought she might explode. Her breath was loud and gasping, and her moans had grown more and more incoherent.

And all the while his hands were moving silently up her legs, first grasping her ankles, then her calves, pushing her skirts up and up, until they settled in a rumpled pool above her knees.

And it was only then that he pulled away and gave her a hint of a reprieve.

She looked at him, her eyes glazed, her lips pink and parted. She didn't say anything; he didn't think she *could* say anything. But he saw the questions in her eyes. She might be beyond speech, but she was several minutes away from total insanity.

"I thought it would be cruel to torture it any longer," he said, lightly taking her nipple between his thumb and forefinger.

She groaned.

"You like that." It was a statement, and not a particularly sophisticated one, but this was Francesca, not some nameless woman he was tupping while he closed his eyes and imagined her face. And every time she mewled with pleasure his heart raced with joy. "You like it," he said again, smiling with satisfaction.

"Yes," she whispered. "Yes."

He leaned in until his lips were brushing her ear. "You'll like this, too."

"What?" she asked, surprising him with her query. He'd thought she was too far gone to question him aloud.

He nudged her skirts a little higher, just enough so that there was no danger of them falling off her lap. "You want to hear it, don't you?" he murmured, sliding his hands until they were just above her knees. He squeezed her thighs gently, circling against her skin with his thumbs. "You want to know."

She nodded.

He moved toward her again, lightly touching his lips to hers, close enough to feel her, yet far enough to speak. "You were always so curious," he murmured. "You asked so many questions."

He slid his lips along her cheek to her ear, whispering all the way. "Michael," he said, softening his voice to mimic hers, "tell me something naughty. Tell me something wicked."

She blushed. He couldn't see it, but he could feel it, sense the hot rush of blood to her skin.

"But I never told you what you wanted to hear, did I?" he asked, lightly nipping at her earlobe. "I always left you outside the bedroom door."

He paused, not because he expected an answer, just because he wanted to hear her breathe.

"Did you wonder?" he whispered. "Did you leave me and wonder what I hadn't told you?" He leaned in, just so she'd feel his lips move whisper-light against her ear. "Did you want to know," he whispered, "what I did when I was wicked?"

He wouldn't make her answer; it wouldn't be fair. But he couldn't stop his own mind from racing back in time, remembering the countless times he'd teased her with hints of his exploits.

He had never been the one to bring them up, however; she had *always* asked.

"Do you want me to tell you?" he murmured. He felt her jerk

slightly in surprise, and he chuckled. "Not about them, Francesca. You. Only you."

She turned, causing his lips to slide along her cheek. He drew back so he could see her face, and her question was clear in her eyes.

What do you mean?

He moved his hands, exerting just enough pressure on her thighs to spread them open one more wicked inch. "Do you want me to tell you what I'm going to do now?" He leaned down, running his tongue along her nipple, which had grown hard and taut in the cool air of the late afternoon. "To you?" he added.

She swallowed convulsively. He decided to take that as a yes.

"There are so many choices," he said huskily, sliding his hands up her legs another few inches. "I scarcely know where to start."

He stopped to look at her for a moment. She was breathing hard, her lips parted and plump from his kisses. And she was mesmerized, completely under his spell.

He dipped closer once again, to her other ear, so he could make sure his words fell hot and moist upon her soul. "I think, however, that I would have to start where you need me most. First I'd kiss you . . ."—he pressed his thumbs into the soft flesh of her inner thighs—". . . *here.*"

He held silent, just for a second, just long enough for her to shiver with desire. "Would you like that?" he murmured, his question intended to torment and tease. "Yes, I can see that you would.

"But that wouldn't be enough," he mused, "for either of us. So clearly, I would then have to kiss you *here.*" His thumbs inched up until they reached the hot crevice between her legs and her torso, and then he pressed gently, so she would know exactly what he was talking about. "I think you would enjoy a kiss right there," he added, "almost as much"—he slid along the crease, down, down, closer to the very center of her, but not quite all the way—"as I would like to kiss you."

Her breath came a little faster.

"I'd have to take my time there," he murmured, "switch, perhaps, from my lips to my tongue. Run it along the edge right here." He used one fingernail to show her what he meant. "And all the while, I would be pushing you farther and farther open. Like that, maybe?"

He drew back, as if to examine his handiwork. The sight of her was stunningly erotic. She was perched on the edge of the table, her legs open to him, although not nearly enough for what he wanted to do. The skirt of her dress still hung down between her thighs, shielding her from his view, but somehow that made her almost more tempting. He didn't need to see her, he realized, not yet, anyway. Her position was sultry enough, made even more wicked by her breast, still bared to his gaze, its nipple pink and taut and begging for more.

But nothing, nothing could have speared him with more desire than the sight of her face. Parted lips, eyes darkened to cobalt with passion. Every breath she took seemed to call to him—

Take me.

And it was almost enough to force him to abandon his wicked seduction and plunge into her right then and there.

But no—he had to do this slowly. He had to tease her and torture her, bring her to the very heights of ecstasy and then keep her there as long as he could. He had to make sure they both understood that this was something they could never, *ever* live without.

But still, it was hard—no, *he* was hard, and it was so damned difficult to exercise restraint.

"What do you think, Francesca?" he murmured, giving her thighs one last squeeze. "I don't think we've opened you enough, do you?"

She made a sound. He would never know how to describe it, but it set him afire.

"Maybe," he said softly, "more like this." And he pushed, slowly, inexorably, until she was spread wide. Her skirt went taut over her thighs, and he tsk tsked at it, murmuring, "That can't be comfortable. Let me help you with that."

He hooked his fingers over the hem, and slid it up until it pooled about her waist.

And she was completely exposed.

He couldn't see her yet, not with his eyes still focused inexorably on her face. But the knowledge of her position made them both shiver, he with desire, she with anticipation, and he had to steel his shoulders just to maintain his control. It wasn't his time yet. It would be soon, to be sure; he was quite certain he'd perish if he didn't make her his that night.

But for now, this was still about Francesca. And what he could make her feel.

He put his lips to her ear. "You're not cold, are you?"

Her only answer was her shivering breath.

He brought one finger to her womanly center and began to stroke. "I would never allow you to remain cold," he whispered. "That would be so ungentlemanly of me."

His strokes slid into circles, slow and hot against her flesh.

"If we were out of doors," he mused, "I would offer my coat. But here"—he slid one fingertip inside, just enough to make her gasp—"I can only offer my mouth."

She made another incoherent sound, this one barely more than a strangled cry.

"Yes," he said wickedly, "that is what I would do to you. I'd kiss you right here, right where it would pleasure you the most."

She could do nothing but breathe.

"I believe I would start with my lips," he murmured, "but then I would have to use my tongue so I could explore you more deeply." He used his fingers to tickle her, demonstrating what he planned to do with his mouth. "Rather like this, I think, but it would be much hotter." He ran his tongue along the inside of her ear. "And wetter."

"Michael," she moaned.

She'd said his name. And nothing more. She was getting closer to the brink.

"I'd taste everything," he whispered. "Every last drop of you. And then, just when I was sure I'd explored you completely, I'd part you further." He spread her with his fingers, pulling her open in the most wicked way possible. Then he tickled her flesh with his fingernail. "Just in case I'd missed some secret corner."

"Michael," she moaned again.

"Who knows how long I'd kiss you?" he murmured. "I might not be able to stop." He moved his face down a little, so that he could nuzzle her neck. "You might not want me to stop." He paused, then slid another finger inside of her. He whispered, "Do you want me to stop?"

He was playing with fire every time he asked her a question, every time he gave her a chance to say no. If he were colder, more calculating, he would just press on with his seduction, and he could sweep her away before she could even begin to consider her actions. She'd be lost on her wave of passion, and before she knew it he would be inside of her, and she would be, finally and indelibly, his.

But something in him could never be quite that ruthless, not with Francesca. And he needed her approval, even if it was nothing more than a nod or a moan. She'd probably regret this later, but even so, he didn't want her to be able to say, even to herself, that she hadn't been thinking, that she hadn't said yes.

And *he* needed the yes. He had loved her for years, dreamed about touching her for so damned long. And now that the moment was finally here, he just didn't know if he could bear it if she didn't really want it. There were only so many ways a man's heart could break, and he had a feeling his couldn't survive another puncture.

"Do you want me to stop?" he whispered again, and this time he did stop. He didn't remove his hands, but he didn't move them either, just held still and allowed her a moment of quiet in which to make her answer. And he pulled his head back, just far enough so that she had to look at him. Or if not that, then at least he would be looking at her.

"No," she whispered, not quite raising her eyes to his.

His heart jumped in his chest. "Then I had better get to doing everything I talked about," he murmured.

And he did. He sank to his knees and he kissed her. He kissed her as she shuddered, he kissed her as he moaned. He kissed her when she grabbed his hair and pulled, and he kissed her when she let go, her hands scrambling wildly for purchase.

He kissed her in every way he'd promised he would, and he kissed her until she almost climaxed.

Almost.

He should have done it, should have followed through, but he just couldn't manage it. He had to have her. He'd wanted this for so long, wanted to make her scream his name and shudder in his arms. But when it happened, for the first time at least, he wanted to be inside her. He wanted to feel her around him, and he wanted to . . .

Hell, he just wanted it this way, and if it meant he was out of control, so be it.

Hands shaking, he tore open his breeches, finally allowing his manhood to spring free.

"Michael?" she whispered. Her eyes had been closed, but when he moved and left her she'd opened them. She looked down at him, her eyes widening. There was no mistaking what was about to happen.

"I need you," he said hoarsely. And when she did nothing but stare at him, he said it again. "I need you now."

But not on the table. Even he wasn't that talented, so he picked her up, shuddering with delight as she wrapped her legs around him, and set her down on the plush carpet. It wasn't a bed, but there was no way he was going to make it to a bed, and frankly, he didn't think either of them would care. He pushed her skirts back up to her waist, and he covered her.

And entered her.

He'd thought to go slowly, but she was so wet and ready for him, that he just slid inside, even as she gasped at the intrusion.

"Did that hurt?" he grunted.

She shook her head. "Don't stop," she moaned. "Please."

"Never," he vowed. "Never."

He moved, and she moved beneath him, and they were both already so aroused that it was a mere moment later that they both exploded.

And he, who had slept with countless women, suddenly realized that he'd been nothing but a green boy.

Because it had *never* been like this.

That had been his body. *This* was his soul.

Chapter 18

. . . absolutely.

—from Michael Stirling to his mother, Helen, three years after his departure for India

The following morning was, to the best of Francesca's recollection, quite the worst of recent memory.

All she wanted to do was cry, but even that seemed beyond her. Tears were for the innocent, and that was an adjective that she could never again use to describe herself.

She hated herself this morning, hated that she'd betrayed her heart, her every last principle, all for a spot of wicked passion.

She hated that she had felt desire for a man other than John, and *really* hated that the desire had gone beyond anything she'd felt with her husband. Her marriage bed had been one of laughter and passion, but nothing, *nothing* could have prepared her for the wicked thrill she had felt when Michael had placed his lips to her ear and told her all the naughty things he wanted to do with her.

Or for the explosion that had followed, when he'd made good on his promises.

She hated that this had all happened, and she hated that it had happened with Michael, because somehow that made it all seem triply wrong.

And most all, she hated *him* because he'd asked her permission, because every step of the way, even as his fingers had teased her mercilessly, he had made sure she was willing, and now she could never claim that she'd been swept away, that she'd been powerless against the force of her own passion.

And now it was the morning after, and Francesca realized that she could no longer differentiate between coward and fool, at least not as the terms pertained to herself.

She clearly was both, quite possibly with an *immature* thrown in for bad measure.

Because all she wanted to do was run.

She could face up to the consequences of her actions.

Truly, that was what she *should* do.

But instead, just like before, she fled.

She couldn't really leave Kilmartin; she'd just got there, after all, and unless she was prepared to carry her northward flight straight past the Orkney Islands into Norway, she was stuck where she was.

But she *could* leave the house, which was precisely what she did at the first streaks of dawn, and this after her pathetic performance the night before, when she'd stumbled out of the rose drawing room some ten minutes after her intimacies with Michael, mumbling incoherencies and apologies, only to barricade herself in her bedroom for the rest of the evening.

She didn't want to face him yet.

Heaven above, she didn't think she *could*.

She, who had always prided herself on her cool and level head, had been reduced to a stammering idiot, muttering to herself like a bedlamite, terrified to face the one man she quite obviously couldn't avoid forever.

But if she could avoid him for one day, she told herself, that was something. And as for tomorrow— Well, she could worry about tomorrow some other time. Tomorrow, maybe. For now all she wanted to do was run from her problems.

Courage, she was now quite certain, was a vastly overrated virtue.

She wasn't sure where she wanted to go; anywhere that could be termed *out* would probably do, any spot where she could tell herself that the odds of running into Michael were slim indeed.

And then, because she was quite convinced that no higher power was inclined to show her benevolence ever again, it began to rain an hour into her hike, starting first as a light sprinkle but quickly developing into a full-fledged downpour. Francesca huddled under a wide-limbed tree for shelter, resigned to wait out the rain, and then finally, after twenty minutes of shifting her weight from foot to foot, she just sat her bottom down onto the damp earth, cleanliness be hanged.

She was going to be here for some time; she might as well be comfortable, since she wasn't going to be either warm or dry.

And of course, that was how Michael found her, just short of two hours later.

Good God, it figured he'd look for her. Couldn't a man be counted on to behave like a cad when it truly mattered?

"Is there room for me under there?" he called out over the rain.

"Not for you *and* your horse," she grumbled.

"What was that?"

"No!" she yelled.

He didn't listen to her, of course, and nudged his mount under the tree, loosely tying the gelding to a low branch after he'd hopped down.

"Jesus, Francesca," he said without preamble. "What the hell are you doing out here?"

"And good day to you, too," she muttered.

"Do you have any idea how long I've been looking for you?"

"About as long as I've been huddled under the tree, I imagine," she retorted. She supposed she should be glad that he'd come to rescue her, and her shivering limbs were just itching to leap onto his horse and ride away, but the rest of her was still in a foul mood and quite willing to be contrary just for the sake of being, well, contrary.

Nothing could put a woman in worse spirits than a nice bout of self-derision.

Although, she thought rather peevishly, *he* was certainly not blameless in the debacle that was last night. And if he assumed that her litany of panicked, after-the-fact *I'm sorrys* the night before meant that she'd absolved him of guilt, he was quite mistaken.

"Well, let's go, then," he said briskly, nodding toward his mount.

She kept her gaze fixed over his shoulder. "The rain is letting up."

"In China, perhaps."

"I'm quite fine," she lied.

"Oh, for God's sake, Francesca," he said in short tones, "hate me all you want, but don't be an idiot."

"It's too late for that," she said under her breath.

"Maybe so," he agreed, demonstrating annoyingly superior hearing, "but I'm damned cold, and I want to go home. Believe what you will, but right now I have a far greater desire for a cup of tea than I do for you."

Which should have reassured her, but instead all she wanted to do was hurl a rock at his head.

But then, perhaps just to prove that her soul wasn't immediately headed for a toasty locale, the rain did let up, not all the way, but enough to lend a hint of truth to her lie.

"The sun will be out in no time," she said, motioning to the drizzle. "I'm fine."

"And do you plan to lie in the middle of the field for six hours until your dress dries off?" he drawled. "Or do you just prefer a slow, lingering case of lung fever?"

She looked him straight in the eye for the first time. "You are a horrible man," she said.

He laughed. "Now *that* is the first truthful thing you've said all morning."

"Is it possible you don't understand that I wish to be alone?" she countered.

"Is it possible you don't understand that I wish for you *not* to die of pneumonia? Get on the horse, Francesca," he ordered, in much the same tone she imagined he'd used on his troops in France. "When we are home you may feel free to lock yourself in your room—for a full two weeks, if it so pleases you—but for now, can we just get the hell out of the rain?"

It was tempting, of course, but even more than that, damned irritating because he was speaking nothing but sense, and the last thing she wanted just now was for him to be *right* about anything. Especially because she had a sinking feeling she needed more than two weeks to get past what had happened the evening before.

She was going to need a lifetime.

"Michael," she whispered, hoping she might be able to appeal to whichever side of him took pity on pathetic, quivering females, "I can't be with you right now."

"For a twenty-minute ride?" he snapped. And then, before she had the presence of mind to even yelp in irritation, he'd hauled her to her feet, and then off her feet, and then onto his horse.

"Michael!" she shrieked.

"Sadly," he said in a dry voice, "not said in the same tones I heard from you last night."

She smacked him.

"I deserved that," he said, mounting the horse behind her, and then doing a devilish wiggle until she was forced by the shape of the saddle to settle partially onto his lap, "but not as much as you deserve to be horsewhipped for your foolishness."

She gasped.

"If you wanted me to kneel at your feet, begging for your forgiveness," he said, his lips scandalously close to her ear, "you shouldn't have behaved like an idiot and run off in the rain."

"It wasn't raining when I left," she said childishly, letting out a little "Oh!" of surprise when he spurred the horse into motion.

Then, of course, she wished she had something else to hold on to for balance besides his thighs.

Or that his arm wasn't wrapped quite so tightly around her, or so high on her ribcage. Good God, her breasts were practically sitting on his forearm.

And never mind that she was nestled quite firmly between his legs, with her backside butted right up against—

Well, she supposed the rain was good for one thing. He had to be shriveled and cold, which was going a long way in her imagination toward keeping her own traitorous body in check.

Except that she'd seen him the night before, seen Michael in a way she'd never thought to see him, of all people, in all of his splendid male glory.

And that was the worst part of all. A phrase like *splendid male glory* ought to be a joke, to be uttered with sarcasm and a cunningly wicked smile.

But with Michael, it fit perfectly.

He'd fit perfectly.

And she'd lost whatever shreds of sanity she'd still possessed.

They rode on in silence, or if not precisely silence, they at least did not speak. But there were other sounds, far more dangerous and unnerving. Francesca was acutely aware of every breath he took, low and whispering across her ear, and she could swear she could hear his heart beating against her back. And then—

"Damn."

"What is it?" she asked, trying to twist around to see his face.

"Felix has gone lame," he muttered, leaping down from the saddle.

"Is he all right?" she inquired, accepting his wordless offer to help her dismount as well.

"He'll be fine," Michael said, kneeling in the rain to inspect the gelding's front left leg. His knees sank instantly into the muddy earth, ruining his riding breeches. "He can't carry the both of us, however. Couldn't even manage just you, I fear." He stood, scanning the horizon, determining just where on the property they were. "We'll have to make for the gardener's cottage," he said, impatiently pushing his sodden hair from his eyes. It slid right back over his brow.

"The gardener's cottage?" Francesca echoed, even though she knew perfectly well what he was talking about. It was a small, one-room structure, uninhabited since the current gardener, whose wife had recently been delivered of twins, had moved into a larger dwelling on the other side of Kilmartin. "Can't we go home?" she asked, a little desperately. She didn't need to be alone with him, trapped in a cozy little cottage with, if she remembered correctly, a rather large bed.

"It will take us over an hour on foot," he said grimly, "and the storm is growing worse."

He was right, drat it all. The sky had taken on a queer, greenish hue, the clouds touched with that strange light that preceded a storm of exquisite violence. "Very well," she said, trying to swallow her apprehension. She didn't know which frightened her more—the thought of being stuck out of doors in the storm or trapped inside a small cottage with Michael.

"If we run, we can be there in just a few minutes," Michael said. "Or rather, you can run. I'll have to lead Felix. I don't know how long it will take for him to make the journey."

Francesca felt her eyes narrowing as she turned to him. "You didn't do this on purpose, did you?"

He turned to her with a thunderous expression, matched rather terrifyingly by the streak of lightning that flashed through the sky.

"Sorry," she said hastily, immediately regretting her words. There were certain things one *never* accused a British gentleman of, the foremost of which was deliberate injury to an animal, for *any* reason. "I apologize," she added, just as a clap of thunder shook the earth. "Truly, I do."

"Do you know how to get there?" he yelled over the storm.

She nodded.

"Can you start a fire while you wait for me?"

"I can try."

"Go, then," he said curtly. "Run and get yourself warm. I'll be there soon enough."

She did, although she wasn't quite sure whether she was running to the cottage or away from him.

And considering the fact that he'd be mere minutes behind her, did it really matter?

But as she ran, her legs aching and her lungs burning, the answer to that question didn't seem terribly important. The pain of the exertion took over, matched only by the sting of the rain against her face. But it all felt strangely appropriate, as if she deserved no more.

And, she thought miserably, she probably didn't.

By the time Michael pushed open the door to the gardener's cottage, he was soaked to the bone and shivering like a madman. It had taken far longer than he had anticipated to lead Felix to the gardener's cottage, and then, of course, he'd been faced with the task of finding a decent spot to tie the injured gelding, since he couldn't very well leave him under a tree in an electrical storm. He'd finally managed to fashion a makeshift stall in what used to be a chicken shed, but the end result was that by the time he made it into the cottage, his hands were bleeding and his boots were dotted with a foul substance that the rain had inexplicably not managed to wash off.

Francesca was kneeling by the fireplace, attempting to spark a flame. From the sound of her mutterings, she wasn't meeting with much success.

"Dear heavens!" she exclaimed. "What happened to you?"

"I had trouble finding a place to tie Felix," he explained gruffly. "I had to build him a shelter."

"With your own two hands?"

"I had no other tools," he said with a shrug.

She glanced nervously out the window. "Will he be all right?"

"I hope so," Michael replied, sitting down on a three-legged stool to remove his boots. "I couldn't very well slap his rump and send him home on that injured leg."

"No," she said, "of course not." And then her face took on a horrified expression, and she jumped to her feet, exclaiming, "Will *you* be all right?"

Normally, he'd have welcomed her concern, but it would have been far easier to milk it if he knew what the devil she was talking about. "I beg your pardon?" he asked politely.

"The malaria," she said, with a touch of urgency. "You're soaked, and you've just had an attack. I don't want you to—" She stopped, clearing her throat and visibly squaring her shoulders. "My concern does not mean that I am more charitably inclined to you than I was an hour ago, but I do not wish for you to suffer a relapse."

He thought briefly about lying to gain her sympathies, but instead he just said, "It doesn't work that way."

"Are you certain?"

"Quite. Chills don't bring on the disease."

"Oh." She took a bit of time to digest that information. "Well, in that case . . ." Her words trailed off, and her lips tightened unpleasantly. "Carry on, then," she finally said.

Michael gave her an insolent salute and then went back to work on his boots, giving the second one a firm yank before gingerly picking up both by the tops and setting them down near the door. "Don't touch those," he said absently, moving over to the fireplace. "They're filthy."

"I couldn't get the fire started," she said, still standing awkwardly near the hearth. "I'm sorry. I haven't much experience in that area, I'm afraid. I did find some dry wood in the corner, though." She motioned to the grate, where she'd set down a couple of logs.

He set to work igniting a flame, his hands still stinging a bit from the scrapes he'd incurred clearing the bramble out of the chicken shed for Felix. He welcomed the pain, actually. Minor as it was, it still gave him something to think about other than the woman standing behind him.

She was angry.

He should have expected that. He did expect it, in truth, but what he didn't expect was how much it would sting his pride, and, in all honesty, his heart. He had known, of course, that she wouldn't suddenly declare her undying love for him after one episode of relentless passion, but he'd been just enough of a fool that a tiny little piece of him had hoped for such an outcome, all the same.

Who would have thought, after all his years of bad behavior, that he'd emerge such a hopeless romantic?

But Francesca would come around, he was fairly certain of that. She'd have to. She'd been compromised—quite thoroughly, he thought with some measure of satisfaction. And while she'd not been a virgin, that still meant something to a principled woman like Francesca.

He was left with a decision—did he wait out her anger, or did he needle and push until she accepted the inevitability of the situation? The latter was sure to leave him bruised and gasping, but he rather thought it presented a greater chance of success.

If he left her alone, she would think the problem into oblivion, maybe find a way to pretend nothing had ever happened.

"Did you get it started?" he heard her ask from across the room.

He fanned a spark for a few more seconds, then let out a satisfied exhale when tiny orange flames began to flicker and lick. "I'll have to nurse it along for a little while longer," he said, turning around to look at her. "But yes, it should be going strong quite soon."

"Good," she said succinctly. She took a few steps backward until she was butted up against the bed. "I'll be right here."

He couldn't help but crack a wry smile at that. The cottage held a single room. Where else did she think she was going to go?

"You," she said, with much the air of an unpopular governess, "can remain over there."

He followed the line of her pointed finger to the opposite corner. "Really?" he drawled.

"I think it's best."

He shrugged. "Fine."

"Fine?"

"Fine." And then he stood and began to strip off his clothing.

"What are you doing?" she gasped.

He smiled to himself, keeping his back to her. "Keeping to my corner," he said, tossing the words lightly over his shoulder.

"You are taking your clothes off," she said, somehow managing to sound shocked and haughty at the same time.

"I suggest you do the same," he said, frowning as he noticed a streak of blood on his sleeve. Damn, but his hands really were a mess.

"I most certainly will not," Francesca said.

"Hold this, will you?" he said, tossing her his shirt. She shrieked as it hit her in the chest, which brought him no small measure of satisfaction.

"Michael!" she exclaimed, hurling the garment back at him.

"Sorry," he said in his most unrepentant voice. "Thought you might like to use it as a cloth to wipe up."

"Put your shirt back on," she ground out.

"And freeze?" he asked, lifting one arrogant brow. "Malaria or no, I have no wish to catch a chill. Besides, it's nothing you haven't seen before." And then, over her gasp, he added, "No, wait. I do beg your pardon. You haven't seen it. I didn't manage to get anything more than my trousers off last night, did I?"

"Get out," she said, her voice low and furious.

He just chuckled and cocked his head toward the window, which was thrumming with the sound of the rain against the glass.

"I don't think so, Francesca. You're stuck with me for the duration, I'm afraid."

As if to prove his point, the small cottage shook down to its foundations with the force of thunder.

"You might want to turn around," Michael said conversationally. Her eyes widened slightly in incomprehension, so he added, "I'm about to remove my breeches."

She let out a little grunt of outrage, but she turned.

"Oh, and get off the blanket," he called out, peeling off his sodden clothing. "You're soaking it."

For a second he thought she would plant her bottom even more firmly against it, just to defy him, but her good sense must have won out, because she stood and yanked the coverlet from the bed, shaking off whatever drops she'd left behind.

He walked over—it took only four steps with his lengthy stride—and pulled the other blanket off for himself. It wasn't as substantial as the one she held, but it would do. "I'm covered," he called out, once he was safely back in his corner.

She turned around. Slowly, and with only one eye open.

Michael fought the urge to shake his head at her. Truly, this all seemed rather after the fact, given what had transpired the night before. But if it made her feel better to grasp at the shreds of her maidenly virtue, he was willing to allow her the boon . . . for the rest of the morning, at least.

"You're shivering," he said.

"I'm cold."

"Of course you are. Your dress is soaked."

She didn't say anything, just shot him a look that told him she did not plan to remove her clothing.

"Do what you wish, then," he said, "but at least come sit near the fire."

She looked hesitant.

"For God's sake, Francesca," he said, his patience growing thin, "I hereby vow not to ravish you. At least not this morning, and not without your permission."

For some reason that made her cheeks burn with even greater ferocity, but she must have still held him and his word in some regard, because she crossed the room and sat near the fire.

"Warmer?" he asked, just to provoke her.

"Quite."

He stoked the fire for the next few minutes, carefully tending it to ensure that the flames would not die out, stealing glances at her profile from time to time. After a while, once her expression had softened a bit, he decided to press his luck, and he said, quite softly, "You never did answer my question last night."

She didn't turn. "What question was that?"

"I believe I asked you to marry me."

"No, you didn't," she replied, her voice quite calm, "you informed me that you believed we should be married and then proceeded to explain why."

"Is that so?" he murmured. "How remiss of me."

"*Don't* take that as an invitation to make your proposal right now," she said sharply.

"You'd have me waste this fabulously romantic moment?" he drawled.

He couldn't be sure, but he thought her lips might have tightened with the barest hint of contained humor.

"Very well," he said, in his most magnanimous tone, "I won't ask you to marry me. Forget that a gentleman would insist upon it, after what happened—"

"If you were a gentleman," she cut in, "it wouldn't have happened."

"There were two of us there, Francesca," he reminded her softly.

"I know," she said, and her tone was so bitter, he regretted having provoked her.

Unfortunately, once he'd made the decision not to taunt her further, he was left with nothing to say. Which didn't seem to speak well of him, but there it was. So he held silent, pulling the woolen blanket more tightly around his barely clad body, surreptitiously eyeing her from time to time, trying to determine if she was becoming overchilled.

He'd hold his tongue, forked though it may be, to spare her feelings, but if she were endangering her health . . . well, then, all bets were off.

But she wasn't shivering, nor did she show any signs of feeling excessively cold, save for the way she was holding up various sections of her skirt toward the fire, vainly attempting to dry the fabric. Every now and then she looked as if she might speak, but then she'd just close her mouth again, wetting her lips with her tongue and letting out little sighs.

And then, without even looking at him, she said, "I will consider it."

He quirked a brow, waiting for her to elaborate.

"Marrying you," she clarified, still keeping her eyes on the fire. "But I won't give you an answer now."

"You might be carrying my child," he said softly.

"I am very much aware of that." She wrapped her arms around her bent knees and hugged. "I will give you an answer once I have that answer."

Michael's nails bit into his palms. He'd made love to her in part to force her hand—he couldn't get around that unsavory fact—but not in an attempt to impregnate her. He'd thought to bind her to him with passion, not with an unplanned pregnancy.

And now she was essentially telling him that the only way she would marry him was for the sake of a baby.

"I see," he said, thinking his voice uncommonly calm, given the hot rush of fury surging through his blood.

Fury he probably had no right to feel, but it was there nevertheless, and he was not enough of a gentleman to ignore it.

"It's too bad I promised not to ravish you this morning, then," he said dangerously, unable to resist a predatory smile.

Her head whipped around to face him.

"I could—how do they say it," he mused, lightly scratching his jawline, "seal the deal. Or at the very least, enjoy myself immensely while I try."

"Michael—"

"But how nice for me," he cut in, "that according to my watch"—he was near enough to where his coat lay on the table to pluck his pocketwatch out into the open—"we've only five minutes to noon."

"You wouldn't," she whispered.

He felt little humor, but he smiled all the same. "You leave me little choice."

"Why?" she asked, and he really didn't know what she was asking, but he answered her, anyway, with the one bit of truth he couldn't escape:

"Because I have to."

Her eyes widened.

"Will you kiss me, Francesca?" he asked.

She shook her head.

She was only five feet from him, and they were both sitting on the floor. He crawled closer, his heart racing when she didn't scoot away. "Will you let me kiss you?" he whispered.

She didn't move.

He leaned toward her.

"I told you I wouldn't seduce you without your permission," he said, his voice husky, his words falling mere inches from her lips.

Still, she didn't move.

"Will you kiss me, Francesca?" he asked again.

She swayed.

And he knew she was his.

Chapter 19

. . . I do believe Michael might be considering a return home. He does not say so directly in his letters, but I cannot discount a mother's intuition. I know that I should not pull him away from all his successes in India, but I think that he misses us. Wouldn't it be lovely to have him home?

—from Helen Stirling to the Countess of Kilmartin, nine months prior to the Earl of Kilmartin's return from India

As she felt his lips touch hers, Francesca could only wonder at the loss of her sanity. Once again, Michael had asked her permission. Once again, he had given her the opportunity to slide away, to reject him and keep herself at a safe distance.

But once again, her mind had been completely enslaved by her body, and she simply was not strong enough to deny the quickening of her breath, or the pounding of her heart.

Or the slow, hot tingle of anticipation she felt as his large, strong hands slid down her body, moving ever closer to the heart of her femininity.

"Michael," she whispered, but they both knew that her plea was not one of rejection. She wasn't asking him to stop—she was begging him to continue, to feed her soul as he had the night before, to remind her of all the reasons she loved being a woman, and to teach her the heady bliss of her own sensual power.

"Mmmm," was his only response. His fingers kept busy with the buttons on her frock, and even though the fabric was still damp and awkward, he divested her of it in record time, leaving her clad only in her thin cotton chemise, made almost transparent by the rain.

"You are so beautiful," he whispered, gazing down at the outline of her breasts, clearly defined under the white cotton. "I can't—I don't—"

He didn't say anything more, which she found puzzling, and she looked at his face. These weren't just words to him, she realized with a jolt of surprise. His throat was working with some emotion she didn't think she'd ever seen on him before.

"Michael?" she whispered. His name was a question, although she wasn't quite sure what she was asking.

And he, she was fairly certain, didn't know how to answer. At least not with words. He scooped her into his arms and then carried her to the bed, stopping at the edge of the mattress to peel away her chemise.

This was where she could stop, Francesca reminded herself. She could end it here. Michael wanted her—badly, she could see quite visibly. But he would stop if she just said the word.

But she couldn't. No matter how hard her brain argued for reason and clarity, her lips could do nothing but sway toward his, leaning in for a kiss, desperate to prolong the contact.

She wanted this. She wanted him. And even though she knew it was wrong, she was too wicked to stop.

He'd made her wicked.

And she wanted to revel in it.

"No," she said, the word crossing her lips with awkward bluntness.

His hands froze.

"I will do it," she said.

His eyes found hers, and she found herself drowning in those quicksilver depths. There were a hundred questions there, not one of which she was prepared to answer. But there was one thing she knew for herself, even if she would never speak the words aloud. If she was going to do this, if she was unable to refuse her own desire, then by God, she would do this in every way. She would take what she wanted, steal what she needed, and at the end of the day, if she managed to come to her senses and put an end to the madness, she would have had one erotic afternoon, one sizzling interlude during which she was in charge.

He'd awakened the wanton within her, and she wanted her revenge.

With one hand on his chest, she pushed him back onto the bed, and he stared up at her with fiery eyes, his lips parted with desire as he watched her in disbelief.

She took a step back, then reached down and lightly grasped the hem of her chemise. "Do you want me to take it off?" she whispered.

He nodded.

"Say it," she demanded. She wanted to know if he was beyond words. She wanted to know if she could reduce him to madness, enslave him to his needs, the way he'd done to her.

"Yes," he gasped, the word coming out hoarse and ripped.

Francesca was no innocent; she'd been married for two years to a man with healthy and active desires, a man who had taught her to celebrate the same in herself. She knew how to be brazen, understood how it could whip up her own urgency, but nothing could have prepared her for the electrical charge of this moment, for the decadent thrill of stripping for Michael.

Or the staggering rush of heat she felt when she raised her gaze to his, and watched him watching her.

This was power.

And she loved it.

With deliberate slowness, she edged the hem up, starting just above her knees, and then sliding up her thighs until she'd nearly reached her hips.

"Enough?" she teased, licking her lips into a sultry half-smile.

He shook his head. "More," he demanded.

Demanded? She didn't like that. "Beg me," she whispered.

"More," he said, more humbly.

She gave him a nod of approval, but just before she let him see the thatch of her womanhood she turned around, wiggling the chemise up and over her bottom, then across her back and finally over her head.

His breath was coming hot and heavy over his lips; she could hear every whisper of it, almost feel it caressing her back. But still she didn't turn around. Instead she let out a slow, seductive moan and slid her hands up the sides of her body, curving slightly to the back as she passed over her derrière, then moving to the front when she reached her breasts. And then, even though she knew he couldn't see her, she squeezed.

He would know what she was doing.

And it would drive him wild.

She heard rustling on the bed, heard the wooden frame creak and groan, and she let out one sharp command:

"Don't move."

"Francesca," he moaned, and his voice was closer. He must've sat up, must've been seconds away from reaching for her.

"Lie down," she said in soft warning.

"Francesca," he said again, but now there was a hint of desperation in his voice.

It made her smile. "Lie down," she repeated, still not looking at him.

She heard him panting, knew that he hadn't moved, that he was still trying to decide what to do.

"Lie down," she said, one last time. "If you want me."

For a second there was silence, and then she heard him settle back against the bed. But she also heard his breath, now tinged with a dangerously ragged edge.

"There you go," she whispered.

She taunted him a little more, running her hands lightly over her skin, her nails skimming the surface, raising goose bumps all along their path. "Mmmm," she moaned, the sound a deliberate tease. "Mmmm."

"Francesca," he whispered.

She moved her hands to her belly, then slid them down, not deeply to touch herself—she wasn't certain she was wicked enough to do that—but just enough to cover her mound, leaving him in the dark, wondering just what it was her fingers were doing.

"Mmmm," she murmured again. "Ohhhh."

He made a sound, guttural, primitive, and entirely inarticulate. He was nearing his breaking point; she wouldn't be able to push him much further.

She looked over her shoulder, licking her lips as she glanced at him. "You should take those off," she said, letting her gaze fall to his still-covered groin. He'd not undressed entirely when he'd removed his wet clothing, and his manhood strained furiously against the fabric. "You don't look very comfortable," she added, infusing her voice with just the barest hint of coy innocence.

He grunted something and then practically tore off his undergarments.

"Oh my," Francesca said, and even though she'd planned the words as a part of her teasing seduction, she found that she very much meant them. He looked huge and powerful, and she knew she was playing a dangerous game, pushing him to his very limits.

But she couldn't stop. She was glorying in her power over him, and she couldn't possibly stop.

"Very nice," she purred, letting her gaze roam up and down his body, settling directly upon his manhood.

"Frannie," he said, "enough."

She let her eyes level onto his. "You answer to *me*, Michael," she said with soft authority. "If you want me, you can have me. But I'm in charge."

"Fr—"

"Those are my terms."

He held still, then settled back slightly in acquiescence. But he did not lie down. He was sitting, leaning back slightly, his hands on the mattress behind him for support. His every muscle was straining, and his eyes held a feline air, as if he were poised to pounce.

He was, she realized, with a shiver of desire, simply magnificent.

And hers for the taking.

"What should I do now?" she wondered aloud.

"Come here," he answered gruffly.

"Not quite yet," she sighed, turning toward him until her body was in profile. She saw his gaze drop to the hardened tips of her breasts, saw his eyes darken as he licked his lips. And she felt herself tauten even more, as the mental image of his tongue on her sent a new rush of heat through her body.

She brought one hand to her breast, curving around the underside, pushing herself up, like some delectable offering. "Is this what you want?" she whispered.

His voice was nothing but a growl. "You know what I want."

"Mmm, yes," she murmured, "but what about in the meantime? Aren't things sweeter when we're forced to wait for them?"

"You have no idea," he said roughly.

She looked down at her breast. "I wonder what would happen if I do . . . this," she said, and then she moved her fingers to her nipple, rolling it about, her body twitching as the motion sent shivers down to the very center of her being.

"Frannie," Michael groaned. She glanced up at him. His lips were parted, and his eyes were glazed with desire.

"I like it," Francesca said, almost in wonderment. She'd never touched herself this way, never even thought to until this very moment, with Michael as her captive audience. "I like it," she said again, then brought her other hand to her other breast and pleasured them in unison. She pushed them up and together, her hands making a sultry corset.

"Oh, my God," Michael moaned.

"I had no idea I could do this," she said, arching her back.

"I can do it better," he gasped.

"Mmm, you probably could," she acceded. "You've had lots of practice, haven't you?" And she shot him a look, one of sophisticated elegance, as if she were comfortable with the fact that he'd seduced scores of women. And the strange truth was, until this very moment, she rather thought she had been.

But now . . .

Now he was hers. Hers to tempt and hers to enjoy, and as long as she had him exactly where she wanted him, she wasn't going to think of those other women. They weren't here in this room. It was just her, and Michael, and the sizzling heat rising between them.

She edged closer to the bed, batting his hand away when he reached toward her. "If I let you touch one, will you make me a promise?" she murmured.

"Anything."

"Nothing more," she said, her tone slightly officious. "You may do what I allow you and nothing more."

He nodded jerkily.

"Lie back," she ordered.

He did as she asked.

She climbed onto the bed, not allowing their bodies to touch in any way. Raising herself onto all fours, she let herself to sway above him, and then softly she said, "One hand, Michael. You may use one hand."

With a groan that sounded as if it were ripped from his throat, he reached for her, his hand large enough to grasp her entire breast. "Oh, my God," he gasped, his body jerking as he squeezed her. "Both hands, please," he begged.

She couldn't resist him. That one simple touch was reducing her to pure flame, and even as she wanted to exert her power over him, she couldn't say no. Nodding because she could barely speak, she arched her back, and then suddenly both of his hands were on her, kneading, caressing, whipping her already heightened senses into a frenzy.

"The tip," she whispered. "Do what I did."

He smiled stealthily, giving her the impression that she might no longer be quite as much in charge as she thought, but he did as she commanded, his fingers torturing her nipples.

And as promised, he was better at it than she was.

Her body bucked, and she almost lost the strength to hold herself up. "Take me in your mouth," she ordered, but her voice was not so authoritative any longer. She was begging him, and they both knew it.

But she wanted it. Oh, how she wanted it. John, for all his ebullience in bed, had never loved her breasts the way Michael had done the night before. He'd never suckled her, never shown her how lips and teeth could make her entire body squirm. Francesca hadn't even known that a man and woman could do such a thing.

But now that she did, she couldn't stop fantasizing about it.

"Come lower," Michael said softly, "if you want me to remain lying down."

Still on her hands and knees, she leaned down, allowing one breast to swing achingly close to his mouth.

He did nothing at first, forcing her to swing lower and lower, until her nipple was brushing lightly across his lips.

"What do you want, Francesca?" he asked, his breath hot and moist over her.

"You know," she whispered.

"Say it again."

She wasn't in charge anymore. She knew it, but she was past caring. His voice held the soft edge of authority, but she was too far gone to do anything but obey.

"Take me in your mouth," she said again.

His head snapped up and his lips nipped her, tugging her down until she was in a position for him to have his leisurely way with her. He tickled and teased, and she felt herself sinking deeper into his spell, losing her will and her strength, wanting nothing but to lie down on her back and allow him to do whatever he wanted to her.

"Now what?" he asked politely, not releasing her from his lips. "More of this? Or"—he swirled his tongue in a particularly wicked fashion—"something else?"

"Something else," she gasped, and she wasn't sure if it was because she wanted something else or because she didn't think she could stand one more minute of what he was doing just then.

"You're in charge," he said, his voice holding the barest hint of mocking. "I'm yours to command."

"I want . . . I want . . ." She was breathing too hard to finish the sentence. Or maybe she just didn't know what she wanted.

"Shall I offer you a few selections?"

She nodded.

He trailed one finger down the center of her belly to her womanhood. "I could touch you here," he said in a devilish whisper, "or if you'd prefer, I could kiss you."

Her body tightened at the thought.

"But that presents new questions," he said. "Do you lie back and allow me to kneel between your legs, or do you remain above me and lower yourself onto my mouth?"

"Oh, my God!" She didn't know. She just didn't know that such things were possible.

"Or," he said thoughtfully, "you could take me into your mouth. I'm quite certain I would enjoy it, although I must say, it's not really in the tenor of the interlude."

Francesca felt her lips part with shock, and she couldn't help but peer down at his manhood, large and ready for her. She had kissed John there once or twice, when she'd felt particularly daring, but to take it into her mouth?

It was too scandalous. Even in her present state of debauchery.

"No," Michael said with an amused smile. "Another time, perhaps. I can tell you'll be a most cunning pupil."

Francesca nodded, unable to believe what she was promising.

"So for now," he said, "those are our options, or . . ."

"Or what?" she asked, her voice more of a harsh whisper.

His hands settled on her hips. "Or we could just proceed right to the main course," he said commandingly, exerting a gentle but steady pressure on her, guiding her down toward the evidence of his desire. "You could ride me. Have you ever done that?"

She shook her head.

"Do you want to?"

She nodded.

One of his hands left her hips and found the back of her head, pulling her down until they were nose to nose. "I'm not a gentle pony," he said softly. "I promise you, you will have to work to keep your seat."

"I want it," she whispered.

"Are you ready for me?"

She nodded.

"Are you certain?" he whispered, his lips curving just enough to taunt her. She wasn't sure what he was asking, and he knew it.

She just looked at him, her eyes widening in question.

"Are you wet?" he murmured.

Her cheeks grew hot—as if they weren't already burning, but she nodded.

"Are you sure?" he mused. "I should probably check, just to make certain."

Francesca's breath caught as she watched his hand curve around her thigh, moving toward her center. He moved slowly, deliberately, drawing out the torture of anticipation. And then, just when she thought she might scream at it all, he touched her, one finger lazily drawing circles against her soft flesh.

"Very nice," he purred, his words echoing her own.

"Michael," she gasped.

But he was enjoying his position too much to allow her to rush things along. "I'm not sure," he said. "You're ready here, but what about . . . here?"

Francesca nearly screamed as one finger slipped inside of her.

"Oh, yes," he murmured. "And you like it, too."

"Michael . . . Michael . . ." It was all she could say.

Another finger slid into place next to the first. "So warm," he whispered. "The very heart of you."

"Michael . . ."

His eyes caught hers. "Do you want me?" he asked, his voice stark and direct.

She nodded.

"Now?"

She nodded again, this time with more vigor.

His fingers slid out, and his hands found her hips again, guiding her down . . . down . . . until she could feel the tip of him at her opening. She tried to move her body down onto him, but he held her in place. "Not too fast," he whispered.

"Please . . ."

"Let me move you," he said, and his hands gently pushed at her hips, edging her down until she felt herself being stretched open by him. He felt huge, and it was all so different in this position.

"Good?" he asked.

She nodded.

"More?"

She nodded again.

And he continued the torture, holding himself still, but moving her body down atop his, each impossible inch of him sliding into her, stealing her breath, her voice, her very ability to think.

"Slide up and down," he commanded.

Her eyes flew to his.

"You can do it," he said softly.

She did, testing the motion, moaning at the pleasure of the friction, then gasping as she realized that she was sliding farther down onto him, that he wasn't yet entirely embedded within her body.

"Take me to the hilt," he said.

"I can't." And she couldn't. She couldn't possibly. She knew she had done so the night before, but this was different. He couldn't possibly fit.

His hands tightened on her, and his hips arched slightly up, and then in one mind-numbing jolt, she found herself seated directly atop him, skin to skin.

And she could barely breathe.

"Oh, my God," he groaned.

She just sat there, rocking back and forth, unsure of what to do.

His breath was coming in fits and starts, and his body began to writhe under hers. She grasped his shoulders in an attempt to hold on, to keep her seat, and as she did, she began to move up and down, to take control, to seek pleasure for herself.

"Michael, Michael," she moaned, her body beginning to sway from side to side, unable to hold itself up, unable to maintain strength against the hot tide of desire sweeping across her.

He just grunted, his body bucking beneath her. As promised, he wasn't gentle, and he wasn't tame. He forced her to work for her pleasure, to hold on tight, to move with him, and then against him, and then . . .

A scream ripped from her throat.

And the world quite simply fell apart.

She didn't know what to do, didn't know what to say. She let go of his shoulders as her body straightened and then arched, every muscle growing impossibly taut.

And beneath her, he exploded. His face contorted, his body lifted them both off the bed, and she knew that he was pouring himself into her. Her name was on his lips, over and over, decreasing in volume until it was the barest of whispers. And when he was done, all he said was, "Lie with me."

She did. And she slept.

For the first time in days, she slept deeply and truly.

And she never knew that he laid awake the whole time, his lips at her temple, his hand against her hair.

Whispering her name.

Whispering other words as well.

Chapter 20

. . . Michael will do what he wishes. He always does.

—from the Countess of Kilmartin to Helen Stirling, three days after the receipt of Helen's missive

The days that followed brought Francesca no peace. When she thought about it rationally—or at least as rationally as she was able—it seemed as if she should have found some answers, should have sensed some sort of logic in the air, something that might tell her what to do, how to act, what sort of choice she needed to make.

But, no. Nothing.

She'd made love to him twice.

Twice.

To Michael.

That alone should have dictated her decisions, convinced her to accept his proposal. It should have been clear. She had lain with him. She might be pregnant, although that did seem a remote possibility, given that it had taken her a full two years to conceive with John.

But even without such consequences, her decision should have been obvious. In her world, in her society, the sort of intimacies in which she'd engaged meant only one thing.

She must marry him.

And yet she couldn't quite summon the *yes* to her lips. Every time she thought she'd convinced herself that it was what she had to do, a little voice inside of her argued for caution, and she stopped, unable to move forward, too scared to delve into her feelings and try to figure out why she felt so paralyzed.

Michael didn't understand, of course. How could he, when she didn't understand herself?

"I shall call upon the vicar tomorrow morning," he'd murmured at her ear as he helped her mount a fresh horse outside the gardener's cottage. She had awakened alone sometime in the late afternoon, a brief note from him on the pillow beside her, explaining that he was taking Felix back to Kilmartin and would return shortly with a new mount.

But he had only brought one horse, forcing her once again to share the saddle, this time perched behind him.

"I'm not ready," she'd said, a sudden rush of panic filling her chest. "Don't go see him. Not yet."

His face had darkened, but he didn't allow his temper to rise any further. "We will discuss it later," he'd said.

And they'd ridden home in silence.

She tried to escape to her room once they reached Kilmartin, mumbling something about needing to bathe, but he caught her hand, his grip firm and unyielding, and she found herself alone with him, back in the rose drawing room of all places, the door shut firmly behind them.

"What is all this about?" he asked.

"What do you mean?" she stalled, trying desperately not to look at the table behind him. It was the one upon which he'd perched her the night before, then done unspeakable things to her.

And the memory alone was enough to make her shiver.

"You know what I mean," he said impatiently.

"Michael, I—"

"Will you marry me?" he demanded.

Dear God, she wished he hadn't just come out and said it. It was all so much easier to avoid when the words weren't right there, hanging between them.

"I—I—"

"Will you marry me?" he repeated, and this time the words were hard, with more of an edge to them.

"I don't know," she finally answered. "I need more time."

"Time for what?" he snapped. "For me to try a little harder to get you pregnant?"

She flinched as if struck.

He advanced upon her. "Because I'll do it," he warned. "I'll take you right now, and then again tonight, and then three times tomorrow if that's what is required."

"Michael, stop . . ." she whispered.

"I have lain with you," he said, his words stark and yet strangely urgent. "Twice. You are no innocent. You know what that means."

And it was *because* she was no innocent—and no one would ever expect her to be—that she was able to say, "I know. But that doesn't matter. Not if I don't conceive."

Michael hissed a word she never dreamed he'd say in her presence.

"I need time," she said, hugging her arms against her body.

"Why?"

"I don't know. To think. To muddle through. I don't know."

"What the devil is there left to think about?" he bit off.

"Well, for one thing, about whether you'll make a good husband," she snapped back, finally goaded into anger.

He drew back. "What the hell is that supposed to mean?"

"Your past behavior, to start with," she replied, narrowing her eyes. "You haven't exactly been the model of Christian rectitude."

"This, coming from the woman who ordered me to strip off my clothing earlier this afternoon?" he taunted.

"Don't be ugly," she said in a low voice.

"Don't push my temper."

Her head began to pound, and she pressed her fingers to her temples. "For God's sake, Michael, can't you let me think? Can't you give me just a little time to think?"

But the truth was, she was terrified to think. Because what would she learn? That she was a wanton, a hussy? That she had felt a primitive thrill with this man, a soaring, scandalous sensation that had never been there with her husband, whom she'd loved with every inch of her heart?

She'd found pleasure with John, but nothing like this.

She'd never even dreamed *this* existed.

And yet she'd found it with Michael.

Her friend, too. Her confidant.

Her lover.

Dear God, what did that make her?

"Please," she finally whispered. "Please. I need to be alone."

Michael stared at her for the longest time, long enough so that she wanted to squirm under his scrutiny, but finally he just swore under his breath and stalked from the room.

She collapsed onto the sofa and let her head hang in her hands. But she didn't cry.

She didn't cry. Not one single tear. And for the life of her, she didn't understand why not.

He would never understand women.

Michael swore viciously as he yanked off his boots, hurling the offending footwear against the door to his wardrobe.

"My lord?" came his valet's tentative voice, poking out through the opened door to the dressing room.

"Not now, Reivers," Michael snapped.

"Right," the valet said quickly, scurrying across the room to gather up the boots. "I'll just take these. You'll want them cleaned."

Michael cursed again.

"Er, or perhaps burned." Reivers gulped.

Michael just looked at him and growled.

Reivers fled, but fool that he was, he forgot to close the door behind him.

Michael kicked it shut, cursing again when he failed to find satisfaction in the slam.

Even the little pleasures in life were denied to him now, it seemed.

He paced restlessly across the deep burgundy carpet, pausing only occasionally at the window.

Forget understanding *women*. He'd never pretended to have that ability. But he thought he'd understood Francesca. At least well enough to safely tell himself that she would marry any man with whom she'd lain twice.

Once, maybe not. *Once* she could call a mistake. But twice—

She would never allow a man to take her twice unless she held him in some regard.

But, he thought with a twisted grimace, apparently not.

Apparently she was willing to use him for her own pleasure—and she had. Dear God, she had. She had assumed the lead, taken what she'd wanted, relinquishing control only when the flames between them spiraled into an inferno.

She had used him.

And he would never have thought she had it in her.

Had she been like this with John? Had she taken charge? Had she—

He stopped, his feet freezing into place on the carpet.

John.

He had forgotten about John.

How was that possible?

For years, every time he'd seen Francesca, every time he'd leaned in for one intoxicating whiff of her, John had been there, first in his thoughts, and then in his memory.

But since the moment she'd entered the rose drawing room last night, when he heard her footsteps behind him and whispered the words, "Marry me," to himself, he'd forgotten about John.

His memory would never disappear. He was too dear, too important—to both of them. But somewhere along the way, somewhere along the way to Scotland, to be precise, Michael finally allowed himself to think—

I could marry her. I could ask her. I really could.

And as he granted himself permission, it felt less and less like he was stealing her from his cousin's memory.

Michael hadn't asked to be placed in this position. He had never looked up to the heavens and wished himself the earldom. He had never even truly wished for Francesca, just accepted that she could never be his.

But John had died. He had *died.*

And it was nobody's fault.

John had died, and Michael's life had been changed in every way imaginable except one.

He still loved Francesca.

God, how he loved her.

There was no reason they couldn't marry. No laws, no customs, nothing but his own conscience, which had, quite suddenly, grown silent on the matter.

And Michael finally allowed himself to ponder, for the very first time, the one question he had never asked himself.

What would John think of all this?

And he realized that his cousin would have given his blessing. John's heart was that big, his love for Francesca—and Michael—that true. He would have wanted Francesca to be loved and cherished the way that Michael loved and cherished her.

And he would have wanted Michael to be happy.

The one emotion Michael had never truly thought he could apply to himself.

Happy.

Imagine that.

Francesca had been waiting for Michael to knock upon her door, but when the rap came, she still jumped with surprise.

Her shock was much greater when she opened the door and found she had to lower her gaze considerably. A full foot, to be precise. Michael wasn't on the other side of her door. It was just one of the housemaids, carrying a supper tray for her.

Eyes narrowing suspiciously, Francesca poked her head into the hall, looking this way and that, fully expecting Michael to be lurking in some darkened corner, just waiting for the right moment to pounce.

But he was nowhere.

"His lordship thought you might be hungry," the maid said, setting the tray down on Francesca's escritoire.

Francesca scanned the contents for a note, a flower, something to indicate Michael's intentions, but there was nothing.

And there was nothing for the rest of the night, and nothing the next morning, either.

Nothing but a breakfast tray, and another bob and curtsy from the housemaid, with another, "His lordship thought you might be hungry."

Francesca had asked for time to think, and that appeared to be exactly what he was giving her.

And it was horrible.

Granted, it would probably have been worse if he'd disregarded her wishes and not allowed her to be alone. Clearly, she could not be trusted in his presence. And she didn't particularly trust him, either, with his sultry looks and whispered questions.

Will you kiss me, Francesca? Will you let me kiss you?

And she couldn't refuse, not when he was standing so close, his eyes—his amazing, silver, heavy-lidded eyes—watching her with such smoldering intensity.

He mesmerized her. That could be the only explanation.

She dressed herself that morning, donning a serviceable day dress which would serve her well out of doors. She didn't want to remain cooped up in her room, but neither did she wish to roam the halls of Kilmartin, holding her breath as she turned each corner, waiting for Michael to appear before her.

She supposed he could find her outside if he really wanted to, but at least he would have to expend a bit of effort to do it.

She ate her breakfast, surprised that she had an appetite under such circumstances, and then slipped out of her room, shaking her head at herself as she peered stealthily down the hall, acting like nothing so much as a burglar, eager to make a clean escape.

This was what she'd been reduced to, she thought grumpily.

But she didn't see him as she made her way down the hall, and she didn't see him on the stairs, either.

He wasn't in any of the drawing rooms or salons, and indeed, by the time she reached the front door, she couldn't help but frown.

Where was he?

She didn't wish to see him, of course, but it did seem rather anticlimactic after all of her worrying.

She placed her hand on the knob.

She *should* run. She should hurry out now, while the coast was clear and she could make her escape.

But she paused.

"Michael?" She only mouthed the word, which shouldn't have counted for anything. But she couldn't shake the feeling that he was there, that he was watching her.

"Michael?" she whispered, looking this way and that.

Nothing.

She gave her head a shake. Good God, what had become of her? She was growing far too fanciful. Paranoid, even.

With one last glance behind her, she left the house.

And never did see him, watching her from under the curved staircase, his face touched with the smallest, and truest, of smiles.

Francesca had remained out of doors as long as she was able, finally giving in to a mixture of weariness and cold. She had wandered the grounds for probably six or seven hours, and she was tired, and hungry, and eager for nothing so much as a cup of tea.

And she couldn't avoid her house forever.

So she slipped back in as quietly as she'd left, planning to make her way up to her room, where she could dine in private. But before she could make it to the bottom of the stairs, she heard her name.

"Francesca!"

It was Michael. Of course it was Michael. She couldn't expect him to leave her alone forever.

But the strange thing was—she wasn't quite certain whether she was annoyed or relieved.

"Francesca," he said again, coming to the doorway of the library, "come join me."

He sounded affable—too affable, if that were possible, and furthermore, Francesca was suspicious at his choice of rooms. Wouldn't he have wanted to draw her into the rose drawing room, where she'd be assaulted by memories of their torrid encounter? Wouldn't he at least have chosen the green salon, which had been decorated in a lush, romantic style, complete with cushioned divans and overstuffed pillows?

What was he doing in the library, which had to be, she was quite certain, the least likely room at Kilmartin in which one might stage a seduction?

"Francesca?" he said again, by now looking amused at her indecision.

"What are you doing in there?" she asked, trying not to sound suspicious.

"Having tea."

"Tea?"

"Leaves boiled in water?" he murmured. "Perhaps you've tried it."

She pursed her lips. "But in the library?"

He shrugged. "It seemed as good a place as any." He stepped aside and swooshed his arm in front of him, indicating that she should enter. "As *innocent* a place as any," he added.

She tried not to blush.

"Did you have a pleasant walk?" he asked, his voice perfectly conversational.

"Er, yes."

"Lovely day out."

She nodded.

"I imagine the ground is still a bit soggy in places, though."

What was he up to?

"Tea?" he asked.

She nodded, her eyes widening when he poured for her. Men *never* did that.

"Had to fend for myself from time to time in India," he explained, reading her thoughts perfectly. "Here you go."

She took the delicate china cup and sat, allowing the warmth of the tea to seep through the china and onto her hands. She blew lightly on it, then took a taste, testing the temperature.

"Biscuit?" He held out a plate laden with all sorts of baked delights.

Her stomach rumbled, and she took one without speaking.

"They're good," he offered. "I ate four while I was waiting for you."

"Were you waiting long?" she asked, almost surprised by the sound of her own voice.

"An hour or so."

She sipped at her tea. "It's still quite hot."

"I had the pot refilled every ten minutes," he said.

"Oh." Such thoughtfulness was, if not precisely surprising, then still unexpected.

One of his brows quirked, but only slightly, and she wasn't sure whether he'd done it on purpose. He was always in such control of his expressions; he'd have been a master gambler, had he had the inclination. But his left brow was different; Francesca had noticed years ago that it sometimes moved when he clearly thought he was keeping his face perfectly impassive. She'd always thought of it as her own little secret, her private window into the workings of his mind.

Except now she wasn't sure she wanted such a window. It implied a closeness with which she wasn't quite comfortable any longer.

Not to mention that she'd clearly been deluded when she'd thought she might ever understand the workings of his mind.

He plucked a biscuit off the tray, idly regarded the dollop of raspberry jam in its center, then popped it into his mouth.

"What is this about?" she asked, unable to contain her curiosity any longer. She felt rather like prey, being fattened up for the kill.

"The tea?" he inquired, once he'd swallowed. "Mostly about tea, if you must know."

"*Michael.*"

"I thought you might be cold," he explained with a shrug. "You were gone quite some time."

"You know when I left?"

He looked at her sardonically. "Of course."

And she wasn't surprised. That was the only thing that surprised her, actually—that she wasn't surprised.

"I have something for you," he said.

Her eyes narrowed. "You do?"

"Is that so remarkable?" he murmured, and he reached down onto the seat beside him.

Her breath caught. *Not a ring. Please, not a ring. Not yet.*

She wasn't ready to say yes.

And she wasn't ready to say no, either.

But instead, he set upon the table a small posy of flowers, each bloom more delicate than the last. She'd never been good with flowers, hadn't bothered to learn the names, but there was stalky white one, and a bit of purple, and something that was almost blue. And it had all been tied rather elegantly with a silver ribbon.

Francesca just stared at it, unable to decide what to make of such a gesture.

"You can touch it," he said, a hint of amusement playing along his voice. "It shan't pass along disease."

"No," she said quickly, reaching out for the tiny bouquet, "of course not. I just . . ." She brought the blooms to her face and inhaled, then set them down, her hands retreating quickly to her lap.

"You just what?" he asked softly.

"I don't really know," she replied. And she didn't. She had no idea how she'd meant to complete that sentence, if indeed she had ever intended to. She looked down at the small bouquet, blinking several times before asking, "What is this?"

"I call them flowers."

She looked up, her eyes meeting his fully and deeply. "No," she said, "*what is this*?"

"The gesture, you mean?" He smiled. "Why, I'm courting you."

Her lips parted.

He took a sip of his tea. "Is it such a surprise?"

After all that had passed between them?

Yes.

"You deserve no less," he said.

"I thought you said you intended to—" She broke off, blushing madly. He'd said he meant to take her until she became pregnant.

Three times today, as a matter of fact. Three times, he'd vowed, and they were still quite at zero and . . .

Her cheeks burned, and she couldn't help but feel the memory of him between her legs.

Dear God.

But—thank heavens—his expression remained innocent, and all he said was, "I've rethought my strategies."

She took a frenetic bite of her biscuit. Any excuse to bring her hands to her face and hide a bit of her embarrassment.

"Of course I still plan to pursue my options in that area," he said, leaning forward with a sultry gaze. "I'm only a man, after all. And you, as I believe we've more than made clear, are very much a woman."

She jammed the rest of the biscuit into her mouth.

"But I thought you deserved more," he finished, sitting back with a mild expression, as if he hadn't just seared her with innuendo. "Don't you think?"

No, she didn't think. Not anymore, at least. It was a bit of a problem, that.

Because as she sat there, furiously stuffing food into her mouth, she couldn't take her eyes off his lips. Those magnificent lips, smiling languidly at her.

She heard herself sigh. Those lips had done such magnificent things to her.

To all of her. Every last inch.

Good God, she could practically feel them now.

And it left her squirming in her seat.

"Are you all right?" he asked solicitously.

"Quite," she somehow managed to say, gulping at her tea.

"Is your chair uncomfortable?"

She shook her head.

"Is there anything I can get for you?"

"Why are you doing this?" she finally burst out.

"Doing what?"

"Being so nice to me."

His brows lifted. "Shouldn't I be?"

"No!"

"I shouldn't be nice." It wasn't a question as he said it, rather an amused statement.

"That's not what I meant," she said, shaking her head. He'd befuddled her, and she hated it. There was nothing she valued more than a cool and clear head, and Michael had managed to steal that from her with a single kiss.

And then he'd done more.

So much more.

She was never going to be the same.

She was never going to be *sane.*

"You look distressed," he said.

She wanted to strangle him.

He cocked his head and smiled.

She wanted to kiss him.

He held up the teapot. "More?"

God yes, and that was the problem.

"Francesca?"

She wanted to jump across the table and onto his lap.

"Are you quite all right?"

It was growing difficult to breathe.

"Frannie?"

Every time he spoke, every time he moved his mouth, even just to breathe, her eyes settled on his lips.

She felt herself licking her own.

And she knew that he knew—with all of his experience, all of his seductive prowess—exactly what she was feeling.

He could reach for her now and she wouldn't refuse.

He could touch her and she'd go up in flames.

"I have to go," she said, but her words were breathless and lacking in conviction. And it didn't help that she couldn't seem to wrench her gaze from his own.

"Important matters to attend to in your bedchamber?" he murmured, his lips curving.

She nodded, even though she knew he was mocking her.

"Go then," he encouraged, but his voice was mild and in fact sounded like nothing so much as a seductive purr.

Somehow she managed to move her hands to the edge of the table. She gripped the wood, telling herself to push away, to do something, to move.

But she was frozen.

"Would you prefer to stay?" he murmured.

She shook her head. Or at least she thought she did.

He stood and came to the back of her chair, leaning down to whisper in her ear, "Shall I help you to rise?"

She shook her head again and nearly jumped to her feet, his nearness somewhat paradoxically breaking the spell he'd cast over her. Her shoulder bumped his chest, and she lurched back, terrified that further contact would cause her to do something she might regret.

As if she hadn't had enough of that already.

"I need to go upstairs," she blurted out.

"Clearly," he said softly.

"Alone," she added.

"I wouldn't dream of forcing you to endure my company for one moment longer."

She narrowed her eyes. Just what was he up to? And why the devil did she feel so disappointed?

"But perhaps . . ." he murmured.

Her heart leapt.

". . . perhaps I should offer you a farewell kiss," he finished. "On the hand, of course. It would only be proper."

As if they hadn't discarded propriety back in London.

He took her fingers lightly in his own. "We are courting, after all," he said. "Aren't we?"

She stared down at him, unable to take her eyes off of his head as he bent down over her hand. His lips brushed her fingers. Once . . . twice . . . and then he was through.

"Dream of me," he said softly.

Her lips parted. She couldn't stop watching his face. He'd mesmerized her, held her soul captive. And she couldn't move.

"Unless you want more than a dream," he said.

She did.

"Will you stay?" he whispered. "Or will you go?"

She stayed. Heaven help her, she stayed.

And Michael showed her just how romantic a library could be.

Chapter 21

. . . a brief note to let you know that I have arrived safely in Scotland. I must say, I am glad to be here. London was stimulating as always, but I believe I needed a bit of quiet. I feel quite more focused and at peace here in the country.

—from the Countess of Kilmartin to her mother,
the dowager Viscountess Bridgerton,
one day after her arrival at Kilmartin

Three weeks later, Francesca still didn't know what she was doing.

Michael had brought up the issue of marriage twice more, and each time she'd managed to dodge the question. If she considered his proposal, she would actually have to think. She'd have to think about him, and she'd have to think about John, and worst of all, she'd have to think about herself.

And she'd have to figure out just what it was she was doing. She kept telling herself she would marry him only if she became pregnant, but then she kept coming back to his bed, allowing him to seduce her at every turn.

But even that wasn't truly accurate any longer. She was delusional if she thought she required any seducing to make room for him in her bed. She'd become the wicked one, however much she tried to hide from the fact by telling herself that she was wandering the house at night in her bedclothes because she was restless, not because she was seeking his company.

But she always found him. Or if not, she placed herself in a position where he might find her.

And she never said no.

Michael was growing impatient. He hid it well, but she knew him well. She knew him better than she knew anyone left on this planet, and even though he insisted he was courting her, wooing her with romantic phrases and gestures, she could see the faint lines of impatience curling around his mouth. He would begin a conversation that she knew would lead to the subject of marriage, and she always dodged it before he mentioned the word.

He allowed her to get away with it, but his eyes would change, and his jaw would tighten, and then, when he took her—and he always did, after moments like those—it was with renewed urgency, and even a touch of anger.

But still, it wasn't quite enough to jolt her into action.

She couldn't say yes. She didn't know why; she just couldn't.

But she couldn't say no, either. Maybe she was wicked, and maybe she was a wanton, but she didn't want this to end. Not the passion, and not, she was forced to acknowledge, his company, either.

It wasn't just the lovemaking, it was the moments after, when she lay curled in his arms, his hand idly stroking her hair. Sometimes they were silent, but sometimes they talked, about anything and everything. He told her about India, and she told him of her childhood. She gave him her opinions about political matters, and he actually listened. And he told her devilish jokes that men were never supposed to tell women, and women certainly weren't supposed to enjoy.

And then, once the bed had stopped shaking with her mirth, his mouth would find hers, a smile embedded on his lips. "I love your laughter," he would murmur, and his hands would curl her to him. She'd sigh, still giggling, and they'd begin their passion anew.

And Francesca would, once again, be able to hold the rest of the world at bay.

And then she bled.

It started as it always did, just a few drops on the cotton of her chemise. She shouldn't have been surprised; her cycles may not have been regular, but they always arrived eventually, and she already knew that hers was not a terribly fertile womb.

But still, somehow she hadn't been expecting it. Not yet, anyway.

It made her cry.

Nothing dramatic, nothing that wracked her body and consumed her soul, but her breath caught when she saw the tiny drops of blood, and before she realized what she was doing, twin tears were trickling down her cheeks.

And she wasn't even sure why.

Was it because there would be no baby, or was it—God help her—because there would be no marriage?

Michael came to her room that night, but she sent him away, explaining that it wasn't the right time. His lips found her ear, and he reminded her of all the wicked things they could still do, blood or no, but she refused, and asked him to leave.

He looked disappointed, but he seemed to understand. Women could be squeamish about such things.

But when she woke in the middle of the night, she wished he was holding her.

Her menses didn't last long; it never did. And when Michael

asked her discreetly if her time was through, she didn't lie. He'd have known if she had, anyway; he always did.

"Good," he said with a secret smile. "I've missed you."

Her lips parted to say that she'd missed him, too, but somehow she was afraid to say the words.

He nudged her toward the bed, and together they tumbled, their bodies a tangle of arms and legs as they fell.

"I dreamed of you," he said hoarsely, his hands pushing her skirt up to her waist. "Every night you came to me in dreams." One finger found her essence and dipped inside. "They were very, very good dreams," he finished, his voice hot and full of the devil.

She caught her lip between her teeth, her breath coming in short gasps as his finger slid out and caressed her right where he knew it would make her melt.

"In my dreams," he murmured, his lips hot at her ear, "you did unspeakable things."

She moaned at the sensation. He could ignite her body with a single touch, but she went up in flames when he spoke like this.

"New things," he murmured, spreading her legs wider. "Things I'm going to have to teach you . . . tonight, I think."

"Oh, God," she gasped. He'd moved his lips to her thigh, and she knew what was coming.

"But first a bit of the tried and true," he continued, his lips tickling their way up toward their destination. "We have all night to explore."

He kissed her then, just as he knew she liked it, holding her immobile with his powerful hands as his lips brought her closer and closer to the peaks of passion.

But before she reached the apex, he moved away, his hands tearing at the fastenings of his trousers. He swore when his fingers trembled, when the button didn't slip free on the first try.

And it gave Francesca just enough time to stop and think.

The one thing she truly didn't want to do.

But her mind was relentless, and it was unkind, and before she knew what she was doing, she'd scrambled from the bed, the word, "Wait!" flying from her lips, even as she flew across the room.

"What?" he gasped.

"I can't do this."

"You can't . . ."—he stopped, unable to finish the question without taking a heaving breath—". . . *what*?"

He'd finally had success with his trousers, and they had fallen to the floor, leaving her with a stunning view of his arousal.

Francesca averted her eyes. She couldn't look at him. Not at his face, not at his . . . "I can't," she said, her voice shaking. "I shouldn't. I don't know."

"*I* know," he growled, stepping toward her.

"No!" she cried out, hurrying toward the door. She'd played with fire for weeks, tempting the fates, and she'd won her gamble. If there was ever a time to escape, this was it. And as hard as it was to leave, she knew that she must. She wasn't this sort of woman. She couldn't be.

"I can't do this," she said, her back now flat against the hard wood of the door. "I can't. I . . . I . . ."

I want to, she thought. Even as she knew she shouldn't, she couldn't escape the fact that she wanted to, anyway. But if she told him that, would he make her change her mind? He could do it, too. She knew he could. One kiss, one touch, and all of her resolve would be lost.

He just swore and yanked his trousers back up.

"I don't know who I am any longer," she said. "I'm not this sort of woman."

"*What* sort of woman?" he snapped.

"A wanton," she whispered. "Fallen."

"Then marry me," he shot back. "I offered to make you respectable from the beginning, but *you* refused."

He had her there, and she knew it. But logic didn't seem to have a place in her heart these days, and all she could think was— How could she marry him? How could she marry *Michael*?

"I wasn't supposed to feel this for another man," she said, barely able to believe that she'd spoken the words aloud.

"Feel *what*?" he asked urgently.

She swallowed, forcing herself to bring her eyes to his face. "The passion," she admitted.

His face took on a strange expression, almost one of disgust. "Right," he drawled. "Of course. It's a damned good thing you have me here to service you."

"No!" she cried out, horrified by the derision lacing his voice. "That's not it."

"Isn't it?"

"No." But she didn't know what was.

He took a ragged breath and turned away from her, his body taut with tension. She watched his back with terrible fascination, unable to take her eyes off of him. His shirt was loose, and even though she couldn't see his face, she knew his body, every last curve of it. He looked desolate, hardened.

Worn out.

"Why do you stay?" he asked in a low voice, leaning on the edge of the mattress with the flats of both hands.

"Wh–what?"

"Why do you stay?" he repeated, his words rising in volume but never losing control. "If you hate me so much, why do you stay?"

"I don't hate you," she said. "You know I—"

"I don't know a damned thing, Francesca," he bit off. "I don't even know you any longer." His shoulders tensed as his fingers bit into the mattress. She could see one of his hands; the knuckles had gone white.

"I don't hate you," she said again, as if saying it twice would somehow turn her words into solid things, palpable and real, that she could force him to hold on to. "I don't. I don't hate you."

He said nothing.

"It's not you, it's me," she said, pleading with him now—for what, she wasn't certain. Maybe for him not to hate *her.* That was the one thing she didn't think she could bear.

But all he did was laugh. It was a horrible sound, bitter and low. "Oh, Francesca," he said, condescension lending his words a brittle flavor. "If I had a pound for every time I've said *that* . . ."

Her mouth settled into a grim line. She didn't like to be reminded of all the women who had gone before her. She didn't want to know about them, didn't even want to recall their existence.

"Why do you stay?" he asked again, finally turning around to face her.

She nearly reeled at the fire in his eyes. "Michael, I—"

"Why?" he demanded, fury pounding his voice into a harsh rumble. His face had tightened into deep, angry lines, and her hand instinctively reached for the doorknob.

"Why do you stay, Francesca?" he persisted, moving toward her with the predatory grace of a tiger. "There is nothing for you here at Kilmartin, nothing but *this.*"

She gasped as his hands landed hard on her shoulders, let out a soft cry of surprise as his lips found hers. It was a kiss of anger, of brutal desperation, but still, her traitorous body wanted nothing more than to melt into him, to let him do what he wished, turn all of his wicked attentions on her.

She wanted him. Dear God, even like this, she wanted him.

And she feared she would never learn to say no.

But he wrenched himself away. *He* did it. Not her.

"Is that what you want?" he asked, his voice ragged and hoarse. "Is that all?"

She did nothing, didn't even move, just looked at him with wild eyes.

"*Why do you stay?*" he demanded, and she knew it was the last time he'd ask.

She didn't have an answer.

He gave her several seconds. He waited for her to speak until the silence rose between them like a gorgon, but every time she opened her mouth, no sound emerged, and she couldn't do anything but stand there, shaking as she watched his face.

With a vicious curse, he turned away. "Leave," he ordered. "Now. I want you out of the house."

"Wh–what?" She couldn't believe it, couldn't believe that he would actually toss her out.

He didn't look at her as he said, "If you can't be with me, if you can't give all of yourself to me, then I want you gone."

"Michael?" It was just a whisper, barely that.

"I can't bear this halfway existence," he said, his voice so low she wasn't certain she'd heard correctly.

All she could manage to say was, "Why?"

At first she didn't think he was going to respond. His posture became impossibly taut, and then he began to shake.

Her hand rose to cover her mouth. Was he crying? Could he be . . .

Laughing?

"Oh, God, Francesca," he said, his voice punctuated with derisive laughter. "Now there's a good one. Why? *Why?* Why?" He gave each one a different tenor, as if he were testing out the word, asking it to different people.

"Why?" he asked again, this time with increased volume as he turned around to face her. "*Why?* It's because I love you, damn me to hell. Because I've always loved you. Because I loved you when you were with John, and I loved you when I was in India, and God only knows I don't deserve you, but I love you, anyway."

Francesca sagged against the door.

"How's that for a witty little joke?" he mocked. "I love *you*. I love *you*, my cousin's wife. I love *you*, the one woman I can never have. I love *you*, Francesca Bridgerton Stirling, who—"

"Stop," she choked out.

"Now? Now that I've finally gotten started? Oh, I don't think so," he said grandly, waving one of his arms through the air like a showman. He leaned in close—painfully, uncomfortably close. And his smile was terrifying as he asked, "Are you scared yet?"

"Michael—"

"Because I haven't nearly begun," he said, his voice skipping over hers. "Do you want to know what I was thinking when you were married to John?"

"No," she said desperately, shaking her head.

He opened his mouth to say more, his eyes still flashing with his contemptuous passion, but then something happened. Something changed. It was in his eyes. They were so angry, so inflamed, and then they simply . . .

Stopped.

Turned cold. Weary.

Then he closed them. He looked exhausted.

"Go," he said. "Now."

She whispered his name.

"Go," he repeated, ignoring her plea. "If you're not mine, I don't want you anymore."

"But I—"

He walked to the window, leaning heavily on the sill. "If this is to end, you will have to do it. You will have to walk away, Francesca. Because now . . . after everything . . . I'm just not strong enough to say goodbye."

She stood motionless for several seconds, and then, just when she was sure the tension between them would tighten and snap her in two, her feet somehow found purchase, and she ran from the room.

She ran.

And she ran.

And she ran.

She ran blindly, without thinking.

She ran outside, into the night, into the rain.

She ran until her lungs burned. She ran until she had no balance, was tripping and sliding in the mud.

She ran until she could run no longer, and then she just sat, finding comfort and shelter in the gazebo John had erected for her years earlier, after throwing up his arms and announcing that he'd given up trying to get her to curb her lengthy hikes, and this way at least she'd have a place outside to call her own.

She sat there for hours, shivering in the cold, but not feeling a thing. And all she could wonder was—

Just what was it she was running from?

Michael had no memory of the moments that followed her departure. It could have been one minute, it could have been ten. All he knew was that he seemed to wake up when he realized he'd nearly put his fist through the wall.

And yet somehow he barely noticed the pain.

"My lord?"

It was Reivers, popping his head in to inquire about the commotion.

"Get out," Michael growled. He didn't want to see anyone, didn't want to hear anyone even breathe.

"But maybe some ice for—"

"Get out!" Michael roared, and it felt as if his body were growing huge and monsterish as he turned. He wanted to hurt someone. He wanted to claw at the air.

Reivers fled.

Michael dug his fingernails into his palms, even as his right fist was beginning to swell. Somehow the motion seemed the only way to keep the devil inside at bay, to prevent him from tearing the room apart with his very fingers.

Six years.

He stood there, stock still, with only one thought in his head.

Six bloody years.

He'd held this inside for six years, scrupulously kept his feelings off of his face when he watched her, never told a soul.

Six years he'd loved her, and it had all come to *this*.

He'd laid his heart on the table. He'd practically handed her a knife and asked her to slice it open.

Oh, no, Francesca, you can do better than that. Hold steady there, you can easily make a few more cuts. And while you're at it, why don't you take these pieces here and dice them up?

Whoever had said it was a good thing to speak the truth was an ass. Michael would have given anything, both his bloody feet, even, to have made this all go away.

But that was the thing about words.

He laughed miserably.

You couldn't take them back.

Spread it on the floor now. There you go, stamp it down. No, harder. Harder than that, Frannie. You can do it.

Six years.

Six bloody years, all lost in a single moment. All because he'd thought he might actually have the right to feel happy.

He should have known better.

And for the grand finale, just set the whole bloody thing aflame. Brava, Francesca!

There went his heart.

He looked down at his hands. His nails had carved half-moons into his palms. One had even broken the skin.

What was he going to do? What the *hell* was he going to do now?

He didn't know how to live his life with her knowing the truth. For six years, his every thought and action had revolved around making sure she didn't know. All men had some guiding principle in their lives, and that had been his.

Make sure Francesca never finds out.

He sat in his chair, barely able to contain his own maniacal laughter.

Oh, Michael, he thought, the chair shaking beneath him as he let his head fall into his hands. *Welcome to the rest of your life.*

His second act, as it happened, opened far sooner than he'd expected, with a soft knock on his door about three hours later.

Michael was still sitting in his chair, his only concession to the passage of time the movement of his head from his hands to the seat back. He'd been leaning like that for some time now, his neck uncomfortable but unmoving, his eyes staring sightlessly at some random spot on the ecru silk fabric covering the wall.

He felt removed, set apart, and when he heard the knock, he didn't even recognize the sound at first.

But it came again, no less timid than the first, but still persistent.

Whoever it was, he wasn't going away.

"Enter!" he barked.

He was a she.

Francesca.

He should have risen. He wanted to. Even after everything, he didn't hate her, didn't wish to offer his disrespect. But she had wrenched everything from him, every last drop of strength and purpose, and all he could manage was a slight lifting of his brows, accompanied by a tired, "What?"

Her lips parted, but she didn't say anything. She was wet, he realized, almost idly. She must have gone outside. Silly fool, it was cold out.

"What is it, Francesca?" he asked.

"I'll marry you," she said, so quietly he more read the words on her lips than did he hear them. "If you'll still have me."

And you'd have thought he'd jump from his chair. Rise, at least, unable to tamp down the joy spreading through his body. You'd have thought he might stride across the room, a man of purpose and resolve, to sweep her from her feet, rain kisses on her face, and lay her on the bed, where he might seal the bargain in the most primitive manner possible.

But instead he just sat there, too heart-weary to do anything other than ask, "Why?"

She flinched at the suspicion in his voice, but he didn't feel particularly charitable at the moment. After what she'd done to him, she could suffer a bit of discomfort herself.

"I don't know," she admitted. She was standing very still, her arms straight at her sides. She wasn't rigid, but he could tell she was trying very hard not to move.

If she did, he suspected, she'd run from the room.

"You'll have to do better than that," he said.

Her lower lip caught between her teeth. "I don't know," she whispered. "Don't make me figure it out."

He lifted one sardonic brow.

"Not yet, at least," she finished.

Words, he thought, almost dispassionately. He'd had his words, and now these were hers.

"You can't take it back," he said in a low voice.

She shook her head.

He rose slowly to his feet. "There will be no backing out. No cold feet. No changed minds."

"No," she said. "I promise."

And that was when he finally let himself believe her. Francesca did not give promises lightly. And she never broke her vows.

He was across the room in an instant, his hands at her back, his arms around her, his mouth raining desperate kisses on her face. "You will be mine," he said. "This is it. Do you understand?"

She nodded, arching her neck as his lips slid down the long column to her shoulder.

"If I want to tie you to the bed, and keep you there until you're heavy with child, I'll do it," he vowed.

"Yes," she gasped.

"And you won't complain."

She shook her head.

His fingers tugged at her gown. It fell to the floor with stunning speed. "And you'll like it," he growled.

"Yes. *Oh, yes.*"

He moved her to the bed. He wasn't gentle or smooth, but she didn't seem to want that, and he fell upon her like a starving man. "You will be mine," he said again, grasping her bottom and pulling her toward him. "Mine."

And she was. For that night, at least, she was.

Chapter 22

. . . I am sure you have everything well in hand. You always do.

—from the dowager Viscountess Bridgerton to her daughter, the Countess of Kilmartin, immediately upon the receipt of Francesca's missive

The hardest part about planning a wedding with Michael, Francesca soon realized, was figuring out how to tell people.

As difficult as it had been for her to accept the idea, she couldn't imagine how everyone else might take it. Good God, what would Janet say? She'd been remarkably supportive of Francesca's decision to remarry, but surely she hadn't considered Michael as a candidate.

And yet even as Francesca sat at her desk, her pen hovering over paper for hours on end, trying to find the right words, something inside of her knew that she was doing the right thing.

She still wasn't sure *why* she'd decided to marry him. And she wasn't sure how she ought to feel about his stunning revelation of love, but somehow she knew she wished to be his wife.

That didn't, however, make it any easier to figure out how to tell everyone else about it.

Francesca was sitting in her study, penning letters to her family—or rather, crumpling the paper of her latest misfire and tossing it on the floor—when Michael entered with the post.

"This arrived from your mother," he said, handing her an elegantly appointed cream-colored envelope.

Francesca slid her letter opener under the flap and removed the missive, which was, she noted with surprise, a full four pages long. "Good heavens," she murmured. Her mother generally managed to say what she needed to say with one sheet of paper, two at the most.

"Is anything amiss?" Michael asked, perching himself on the edge of her desk.

"No, no," Francesca said distractedly. "I just . . . Good heavens!"

He twisted and stretched a bit, trying to get a look at the words. "What is it?"

Francesca just waved a shushing hand in his direction.

"Frannie?"

She flipped to the next page. "Good heavens!"

"Give me that," he said, reaching for the paper.

She turned quickly to the side, refusing to relinquish it. "Oh, my God," she breathed.

"Francesca Stirling, if you don't—"

"Colin and Penelope got married."

Michael rolled his eyes. "We already knew—"

"No, I mean they moved up the wedding date by . . . well, goodness, it must have been by over a month, I would think."

Michael just shrugged. "Good for them."

Francesca looked up at him with annoyed eyes. "Someone might have *told* me."

"I imagine there wasn't time."

"But that," she said with great irritation, "is not the worst of it."

"I can't imagine—"

"*Eloise* is getting married as well."

"Eloise?" Michael asked with some surprise. "Was she even being courted by anyone?"

"No," Francesca said, quickly flipping to the third sheet of her mother's letter. "It's someone she's never met."

"Well, I imagine she's met him now," Michael said in a dry voice.

"I can't believe no one *told* me."

"You *have* been in Scotland."

"Still," she said grumpily.

Michael just chuckled at her annoyance, drat the man.

"It's as if I don't exist," she said, irritated enough to shoot him her most ferocious glare.

"Oh, I wouldn't say—"

"Oh, yes," she said with great flair, "*Francesca.*"

"Frannie . . ." He sounded quite amused now.

"Has someone told Francesca?" she said, doing a rather fine group impression of her family. "Remember her? Sixth of eight? The one with the blue eyes?"

"Frannie, don't be daft."

"I'm not daft, I'm just ignored."

"I rather thought you liked being a bit removed from your family."

"Well, yes," she grumbled, "but that's beside the fact."

"Of course," he murmured.

She glared at him for his sarcasm.

"Shall we prepare to leave for the wedding?" he inquired.

"As if I *could*," she said with a great huff. "It's in three days' time."

"My felicitations," Michael said admiringly.

Her eyes narrowed suspiciously. "What is that supposed to mean?"

"One can't help but feel a great respect for any man who manages to get the deed done with such swiftness," he said with a shrug.

"Michael!"

He positively leered at her. "I did."

"I haven't married you yet," she pointed out.

He grinned. "The deed I was referring to wasn't marriage."

She felt her face go red. "Stop it," she muttered.

His fingers tickled along her hand. "Oh, I don't think so."

"Michael, this is not the time," she said, yanking her hand away.

He sighed. "It starts already."

"What does *that* mean?"

"Oh, nothing," he said, plopping down in a nearby chair. "Just that we're not even wed, and already we're an old married couple."

She gave him an arch look, then turned back to her mother's letter. They did sound like an old married couple, not that she wished to give him the satisfaction of her agreement. She supposed it was because unlike most newly affianced pairs, they had known each other for years. He was, despite the amazing changes of the past few weeks, her very best friend.

She stopped. Froze.

"Is something wrong?" Michael asked.

"No," she said, giving her head a little shake. Somehow, in the midst of her confusion, she'd lost sight of that. Michael may have been the last person she'd have thought she'd marry, but that was for a good reason, wasn't it?

Who'd have thought she'd marry her best friend?

Surely that had to bode well for the union.

"Let's get married," he said suddenly.

She looked up questioningly. "Wasn't that already on the agenda?"

"No," he said, grasping her hand, "let's do it today."

"Today?" she exclaimed. "Are you mad?"

"Not at all. We're in Scotland. We don't need banns."

"Well, yes, but—"

He knelt before her, his eyes aglow. "Let's do it, Frannie. Let's be mad, bad, and rash."

"No one will believe it," she said slowly.

"No one is going to believe it, anyway."

He had a point there. "But my family . . ." she added.

"You just said they left you out of their festivities."

"Yes, but it was hardly on purpose!"

He shrugged. "Does it matter?"

"Well, yes, if one really thinks about—"

He yanked her to his feet. "Let's go."

"Michael . . ." And she didn't know why she was dragging her feet, except maybe that she felt she ought. It was a wedding, after all, and such haste was a bit unseemly.

He quirked a brow. "Do you really want a lavish wedding?"

"No," she said, quite honestly. She'd done that once. It didn't seem appropriate the second time around.

He leaned in, his lips touching her ear. "Are you willing to risk an eight-month baby?"

"Obviously I *was*," she said pertly.

"Let's give our child a respectable nine months of gestation," he said jauntily.

She swallowed uncomfortably. "Michael, you must be aware that I may not conceive. With John, it took—"

"I don't care," he cut in.

"I think you do," she said softly, worried about his response, but unwilling to enter into marriage without a clear conscience. "You've mentioned it several times, and—"

"To trap you into marriage," he interrupted. And then, with stunning speed, he had her back against the wall, his body pressed up against hers with startling intimacy. "I don't care if you're barren," he said, his voice hot against her ear. "I don't care if you deliver a litter of puppies."

His hand crept under her dress, sliding right up her thigh. "All I care about," he said thickly, one finger turning very, very wicked, "is that you're *mine*."

"Oh!" Francesca yelped, feeling her limbs go molten. "Oh, yes."

"Yes on this?" he asked devilishly, wiggling his finger just enough to drive her wild, "or yes on getting married today?"

"On this," she gasped. "Don't stop."

"What about the marriage?"

Francesca grabbed his shoulders for support.

"What about the marriage?" he asked again, quickly withdrawing his finger.

"Michael!" she wailed.

His lips spread into a slow, feral smile. "What about the marriage?"

"Yes!" she begged. "Yes! Whatever you want."

"Anything?"

"Anything," she sighed.

"Good," he said, and then, abruptly, he stepped away.

Leaving her slackjawed and rather mussed.

"Shall I retrieve your coat?" he inquired, adjusting his cuffs. He was the perfect picture of elegant manhood, not a hair out of place, utterly calm and composed.

She, on the other hand, was quite certain she resembled a banshee. "Michael?" she managed to ask, trying to ignore the extremely uncomfortable sensation he'd left down in her lower regions.

"If you want to finish," he said, in much the same tone he might have used while discussing grouse hunting, "you'll have to do so as the Countess of Kilmartin."

"I *am* the Countess of Kilmartin," she growled.

He gave her a nod of acknowledgment. "You'll have to do it as *my* Countess of Kilmartin," he corrected. He gave her a moment to respond, and when she did not, he asked again, "Shall I get your coat?"

She nodded.

"Excellent choice," he murmured. "Will you wait here or accompany me to the hall?"

She pried her teeth apart to say, "I'll come out to the hall."

He took her arm and guided her to the door, leaning down to murmur, "Eager little thing, aren't we?"

"Just get my coat," she ground out.

He chuckled, but the sound was warm and rich, and already she felt her irritation beginning to melt away. He was a rogue and scoundrel, and probably a hundred other things as well, but he was her rogue and scoundrel, and she knew he possessed a heart as fine and true as any man she could ever hope to meet. Except for . . .

She stopped short and jabbed one finger against his chest.

"There will be no other women," she said sharply.

He just looked at her with one arched brow.

"I mean it. No mistresses, no dalliances, no—"

"Good God, Francesca," he cut in, "do you really think I could? No, scratch that. Do you really think I *would*?"

She'd been so caught up in her own intentions that she hadn't really looked at his face, and she was stunned by the expression she saw there. He was angry, she realized, irked that she'd even asked.

But she couldn't dismiss out of hand a decade of bad behavior, and she didn't think he had the right to expect her to, so she said, lowering her voice slightly, "You don't have the finest reputation."

"For God's sake," he grunted, yanking her out into the hall. "They were all just to get you out of my mind, anyway."

Francesca was shocked into stumbling silence as she followed him toward the front door.

"Any other questions?" he asked, turning to her with such a supercilious expression that one would have thought he'd been born to the earldom, rather than fallen into it by chance.

"Nothing," she squeaked.

"Good. Now let's go. I have a wedding to attend."

Later that night, Michael couldn't help but be pleased by the day's turn of events. "Thank you, Colin," he said rather jovially to himself as he undressed for bed, "and thank you, too, whomever you are, for marrying Eloise on a moment's notice."

Michael rather doubted that Francesca would have agreed to a rushed wedding if her two siblings hadn't up and gotten married without her.

And now she was his wife.

His wife.

It was almost impossible to believe.

It had been his goal for weeks, and she'd finally agreed the night before, but it wasn't until he'd slid the ancient gold band onto her finger that it had sunk in.

She was his.

Until death do they part.

"Thank you, John," Michael added, the levity leaving his voice. Not for dying, never for that. But rather for releasing him of the guilt. Michael still wasn't quite certain how it had come about, but ever since that fateful night, after he and Francesca had made love at the gardener's cottage, Michael had known, in his heart of hearts, that John would have approved.

He would have given his blessing and in his more fanciful moments, Michael liked to think that if John could have chosen a new husband for Francesca, he would have selected him.

Clad in a burgundy robe, Michael walked to the connecting door between his and Francesca's rooms. Even though they had been intimate since his arrival at Kilmartin, it was only today that he had moved into the earl's bedchamber. It was odd; in London, he hadn't been so worried about appearances. They'd taken residence in the official bedrooms of the earl and countess and simply made sure the entire household was aware that the connecting door was firmly locked from both sides.

But here in Scotland, where they were behaving in a manner deserving of gossip, he'd been careful to unpack his belongings in a room as far down the hall from Francesca's as was available. It didn't matter that one or the other of them had been sneaking back and forth the whole time; at least they gave the appearance of respectability.

The servants weren't stupid; Michael was quite sure they'd all known what was going on, but they adored Francesca, and they wanted her to be happy, and they would never breathe a word against her to anyone.

Still, it was rather nice to put all of that nonsense behind them.

He reached for the doorknob but didn't grasp it right away, stopping instead to listen for sounds in the next room. He didn't hear much. He didn't know why he'd thought he might; the door was solid and ancient and not inclined to give up secrets. Still, there was something about the moment that called to him, that begged for savoring.

He was about to enter Francesca's bedchamber.

And he had every right to be there.

The only thing that might have made it better would be if she had told him she loved him.

The omission left a small, niggling spot on his heart, but that was more than overshadowed by his newfound joy. He didn't want her to say words she did not feel, and even if she never loved him as a wife ought to love her husband, he knew that her feelings were stronger and more noble than what most wives felt for their husbands.

He knew that she cared for him, loved him deeply as a friend. And if anything were to happen to him, she would mourn him with every inch of her heart.

He really couldn't ask for more.

He might *want* more, but he already had so much more than he'd ever hoped for. He shouldn't be greedy. Not when, on top of everything, he had the passion.

And there was passion.

It was almost amusing how much it had surprised her, how much it continued to surprise her each and every day. He had used it to his advantage; he knew that and he wasn't ashamed. He'd used it that very afternoon, while trying to convince her to marry him right then and there.

And it had worked.

Thank God, it had worked.

He felt giddy, like a green boy. When the idea had come to him—to wed that day—it had been like a strange shot of electricity through his veins, and he'd barely been able to contain himself. It had been one of those moments when he knew he had to succeed, would have done anything to win her over.

Now, as he stood on the threshold of his marriage, he couldn't help but wonder if it would be different now. Would she feel different in his arms as his wife than she had as his lover? When he looked upon her face in the morning, would the air feel changed? When he saw her across a crowded room—

He gave his head a little shake. He was turning into a sentimental fool. His heart had always skipped a beat when he saw her across a crowded room. Anything more, and he didn't think the organ could take the strain.

He pushed open the door. "Francesca?" he called out, his voice soft and husky in the night air.

She was standing by the window, clad in a nightgown of deep blue. The cut was modest, but the fabric clung, and for a moment, Michael couldn't breathe.

And he knew—he didn't know how, but he knew—that it would always be like this.

"Frannie?" he whispered, moving slowly toward her.

She turned, and there was hesitation on her face. Not nervousness, precisely, but rather an endearing expression of apprehension, as if she, too, realized that it was all different now.

"We did it," he said, unable to keep a loopy smile off of his face.

"I still can't believe it," she said.

"Nor can I," he admitted, reaching out to touch her cheek, "but it's true."

"I—" She shook her head. "Never mind."

"What were you going to say?"

"It's nothing."

He took both of her hands and tugged her toward him. "It's not nothing," he murmured. "When it's you, and when it's me, it's never nothing."

She swallowed, shadows playing across the delicate lines of her throat, and she finally said, "I just . . . I wanted to say . . ."

His fingers tightened around hers, lending her encouragement. He wanted her to say it. He hadn't thought he needed the words, not yet, anyway, but dear God, how much he wanted to hear them.

"I'm very glad I married you," she finished, her voice matching the uncharacteristically shy expression on her face. "It was the right thing to do."

He felt his toes clench slightly, gripping the carpet as he tamped down his disappointment. It was more than he'd ever thought to hear from her, and yet so much less than he'd hoped.

And yet, even with that, she was still here in his arms, and she was his wife, and that, he vowed fiercely to himself, had to count for something.

"I'm glad, too," he said softly, and pulled her close. His lips touched hers, and it *was* different when he kissed her. There was a new sense of belonging, and lack of furtiveness and desperation.

He kissed her slowly, gently, taking the time to explore her, to relish every moment. His hands slid along the silk of her nightgown, and she moaned as the fabric bunched under his fingers.

"I love you," he whispered, deciding there was no use in holding the words to himself any longer, even if she wasn't inclined to say the same. His lips moved across her cheek to her ear, and he nibbled gently on her lobe before moving down her neck to the delectable hollow at the base of her throat.

"Michael," she sighed, swaying into him. "Oh, Michael."

He cupped her bottom and pressed her to him, a groan slipping across his lips as he felt her tight and warm against his arousal.

He'd thought he'd wanted her before, but this . . . this was different.

"I need you," he said hoarsely, dropping to his knees as his lips slid down the center of her, over the silk. "I need you so much."

She whispered his name, and she sounded confused as she looked down at him, at his position of supplication.

"Francesca," he said, and he had no idea why he was saying it, just that her name was the most important thing in the world right then. Her name, and her body, and the beauty of her soul.

"Francesca," he whispered again, burying his face against her belly.

Her hands settled on his head, fingers entwined in his hair. He could have remained like that for hours, on his knees before her, but then she dropped down, too, and she moved toward him, arching her neck as she kissed him. "I want you," she said. "Please."

Michael groaned, pulling her toward him, and then pulling her to her feet before tugging her toward the bed. In moments they were on the mattress, the soft down of it drawing them in, embracing them even as they embraced each other.

"Frannie," he said, his trembling fingers sliding her silk gown up and over her waist.

One of her hands cupped the back of his head, and she pulled him down for another kiss, this one deep and hot. "I need you," she said, her voice almost a groan of need. "I need you so much."

"I want to see all of you," he said, practically tearing the silk from her body. "I need to *feel* all of you."

Francesca was as eager as he was, and her fingers went to the sash on his robe, untying the loose knot before pushing it open, revealing the broad expanse of his chest. She touched the light dusting of hair, almost feeling a sense of wonder as her hand moved across his skin.

She'd never thought to be in this place, in this moment. This certainly wasn't the first time she'd seen him this way, touched him in this manner, but somehow it was different now.

He was her husband.

It was so hard to believe, and yet it felt so perfect and right.

"Michael," she murmured, tugging the robe over his shoulders.

"Mmmm?" was his reply. He was busy doing something delectable to the back of her knee.

She fell back against the pillows, completely forgetting what she'd been about to say, if there had been anything at all.

His hand wrapped lightly around the front of her thigh, then slid up toward her hip, to her waist, and then finally to the side of her breast. Francesca wanted to take part, wanted to be adventurous and touch him as he was touching her, but his caresses were making her languid and lazy, and all she could do was lie back and enjoy his ministrations, occasionally reaching out to trail her fingers along whichever part of his skin they were able to reach.

She felt cherished.

Worshipped.

Loved.

It was humbling.

It was exquisite.

It was sacred and seductive, and it took her breath away.

His lips followed the trail his hands had forged, sending tingles of desire up and across her belly, coming to rest in the flattened hollow between her breasts.

"Francesca," he murmured, kissing his way to her nipple. He teased it first with his tongue, then took it in his mouth, biting it gently.

The sensation was intense and immediate. Her body convulsed, and her fingers gripped frantically into the bedsheets, desperate for purchase in a world that had suddenly tilted right off its axis.

"Michael," she gasped, arching her back. His fingers had slipped between her legs, not that she needed anything more to ready her for his eventual entry. She wanted this, and she wanted him, and she wanted it to last forever.

"You feel so good," he said hoarsely, his breath hot on her skin. He moved then, positioning himself at her entrance. His face was over hers, nose to nose, and his eyes glowed hot and intense.

Francesca wiggled beneath him, the movement tipping her hips to welcome him more deeply. "Now," she said, the word a cross between an order and a plea.

He moved slowly, inching his way inside with tantalizing deliberation. She felt herself opening, stretching to greet him until their bodies touched, and she knew that he was embedded fully.

"Oh, my God," he grunted, his face stretched taut with passion. "I can't . . . I have to . . ."

She answered by arching her hips, pressing herself even more firmly against him.

He began to move within her, each stroke bringing a new wave of sensation that spread and burned through her body. She said his name, and then she could not speak, could do nothing but gasp for air as their movements grew more frenzied and desperate.

And then it came upon her, in a lightning wave of pleasure. Her body exploded, and she cried out, unable to contain the intensity of the experience. Michael thrust into her harder, and then again, and again. He called out as he climaxed, her name a prayer and a benediction on his lips, and then he collapsed atop her.

"I'm too heavy," he said, making a halfhearted attempt to move off of her.

"Don't," she said, stilling him with her hand. She didn't want him to move, not yet. Soon it would be hard to breathe, and he'd have to adjust, but for now there was something elemental in their position, something to which she wasn't ready to bid farewell.

"No," he said, and she could hear a smile in his voice, "I'll crush you." He slid off of her, but he didn't relinquish their closeness, and she found herself curled next to him like a nested spoon, her back warmed by his skin, her body held snugly in place by his arm under her breasts.

He murmured something against her neck, and she couldn't really understand the words, but that didn't matter; she knew what he'd said.

He nodded off soon after, his breath a slow and steady lullaby at her ear. But Francesca did not sleep. She was tired, she was drowsy, and she was sated, but she did not sleep.

It had been different tonight.

And she was left wondering why.

Chapter 23

. . . I am sure that Michael will be penning a letter as well, but as I count you as a dear, dear friend, I wanted to write to you myself to inform you that we have married. Are you surprised? I must confess that I was.

—from the Countess of Kilmartin to Helen Stirling, three days after her marriage to the Earl of Kilmartin

"You look terrible."

Michael turned to Francesca with a somewhat dry expression. "And good morning to you, too," he remarked, turning his attention back to his eggs and toast.

Francesca slid into place across the breakfast table from him. It was two weeks into their marriage; Michael had risen early that morning, and when she'd awakened, his side of the bed had been cold.

"I'm not joking," she said, feeling her concern knit her brows into a wrinkled line. "You look quite pasty, and you're not even sitting up straight. You should go back to bed and get some rest."

He coughed, then coughed again, the second spasm wracking

his body. "I'm fine," he said, although the words came out rather like a gasp.

"You're not fine."

He rolled his eyes. "Married a fortnight, and already—"

"If you didn't wish for a nagging wife, you shouldn't have married me," Francesca said, judging the distance across the table and deciding that she couldn't reach far enough to touch his forehead to check for fever.

"I'm fine," he said firmly, and this time he picked up his copy of *The London Times*—several days old but as current as they could expect in the Scottish border counties—and proceeded to ignore her.

Two could play at that game, Francesca decided, and she devoted her attention to the always challenging task of spreading jam on her muffin.

Except he coughed.

She shifted in her seat, trying not to say anything.

He coughed again, this time turning away from the table so that he could bend over a bit.

"M—"

He gave her a look of such ferocity that she shut her mouth.

She narrowed her eyes.

He inclined his head in an annoyingly condescending manner, then had the effect ruined when his body convulsed with another spasm.

"That's it," Francesca announced, rising to her feet. "You are going back to bed. Now."

"I'm fine," he grunted.

"You're not fine."

"I'm—"

"Sick," she interrupted. "You're sick, Michael. Diseased, ill, plague-ridden, you're sick. As a dog. I don't see how I could possibly make it any more clear."

"I haven't got the plague," he muttered.

"No," she said, coming around the table to grasp his arm, "but you do have malaria, and—"

"It's not malaria," he said, whacking his chest as he coughed again.

She pulled him to his feet, a task she couldn't have completed without at least a bit of assistance on his part. "How do you know that?" she asked.

"I just do."

She pursed her lips. "And you speak with the medical expertise that comes from—"

"Having had the disease for the better part of a year," he cut in. "It's not malaria."

She nudged him toward the door.

"Besides," he protested, "it's too soon."

"Too soon for what?"

"For another attack," he explained wearily. "I just had one in London, what was it—two months ago? It's too soon."

"Why is it too soon?" she asked, her voice strangely quiet.

"It just is," he muttered, but inside, he knew a different truth. It wasn't too soon; he'd known plenty of people who'd had their malarial attacks two months apart.

They'd all been sick. Really sick.

Quite a few of them had died.

If his attacks were coming closer together, did that mean the disease was winning?

Now there was irony for you. He'd finally married Francesca, and now he might be dying.

"It isn't malaria," he said again, this time with enough force to make her stop walking and look up at him.

"It isn't," he said.

She just nodded.

"It's probably a cold," he said.

She nodded again, but he got the distinct impression that she was placating him.

"I'll take you to bed," she said softly.

And he let her.

Ten hours later, Francesca was terrified. Michael's fever was rising, and although he was not delirious or incoherent, it was clear that he was very, very ill. He kept saying that it wasn't malaria, that it didn't *feel* like malaria, but every time she pressed him for details, he couldn't explain why—at least not to her satisfaction.

She didn't know much about the disease; the fashionable ladies' bookshops in London declined to carry medical texts. She'd wanted to ask her own doctor, or even seek an expert at the Royal College of Physicians, but she had made a promise to Michael that she would keep his illness a secret. If she ran around town making inquiries about malaria, eventually someone would want to know why. Thus, most of what she knew she had learned from Michael during the few short months he'd been back from India.

But it didn't seem right that the attacks were coming closer together. Not, she had to allow, that she possessed any medical knowledge upon which to base that assumption. When he'd fallen ill in London, he'd said that it had been six months since his last set of fevers, and three before that.

Why would the disease suddenly change course and attack again so quickly? It just didn't make sense. Not if he was getting better.

And he had to be getting better. He had to be.

She sighed, reaching out to touch his forehead. He was sleeping now, snoring slightly, as he tended to when he was congested. Or so he'd told her. They hadn't been married long enough for her to have gained that knowledge firsthand.

His skin was hot, although not burningly so. His mouth looked parched, so she spooned some tepid tea over his lips, tilting up his chin to try to help him swallow in his sleep.

Instead, he choked and came awake, spewing the tea across the bed.

"Sorry," Francesca said, surveying the damage. At least it had been a small spoonful.

"What the devil are you doing to me?" he sputtered.

"I don't know," she admitted. "I haven't much experience nursing. You looked thirsty."

"Next time I'm thirsty, I'll tell you," he grumbled.

She nodded her agreement and watched as he tried to make himself comfortable again. "You wouldn't happen to be thirsty right now?" she asked in a mild voice.

"Just a bit," he said, his syllables slightly clipped.

Without a word, she held out the cup of tea. He downed it all in one long gulp.

"Would you like another cup?"

He shook his head. "Any more and I'm going to have to pi—" He broke off and cleared his throat. "Sorry," he mumbled.

"I have four brothers," she said. "Pay it no mind. Would you like me to fetch you the chamberpot?"

"I can do it myself."

He didn't look well enough to cross the room on his own, but she knew better than to argue with a man in that irritable a state. He would come to his senses when he tried to stand and fell right back down against the bed. No amount of argument or reason on her part would convince him otherwise.

"You're quite feverish," she said softly.

"It isn't malaria."

"I didn't say—"

"You were thinking it."

"What happens if it *is* malaria?" she asked.

"It's not—"

"But what if it is?" she cut in, and to her horror, her voice had that awful pitch to it, that roundish sound of terror it made just before it actually choked.

Michael looked at her for several seconds, his eyes grim. Finally, he just rolled over and said, "It's not."

Francesca swallowed. She had her answer now. "Do you mind if I leave?" she blurted out, standing up so quickly the blood rushed from her head.

He didn't say anything, but she could see him shrug under the covers.

"It's just for a walk," she explained haltingly, making her way to the door. "Before the sun goes down."

"I'll be fine," he grunted.

She nodded, even though he wasn't looking at her. "I'll see you soon," she said.

But he'd already fallen back asleep.

The air was misty and threatened more precipitation, so Francesca grabbed a rain parasol and made her way to the gazebo. The sides were open to the elements, but it had a roof, and should the heavens open, she would remain at least nominally dry.

But with every step, it felt as if her breathing was growing more labored, and by the time she reached her destination, she was heaving with exertion, not from the walk, but just from keeping the tears at bay.

The minute she sat down, she stopped trying.

Each sob was huge, and hugely unladylike, but she didn't care.

Michael might be dying. For all she knew, he *was* dying, and she was going to be a widow twice over.

It had nearly killed her last time.

And she just didn't know if she was strong enough to go through it all again. She didn't know if she wanted to be strong enough.

It wasn't right, and it wasn't fair, damn it all, that she should have to lose two husbands when so many women got to hold on to one for an entire lifetime. And most of those women didn't even like their spouses, whereas *she*, who actually loved them both—

Francesca's breath caught.

She loved him? Michael?

No, no, she assured herself, she didn't *love* him. Not like that. When she'd thought it, when the word had echoed through her brain, she'd meant in friendship. Of course she loved Michael *that* way. She'd always loved him, right? He was her best friend, had been even back when John was alive.

She pictured him, saw his face, his smile.

She closed her eyes, remembered his kiss and the perfect feeling of his hand at the small of her back as they walked through the house.

And she finally figured out why everything had seemed different between them of late. It wasn't, as she'd originally supposed, just because they'd married. It wasn't because he was her husband, because she wore his ring on her finger.

It was because she loved him.

This thing between them, this bond—it wasn't just passion, and it wasn't wicked.

It was love, and it was divine.

And Francesca could not have been more surprised if John had materialized before her and started to dance an Irish reel.

Michael.

She loved Michael.

Not just as a friend, but as a husband and a lover. She loved him with the depth and intensity she'd felt for John. It was different, because they were different men, and she was different now, too, but it was also the same. It was the love of a woman for a man, and it filled every corner of her heart.

And by God, she didn't want him to die.

"You can't do this to me," she yelled, hanging over the side of the gazebo bench and looking up at the sky. A fat raindrop landed on the bridge of her nose, splashing into her eye.

"Oh, no you don't," she growled, wiping the moisture away. "Don't think you can—"

Three more drops, in rapid succession.

"Damn," Francesca muttered, followed by a "Sorry," aimed back up at the clouds.

She pulled her head back into the gazebo, taking refuge under the wooden roof as the rain grew in intensity.

What was she supposed to do now? Charge forth with all the single-minded purpose of an avenging angel, or have a good cry and feel sorry for herself?

Or maybe a little of both.

She looked out at the rain, which was now thundering down with enough force to strike fear in the heart of even the most determined of avenging angels.

Definitely a little of both.

Michael opened his eyes, surprised to discover that it was morning. He blinked a few times, just to verify this fact. The curtains were drawn shut, but not all the way, and there was a clear streak of light making a stripe along the carpet.

Morning. Well. He must have been really tired. The last thing he remembered was Francesca dashing out the door, stating her intention to go for a walk, despite the fact that any fool would have realized that it was going to rain.

Silly woman.

He tried to sit up, then quickly flopped back down on the covers. Damn, he felt like death. Not, he allowed, the finest metaphor under the circumstances, but he couldn't think of much else that would adequately describe the ache that permeated his body. He felt exhausted, nearly glued to the sheets. The mere thought of sitting up was enough to make him groan.

Damn, he was miserable.

He touched his forehead, trying to ascertain if he still had a fever, but if his brow was hot, then so was his hand; he couldn't tell a thing other than the fact that he was damned sweaty and certainly in need of a good bath.

He tried to sniff the air around him, but he was so congested that he ended up coughing.

He sighed. Well, if he stank, at least *he* didn't have to smell it.

He heard a soft sound at the door and looked up to see Francesca entering the room. She moved quietly on stockinged feet, clearly trying to avoid disturbing him. As she approached the bed, however, she finally looked at him and let out a little, "Oh!" of surprise.

"You're awake," she said.

He nodded. "What time is it?"

"Half eight. Not too late, really, except that you fell asleep last evening before the supper hour."

He nodded again, since he didn't really have anything pertinent to add to the conversation. And besides that, he was too tired to speak.

"How are you feeling?" she asked, sitting down beside him. "And would you like something to eat?"

"Like hell, and no, thank you."

Her lips curved slightly. "Something to drink?"

He nodded.

She picked up a small bowl that had been sitting on a nearby table. A saucer had been resting on top of it, presumably to keep the contents warm. "It's from last night," she said apologetically, "but I've had it covered, so it shouldn't be too dreadful."

"Broth?" he asked.

She nodded, holding a spoon to his lips. "Is it too cold?"

He sipped a little, then shook his head. It was barely lukewarm, but he didn't think he could stand anything overheated, anyway.

She fed him in silence for a minute or so, and then, once he said he'd had enough, she set the bowl back down, carefully replacing the lid, even though he imagined she would wish to order up a new bowl for his next meal. "Do you have a fever?" she whispered.

He tried to summon a devil-may-care smile. "I have no idea."

She reached out to touch his forehead.

"Didn't have time to bathe," he mumbled, apologizing for his slippery visage without actually uttering the word *sweat* in her presence.

She made no sign of having heard his attempt at a joke, instead just furrowed her brow as she pressed her hand against him more closely. And then, surprising him with her swiftness, she stood and leaned over him, touching her lips to his forehead.

"Frannie?"

"You're hot," she said, barely breathing the words. "You're hot!"

He did nothing but blink.

"You still have a fever," she said excitedly. "Don't you understand? If you still have a fever, it can't be malaria!"

For a moment he couldn't breathe. She was right. He couldn't believe it had not occurred to him, but she was right. The malarial fevers always disappeared by morning. They hit again the next day, of course, often with horrible force, but they always dissipated, giving him a day's respite before once again laying him low.

"It's not malaria," she said again, her eyes suspiciously bright.

"I told you it wasn't," he said, but inside, he knew the truth— He hadn't been so sure.

"You're not going to die," she whispered, her lower lip catching in her teeth.

His eyes flew to hers. "Were you worried I would?" he asked quietly.

"Of course I was," she returned, no longer trying to hide the choking sound in her voice. "My God, Michael, I can't believe you— Do you have any idea how I— Oh, for God's sake."

He had no idea what she'd just said, but he had a feeling it was good.

She stood, the back of her chair bumping against the wall. A cloth napkin had been sitting beside the broth; she snatched it up and used it to dab at her eyes.

"Frannie?" he murmured.

"You're such a *man*," she said with a scowl.

He could do nothing but raise his eyebrows at that.

"You should know I—" But she stopped, broke herself off.

"What is it, Frannie?"

She shook her head. "Not yet," she said, and he got the impression she was talking more to herself than to him. "Soon, but not yet."

He blinked. "I beg your pardon?"

"I have to go out," she said, her words oddly curt and abrupt. "There's something I need to do."

"At half eight in the morning?"

"I'll be back soon," she said, hurrying toward the door. "Don't go anywhere."

"Well, damn," he tried to joke, "there go my plans to visit the King."

But Francesca was so distracted she didn't even bother to poke at his rather pathetic attempt at humor. "Soon," she said, the word coming out strangely like a promise. "I'll be back soon."

All he could do was shrug and watch the door as she shut it behind her.

Chapter 24

. . . I am not certain how to tell you this, and moreover, I am not certain how the news will be received, but Michael and I were married three days ago. I don't know how to describe the events leading up to the marriage, except to say that it simply felt like the right thing to do. Please know that this in no way diminishes the love I felt for John. He will always hold a special and cherished place in my heart, as do you . . .

—from the Countess of Kilmartin to the dowager Countess of Kilmartin, three days after her marriage to the Earl of Kilmartin

A quarter of an hour later, Michael was feeling remarkably better. Not well, of course; not by any stretch of the imagination could he have convinced himself—or anyone else for that matter—that he was his regular hale and hearty self. But the broth must have restored him a bit, as had the conversation, and when he got up to use the chamberpot, he found he was steadier on his legs than he would have thought. He followed this task with a bit of a makeshift bath, using a dampened cloth to wash the worst of the perspiration from his body. After donning a clean dressing gown, he felt almost human again.

He started to walk back to his bed, but he just couldn't bring himself to slide his body back between those sweaty sheets, so instead he rang for a servant and sat down in his leather wingbacked chair, turning it slightly so that he might gaze out the window.

It was sunny. That was a nice change. The weather had been dismal for both the weeks of his marriage. He hadn't particularly minded; when one spent as much time making love to one's wife as he had done, one didn't particularly care if the sun was shining.

But now, escaping his sickbed, he found that his spirits were buoyed by the sparkle of the sunlight on the dewy grass.

A movement out the window caught his eye, and he realized that it was Francesca, hurrying across the lawn. She was too far away to see clearly, but she was bundled up in her most serviceable coat, and was clutching something in her hand.

He leaned forward for a better look, but she disappeared from view, slipping behind a hedgerow.

Just then, Reivers entered the room. "You rang, my lord?"

Michael turned to face him. "Yes. Could you see to having someone come and change the sheets?"

"Of course, my lord."

"And—" Michael had been about to ask him to have a bath drawn as well, but for some reason the following words slipped out of his mouth instead: "Do you happen to know where Lady Kilmartin went? I saw her walking across the lawn."

Reivers shook his head. "No, my lord. She did not see fit to confide in me, although Davies did tell me that she asked him to ask the gardener to cut her some flowers."

Michael nodded his head as he mentally followed the chain of people. He really ought to have more respect for the sheer efficiency of servants' gossip. "Flowers, you say," he murmured. That must have been what she was holding as she crossed the lawn a few minutes earlier.

"Peonies," Reivers confirmed.

"Peonies," Michael echoed, leaning forward with interest. They were John's favorite bloom, and had been the centerpiece of Francesca's wedding bouquet. It was almost appalling that he remembered such a detail, but while he'd gone and gotten himself rippingly drunk as soon as John and Francesca had departed the party, he remembered the actual ceremony with blinding detail.

Her dress had been blue. Ice blue. And the flowers had been peonies. They'd had to get them from a hothouse, but Francesca had insisted upon it.

And suddenly he knew exactly where she was going, bundled up against the slight nip in the air.

She was going to John's grave.

Michael had visited the site once since his return. He'd gone alone, a few days after that extraordinary moment in his bedchamber, when he'd suddenly realized that John would have approved of his marrying Francesca. More than that, he almost thought John was up there somewhere, having a good chuckle over the whole thing.

And Michael couldn't help but wonder— Did Francesca realize? Did she realize that John would have wanted this? For both of them?

Or was she still gripped by guilt?

Michael felt himself rise from his chair. He knew guilt, knew how it ate at one's heart, tore at one's soul. He knew the pain, and he knew the way it felt like acid in one's belly.

And he never wanted that for Francesca. Never.

She might not love him. She might not *ever* love him. But she was happier now than she had been before they'd married; he was sure of it. And it would kill him if she felt any shame for that happiness.

John would have wanted her to be happy. He would have wanted her to love and be loved. And if Francesca somehow didn't realize that—

Michael started pulling on his clothing. He might still be weak, and he might still be feverish, but by God he could make it down to the chapel graveyard. It would half kill him, but he would not allow her to sink into the same sort of guilty despair he'd suffered for so long.

She didn't have to love him. She didn't. He'd said those words to himself so many times during their brief marriage that he almost believed them.

She didn't have to love him. But she did have to feel free. Free to be happy.

Because if she wasn't happy . . .

Well, that *would* kill him. He could live without her love, but not without her happiness.

Francesca had known the ground would be damp, so she'd brought along a small blanket, the green and gold of the Stirling plaid making her smile wistfully as she spread it out over the grass.

"Hello, John," she said, kneeling as she carefully arranged the peonies at the base of his headstone. His grave was a simple affair, far less ostentatious than the monuments many of the nobility erected to honor their dead.

But it was what John would have wanted. She'd known him so well, been able to predict his words half the time.

He would have wanted something simple, and he would have wanted it here, in the far corner of the churchyard, closer to the rolling fields of Kilmartin, his favorite place in the world.

And so that was what she'd given him.

"It's a nice day," she said, sitting back on her bottom. She hiked up her skirts so that she could sit cross-legged, then carefully arranged them back over her legs. It wasn't the sort of position she could ever assume in polite company, but this was different.

John would have wanted her to be comfortable.

"It's been raining for weeks," she said. "Some days worse than others, of course, but never a day without at least a few minutes of moisture. You wouldn't have minded it, but I must confess, I've been longing for the sun."

She noticed that one of the stems wasn't quite where she wanted it, so she leaned forward and reset it into place.

"Of course, it hasn't really stopped me from going out," she said with a nervous laugh. "I seem to get caught out in the rain quite a bit lately. I'm not really certain what it is—I used to be more heedful of the weather."

She sighed. "No, I do know what it is. I'm just afraid to tell you. Silly of me, I know, but . . ." She laughed again, that strained noise that sounded all wrong from her lips. It was the one thing she'd never felt around John—nervous. From the moment they'd met, she'd felt so comfortable in his presence, so utterly at ease, both with him and herself.

But now . . .

Now she finally had cause for nerves.

"Something has happened, John," she said, her fingers plucking at the fabric of her coat. "I . . . started feeling something for someone that perhaps I shouldn't have done."

She looked around, half expecting some sort of divine sign from above. But there was nothing, just the gentle ruffle of wind against the leaves.

She swallowed, focusing her attention back on John's headstone.

It was silly that a piece of rock might come to symbolize a man, but she had no idea where else to look when she spoke to his memory. "Maybe I shouldn't have felt it," she said, "or maybe I should have, and I just thought I shouldn't have. I don't know. All I know is it happened. I didn't expect it, but then, there it was, and . . . with . . ."

She stopped, her mouth curving into a smile that was almost rueful. "Well, I suppose you know who it was with. Can you imagine?"

And then something remarkable happened. In retrospect, she rather thought the earth should have moved, or a shaft of light come sparkling down from the heavens across the gravesite. But there was none of that. Nothing palpable, nothing audible or visible, just an odd sense of shifting within herself, almost as if something had finally nudged itself into place.

And she knew—truly, fully knew—that John could have imagined it. And more than that, he would have wanted it.

He would have wanted her to marry Michael. He would have wanted her to marry any man with whom she'd fallen in love, but she rather thought he'd be almost tickled that it had happened with Michael.

They were his two favorite people, and he would have liked knowing that they were together.

"I love him," she said, and she realized it was the first time she'd said it aloud. "I love Michael. I do, and John—" She touched his name, etched in the headstone. "I think you would approve," she whispered. "Sometimes I almost think you arranged the whole thing.

"It's so strange," she continued, tears now filling her eyes. "I spent so much time thinking to myself that I would never fall in love again. How could I possibly? And when anyone asked me what you would have wanted for me, of course I replied that you would wish for me to find someone else. But inside—" She smiled wistfully. "Inside I knew it wouldn't happen. I wasn't going to fall in love. I knew it. I absolutely *knew* it. So it didn't really matter what you wanted for me, did it?

"Except it did happen," she said softly. "It happened, and I never expected it. It happened, and it happened with Michael. I love him so much, John," she said, her voice breaking with emotion. "I kept trying to tell myself that I didn't, but when I thought he was dying, it was just too much, and I knew . . . oh God, I knew it, John. I need him. I love him. I can't live without him, and I just needed to tell you, to know that you . . . that you . . ."

She couldn't go on. There was too much inside of her, too many emotions, all desperately pushing to get out. She put her face in her hands and cried, not out of sorrow, and not out of joy, but just because she couldn't keep it inside.

"John," she gasped. "I love him. And I think this is what you would have wanted. I really do, but—"

And then, from behind her, she heard a noise. A footstep, a breath. She turned, but she already knew who it would be. She could feel him in the air.

"Michael," she whispered, staring at him like he was a specter. He was pale and gaunt and had to lean on a tree for support, but to her he looked perfect.

"Francesca," he said, the word awkwardly passing over his lips. "Frannie."

She rose to her feet, her eyes never leaving his. "Did you hear me?" she whispered.

"I love you," he said hoarsely.

"But did you hear me?" she persisted. She had to know, and if he hadn't heard her, she had to tell him.

He nodded jerkily.

"I love you," she said. She wanted to go to him, she wanted to throw her arms around him, but somehow she was rooted to her spot. "I love you," she said again. "I love you."

"You don't have to—"

"No, I do. I have to say it. I have to tell you. I love you. I do. I love you so much."

And then the distance between them was gone, and his arms came around her. She buried her face against his chest, her tears soaking his shirt. She wasn't sure why she was crying, but she didn't really care. All she wanted was the warmth of his embrace.

In his arms she could feel the future, and it was wonderful.

Michael's chin came to rest on her head. "I didn't mean that you didn't need to say it," he murmured, "just that you didn't have to repeat it."

She laughed at that, even as the tears kept flowing, and both of their bodies shook.

"You have to say it," he said. "If you feel it, then you have to say it. I'm a greedy bastard, and I want it all."

She looked up at him, her eyes bright. "I love you."

Michael touched her cheek. "I have no idea what I did to deserve you," he said.

"You didn't have to do anything," she whispered. "You just had to be." She reached up and touched his cheek, the gesture a perfect mirror of his own. "It just took me a while to realize it, that's all."

He turned his face into her hand, then brought both of his up to cover it. He pressed a kiss against her palm, stopping just to inhale the scent of her skin. He'd tried so hard to convince himself that it didn't matter if she loved him, that having her as his wife was enough. But now . . .

Now that she'd said it, now that he knew, now that his heart had soared, he knew better.

This was heaven.

This was bliss.

This was something he'd never dared hope to feel, something he never could have dreamed existed.

This was love.

"For the rest of my life," he vowed, "I will love you. For the rest of my life. I promise you. I will lay down my life for you. I will honor and cherish you. I will—" He was choking on the words, but he didn't care. He just wanted to tell her. He just wanted her to know.

"Let's go home," she said softly.

He nodded.

She took his hand, gently pulling him away from the clearing, back toward the wooded area that lay between the churchyard and Kilmartin. Michael leaned into her tug, but before his feet lifted from the earth, he turned back toward John's grave and mouthed the words, *Thank you.*

And then he let his wife lead him home.

"I wanted to tell you later," she was saying. Her voice was still shaky with emotion, but she was starting to sound a bit more like her usual self. "I'd planned a big romantic gesture. Something huge. Something . . ." She turned to him, offering him a rueful smile. "Well, I don't know what, but it would have been grand."

He just shook his head. "I don't need that," he said. "All I need . . . I just need . . ."

And it didn't matter that he didn't know how to finish the sentence, because somehow she knew, anyway.

"I know," she whispered. "I need the exact same thing."

Epilogue

My dear nephew,

Although Helen insists that she was not surprised at the announcement of your marriage to Francesca, I shall own up to a less clever imagination and confess that to me, it came as a complete shock.

I implore you, however, not to confuse shock with lack of acceptance. It did not require much time or thought to realize that you and Francesca are an ideal match. I don't know how I did not see it before. I do not profess to understand metaphysics, and in truth, I rarely have patience for those who claim that they do, but there is an understanding between the two of you, a meeting of the minds and souls that exists on a higher plane.

You were, it is clear, born for each other.

These are not easy words for me to write. John still lives on in my heart, and I feel his presence every day. I mourn my son, and I shall always do so. I cannot tell you what comfort it gives me to know that you and Francesca feel the same.

I hope you will not think me self-important when I offer you my blessing.

And I hope you will not think me foolish when I also extend my thanks.

Thank you, Michael, for letting my son love her first.

—from Janet Stirling,
dowager Countess of Kilmartin,
to Michael Stirling,
Earl of Kilmartin, June 1824

Author's Note

Dear Reader,

I have subjected the characters of *When He Was Wicked* to more than their fair share of medical misfortune. Researching the conditions of both John and Michael was complicated; I had to make sure that their disease processes made scientific sense, while at the same time revealing only what was known by medical science in 1824 England.

John died of a ruptured cerebral aneurysm. Cerebral aneurysms are congenital weak spots in the walls of blood vessels within the brain. They may lie dormant for many years or they may rapidly enlarge and then rupture, leading to bleeding in the brain, which can be followed by unconsciousness, coma, and death. Headaches brought on by ruptured cerebral aneurysms are sudden and explosive but can be preceded by a lingering headache for some time prior to the actual rupture.

Nothing could have been done to save him; even today approximately one-half of ruptured cerebral aneurysms lead to death.

During the 19th century, the only way to make a definitive diagnosis of a ruptured cerebral aneurysm was at autopsy. It is extremely unlikely, however, that an earl would have undergone a postmortem dissection; therefore, John's death would have remained a mystery to those who loved him. All Francesca would ever know was that her husband had a headache, lay down, and died.

The turning point in the treatment of cerebral aneurysms came with the widespread use of angiography in the 1950s. This technique, which consists of the injection of radiopaque dye into the vessels feeding the brain to give an X-ray picture of the vascular anatomy, was developed by Egas Moniz in Portugal in 1927. An interesting historical footnote: Moniz won the Nobel Prize for Medicine in 1949, but not for his work in the groundbreaking and life-saving field of angiography. Rather, he was honored for his discovery of the frontal lobotomy as a treatment for psychiatric illness.

As for malaria, it is an ancient disease. Throughout recorded history, it has been observed that exposure to warm, moist, humid air is associated with periodic fevers, weakness, anemia, kidney failure, coma, and death. The name of the disease comes from the Italian for "bad air," and reflects the belief of our ancestors that the air itself was to blame. In *When He Was Wicked*, Michael cites "putrid air" as the source of his illness.

Today we understand that malaria is in fact a parasitic disease. The hot, swampy conditions themselves are not to blame, but rather serve as breeding grounds for mosquitoes of the genus *Anopheles*, the vector of the infection. During an insect bite, female *Anopheles* mosquitoes unwittingly inject microscopic organisms into the hapless human host. These organisms are single-celled parasites of the genus *Plasmodium*. There are four species of *Plasmodium* that can infect people: *falciparum*, *vivax*, *ovale*, and *malariae*. Once in the bloodstream, these microorganisms are swept into the liver, where they multiply at a furious pace; within a week, tens of thousands of parasites are released back into the bloodstream, where they infect red blood cells and feed upon the oxygen-carrying hemoglobin inside. Every two or three days, through a synchronized process that is poorly understood, the offspring of these parasites erupt from the red cells, leading to high fevers and violent chills. In the case of *falciparum* malaria, the infected cells can become sticky, and glom on to the inside of blood vessels in the kidney and brain, leading to renal failure and coma—and death, if treatment is delayed.

Michael was fortunate. Although he did not know it, he suffered from *vivax* malaria, which can persist in patients' livers for decades but rarely kills its victims. The exhaustion and fevers caused by *vivax* malaria, however, are severe.

At the end of the book, both Michael and Francesca worry that a higher frequency of attacks might indicate that he was losing his battle with the disease. In truth, with *vivax* malaria, this would not have mattered. There is little rhyme or reason to when a *vivax* patient might suffer an episode of malarial fevers (except in the case of immunosuppression, such as cancer, pregnancy, or AIDS). In fact, some patients experience a complete cessation of fevers and remain healthy for the rest of their lives. I'd like to think that Michael was one of the lucky ones, but even if not, there is no reason to think that he did not live to a ripe old age. Furthermore, since malaria is strictly a blood borne disease, he could not have transmitted it to members of his family.

The cause of malaria would not be understood for decades after *When He Was Wicked* took place, but the fundamentals of treatment were already known: A cure could be achieved by consuming the bark of the tropical cinchona tree. This was usually mixed with water, yielding "quinine water." Quinine was first sold commercially in France in 1820, but its use was fairly widespread for some time prior.

Malaria has been mostly eradicated from the developed world, in large part because of mosquito control efforts. However, it remains a leading cause of death and disability among people who live in the developing world. Between 1 million and 3 million people die of *falciparum* malaria every year. That averages one death every thirty seconds. Most of the dead are in sub-Saharan Africa, and most are children under five years of age.

A portion of the proceeds of this book will be donated to malarial drug development research.

Sincerely,

Dear Reader,

Have you ever wondered what happened to your favorite characters after you closed the final page? Wanted just a little bit more of a favorite novel? I have, and if the questions from my readers are any indication, I'm not the only one. So after countless requests from Bridgerton fans, I decided to try something a little different, and I wrote a "2nd Epilogue" for each of the novels. These are the stories that come after the stories.

At first, the Bridgerton 2nd Epilogues were available exclusively online; later they were published (along with a novella about Violet Bridgerton) in a collection called The Bridgertons: Happily Ever After. Now, for the first time, each 2nd Epilogue is being included with the novel it follows. I hope you enjoy Michael and Francesca as they continue their journey.

Warmly,
Julia Quinn

When He Was Wicked: The 2nd Epilogue

She was counting again.

Counting, always counting.

Seven days since her last menses.

Six until she might be fertile.

Twenty-four to thirty-one until she might expect to bleed again, provided she didn't conceive.

Which she probably wouldn't.

It had been three years since she'd married Michael. Three years. She'd suffered through her courses thirty-three times. She'd counted them, of course; made depressing little hatch marks on a piece of paper she kept tucked away in her desk, in the far back corner of the middle drawer, where Michael wouldn't see.

It would pain him. Not because he wanted a child, which he did, but rather because *she* wanted one so desperately.

And he wanted it for her. Maybe even more than he wanted one himself.

She tried to hide her sorrow. She tried to smile at the breakfast table and pretend that it didn't *matter* that she'd a wad of cloth between her legs, but Michael always saw it in her eyes, and he seemed to hold her closer through the day, kiss her brow more often.

She tried to tell herself that she should count her blessings. And she did. Oh, how she did. Every day. She was Francesca Bridgerton Stirling, Countess of Kilmartin, blessed with two loving families—the one she'd been born into, and the one she'd acquired—twice—through marriage.

She had a husband most women only dreamed of. Handsome, funny, intelligent, and as desperately in love with her as she was with him. Michael made her laugh. He made her days a joy and her nights an adventure. She loved to talk with him, to walk with him, to simply sit in the same room with him and steal glances while they were each pretending to read a book.

She was happy. Truly, she was. And if she never had a baby, at least she had this man—this wonderful, marvelous, miraculous man who understood her in a way that left her breathless.

He knew her. He knew every inch of her, and still, he never ceased to amaze and challenge her.

She loved him. With every breath in her body, she loved him.

And most of the time, it was enough. Most of the time, it was more than enough.

But late at night, after he'd fallen asleep, and she still lay awake, curled up against him, she felt an emptiness that she feared neither of them could ever fill. She would touch her abdomen, and there it was, flat as always, mocking her with its refusal to do the one thing she wanted more than anything else.

And that was when she cried.

There had to be a name for it, Michael thought as he stood at his window, watching Francesca disappear over the hillside toward the Kilmartin family plot. There had to be a name for this particular brand of pain, of torture, really. All he wanted in the world was to make her happy. Oh, for certain there were other things—peace, health, prosperity for his tenants, right-minded men in the seat of prime minister for the next hundred years. But when all was said and done, what he wanted was Francesca's happiness.

He loved her. He always had. It was, or at least it should have been, the most uncomplicated thing in the world. He loved her. Period. And he would have moved heaven and earth, if it were only in his power, to make her happy.

Except the one thing she wanted most of all, the one thing she craved so desperately and fought so valiantly to hide her pain about, he could not seem to give her.

A child.

And the funny thing was, he was beginning to feel the same pain.

At first, he had felt it just for her. She wanted a child, and therefore he wanted one as well. She wanted to be a mother, and therefore he wanted her to be one. He wanted to see her holding a child, not because it would be his child, but because it would be hers.

He wanted her to have what she desired. And selfishly, he wanted to be the man to give it to her.

But lately, he'd felt the pangs himself. They would visit one of her many brothers or sisters and be immediately surrounded by the next generation of offspring. They would tug on his leg, shriek, "Uncle Michael!" and howl with laughter when he would toss them in the air, always begging for one more minute, one more twirl, one more secret peppermint candy.

The Bridgertons were marvelously fertile. They all seemed to produce exactly the number of offspring they desired. And then perhaps one more, just for good measure.

Except Francesca.

Five hundred and eighty-four days later, Francesca stepped out of the Kilmartin carriage and breathed the fresh, clean air of the Kent countryside. Spring was well under way, and the sun was warm on her cheeks, but when the wind blew, it carried with it the last hints of winter. Francesca didn't mind, though. She'd always liked the tingle of a cold wind on her skin. It drove Michael mad—he was always complaining that he'd never quite readjusted to life in a cold climate after so many years in India.

She was sorry he had not been able to accompany her on the long ride down from Scotland for the christening of Hyacinth's baby daughter, Isabella. He would be there, of course; she and Michael never missed the christening of any of their nieces and nephews. But affairs in Edinburgh had delayed his arrival. Francesca could have delayed her trip as well, but it had been many months since she had seen her family, and she missed them.

It was funny. When she was younger, she'd always been so eager to get away, to set up her own household, her own identity. But now, as she watched her nieces and nephews grow, she found herself visiting more often. She didn't want to miss the milestones. She had just happened to be visiting when Colin's daughter Agatha had taken her first steps. It had been breathtaking. And although she had wept quietly in her bed that night, the tears in her eyes as she'd watched Aggie lurch forward and laugh had been ones of pure joy.

If she wasn't going to be a mother, then by God, at least she would have those moments. She couldn't bear to think of life without them.

Francesca smiled as she handed her cloak to a footman and walked down the familiar corridors of Aubrey Hall. She'd spent much of her childhood here, and at Bridgerton House in London. Anthony and his wife had made some changes, but much was still just as it had always been. The walls were still painted the same creamy white, with the barest undertone of peach. And the Fragonard her father had bought her mother for her thirtieth birthday still hung over the table just outside the door to the rose salon.

"Francesca!"

She turned. It was her mother, rising from her seat in the salon.

"How long have you been standing out there?" Violet asked, coming to greet her.

Francesca embraced her mother. "Not long. I was admiring the painting."

Violet stood beside her and together they regarded the Fragonard. "It's marvelous, isn't it?" she murmured, a soft, wistful smile touching her face.

"I love it," Francesca said. "I always have. It makes me think of Father."

Violet turned to her in surprise. "It does?"

Francesca could understand her reaction. The painting was of a young woman holding a bouquet of flowers with a note attached. Not a very masculine subject. But she was looking over her shoulder, and her expression was a little bit mischievous, as if, given the correct provocation, she might laugh. Francesca could not remember much of her parents' relationship; she had been but six at the time of her father's death. But she remembered the laughter. The sound of her father's deep, rich chuckle—it lived within her.

"I think your marriage must have been like that," Francesca said, motioning to the painting.

Violet took a half step back and cocked her head to the side. "I think you're right," she said, looking rather delighted by the realization. "I never thought of it quite that way."

"You should take the painting back with you to London," Francesca said. "It's yours, isn't it?"

Violet blushed, and for a brief moment, Francesca saw the young girl she must have been shining out from her eyes. "Yes," she said, "but it belongs here. This was where he gave it to me. And this"—she motioned to its spot of honor on the wall—"was where we hung it together."

"You were very happy," Francesca said. It wasn't a question, just an observation.

"As are you."

Francesca nodded.

Violet reached out and took her hand, patting it gently as they both continued to study the painting. Francesca knew exactly what her mother was thinking about—her infertility, and the fact that they seemed to have an unspoken agreement never to talk about it, and really, why should they? What could Violet possibly say that would make it better?

Francesca couldn't say anything, because that would just make her mother feel even worse, and so instead they stood there as they always did, thinking the same thing but never speaking of it, wondering which of them hurt more.

Francesca thought it might be her—hers was the barren womb, after all. But maybe her mother's pain was more acute. Violet was her *mother*, and she was grieving for the lost dreams of her child. Wouldn't that be painful? And the irony was, Francesca would never know. She'd never know what it felt like to hurt for a child because she'd never know what it was to be a mother.

She was almost three and thirty. She did not know any married lady who had reached that age without conceiving a child. It seemed that children either arrived right away or not at all.

"Has Hyacinth arrived?" Francesca asked, still looking at the painting, still staring at the twinkle in the woman's eye.

"Not yet. But Eloise will be here later this afternoon. She—"

But Francesca heard the catch in her mother's voice before she'd cut herself off. "Is she expecting, then?" she asked.

There was a beat of silence, and then: "Yes."

"That's wonderful." And she meant it. She did, with every last bit of her being. She just didn't know how to make it sound that way.

She didn't want to look at her mother's face. Because then she would cry.

Francesca cleared her throat, tilting her head to the side as if there were an inch of the Fragonard she hadn't yet perused. "Anyone else?" she queried.

She felt her mother stiffen slightly beside her, and she wondered if Violet was deciding whether it was worth it to pretend that she didn't know exactly what she meant.

"Lucy," her mother said quietly.

Francesca finally turned and faced Violet, pulling her hand out of her mother's grasp. "Again?" she asked. Lucy and Gregory had been married for less than two years, but this would be their second child.

Violet nodded. "I'm sorry."

"Don't say that," Francesca said, horrified by how thick her voice sounded. "Don't say you're sorry. It's not something to be sorry about."

"No," her mother said quickly. "That wasn't what I meant."

"You should be delighted for them."

"I am!"

"More delighted for them than you are sorry for me," Francesca choked out.

"Francesca . . ."

Violet tried to reach for her, but Francesca pulled away. "Promise me," she said. "You have to promise me that you will always be more happy than you are sorry."

Violet looked at her helplessly, and Francesca realized that her mother did not know what to say. For her entire life, Violet Bridgerton had been the most sensitive and wonderful of mothers. She always seemed to know what her children needed, exactly when they needed it—whether it was a kind word or a gentle prod, or even a giant proverbial kick in the breeches.

But now, in this moment, Violet was lost. And Francesca was the one who had done it to her.

"I'm sorry, Mother," she said, the words spilling out. "I'm so sorry, I'm so sorry."

"No." Violet rushed forward to embrace her, and this time Francesca did not pull away. "No, darling," Violet said again, softly stroking her hair. "Don't say that, please don't say that."

She shushed and she crooned, and Francesca let her mother hold her. And when Francesca's hot, silent tears fell on her mother's shoulder, neither one of them said a word.

By the time Michael arrived two days later, Francesca had thrown herself into the preparations for little Isabella's christening, and her conversation with her mother was, if not forgotten, at least not at the forefront of her mind. It wasn't as if any of this was new, after all. Francesca was just as barren as she'd been every time she came to England to see her family. The only difference this time was that she'd actually talked to someone about it. A little bit.

As much as she was able.

And yet, somehow, something had been lifted from her. When she'd stood there in the hall, her mother's arms around her, something had poured out from her along with her tears.

And while she still grieved for the babies she would never have, for the first time in a long time, she felt unreservedly happy.

It was strange and wonderful, and she positively refused to question it.

"Aunt Francesca! Aunt Francesca!"

Francesca smiled as she looped her arm through that of her niece. Charlotte was Anthony's youngest, due to turn eight in a month's time. "What is it, poppet?"

"Did you see the baby's dress? It's so *long*."

"I know."

"And frilly."

"Christening dresses are meant to be frilly. Even the boys are covered in lace."

"It seems a waste," Charlotte said with a shrug. "Isabella doesn't *know* she's wearing anything so pretty."

"Ah, but we do."

Charlotte pondered this for a moment. "But I don't care, do you?"

Francesca chuckled. "No, I don't suppose I do. I should love her no matter what she was wearing."

The two of them continued their stroll through the gardens, picking the grape hyacinths to decorate the chapel. They had nearly filled the basket when they heard the unmistakable sound of a carriage coming down the drive.

"I wonder who it is now," Charlotte said, rising to her toes as if that might actually help her see the carriage any better.

"I'm not sure," Francesca replied. Any number of relations were due that afternoon.

"Uncle Michael, maybe."

Francesca smiled. "I hope so."

"I *adore* Uncle Michael," Charlotte said with a sigh, and Francesca almost laughed, because the look in her niece's eyes was one she'd seen a thousand times before.

Women adored Michael. It seemed even seven-year-old girls were not immune to his charm.

"Well, he is very handsome," Francesca demurred.

Charlotte shrugged. "I suppose."

"You suppose?" Francesca replied, trying very hard not to smile.

"*I* like him because he tosses me in the air when Father isn't looking."

"He does like to bend the rules."

Charlotte grinned. "I know. It's why I don't tell Father."

Francesca had never thought of Anthony as particularly stern, but he had been the head of the family for over twenty years, and she supposed the experience had endowed him with a certain love of order and tidiness.

And it had to be said—he *did* like to be in charge.

"It shall be our secret," Francesca said, leaning down to whisper in her niece's ear. "And anytime you wish to come visit us in Scotland, you may. We bend rules all the time."

Charlotte's eyes grew huge. "You do?"

"Sometimes we have breakfast for supper."

"Brilliant."

"And we walk in the rain."

Charlotte shrugged. "Everybody walks in the rain."

"Yes, I suppose, but sometimes we *dance*."

Charlotte stepped back. "May I go back with you *now*?"

"That's up to your parents, poppet." Francesca laughed and reached for Charlotte's hand. "But we can dance right now."

"Here?"

Francesca nodded.

"Where everyone can see?"

Francesca looked around. "I don't see anyone watching. And even if there were, who cares?"

Charlotte's lips pursed, and Francesca could practically *see* her mind at work. "Not me!" she announced, and she linked her arm through Francesca's. Together they did a little jig, followed by a Scottish reel, twisting and twirling until they were both breathless.

"Oh, I wish it would rain!" Charlotte laughed.

"Now what would be the fun in that?" came a new voice.

"Uncle Michael!" Charlotte shrieked, launching herself at him.

"And I am instantly forgotten," Francesca said with a wry smile.

Michael looked at her warmly over Charlotte's head. "Not by me," he murmured.

"Aunt Francesca and I have been dancing," Charlotte told him.

"I know. I saw you from inside the house. I especially enjoyed the new one."

"What new one?"

Michael pretended to look confused. "The new dance you were doing."

"We weren't doing any new dances," Charlotte replied, her brows knitting together.

"Then what was that one that involved throwing yourself on the grass?"

Francesca bit her lip to keep from smiling.

"We *fell*, Uncle Michael."

"No!"

"We did!"

"It was a vigorous dance," Francesca confirmed.

"You must be exceptionally graceful, then, because it looked *completely* as if you'd done it on purpose."

"We didn't! We didn't!" Charlotte said excitedly. "We really did just fall. By accident!"

"I suppose I will believe you," he said with a sigh, "but only because I know you are far too trustworthy to lie."

She looked him in the eye with a melting expression. "I would never lie to you, Uncle Michael," she said.

He kissed her cheek and set her down. "Your mother says it's time for dinner."

"But you just got here!"

"I'm not going anywhere. You need your sustenance after all the dancing."

"I'm not hungry," she offered.

"Pity, then," he said, "because I was going to teach you to waltz this afternoon, and you certainly cannot do that on an empty stomach."

Charlotte's eyes grew to near circles. "Really? Father said I cannot learn until I am ten."

Michael gave her one of those devastating half smiles that still made Francesca tingle. "We don't have to tell him, do we?"

"Oh, Uncle Michael, I *love* you," she said fervently, and then, after one extremely vigorous hug, Charlotte ran off to Aubrey Hall.

"And another one falls," Francesca said with a shake of her head, watching her niece dash across the fields.

Michael took her hand and tugged her toward him. "What is that supposed to mean?"

Francesca grinned a little and sighed a little and said, "I would *never* lie to you."

He kissed her soundly. "I certainly hope not."

She looked up into his silvery eyes and let herself ease against the warmth of his body. "It seems no woman is immune."

"How lucky I am, then, that I fall under the spell of only one."

"Lucky for *me*."

"Well, yes," he said with affected modesty, "but I wasn't going to say it."

She swatted him on the arm.

He kissed her in return. "I missed you."

"I missed you, too."

"And how is the clan Bridgerton?" he asked, linking his arm through hers.

"Rather wonderful," Francesca replied. "I am having a splendid time, actually."

"Actually?" he echoed, looking vaguely amused.

Francesca steered him away from the house. It had been over a week since she'd had his company, and she didn't wish to share him just then. "What do you mean?" she asked.

"You said 'actually.' As if you were surprised."

"Of course not," she said. But then she thought. "I always have a lovely time when I visit my family," she said carefully.

"But . . ."

"But it's better this time." She shrugged. "I don't know why."

Which wasn't precisely the truth. That moment with her mother—there had been magic in those tears.

But she couldn't tell him that. He'd hear the bit about crying and nothing else, and then he'd worry, and she'd feel terrible for worrying him, and she was *tired* of all that.

Besides, he was a man. He'd never understand, anyway.

"I feel happy," she announced. "Something in the air."

"The sun *is* shining," he observed.

She gave him a jaunty, single-shouldered shrug and leaned back against a tree. "Birds are singing."

"Flowers blooming?"

"Just a few," she admitted.

He regarded the landscape. "All the moment needs is a cherubic little bunny hopping across the field."

She smiled blissfully and leaned into him for a kiss. "Bucolic splendor is a marvelous thing."

"Indeed." His lips found hers with familiar hunger. "I missed you," he said, his voice husky with desire.

She let out a little moan as he nipped her ear. "I know. You said that."

"It bears repeating."

Francesca meant to say something witty about never tiring of hearing it, but at that moment she found herself pressed rather breathlessly against a tree, one of her legs lifted up around his hips.

"You wear *far* too many clothes," he growled.

"We're a little too close to the house," she gasped, her belly clenching with need as he pressed more intimately against her.

"How far," he murmured, one of his hands stealing under her skirts, "is 'not too close'?"

"Not far."

He drew back and gazed at her. "Really?"

"Really." Her lips curved, and she felt devilish. She felt powerful. And she wanted to take charge. Of him. Of her life. Of everything.

"Come with me," she said impulsively, and she grabbed his hand and ran.

Michael had missed his wife. At night, when she was not beside him, the bed felt cold, and the air felt empty. Even when he was tired, and his body was not hungry for her, he craved her presence, her scent, her warmth.

He missed the sound of her breathing. He missed the way the mattress moved differently when there was a second body on it.

He knew, even though she was more reticent than he, and far

less likely to use such passionate words, that she felt the same way. But even so, he was pleasantly surprised to be racing across a field, letting her take the lead, knowing that in a few short minutes he would be buried deep within her.

"Here," she said, skidding to a halt at the bottom of a hill.

"Here?" he asked dubiously. There was no cover of trees, nothing to block them from sight should anyone stroll by.

She sat. "No one comes this way."

"No one?"

"The grass is very soft," she said seductively, patting a spot beside her.

"I'm not even going to ask how you know that," he muttered.

"Picnics," she said, her expression delightfully outraged, "with my *dolls*."

He took off his coat and laid it like a blanket on the grass. The ground was softly sloped, which he would imagine would be more comfortable for her than horizontal.

He looked at her. He looked at the coat. She didn't move.

"You," she said.

"Me?"

"Lie down," she ordered.

He did. With alacrity.

And then, before he'd had time to make a comment, to tease or cajole, or even really to breathe, she'd straddled him.

"Oh, dear G—" he gasped, but he couldn't finish. She was kissing him now, her mouth hot and hungry and aggressive. It was all deliciously familiar—he loved knowing every little bit of her, from the slope of her breast to the rhythm of her kisses—and yet this time, she felt a little . . .

New.

Renewed.

One of his hands moved to the back of her head. At home he liked to pull the pins out one by one, watching each lock tumble from her coiffure. But today he was too needy, too urgent, and he didn't have patience for—

"What was that for?" he asked. She had yanked his hand away.

Her eyes narrowed languidly. "I'm in charge," she whispered.

His body tightened. More. Dear God, she was going to kill him.

"Don't go slow," he gasped.

But he didn't think she was listening. She was taking her time, undoing his breeches, letting her hands flutter along his belly until she found him.

"Frannie . . ."

One finger. That's all she gave him. One featherlight finger along his shaft.

She turned, looked at him. "This is fun," she remarked.

He just focused on trying to breathe.

"I love you," she said softly, and he felt her rise. She hoisted her skirts to her thighs as she positioned herself, and then, with one spectacularly swift stroke, she took him within her, her body coming to rest against his, leaving him embedded to the hilt.

He wanted to move then. He wanted to thrust up, or flip her over and pound until they were both nothing but dust, but her hands were firm on his hips, and when he looked up at her, her eyes were closed, and she almost looked as if she were concentrating.

Her breathing was slow and steady, but it was loud, too, and with each exhale she seemed to bear down on him just a little bit heavier.

"Frannie," he groaned, because he didn't know what else to do. He wanted her to move faster. Or harder. Or something, but all she did was rock back and forth, her hips arching and curving in delicious torment. He clutched her hips, intending to move her up and down, but she opened her eyes and shook her head with a soft, blissful smile.

"I like it this way," she said.

He wanted something different. He *needed* something different, but when she looked down at him, she looked so damned happy that he could deny her nothing. And then, sure enough, she began to shudder, and it was strange, because he knew the feel of her climax so well, and yet this time it seemed softer . . . and stronger, at the same time.

She swayed, and she rocked, and then she let out a little scream and sagged against him.

And then, to his utter and complete surprise, he came. He hadn't thought he was ready. He hadn't thought he was remotely near climax, not that it would have taken long had he been able to move beneath her. But then, without warning, he had simply exploded.

They lay that way for some time, the sun falling gently on them. She burrowed her face in his neck, and he held her, wondering how it was possible that such moments existed.

Because it was perfect. And he would have stayed there forever, had he been able. And even though he didn't ask her, he knew she felt the same.

They'd meant to go home two days after the christening, Francesca thought as she watched one of her nephews tackle the other to the ground, but here it was, three weeks out, and they had not even begun to pack.

"No broken bones, I hope."

Francesca smiled up at her sister Eloise, who had also elected to stay on at Aubrey Hall for an extended visit. "No," she answered, wincing slightly when the future Duke of Hastings—otherwise known as Davey, aged eleven—let out a war whoop as he jumped from a tree. "But it's not for lack of trying."

Eloise took a seat beside her and tilted her face to the sun. "I'll put my bonnet on in a minute, I swear it," she said.

"I can't quite determine the rules of the game," Francesca remarked.

Eloise didn't bother to open her eyes. "That's because there are none."

Francesca watched the chaos with fresh perspective. Oliver, Eloise's twelve-year-old stepson, had grabbed hold of a ball—since when had there been a ball?—and was racing across the lawn. He appeared to reach his goal—not that Francesca would ever be sure whether that was the giant oak stump that had been there since she was a child or Miles, Anthony's second son, who had been sitting cross-legged and cross-armed since Francesca had come outside ten minutes earlier.

But whichever was the case, Oliver must have won a point, because he slammed the ball against the ground and then jumped up and down with a triumphant cry. Miles must have been on his team—this was the first indication Francesca had that there were teams—because he hopped to his feet and celebrated in kind.

Eloise opened one eye. "My child didn't kill anyone, did he?"

"No."

"No one killed him?"

Francesca smiled. "No."

"Good." Eloise yawned and resettled into her chaise.

Francesca thought about her words. "Eloise?"

"Mmmm?"

"Do you ever . . ." She frowned. There really wasn't any right way to ask this. "Do you ever love Oliver and Amanda . . ."

"Less?" Eloise supplied.

"Yes."

Eloise sat up straighter and opened her eyes. "No."

"Really?" It wasn't that Francesca didn't believe her. She loved her nieces and nephews with every breath in her body; she would have laid down her life for any one of them—Oliver and Amanda included—without even a moment's hesitation. But she hadn't ever given birth. She had never carried a child in her womb—not for long, anyway—and didn't know if somehow that made it different. Made it more.

If she had a baby, one of her own, born of her blood and Michael's, would she suddenly realize that this love she felt now for Charlotte and Oliver and Miles and all the others— Would it suddenly feel like a wisp next to what was in her heart for her own child?

Did it make a difference?

Did she want it to make a difference?

"I thought it would," Eloise admitted. "Of course I loved Oliver and Amanda long before I had Penelope. How could I not? They are pieces of Phillip. And," she continued, her face growing thoughtful, as if she had never quite delved into this before, "they are . . . themselves. And I am their mother."

Francesca smiled wistfully.

"But even so," Eloise continued, "before I had Penelope, and even when I was carrying her, I thought it would be different." She paused. "It *is* different." She paused again. "But it's not less. It's not a question of levels or amounts, or even . . . really . . . the nature of it." Eloise shrugged. "I can't explain it."

Francesca looked back to the game, which had resumed with new intensity. "No," she said softly, "I think you did."

There was a long silence, and then Eloise said, "You don't . . . talk about it much."

Francesca shook her head gently. "No."

"Do you want to?"

She thought about that for a moment. "I don't know." She turned to her sister. They had been at sixes and sevens for much of their childhood, but in so many ways Eloise was like the other half of her coin. They looked so alike, save for the color of their eyes, and they even shared the same birthday, just one year apart.

Eloise was watching her with a tender curiosity, a sympathy that, just a few weeks ago, would have been heartbreaking. But now it was simply comforting. Francesca didn't feel pitied, she felt loved.

"I'm happy," Francesca said. And she was. She really was. For once she didn't feel that aching emptiness hiding underneath. She'd even forgotten to count. She didn't know how many days it had been since her last menses, and it felt so bloody *good.*

"I hate numbers," she muttered.

"I beg your pardon?"

She bit back a smile. "Nothing."

The sun, which had been obscured behind a thin layer of cloud, suddenly popped into the open. Eloise shaded her eyes with her hand as she sat back. "Good heavens," she remarked. "I think Oliver just *sat* on Miles."

Francesca laughed, and then, before she even knew what she was about, stood. "Do you think they'll let me play?"

Eloise looked at her as if she'd gone mad, which, Francesca thought with a shrug, perhaps she had.

Eloise looked at Francesca, and then at the boys, and then back at Francesca. And then she stood. "If you do it, I'll do it."

"You can't do it," Francesca said. "You're pregnant."

"Barely," Eloise said with a scoff. "Besides, Oliver wouldn't dare sit on *me*." She held out her arm. "Shall we?"

"I believe we shall." Francesca linked her arm through her sister's, and together they ran down the hill, shouting like banshees and loving every minute of it.

"I heard you made quite a scene this afternoon," Michael said, perching on the edge of the bed.

Francesca did not move. Not even an eyelid. "I'm exhausted" was all she said.

He took in the dusty hem of her dress. "And dirty, too."

"Too tired to wash."

"Anthony said that Miles said that he was quite impressed. Apparently you throw quite well for a girl."

"It would have been brilliant," she replied, "had I been informed that I wasn't meant to use my hands."

He chuckled. "What game, exactly, were you playing?"

"I have no idea." She let out an exhausted little moan. "Would you rub my feet?"

He pushed himself farther onto the bed and slid her dress up to mid-calf. Her feet were filthy. "Good Lord," he exclaimed. "Did you go barefoot?"

"I couldn't very well play in my slippers."

"How did Eloise fare?"

"She, apparently, throws like a boy."

"I thought you weren't meant to use your hands."

At that, she pushed herself indignantly up on her elbows. "I *know*. It depended on what end of the field one was at. Whoever heard of such a thing."

He took her foot in his hands, making a mental note to wash them later—his hands that was, she could take care of her own feet. "I had no idea you were so competitive," he remarked.

"It runs in the family," she mumbled. "No, no, there. Yes, right there. Harder. Oooooohhhh . . ."

"Why do I feel as if I heard this before," he mused, "except that I was having much more fun?"

"Just be quiet and keep rubbing my feet."

"At your service, Your Majesty," he murmured, smiling when she realized she was perfectly content to be referred to as such. After a minute or two of silence, save for the occasional moan from Francesca, he asked, "How much longer do you wish to stay?"

"Are you eager to return home?"

"I do have matters to attend to," he replied, "but nothing that cannot wait. I'm rather enjoying your family, actually."

She quirked a brow—and a smile. "Actually?"

"Indeed. Although it was a bit daunting when your sister beat me at the shooting match."

"She beats everyone. She always has. Shoot with Gregory next time. He can't hit a tree."

Michael moved on to the other foot. Francesca looked so happy and relaxed. Not just now, but at the supper table, and in the drawing room, and when she was chasing her nieces and nephews, and even at night, when he was making love to her in their huge four-poster bed. He was ready to go home, back to Kilmartin, which was ancient and drafty but indelibly theirs. But he'd happily remain here forever, if it meant Francesca would always look like this.

"I think you're right," she said.

"Of course," he replied, "but about what, exactly?"

"It's time to go home."

"I didn't say that it was. I merely inquired as to your intentions."

"You didn't have to say it," she said.

"If you want to stay—"

She shook her head. "I don't. I want to go home. Our home." With a stiff groan, she sat up all the way, curling her legs beneath her. "This has been lovely, and I have had such a wonderful time, but I miss Kilmartin."

"Are you certain?"

"I miss you."

He lifted his brows. "I'm right here."

She smiled and leaned forward. "I miss having you to myself."

"You need only say the word, my lady. Anytime, anywhere. I'll whisk you off and let you have your way with me."

She chuckled. "Perhaps right now."

He thought that was an excellent idea, but chivalry forced him to say, "I thought you were sore."

"Not that sore. Not if you do all the work."

"That, my dear, is not a problem." He pulled his shirt over his head and lay down beside her, giving her a long, delicious kiss. He pulled back with a contented sigh and then just gazed at her. "You're beautiful," he whispered. "More than ever."

She smiled—that lazy, warm smile that meant she'd been recently pleasured, or knew she was about to be.

He loved that smile.

He went to work on the buttons at the back of her frock and was halfway down when all of a sudden a thought popped into his head. "Wait," he said. "Can you?"

"Can I what?"

He stopped, frowning as he tried to count it out in his head. Oughtn't she be bleeding? "Isn't it your time?" he asked.

Her lips parted, and she blinked. "No," she said, sounding a little bit startled—not by his question but by her answer. "No, I'm not."

He shifted position, moving back a few inches so that he could better see her face. "Do you think . . . ? "

"I don't know." She was blinking rapidly now, and he could hear that her breathing had grown more rapid. "I suppose. I could . . ."

He wanted to whoop with joy, but he dared not. Not yet. "When do you think—"

"—I'll know? I don't know. Maybe—"

"—in a month? Two?"

"Maybe two. Maybe sooner. I don't know." Her hand flew to her belly. "It might not take."

"It might not," he said carefully.

"But it might."

"It might."

He felt laughter bubbling within him, a strange giddiness in his belly, growing and tickling until it burst from his lips.

"We can't be sure," she warned, but he could see that she was excited, too.

"No," he said, but somehow he knew they were.

"I don't want to get my hopes up."

"No, no, of course we mustn't."

Her eyes grew wide, and she placed both hands on her belly, still absolutely, completely flat.

"Do you feel anything?" he whispered.

She shook her head. "It would be too early, anyway."

He knew that. He knew that he knew that. He didn't know why he'd asked.

And then Francesca said the damnedest thing. "But he's there," she whispered. "I know it."

"Frannie . . ." If she was wrong, if her heart was broken again—he just didn't think he could bear it.

But she was shaking her head. "It's true," she said, and she wasn't insisting. She wasn't trying to convince him, or even herself. He could hear it in her voice. Somehow she knew.

"Have you been feeling ill?" he asked.

She shook her head.

"Have you—Good God, you shouldn't have been playing with the boys this afternoon."

"Eloise did."

"Eloise can do what she damned well pleases. She isn't *you*."

She smiled. Like a Madonna, she smiled, he would have sworn it. And she said, "I won't break."

He remembered when she'd miscarried years ago. It had not been his child, but he had felt her pain, hot and searing, like a fist around his heart. His cousin—her first husband—had been dead a scant few weeks, and they were both reeling from that loss. When she'd lost John's baby . . .

He didn't think either one of them could survive another loss like that.

"Francesca," he said urgently, "you must take care. *Please*."

"It won't happen again," she said, shaking her head.

"How do you *know*?"

She gave him a bewildered shrug. "I don't know. I just do."

Dear God, he prayed she was not deluding herself. "Do you want to tell your family?" he asked quietly.

She shook her head. "Not yet. Not because I have any fears," she hastened to add. "I just want—" Her lips pressed together in the most adorably giddy little smile. "I just want it to be mine for a little while. Ours."

He brought her hand to his lips. "How long is a little while?"

"I'm not sure." But her eyes were growing crafty. "I'm not quite sure . . ."

One year later . . .

Violet Bridgerton loved all her children equally, but she loved them *differently* as well. And when it came to missing them, she did so in what she considered a most logical manner. Her heart pined the most for the one she'd seen the least. And that was why, as she waited in the drawing room at Aubrey Hall, waiting for a carriage bearing the Kilmartin crest to roll down the drive, she found herself fidgety and eager, jumping up every five minutes to watch through the window.

"She wrote that they would arrive today," Kate reassured her.

"I know," Violet replied with a sheepish smile. "It's just that I haven't seen her for an entire year. I know Scotland is far, but I've never gone an entire year without seeing one of my children before."

"Really?" Kate asked. "That's remarkable."

"We all have our priorities," Violet said, deciding there was no point in trying to pretend she wasn't champing at the bit. She set down her embroidery and moved to the window, craning her neck when she thought she saw something glinting in the sunlight.

"Even when Colin was traveling so much?" Kate asked.

"The longest he was gone was three hundred and forty-two days," Violet replied. "When he was traveling in the Mediterranean."

"You counted?"

Violet shrugged. "I can't help myself. I like to count." She thought of all the counting she'd done when her children were growing up, making sure she had as many offspring at the end of an outing as she'd had at the beginning. "It helps to keep track of things."

Kate smiled as she reached down and rocked the cradle at her feet. "I shall never complain about the logistics of managing four."

Violet crossed the room to peek down at her newest grandchild. Little Mary had been a bit of a surprise, coming so many years after Charlotte. Kate had thought herself done with childbearing, but then, ten months earlier, she'd got out of bed, walked calmly to the chamber pot, emptied the contents of her stomach, and announced to Anthony, "I believe we're expecting again."

Or so they'd told Violet. She made it a point to stay out of her grown children's bedrooms except in the case of illness or childbirth.

"I never complained," Violet said softly. Kate didn't hear, but Violet hadn't meant her to. She smiled down at Mary, sleeping sweetly under a purple blanket. "I think your mother would have been delighted," she said, looking up at Kate.

Kate nodded, her eyes misting over. Her mother—actually her stepmother, but Mary Sheffield had raised her from a little girl—had passed away a month before Kate realized that she was pregnant. "I know it makes no sense," Kate said, leaning down to examine her child's face more closely, "but I would swear she looks a bit like her."

Violet blinked and tilted her head to the side. "I think you're right."

"Something about the eyes."

"No, it's the nose."

"Do you think? I rather thought— Oh look!" Kate pointed toward the window. "Is that Francesca?"

Violet straightened and rushed to the window. "It is!" she exclaimed. "Oh, and the sun is shining. I'm going to wait outside."

With nary a backward glance she grabbed her shawl off a side table and dashed into the hall. It had been so long since she'd seen Frannie, but that wasn't the only reason she was so eager to see her. Francesca had changed during her last visit, back at Isabella's christening. It was hard to explain, but Violet had sensed that something had shifted within her.

Of all her children, Francesca had always been the most quiet, the most private. She loved her family, but she also loved being apart from them, forging her own identity, making her own life. It was not surprising that she had never chosen to share her feelings about the most painful corner of her life—her infertility. But last time, even though they had not spoken about it explicitly, something had still passed between them, and Violet had almost felt as if she'd been able to absorb some of her grief.

When Francesca had departed, the clouds behind her eyes had been lifted. Violet didn't know whether she had finally accepted her fate, or whether she had simply learned how to rejoice in what she had, but Francesca had seemed, for the first time in Violet's recent memory, unreservedly happy.

Violet ran through the hall—really, at her age!—and pushed open the front door so that she could wait in the drive. Francesca's carriage was nearly there, starting the final turn so that one of the doors would be facing the house.

Violet could see Michael through the window. He waved. She beamed.

"Oh, I've missed you!" she exclaimed, hurrying forward as he hopped down. "You must promise never to wait so long again."

"As if I could refuse you anything," he said, leaning down to kiss her cheek. He turned then, holding his arm out to assist Francesca.

Violet embraced her daughter, then stepped back to look at her. Frannie was . . .

Glowing.

She was positively radiant.

"I missed you, Mother," she said.

Violet would have made a reply, but she found herself unexpectedly choked up. She felt her lips press together, then twitch at the corners as she fought to contain her tears. She didn't know why she was so emotional. Yes, it had been over a year, but hadn't she gone three hundred and forty-two days before? This was not so very different.

"I have something for you," Francesca said, and Violet could have sworn her eyes were glistening, too.

Francesca turned back to the carriage and held out her arms. A maid appeared in the doorway, holding some sort of bundle, which she then handed down to her mistress.

Violet gasped. Dear God, it couldn't be . . .

"Mother," Francesca said softly, cradling the precious little bundle, "this is John."

The tears, which had been waiting patiently in Violet's eyes, began to roll. "Frannie," she whispered, taking the baby into her arms, "why didn't you tell me?"

And Francesca—her maddening, inscrutable third daughter—said, "I don't know."

"He's beautiful," Violet said, not caring that she'd been kept in the dark. She didn't care about anything in that moment—nothing but the tiny boy in her arms, gazing up at her with an impossibly wise expression.

"He has your eyes," Violet said, looking up at Francesca.

Frannie nodded, and her smile was almost silly, as if she couldn't quite believe it. "I know."

"And your mouth."

"I think you're right."

"And your—oh, my, I think he has your nose as well."

"I'm told," Michael said in an amused voice, "that I was involved in his creation, too, but I have yet to see any evidence."

Francesca looked at him with so much love that it nearly took Violet's breath away. "He has your charm," she said.

Violet laughed, and then she laughed again. There was too much happiness inside of her—she couldn't possibly hold it in. "I think it's time we introduced this little fellow to his family," she said. "Don't you?"

Francesca held out her arms to take the baby, but Violet turned away. "Not just yet," she said. She wanted to hold him a while longer. Maybe until Tuesday.

"Mother, I think he might be hungry."

Violet assumed an arch expression. "He'll let us know."

"But—"

"I know a thing or two about babies, Francesca Bridgerton Stirling." Violet grinned down at John. "They adore their grandmamas, for example."

He gurgled and cooed, and then—she was positive—he smiled.

"Come with me, little one," she whispered, "I have so much to tell you."

And behind her, Francesca turned to Michael and said, "Do you think we'll get him back for the duration of the visit?"

He shook his head, then added, "It'll give us more time to see about getting the little fellow a sister."

"Michael!"

"Listen to the man," Violet called, not bothering to turn around.

"Good heavens," Francesca muttered.

But she did listen.

And she did enjoy.

And nine months later, she said good morning to Janet Helen Stirling.

Who looked *exactly* like her father.

About the Author

#1 *New York Times* bestselling author JULIA QUINN began writing one month after graduating from college and, aside from a brief stint in medical school, she has been tapping away at her keyboard ever since. Her novels have been translated into forty-three languages and are beloved the world over. A graduate of Harvard and Radcliffe Colleges, she lives with her family in the Pacific Northwest.